In the Shadow of
Frankenstein

In the Shadow of Frankenstein

Tales of the Modern Prometheus

EDITED BY STEPHEN JONES

Foreword by Neil Gaiman

PEGASUS BOOKS

NEW YORK LONDON

IN THE SHADOW OF FRANKENSTEIN

Pegasus Books Ltd.
148 W 37th Street, 13th Floor
New York, NY 10018

Copyright © 1994, 2015 by Stephen Jones

First Pegasus Books cloth edition July 2016

Published in conjunction with Robinson Publishing,
an imprint of Constable & Robinson.
Originally published as *The Mammoth Book of Frankenstein.*

Interior design by Maria Fernandez

Library of Congress Cataloging-in-Publication Data is available.

ISBN: 978-1-68177-145-8

10 9 8 7 6 5 4 3 2 1

Printed in the United States of America
Distributed by W. W. Norton & Company

*This one is of course for Kim,
in friendship and admiration.*

CONTENTS

In the Shadow of
Frankenstein

NEIL GAIMAN

Foreword

c—✦—ɔ

The cold, wet summer of 1816, a night of ghost stories and a challenge allowed a young woman to delineate the darkness, and give us a way of looking at the world.

They were in a villa on the shores of Lake Geneva: Lord Byron—the best-selling poet, too dangerous for the drawing rooms of England and in exile; his doctor, John William Polidori; Percy Shelley, poet and atheist, and his soon-to-be wife, eighteen-year-old Mary Wollstonecraft Godwin. Ghost stories were read, and then Byron challenged the group to come up with a new ghost story.

He started, but did not complete, a vampire story; Dr. Polidori completed a story about the first Byronesque vampire, "The Vampyre"; and young Mary, already the mother of a living child and a dead one, after several days of frustration, imagined a story about a man who fabricated a living creature, a monster, and brought it to life.

The book she wrote over the following year, initially published anonymously, was *Frankenstein or, The Modern Prometheus*, and it slowly changed everything.

Ideas happen when the time is right for them ("In steam engine time, people make steam engines," as Charles Fort put it). The ground had been prepared.

Gothic fiction had been all the rage for some time: dark, driven men had wandered the corridors of their ancestral homes, finding secret passages and dead relatives, magical, miserable, occasionally immortal; while the questing urge of science had discovered that frogs could twitch and spasm, after death, when current was applied. In an era of change, so much more was waiting to be discovered.

Brian Aldiss points to *Frankenstein* as the first work of science fiction (which he defines as hubris clobbered by nemesis) and he may be right. It was the place that people learned we could bring life back from death— but a dark and dangerous and untamable form of life, one that would, in the end, turn on us and harm us.

That idea, the cross-breeding of the Gothic and the scientific romance, was released from into the world, and would become a key metaphor for our times: the glittering promise of science, offering life and miracles, and the nameless creature in the shadows, monster and miracle all in one—back from the dead, needing knowledge and love but able, in the end, only to destroy.

It was Mary Shelley's gift to us, and we would be infinitely poorer without it.

INTRODUCTION

It's Alive!

❦

Frankenstein . . . his very name conjures up images of plundered graves, secret laboratories, electrical experiments and reviving the dead. Within these pages, the maddest doctor of them all and his demented disciples once again delve into the Secrets of Life, as science fiction meets horror when the world's most famous Monster lives again!

Both maker and Monster were originally conceived in the imagination of Mary W. Shelley during the summer of 1816 in Switzerland. Along with her lover Percy Bysshe Shelley, Dr. John Polidori and Lord Byron, who were staying in neighboring households on the shores of Lake Geneva, the eighteen-year-old Mary decided to try her hand at writing a ghost story. Urged by Percy to develop the result into a booklength work, *Frankenstein; or, The Modern Prometheus* was published anonymously a year-and-a-half later.

It was a huge success, and by 1823 at least five different adaptations were being staged in London. The story first reached the screen in 1910 when Charles Ogle portrayed the misshapen creation. At least two more versions were filmed before Universal cast the relatively unknown Boris Karloff in the role of the Monster for James Whale's classic 1931 adaptation of *Frankenstein*. With his square-shaped skull, corpse-like pallor and distinctive neck bolts, it's Karloff's (and make-up maestro Jack Pierce's) sympathetic interpretation of the creature which most people still remember.

Karloff recreated his role through two sequels before tiring of the part, but Universal kept the series going for another five episodes. Lon Chaney, Jr., Bela Lugosi and Glenn Strange all donned the distinctive make-up, until finally Abbott and Costello met Frankenstein in 1948 and the series was brought to a satisfactory, if somewhat overdue conclusion.

Boris Karloff went on to play the creator in *Frankenstein 1970* (1958) and appeared as the Monster one last time on television's *Route 66* in the early 1960s. However, Mary Shelley's immortal creation continued to live on in numerous low budget variations involving Frankenstein and his apparently limitless offspring and prodigies.

In 1957 Britain's Hammer Films revived the characters, this time in color, with *The Curse of Frankenstein*; but instead of following the exploits of the Creature, the series of six loosely-connected films concentrated instead on Peter Cushing's pitiless Baron and his failed experiments.

There have been numerous screen and television adaptations since. From Peter Boyle's tap-dancing Monster in Mel Brooks' *Young Frankenstein* (1974), through Robert De Niro's dignified creature in Kenneth Branagh's *Mary Shelley's Frankenstein* (1994), to Aaron Eckhart's vampire-killing anti-hero in Stuart Beattie's *I, Frankenstein* (2014), film-makers have continued to expand and develop the original story and characters in often unusual and unexpected ways.

Paul McGuigan's *Victor Frankenstein* (2015), which explores the relationship between the young scientist (James McAvoy) and his troubled assistant Igor (Daniel Radcliffe), is unlikely to be the final interpretation.

There have also been many literary succesors to Mary Shelley's novel, from Donald F. Glut's pulp series "The New Adventures of Frankenstein" to Brian Aldiss' *Frankenstein Unbound* (filmed in 1990), in which Mary and her literary creations co-exist in the same alternate world.

More recently, Dean R. Koontz created a series of contemporary Frankenstein novels (which were also the basis for a failed TV pilot), and there have been illustrated versions of the story by everyone from Bernie Wrightson to Gris Grimly.

For many people, the name of Shelley's scientist and his Monster have become synonymous over the years (and there is an argument to be made that they are two representations of the same man).

Director Danny Boyle explored this duality between the creator and his creation in 2011 in the Royal National Theatre production of *Frankenstein*, in which Benedict Cumberbatch and Johnny Lee Miller alternated the roles on stage in award-winning performances.

Now this revised and updated edition of *The Mammoth Book of Frankenstein* collects together one poem and twenty-four electrifying tales of cursed creation that are guaranteed to spark the interest of any reader—classics from the pulp magazines by Robert Bloch and Manly Wade Wellman, modern masterpieces from Ramsey Campbell, Dennis Etchison, Karl Edward Wagner, Stephen Volk, David J. Schow and R. Chetwynd-Hayes, and original contributions by Graham Masterton, Basil Copper, John Brunner, Guy N. Smith, Kim Newman, Paul McAuley, Roberta Lannes, Michael Marshall Smith, Daniel Fox, Adrian Cole, Nancy Kilpatrick, Brian Mooney and Lisa Morton.

Also included are three short novels: *The Hound of Frankenstein* by Peter Tremayne, *The Dead End* by David Case and, as a special bonus, the full and unabridged text of Mary Shelley's original masterpiece, *Frankenstein; or, The Modern Prometheus*, while a new Foreword by Neil Gaiman discusses the enduring influence of Shelley's monstrous creation.

So, as an electrical storm rages overhead, the generators are charged up, and under the sheet a cold form awaits its miraculous rebirth. Now it's time to throw that switch and discover all that Man Was Never Meant to Know . . .

—STEPHEN JONES,
LONDON, ENGLAND

MARY W. SHELLEY

Frankenstein; or, The Modern Prometheus

❦

Mary Wollstonecraft Shelley (1797–1851) was born in London, the only child of novelist and political philosopher William Godwin and the early female emancipator Mary Wollstonecraft, who died ten days after the birth of her daughter. While still a teenager, Mary eloped to Europe with the English poet Percy Bysshe Shelley in 1814, finally marrying him in December 1816—the same year she wrote the original version of the novel which follows.

Although she never repeated the success of Frankenstein, *her later novels included* Valperga *(1823);* The Last Man *(1826), about the only survivor of a future plague which wipes out the world's population;* The Fortunes of Perkin Warbeck *(1830);* Lodore *(1835); and* Falkner *(1837). She also published* Rambles in Germany and Italy *in 1844, which was well received. Richard Garnett collected most of her short fiction in the posthumous collection* Tales and Stories *(1891), while another tale, "The Heir of Mondolfo," did not see print until 1877.*

In her introduction to the 1831 edition of Frankenstein, *Mary Shelley recalls how the story first came to her: "When I placed my head on my pillow I did not sleep, nor could I be said to think. My imagination, unbidden, possessed and guided me, gifting the successive images that arose in my mind with a vividness far beyond the usual bounds of reverie. I saw—with shut eyes, but acute mental vision—I saw the pale student of unhallowed arts kneeling beside the thing he had put together. I saw the hideous phantasm of a man stretched out, and then, on the working of some powerful engine, show signs of life, and stir with an uneasy, half vital motion. Frightful must it be; for supremely frightful would be the effect of any human endeavor to mock the stupendous mechanism of the Creator of the world . . ."*

After almost 190 years, the novel which follows still remains a classic of science fiction and horror . . .

PREFACE

The event on which this fiction is founded has been supposed, by Dr. Darwin, and some of the physiological writers of Germany, as not of impossible occurrence. I shall not be supposed as according the remotest degree of serious faith to such an imagination; yet, in assuming it as the basis of a work of fancy, I have not considered myself as merely weaving a series of supernatural terrors. The event on which the interest of the story depends is exempt from the disadvantages of a mere tale of spectres or enchantment. It was recommended by the novelty of the situations which it develops; and, however impossible as a physical fact, affords a point of view to the imagination for the delineating of human passions more comprehensive and commanding than any which the ordinary relations of existing events can yield.

I have thus endeavored to preserve the truth of the elementary principles of human nature, while I have not scrupled to innovate upon their combinations. *The Iliad*, the tragic poetry of Greece—Shakspeare, in the *Tempest* and *Midsummer Night's Dream*—and most especially Milton, in *Paradise Lost*, conform to this rule; and the most humble novelist, who seeks to confer or receive amusement from his labors, may, without presumption, apply to prose fiction a license, or rather a rule, from the adoption of which so many exquisite combinations of human feeling have resulted in the highest specimens of poetry.

The circumstance on which my story rests was suggested in casual conversation. It was commenced partly as a source of amusement, and partly as an expedient for exercising any untried resources of mind. Other motives were mingled with these as the work proceeded. I am by no means indifferent to the manner in which whatever moral tendencies exist in the sentiments or characters it contains shall affect the reader; yet my chief concern in this respect has been limited to the avoiding the enervating effects of the novels of the present day and to the exhibition of the amiableness of domestic affection, and the excellence of universal virtue. The opinions which naturally spring from the character and situation of the hero are by no means to be conceived as existing always in my own conviction; nor is any inference justly to be drawn from the following pages as prejudicing any philosophical doctrine of whatever kind.

It is a subject also of additional interest to the author that this story was begun in the majestic region where the scene is principally laid, and in society which cannot cease to be regretted. I passed the summer of 1816 in the environs of Geneva. The season was cold and rainy, and in the evenings we crowded around a blazing wood fire, and occasionally amused ourselves with some German stories of ghosts, which happened to fall into our hands. These tales excited in us a playful desire of imitation. Two other friends (a tale from the pen of one of whom would be far more acceptable to the public than anything I can ever hope to produce) and myself agreed to write each a story founded on some supernatural occurrence.

The weather, however, suddenly became serene; and my two friends left me on a journey among the Alps, and lost, in the magnificent scenes which they present, all memory of their ghostly visions. The following tale is the only one which has been completed.

MARLOW, September 1817.

LETTER I
To Mrs. Saville, England

PETERSBURGH, *Dec. 11th, 17—.*

You will rejoice to hear that no disaster has accompanied the commencement of an enterprise which you have regarded with such evil forebodings. I arrived here yesterday; and my first task is to assure my dear sister of my welfare, and increasing confidence in the success of my undertaking.

I am already far north of London; and as I walk in the streets of Petersburgh, I feel a cold northern breeze play upon my cheeks, which braces my nerves, and fills me with delight. Do you understand this feeling? This breeze, which has traveled from the regions towards which I am advancing, gives me a foretaste of those icy climes. Inspirited by this wind of promise, my day dreams become more fervent and vivid. I try in vain to be persuaded that the pole is the seat of frost and desolation; it ever presents itself to my imagination as the region of beauty and delight. There, Margaret, the sun is for ever visible; its broad disk just skirting the horizon, and diffusing a perpetual splendor. There—for with your leave, my sister, I will put some trust in preceding navigators—there snow and frost are banished; and, sailing over a calm sea, we may be wafted to a land surpassing in wonders and in beauty every region hitherto discovered on the habitable globe. Its productions and features may be without example, as the phenomena of the heavenly bodies undoubtedly are in those undiscovered solitudes. What may not be expected in a country of eternal light? I may there discover the wondrous power which attracts the needle; and may regulate a thousand celestial observations, that require only this voyage to render their seeming eccentricities consistent for ever. I shall satiate my ardent curiosity with the sight of a part of the world never before visited, and may tread a land never before imprinted by the foot of man. These are my enticements, and they are sufficient to conquer all fear of danger or death, and to induce me to commence this laborious voyage with the joy a child feels when he embarks in a little boat, with his holiday mates, on an expedition of discovery up his native river. But, supposing all these conjectures to be false, you cannot contest the inestimable benefit which I shall confer on all mankind to the last generation, by discovering a passage near the pole to those countries, to reach which at present so many months are requisite; or by ascertaining the secret of the magnet, which, if at all possible, can only be effected by an undertaking such as mine.

These reflections have dispelled the agitation with which I began my letter, and I feel my heart glow with an enthusiasm which elevates me to heaven; for nothing contributes so much to tranquilize the mind as a steady purpose—a point on which the soul may fix its intellectual eye. This expedition has been the favorite dream of my early years. I have read with ardor the accounts of the various voyages which have been made in the prospect of arriving at the North Pacific Ocean through the seas which surround the pole. You may remember that a history of all the voyages made for purposes of discovery composed the whole of our good uncle Thomas's library. My education was neglected, yet I was passionately fond of reading. These volumes were my study day and night, and my familiarity with them increased that regret which I had felt, as a child, on learning that my father's dying injunction had forbidden my uncle to allow me to embark in a seafaring life.

These visions faded when I perused, for the first time, those poets whose effusions entranced my soul, and lifted it to heaven. I also became a poet, and for one year lived in a Paradise of my own creation; I imagined that I also might obtain a niche in the temple where the names of Homer and Shakespeare are consecrated. You are well acquainted with my failure, and how heavily I bore the disappointment. But just at that time I inherited the fortune of my cousin, and my thoughts were turned into the channel of their earlier bent.

Six years have passed since I resolved on my present undertaking. I can, even now, remember the hour from which I dedicated myself to this great enterprise. I commenced by inuring my body to hardship. I accompanied the whale-fishers on several expeditions to the North Sea; I voluntarily endured cold, famine, thirst, and want of sleep; I often worked harder than the common sailors during the day, and devoted my nights to the study of mathematics, the theory of medicine, and those branches of physical science from which a naval adventurer might derive the greatest practical advantage. Twice I actually hired myself as an under-mate in a Greenland whaler, and acquitted myself to admiration. I must own I felt a little proud when my captain offered me the second dignity in the vessel, and entreated me to remain with the greatest earnestness; so valuable did he consider my services.

And now, dear Margaret, do I not deserve to accomplish some great purpose? My life might have been passed in ease and luxury; but I preferred glory to every enticement that wealth placed in my path. Oh, that some encouraging voice would answer in the affirmative! My courage and my resolution is firm; but my hopes fluctuate and my spirits are often depressed. I am about to proceed on a long and difficult voyage, the emergencies of which will demand all my fortitude: I am required not only to raise the spirits of others, but sometimes to sustain my own, when theirs are failing.

This is the most favorable period for traveling in Russia. They fly quickly over the snow in their sledges; the motion is pleasant, and, in my opinion, far more agreeable than that of an English stage-coach. The cold is not excessive, if you are wrapped in furs—a dress which I have already adopted; for there is a great difference between walking the deck and remaining seated motionless for hours, when no exercise prevents the blood from actually freezing in your veins. I have no ambition to lose my life on the post-road between St Petersburgh and Archangel.

I shall depart for the latter town in a fortnight or three weeks; and my intention is to hire a ship there, which can easily be done by paying the insurance for the owner, and to engage as many sailors as I think necessary among those who are accustomed to the whale-fishing. I do not intend to sail until the month of June; and when shall I return? Ah, dear sister, how can I answer this question? If I succeed, many many months, perhaps years, will pass before you and I may meet. If I fail, you will see me again soon, or never.

Farewell, my dear, excellent Margaret. Heaven shower down blessings on you, and save me, that I may again and again testify my gratitude for all your love and kindness.—Your affectionate brother,

R. WALTON.

LETTER II
To Mrs. Saville, England

ARCHANGEL, *March 28th, 17—.*

How slowly the time passes here, encompassed as I am by frost and snow! yet a second step is taken towards my enterprise. I have hired a vessel, and am occupied in collecting my sailors; those whom I have already engaged appear to be men on whom I can depend, and are certainly possessed of dauntless courage.

But I have one want which I have never yet been able to satisfy; and the absence of the object of which I now feel as a most severe evil. I have no friend, Margaret: when I am glowing with the enthusiasm of success, there will be none to participate my joy; if I am assailed by disappointment, no one will endeavor to sustain me in dejection. I shall commit my thoughts to paper, it is true; but that is a poor medium for the communication of feeling. I desire the company of a man who could sympathize with me; whose eyes would reply to mine. You may deem me romantic, my dear sister, but I bitterly feel the want of a friend. I have no one near me, gentle yet courageous, possessed of a cultivated as well as of a capacious mind, whose tastes are like my own, to approve or amend my plans. How would such a friend repair the faults of your poor brother! I am too ardent in execution, and too impatient of difficulties. But it is a still greater evil to me that I am self-educated: for the first fourteen years of my life I ran wild on a common, and read nothing but our uncle Thomas's books of voyages. At that age I became acquainted with the celebrated poets of our own country; but it was only when it had ceased to be in my power to derive its most important benefits from such a conviction that I perceived the necessity of becoming acquainted with more languages than that of my native country. Now I am twenty-eight, and am in reality more illiterate than many schoolboys of fifteen. It is true that I have thought more, and that my day dreams are more extended and magnificent; but they want (as the painters call it) *keeping*; and I greatly need a friend who would have sense enough not to despise me as romantic, and affection enough for me to endeavor to regulate my mind.

Well, these are useless complaints; I shall certainly find no friend on the wide ocean; nor even here in Archangel, among merchants and seamen. Yet some feelings, unallied to the dross of human nature, beat even in these rugged bosoms. My lieutenant, for instance, is a man of wonderful courage and enterprise; he is madly desirous of glory: or rather, to word my phrase more characteristically, of advancement in his profession. He is an Englishman, and in the midst of national and professional prejudices, unsoftened by cultivation, retains some of the noblest endowments of humanity. I first became acquainted with him on board a whale vessel: finding that he was unemployed in this city, I easily engaged him to assist in my enterprise.

The master is a person of an excellent disposition, and is remarkable in the ship for his gentleness and the mildness of his discipline. This circumstance, added to his well known integrity and dauntless courage, made me very desirous to engage him. A youth passed in solitude, my best years spent under your gentle and feminine fosterage, has so refined the groundwork of my character that I cannot overcome an intense distaste to the usual brutality exercised on board ship: I have never believed it to be necessary; and when I heard of a mariner equally noted for his kindliness of heart, and the respect and obedience paid to him by his crew, I felt myself peculiarly fortunate in being able to secure his services. I heard of him first in rather a romantic manner, from a lady who owes to him the happiness of her life. This, briefly, is his story. Some years ago he loved a young Russian lady of moderate fortune; and having amassed a considerable sum in prize-money, the father of the girl consented to the match. He saw his mistress once before the destined ceremony; but she was bathed in tears, and, throwing herself at his feet, entreated him to spare her, confessing at the same time that she loved another, but that he was poor, and that her father would never consent to the union. My generous friend reassured the suppliant, and on being informed of the name of her lover, instantly abandoned his pursuit. He had already bought a farm with his money, on which he had designed to pass the remainder of his life; but he bestowed the whole on his rival, together with the remains of his prize-money to purchase stock, and then himself solicited the young woman's father to consent to her marriage with her lover. But the old man decidedly refused, thinking himself bound in honor to my friend; who, when he found the father inexorable, quitted his country, nor returned until he heard that his former mistress was married according to her inclinations. "What a noble fellow!" you will exclaim. He is so; but then he is wholly uneducated: he is as silent as a Turk, and a kind of ignorant carelessness attends him, which, while it renders his conduct the more astonishing, detracts from the interest and sympathy which otherwise he would command.

Yet do not suppose, because I complain a little, or because I can conceive a consolation for my toils which I may never know, that I am wavering in my resolutions. Those are as fixed as fate; and my voyage is only now delayed until the weather shall permit my embarkation. The winter has been dreadfully severe; but the spring promises well, and it is considered as a remarkably early season; so that perhaps I may sail sooner than I expected. I shall do nothing rashly: you know me sufficiently to confide in my prudence and considerateness whenever the safety of others is committed to my care.

I cannot describe to you my sensations on the near prospect of my undertaking. It is impossible to communicate to you a conception of the trembling sensation, half pleasurable and half fearful, with which I am preparing to depart. I am going to unexplored regions, to "the land of mist and snow"; but I shall kill no albatross, therefore do not be alarmed for my safety, or if I should come back to you as worn and woeful as the "Ancient Mariner"? You will smile at my allusion; but I will disclose a secret. I have often attributed my attachment to, my passionate enthusiasm for, the dangerous mysteries of ocean, to that production of the most imaginative of modern poets. There is something at work in my soul which I do not understand. I am practically industrious—painstaking;—a workman to execute with perseverance and labor:—but besides this, there is a love for the marvelous, a belief in the marvelous, intertwined in all my projects, which hurries me out of the common pathways of men, even to the wild sea and unvisited regions I am about to explore.

But to return to dearer considerations. Shall I meet you again, after having traversed immense seas, and returned by the most southern cape of Africa or America? I dare not expect such success, yet I cannot bear to look on the reverse of the picture. Continue for the present to write to me by every opportunity: I may receive your letters on some occasions when I need them most to support my spirits. I love you very tenderly. Remember me with affection, should you never hear from me again.—Your affectionate brother,

ROBERT WALTON.

LETTER III
To Mrs. Saville, England

July 7th, 17—

My dear Sister,—I write a few lines in haste, to say that I am safe, and well advanced on my voyage. This letter will reach England by a merchantman now on its homeward voyage from Archangel; more fortunate than I, who may not see my native land, perhaps, for many years. I am, however, in good spirits: my men are bold, and apparently firm of purpose; nor do the floating sheets of ice that continually pass us, indicating the dangers of the region towards which we are advancing, appear to dismay them. We have already reached a very high latitude; but it is the height of summer, and although not so warm as in England, the southern gales, which blow us speedily towards those shores which I so ardently desire to attain, breathe a degree of renovating warmth which I had not expected.

No incidents have hitherto befallen us that would make a figure in a letter. One or two stiff gales, and the springing of a leak, are accidents which experienced navigators scarcely remember to record; and I shall be well content if nothing worse happen to us during our voyage.

Adieu, my dear Margaret. Be assured that for my own sake, as well as yours, I will not rashly encounter danger. I will be cool, persevering, and prudent.

But success *shall* crown my endeavors. Wherefore not? Thus far I have gone, tracing a secure way over the pathless seas: the very stars themselves being witnesses and testimonies of my triumph. Why not still proceed over the untamed yet obedient element? What can stop the determined heart and resolved will of man?

My swelling heart involuntarily pours itself out thus. But I must finish. Heaven bless my beloved sister!

R.W.

LETTER IV
To Mrs. Saville, England

August 5th, 17—.

So strange an accident has happened to us that I cannot forbear recording it, although it is very probable that you will see me before these papers can come into your possession.

Last Monday (July 31st), we were nearly surrounded by ice, which closed in the ship on all sides, scarcely leaving her the sea-room in which she floated. Our situation was somewhat dangerous, especially as we were compassed round by a very thick fog. We accordingly lay to, hoping that some change would take place in the atmosphere and weather.

About two o'clock the mist cleared away, and we beheld, stretched out in every direction, vast and irregular plains of ice, which seemed to have no end. Some of my comrades groaned, and my own mind began to grow watchful with anxious thoughts, when a strange sight suddenly attracted our attention, and diverted our solicitude from our own situation. We perceived a low carriage, fixed on a sledge and drawn by dogs, pass on towards the north, at the distance of half a mile: a being which had the shape of a man, but apparently of gigantic stature, sat in the sledge, and guided the dogs. We watched the rapid progress of the traveler with our telescopes, until he was lost among the distant inequalities of the ice.

This appearance excited our unqualified wonder. We were, as we believed, many hundred miles from any land; but this apparition seemed to denote that it was not, in reality, so distant as we had supposed. Shut in, however, by ice, it was impossible to follow his track, which we had observed with the greatest attention.

About two hours after this occurrence, we heard the ground sea; and before night the ice broke, and freed our ship. We, however, lay to until the morning, fearing to encounter in the dark those large loose masses which float about after the breaking up of the ice. I profited of this time to rest for a few hours.

In the morning, however, as soon as it was light, I went upon deck, and found all the sailors busy on one side of the vessel, apparently talking to some one in the sea. It was, in fact, a sledge, like that we had seen before, which had drifted towards us in the night, on a large fragment of ice. Only one dog remained alive; but there was a human being within it, whom the sailors were persuading to enter the vessel. He was not, as the other traveler seemed to be, a savage inhabitant of some undiscovered island, but an European. When I appeared on deck, the master said, "Here is our captain, and he will not allow you to perish on the open sea."

On perceiving me, the stranger addressed me in English, although with a foreign accent. "Before I come on board your vessel," said he, "will you have the kindness to inform me whither you are bound?"

You may conceive my astonishment on hearing such a question addressed to me from a man on the brink of destruction, and to whom I should have supposed that my vessel would have been a resource which he would not have exchanged for the most precious wealth the earth can afford. I replied, however, that we were on a voyage of discovery towards the northern pole.

Upon hearing this he appeared satisfied, and consented to come on board. Good God! Margaret, if you had seen the man who thus capitulated for his safety, your surprise would have been boundless. His limbs were nearly frozen, and his body dreadfully emaciated by fatigue and suffering. I never saw a man in so wretched a condition. We attempted to carry him into the cabin; but as soon as he had quitted the fresh air, he fainted. We accordingly brought him back to the deck, and restored him to animation by rubbing him with brandy, and forcing him to swallow a small quantity. As soon as he showed signs of life we wrapped him up in blankets, and placed him near the chimney of the kitchen stove. By slow degrees he recovered, and ate a little soup, which restored him wonderfully.

Two days passed in this manner before he was able to speak; and I often feared that his sufferings had deprived him of understanding. When he had in some measure recovered, I removed him to my own cabin, and attended on him as much as my duty would permit. I never saw a more interesting creature: his eyes have generally an expression of wildness, and even madness; but there are moments when, if any one performs an act of kindness towards him, or does him any the most trifling service, his whole countenance is lighted up, as it were, with a beam of benevolence and sweetness that I never saw equalled. But he is generally melancholy and despairing; and sometimes he gnashes his teeth, as if impatient of the weight of woes that oppresses him.

When my guest was a little recovered, I had great trouble to keep off the men, who wished to ask him a thousand questions; but I would not allow him to be tormented by their idle curiosity, in a state of body and mind whose restoration evidently depended upon entire repose. Once, however, the lieutenant asked, Why he had come so far upon the ice in so strange a vehicle?

His countenance instantly assumed an aspect of the deepest gloom; and he replied, "To seek one who fled from me."

"And did the man whom you pursued travel in the same fashion?"

"Yes."

"Then I fancy we have seen him; for the day before we picked you up, we saw some dogs drawing a sledge, with a man in it, across the ice."

This aroused the stranger's attention; and he asked a multitude of questions concerning the route which the dæmon, as he called him, had pursued. Soon after, when he was alone with me, he said,—"I have, doubtless, excited your curiosity, as well as that of these good people; but you are too considerate to make inquiries."

"Certainly; it would indeed be very impertinent and inhuman in me to trouble you with any inquisitiveness of mine."

"And yet you rescued me from a strange and perilous situation; you have benevolently restored me to life."

Soon after this he inquired if I thought that the breaking up of the ice had destroyed the other sledge? I replied that I could not answer with any degree of certainty; for the ice had not broken until near midnight, and the traveler might have arrived at a place of safety before that time; but of this I could not judge.

From this time a new spirit of life animated the decaying frame of the stranger. He manifested the greatest eagerness to be upon deck, to watch for the sledge which had before appeared; but I have persuaded him to remain in the cabin, for he is far too weak to sustain the rawness of the atmosphere. I have promised that some one should watch for him, and give him instant notice if any new object should appear in sight.

Such is my journal of what relates to this strange occurrence up to the present day. The stranger has gradually improved in health, but is very silent, and appears uneasy when any one except myself enters his cabin. Yet his manners are so conciliating and gentle that the sailors are all interested in him, although they have had very little communication with him. For my own part, I begin to love him as a brother; and his constant and deep grief fills me with sympathy and compassion. He must have been a noble creature in his better days, being even now in wreck so attractive and amiable.

I said in one of my letters, my dear Margaret, that I should find no friend on the wide ocean; yet I have found a man who, before his spirit had been broken by misery, I should have been happy to have possessed as the brother of my heart.

I shall continue my journal concerning the stranger at intervals, should I have any fresh incidents to record.

August 13th, 17—.

My affection for my guest increases every day. He excites at once my admiration and my pity to an astonishing degree. How can I see so noble a creature destroyed by misery, without feeling the most poignant grief? He is so gentle, yet so wise; his mind is so cultivated; and when he speaks, although his words are culled with the choicest art, yet they flow with rapidity and unparalleled eloquence.

He is now much recovered from his illness, and is continually on the deck, apparently watching for the sledge that preceded his own. Yet, although unhappy, he is not so utterly occupied by his own misery but that he interests himself deeply in the projects of others. He has frequently conversed with me on mine, which I have communicated to him without disguise. He entered attentively into all my arguments in favor of my eventual success, and into every minute detail of the measures I had taken to secure it. I was easily led by the sympathy which he evinced to use the language of my heart; to give utterance to the burning ardor of my soul; and to say, with all the fervor that warmed me, how gladly I would sacrifice my fortune, my existence, my every hope, to the furtherance of my enterprise. One man's life or death were but a small price to pay for the acquirement of the knowledge which I sought; for the dominion I should acquire and transmit over the elemental foes of our race. As I spoke, a dark gloom spread over my listener's countenance. At first I perceived that he tried to suppress his emotion; he placed his hands before his eyes; and my voice quivered and failed me, as I beheld tears trickle fast from between his fingers—a groan burst from his heaving breast. I paused;—at length he spoke, in broken accents:—"Unhappy man! Do you share my madness? Have you drank also of the intoxicating draught? Hear me—let me reveal my tale, and you will dash the cup from your lips!"

Such words, you may imagine, strongly excited my curiosity; but the paroxysm of grief that had seized the stranger overcame his weakened powers, and many hours of repose and tranquil conversation were necessary to restore his composure.

Having conquered the violence of his feelings, he appeared to despise himself for being the slave of passion; and quelling the dark tyranny of despair, he led me again to converse concerning myself personally. He asked me the history of my earlier years. The tale was quickly told: but it awakened various trains of reflection. I spoke of my desire of finding a friend—of my thirst for a more intimate sympathy with a fellow mind than had ever fallen to my lot; and expressed my conviction that a man could boast of little happiness, who did not enjoy this blessing.

"I agree with you," replied the stranger; "we are unfashioned creatures, but half made up, if one wiser, better, dearer than ourselves—such a friend ought to be—do not lend his aid to perfectionate our weak and faulty natures. I once had a friend, the most noble of human creatures, and am entitled, therefore, to judge respecting friendship. You have hope, and the world before you, and have no cause for despair. But I—I have lost everything, and cannot begin life anew."

As he said this, his countenance became expressive of a calm settled grief that touched me to the heart. But he was silent, and presently retired to his cabin.

Even broken in spirit as he is, no one can feel more deeply than he does the beauties of nature. The starry sky, the sea, and every sight afforded by these wonderful regions, seems still to have the power of elevating his soul from earth. Such a man has a double existence: he may suffer misery, and be overwhelmed by disappointments; yet, when he has retired into himself, he will be like a celestial spirit that has a halo around him, within whose circle no grief or folly ventures.

Will you smile at the enthusiasm I express concerning this divine wanderer? You would not if you saw him. You have been tutored and refined by books and retirement from the world, and you are, therefore, somewhat fastidious; but this only renders you the more fit to appreciate the extraordinary merits of this wonderful man. Sometimes I have endeavored to discover what quality it is which he possesses that elevates him so immeasurably above any other person I ever knew. I believe it to be an intuitive discernment; a quick but neverfailing power of judgement; a penetration into the causes of things, unequalled for clearness and precision; add to this a facility of expression, and a voice whose varied intonations are soul-subduing music.

August 19th, 17—.

Yesterday the stranger said to me, "You may easily perceive, Captain Walton, that I have suffered great and unparalleled misfortunes. I had determined, at one time, that the memory of these evils should die with me; but you have won me to alter my determination. You seek for

knowledge and wisdom, as I once did; and I ardently hope that the gratification of your wishes may not be a serpent to sting you, as mine has been.
I do not know that the relation of my disasters will be useful to you; yet,
when I reflect that you are pursuing the same course, exposing yourself
to the same dangers which have rendered me what I am, I imagine that
you may deduce an apt moral from my tale; one that may direct you if you
succeed in your undertaking, and console you in case of failure. Prepare
to hear of occurrences which are usually deemed marvelous. Were we
among the tamer scenes of nature, I might fear to encounter your unbe-
lief, perhaps your ridicule; but many things will appear possible in these
wild and mysterious regions which would provoke the laughter of those
unacquainted with the ever-varied powers of nature:—nor can I doubt
but that my tale conveys in its series internal evidence of the truth of the
events of which it is composed."

You may easily imagine that I was much gratified by the offered communication; yet I could not endure that he should renew his grief by a
recital of his misfortunes. I felt the greatest eagerness to hear the promised narrative, partly from curiosity, and partly from a strong desire to
ameliorate his fate, if it were in my power. I expressed these feelings in
my answer.

"I thank you," he replied, "for your sympathy, but it is useless; my
fate is nearly fulfilled. I wait but for one event, and then I shall repose in
peace. I understand your feeling," continued he, perceiving that I wished
to interrupt him; "but you are mistaken, my friend, if thus you will allow
me to name you; nothing can alter my destiny: listen to my history, and
you will perceive how irrevocably it is determined."

He then told me that he would commence his narrative the next day
when I should be at leisure. This promise drew from me the warmest
thanks. I have resolved every night, when I am not imperatively occupied
by my duties, to record, as nearly as possible in his own words, what he
has related during the day. If I should be engaged, I will at least make
notes. This manuscript will doubtless afford you the greatest pleasure;
but to me, who know him, and who hear it from his own lips, with what
interest and sympathy shall I read it in some future day! Even now, as
I commence my task, his fulltoned voice swells in my ears; his lustrous

eyes dwell on me with all their melancholy sweetness; I see his thin hand raised in animation, while the lineaments of his face are irradiated by the soul within. Strange and harrowing must be his story; frightful the storm which embraced the gallant vessel on its course, and wrecked it—thus!

I

I am by birth a Genevese; and my family is one of the most distinguished of that republic. My ancestors had been for many years counselors and syndics; and my father had filled several public situations with honor and reputation. He was respected by all who knew him for his integrity and indefatigable attention to public business. He passed his younger days perpetually occupied by the affairs of his country; a variety of circumstances had prevented his marrying early, nor was it until the decline of life that he became a husband and the father of a family.

As the circumstances of his marriage illustrate his character, I cannot refrain from relating them. One of his most intimate friends was a merchant, who, from a flourishing state, fell, through numerous mischances, into poverty. This man, whose name was Beaufort, was of a proud and unbending disposition, and could not bear to live in poverty and oblivion in the same country where he had formerly been distinguished for his rank and magnificence. Having paid his debts, therefore, in the most honorable manner, he retreated with his daughter to the town of Lucerne, where he lived unknown and in wretchedness. My father loved Beaufort with the truest friendship, and was deeply grieved by his retreat in these unfortunate circumstances. He bitterly deplored the false pride which led his friend to a conduct so little worthy of the affection that united them. He lost no time in endeavoring to seek him out, with the hope of persuading him to begin the world again through his credit and assistance.

Beaufort had taken effectual measures to conceal himself; and it was ten months before my father discovered his abode. Overjoyed at this discovery, he hastened to the house, which was situated in a mean street, near the Reuss. But when he entered, misery and despair alone welcomed him. Beaufort had saved but a very small sum of money from the wreck of his fortunes; but it was sufficient to provide him with sustenance for some months, and in the meantime he hoped to procure some respectable employment in a merchant's house. The interval was, consequently, spent in inaction; his grief only became more deep and rankling when he had leisure for reflection; and at length it took so fast hold of his mind that at the end of three months he lay on a bed of sickness, incapable of any exertion.

His daughter attended him with the greatest tenderness; but she saw with despair that their little fund was rapidly decreasing, and that there was no other prospect of support. But Caroline Beaufort possessed a mind of an uncommon mold; and her courage rose to support her in her adversity. She procured plain work; she plaited straw; and by various means contrived to earn a pittance scarcely sufficient to support life.

Several months passed in this manner. Her father grew worse; her time was more entirely occupied in attending him; her means of subsistence decreased; and in the tenth month her father died in her arms, leaving her an orphan and a beggar. This last blow overcame her; and she knelt by Beaufort's coffin, weeping bitterly, when my father entered the chamber. He came like a protecting spirit to the poor girl, who committed herself to his care; and after the interment of his friend, he conducted her to Geneva, and placed her under the protection of a relation. Two years after this event Caroline became his wife.

There was a considerable difference between the ages of my parents, but this circumstance seemed to unite them only closer in bonds of devoted affection. There was a sense of justice in my father's upright mind, which rendered it necessary that he should approve highly to love strongly. Perhaps during former years he had suffered from the late-discovered unworthiness of one beloved, and so was disposed to set a greater value on tried worth. There was a show of gratitude and worship in his attachment to my mother, differing wholly from the doting fondness of age, for it was inspired by reverence for her virtues, and a desire to be the means of, in some degree, recompensing her for the sorrows she had endured, but which gave inexpressible grace to his behavior to her. Everything was made to yield to her wishes and her convenience. He strove to shelter her, as a fair exotic is sheltered by the gardener, from every rougher wind, and to surround her with all that could tend to excite pleasurable emotion in her soft and benevolent mind. Her health, and even the tranquility of her hitherto constant spirit, had been shaken by what she had gone through. During the two years that had elapsed previous to their marriage my father had gradually relinquished all his public functions; and immediately after their union they sought the pleasant climate of Italy, and the change of scene and interest attendant on a tour through that land of wonders, as a restorative for her weakened frame.

From Italy they visited Germany and France. I, their eldest child, was born in Naples, and as an infant accompanied them in their rambles. I remained for several years their only child. Much as they were attached to each other, they seemed to draw inexhaustible stores of affection from a very mine of love to bestow them upon me. My mother's tender caresses, and my father's smile of benevolent pleasure while regarding me, are my first recollections. I was their plaything and their idol, and something better—their child, the innocent and helpless creature bestowed on them by Heaven, whom to bring up to good, and whose future lot it was in their hands to direct to happiness or misery, according as they fulfilled their duties towards me. With this deep consciousness of what they owed towards the being to which they had given life, added to the active spirit of tenderness that animated both, it may be imagined that while during every hour of my infant life I received a lesson of patience, of charity, and of self-control, I was so guided by a silken cord that all seemed but one train of enjoyment to me.

For a long time I was their only care. My mother had much desired to have a daughter, but I continued their single offspring. When I was about five years old, while making an excursion beyond the frontiers of Italy, they passed a week on the shores of the Lake of Como. Their benevolent disposition often made them enter the cottages of the poor. This, to my mother, was more than a duty; it was a necessity, a passion—remembering what she had suffered, and how she had been relieved—for her to act in her turn the guardian angel to the afflicted. During one of their walks a poor cot in the foldings of a vale attracted their notice as being singularly disconsolate, while the number of half-clothed children gathered about it spoke of penury in its worst shape. One day, when my father had gone by himself to Milan, my mother, accompanied by me, visited this abode.

She found a peasant and his wife, hard working, bent down by care and labor, distributing a scanty meal to five hungry babes. Among these there was one which attracted my mother far above all the rest. She appeared of a different stock. The four others were dark-eyed, hardy little vagrants; this child was thin, and very fair. Her hair was the brightest living gold, and, despite the poverty of her clothing, seemed to set a crown of distinction on her head. Her brow was clear and ample, her blue eyes cloudless, and her lips and the molding of her face so expressive of sensibility and sweetness, that none could behold her without looking on her as of a distinct species, a being heaven-sent, and bearing a celestial stamp in all her features.

The peasant woman, perceiving that my mother fixed eyes of wonder and admiration on this lovely girl, eagerly communicated her history. She was not her child, but the daughter of a Milanese nobleman. Her mother was a German, and had died on giving her birth. The infant had been placed with these good people to nurse: they were better off then. They had not been long married, and their eldest child was but just born. The father of their charge was one of those Italians nursed in the memory of the antique glory of Italy—one among the *schiavi ognor frementi*, who exerted himself to obtain the liberty of his country. He became the victim of its weakness. Whether he had died, or still lingered in the dungeons of Austria, was not known. His property was confiscated, his child became an orphan and a beggar. She continued with her foster parents, and bloomed in their rude abode, fairer than a garden rose among darkleaved brambles.

When my father returned from Milan, he found playing with me in the hall of our villa a child fairer than pictured cherub—a creature who seemed to shed radiance from her looks, and whose form and motions were lighter than the chamois of the hills. The apparition was soon explained. With his permission my mother prevailed on her rustic guardians to yield their charge to her. They were fond of the sweet orphan. Her presence had seemed a blessing to them; but it would be unfair to her to keep her in poverty and want, when Providence afforded her such powerful protection. They consulted their village priest, and the result was that Elizabeth Lavenza became the inmate of my parents' house—my more than sister—the beautiful and adored companion of all my occupations and my pleasures.

Every one loved Elizabeth. The passionate and almost reverential attachment with which all regarded her became, while I shared it, my pride and my delight. On the evening previous to her being brought to my home, my mother had said playfully—"I have a pretty present for my Victor—to-morrow he shall have it." And when, on the morrow, she presented Elizabeth to me as her promised gift, I, with childish seriousness, interpreted her words literally, and looked upon Elizabeth as mine—mine to protect, love, and cherish. All praises bestowed on her, I received as made to a possession of my own. We called each other familiarly by the name of cousin. No word, no expression could body forth the kind of relation in which she stood to me—my more than sister, since till death she was to be mine only.

II

We were brought up together; there was not quite a year difference in our ages. I need not say that we were strangers to any species of disunion or dispute. Harmony was the soul of our companionship, and the diversity and contrast that subsisted in our characters drew us nearer together. Elizabeth was of a calmer and more concentrated disposition; but, with all my ardor, I was capable of a more intense application, and was more deeply smitten with the thirst for knowledge. She busied herself with following the aerial creations of the poets; and in the majestic and wondrous scenes which surrounded our Swiss home—the sublime shapes of the mountains; the changes of the seasons; tempest and calm; the silence of winter, and the life and turbulence of our Alpine summers—she found ample scope for admiration and delight. While my companion contemplated with a serious and satisfied spirit the magnificent appearances of things, I delighted in investigating their causes. The world was to me a secret which I desired to divine. Curiosity, earnest research to learn the hidden laws of nature, gladness akin to rapture, as they were unfolded to me, are among the earliest sensations I can remember.

On the birth of a second son, my junior by seven years, my parents gave up entirely their wandering life, and fixed themselves in their native country. We possessed a house in Geneva, and a *campagne* on Belrive, the eastern shore of the lake, at the distance of rather more than a league from the city. We resided principally in the latter, and the lives of my parents were passed in considerable seclusion. It was my temper to avoid a crowd, and to attach myself fervently to a few. I was indifferent, therefore, to my schoolfellows in general; but I united myself in the bonds of the closest friendship to one among them. Henry Clerval was the son of a merchant of Geneva. He was a boy of singular talent and fancy. He loved enterprise, hardship, and even danger, for its own sake. He was deeply read in books of chivalry and romance. He composed heroic songs, and began to write many a tale of enchantment and knightly adventure. He tried to make us act plays, and to enter into masquerades, in which the characters were drawn from the heroes of Roncesvalles, of the Round Table of King Arthur, and the chivalrous train who shed their blood to redeem the holy sepulchre from the hands of the infidels.

No human being could have passed a happier childhood than myself. My parents were possessed by the very spirit of kindness and indulgence. We felt that they were not the tyrants to rule our lot according to their caprice, but the agents and creators of all the many delights which we enjoyed. When I mingled with other families, I distinctly discerned how peculiarly fortunate my lot was, and gratitude assisted the development of filial love.

My temper was sometimes violent, and my passions vehement; but by some law in my temperature they were turned, not towards childish pursuits, but to an eager desire to learn, and not to learn all things indiscriminately. I confess that neither the structure of languages, nor the code of governments, nor the politics of various states, possessed attractions for me. It was the secrets of heaven and earth that I desired to learn; and whether it was the outward substance of things, or the inner spirit of nature and the mysterious soul of man that occupied me, still my inquiries were directed to the metaphysical, or, in its highest sense, the physical secrets of the world.

Meanwhile Clerval occupied himself, so to speak, with the moral relations of things. The busy stage of life, the virtues of heroes, and the actions of men, were his theme; and his hope and his dream was to become one among those whose names are recorded in story, as the gallant and adventurous benefactors of our species. The saintly soul of Elizabeth shone like a shrine-dedicated lamp in our peaceful home. Her sympathy was ours; her smile, her soft voice, the sweet glance of her celestial eyes, were ever there to bless and animate us. She was the living spirit of love to soften and attract: I might have become sullen in my study, rough through the ardor of my nature, but that she was there to subdue me to a semblance of her own gentleness. And Clerval—could aught ill entrench on the noble spirit of Clerval?—yet he might not have been so perfectly humane, so thoughtful in his generosity—so full of kindness and tenderness amidst his passion for adventurous exploit, had she not unfolded to him the real loveliness of beneficence, and made the doing good the end and aim of his soaring ambition.

I feel exquisite pleasure in dwelling on the recollections of childhood, before misfortune had tainted my mind, and changed its bright visions of extensive usefulness into gloomy and narrow reflections upon self. Besides, in drawing the picture of my early days, I also record those events which led, by insensible steps, to my after tale of misery: for when I would account to myself for the birth of that passion, which afterwards ruled my destiny, I find it arise, like a mountain river, from ignoble and almost forgotten sources; but, swelling as it proceeded, it became the torrent which, in its course, has swept away all my hopes and joys.

Natural philosophy is the genius that has regulated my fate; I desire, therefore, in this narration, to state those facts which led to my predilection for that science. When I was thirteen years of age, we all went on a party of pleasure to the baths near Thonon: the inclemency of the weather obliged us to remain a day confined to the inn. In this house I chanced to find a volume of the works of Cornelius Agrippa. I opened it with apathy; the theory which he attempts to demonstrate, and the wonderful facts which he relates, soon changed this feeling into enthusiasm. A new light seemed to dawn upon my mind; and, bounding with joy, I communicated my discovery to my father. My father looked carelessly at the title page of my book, and said, "Ah! Cornelius Agrippa! My dear Victor, do not waste your time upon this; it is sad trash."

If, instead of this remark, my father had taken the pains to explain to me that the principles of Agrippa had been entirely exploded, and that a modern system of science had been introduced, which possessed much greater powers than the ancient, because the powers of the latter were chimerical, while those of the former were real and practical; under such circumstances, I should certainly have thrown Agrippa aside, and have contented my imagination, warmed as it was, by returning with greater ardor to my former studies. It is even possible that the train of my ideas would never have received the fatal impulse that led to my ruin. But the cursory glance my father had taken of my volume by no means assured me that he was acquainted with its contents; and I continued to read with the greatest avidity.

When I returned home, my first care was to procure the whole works of this author, and afterwards of Paracelsus and Albertus Magnus. I read and studied the wild fancies of these writers with delight; they appeared to me treasures known to few beside myself. I have described myself as always having been embued with a fervent longing to penetrate the secrets of nature. In spite of the intense labor and wonderful discoveries of modern philosophers, I always came from my studies discontented and unsatisfied. Sir Isaac Newton is said to have avowed that he felt like a child picking up shells beside the great and unexplored ocean of truth. Those of his successors in each branch of natural philosophy with whom I was acquainted appeared, even to my boy's apprehensions, as tyros engaged in the same pursuit.

The untaught peasant beheld the elements around him, and was acquainted with their practical uses. The most learned philosopher knew little more. He had partially unveiled the face of Nature, but her immortal lineaments were still a wonder and a mystery. He might dissect, anatomize, and give names; but, not to speak of a final cause, causes in their secondary and tertiary grades were utterly unknown to him. I had gazed upon the fortifications and impediments that seemed to keep human beings from entering the citadel of nature, and rashly and ignorantly I had repined.

But here were books, and here were men who had penetrated deeper and knew more. I took their word for all that they averred, and I became their disciple. It may appear strange that such should arise in the eighteenth century; but while I followed the routine of education in the schools of Geneva, I was, to a great degree, self taught with regard to my favorite studies. My father was not scientific, and I was left to struggle with a child's blindness, added to a student's thirst for knowledge. Under the guidance of my new preceptors, I entered with the greatest diligence into the search of the philosopher's stone and the elixir of life; but the latter soon obtained my undivided attention. Wealth was an inferior object; but what glory would attend the discovery, if I could banish disease from the human frame, and render man invulnerable to any but a violent death!

Nor were these my only visions. The raising of ghosts or devils was a promise liberally accorded by my favorite authors, the fulfillment of which I most eagerly sought; and if my incantations were always unsuccessful, I attributed the failure rather to my own inexperience and mistake than to a want of skill or fidelity in my instructors. And thus for a time I was occupied by exploded systems, mingling, like an unadept, a thousand contradictory theories, and floundering desperately in a very slough of multifarious knowledge, guided by an ardent imagination and childish reasoning, till an accident again changed the current of my ideas.

When I was about fifteen years old we had retired to our house near Belrive, when we witnessed a most violent and terrible thunderstorm. It advanced from behind the mountains of Jura; and the thunder burst at once with frightful loudness from various quarters of the heavens. I remained, while the storm lasted, watching its progress with curiosity and delight. As I stood at the door, on a sudden I beheld a stream of fire issue from an old and beautiful oak which stood about twenty yards from our house; and so soon as the dazzling light vanished the oak had disappeared, and nothing remained but a blasted stump. When we visited it the next morning, we found the tree shattered in a singular manner. It was not splintered by the shock, but entirely reduced to thin ribands of wood. I never beheld anything so utterly destroyed.

Before this I was not unacquainted with the more obvious laws of electricity. On this occasion a man of great research in natural philosophy was with us, and, excited by this catastrophe, he entered on the explanation of a theory which he had formed on the subject of electricity and galvanism, which was at once new and astonishing to me. All that he said threw greatly into the shade Cornelius Agrippa, Albertus Magnus, and Paracelsus, the lords of my imagination; but by some fatality the overthrow of these men disinclined me to pursue my accustomed studies. It seemed to me as if nothing would or could ever be known. All that had so long engaged my attention suddenly grew despicable. By one of those caprices of the mind, which we are perhaps most subject to in early youth, I at once gave up my former occupations; set down natural history and all its progeny as a deformed and abortive creation; and entertained the greatest disdain for a would-be science, which could never even step within the threshold of real knowledge. In this mood of mind I betook myself to the mathematics, and the branches of study appertaining to that science, as being built upon secure foundations, and so worthy of my consideration.

Thus strangely are our souls constructed, and by such slight ligaments are we bound to prosperity or ruin. When I look back, it seems to me as if this almost miraculous change of inclination and will was the immediate suggestion of the guardian angel of my life—the last effort made by the spirit of preservation to avert the storm that was even then hanging in the stars, and ready to envelope me. Her victory was announced by an unusual tranquility and gladness of soul, which followed the relinquishing of my ancient and latterly tormenting studies. It was thus that I was to be taught to associate evil with their prosecution, happiness with their disregard.

It was a strong effort of the spirit of good; but it was ineffectual. Destiny was too potent, and her immutable laws had decreed my utter and terrible destruction.

III

When I had attained the age of seventeen, my parents resolved that I should become a student at the university of Ingolstadt. I had hitherto attended the schools of Geneva; but my father thought it necessary, for the completion of my education, that I should be made acquainted with other customs than those of my native country. My departure was therefore fixed at an early date; but before the day resolved upon could arrive, the first misfortune of my life occurred—an omen, as it were, of my future misery.

Elizabeth had caught the scarlet fever; her illness was severe, and she was in the greatest danger. During her illness, many arguments had been urged to persuade my mother to refrain from attending upon her. She had, at first, yielded to our entreaties; but when she heard that the life of her favorite was menaced, she could no longer control her anxiety. She attended her sick bed—her watchful attentions triumphed over the malignity of the distemper—Elizabeth was saved, but the consequences of this imprudence were fatal to her preserver. On the third day my mother sickened; her fever was accompanied by the most alarming symptoms, and the looks of her medical attendants prognosticated the worst event. On her death-bed the fortitude and benignity of this best of women did not desert her. She joined the hands of Elizabeth and myself:—"My children," she said, "my firmest hopes of future happiness were placed on the prospect of your union. This expectation will now be the consolation of your father. Elizabeth, my love, you must supply my place to my younger children. Alas! I regret that I am taken from you; and, happy and beloved as I have been, is it not hard to quit you all? But these are not thoughts befitting me; I will endeavor to resign myself cheerfully to death, and will indulge a hope of meeting you in another world."

She died calmly; and her countenance expressed affection even in death. I need not describe the feelings of those whose dearest ties are rent by that most irreparable evil; the void that presents itself to the soul; and the despair that is exhibited on the countenance. It is so long before the mind can persuade itself that she, whom we saw every day, and whose very existence appeared a part of our own, can have departed for ever—that the brightness of a beloved eye can have been extinguished, and the sound of a voice so familiar, and dear to the ear, can be hushed, never more to be heard. These are the reflections of the first days; but when the lapse of time proves the reality of the evil, then the actual bitterness of grief commences. Yet from whom has not that rude hand rent away some dear connection? And why should I describe a sorrow which all have felt, and must feel? The time at length arrives, when grief is rather an indulgence than a necessity; and the smile that plays upon the lips, although it may be deemed a sacrilege, is not banished. My mother was dead, but we had still duties which we ought to perform; we must continue our course with the rest, and learn to think ourselves fortunate, whilst one remains whom the spoiler has not seized.

My departure for Ingolstadt, which had been deferred by these events, was now again determined upon. I obtained from my father a respite of some weeks. It appeared to me sacrilege so soon to leave the repose, akin to death, of the house of mourning, and to rush into the thick of life. I was new to sorrow, but it did not the less alarm me. I was unwilling to quit the sight of those that remained to me; and, above all, I desired to see my sweet Elizabeth in some degree consoled.

She indeed veiled her grief, and strove to act the comforter to us all. She looked steadily on life, and assumed its duties with courage and zeal. She devoted herself to those whom she had been taught to call her uncle and cousins. Never was she so enchanting as at this time when she recalled the sunshine of her smiles and spent them upon us. She forgot even her own regret in her endeavors to make us forget.

The day of my departure at length arrived. Clerval spent the last evening with us. He had endeavored to persuade his father to permit him to accompany me, and to become my fellow student; but in vain. His father was a narrow-minded trader, and saw idleness and ruin in the aspirations and ambition of his son. Henry deeply felt the misfortune of being debarred from a liberal education. He said little; but when he spoke, I read in his kindling eye and in his animated glance a restrained but firm resolve not to be chained to the miserable details of commerce.

We sat late. We could not tear ourselves away from each other, nor persuade ourselves to say the word "Farewell!" It was said; and we retired under the pretense of seeking repose, each fancying that the other was deceived: but when at morning's dawn I descended to the carriage which was to convey me away, they were all there—my father again to bless me, Clerval to press my hand once more, my Elizabeth to renew her entreaties that I would write often, and to bestow the last feminine attentions on her playmate and friend.

I threw myself into the chaise that was to convey me away, and indulged in the most melancholy reflections. I, who had ever been surrounded by amiable companions, continually engaged in endeavoring to bestow mutual pleasure, I was now alone. In the university, whither I was going, I must form my own friends, and be my own protector. My life had hitherto been remarkably secluded and domestic; and this had given me invincible repugnance to new countenances. I loved my brothers, Elizabeth, and Clerval; these were "old familiar faces"; but I believed myself totally unfitted for the company of strangers. Such were my reflections as I commenced my journey; but as I proceeded my spirits and hopes rose. I ardently desired the acquisition of knowledge. I had often, when at home, thought it hard to remain during my youth cooped up in one place, and had longed to enter the world, and take my station among other human beings. Now my desires were complied with, and it would, indeed, have been folly to repent.

I had sufficient leisure for these and many other reflections during my journey to Ingolstadt, which was long and fatiguing. At length the high white steeple of the town met my eyes. I alighted, and was conducted to my solitary apartment, to spend the evening as I pleased.

The next morning I delivered my letters of introduction and paid a visit to some of the principal professors. Chance—or rather the evil influence, the Angel of Destruction, which asserted omnipotent sway over me from the moment I turned my reluctant steps from my father's door—led me first to M. Krempe, professor of natural philosophy. He was an uncouth man, but deeply embued in the secrets of his science. He asked me several questions concerning my progress in the different branches of science appertaining to natural philosophy. I replied carelessly; and, partly in contempt, mentioned the names of my alchymists as the principal authors I had studied. The professor stared: "Have you," he said, "really spent your time in studying such nonsense?"

I replied in the affirmative. "Every minute," continued M. Krempe with warmth, "every instant that you have wasted on those books is utterly and entirely lost. You have burdened your memory with exploded systems and useless names. Good God! in what desert land have you lived, where no one was kind enough to inform you that these fancies, which you have so greedily imbibed, are a thousand years old, and as musty as they are ancient? I little expected, in this enlightened and scientific age, to find a disciple of Albertus Magnus and Paracelsus. My dear sir, you must begin your studies entirely anew."

So saying, he stepped aside, and wrote down a list of several books treating of natural philosophy, which he desired me to procure; and dismissed me, after mentioning that in the beginning of the following week he intended to commence a course of lectures upon natural philosophy in its general relations, and that M. Waldman, fellow-professor, would lecture upon chemistry the alternate days that he omitted.

I returned home, not disappointed, for I have said that I had long considered those authors useless whom the professor reprobated; but I returned, not at all the more inclined to recur to these studies in any shape. M. Krempe was a little squat man, with a gruff voice and a repulsive countenance; the teacher, therefore, did not prepossess me in favor of his pursuits. In rather a too philosophical and connected a strain, perhaps, I have given an account of the conclusions I had come to concerning them in my early years. As a child, I had not been content with the results promised by the modern professors of natural science. With a confusion of ideas only to be accounted for by my extreme youth, and my want of a guide on such matters, I had retrod the steps of knowledge along the paths of time, and exchanged the discoveries of recent inquirers for the dreams of forgotten alchymists. Besides, I had a contempt for the uses of modern natural philosophy. It was very different when the masters of the science sought immortality and power; such views, although futile, were grand: but now the scene was changed. The ambition of the inquirer seemed to limit itself to the annihilation of those visions on which my interest in science was chiefly founded. I was required to exchange chimeras of boundless grandeur for realities of little worth.

Such were my reflections during the first two or three days of my residence at Ingolstadt, which were chiefly spent in becoming acquainted with the localities, and the principal residents in my new abode. But as the ensuing week commenced, I thought of the information which M. Krempe had given me concerning the lectures. And although I could not consent to go and hear that little conceited fellow deliver sentences out of a pulpit, I recollected what he had said of M. Waldman, whom I had never seen, as he had hitherto been out of town.

Partly from curiosity, and partly from idleness, I went into the lecturing room, which M. Waldman entered shortly after. This professor was very unlike his colleague. He appeared about fifty years of age, but with an aspect expressive of the greatest benevolence; a few grey hairs covered his temples, but those at the back of his head were nearly black. His person was short, but remarkably erect; and his voice the sweetest I had ever heard. He began his lecture by a recapitulation of the history of chemistry, and the various improvements made by different men of learning, pronouncing with fervor the names of the most distinguished discoverers. He then took a cursory view of the present state of the science, and explained many of its elementary terms. After having made a few preparatory experiments, he concluded with a panegyric upon modern chemistry, the terms of which I shall never forget:—

"The ancient teachers of this science," said he, "promised impossibilities, and performed nothing. The modern masters promise very little; they know that metals cannot be transmuted, and that the elixir of life is a chimera. But these philosophers, whose hands seem only made to dabble in dirt, and their eyes to pore over the microscope or crucible, have indeed performed miracles. They penetrate into the recesses of nature, and show how she works in her hiding places. They ascend into the heavens: they have discovered how the blood circulates, and the nature of the air we breathe. They have acquired new and almost unlimited powers; they can command the thunders of heaven, mimic the earthquake, and even mock the invisible world with its own shadows."

Such were the professor's words—rather let me say such the words of fate, enounced to destroy me. As he went on, I felt as if my soul were grappling with a palpable enemy; one by one the various keys were touched which formed the mechanism of my being: chord after chord was sounded, and soon my mind was filled with one thought, one conception, one purpose. So much has been done, exclaimed the soul of Frankenstein—more, far more, will I achieve: treading in the steps already marked, I will pioneer a new way, explore unknown powers, and unfold to the world the deepest mysteries of creation.

I closed not my eyes that night. My internal being was in a state of insurrection and turmoil; I felt that order would thence arise, but I had no power to produce it. By degrees, after the morning's dawn, sleep came. I awoke, and my yesternight's thoughts were as a dream. There only remained a resolution to return to my ancient studies, and to devote myself to a science for which I believed myself to possess a natural talent. On the same day, I paid M. Waldman a visit. His manners in private were even more mild and attractive than in public; for there was a certain dignity in his mien during his lecture, which in his own house was replaced by the greatest affability and kindness. I gave him pretty nearly the same account of my former pursuits as I had given to his fellow-professor. He heard with attention the little narration concerning my studies, and smiled at the names of Cornelius Agrippa and Paracelsus, but without the contempt that M. Krempe had exhibited. He said, that "these were men to whose indefatigable zeal modern philosophers were indebted for most of the foundations of their knowledge. They had left to us, as an easier task, to give new names, and arrange in connected classifications, the facts which they in a great degree had been the instruments of bringing to light. The labors of men of genius, however erroneously directed, scarcely ever fail in ultimately turning to the solid advantage of mankind." I listened to his statement, which was delivered without any presumption or affectation; and then added, that his lecture had removed my prejudices against modern chemists; I expressed myself in measured terms, with the modesty and deference due from a youth to his instructor, without letting escape (inexperience in life would have made me ashamed) any of the enthusiasm which stimulated my intended labors. I requested his advice concerning the books I ought to procure.

"I am happy," said M. Waldman, "to have gained a disciple; and if your application equals your ability, I have no doubt of your success. Chemistry is that branch of natural philosophy in which the greatest improvements have been and may be made: it is on that account that I have made it my peculiar study; but at the same time I have not neglected the other branches of science. A man would make but a very sorry chemist if he attended to that department of human knowledge alone. If your wish is to become really a man of science, and not merely a petty experimentalist, I should advise you to apply to every branch of natural philosophy, including mathematics."

He then took me into his laboratory, and explained to me the uses of his various machines; instructing me as to what I ought to procure, and promising me the use of his own when I should have advanced far enough in the science not to derange their mechanism. He also gave me the list of books which I had requested; and I took my leave.

Thus ended a day memorable to me: it decided my future destiny.

IV

From this day natural philosophy, and particularly chemistry, in the most comprehensive sense of the term, became nearly my sole occupation. I read with ardor those works, so full of genius and discrimination, which modern inquirers have written on these subjects. I attended the lectures, and cultivated the acquaintance, of the men of science of the university; and I found even in M. Krempe a great deal of sound sense and real information, combined, it is true, with a repulsive physiognomy and manners, but not on that account the less valuable. In M. Waldman I found a true friend. His gentleness was never tinged by dogmatism; and his instructions were given with an air of frankness and good nature that banished every idea of pedantry. In a thousand ways he smoothed for me the path of knowledge, and made the most abstruse inquiries clear and facile to my apprehension. My application was at first fluctuating and uncertain; it gained strength as I proceeded, and soon became so ardent and eager that the stars often disappeared in the light of morning whilst I was yet engaged in my laboratory.

As I applied so closely, it may be easily conceived that my progress was rapid. My ardor was indeed the astonishment of the students, and my proficiency that of the masters. Professor Krempe often asked me, with a sly smile, how Cornelius Agrippa went on? whilst M. Waldman expressed the most heartfelt exultation in my progress. Two years passed in this manner, during which I paid no visit to Geneva, but was engaged, heart and soul, in the pursuit of some discoveries, which I hoped to make. None but those who have experienced them can conceive of the enticements of science. In other studies you go as far as others have gone before you, and there is nothing more to know; but in a scientific pursuit there is continual food for discovery and wonder. A mind of moderate capacity, which closely pursues one study, must infallibly arrive at great proficiency in that study; and I, who continually sought the attainment of one object of pursuit, and was solely wrapt up in this, improved so rapidly that, at the end of two years, I made some discoveries in the improvement of some chemical instruments which procured me great esteem and admiration at the university. When I had arrived at this point, and had become as well acquainted with the theory and practice of natural philoosphy as depended on the lessons of any of the professors at Ingolstadt, my residence there being no longer conducive to my improvement, I thought of returning to my friends and my native town, when an incident happened that protracted my stay.

One of the phenomena which had peculiarly attracted my attention was the structure of the human frame, and, indeed, any animal endued with life. Whence, I often asked myself, did the principle of life proceed? It was a bold question, and one which has ever been considered as a mystery; yet with how many things are we upon the brink of becoming acquainted, if cowardice or carelessness did not restrain our inquiries. I revolved these circumstances in my mind, and determined thenceforth to apply myself more particularly to those branches of natural philosophy which relate to physiology. Unless I had been animated by an almost supernatural enthusiasm, my application to this study would have been irksome, and almost intolerable. To examine the causes of life, we must first have recourse to death. I became acquainted with the science of anatomy: but this was not sufficient; I must also observe the natural decay and corruption of the human body. In my education my father had taken the greatest precautions that my mind should be impressed with no supernatural horrors. I do not ever remember to have trembled at a tale of superstition, or to have feared the apparition of a spirit. Darkness had no effect upon my fancy; and a churchyard was to me merely the receptacle of bodies deprived of life, which, from being the seat of beauty and strength, had become food for the worm. Now I was led to examine the cause and progress of this decay, and forced to spend days and nights in vaults and charnel-houses. My attention was fixed upon every object the most insupportable to the delicacy of the human feelings. I saw how the fine form of man was degraded and wasted; I beheld the corruption of death succeed to the blooming cheek of life; I saw how the worm inherited the wonders of the eye and brain. I paused, examining and analyzing all the minutiæ of causation, as exemplified in the change from life to death, and death to life, until from the midst of this darkness a sudden light broke in upon me—a light so brilliant and wondrous, yet so simple, that while I became dizzy with the immensity of the prospect which it illustrated, I was surprised, that among so many men of genius who had directed their inquiries towards the same science, that I alone should be reserved to discover so astonishing a secret.

Remember, I am not recording the vision of a madman. The sun does not more certainly shine in the heavens, than that which I now affirm is true. Some miracle might have produced it, yet the stages of the discovery were distinct and probable. After days and nights of incredible labor and fatigue, I succeeded in discovering the cause of generation and life; nay, more, I became myself capable of bestowing animation upon lifeless matter.

The astonishment which I had at first experienced on this discovery soon gave place to delight and rapture. After so much time spent in painful labor, to arrive at once at the summit of my desires was the most gratifying consummation of my toils. But this discovery was so great and overwhelming that all the steps by which I had been progressively led to it were obliterated, and I beheld only the result. What had been the study and desire of the wisest men since the creation of the world was now within my grasp. Not that, like a magic scene, it all opened upon me at once: the information I had obtained was of a nature rather to direct my endeavors so soon as I should point them towards the object of my search, than to exhibit that object already accomplished. I was like the Arabian who had been buried with the dead, and found a passage to life, aided only by one glimmering, and seemingly ineffectual, light.

I see by your eagerness, and the wonder and hope which your eyes express, my friend, that you expect to be informed of the secret with which I am acquainted; that cannot be: listen patiently until the end of my story, and you will easily perceive why I am reserved upon that subject. I will not lead you on, unguarded and ardent as I then was, to your destruction and infallible misery. Learn from me, if not by my precepts, at least by my example, how dangerous is the acquirement of knowledge, and how much happier that man is who believes his native town to be the world, than he who aspires to become greater than his nature will allow.

When I found so astonishing a power placed within my hands, I hesitated a long time concerning the manner in which I should employ it. Although I possessed the capacity of bestowing animation, yet to prepare a frame for the reception of it, with all its intricacies of fibers, muscles, and veins, still remained a work of inconceivable difficulty and labor. I doubted at first whether I should attempt the creation of a being like myself, or one of simpler organization; but my imagination was too much exalted by my first success to permit me to doubt of my ability to give life to an animal as complex and wonderful as man. The materials at present within my command hardly appeared adequate to so arduous an undertaking; but I doubted not that I should ultimately succeed. I prepared myself for a multitude of reverses; my operations might be incessantly baffled, and at last my work be imperfect: yet, when I considered the improvement which every day takes place in science and mechanics, I was encouraged to hope my present attempts would at least lay the foundations of future success. Nor could I consider the magnitude and complexity of my plan as any argument of its impracticability. It was with these feelings that I began the creation of a human being. As the minuteness of the parts formed a great hinderance to my speed, I resolved, contrary to my first intention, to make the being of a gigantic stature; that is to say, about eight feet in height, and proportionably large. After having formed this determination, and having spent some months in successfully collecting and arranging my materials, I began.

No one can conceive the variety of feelings which bore me onwards, like a hurricane, in the first enthusiasm of success. Life and death appeared to me ideal bounds, which I should first break through, and pour a torrent of light into our dark world. A new species would bless me as its creator and source; many happy and excellent natures would owe their being to me. No father could claim the gratitude of his child so completely as I should deserve theirs. Pursuing these reflections, I thought, that if I could bestow animation upon lifeless matter, I might in process of time (although I now found it impossible) renew life where death had apparently devoted the body to corruption.

These thoughts supported my spirits, while I pursued my undertaking with unremitting ardor. My cheek had grown pale with study, and my person had become emaciated with confinement. Sometimes, on the very brink of certainty, I failed; yet still I clung to the hope which the next day or the next hour might realize. One secret which I alone possessed was the hope to which I had dedicated myself; and the moon gazed on my midnight labors, while, with unrelaxed and breathless eagerness, I pursued nature to her hiding-places. Who shall conceive the horrors of my secret toil, as I dabbled among the unhallowed damps of the grave, or tortured the living animal to animate the lifeless clay? My limbs now tremble and my eyes swim with the remembrance; but then a resistless, and almost frantic, impulse urged me forward; I seemed to have lost all soul or sensation but for this one pursuit. It was indeed but a passing trance that only made me feel with renewed acuteness so soon as, the unnatural stimulus ceasing to operate, I had returned to my old habits. I collected bones from charnel-houses; and disturbed, with profane fingers, the tremendous secrets of the human frame. In a solitary chamber, or rather cell, at the top of the house, and separated from all the other apartments by a gallery and staircase, I kept my workshop of filthy creation: my eye-balls were starting from their sockets in attending to the details of my employment. The dissecting room and the slaughter-house furnished many of my materials; and often did my human nature turn with loathing from my occupation, whilst, still urged on by an eagerness which perpetually increased, I brought my work near to a conclusion.

The summer months passed while I was thus engaged, heart and soul, in one pursuit. It was a most beautiful season; never did the fields bestow a more plentiful harvest, or the vines yield a more luxuriant vintage: but my eyes were insensible to the charms of nature. And the same feelings which made me neglect the scenes around me caused me also to forget those friends who were so many miles absent, and whom I had not seen for so long a time. I knew my silence disquieted them; and I well remembered the words of my father: "I know that while you are pleased with yourself, you will think of us with affection, and we shall hear regularly from you.

38

You must pardon me if I regard any interruption in your correspondence as a proof that your other duties are equally neglected."

I knew well, therefore, what would be my father's feelings; but I could not tear my thoughts from my employment, loathsome in itself, but which had taken an irresistible hold of my imagination. I wished, as it were, to procrastinate all that related to my feelings of affection until the great object, which swallowed up every habit of my nature, should be completed.

I then thought that my father would be unjust if he ascribed my neglect to vice, or faultiness on my part; but I am now convinced that he was justified in conceiving that I should not be altogether free from blame. A human being in perfection ought always to preserve a calm and peaceful mind, and never to allow passion or a transitory desire to disturb his tranquility. I do not think that the pursuit of knowledge is an exception to this rule. If the study to which you apply yourself has a tendency to weaken your affections, and to destroy your taste for those simple pleasures in which no alloy can possibly mix, then that study is certainly unlawful, that is to say, not befitting the human mind. If this rule were always observed; if no man allowed any pursuit whatsoever to interfere with the tranquility of his domestic affections, Greece had not been enslaved; Cæsar would have spared his country; America would have been discovered more gradually; and the empires of Mexico and Peru had not been destroyed.

But I forget that I am moralizing in the most interesting part of my tale; and your looks remind me to proceed.

My father made no reproach in his letters, and only took notice of my silence by inquiring into my occupations more particularly than before. Winter, spring, and summer passed away during my labors; but I did not watch the blossom or the expanding leaves—sights which before always yielded me supreme delight—so deeply was I engrossed in my occupation. The leaves of that year had withered before my work drew near to a close; and now every day showed me more plainly how well I had succeeded. But my enthusiasm was checked by my anxiety, and I appeared rather like one doomed by slavery to toil in the mines, or any other unwholesome trade, than an artist occupied by his favorite employment. Every night I was oppressed by a slow fever, and I became nervous to a most painful degree; the fall of a leaf startled me, and I shunned my fellow-creatures as if I had been guilty of a crime. Sometimes I grew alarmed at the wreck I perceived that I had become; the energy of my purpose alone sustained me: my labors would soon end, and I believed that exercise and amusement would then drive away incipient disease; and I promised myself both of these when my creation should be complete.

V

It was on a dreary night of November that I beheld the accomplishment of my toils. With an anxiety that almost amounted to agony, I collected the instruments of life around me, that I might infuse a spark of being into the lifeless thing that lay at my feet. It was already one in the morning; the rain pattered dismally against the panes, and my candle was nearly burnt out, when, by the glimmer of the half-extinguished light, I saw the dull yellow eye of the creature open; it breathed hard, and a convulsive motion agitated its limbs.

How can I describe my emotions at this catastrophe, or how delineate the wretch whom with such infinite pains and care I had endeavored to form? His limbs were in proportion, and I had selected his features as beautiful. Beautiful!—Great God! His yellow skin scarcely covered the work of muscles and arteries beneath; his hair was of a lustrous black, and flowing; his teeth of a pearly whiteness; but these luxuriances only formed a more horrid contrast with his watery eyes, that seemed almost of the same color as the dun white sockets in which they were set, his shrivelled complexion and straight black lips.

The different accidents of life are not so changeable as the feelings of human nature. I had worked hard for nearly two years, for the sole purpose of infusing life into an inanimate body. For this I had deprived myself of rest and health. I had desired it with an ardor that far exceeded moderation; but now that I had finished, the beauty of the dream vanished, and breathless horror and disgust filled my heart. Unable to endure the aspect of the being I had created, I rushed out of the room, and continued a long time traversing my bedchamber, unable to compose my mind to sleep. At length lassitude succeeded to the tumult I had before endured;

and I threw myself on the bed in my clothes, endeavoring to seek a few moments of forgetfulness. But it was in vain: I slept, indeed, but I was disturbed by the wildest dreams. I thought I saw Elizabeth, in the bloom of health, walking in the streets of Ingolstadt. Delighted and surprised, I embraced her; but as I imprinted the first kiss on her lips, they became livid with the hue of death; her features appeared to change, and I thought that I held the corpse of my dead mother in my arms; a shroud enveloped her form, and I saw the grave worms crawling in the folds of the flannel. I started from my sleep with horror; a cold dew covered my forehead, my teeth chattered, and every limb became convulsed: when, by the dim and yellow light of the moon, as it forced its way through the window shutters, I beheld the wretch—the miserable monster whom I had created. He held up the curtain of the bed; and his eyes, if eyes they may be called, were fixed on me. His jaws opened, and he muttered some inarticulate sounds, while a grin wrinkled his cheeks. He might have spoken, but I did not hear; one hand was stretched out, seemingly to detain me, but I escaped, and rushed down stairs. I took refuge in the courtyard belonging to the house which I inhabited; where I remained during the rest of the night, walking up and down in the greatest agitation, listening attentively, catching and fearing each sound as if it were to announce the approach of the demoniacal corpse to which I had so miserably given life.

Oh! no mortal could support the horror of that countenance. A mummy again endued with animation could not be so hideous as that wretch. I had gazed on him while unfinished; he was ugly then; but when those muscles and joints were rendered capable of motion, it became a thing such as even Dante could not have conceived.

I passed the night wretchedly. Sometimes my pulse beat so quickly and hardly that I felt the palpitation of every artery; at others, I nearly sank to the ground through languor and extreme weakness. Mingled with this horror, I felt the bitterness of disappointment; dreams that had been my food and pleasant rest for so long a space were now become a hell to me; and the change was so rapid, the overthrow so complete!

Morning, dismal and wet, at length dawned, and discovered to my sleepless and aching eyes the church of Ingolstadt, its white steeple and clock, which indicated the sixth hour. The porter opened the gates of the court, which had that night been my asylum, and I issued into the streets, pacing them with quick steps, as if I sought to avoid the wretch whom I feared every turning of the street would present to my view. I did not dare return to the apartment which I inhabited, but felt impelled to hurry on, although drenched by the rain which poured from a black and comfortless sky.

I continued walking in this manner for some time, endeavoring, by bodily exercise, to ease the load that weighed upon my mind. I traversed the streets, without any clear conception of where I was, or what I was doing. My heart palpitated in the sickness of fear; and I hurried on with irregular steps, not daring to look about me:—

> Like one who, on a lonely road,
> Doth walk in fear and dread,
> And, having once turned round, walks on,
> And turns no more his head;
> Because he knows a frightful fiend
> Doth close behind him tread.*

Continuing thus, I came at length opposite to the inn at which the various diligences and carriages usually stopped. Here I paused, I knew not why; but I remained some minutes with my eyes fixed on a coach that was coming towards me from the other end of the street. As it drew nearer, I observed that it was the Swiss diligence: it stopped just where I was standing, and, on the door being opened, I perceived Henry Clerval, who, on seeing me, instantly sprung out. "My dear Frankenstein," exclaimed he, "how glad I am to see you! how fortunate that you should be here at the very moment of my alighting!"

Nothing could equal my delight on seeing Clerval; his presence brought back to my thoughts my father, Elizabeth, and all those scenes of home so dear to my recollection. I grasped his hand, and in a moment forgot my horror and misfortune; I felt suddenly, and for the first time during many months, calm and serene joy. I welcomed my friend, therefore, in the most

---

* Coleridge's *The Rime of the Ancient Mariner.*

cordial manner, and we walked towards my college. Clerval continued talking for some time about our mutual friends, and his own good fortune in being permitted to come to Ingolstadt. "You may easily believe," said he, "how great was the difficulty to persuade my father that all necessary knowledge was not comprised in the noble art of bookkeeping; and, indeed, I believe I left him incredulous to the last, for his constant answer to my unwearied entreaties was the same as that of the Dutch schoolmaster in the *Vicar of Wakefield*. 'I have ten thousand florins a year without Greek, I eat heartily without Greek.' But his affection for me at length overcame his dislike of learning, and he has permitted me to undertake a voyage of discovery to the land of knowledge."

"It gives me the greatest delight to see you; but tell me how you left my father, brothers, and Elizabeth."

"Very well, and very happy, only a little uneasy that they hear from you so seldom. By the by, I mean to lecture you a little upon their account myself.—But, my dear Frankenstein," continued he, stopping short, and gazing full in my face, "I did not before remark how very ill you appear; so thin and pale; you look as if you had been watching for several nights."

"You have guessed right; I have lately been so deeply engaged in one occupation that I have not allowed myself sufficient rest, as you see: but I hope, I sincerely hope, that all these employments are now at an end, and that I am at length free."

I trembled excessively; I could not endure to think of, and far less to allude to, the occurrences of the preceding night. I walked with a quick pace, and we soon arrived at my college. I then reflected, and the thought made me shiver, that the creature whom I had left in my apartment might still be there, alive, and walking about. I dreaded to behold this monster; but I feared still more that Henry should see him. Entreating him, therefore, to remain a few minutes at the bottom of the stairs, I darted up towards my own room. My hand was already on the lock of the door before I recollected myself. I then paused; and a cold shivering came over me. I threw the door forcibly open, as children are accustomed to do when they expect a spectre to stand in waiting for them on the other side; but nothing appeared. I stepped fearfully in: the apartment was empty; and my bedroom was also freed from its hideous guest. I could hardly believe that so great a good fortune could have befallen me; but when I became assured that my enemy had indeed fled, I clapped my hands for joy, and ran down to Clerval.

We ascended into my room, and the servant presently brought breakfast; but I was unable to contain myself. It was not joy only that possessed me; I felt my flesh tingle with excess of sensitiveness, and my pulse beat rapidly. I was unable to remain for a single instant in the same place; I jumped over the chairs, clapped my hands, and laughed aloud. Clerval at first attributed my unusual spirits to joy on his arrival; but when he observed me more attentively he saw a wildness in my eyes for which he could not account; and my loud, unrestrained heartless laughter, frightened and astonished him.

"My dear Victor," cried he, "what, for God's sake, is the matter? Do not laugh in that manner. How ill you are! What is the cause of all this?"

"Do not ask me," cried I, putting my hands before my eyes, for I thought I saw the dreaded spectre glide into the room; "*he* can tell.—Oh, save me! save me!" I imagined that the monster seized me; I struggled furiously, and fell down in a fit.

Poor Clerval! what must have been his feelings? A meeting, which he anticipated with such joy, so strangely turned to bitterness. But I was not the witness of his grief; for I was lifeless, and did not recover my senses for a long, long time.

This was the commencement of a nervous fever, which confined me for several months. During all that time Henry was my only nurse. I afterwards learned that, knowing my father's advanced age, and unfitness for so long a journey, and how wretched my sickness would make Elizabeth, he spared them this grief by concealing the extent of my disorder. He knew that I could not have a more kind and attentive nurse than himself; and, firm in the hope he felt of my recovery, he did not doubt that, instead of doing harm, he performed the kindest action that he could towards them.

But I was in reality very ill; and surely nothing but the unbounded and unremitting attentions of my friend could have restored me to life. The form of the monster on whom I had bestowed existence was for ever before my eyes, and I raved incessantly concerning him. Doubtless my words surprised Henry: he at first believed them to be the wanderings of my disturbed imagination; but the pertinacity with which I continually recurred to the same subject, persuaded him that my disorder indeed owed its origin to some uncommon and terrible event.

By very slow degrees, and with frequent relapses that alarmed and grieved my friend, I recovered. I remember the first time I became capable of observing outward objects with any kind of pleasure, I perceived that the fallen leaves had disappeared, and that the young buds were shooting forth from the trees that shaded my window. It was a divine spring; and the season contributed greatly to my convalescence. I felt also sentiments of joy and affection revive in my bosom; my gloom disappeared, and in a short time I became as cheerful as before I was attacked by the fatal passion.

"Dearest Clerval," exclaimed I, "how kind, how very good you are to me. This whole winter, instead of being spent in study, as you promised yourself, has been consumed in my sick room. How shall I ever repay you? I feel the greatest remorse for the disappointment of which I have been the occasion; but you will forgive me."

"You will repay me entirely, if you do not discompose yourself, but get well as fast as you can; and since you appear in such good spirits, I may speak to you on one subject, may I not?"

I trembled. One subject! what could it be? Could he allude to an object on whom I dared not even think?

"Compose yourself," said Clerval, who observed my change of color, "I will not mention it, if it agitates you; but your father and cousin would be very happy if they received a letter from you in your own handwriting. They hardly know how ill you have been, and are uneasy at your long silence."

"Is that all, my dear Henry? How could you suppose that my first thoughts would not fly towards those dear, dear friends whom I love, and who are so deserving of my love."

"If this is your present temper, my friend, you will perhaps be glad to see a letter that has been lying here some days for you; it is from your cousin, I believe."

VI

Clerval then put the following letter into my hands. It was from my own Elizabeth:—

"My dearest Cousin,—You have been ill, very ill, and even the constant letters of dear kind Henry are not sufficient to reassure me on your account. You are forbidden to write—to hold a pen; yet one word from you, dear Victor, is necessary to calm our apprehensions. For a long time I have thought that each post would bring this line, and my persuasions have restrained my uncle from undertaking a journey to Ingolstadt. I have prevented his encountering the inconveniences and perhaps dangers of so long a journey; yet how often have I regretted not being able to perform it myself! I figure to myself that the task of attending on your sick bed has devolved on some mercenary old nurse, who could never guess your wishes, nor minister to them with the care and affection of your poor cousin. Yet that is over now: Clerval writes that indeed you are getting better. I eagerly hope that you will confirm this intelligence soon in your own handwriting.

"Get well—and return to us. You will find a happy, cheerful home, and friends who love you dearly. Your father's health is vigorous, and he asks but to see you—but to be assured that you are well; and not a care will ever cloud his benevolent countenance. How pleased you would be to remark the improvement of our Ernest! He is now sixteen, and full of activity and spirit. He is desirous to be a true Swiss, and to enter into foreign service; but we cannot part with him, at least until his elder brother returns to us. My uncle is not pleased with the idea of a military career in a distant country; but Ernest never had your powers of application. He looks upon study as an odious fetter;—his time is spent in the open air, climbing the hills or rowing on the lake. I fear that he will become an idler, unless we yield the point, and permit him to enter on the profession which he has selected.

"Little alteration, except the growth of our dear children, has taken place since you left us. The blue lake, and snow-clad mountains, they never change;—and I think our placid home and our contented hearts are regulated by the same immutable laws. My trifling occupations take up my time and amuse me, and I am rewarded for any exertions by seeing none but happy, kind faces around me. Since you left us, but one change has taken place in our little household. Do you remember on what occasion Justine Moritz entered our family? Probably you do not; I will relate her history, therefore, in a few words. Madame Moritz, her mother, was a widow with four children, of whom Justine was the third. This girl had always been the favorite of her father; but, through a strange perversity, her mother could not endure her, and after the death of M. Moritz, treated her very ill. My aunt observed this; and, when Justine was twelve years of age, prevailed on her mother to allow her to live at our house. The republican institutions of our country have produced simpler and happier manners than those which prevail in the great monarchies that surround it. Hence there is less distinction between the several classes of its inhabitants; and the lower orders, being neither so poor nor so despised, their manners are more refined and moral. A servant in Geneva does not mean the same thing as a servant in France and England. Justine, thus received in our family, learned the duties of a servant; a condition which, in our fortunate country, does not include the idea of ignorance, and a sacrifice of the dignity of a human being.

"Justine, you may remember, was a great favorite of yours; and I recollect you once remarked, that if you were in an ill-humor, one glance from Justine could dissipate it, for the same reason that Ariosto gives concerning the beauty of Angelica—she looked so frank-hearted and happy. My aunt conceived a great attachment for her, by which she was induced to give her an education superior to that which she had at first intended. This benefit was fully repaid; Justine was the most grateful little creature in the world: I do not mean that she made any professions; I never heard one pass her lips; but you could see by her eyes that she almost adored her protectress. Although her disposition was gay, and in many respects inconsiderate, yet she paid the greatest attention to every gesture of my aunt. She thought her the model of all excellence, and endeavored to imitate her phraseology and manners, so that even now she often reminds me of her.

"When my dearest aunt died, every one was too much occupied in their own grief to notice poor Justine, who had attended her during her illness with the most anxious affection. Poor Justine was very ill; but other trials were reserved for her.

"One by one, her brothers and sister died; and her mother, with the exception of her neglected daughter, was left childless. The conscience of the woman was troubled; she began to think that the deaths of her favorites was a judgment from heaven to chastise her partiality. She was a Roman Catholic; and I believe her confessor confirmed the idea which she had conceived. Accordingly, a few months after your departure for Ingolstadt, Justine was called home by her repentant mother. Poor girl! she wept when she quitted our house; she was much altered since the death of my aunt; grief had given softness and a winning mildness to her manners, which had before been remarkable for vivacity. Nor was her residence at her mother's house of a nature to restore her gaiety. The poor woman was very vacillating in her repentance. She sometimes begged Justine to forgive her unkindness, but much oftener accused her of having caused the deaths of her brothers and sister. Perpetual fretting at length threw Madame Moritz into a decline, which at first increased her irritability, but she is now at peace for ever. She died on the first approach of cold weather, at the beginning of this last winter. Justine has returned to us; and I assure you I love her tenderly. She is very clever and gentle, and extremely pretty; as I mentioned before, her mien and her expressions continually remind me of my dear aunt.

"I must say also a few words to you, my dear cousin, of little darling William. I wish you could see him; he is very tall of his age, with sweet laughing blue eyes, dark eyelashes, and curling hair. When he smiles, two little dimples appear on each cheek, which are rosy with health. He has already had one or two little *wives*, but Louisa Biron is his favorite, a pretty little girl of five years of age.

"Now, dear Victor, I dare say you wish to be indulged in a little gossip concerning the good people of Geneva. The pretty Miss Mansfield has already received the congratulatory visits on her approaching marriage with a young Englishman, John Melborne, Esq. Her ugly sister, Manon, married M. Duvillard, the rich banker, last autumn. Your favorite school-fellow, Louis Manoir, has suffered several misfortunes since the departure of Clerval from Geneva. But he has already recovered his spirits, and is reported to be on the point of marrying a very lively pretty Frenchwoman, Madame Tavernier. She is a widow, and much older than Manoir; but she is very much admired, and a favorite with everybody.

"I have written myself into better spirits, dear cousin; but my anxiety returns upon me as I conclude. Write, dearest Victor—one line—one word will be a blessing to us. Ten thousand thanks to Henry for his kindness, his affection, and his many letters: we are sincerely grateful. Adieu! my cousin; take care of yourself; and, I entreat you, write!

ELIZABETH LAVENZA.

"GENEVA, *March 18th, 17—.*"

"Dear, dear Elizabeth!" I exclaimed, when I had read her letter, "I will write instantly, and relieve them from the anxiety they must feel." I wrote, and this exertion greatly fatigued me; but my convalescence had commenced, and proceeded regularly. In another fortnight I was able to leave my chamber.

One of my first duties on my recovery was to introduce Clerval to the several professors of the university. In doing this, I underwent a kind of rough usage, ill befitting the wounds that my mind had sustained. Ever since the fatal night, the end of my labors, and the beginning of my misfortunes, I had conceived a violent antipathy even to the name of natural philosophy. When I was otherwise quite restored to health, the sight of a chemical instrument would renew all the agony of my nervous symptoms. Henry saw this, and had removed all my apparatus from my view. He had also changed my apartment; for he perceived that I had acquired a dislike for the room which had previously been my laboratory. But these cares of Clerval were made of no avail when I visited the professors. M. Waldman inflicted torture when he praised, with kindness and warmth, the astonishing progress I had made in the sciences. He soon perceived that I disliked the subject; but not guessing the real cause, he attributed my feelings to modesty, and changed the subject from my improvement, to the science itself, with a desire, as I evidently saw, of drawing me out. What could I do? He meant to please, and he tormented me. I felt as if he had placed carefully, one by one, in my view those instruments which were to be afterwards used in putting me to a slow and cruel death. I writhed under his words; yet dared not exhibit the pain I felt. Clerval, whose eyes and feelings were always quick in discerning the sensations of others, declined the subject, alleging, in excuse, his total ignorance; and the conversation took a more general turn. I thanked my friend from my heart, but I did not speak. I saw plainly that he was surprised, but he never attempted to draw my secret from me; and although I loved him with a mixture of affection and reverence that knew no bounds, yet I could never persuade myself to confide to him that event which was so often present to my recollection, but which I feared the detail to another would only impress more deeply.

M. Krempe was not equally docile; and in my condition at that time, of almost insupportable sensitiveness, his harsh blunt encomiums gave me even more pain than the benevolent approbation of M. Waldman. "D—n the fellow!" cried he; "why, M. Clerval, I assure you he has outstript us all. Ay, stare if you please; but it is nevertheless true. A youngster who, but a few years ago, believed in Cornelius Agrippa as firmly as in the gospel, has now set himself at the head of the university; and if he is not soon pulled down, we shall all be out of countenance.—Ay, ay," continued he, observing my face expressive of suffering, "M. Frankenstein is modest; an excellent quality in a young man. Young men should be diffident of themselves, you know, M. Clerval: I was myself when young; but that wears out in a very short time."

M. Krempe had now commenced an eulogy on himself, which happily turned the conversation from a subject that was so annoying to me.

Clerval had never sympathized in my tastes for natural science; and his literary pursuits differed wholly from those which had occupied me. He came to the university with the design of making himself complete master of the oriental languages, as thus he should open a field for the plan of life he had marked out for himself. Resolved to pursue no inglorious career, he turned his eyes toward the East, as affording scope for his spirit of enterprise. The Persian, Arabic, and Sanscrit languages engaged his attention, and I was easily induced to enter on the same studies. Idleness had ever been irksome to me, and now that I wished to fly from reflection, and hated my former studies, I felt great relief in being the fellow-pupil with my friend, and found not only instruction but consolation in the works of the orientalists. I did not, like him, attempt a critical knowledge of their dialects, for I did not contemplate making any other use of them than temporary amusement. I read merely to understand their meaning, and they well repaid my labors. Their melancholy is soothing, and their joy elevating, to a degree I never experienced in studying the authors of any other country. When you read their writings, life appears to consist in a warm sun and a garden of roses—in the smiles and frowns of a fair enemy, and the fire that consumes your own heart. How different from the manly and heroical poetry of Greece and Rome!

Summer passed away in these occupations, and my return to Geneva was fixed for the latter end of autumn; but being delayed by several accidents, winter and snow arrived, the roads were deemed impassable, and my journey was retarded until the ensuing spring. I felt this delay very bitterly; for I longed to see my native town and my beloved friends. My return had only been delayed so long from an unwillingness to leave Clerval in a strange place, before he had become acquainted with any of its inhabitants. The winter, however, was spent cheerfully; and although the spring was uncommonly late, when it came its beauty compensated for its dilatoriness.

The month of May had already commenced, and I expected the letter daily which was to fix the date of my departure, when Henry proposed a pedestrian tour in the environs of Ingolstadt, that I might bid a personal farewell to the country I had so long inhabited. I acceded with pleasure to this proposition: I was fond of exercise, and Clerval had always been my favorite companion in the rambles of this nature that I had taken among the scenes of my native country.

We passed a fortnight in these perambulations: my health and spirits had long been restored, and they gained additional strength from the salubrious air I breathed, the natural incidents of our progress, and the conversation of my friend. Study had before secluded me from the intercourse of my fellow-creatures, and rendered me unsocial; but Clerval called forth the better feelings of my heart; he again taught me to love the aspect of nature, and the cheerful faces of children. Excellent friend! how sincerely did you love me, and endeavor to elevate my mind until it was on a level with your own! A selfish pursuit had cramped and narrowed me, until your gentleness and affection warmed and opened my senses; I became the same happy creature who, a few years ago, loved and beloved by all, had no sorrow or care. When happy, inanimate nature had the power of bestowing on me the most delightful sensations. A serene sky and verdant fields filled me with ecstasy. The present season was indeed divine; the flowers of spring bloomed in the hedges, while those of summer were already in bud. I was undisturbed by thoughts which during the preceding year had pressed upon me, notwithstanding my endeavors to throw them off, with an invincible burden.

Henry rejoiced in my gaiety, and sincerely sympathized in my feelings: he exerted himself to amuse me, while he expressed the sensations that filled his soul. The resources of his mind on this occasion were truly astonishing: his conversation was full of imagination; and very often, in imitation of the Persian and Arabic writers, he invented tales of wonderful fancy and passion. At other times he repeated my favorite poems, or drew me out into arguments, which he supported with great ingenuity.

We returned to our college on a Sunday afternoon: the peasants were dancing, and every one we met appeared gay and happy. My own spirits were high, and I bounded along with feelings of unbridled joy and hilarity.

VII

On my return, I found the following letter from my father:—

"My dear Victor,—You have probably waited impatiently for a letter to fix the date of your return to us; and I was at first tempted to write only a few lines, merely mentioning the day on which I should expect you. But that would be a cruel kindness, and I dare not do it. What would be your surprise, my son, when you expected a happy and glad welcome, to behold, on the contrary, tears and wretchedness? And how, Victor, can I relate our misfortune? Absence cannot have rendered you callous to our joys and griefs; and how shall I inflict pain on my long absent son? I wish to prepare you for the woeful news, but I know it is impossible; even now your eye skims over the page, to seek the words which are to convey to you the horrible tidings.

"William is dead!—that sweet child, whose smiles delighted and warmed my heart, who was so gentle, yet so gay! Victor, he is murdered!

"I will not attempt to console you; but will simply relate the circumstances of the transaction.

"Last Thursday (May 7th), I, my niece, and your two brothers, went to walk in Plainpalais. The evening was warm and serene, and we prolonged our walk farther than usual. It was already dusk before we thought of returning; and then we discovered that William and Ernest, who had gone on before, were not to be found. We accordingly rested on a seat until they should return. Presently Ernest came, and inquired if we had seen his brother: he said, that he had been playing with him, that William had run away to hide himself, and that he vainly sought for him, and afterwards waited for him a long time, but that he did not return.

"This account rather alarmed us, and we continued to search for him until night fell, when Elizabeth conjectured that he might have returned to the house. He was not there. We returned again, with torches; for I could not rest, when I thought that my sweet boy had lost himself, and was exposed to all the damps and dews of night; Elizabeth also suffered extreme anguish. About five in the morning I discovered my lovely boy, whom the night before I had seen blooming and active in health, stretched on the grass livid and motionless: the print of the murderer's finger was on his neck.

"He was conveyed home, and the anguish that was visible in my countenance betrayed the secret to Elizabeth. She was very earnest to see the corpse. At first I attempted to prevent her; but she persisted, and entering the room where it lay, hastily examined the neck of the victim, and clasping her hands exclaimed, 'O God! I have murdered my darling child!'

"She fainted, and was restored with extreme difficulty. When she again lived, it was only to weep and sigh. She told me that that same evening William had teased her to let him wear a very valuable miniature that she possessed of your mother. This picture is gone, and was doubtless the temptation which urged the murderer to the deed. We have no trace of him at present, although our exertions to discover him are unremitted; but they will not restore my beloved William!

"Come, dearest Victor; you alone can console Elizabeth. She weeps continually, and accuses herself unjustly as the cause of his death; her words pierce my heart. We are all unhappy; but will not that be an additional motive for you, my son, to return and be our comforter? Your dear mother! Alas, Victor! I now say, Thank God she did not live to witness the cruel, miserable death of her youngest darling!

"Come, Victor; not brooding thoughts of vengeance against the assassin, but with feelings of peace and gentleness, that will heal, instead of festering, the wounds of our minds. Enter the house of mourning, my friend, but with kindness and affection for those who love you, and not with hatred for your enemies.—Your affectionate and afflicted father,

ALPHONSE FRANKENSTEIN.

"GENEVA, *May 12th, 17—*."

Clerval, who had watched my countenance as I read this letter, was surprised to observe the despair that succeeded to the joy I at first expressed on receiving news from my friends. I threw the letter on the table, and covered my face with my hands.

"My dear Frankenstein," exclaimed Henry, when he perceived me weep with bitterness, "are you always to be unhappy? My dear friend, what has happened?"

I motioned to him to take up the letter, while I walked up and down the room in the extremest agitation. Tears also gushed from the eyes of Clerval, as he read the account of my misfortune.

"I can offer you no consolation, my friend," said he; "your disaster is irreparable. What do you intend to do?"

"To go instantly to Geneva: come with me, Henry, to order the horses."

During our walk, Clerval endeavored to say a few words of consolation; he could only express his heartfelt sympathy. "Poor William!" said he, "dear lovely child, he now sleeps with his angel mother! Who that had seen him bright and joyous in his young beauty, but must weep over his untimely loss! To die so miserably; to feel the murderer's grasp! How much more a murderer, that could destroy such radiant innocence! Poor little fellow! one only consolation have we; his friends mourn and weep, but he is at rest. The pang is over, his sufferings are at an end for ever. A sod covers his gentle form, and he knows no pain. He can no longer be a subject for pity; we must reserve that for his miserable survivors."

Clerval spoke thus as we hurried through the streets; the words impressed themselves on my mind, and I remembered them afterwards in solitude. But now, as soon as the horses arrived, I hurried into a cabriolet, and bade farewell to my friend.

My journey was very melancholy. At first I wished to hurry on, for I longed to console and sympathize with my loved and sorrowing friends; but when I drew near my native town, I slackened my progress. I could hardly sustain the multitude of feelings that crowded into my mind. I passed through scenes familiar to my youth, but which I had not seen for nearly six years. How altered everything might be during that time! One sudden and desolating change had taken place; but a thousand little circumstances might have by degrees worked other alterations, which, although they were done more tranquily, might not be the less decisive. Fear overcame me; I dared not advance, dreading a thousand nameless evils that made me tremble, although I was unable to define them.

I remained two days at Lausanne, in this painful state of mind. I contemplated the lake: the waters were placid; all around was calm; and the snowy mountains, "the palaces of nature," were not changed. By degrees the calm and heavenly scene restored me, and I continued my journey towards Geneva.

The road ran by the side of the lake, which became narrower as I approached my native town. I discovered more distinctly the black sides of Jura, and the bright summit of Mont Blanc. I wept like a child. "Dear mountains! my own beautiful lake! how do you welcome your wanderer? Your summits are clear; the sky and lake are blue and placid. Is this to prognosticate peace, or to mock at my unhappiness?"

I fear, my friend, that I shall render myself tedious by dwelling on these preliminary circumstances; but they were days of comparative happiness, and I think of them with pleasure. My country, my beloved country! who but a native can tell the delight I took in again beholding thy streams, thy mountains, and, more than all, thy lovely lake!

Yet, as I drew nearer home, grief and fear again overcame me. Night also closed around; and when I could hardly see the dark mountains, I felt still more gloomily. The picture appeared a vast and dim scene of evil, and I foresaw obscurely that I was destined to become the most wretched of human beings. Alas! I prophesied truly, and failed only in one single circumstance, that in all the misery I imagined and dreaded, I did not conceive the hundredth part of the anguish I was destined to endure.

It was completely dark when I arrived in the environs of Geneva; the gates of the town were already shut; and I was obliged to pass the night at Secheron, a village at the distance of half a league from the city. The sky was serene; and, as I was unable to rest, I resolved to visit the spot where my poor William had been murdered. As I could not pass through the town, I was obliged to cross the lake in a boat to arrive at Plainpalais. During this short voyage I saw the lightnings playing on the summit of Mont Blanc in the most beautiful figures. The storm appeared to approach rapidly; and, on landing, I ascended a low hill, that I might observe its progress. It advanced; the heavens were clouded, and I soon felt the rain coming slowly in large drops, but its violence quickly increased.

I quitted my seat, and walked on, although the darkness and storm increased every minute, and the thunder burst with a terrific crash over my head. It was echoed from Salêve, the Juras, and the Alps of Savoy; vivid flashes of lightning dazzled my eyes, illuminating the lake, making it appear like a vast sheet of fire; then for an instant everything seemed of a pitchy darkness, until the eye recovered itself from the preceding flash. The storm, as is often the case in Switzerland, appeared at once in various parts of the heavens. The most violent storm hung exactly north of the town, over that part of the lake which lies between the promontory of Belrive and the village of Copêt. Another storm enlightened Jura with faint flashes; and another darkened and sometimes disclosed the Môle, a peaked mountain to the east of the lake.

While I watched the tempest, so beautiful yet terrific, I wandered on with a hasty step. This noble war in the sky elevated my spirits; I clasped my hands, and exclaimed aloud, "William, dear angel! this is thy funeral, this thy dirge!" As I said these words, I perceived in the gloom a figure which stole from behind a clump of trees near me; I stood fixed, gazing intently: I could not be mistaken. A flash of lightning illuminated the object, and discovered its shape plainly to me; its gigantic stature, and the deformity of its aspect, more hideous than belongs to humanity, instantly informed me that it was the wretch, the filthy dæmon, to whom I had given life. What did he there? Could he be (I shuddered at the conception) the murderer of my brother? No sooner did that idea cross my imagination, than I became convinced of its truth; my teeth chattered, and I was forced to lean against a tree for support. The figure passed me quickly, and I lost it in the gloom. Nothing in human shape could have destroyed that fair child. *He* was the murderer! I could not doubt it. The mere presence of the idea was an irresistible proof of the fact. I thought of pursuing the devil; but it would have been in vain, for another flash discovered him to me hanging among the rocks of the nearly perpendicular ascent of Mont Salêve, a hill that bounds Plainpalais on the south. He soon reached the summit, and disappeared.

I remained motionless. The thunder ceased; but the rain still continued, and the scene was enveloped in an impenetrable darkness. I revolved in my mind the events which I had until now sought to forget: the whole train of my progress towards the creation; the appearance of the work of my own hands alive at my bedside; its departure. Two years had now nearly elapsed since the night on which he first received life; and was this his first crime? Alas! I had turned loose into the world a depraved wretch, whose delight was in carnage and misery; had he not murdered my brother?

No one can conceive the anguish I suffered during the remainder of the night, which I spent, cold and wet, in the open air. But I did not feel the inconvenience of the weather; my imagination was busy in scenes of evil and despair. I considered the being whom I had cast among mankind, and endowed with the will and power to effect purposes of horror, such as the deed which he had now done, nearly in the light of my own vampire, my own spirit let loose from the grave, and forced to destroy all that was dear to me.

Day dawned; and I directed my steps towards the town. The gates were open, and I hastened to my father's house. My first thought was to discover what I knew of the murderer, and cause instant pursuit to be made. But I paused when I reflected on the story that I had to tell. A being whom I myself had formed, and endued with life, had met me at midnight among the precipices of an inaccessible mountain. I remembered also the nervous fever with which I had been seized just at the time that I dated my creation, and which would give an air of delirium to a tale otherwise so utterly improbable. I well knew that if any other had communicated such a relation to me, I should have looked upon it as the ravings of insanity. Besides, the strange nature of the animal would elude all pursuit, even if I were so far credited as to persuade my relatives to commence it. And then of what use would be pursuit? Who could arrest a creature capable of scaling the overhanging sides of Mont Salêve? These reflections determined me, and I resolved to remain silent.

It was about five in the morning when I entered my father's house. I told the servants not to disturb the family, and went into the library to attend their usual hour of rising.

Six years had elapsed, passed as a dream but for one indelible trace, and I stood in the same place where I had last embraced my father before my departure for Ingolstadt. Beloved and venerable parent! He still remained to me. I gazed on the picture of my mother, which stood over the mantel-piece. It was an historical subject, painted at my father's desire, and represented Caroline Beaufort in an agony of despair, kneeling by the coffin of her dead father. Her garb was rustic, and her cheek pale; but there was an air of dignity and beauty, that hardly permitted the sentiment of pity. Below this picture was a miniature of William; and my tears flowed when I looked upon it. While I was thus engaged, Ernest entered: he had heard me arrive, and hastened to welcome me. He expressed a sorrowful delight to see me: "Welcome, my dearest Victor," said he. "Ah! I wish you had come three months ago, and then you would have found us all joyous and delighted! You come to us now to share a misery which nothing can alleviate; yet your presence will, I hope, revive our father, who seems sinking under his misfortune; and your persuasions will induce poor Elizabeth to cease her vain and tormenting self-accusations.—Poor William! he was our darling and our pride!"

Tears, unrestrained, fell from my brother's eyes; a sense of mortal agony crept over my frame. Before, I had only imagined the wretchedness of my desolated home; the reality came on me as a new, and a not less terrible, disaster. I tried to calm Ernest; I inquired more minutely concerning my father and her I named my cousin.

"She most of all," said Ernest, "requires consolation; she accused herself of having caused the death of my brother, and that made her very wretched. But since the murderer has been discovered—"

"The murderer discovered! Good God! how can that be? Who could attempt to pursue him? It is impossible; one might as well try to overtake the winds, or confine a mountainstream with a straw. I saw him too; he was free last night!"

"I do not know what you mean," replied my brother, in accents of wonder, "but to us the discovery we have made completes our misery. No one would believe it at first; and even now Elizabeth will not be convinced, notwithstanding all the evidence. Indeed, who would credit that Justine Moritz, who was so amiable, and fond of all the family, could suddenly become capable of so frightful, so appalling a crime?"

"Justine Moritz! Poor, poor girl, is she the accused? But it is wrongfully; every one knows that; no one believes it, surely, Ernest?"

"No one did at first; but several circumstances came out, that have almost forced conviction upon us; and her own behavior has been so confused, as to add to the evidence of facts a weight that, I fear, leaves no hope for doubt. But she will be tried to-day, and you will then hear all."

He related that, the morning on which the murder of poor William had been discovered, Justine had been taken ill, and confined to her bed for several days. During this interval, one of the servants, happening to examine the apparel she had worn on the night of the murder, had discovered in her pocket the picture of my mother, which had been judged to be the temptation of the murderer. The servant instantly showed it to one of the others, who, without saying a word to any of the family, went to a magistrate; and, upon their deposition, Justine was apprehended. On being charged with the fact, the poor girl confirmed the suspicion in a great measure by her extreme confusion of manner.

This was a strange tale, but it did not shake my faith; and I replied earnestly, "You are all mistaken; I know the murderer. Justine, poor, good Justine, is innocent."

At that instant my father entered. I saw unhappiness deeply impressed on his countenance, but he endeavored to welcome me cheerfully; and, after we had exchanged our mournful greeting, would have introduced some other topic than that of our disaster, had not Ernest exclaimed, "Good God, papa! Victor says that he knows who was the murderer of poor William."

"We do also, unfortunately," replied my father; "for indeed I had rather have been for ever ignorant than have discovered so much depravity and ingratitude in one I valued so highly."

"My dear father, you are mistaken; Justine is innocent."

"If she is, God forbid that she should suffer as guilty. She is to be tried to-day, and I hope, I sincerely hope, that she will be acquitted."

This speech calmed me. I was firmly convinced in my own mind that Justine, and indeed every human being, was guiltless of this murder. I had no fear, therefore, that any circumstantial evidence could be brought forward strong enough to convict her. My tale was not one to announce publicly; its astounding horror would be looked upon as madness by the vulgar. Did any one indeed exist, except I, the creator, who would believe, unless his senses convinced him, in the existence of the living monument of presumption and rash ignorance which I had let loose upon the world?

We were soon joined by Elizabeth. Time had altered her since I last beheld her; it had endowed her with loveliness surpassing the beauty of her childish years. There was the same candor, the same vivacity, but it was allied to an expression more full of sensibility and intellect. She welcomed me with the greatest affection. "Your arrival, my dear cousin," said she, "fills me with hope. You perhaps will find some means to justify my poor guiltless Justine. Alas! who is safe, if she be convicted of crime? I rely on her innocence as certainly as I do upon my own. Our misfortune is doubly hard to us; we have not only lost that lovely darling boy, but this poor girl, whom I sincerely love, is to be torn away by even a worse fate. If she is condemned, I never shall know joy more. But she will not, I am sure she will not; and then I shall be happy again, even after the sad death of my little William."

"She is innocent, my Elizabeth," said I, "and that shall be proved; fear nothing, but let your spirits be cheered by the assurance of her acquittal."

"How kind and generous you are! every one else believes in her guilt, and that made me wretched, for I knew that it was impossible: and to see every one else prejudiced in so deadly a manner rendered me hopeless and despairing." She wept.

"Dearest niece," said my father, "dry your tears. If she is, as you believe, innocent, rely on the justice of our laws, and the activity with which I shall prevent the slightest shadow of partiality."

VIII

We passed a few sad hours, until eleven o'clock, when the trial was to commence. My father and the rest of the family being obliged to attend as witnesses, I accompanied them to the court. During the whole of this wretched mockery of justice I suffered living torture. It was to be decided, whether the result of my curiosity and lawless devices would cause the death of two of my fellow-beings: one a smiling babe, full of innocence and joy; the other far more dreadfully murdered, with every aggravation of infamy that could make the murder memorable in horror. Justine also was a girl of merit, and possessed qualities which promised to render her life happy: now all was to be obliterated in an ignominious grave; and I the cause! A thousand times rather would I have confessed myself guilty of the crime ascribed to Justine; but I was absent when it was committed, and such a declaration would have been considered as the ravings of a madman, and would not have exculpated her who suffered through me.

The appearance of Justine was calm. She was dressed in mourning; and her countenance, always engaging, was rendered, by the solemnity of her feelings, exquisitely beautiful. Yet she appeared confident in innocence, and did not tremble, although gazed on and execrated by thousands; for all the kindness which her beauty might otherwise have excited, was obliterated in the minds of the spectators by the imagination of the enormity she was supposed to have committed. She was tranquil, yet her tranquility was evidently constrained; and as her confusion had before been adduced as a proof of her guilt, he worked up her mind to an appearance of courage. When she entered the court, she threw her eyes round it, and quickly discovered where we were seated. A tear seemed to dim her eye when she saw us; but she quickly recovered herself, and a look of sorrowful affection seemed to attest her utter guiltlessness.

The trial began; and, after the advocate against her had stated the charge, several witnesses were called. Several strange facts combined against her, which might have staggered any one who had not such proof of her innocence as I had. She had been out the whole of the night on which the murder had been committed, and towards morning had been perceived by a market-woman not far from the spot where the body of the murdered child had been afterwards found. The woman asked her what she did there; but she looked very strangely, and only returned a confused and unintelligible answer. She returned to the house about eight o'clock; and, when one inquired where she had passed the night, she replied that she had been looking for the child, and demanded earnestly if anything had been heard concerning him. When shown the body, she fell into violent hysterics, and kept her bed for several days. The picture was then produced, which the servant had found in her pocket; and when Elizabeth, in a faltering voice, proved that it was the same which, an hour before the child had been missed, she had placed round his neck, a murmur of horror and indignation filled the court.

Justine was called on for her defense. As the trial had proceeded, her countenance had altered. Surprise, horror, and misery were strongly expressed. Sometimes she struggled with her tears; but, when she was desired to plead, she collected her powers, and spoke, in an audible, although variable voice.

"God knows," she said, "how entirely I am innocent. But I do not pretend that my protestations should acquit me: I rest my innocence on a plain and simple explanation of the facts which have been adduced against me; and I hope the character I have always borne will incline my judges to a favorable interpretation, where any circumstance appears doubtful or suspicious."

She then related that, by the permission of Elizabeth, she had passed the evening of the night on which the murder had been committed at the house of an aunt at Chêne, a village situated at about a league from Geneva. On her return, at about nine o'clock, she met a man, who asked her if she had seen anything of the child who was lost. She was alarmed by this account, and passed several hours in looking for him, when the gates of Geneva were shut, and she was forced to remain several hours of the night in a barn belonging to a cottage, being unwilling to call up the inhabitants, to whom she was well known. Most of the night she spent here watching; towards morning she believed that she slept for a few minutes; some steps disturbed her, and she awoke. It was dawn, and she quitted her asylum, that she might again endeavor to find my brother. If she had gone near the spot where his body lay, it was without her knowledge. That she had been bewildered when questioned by the market-woman was not surprising, since she had passed a sleepless night, and the fate of poor William was yet uncertain. Concerning the picture she could give no account.

"I know," continued the unhappy victim, "how heavily and fatally this one circumstance weighs against me, but I have no power of explaining it; and when I have expressed my utter ignorance, I am only left to conjecture concerning the probabilities by which it might have been placed in my pocket. But here also I am checked. I believe that I have no enemy on earth, and none surely would have been so wicked as to destroy me wantonly. Did the murderer place it there? I know of no opportunity afforded him for so doing; or, if I had, why should he have stolen the jewel, to part with it again so soon?

"I commit my cause to the justice of my judges, yet I see no room for hope. I beg permission to have a few witnesses examined concerning my character; and if their testimony shall not overweigh my supposed guilt, I must be condemned, although I would pledge my salvation on my innocence."

Several witnesses were called, who had known her for many years, and they spoke well of her; but fear and hatred of the crime of which they supposed her guilty rendered them timorous, and unwilling to come forward. Elizabeth saw even this last resource, her excellent dispositions and irreproachable conduct, about to fail the accused, when, although violently agitated, she desired permission to address the court.

"I am," said she, "the cousin of the unhappy child who was murdered, or rather his sister, for I was educated by, and have lived with his parents ever since and even long before, his birth. It may, therefore, be judged indecent in me to come forward on this occasion; but when I see a fellow-creature about to perish through the cowardice of her pretended friends, I wish to be allowed to speak, that I may say what I know of her character. I am well acquainted with the accused. I have lived in the same house with her, at one time for five and at another for nearly two years. During all that period she appeared to me the most amiable and benevolent of human creatures. She nursed Madame Frankenstein, my aunt, in her last illness, with the greatest affection and care; and afterwards attended her own mother during a tedious illness, in a manner that excited the admiration of all who knew her; after which she again lived in my uncle's house, where she was beloved by all the family. She was warmly attached to the child who is now dead, and acted towards him like a most affectionate mother. For my own part, I do not hesitate to say, that, notwithstanding all the evidence produced against her, I believe and rely on her perfect innocence. She had no temptation for such an action: as to the bauble on which the chief proof rests, if she had earnestly desired it, I should have willingly given it to her; so much do I esteem and value her."

A murmur of approbation followed Elizabeth's simple and powerful appeal; but it was excited by her generous interference, and not in favor of poor Justine, on whom the public indignation was turned with renewed violence, charging her with the blackest ingratitude. She herself wept as Elizabeth spoke, but she did not answer. My own agitation and anguish was extreme during the whole trial. I believed in her innocence; I knew it. Could the dæmon, who had (I did not for a minute doubt) murdered my brother, also in his hellish sport have betrayed the innocent to death and ignominy? I could not sustain the horror of my situation; and when I perceived that the popular voice, and the countenances of the judges, had already condemned my unhappy victim, I rushed out of the court in agony. The tortures of the accused did not equal mine; she was sustained by innocence, but the fangs of remorse tore my bosom, and would not forego their hold.

I passed a night of unmingled wretchedness. In the morning I went to the court; my lips and throat were parched. I dared not ask the fatal question; but I was known, and the officer guessed the cause of my visit. The ballots had been thrown; they were all black, and Justine was condemned.

I cannot pretend to describe what I then felt. I had before experienced sensations of horror; and I have endeavored to bestow upon them adequate expressions, but words cannot convey an idea of the heart-sickening despair that I then endured. The person to whom I addressed myself added, that Justine had already confessed her guilt. "That evidence," he observed, "was hardly required in so glaring a case, but I am glad of it; and, indeed, none of our judges like to condemn a criminal upon circumstantial evidence, be it ever so decisive."

This was strange and unexpected intelligence; what could it mean? Had my eyes deceived me and was I really as mad as the whole world would believe me to be, if I disclosed the object of my suspicions? I hastened to return home, and Elizabeth eagerly demanded the result.

"My cousin," replied I, "it is decided as you may have expected; all judges had rather that ten innocent should suffer, than that one guilty should escape. But she has confessed."

This was a dire blow to poor Elizabeth, who had relied with firmness upon Justine's innocence. "Alas!" said she, "how shall I ever again believe in human goodness? Justine, whom I loved and esteemed as my sister, how could she put on those smiles of innocence only to betray? Her mild eyes seemed incapable of any severity or guile, and yet she has committed a murder."

Soon after we heard that the poor victim had expressed a desire to see my cousin. My father wished her not to go; but said, that he left it to her own judgement and feelings to decide. "Yes," said Elizabeth, "I will go, although she is guilty; and you, Victor, shall accompany me: I cannot go alone." The idea of this visit was torture to me, yet I could not refuse.

We entered the gloomy prison-chamber, and beheld Justine sitting on some straw at the farther end; her hands were manacled, and her head rested on her knees. She rose on seeing us enter; and when we were left alone with her, she threw herself at the feet of Elizabeth, weeping bitterly. My cousin wept also.

"Oh, Justine!" said she, "why did you rob me of my last consolation? I relied on your innocence; and although I was then very wretched, I was not so miserable as I am now."

"And do you also believe that I am so very, very wicked? Do you also join with my enemies to crush me, to condemn me as a murderer?" Her voice was suffocated with sobs.

"Rise, my poor girl," said Elizabeth, "why do you kneel, if you are innocent? I am not one of your enemies; I believed you guiltless, notwithstanding every evidence, until I heard that you had yourself declared your guilt. That report, you say, is false; and be assured, dear Justine, that nothing can shake my confidence in you for a moment, but your own confession."

"I did confess; but I confessed a lie. I confessed, that I might obtain absolution; but now that falsehood lies heavier at my heart than all my other sins. The God of heaven forgive me! Ever since I was condemned, my confessor has besieged me; he threatened and menaced, until I almost began to think that I was the monster that he said I was. He threatened excommunication and hell fire in my last moments, if I continued obdurate. Dear lady, I had none to support me; all looked on me as a wretch doomed to ignominy and perdition. What could I do? In an evil hour I subscribed to a lie; and now only am I truly miserable."

She paused, weeping, and then continued—"I thought with horror, my sweet lady, that you should believe your Justine, whom your blessed aunt had so highly honored, and whom you loved, was a creature capable of a crime which none but the devil himself could have perpetrated. Dear William! dearest blessed child! I soon shall see you again in heaven, where we shall all be happy; and that consoles me, going as I am to suffer ignominy and death."

"Oh, Justine! forgive me for having for one moment distrusted you. Why did you confess? But do not mourn, dear girl. Do not fear. I will proclaim, I will prove your innocence. I will melt the stony hearts of your enemies by my tears and prayers. You shall not die!—You, my playfellow, my companion, my sister, perish on the scaffold! No! no! I never could survive so horrible a misfortune."

Justine shook her head mournfully. "I do not fear to die," she said; "that pang is past. God raises my weakness, and gives me courage to endure the worst. I leave a sad and bitter world; and if you remember me, and think of me as of one unjustly condemned, I am resigned to the fate awaiting me. Learn from me, dear lady, to submit in patience to the will of Heaven!"

During this conversation I had retired to a corner of the prison-room, where I could conceal the horrid anguish that possessed me. Despair! Who dared talk of that? The poor victim, who on the morrow was to pass the awful boundary between life and death, felt not as I did, such deep and bitter agony. I gnashed my teeth, and ground them together, uttering a groan that came from my inmost soul. Justine started. When she saw who it was, she approached me, and said, "Dear sir, you are very kind to visit me; you, I hope, do not believe that I am guilty?"

I could not answer. "No, Justine," said Elizabeth; "he is more convinced of your innocence than I was; for even when he heard that you had confessed, he did not credit it."

"I truly thank him. In these last moments I feel the sincerest gratitude towards those who think of me with kindness. How sweet is the affection of others to such a wretch as I am! It removes more than half my misfortune; and I feel as if I could die in peace, now that my innocence is acknowledged by you, dear lady, and your cousin."

Thus the poor sufferer tried to comfort others and herself. She indeed gained the resignation she desired. But I, the true murderer, felt the never-dying worm alive in my bosom, which allowed of no hope or consolation. Elizabeth also wept, and was unhappy; but her's also was the misery of innocence, which, like a cloud that passes over the fair moon, for a while hides but cannot tarnish its brightness. Anguish and despair had penetrated into the core of my heart; I bore a hell within me, which nothing could extinguish. We stayed several hours with Justine; and it was with great difficulty that Elizabeth could tear herself away. "I wish," cried she, "that I were to die with you; I cannot live in this world of misery."

Justine assumed an air of cheerfulness, while she with difficulty repressed her bitter tears. She embraced Elizabeth, and said, in a voice of half-suppressed emotion, "Farewell, sweet lady, dearest Elizabeth, my beloved and only friend; may Heaven, in its bounty, bless and preserve you; may this be the last misfortune that you will ever suffer! Live, and be happy, and make others so."

And on the morrow Justine died. Elizabeth's heart-rending eloquence failed to move the judges from their settled conviction in the criminality of the saintly sufferer. My passionate and indignant appeals were lost upon them. And when I received their cold answers, and heard the harsh unfeeling reasoning of these men, my purposed avowal died away on my lips. Thus I might proclaim myself a madman, but not revoke the sentence passed upon my wretched victim. She perished on the scaffold as a murderess!

From the tortures of my own heart, I turned to contemplate the deep and voiceless grief of my Elizabeth. This also was my doing! And my father's woe, and the desolation of that late so smiling home—all was the work of my thrice-accursed hands! Ye weep, unhappy ones; but these are not your last tears! Again shall you raise the funeral wail, and the sound of your lamentations shall again and again be heard! Frankenstein, your son, your kinsman, your early, muchloved friend; he who would spend each vital drop of blood for your sakes—who has no thought nor sense of joy, except as it is mirrored also in your dear countenances—who would fill the air with blessings, and spend his life in serving you—he bids you weep—to shed countless tears; happy beyond his hopes, if thus inexorable fate be satisfied, and if the destruction pause before the peace of the grave have succeeded to your sad torments!

Thus spoke my prophetic soul, as, torn by remorse, horror, and despair, I beheld those I loved spend vain sorrow upon the graves of William and Justine, the first hapless victims to my unhallowed arts.

IX

Nothing is more painful to the human mind, than, after the feelings have been worked up by a quick succession of events, the dead calmness of inaction and certainty which follows, and deprives the soul both of hope and fear. Justine died; she rested; and I was alive. The blood flowed freely in my veins, but a weight of despair and remorse pressed on my heart, which nothing could remove. Sleep fled from my eyes; I wandered like an evil spirit, for I had committed deeds of mischief beyond description horrible, and more, much more (I persuaded myself), was yet behind. Yet my heart overflowed with kindness, and the love of virtue. I had begun life with benevolent intentions, and thirsted for the moment when I should put them in practice, and make myself useful to my fellow-beings. Now all was blasted: instead of that serenity of conscience, which allowed me to look back upon the past with self-satisfaction, and from thence to gather promise of new hopes, I was seized by remorse and the sense of guilt, which hurried me away to a hell of intense tortures, such as no language can describe.

This state of mind preyed upon my health, which had perhaps never entirely recovered from the first shock it had sustained. I shunned the face of man; all sound of joy or complacency was torture to me; solitude was my only consolation—deep, dark, deathlike solitude.

My father observed with pain the alteration perceptible in my disposition and habits, and endeavored by arguments deduced from the feelings of his serene conscience and guiltless life, to inspire me with fortitude, and awaken in me the courage to dispel the dark cloud which brooded over me. "Do you think, Victor," said he, "that I do not suffer also? No one could love a child more than I loved your brother" (tears came into his eyes as he spoke); "but is it not a duty to the survivors, that we should refrain from augmenting their unhappiness by an appearance of immoderate grief? It is also a duty owed to yourself; for excessive sorrow prevents improvement or enjoyment, or even the discharge of daily usefulness, without which no man is fit for society."

This advice, although good, was totally inapplicable to my case; I should have been the first to hide my grief, and console my friends, if remorse had not mingled its bitterness, and terror its alarm with my other sensations. Now I could only answer my father with a look of despair, and endeavor to hide myself from his view.

About this time we retired to our house at Belrive. This change was particularly agreeable to me. The shutting of the gates regularly at ten o'clock, and the impossibility of remaining on the lake after that hour, had rendered our residence within the walls of Geneva very irksome to me. I was now free. Often, after the rest of the family had retired for the night, I took the boat, and passed many hours upon the water. Sometimes, with my sails set, I was carried by the wind; and sometimes, after rowing into the middle of the lake, I left the boat to pursue its own course, and gave way to my own miserable reflections. I was often tempted, when all was at peace around me, and I the only unquiet thing that wandered restless in a scene so beautiful and heavenly—if I except some bat, or the frogs, whose harsh and interrupted croaking was heard only when I approached the shore—often, I say, I was tempted to plunge into the silent lake, that the waters might close over me and my calamities for ever. But I was restrained, when I thought of the heroic and suffering Elizabeth, whom I tenderly loved, and whose existence was bound up in mine. I thought also of my father and surviving brother: should I by my base desertion leave them exposed and unprotected to the malice of the fiend whom I had let loose among them?

At these moments I wept bitterly, and wished that peace would revisit my mind only that I might afford them consolation and happiness. But that could not be. Remorse extinguished every hope. I had been the author of unalterable evils; and I lived in daily fear, lest the monster whom I had created should perpetrate some new wickedness. I had an obscure feeling that all was not over, and that he would still commit some signal crime, which by its enormity should almost efface the recollection of the past. There was always scope for fear, so long as anything I loved remained behind. My abhorrence of this fiend cannot be conceived. When I thought of him, I gnashed my teeth, my eyes became inflamed, and I ardently wished to extinguish that life which I had so thoughtlessly bestowed. When I reflected on his crimes and malice, my hatred and revenge burst all bounds of moderation. I would have made a pilgrimage to the highest peak of the Andes, could I, when there, have precipitated him to their base. I wished to see him again, that I might wreak the utmost extent of abhorrence on his head, and avenge the deaths of William and Justine.

Our house was the house of mourning. My father's health was deeply shaken by the horror of the recent events. Elizabeth was sad and desponding; she no longer took delight in her ordinary occupations; all pleasure seemed to her sacrilege toward the dead; eternal woe and tears she then thought was the just tribute she should pay to innocence so blasted and destroyed. She was no longer that happy creature, who in earlier youth wandered with me on the banks of the lake, and talked with ecstasy of our future prospects. The first of those sorrows which are sent to wean us from the earth, had visited her, and its dimming influence quenched her dearest smiles.

"When I reflect, my dear cousin," said she, "on the miserable death of Justine Moritz, I no longer see the world and its works as they before appeared to me. Before, I looked upon the accounts of vice and injustice, that I read in books or heard from others, as tales of ancient days, or imaginary evils; at least they were remote, and more familiar to reason than to the imagination; but now misery has come home, and men appear to me as monsters thirsting for each other's blood. Yet I am certainly unjust. Everybody believed that poor girl to be guilty; and if she could have committed the crime for which she suffered, assuredly she would have been the most depraved of human creatures. For the sake of a few jewels, to have murdered the son of her benefactor and friend, a child whom she had nursed from its birth, and appeared to love as if it had been her own! I could not consent to the death of any human being; but certainly I should have thought such a creature unfit to remain in the society of men. But she was innocent. I know, I feel she was innocent; you are of the same opinion, and that confirms me. Alas! Victor, when falsehood can look so like the truth, who can assure themselves of certain happiness? I feel as if I were walking on the edge of a precipice, towards which thousands are crowding, and endeavoring to plunge me into the abyss. William and Justine were assassinated, and the murderer escapes; he walks about the world free, and perhaps respected. But even if I were condemned to suffer on the scaffold for the same crimes, I would not change places with such a wretch."

I listened to this discourse with the extremest agony. I, not in deed, but in effect, was the true murderer. Elizabeth read my anguish in my countenance, and kindly taking my hand, said, "My dearest friend, you must calm yourself. These events have affected me, God knows how deeply; but I am not so wretched as you are. There is an expression of despair, and sometimes of revenge, in your countenance, that makes me tremble. Dear Victor, banish these dark passions. Remember the friends around you, who center all their hopes in you. Have we lost the power of rendering you happy? Ah! while we love—while we are true to each other, here in this land of peace and beauty, your native country, we may reap every tranquil blessing—what can disturb our peace?"

And could not such words from her whom I fondly prized before every other gift of fortune, suffice to chase away the fiend that lurked in my heart? Even as she spoke I drew near to her, as if in terror; lest at that very moment the destroyer had been near to rob me of her.

Thus not the tenderness of friendship, nor the beauty of earth, nor of heaven, could redeem my soul from woe: the very accents of love were ineffectual. I was encompassed by a cloud which no beneficial influence could penetrate. The wounded deer dragging its fainting limbs to some untrodden brake, there to gaze upon the arrow which had pierced it, and to die—was but a type of me.

Sometimes I could cope with the sullen despair that overwhelmed me: but sometimes the whirlwind passions of my soul drove me to seek, by bodily exercise and by change of place, some relief from my intolerable sensations. It was during an access of this kind that I suddenly left my home, and bending my steps towards the near Alpine valleys, sought in the magnificence, the eternity of such scenes, to forget myself and my ephemeral, because human, sorrows. My wanderings were directed towards the valley of Chamounix. I had visited it frequently during my boyhood. Six years had passed since then: *I* was a wreck—but nought had changed in those savage and enduring scenes.

I performed the first part of my journey on horseback. I afterwards hired a mule, as the more sure-footed, and least liable to receive injury on these rugged roads. The weather was fine: it was about the middle of the month of August, nearly two months after the death of Justine; that miserable epoch from which I dated all my woe. The weight upon my spirit was sensibly lightened as I plunged yet deeper in the ravine of Arve. The immense mountains and precipices that overhung me on every side—the sound of the river raging among the rocks, and the dashing of the waterfalls around, spoke of a power mighty as Omnipotence—and I ceased to fear, or to bend before any being less almighty than that which had created and ruled the elements, here displayed in their most terrific guise. Still, as I ascended higher, the valley assumed a more magnificent and astonishing character. Ruined castles hanging on the precipices of piny mountains; the impetuous Arve, and cottages every here and there peeping forth from among the trees, formed a scene of singular beauty. But it was augmented and rendered sublime by the mighty Alps, whose white and shining pyramids and domes towered above all, as belonging to another earth, the habitations of another race of beings.

I passed the bridge of Pélissier, where the ravine, which the river forms, opened before me, and I began to ascend the mountain that overhangs it. Soon after I entered the valley of Chamounix. This valley is more wonderful and sublime, but not so beautiful and picturesque, as that of Servox, through which I had just passed. The high and snowy mountains were its immediate boundaries; but I saw no more ruined castles and fertile fields. Immense glaciers approached the road; I heard the rumbling thunder of the falling avalanche, and marked the smoke of its passage. Mont Blanc, the supreme and magnificent Mont Blanc, raised itself from the surrounding *aiguilles*, and its tremendous *dôme* overlooked the valley.

A tingling long-lost sense of pleasure often came across me during this journey. Some turn in the road, some new object suddenly perceived and recognized, reminded me of days gone by, and were associated with the light-hearted gaiety of boyhood. The very winds whispered in soothing accents, and maternal nature bade me weep no more. Then again the kindly influence ceased to act—I found myself fettered again to grief, and indulging in all the misery of reflection. Then I spurred on my animal, striving so to forget the world, my fears, and, more than all, myself—or, in a more desperate fashion, I alighted, and threw myself on the grass, weighed down by horror and despair.

At length I arrived at the village of Chamounix. Exhaustion succeeded to the extreme fatigue both of body and of mind which I had endured. For a short space of time I remained at the window, watching the pallid lightnings that played above Mont Blanc, and listening to the rushing of the Arve, which pursued its noisy way beneath. The same lulling sounds acted as a lullaby to my too keen sensations: when I placed my head upon my pillow, sleep crept over me; I felt it as it came, and blest the giver of oblivion.

X

I spent the following day roaming through the valley. I stood beside the sources of the Arveiron, which take their rise in a glacier, that with slow pace is advancing down from the summit of the hills, to barricade the valley. The abrupt sides of vast mountains were before me; the icy wall of the glacier overhung me; a few shattered pines were scattered around; and the solemn silence of this glorious presence-chamber of imperial Nature was broken only by the brawling waves, or the fall of some vast fragment, the thunder sound of the avalanche, or the cracking reverberated along the mountains of the accumulated ice, which, through the silent working of immutable laws, was ever and anon rent and torn, as if it had been but a plaything in their hands. These sublime and magnificent scenes afforded me the greatest consolation that I was capable of receiving. They elevated me from all littleness of feeling; and although they did not remove my grief, they subdued and tranquilized it. In some degree, also, they diverted my mind from the thoughts over which it had brooded for the last month. I retired to rest at night; my slumbers, as it were, waited on and ministered to by the assemblance of grand shapes which I had contemplated during the day. They congregated round me; the unstained snowy mountaintop, the glittering pinnacle, the pine woods, and ragged bare ravine; the eagle, soaring amidst the clouds—they all gathered round me, and bade me be at peace.

Where had they fled when the next morning I awoke? All of soul-inspiriting fled with sleep, and dark melancholy clouded every thought. The rain was pouring in torrents, and thick mists hid the summits of the mountains, so that I even saw not the faces of those mighty friends. Still I would penetrate their misty veil, and seek them in their cloudy retreats. What were rain and storm to me? My mule was brought to the door, and I resolved to ascend to the summit of Montanvert. I remembered the effect that the view of the tremendous and ever-moving glacier had produced upon my mind when I first saw it. It had then filled me with a sublime ecstasy that gave wings to the soul, and allowed it to soar from the obscure world to light and joy. The sight of the awful and majestic in nature had indeed always the effect of solemnizing my mind, and causing me to forget the passing cares of life. I determined to go without a guide, for I was well acquainted with the path, and the presence of another would destroy the solitary grandeur of the scene.

The ascent is precipitous, but the path is cut into continual and short windings, which enable you to surmount the perpendicularity of the mountain. It is a scene terrifically desolate. In a thousand spots the traces of the winter avalanche may be perceived, where trees lie broken and strewed on the ground; some entirely destroyed, others bent, leaning upon the jutting rocks of the mountain, or transversely upon other trees. The path, as you ascend higher, is intersected by ravines of snow, down which stones continually roll from above; one of them is particularly dangerous, as the slightest sound, such as even speaking in a loud voice, produces a concussion of air sufficient to draw destruction upon the head of the speaker. The pines are not tall or luxuriant, but they are sombre, and add an air of severity to the scene. I looked on the valley beneath; vast mists were rising from the rivers which ran through it, and curling in thick wreaths around the opposite mountains, whose summits were hid in the uniform clouds, while rain poured from the dark sky, and added to the melancholy impression I received from the objects around me. Alas! why does man boast of sensibilities superior to those apparent in the brute; it only renders them more necessary beings. If our impulses were confined to hunger, thirst, and desire, we might be nearly free; but now we are moved by every wind that blows, and a chance word or scene that that word may convey to us.

> We rest; a dream has power to poison sleep.
>   We rise; one wandering thought pollutes the day.
> We feel, conceive, or reason; laugh or weep,
>   Embrace fond woe, or cast our cares away;
> It is the same: for, be it joy or sorrow,
>   The path of its departure still is free.
> Man's yesterday may ne'er be like his morrow;
>   Nought may endure but mutability!

It was nearly noon when I arrived at the top of the ascent. For some time I sat upon the rock that overlooks the sea of ice. A mist covered both that and the surrounding mountains. Presently a breeze dissipated the cloud, and I descended upon the glacier. The surface is very uneven, rising like the waves of a troubled sea, descending low, and interspersed by rifts that sink deep. The field of ice is almost a league in width, but I spent nearly two hours in crossing it. The opposite mountain is a bare perpendicular rock. From the side where I now stood Montanvert was exactly opposite, at the distance of a league; and above it rose Mont Blanc, in awful majesty. I remained in a recess of the rock, gazing on this wonderful and stupendous scene. The sea, or rather the vast river of ice, wound among its dependent mountains, whose aerial summits hung over its recesses. Their icy and glittering peaks shone in the sunlight over the clouds. My heart, which was before sorrowful, now swelled with something like joy;

I exclaimed—"Wandering spirits, if indeed ye wander, and do not rest in your narrow beds, allow me this faint happiness, or take me, as your companion, away from the joys of life."

As I said this, I suddenly beheld the figure of a man, at some distance, advancing towards me with superhuman speed. He bounded over the crevices in the ice, among which I had walked with caution; his stature, also, as he approached, seemed to exceed that of man. I was troubled: a mist came over my eyes, and I felt a faintness seize me; but I was quickly restored by the cold gale of the mountains. I perceived, as the shape came nearer (sight tremendous and abhorred!) that it was the wretch whom I had created. I trembled with rage and horror, resolving to wait his approach, and then close with him in mortal combat. He approached; his countenance bespoke bitter anguish, combined with disdain and malignity, while its unearthly ugliness rendered it almost too horrible for human eyes. But I scarcely observed this; rage and hatred had at first deprived me of utterance, and I recovered only to overwhelm him with words expressive of furious detestation and contempt.

"Devil," I exclaimed, "do you dare approach me and do not you fear the fierce vengeance of my arm wreaked on your miserable head? Begone, vile insect! or rather, stay, that I may trample you to dust! and, oh! that I could, with the extinction of your miserable existence, restore those victims whom you have so diabolically murdered!"

"I expected this reception," said the dæmon. "All men hate the wretched; how, then, must I be hated, who am miserable beyond all living things! Yet you, my creator, detest and spurn me, thy creature, to whom thou art bound by ties only dissoluble by the annihilation of one of us. You purpose to kill me. How dare you sport thus with life? Do your duty towards me, and I will do mine towards you and the rest of mankind. If you will comply with my conditions, I will leave them and you at peace; but if you refuse, I will glut the maw of death, until it be satiated with the blood of your remaining friends."

"Abhorred monster! fiend that thou art! the tortures of hell are too mild a vengeance for thy crimes. Wretched devil! you reproach me with your creation; come on, then, that I may extinguish the spark which I so negligently bestowed."

My rage was without bounds; I sprang on him, impelled by all the feelings which can arm one being against the existence of another.

He easily eluded me, and said—

"Be calm! I entreat you to hear me, before you give vent to your hatred on my devoted head. Have I not suffered enough that you seek to increase my misery? Life, although it may only be an accumulation of anguish, is dear to me, and I will defend it. Remember, thou hast made me more powerful than thyself; my height is superior to thine; my joints more supple. But I will not be tempted to set myself in opposition to thee. I am thy creature, and I will be even mild and docile to my natural lord and king, if thou wilt also perform thy part, the which thou owest me. Oh, Frankenstein, be not equitable to every other, and trample upon me alone, to whom thy justice, and even thy clemency and affection, is most due. Remember, that I am thy creature; I ought to be thy Adam; but I am rather the fallen angel, whom thou drivest from joy for no misdeed. Everywhere I see bliss, from which I alone am irrevocably excluded. I was benevolent and good; misery made me a fiend. Make me happy, and I shall again be virtuous."

"Begone! I will not hear you. There can be no community between you and me; we are enemies. Begone; or let us try our strength in a fight, in which one must fall."

"How can I move thee? Will no entreaties cause thee to turn a favorable eye upon thy creature, who implores thy goodness and compassion? Believe me, Frankenstein: I was benevolent; my soul glowed with love and humanity: but am I not alone, miserably alone? You, my creator, abhor me; what hope can I gather from your fellow-creatures, who owe me nothing? they spurn and hate me. The desert mountains and dreary glaciers are my refuge. I have wandered here many days; the caves of ice, which I only do not fear, are a dwelling to me, and the only one which man does not grudge. These bleak skies I hail, for they are kinder to me than your fellow-beings. If the multitude of mankind knew of my existence, they would do as you do, and arm themselves for my destruction. Shall I not then hate them who abhor me? I will keep no terms with my enemies. I am miserable, and they shall share my wretchedness. Yet it is in your power to recompense me, and deliver them from an evil which it only remains for you to make so great that not only you and your family, but thousands of others, shall be swallowed up in the whirlwinds of its rage. Let your compassion be moved, and do not disdain me. Listen to my tale: when you have heard that, abandon or commiserate me, as you shall judge that I deserve. But hear me. The guilty are allowed, by human laws, bloody as they are, to speak in their own defense before they are condemned. Listen to me, Frankenstein. You accuse me of murder; and yet you would, with a satisfied conscience, destroy your own creature. Oh, praise the eternal justice of man! Yet I ask you not to spare me: listen to me; and then, if you can, and if you will, destroy the work of your hands."

"Why do you call to my remembrance," I rejoined, "circumstances, of which I shudder to reflect, that I have been the miserable origin and author? Cursed be the day, abhorred devil, in which you first saw light! Cursed (although I curse myself) be the hands that formed you! You have made me wretched beyond expression. You have left me no power to consider whether I am just to you or not. Begone! relieve me from the sight of your detested form."

"Thus I relieve thee, my creator," he said, and placed his hated hands before my eyes, which I flung from me with violence; "thus I take from thee a sight which you abhòr. Still thou canst listen to me, and grant me thy compassion. By the virtues that I once possessed, I demand this from you. Hear my tale; it is long and strange, and the temperature of this place is not fitting to your fine sensations; come to the hut upon the mountain. The sun is yet high in the heavens; before it descends to hide itself behind yon snowy precipices, and illuminate another world, you will have heard my story, and can decide. On you it rests whether I quit for ever the neighborhood of man, and lead a harmless life, or become the scourge of your fellow-creatures, and the author of your own speedy ruin."

As he said this, he led the way across the ice: I followed. My heart was full, and I did not answer him; but, as I proceeded, I weighed the various arguments that he had used, and determined at least to listen to his tale. I was partly urged by curiosity, and compassion confirmed my resolution. I had hitherto supposed him to be the murderer of my brother, and I eagerly sought a confirmation or denial of this opinion. For the first time, also, I felt what the duties of a creator towards his creature were, and that I ought to render him happy before I complained of his wickedness. These motives urged me to comply with his demand. We crossed the ice, therefore, and ascended the opposite rock. The air was cold, and the rain again began to descend: we entered the hut, the fiend with an air of exultation, I with a heavy heart and depressed spirits. But I consented to listen; and, seating myself by the fire which my odious companion had lighted, he thus began his tale.

XI

"It is with considerable difficulty that I remember the original era of my being: all the events of that period appear confused and indistinct. A strange multiplicity of sensations seized me, and I saw, felt, heard, and smelt, at the same time; and it was, indeed, a long time before I learned to distinguish between the operations of my various senses. By degrees, I remember, a stronger light pressed upon my nerves, so that I was obliged to shut my eyes. Darkness then came over me, and troubled me; but hardly had I felt this, when, by opening my eyes, as I now suppose, the light poured in upon me again. I walked, and, I believe, descended; but I presently found a great alteration in my sensations. Before, dark and opaque bodies had surrounded me, impervious to my touch or sight; but I now found that I could wander on at liberty, with no obstacles which I could not either surmount or avoid. The light became more and more oppressive to me; and, the heat wearying me as I walked, I sought a place where I could receive shade. This was the forest near Ingolstadt; and here I lay by the side of a brook resting from my fatigue, until I felt tormented by hunger and thirst. This roused me from my nearly dormant state, and I ate some berries which I found hanging on the trees, or lying on the ground. I slaked my thirst at the brook; and then lying down, was overcome by sleep.

"It was dark when I awoke; I felt cold also, and half-frightened, as it were instinctively, finding myself so desolate. Before I had quitted your apartment, on a sensation of cold, I had covered myself with some clothes; but these were insufficient to secure me from the dews of night. I was a poor, helpless, miserable wretch; I knew, and could distinguish, nothing; but feeling pain invade me on all sides, I sat down and wept.

"Soon a gentle light stole over the heavens, and gave me a sensation of pleasure. I started up, and beheld a radiant form rise from among the trees.* I gazed with a kind of wonder. It moved slowly, but it enlightened my path; and I again went out in search of berries. I was still cold, when under one of the trees I found a huge cloak, with which I covered myself, and sat down upon the ground. No distinct ideas occupied my mind; all was confused. I felt light, and hunger, and thirst, and darkness; innumerable sounds rung in my ears, and on all sides various scents saluted me: the only object that I could distinguish was the bright moon, and I fixed my eyes on that with pleasure.

"Several changes of day and night passed, and the orb of night had greatly lessened, when I began to distinguish my sensations from each other. I gradually saw plainly the clear stream that supplied me with drink, and the trees that shaded me with their foliage. I was delighted when I first discovered that a pleasant sound, which often saluted my ears, proceeded from the throats of the little winged animals who had often intercepted the light from my eyes. I began also to observe, with greater accuracy, the forms that surrrounded me, and to perceive the boundaries of the radiant roof of light which canopied me. Sometimes I tried to imitate the pleasant songs of the birds, but was unable. Sometimes I wished to express my sensations in my own mode, but the uncouth and inarticulate sounds which broke from me frightened me into silence again.

"The moon had disappeared from the night, and again, with a lessened form, showed itself, while I still remained in the forest. My sensations had, by this time, become distinct, and my mind received every day additional ideas. My eyes became accustomed to the light, and to perceive objects in their right forms; I distinguished the insect from the herb, and, by degrees, one herb from another. I found that the sparrow uttered none but harsh notes, whilst those of the blackbird and thrush were sweet and enticing.

"One day, when I was oppressed by cold, I found a fire which had been left by some wandering beggars, and was overcome with delight at the

---

* The Moon

warmth I experienced from it. In my joy I thrust my hand into the live embers, but quickly drew it out again with a cry of pain. How strange, I thought, that the same cause should produce such opposite effects! I examined the materials of the fire, and to my joy found it to be composed of wood. I quickly collected some branches; but they were wet, and would not burn. I was pained at this, and sat still watching the operation of the fire. The wet wood which I had placed near the heat dried, and itself became inflamed. I reflected on this; and, by touching the various branches, I discovered the cause, and busied myself in collecting a great quantity of wood, that I might dry it, and have a plentiful supply of fire. When night came on, and brought sleep with it, I was in the greatest fear lest my fire should be extinguished. I covered it carefully with dry wood and leaves, and placed wet branches upon it; and then, spreading my cloak, I lay on the ground, and sunk into sleep.

"It was morning when I awoke, and my first care was to visit the fire. I uncovered it, and a gentle breeze quickly fanned it into a flame. I observed this also, and contrived a fan of branches, which roused the embers when they were nearly extinguished. When night came again, I found, with pleasure, that the fire gave light as well as heat; and that the discovery of this element was useful to me in my food; for I found some of the offals that the travelers had left had been roasted, and tasted much more savory than the berries I gathered from the trees. I tried, therefore, to dress my food in the same manner, placing it on the live embers. I found that the berries were spoiled by this operation, and the nuts and roots much improved.

"Food, however, became scarce; and I often spent the whole day searching in vain for a few acorns to assuage the pangs of hunger. When I found this, I resolved to quit the place that I had hitherto inhabited, to seek for one where the few wants I experienced would be more easily satisfied. In this emigration, I exceedingly lamented the loss of the fire which I had obtained through accident, and knew not how to reproduce it. I gave several hours to the serious consideration of this difficulty; but I was obliged to relinquish all attempt to supply it; and, wrapping myself up in my cloak, I struck across the wood towards the setting sun. I passed three days in these rambles, and at length discovered the open country.

A great fall of snow had taken place the night before, and the fields were of one uniform white; the appearance was disconsolate, and I found my feet chilled by the cold damp substance that covered the ground.

"It was about seven in the morning, and I longed to obtain food and shelter; at length I perceived a small hut, on a rising ground, which had doubtless been built for the convenience of some shepherd. This was a new sight to me; and I examined the structure with great curiosity. Finding the door open, I entered. An old man sat in it, near a fire, over which he was preparing his breakfast. He turned on hearing a noise; and, perceiving me, shrieked loudly, and, quitting the hut, ran across the fields with a speed of which his debilitated form hardly appeared capable. His appearance, different from any I had ever before seen, and his flight, somewhat surprised me. But I was enchanted by the appearance of the hut: here the snow and rain could not penetrate; the ground was dry; and it presented to me then as exquisite and divine a retreat as Pandaemonium appeared to the dæmons of hell after their sufferings in the lake of fire. I greedily devoured the remnants of the shepherd's breakfast, which consisted of bread, cheese, milk, and wine; the latter, however, I did not like. Then, overcome by fatigue, I lay down among some straw, and fell asleep.

"It was noon when I awoke; and, allured by the warmth of the sun, which shone brightly on the white ground, I determined to recommence my travels; and, depositing the remains of the peasant's breakfast in a wallet I found, I proceeded across the fields for several hours, until at sunset I arrived at a village. How miraculous did this appear! the huts, the neater cottages, and stately houses, engaged my admiration by turns. The vegetables in the gardens, the milk and cheese that I saw placed at the windows of some of the cottages, allured my appetite. One of the best of these I entered; but I had hardly placed my foot within the door, before the children shrieked, and one of the women fainted. The whole village was roused; some fled, some attacked me, until, grievously bruised by stones and many other kinds of missile weapons, I escaped to the open country, and fearfully took refuge in a low hovel, quite bare, and making a wretched appearance after the palaces I had beheld in the village. This hovel, however, joined a cottage of a neat and pleasant appearance; but, after my late dearly bought experience, I dared not enter it. My place of refuge was constructed of wood, but so low that I could with difficulty sit upright in it. No wood, however, was placed on the earth, which formed the floor, but it was dry; and although the wind entered it by innumerable chinks, I found it an agreeable asylum from the snow and rain.

"Here then I retreated, and lay down happy to have found a shelter, however miserable, from the inclemency of the season, and still more from the barbarity of man.

"As soon as morning dawned, I crept from my kennel, that I might view the adjacent cottage, and discover if I could remain in the habitation I had found. It was situated against the back of the cottage, and surrounded on the sides which were exposed by a pig-sty and a clear pool of water. One part was open, and by that I had crept in; but now I covered every crevice by which I might be perceived with stones and wood, yet in such a manner that I might move them on occasion to pass out: all the light I enjoyed came through the sty, and that was sufficient for me.

"Having thus arranged my dwelling, and carpeted it with clean straw, I retired; for I saw the figure of a man at a distance, and I remembered too well my treatment the night before to trust myself in his power. I had first, however, provided for my sustenance for that day, by a loaf of coarse bread, which I purloined, and a cup with which I could drink, more conveniently than from my hand, of the pure water which flowed by my retreat. The floor was a little raised, so that it was kept perfectly dry, and by its vicinity to the chimney of the cottage it was tolerably warm.

"Being thus provided, I resolved to reside in this hovel until something should occur which might alter my determination. It was indeed a paradise compared to the bleak forest, my former residence, the rain-dropping branches, and dank earth. I ate my breakfast with pleasure, and was about to remove a plank to procure myself a little water, when I heard a step, and looking through a small chink, I beheld a young creature, with a pail on her head, passing before my hovel. The girl was young, and of gentle demeanor, unlike what I have since found cottagers and farmhouse servants to be. Yet she was meanly dressed, a coarse blue petticoat and a linen jacket being her only garb; her fair hair was plaited, but not adorned: she looked patient, yet sad. I lost sight of her; and in about a quarter of an hour she returned, bearing the pail, which was now partly filled with milk. As she walked along, seemingly incommoded by the burden, a young man met her, whose countenance expressed a deeper despondence. Uttering a few sounds with an air of melancholy, he took the pail from her head, and bore it to the cottage himself. She followed, and they disappeared. Presently I saw the young man again, with some tools in his hand, cross the field behind the cottage; and the girl was also busied, sometimes in the house, and sometimes in the yard.

"On examining my dwelling, I found that one of the windows of the cottage had formerly occupied a part of it, but the panes had been filled up with wood. In one of these was a small and almost imperceptible chink, through which the eye could just penetrate. Through this crevice a small room was visible, whitewashed and clean, but very bare of furniture. In one corner, near a small fire, sat an old man, leaning his head on his hands in a disconsolate attitude. The young girl was occupied in arranging the cottage; but presently she took something out of a drawer, which employed her hands, and she sat down beside the old man, who, taking up an instrument, began to play, and to produce sounds sweeter than the voice of the thrush or the nightingale. It was a lovely sight, even to me, poor wretch! who had never beheld aught beautiful before. The silver hair and benevolent countenance of the aged cottager won my reverence, while the gentle manners of the girl enticed my love. He played a sweet mournful air, which I perceived drew tears from the eyes of his amiable companion, of which the old man took no notice, until she sobbed audibly; he then pronounced a few sounds, and the fair creature, leaving her work, knelt at his feet. He raised her, and smiled with such kindness and affection that I felt sensations of a peculiar and overpowering nature: they were a mixture of pain and pleasure, such as I had never before experienced, either from hunger or cold, warmth or food; and I withdrew from the window, unable to bear these emotions.

"Soon after this the young man returned, bearing on his shoulders a load of wood. The girl met him at the door, helped to relieve him of his burden, and, taking some of the fuel into the cottage, placed it on the fire; then she and the youth went apart into a nook of the cottage and he showed her a large loaf and a piece of cheese. She seemed pleased, and went into the garden for some roots and plants, which she placed in water, and then upon the fire. She afterwards continued her work, whilst the young man went into the garden, and appeared busily employed in digging and pulling up roots. After he had been employed thus about an hour, the young woman joined him, and they entered the cottage together.

"The old man had, in the meantime, been pensive; but, on the appearance of his companions, he assumed a more cheerful air, and they sat down to eat. The meal was quickly despatched. The young woman was again occupied in arranging the cottage; the old man walked before the cottage in the sun for a few minutes, leaning on the arm of the youth. Nothing could exceed in beauty the contrast between these two excellent creatures. One was old, with silver hairs and a countenance beaming with benevolence and love: the younger was slight and graceful in his figure, and his features were molded with the finest symmetry; yet his eyes and attitude expressed the utmost sadness and despondency. The old man returned to the cottage; and the youth, with tools different from those he had used in the morning, directed his steps across the fields.

"Night quickly shut in; but, to my extreme wonder, I found that the cottagers had a means of prolonging light by the use of tapers, and was delighted to find that the setting of the sun did not put an end to the pleasure I experienced in watching my human neighbors. In the evening, the young girl and her companion were employed in various occupations which I did not understand; and the old man again took up the instrument which produced the divine sounds that had enchanted me in the morning. So soon as he had finished, the youth began, not to play, but to utter sounds that were monotonous, and neither resembling the harmony of the old man's instrument nor the songs of the birds: I since found that he read aloud, but at that time I knew nothing of the science of words or letters.

"The family, after having been thus occupied for a short time, extinguished their lights, and retired, as I conjectured, to rest."

XII

"I lay on my straw, but I could not sleep. I thought of the occurrences of the day. What chiefly struck me was the gentle manners of these people; and I longed to join them, but dared not. I remembered too well the treatment I had suffered the night before from the barbarous villagers, and resolved, whatever course of conduct I might hereafter think it right to pursue, that for the present I would remain quietly in my hovel, watching, and endeavoring to discover the motives which influenced their actions.

"The cottagers arose the next morning before the sun. The young woman arranged the cottage, and prepared the food; and the youth departed after the first meal.

"This day was passed in the same routine as that which preceded it. The young man was constantly employed out of doors, and the girl in various laborious occupations within. The old man, whom I soon perceived to be blind, employed his leisure hours on his instrument or in contemplation. Nothing could exceed the love and respect which the younger cottagers exhibited towards their venerable companion. They performed towards him every little office of affection and duty with gentleness; and he rewarded them by his benevolent smiles.

"They were not entirely happy. The young man and his companion often went apart, and appeared to weep. I saw no cause for their unhappiness; but I was deeply affected by it. If such lovely creatures were miserable, it was less strange that I, an imperfect and solitary being, should be wretched. Yet why were these gentle beings unhappy? They possessed a delightful house (for such it was in my eyes) and every luxury; they had a fire to warm them when chill, and delicious viands when hungry; they were dressed in excellent clothes; and, still more, they enjoyed one another's company and speech, interchanging each day looks of affection and kindness. What did their tears imply? Did they really express pain? I was at first unable to solve these questions; but perpetual attention and time explained to me many appearances which were at first enigmatic.

"A considerable period elapsed before I discovered one of the causes of the uneasiness of this amiable family: it was poverty; and they suffered that evil in a very distressing degree. Their nourishment consisted entirely of the vegetables of their garden, and the milk of one cow, which gave very little during the winter, when its masters could scarcely procure food to support it. They often, I believe, suffered the pangs of hunger very poignantly, especially the two younger cottagers; for several times they placed food before the old man when they reserved none for themselves.

"This trait of kindness moved me sensibly. I had been accustomed, during the night, to steal a part of their store for my own consumption; but when I found that in doing this I inflicted pain on the cottagers, I abstained, and satisfied myself with berries, nuts, and roots, which I gathered from a neighboring wood.

"I discovered also another means through which I was enabled to assist their labors. I found that the youth spent a great part of each day in collecting wood for the family fire; and, during the night, I often took his tools, the use of which I quickly discovered, and brought home firing sufficient for the consumption of several days.

"I remember the first time that I did this the young woman, when she opened the door in the morning, appeared greatly astonished on seeing a great pile of wood on the outside. She uttered some words in a loud voice, and the youth joined her, who also expressed surprise. I observed, with pleasure, that he did not go to the forest that day, but spent it in repairing the cottage and cultivating the garden.

"By degrees I made a discovery of still greater moment. I found that these people possessed a method of communicating their experience and feelings to one another by articulate sounds. I perceived that the words they spoke sometimes produced pleasure or pain, smiles or sadness, in the minds and countenances of the hearers. This was indeed a godlike science, and I ardently desired to become acquainted with it. But I was baffled in every attempt I made for this purpose. Their pronunciation was quick; and the words they uttered, not having any apparent connection with visible objects, I was unable to discover any clue by which I could unravel the mystery of their reference. By great application, however, and after having remained during the space of several revolutions of the moon in my hovel, I discovered the names that were given to some of the most familiar objects of discourse; I learned and applied the words, *fire*, *milk*, *bread*, and *wood*. I learned also the names of the cottagers themselves. The youth and his companion had each of them several names, but the old man had only one, which was *father*. The girl was called *sister*, or *Agatha*; and the youth *Felix*, *brother*, or *son*. I cannot describe the delight I felt when I learned the ideas appropriated to each of these sounds, and was able to pronounce them. I distinguished several other words, without being able as yet to understand or apply them; such as *good, dearest, unhappy*.

"I spent the winter in this manner. The gentle manners and beauty of the cottagers greatly endeared them to me: when they were unhappy, I felt depressed; when they rejoiced, I sympathized in their joys. I saw few human beings beside them; and if any other happened to enter the cottage, their harsh manners and rude gait only enhanced to me the superior accomplishments of my friends. The old man, I could perceive, often endeavored to encourage his children, as sometimes I found that he called them, to cast off their melancholy. He would talk in a cheerful accent, with an expression of goodness that bestowed pleasure even upon me. Agatha listened with respect, her eyes sometimes filled with tears, which she endeavored to wipe away unperceived; but I generally found that her countenance and tone were more cheerful after having listened to the exhortations of her father. It was not thus with Felix. He was always the saddest of the group; and, even to my unpracticed senses, he appeared to have suffered more deeply than his friends. But if his countenance was more sorrowful, his voice was more cheerful than that of his sister, especially when he addressed the old man.

"I could mention innumerable instances, which, although slight, marked the dispositions of these amiable cottagers. In the midst of poverty and want, Felix carried with pleasure to his sister the first little white flower that peeped out from beneath the snowy ground. Early in the morning, before she had risen, he cleared away the snow that obstructed her path to the milk-house, drew water from the well, and brought the wood from the out-house, where, to his perpetual astonishment, he found his store always replenished by an invisible hand. In the day, I believe, he worked sometimes for a neighboring farmer, because he often went forth, and did not return until dinner, yet brought no wood with him. At other times he worked in the garden; but, as there was little to do in the frosty season, he read to the old man and Agatha.

"This reading had puzzled me extremely at first; but, by degrees, I discovered that he uttered many of the same sounds when he read as when he talked. I conjectured, therefore, that he found on the paper signs for speech which he understood, and I ardently longed to comprehend these also; but how was that possible, when I did not even understand the sounds for which they stood as signs? I improved, however, sensibly in this science, but not sufficiently to follow up any kind of conversation, although I applied my whole mind to the endeavor: for I easily perceived that, although I eagerly longed to discover myself to the cottagers, I ought not to make the attempt until I had first become master of their language; which knowledge might enable me to make them overlook the deformity of my figure; for with this also the contrast perpetually presented to my eyes had made me acquainted.

"I had admired the perfect forms of my cottagers—their grace, beauty, and delicate complexions: but how was I terrified when I viewed myself in a transparent pool! At first I started back, unable to believe that it was indeed I who was reflected in the mirror; and when I became fully convinced that I was in reality the monster that I am, I was filled with the bitterest sensations of despondence and mortification. Alas! I did not yet entirely know the fatal effects of this miserable deformity.

"As the sun became warmer, and the light of day longer, the snow vanished, and I beheld the bare trees and the black earth. From this time Felix was more employed; and the heartmoving indications of impending famine disappeared. Their food, as I afterwards found, was coarse, but it was wholesome; and they procured a sufficiency of it. Several new kinds of plants sprung up in the garden, which they dressed; and these signs of comfort increased daily as the season advanced.

"The old man, leaning on his son, walked each day at noon, when it did not rain, as I found it was called when the heavens poured forth its waters. This frequently took place; but a high wind quickly dried the earth, and the season became far more pleasant than it had been.

"My mode of life in my hovel was uniform. During the morning, I attended the motions of the cottagers; and when they were dispersed in various occupations I slept: the remainder of the day was spent in observing my friends. When they had retired to rest, if there was any moon, or the night was star-light, I went into the woods, and collected my own food and fuel for the cottage. When I returned, as often as it was necessary, I cleared their path from the snow, and performed those offices that I had seen done by Felix. I afterwards found that these labors, performed by an invisible hand, greatly astonished them; and once or twice

I heard them, on these occasions, utter the words *good spirit, wonderful*; but I did not then understand the signification of these terms.

"My thoughts now became more active, and I longed to discover the motives and feelings of these lovely creatures; I was inquisitive to know why Felix appeared so miserable and Agatha so sad. I thought (foolish wretch!) that it might be in my power to restore happiness to these deserving people. When I slept, or was absent, the forms of the venerable blind father, the gentle Agatha, and the excellent Felix flitted before me. I looked upon them as superior beings, who would be the arbiters of my future destiny. I formed in my imagination a thousand pictures of presenting myself to them, and their reception of me. I imagined that they would be disgusted, until, by my gentle demeanor and conciliating words, I should first win their favor, and afterwards their love.

"These thoughts exhilarated me, and led me to apply with fresh ardor to the acquiring the art of language. My organs were indeed harsh, but supple; and although my voice was very unlike the soft music of their tones, yet I pronounced such words as I understood with tolerable ease. It was as the ass and the lap-dog; yet surely the gentle ass whose intentions were affectionate, although his manners were rude, deserved better treatment than blows and execration.

"The pleasant showers and genial warmth of spring greatly altered the aspect of the earth. Men, who before this change seemed to have been hid in caves, dispersed themselves, and were employed in various arts of cultivation. The birds sang in more cheerful notes, and the leaves began to bud forth on the trees. Happy, happy earth! fit habitation for gods, which, so short a time before, was bleak, damp, and unwholesome. My spirits were elevated by the enchanting appearance of nature; the past was blotted from my memory, the present was tranquil, and the future gilded by bright rays of hope and anticipations of joy.

XIII

"I now hasten to the more moving part of my story. I shall relate events that impressed me with feelings which from what I had been, have made me what I am.

"Spring advanced rapidly; the weather became fine and the skies cloudless. It surprised me that what before was desert and gloomy should now bloom with the most beautiful flowers and verdure. My senses were gratified and refreshed by a thousand scents of delight, and a thousand sights of beauty.

"It was on one of these days, when my cottagers periodically rested from labor—the old man played on his guitar, and the children listened to him—that I observed the countenance of Felix was melancholy beyond expression; he sighed frequently; and once his father paused in his music, and I conjectured by his manner that he inquired the cause of his son's sorrow. Felix replied in a cheerful accent, and the old man was recommencing his music when some one tapped at the door.

"It was a lady on horseback, accompanied by a countryman as a guide. The lady was dressed in a dark suit, and covered with a thick black veil. Agatha asked a question; to which the stranger only replied by pronouncing, in a sweet accent, the name of Felix. Her voice was musical, but unlike that of either of my friends. On hearing this word, Felix came up hastily to the lady; who, when she saw him, threw up her veil, and I beheld a countenance of angelic beauty and expression. Her hair of a shining raven black, and curiously braided; her eyes were dark, but gentle, although animated; her features of a regular proportion, and her complexion wondrously fair, each cheek tinged with a lovely pink.

"Felix seemed ravished with delight when he saw her, every trait of sorrow vanished from his face, and it instantly expressed a degree of ecstatic joy, of which I could hardly have believed it capable; his eyes sparkled as his cheek flushed with pleasure; and at that moment I thought him as beautiful as the stranger. She appeared affected by different feelings; wiping a few tears from her lovely eyes, she held out her hand to Felix, who kissed it rapturously, and called her, as well as I could distinguish, his sweet Arabian. She did not appear to understand him, but smiled. He assisted her to dismount, and dismissing her guide, conducted her into the cottage. Some conversation took place between him and his father; and the young stranger knelt at the old man's feet, and would have kissed his hand, but he raised her, and embraced her affectionately.

"I soon perceived that, although the stranger uttered articulate sounds, and appeared to have a language of her own, she was neither understood by, nor herself understood, the cottagers. They made many signs which I did not comprehend; but I saw that her presence diffused gladness through the cottage, dispelling their sorrow as the sun dissipates the morning mists. Felix seemed peculiarly happy, and with smiles of delight welcomed his Arabian. Agatha, the ever-gentle Agatha, kissed the hands of the lovely stranger; and, pointing to her brother, made signs which appeared to me to mean that he had been sorrowful until she came. Some hours passed thus, while they, by their countenances, expressed joy, the cause of which I did not comprehend. Presently I found, by the frequent recurrence of some sound which the stranger repeated after them, that she was endeavoring to learn their language; and the idea instantly occurred to me that I should make use of the same instructions to the same end. The stranger learned about twenty words at the first lesson, most of them, indeed, were those which I had before understood, but I profited by the others.

"As night came on, Agatha and the Arabian retired early. When they separated, Felix kissed the hand of the stranger, and said, 'Good night, sweet Safie.' He sat up much longer, conversing with his father; and, by the frequent repetition of her name, I conjectured that their lovely guest was the subject of their conversation. I ardently desired to understand them, and bent every faculty towards that purpose, but found it utterly impossible.

"The next morning Felix went out to his work; and, after the usual occupations of Agatha were finished, the Arabian sat at the feet of the old man, and, taking his guitar, played some airs so entrancingly beautiful that they at once drew tears of sorrow and delight from my eyes. She sang, and her voice flowed in a rich cadence, swelling or dying away, like a nightingale of the woods.

"When she had finished, she gave the guitar to Agatha, who at first declined it. She played a simple air, and her voice accompanied it in sweet accents, but unlike the wondrous strain of the stranger. The old man appeared enraptured, and said some words, which Agatha endeavored to explain to Safie, and by which he appeared to wish to express that she bestowed on him the greatest delight by her music.

"The days now passed as peaceably as before, with the sole alteration that joy had taken place of sadness in the countenances of my friends. Safie was always gay and happy; she and I improved rapidly in the knowledge of language, so that in two months I began to comprehend most of the words uttered by my protectors.

"In the meanwhile also the black ground was covered with herbage, and the green banks interspersed with innumerable flowers, sweet to the scent and the eyes, stars of pale radiance among the moonlight woods; the sun became warmer, the nights clear and balmy; and my nocturnal rambles were an extreme pleasure to me, although they were considerably shortened by the late setting and early rising of the sun; for I never ventured abroad during daylight, fearful of meeting with the same treatment I had formerly endured in the first village which I entered.

"My days were spent in close attention, that I might more speedily master the language; and I may boast that I improved more rapidly than the Arabian, who understood very little, and conversed in broken accents, whilst I comprehended and could imitate almost every word that was spoken.

"While I improved in speech, I also learned the science of letters, as it was taught to the stranger; and this opened before me a wide field for wonder and delight.

"The book from which Felix instructed Safie was Volney's *Ruins of Empires*. I should not have understood the purport of this book, had not Felix, in reading it, given very minute explanations. He had chosen this work, he said, because the declamatory style was framed in imitation of the eastern authors. Through this work I obtained a cursory knowledge of history, and a view of the several empires at present existing in the world; it gave me an insight into the manners, governments, and religions of the different nations of the earth. I heard of the slothful Asiatics; of the stupendous genius and mental activity of the Grecians; of the wars and wonderful virtue of the early Romans—of their subsequent degenerating—of the decline of that mighty empire; of chivalry, Christianity, and kings. I heard of the discovery of the American hemisphere, and wept with Safie over the hapless fate of its original inhabitants.

"These wonderful narrations inspired me with strange feelings. Was man, indeed, at once so powerful, so virtuous and magnificent, yet so vicious and base? He appeared at one time a mere scion of the evil principle, and at another as all that can be conceived of noble and godlike. To be a great and virtuous man appeared the highest honor that can befall a sensitive being; to be base and vicious, as many on record have been, appeared the lowest degradation, a condition more abject than that of the blind mole or harmless worm. For a long time I could not conceive how one man could go forth to murder his fellow, or even why there were laws and governments; but when I heard details of vice and bloodshed, my wonder ceased, and I turned away with disgust and loathing.

"Every conversation of the cottagers now opened new wonders to me. While I listened to the instructions which Felix bestowed upon the Arabian, the strange system of human society was explained to me. I heard of the division of property, of immense wealth and squalid poverty; of rank, descent, and noble blood.

"The words induced me to turn towards myself. I learned that the possessions most esteemed by your fellow-creatures were high and unsullied descent united with riches. A man might be respected with only one of these advantages; but, without either, he was considered, except in very rare instances, as a vagabond and a slave, doomed to waste his powers for the profits of the chosen few! And what was I? Of my creation and creator I was absolutely ignorant; but I knew that I possessed no money, no friends, no kind of property. I was, besides, endued with a figure hideously deformed and loathsome; I was not even of the same nature as man. I was more agile than they, and could subsist upon coarser diet; I bore the extremes of heat and cold with less injury to my frame; my stature far exceeded theirs. When I looked around, I saw and heard of none like me. Was I then a monster, a blot upon the earth, from which all men fled, and whom all men disowned?

"I cannot describe to you the agony that these reflections inflicted upon me: I tried to dispel them, but sorrow only increased with knowledge. Oh, that I had for ever remained in my native wood, nor known nor felt beyond the sensations of hunger, thirst, and heat!

"Of what a strange nature is knowledge! It clings to the mind, when it has once seized on it, like a lichen on the rock. I wished sometimes to shake off all thought and feeling; but I learned that there was but one means to overcome the sensation of pain, and that was death—a state which I feared yet did not understand. I admired virtue and good feelings, and loved the gentle manners and amiable qualities of my cottagers; but I was shut out from intercourse with them, except through means which I obtained by stealth, when I was unseen and unknown, and which rather increased than satisfied the desire I had of becoming one among my fellows. The gentle words of Agatha, and the animated smiles of the charming Arabian, were not for me. The mild exhortations of the old man, and the lively conversation of the loved Felix, were not for me. Miserable, unhappy wretch!

"Other lessons were impressed upon me even more deeply. I heard of the difference of sexes; and the birth and growth of children; how the father doted on the smiles of the infant, and the lively sallies of the older child; how all the life and cares of the mother were wrapped up in the precious charge; how the mind of youth expanded and gained knowledge; of brother, sister, and all the various relationships which bind one human being to another in mutual bonds.

"But where were my friends and relations? No father had watched my infant days, no mother had blessed me with smiles and caresses; or if they had, all my past life was now a blot, a blind vacancy in which I distinguished nothing. From my earliest remembrance I had been as I then was in height and proportion. I had never yet seen a being resembling me, or who claimed any intercourse with me. What was I? The question again recurred, to be answered only with groans.

"I will soon explain to what these feelings tended; but allow me now to return to the cottagers, whose story excited in me such various feelings of indignation, delight, and wonder, but which all terminated in additional love and reverence for my protectors (for so I loved, in an innocent, half painful self-deceit, to call them)."

XIV

"Some time elapsed before I learned the history of my friends. It was one which could not fail to impress itself deeply on my mind, unfolding as it did a number of circumstances, each interesting and wonderful to one so utterly inexperienced as I was.

"The name of the old man was De Lacey. He was descended from a good family in France, where he had lived for many years in affluence, respected by his superiors and beloved by his equals. His son was bred in the service of his country; and Agatha had ranked with ladies of the highest distinction. A few months before my arrival they had lived in a large and luxurious city called Paris, surrounded by friends, and possessed of every enjoyment which virtue, refinement of intellect, or taste, accompanied by a moderate fortune, could afford.

"The father of Safie had been the cause of their ruin. He was a Turkish merchant, and had inhabited Paris for many years, when, for some reason which I could not learn, he became obnoxious to the government. He was seized and cast into prison the very day that Safie arrived from Constantinople to join him. He was tried and condemned to death. The injustice of his sentence was very flagrant; all Paris was indignant; and it was judged that his religion and wealth, rather than the crime alleged against him, had been the cause of his condemnation.

"Felix had accidentally been present at the trial; his horror and indignation were uncontrollable when he heard the decision of the court. He made, at that moment, a solemn vow to deliver him, and then looked around for the means. After many fruitless attempts to gain admittance to the prison, he found a strongly grated window in an unguarded part of the building which lighted the dungeon of the unfortunate Mahometan; who, loaded with chains, waited in despair the execution of the barbarous sentence. Felix visited the grate at night, and made known to the prisoner his intentions in his favor. The Turk, amazed and delighted, endeavored to kindle the zeal of his deliverer by promises of reward and wealth. Felix rejected his offers with contempt; yet when he saw the lovely Safie, who was allowed to visit her father, and who, by her gestures, expressed her lively gratitude, the youth could not help owning to his own mind that the captive possessed a treasure which would fully reward his toil and hazard.

"The Turk quickly perceived the impression that his daughter had made on the heart of Felix, and endeavored to secure him more entirely in his interests by the promise of her hand in marriage, so soon as he should be conveyed to a place of safety. Felix was too delicate to accept this offer; yet he looked forward to the probability of the event as to the consummation of his happiness.

"During the ensuing days, while the preparations were going forward for the escape of the merchant, the zeal of Felix was warmed by several letters that he received from this lovely girl, who found means to express her thoughts in the language of her lover by the aid of an old man, a servant of her father, who understood French. She thanked him in the most ardent terms for his intended services towards her parent; and at the same time she gently deplored her own fate.

"I have copies of these letters; for I found means, during my residence in the hovel, to procure the implements of writing; and the letters were often in the hands of Felix or Agatha. Before I depart, I will give them to you, they will prove the truth of my tale; but at present, as the sun is already far declined, I shall only have time to repeat the substance of them to you.

"Safie related that her mother was a Christian Arab, seized and made a slave by the Turks; recommended by her beauty, she had won the heart of the father of Safie, who married her. The young girl spoke in high and enthusiastic terms of her mother, who, born in freedom, spurned the bondage to which she was now reduced. She instructed her daughter in the tenets of her religion, and taught her to aspire to higher powers of intellect, and an independence of spirit, forbidden to the female followers of Mahomet. This lady died; but her lessons were indelibly impressed on the mind of Safie, who sickened at the prospect of again returning to Asia and being immured within the walls of a harem, allowed only to occupy herself with infantile amusements, ill suited to the temper of her soul, now accustomed to grand ideas and a noble emulation for virtue. The prospect of marrying a Christian, and remaining in a country where women were allowed to take a rank in society, was enchanting to her.

"The day for the execution of the Turk was fixed; but, on the night previous to it, he quitted his prison, and before morning was distant many leagues from Paris. Felix had procured passports in the name of his father, sister and himself. He had previously communicated his plan to the former, who aided the deceit by quitting his house, under the pretence of a journey, and concealed himself, with his daughter, in an obscure part of Paris.

"Felix conducted the fugitives through France to Lyons, and across Mont Cenis to Leghorn, where the merchant had decided to wait a favorable opportunity of passing into some part of the Turkish dominions.

"Safie resolved to remain with her father until the moment of his departure, before which time the Turk renewed his promise that she should be united to his deliverer; and Felix remained with them in expectation of that event; and in the meantime he enjoyed the society of the Arabian, who exhibited towards him the simplest and tenderest affection. They conversed with one another through the means of an interpreter, and sometimes with the interpretation of looks; and Safie sang to him the divine airs of her native country.

"The Turk allowed this intimacy to take place, and encouraged the hopes of the youthful lovers, while in his heart he had formed far other plans. He loathed the idea that his daughter should be united to a Christian; but he feared the resentment of Felix, if he should appear lukewarm; for he knew that he was still in the power of his deliverer, if he should choose to betray him to the Italian state which they inhabited. He revolved a thousand plans by which he should be enabled to prolong the deceit until it might be no longer necessary, and secretly to take his daughter with him when he departed. His plans were facilitated by the news which arrived from Paris.

"The government of France were greatly enraged at the escape of their victim, and spared no pains to detect and punish his deliverer. The plot of Felix was quickly discovered, and De Lacey and Agatha were thrown into prison. The news reached Felix, and roused him from his dream of pleasure. His blind and aged father, and his gentle sister, lay in a noisome dungeon, while he enjoyed the free air and the society of her whom he loved. This idea was torture to him. He quickly arranged with the Turks that if the latter should find a favorable opportunity for escape before Felix could return to Italy, Safie should remain as a boarder at a convent at Leghorn; and then, quitting the lovely Arabian, he hastened to Paris, and delivered himself up to the vengeance of the law, hoping to free De Lacey and Agatha by this proceeding.

"He did not succeed. They remained confined for five months before the trial took place; the result of which deprived them of their fortune, and condemned them to a perpetual exile from their native country.

"They found a miserable asylum in the cottage in Germany where I discovered them. Felix soon learned that the treacherous Turk, for whom he and his family endured such unheard-of oppression, on discovering that his deliverer was thus reduced to poverty and ruin, became a traitor to good feeling and honor, and had quitted Italy with his daughter, insultingly sending Felix a pittance of money, to aid him, as he said, in some plan of future maintenance.

"Such were the events that preyed on the heart of Felix, and rendered him, when I first saw him, the most miserable of his family. He could have endured poverty; and while this distress had been the meed of his virtue, he gloried in it: but the ingratitude of the Turk, and the loss of his beloved Safie, were misfortunes more bitter and irreparable. The arrival of the Arabian now infused new life into his soul.

"When the news reached Leghorn that Felix was deprived of his wealth and rank, the merchant commanded his daughter to think no more of her lover, but to prepare to return to her native country. The generous nature of Safie was outraged by this command; she attempted to expostulate with her father, but he left her angrily, reiterating his tyrannical mandate

"A few days after, the Turk entered his daughter's apartment, and told her hastily that he had reason to believe that his residence at Leghorn had been divulged, and that he should speedily be delivered up to the French government; he had, consequently, hired a vessel to convey him to Constantinople, for which city he should sail in a few hours. He intended to leave his daughter under the care of a confidential servant, to follow at her leisure with the greater part of his property, which had not yet arrived at Leghorn.

"When alone, Safie resolved in her own mind the plan of conduct that it would become her to pursue in this emergency. A residence in Turkey was abhorrent to her; her religion and her feelings were alike adverse to it. By some papers of her father, which fell into her hands, she heard of the exile of her lover, and learnt the name of the spot where he then resided. She hesitated some time, but at length she formed her determination. Taking with her some jewels that belonged to her, and a sum of money, she quitted Italy with an attendant, a native of Leghorn, but who understood the common language of Turkey, and departed for Germany.

"She arrived in safety at a town about twenty leagues from the cottage of De Lacey, when her attendant fell dangerously ill. Safie nursed her with the most devoted affection; but the poor girl died, and the Arabian was left alone, unacquainted with the language of the country, and utterly ignorant of the customs of the world. She fell, however, into good hands. The Italian had mentioned the name of the spot for which they were bound; and, after her death, the woman of the house in which they had lived took care that Safie should arrive in safety at the cottage of her lover.

XV

"Such was the history of my beloved cottagers. It impressed me deeply. I learned, from the views of social life which it developed, to admire their virtues, and to deprecate the vices of mankind.

"As yet I looked upon crime as a distant evil; benevolence and generosity were ever present before me, inciting within me a desire to become an actor in the busy scene where so many admirable qualities were called forth and displayed. But, in giving an account of the progress of my intellect, I must not omit a circumstance which occurred in the beginning of the month of August of the same year.

"One night, during my accustomed visit to the neighboring wood, where I collected my own food, and brought home firing for my protectors, I found on the ground a leathern portmanteau, containing several articles of dress and some books. I eagerly seized the prize, and returned with it to my hovel. Fortunately the books were written in the language the elements of which I had acquired at the cottage; they consisted of *Paradise Lost*, a volume of *Plutarch's Lives*, and the *Sorrows of Werter*. The possession of these treasures gave me extreme delight; I now continually studied and exercised my mind upon these histories, whilst my friends were employed in their ordinary occupations.

"I can hardly describe to you the effect of these books. They produced in me an infinity of new images and feelings that sometimes raised me to ecstasy, but more frequently sunk me into the lowest dejection. In the *Sorrows of Werter*, besides the interest of its simple and affecting story, so many opinions are canvassed, and so many lights thrown upon what had hitherto been to me obscure subjects, that I found in it a never-ending source of speculation and astonishment. The gentle and domestic manners it described, combined with lofty sentiments and feelings, which had for their object something out of self, accorded well with my experience among my protectors, and with the wants which were for ever alive in my own bosom. But I thought Werter himself a more divine being than I had ever beheld or imagined; his character contained no pretension, but it sunk deep. The disquisitions upon death and suicide were calculated to fill me with wonder. I did not pretend to enter into the merits of the case, yet I inclined towards the opinions of the hero, whose extinction I wept, without precisely understanding it.

"As I read, however, I applied much personally to my own feelings and condition. I found myself similar, yet at the same time strangely unlike to the beings concerning whom I read, and to whose conversation I was a listener. I sympathized with, and partly understood them, but I was unformed in mind; I was dependent on none and related to none. 'The path of my departure was free'; and there was none to lament my annihilation. My person was hideous and my stature gigantic. What did this mean? Who was I? What was I? Whence did I come? What was my destination? These questions continually recurred, but I was unable to solve them.

"The volume of *Plutarch's Lives*, which I possessed, contained the histories of the first founders of the ancient republics. This book had a far different effect upon me from the *Sorrows of Werter*. I learned from Werter's imaginations despondency and gloom: but Plutarch taught me high thoughts; he elevated me above the wretched sphere of my own reflections to admire and love the heroes of past ages. Many things I read surpassed my understanding and experience. I had a very confused knowledge of kingdoms, wide extents of country, mighty rivers, and boundless seas. But I was perfectly unacquainted with towns, and large assemblages of men. The cottage of my protectors had been the only school in which I had studied human nature; but this book developed new and mightier scenes of action. I read of men concerned in public affairs, governing or massacring their species. I felt the greatest ardor for virtue rise within me, and abhorrence for vice, as far as I understood the signification of those terms, relative as they were, as I applied them, to pleasure and pain alone. Induced by these feelings, I was of course led to admire peaceable lawgivers, Numa, Solon, and Lycurgus, in preference to Romulus and Theseus. The patriarchal lives of my protectors caused these impressions to take a firm hold on my mind; perhaps, if my first introduction to humanity had been made by a young soldier, burning for glory and slaughter, I should have been imbued with different sensations.

"But *Paradise Lost* excited different and far deeper emotions. I read it, as I had read the other volumes which had fallen into my hands, as a true history. It moved every feeling of wonder and awe that the picture of an omnipotent God warring with his creatures was capable of exciting. I often referred the several situations, as their similarity struck me, to my own. Like Adam, I was apparently united by no link to any other being in existence; but his state was far different from mine in every other respect. He had come forth from the hands of God a perfect creature, happy and prosperous, guarded by the especial care of his Creator; he was allowed to converse with, and acquire knowledge from, beings of a superior nature: but I was wretched, helpless, and alone. Many times I considered Satan as the fitter emblem of my condition; for often, like him, when I viewed the bliss of my protectors, the bitter gall of envy rose within me.

"Another circumstance strengthened and confirmed these feelings. Soon after my arrival in the hovel, I discovered some papers in the pocket of the dress which I had taken from your laboratory. At first I had neglected them; but now that I was able to decipher the characters in which they were written, I began to study them with diligence. It was your journal of the four months that preceded my creation. You minutely described in these papers every step you took in the progress of your work; this history was mingled with accounts of domestic occurrences. You, doubtless, recollect these papers. Here they are. Everything is related in them which bears reference to my accursed origin; the whole detail of that series of disgusting circumstances which produced it is set in view; the minutest description of my odious and loathsome person is given, in language which painted your own horrors and rendered mine indelible. I sickened as I read. 'Hateful day when I received life!' I exclaimed in agony. 'Accursed creator! Why did you form a monster so hideous that even *you* turned from me in disgust? God, in pity, made man beautiful and alluring, after his own image; but my form is a filthy type of yours, more horrid even from the very resemblance. Satan had his companions, fellow-devils, to admire and encourage him; but I am solitary and abhorred.'

"These were the reflections of my hours of despondency and solitude; but when I contemplated the virtues of the cottagers, their amiable and benevolent dispositions, I persuaded myself that when they should become acquainted with my admiration of their virtues, they would compassionate me, and overlook my personal deformity. Could they turn from their door one, however monstrous, who solicited their compassion and friendship? I resolved, at least, not to despair, but in every way to fit myself for an interview with them which would decide my fate. I postponed this attempt for some months longer; for the importance attached to its success inspired me with a dread lest I should fail. Besides, I found that my understanding improved so much with every day's experience that I was unwilling to commence this undertaking until a few more months should have added to my sagacity.

"Several changes, in the meantime, took place in the cottage. The presence of Safie diffused happiness among its inhabitants; and I also found that a greater degree of plenty reigned there. Felix and Agatha spent more time in amusement and conversation, and were assisted in their labors by servants. They did not appear rich, but they were contented and happy; their feelings were serene and peaceful, while mine became every day more tumultuous. Increase of knowledge only discovered to me more clearly what a wretched outcast I was. I cherished hope, it is true; but it vanished when I beheld my person reflected in water, or my shadow in the moonshine, even as that frail image and that inconstant shade.

"I endeavored to crush these fears, and to fortify myself for the trial which in a few months I resolved to undergo; and sometimes I allowed my thoughts, unchecked by reason, to ramble in the fields of Paradise, and dared to fancy amiable and lovely creatures sympathizing with my feelings, and cheering my gloom; their angelic countenances breathed smiles of consolation. But it was all a dream; no Eve soothed my sorrows, nor shared my thoughts; I was alone. I remembered Adam's supplication to his Creator. But where was mine? He had abandoned me: and, in the bitterness of my heart, I cursed him.

"Autumn passed thus. I saw, with surprise and grief, the leaves decay and fall, and nature again assume the barren and bleak appearance it had worn when I first beheld the woods and the lovely moon. Yet I did not heed the bleakness of the weather; I was better fitted by my conformation for the endurance of cold than heat. But my chief delights were the sight of the flowers, the birds, and all the gay apparel of summer; when those deserted me, I turned with more attention towards the cottagers. Their happiness was not decreased by the absence of summer. They loved, and sympathized with one another; and their joys, depending on each other, were not interrupted by the casualties that took place around them. The more I saw of them, the greater became my desire to claim their protection and kindness; my heart yearned to be known and loved by these amiable creatures: to see their sweet looks directed towards me with affection was the utmost limit of my ambition. I dared not think that they would turn them from me with disdain and horror. The poor that stopped at their door were never driven away. I asked, it is true, for greater treasures than a little food or rest: I required kindness and sympathy; but I did not believe myself utterly unworthy of it.

"The winter advanced, and an entire revolution of the seasons had taken place since I awoke into life. My attention, at this time, was solely directed towards my plan of introducing myself into the cottage of my protectors. I revolved many projects; but that on which I finally fixed was, to enter the dwelling when the blind old man should be alone. I had sagacity enough to discover that the unnatural hideousness of my person was the chief object of horror with those who had formerly beheld me. My voice, although harsh, had nothing terrible in it; I thought, therefore, that if, in the absence of his children, I could gain the good-will and mediation of the old De Lacey, I might, by his means, be tolerated by my younger protectors.

"One day, when the sun shone on the red leaves that strewed the ground, and diffused cheerfulness, although it denied warmth, Safie, Agatha, and Felix departed on a long country walk, and the old man, at his own desire, was left alone in the cottage. When his children had departed, he took up his guitar, and played several mournful but sweet airs, more sweet and mournful than I had ever heard him play before. At first his countenance was illuminated with pleasure, but, as he continued, thoughtfulness and sadness succeeded; at length, laying aside the instrument, he sat absorbed in reflection.

"My heart beat quick; this was the hour and moment of trial which would decide my hopes or realize my fears. The servants were gone to a neighboring fair. All was silent in and around the cottage: it was an excellent opportunity; yet, when I proceeded to execute my plan, my limbs failed me, and I sank to the ground. Again I rose; and, exerting all the firmness of which I was master, removed the planks which I had placed before my hovel to conceal my retreat. The fresh air revived me, and, with renewed determination, I approached the door of their cottage.

"I knocked. 'Who is there?' said the old man—'Come in.'

"I entered; 'Pardon this intrusion,' said I: 'I am a traveler in want of a little rest; you would greatly oblige me if you would allow me to remain a few minutes before the fire.'

"'Enter,' said De Lacey; 'and I will try in what manner I can relieve your wants; but, unfortunately, my children are from home, and, as I am blind, I am afraid I shall find it difficult to procure food for you.'

"'Do not trouble yourself, my kind host, I have food; it is warmth and rest only that I need.'

"I sat down, and a silence ensued. I knew that every minute was precious to me, yet I remained irresolute in what manner to commence the interview; when the old man addressed me—

"'By your language, stranger, I suppose you are my countryman;—are you French?'

"'No; but I was educated by a French family, and understand that language only. I am now going to claim the protection of some friends, whom I sincerely love, and of whose favor I have some hopes.'

"'Are they Germans?'

"'No, they are French. But let us change the subject. I am an unfortunate and deserted creature; I look around, and I have no relation or friend upon earth. These amiable people to whom I go have never seen me, and know little of me. I am full of fears; for if I fail there, I am an outcast in the world for ever.'

"'Do not despair. To be friendless is indeed to be unfortunate; but the hearts of men, when unprejudiced by any obvious self-interest, are full of brotherly love and charity. Rely, therefore, on your hopes; and if these friends are good and amiable, do not despair.'

"'They are kind—they are the most excellent creatures in the world; but, unfortunately, they are prejudiced against me. I have good dispositions; my life has been hitherto harmless, and in some degree beneficial; but a fatal prejudice clouds their eyes, and where they ought to see a feeling and kind friend, they behold only a detestable monster.'

"'That is indeed unfortunate; but if you are really blameless, cannot you undeceive them?'

"'I am about to undertake that task; and it is on that account that I feel so many overwhelming terrors. I tenderly love these friends; I have, unknown to them, been for many months in the habits of daily kindness towards them; but they believe that I wish to injure them, and it is that prejudice which I wish to overcome.'

"'Where do these friends reside?'

"'Near this spot.'

"The old man paused, and then continued, 'If you will unreservedly confide to me the particulars of your tale, I perhaps may be of use in undeceiving them. I am blind, and cannot judge of your countenance, but there is something in your words which persuades me that you are sincere. I am poor, and an exile; but it will afford me true pleasure to be in any way serviceable to a human creature.'

"'Excellent man! I thank you, and accept your generous offer. You raise me from the dust by this kindness; and I trust that, by your aid, I shall not be driven from the society and sympathy of your fellow-creatures.'

"'Heaven forbid! even if you were really criminal; for that can only drive you to desperation, and not instigate you to virtue. I also am unfortunate; I and my family have been condemned, although innocent: judge, therefore, if I do not feel for your misfortunes.'

"'How can I thank you, my best and only benefactor? From your lips first have I heard the voice of kindness directed towards me; I shall be for ever grateful; and your present humanity assures me of success with those friends whom I am on the point of meeting.'

"'May I know the names and residence of those friends?'

"I paused. This, I thought, was the moment of decision, which was to rob me of, or bestow happiness on me for ever. I struggled vainly for firmness sufficient to answer him, but the effort destroyed all my remaining strength; I sank on the chair, and sobbed aloud. At that moment I heard the steps of my younger protectors. I had not a moment to lose; but, seizing the hand of the old man, I cried, 'Now is the time!—save and protect me! You and your family are the friends whom I seek. Do not you desert me in the hour of trial!'

"'Great God!' exclaimed the old man, 'who are you?'

"At that instant the cottage door was opened, and Felix, Safie, and Agatha entered. Who can describe their horror and consternation on beholding me? Agatha fainted; and Safie, unable to attend to her friend, rushed out of the cottage. Felix darted forward, and with supernatural force tore me from his father, to whose knees I clung: in a transport of fury, he dashed me to the ground and struck me violently with a stick. I could have torn him limb from limb, as the lion rends the antelope. But my heart sunk within me as with bitter sickness, and I refrained. I saw him on the point of repeating his blow, when, overcome by pain and anguish, I quitted the cottage and in the general tumult escaped unperceived to my hovel."

XVI

"Cursed, cursed creator! Why did I live? Why, in that instant, did I not extinguish the spark of existence which you had so wantonly bestowed? I know not; despair had not yet taken possession of me; my feelings were those of rage and revenge. I could with pleasure have destroyed the cottage and its inhabitants, and have glutted myself with their shrieks and misery.

"When night came, I quitted my retreat, and wandered in the wood; and now, no longer restrained by the fear of discovery, I gave vent to my anguish in fearful howlings. I was like a wild beast that had broken the toils; destroying the objects that obstructed me, and ranging through the wood with a stag-like swiftness. O! what a miserable night I passed! the cold stars shone in mockery, and the bare trees waved their branches above me: now and then the sweet voice of a bird burst forth amidst the universal stillness. All, save I, were at rest or in enjoyment: I, like the arch-fiend, bore a hell within me; and, finding myself unsympathized with, wished to tear up the trees, spread havoc and destruction around me, and then to have sat down and enjoyed the ruin.

"But this was a luxury of sensation that could not endure; I became fatigued with excess of bodily exertion, and sank on the damp grass in the sick impotence of despair. There was none among the myriads of men that existed who would pity or assist me; and should I feel kindness towards my enemies? No: from that moment I declared everlasting war against the species, and, more than all, against him who had formed me, and sent me forth to this insupportable misery.

"The sun rose; I heard the voices of men, and knew that it was impossible to return to my retreat during that day. Accordingly I hid myself in some thick underwood, determining to devote the ensuing hours to reflection on my situation.

"The pleasant sunshine, and the pure air of day, restored me to some degree of tranquility; and when I considered what had passed at the cottage, I could not help believing that I had been too hasty in my conclusions. I had certainly acted imprudently. It was apparent that my conversation had interested the father in my behalf, and I was a fool in having exposed my person to the horror of his children. I ought to have familiarized the old De Lacey to me, and by degrees to have discovered myself to the rest of his family, when they should have been prepared for my approach. But I did not believe my errors to be irretrievable; and, after much consideration, I resolved to return to the cottage, seek the old man, and by my representations win him to my party.

"These thoughts calmed me, and in the afternoon I sank into a profound sleep; but the fever of my blood did not allow me to be visited by peaceful dreams. The horrible scene of the preceding day was for ever acting before my eyes; the females were flying, and the enraged Felix tearing me from his father's feet. I awoke exhausted; and, finding that it was already night, I crept forth from my hiding-place, and went in search of food.

"When my hunger was appeased, I directed my steps towards the well-known path that conducted to the cottage. All there was at peace. I crept into my hovel, and remained in silent expectation of the accustomed hour when the family arose. That hour passed, the sun mounted high in the heavens, but the cottagers did not appear. I trembled violently, apprehending some dreadful misfortune. The inside of the cottage was dark, and I heard no motion; I cannot describe the agony of this suspense.

"Presently two countrymen passed by; but, pausing near the cottage, they entered into conversation, using violent gesticulations; but I did not understand what they said, as they spoke the language of the country, which differed from that of my protectors. Soon after, however, Felix approached with another man: I was surprised, as I knew that he had not quitted the cottage that morning, and waited anxiously to discover, from his discourse, the meaning of these unusual appearances.

"'Do you consider,' said his companion to him, 'that you will be obliged to pay three months' rent, and to lose the produce of your garden? I do not wish to take any unfair advantage, and I beg therefore that you will take some days to consider of your determination.'

"'It is utterly useless,' replied Felix; 'we can never again inhabit your cottage. The life of my father is in the greatest danger, owing to the dreadful circumstance that I have related. My wife and my sister will never recover their horror. I entreat you not to reason with me any more. Take possession of your tenement, and let me fly from this place.'

"Felix trembled violently as he said this. He and his companion entered the cottage, in which they remained for a few minutes, and then departed. I never saw any of the family of De Lacey more.

"I continued for the remainder of the day in my hovel in a state of utter and stupid despair. My protectors had departed, and had broken the only link that held me to the world. For the first time the feelings of revenge and hatred filled my bosom, and I did not strive to control them; but, allowing myself to be borne away by the stream, I bent my mind towards injury and death. When I thought of my friends, of the mild voice of De Lacey, the gentle eyes of Agatha, and the exquisite beauty of the Arabian, these thoughts vanished, and a gush of tears somewhat soothed me. But again, when I reflected that they had spurned and deserted me, anger returned, a rage of anger; and, unable to injure anything human, I turned my fury towards inanimate objects. As night advanced, I placed a variety of combustibles around the cottage; and, after having destroyed every vestige of cultivation in the garden, I waited with forced impatience until the moon had sunk to commence my operations.

"As the night advanced, a fierce wind arose from the woods, and quickly dispersed the clouds that had loitered in the heavens: the blast tore along like a mighty avalanche, and produced a kind of insanity in my spirits that burst all bounds of reason and reflection. I lighted the dry branch of a tree, and danced with fury around the devoted cottage, my eyes still fixed on the western horizon, the edge of which the moon nearly touched. A part of its orb was at length hid, and I waved my brand; it sunk, and, with a loud scream, I fired the straw, and heath, and bushes, which I had collected. The wind fanned the fire, and the cottage was quickly enveloped by the flames, which clung to it, and licked it with their forked and destroying tongues.

"As soon as I was convinced that no assistance could save any part of the habitation, I quitted the scene and sought for refuge in the woods.

"And now, with the world before me, whither should I bend my steps? I resolved to fly far from the scene of my misfortunes; but to me, hated and despised, every country must be equally horrible. At length the thought of you crossed my mind. I learned from your papers that you were my father, my creator; and to whom could I apply with more fitness than to him who had given me life? Among the lessons that Felix had bestowed upon Safie, geography had not been omitted. I had learned from these the relative situations of the different countries of the earth. You had mentioned Geneva as the name of your native town; and towards this place I resolved to proceed.

"But how was I to direct myself? I knew that I must travel in a south-westerly direction to reach my destination; but the sun was my only guide. I did not know the names of the towns that I was to pass through, nor could I ask information from a single human being; but I did not despair. From you only could I hope for succor, although towards you I felt no sentiment but that of hatred. Unfeeling, heartless creator! you had endowed me with perceptions and passions, and then cast me abroad an object for the scorn and horror of mankind. But on you only had I any claim for pity and redress, and from you I determined to seek that justice which I vainly attempted to gain from any other being that wore the human form.

"My travels were long, and the sufferings I endured intense. It was late in autumn when I quitted the district where I had so long resided. I traveled only at night, fearful of encountering the visage of a human being. Nature decayed around me, and the sun became heatless; rain and snow poured around me; mighty rivers were frozen; the surface of the earth was hard, and chill, and bare, and I found no shelter. Oh, earth! how often did I imprecate curses on the cause of my being! The mildness of my nature had fled, and all within me was turned to gall and bitterness. The nearer I approached to your habitation, the more deeply did I feel the spirit of revenge enkindled in my heart. Snow fell, and the waters were hardened; but I rested not. A few incidents now and then directed me, and I possessed a map of the country; but I often wandered wide from my path. The agony of my feelings allowed me no respite: no incident occurred from which my rage and misery could not extract its food; but a circumstance that happened when I arrived on the confines of Switzerland, when the sun had recovered its warmth, and the earth again began to look green, confirmed in an especial manner the bitterness and horror of my feelings.

"I generally rested during the day, and traveled only when I was secured by night from the view of man. One morning, however, finding that my path lay through a deep wood, I ventured to continue my journey after the sun had risen; the day, which was one of the first of spring, cheered even me by the loveliness of its sunshine and the balminess of the air. I felt emotions of gentleness and pleasure, that had long appeared dead, revive within me. Half surprised by the novelty of these sensations, I allowed myself to be borne away by them; and, forgetting my solitude and deformity, dared to be happy. Soft tears again bedewed my cheeks, and I even raised my humid eyes with thankfulness towards the blessed sun which bestowed such joy upon me.

"I continued to wind among the paths of the wood, until I came to its boundary, which was skirted by a deep and rapid river, into which many of the trees bent their branches, now budding with the fresh spring. Here I paused, not exactly knowing what path to pursue, when I heard the sound of voices that induced me to conceal myself under the shade of a cypress. I was scarcely hid, when a young girl came running towards the spot where I was concealed, laughing, as if she ran from some one in sport. She continued her course along the precipitous sides of the river, when suddenly her foot slipped, and she fell into the rapid stream. I rushed from my hiding place; and, with extreme labor from the force of the current, saved her, and dragged her to shore. She was senseless; and I endeavored by every means in my power to restore animation, when I was suddenly interrupted by the approach of a rustic, who was probably the person from whom she had playfully fled. On seeing me, he darted towards me, and tearing the girl from my arms, hastened towards the deeper parts of the wood. I followed speedily, I hardly knew why; but when the man saw me draw near, he aimed a gun, which he carried, at my body, and fired. I sunk to the ground, and my injurer, with increased swiftness, escaped into the wood.

"This was then the reward of my benevolence! I had saved a human being from destruction, and, as a recompense, I now writhed under the miserable pain of a wound, which shattered the flesh and bone. The feelings of kindness and gentleness which I had entertained but a few moments before gave place to hellish rage and gnashing of teeth. Inflamed by pain, I vowed eternal hatred and vengeance to all mankind. But the agony of my wound overcame me; my pulses paused, and I fainted.

"For some weeks I led a miserable life in the woods, endeavoring to cure the wound which I had received. The ball had entered my shoulder, and I knew not whether it had remained there or passed through; at any rate I had no means of extracting it. My sufferings were augmented also by the oppressive sense of the injustice and ingratitude of their infliction. My daily vows rose for revenge—a deep and deadly revenge, such as would alone compensate for the outrages and anguish I had endured.

"After some weeks my wound healed, and I continued my journey. The labors I endured were no longer to be alleviated by the bright sun or gentle breezes of spring; all joy was but a mockery, which insulted my desolate state, and made me feel more painfully that I was not made for the enjoyment of pleasure.

"But my toils now drew near a close; and in two months from this time I reached the environs of Geneva.

"It was evening when I arrived, and I retired to a hiding place among the fields that surround it, to meditate in what manner I should apply to you. I was oppressed by fatigue and hunger, and far too unhappy to enjoy the gentle breezes of evening, or the prospect of the sun setting behind the stupendous mountains of Jura.

"At this time a slight sleep relieved me from the pain of reflection, which was disturbed by the approach of a beautiful child, who came running into the recess I had chosen, with all the sportiveness of infancy. Suddenly, as I gazed on him, an idea seized me, that this little creature was unprejudiced, and had lived too short a time to have imbibed a horror of deformity. If, therefore, I could seize him, and educate him as my companion and friend, I should not be so desolate in this peopled earth.

"Urged by this impulse, I seized on the boy as he passed and drew him towards me. As soon as he beheld my form, he placed his hands before his eyes and uttered a shrill scream: I drew his hand forcibly from his face, and said, 'Child, what is the meaning of this? I do not intend to hurt you; listen to me.'

"He struggled violently. 'Let me go,' he cried; 'monster! ugly wretch! you wish to eat me, and tear me to pieces—You are an ogre—Let me go, or I will tell my papa.'

"'Boy, you will never see your father again; you must come with me.'

"'Hideous monster! let me go. My papa is a Syndic—he is M. Frankenstein—he will punish you. You dare not keep me.'

"'Frankenstein! you belong then to my enemy—to him towards whom I have sworn eternal revenge; you shall be my first victim.'

"The child still struggled, and loaded me with epithets which carried despair to my heart; I grasped his throat to silence him, and in a moment he lay dead at my feet.

"I gazed on my victim, and my heart swelled with exultation and hellish triumph: clapping my hands, I exclaimed, 'I, too, can create desolation; my enemy is not invulnerable; this death will carry despair to him and a thousand other miseries shall torment and destroy him.'

"As I fixed my eyes on the child, I saw something glittering on his breast. I took it; it was a portrait of a most lovely woman. In spite of my malignity, it softened and attracted me. For a few moments I gazed with delight on her dark eyes, fringed by deep lashes, and her lovely lips; but presently my rage returned: I remembered that I was for ever deprived of the delights that such beautiful creatures could bestow; and that she whose resemblance I contemplated would, in regarding me, have changed that air of divine benignity to one expressive of disgust and affright.

"Can you wonder that such thoughts transported me with rage? I only wonder that at that moment, instead of venting my sensations in exclamations and agony, I did not rush among mankind and perish in the attempt to destroy them.

"While I was overcome by these feelings, I left the spot where I had committed the murder, and seeking a more secluded hiding place, I entered a barn which had appeared to me to be empty. A woman was sleeping on some straw; she was young: not indeed so beautiful as her whose portrait I held; but of an agreeable aspect, and blooming in the loveliness of youth and health. Here, I thought, is one of those whose joy-imparting smiles are bestowed on all but me. And then I bent over her, and whispered, 'Awake, fairest, thy lover is near—he who would give his life but to obtain one look of affection from thine eyes: my beloved, awake!'

"The sleeper stirred; a thrill of terror ran through me. Should she indeed awake, and see me, and curse me, and denounce the murderer? Thus would she assuredly act, if her darkened eyes opened and she beheld me. The thought was madness; it stirred the fiend within me—not I, but she shall suffer: the murder I have committed because I am for ever robbed of all that she could give me, she shall atone. The crime had its source in her: be hers the punishment! Thanks to the lessons of Felix and the sanguinary laws of man, I had learned now to work mischief. I bent over her, and placed the portrait securely in one of the folds of her dress. She moved again, and I fled.

"For some days I haunted the spot where these scenes had taken place; sometimes wishing to see you, sometimes resolved to quit the world and its miseries for ever. At length I wandered towards these mountains, and have ranged through their immense recesses, consumed by a burning passion which you alone can gratify. We may not part until you have promised to comply with my requisition. I am alone, and miserable; man will not associate with me; but one as deformed and horrible as myself would not deny herself to me. My companion must be of the same species, and have the same defects. This being you must create."

XVII

The being finished speaking, and fixed his looks upon me in expectation of a reply. But I was bewildered, perplexed, and unable to arrange my ideas sufficiently to understand the full extent of his proposition. He continued—

"You must create a female for me, with whom I can live in the interchange of those sympathies necessary for my being. This you alone can do; and I demand it of you as a right which you must not refuse to concede."

The latter part of his tale had kindled anew in me the anger that had died away while he narrated his peaceful life among the cottagers, and, as he said this, I could no longer suppress the rage that burned within me.

"I do refuse it," I replied; "and no torture shall ever extort a consent from me. You may render me the most miserable of men, but you shall never make me base in my own eyes. Shall I create another like yourself, whose joint wickedness might desolate the world! Begone! I have answered you; you may torture me, but I will never consent."

"You are in the wrong," replied the fiend; "and, instead of threatening, I am content to reason with you. I am malicious because I am miserable. Am I not shunned and hated by all mankind? You, my creator, would tear me to pieces, and triumph; remember that, and tell me why I should pity man more than he pities me? You would not call it murder if you could precipitate me into one of those ice-rifts, and destroy my frame, the work of your own hands. Shall I respect man when he condemns me? Let him live with me in the interchange of kindness; and, instead of injury, I would bestow every benefit upon him with tears of gratitude at his acceptance. But that cannot be; the human senses are insurmountable barriers to our union. Yet mine shall not be the submission of abject slavery. I will revenge my injuries: if I cannot inspire love, I will cause fear; and chiefly towards you my archenemy, because my creator, do I swear inextinguishable hatred. Have a care: I will work at your destruction, nor finish until I desolate your heart, so that you shall curse the hour of your birth."

A fiendish rage animated him as he said this; his face was wrinkled into contortions too horrible for human eyes to behold; but presently he calmed himself and proceeded—

"I intended to reason. This passion is detrimental to me; for you do not reflect that *you* are the cause of its excess. If any being felt emotions of benevolence towards me, I should return them an hundred and an hundred fold; for that one creature's sake, I would make peace with the whole kind! But I now indulge in dreams of bliss that cannot be realized. What I ask of you is reasonable and moderate; I demand a creature of another sex, but as hideous as myself; the gratification is small, but it is all that I can receive, and it shall content me. It is true we shall be monsters, cut off from all the world; but on that account we shall be more attached to one another. Our lives will not be happy, but they will be harmless, and free from the misery I now feel. Oh! my creator, make me happy; let me feel gratitude towards you for one benefit! Let me see that I excite the sympathy of some existing thing; do not deny me my request!"

I was moved. I shuddered when I thought of the possible consequences of my consent; but I felt that there was some justice in his argument. His tale, and the feelings he now expressed, proved him to be a creature of fine sensations; and did I not as his maker owe him all the portion of happiness that it was in my power to bestow? He saw my change of feeling and continued—

"If you consent, neither you nor any other human being shall ever see us again: I will go to the vast wilds of South America. My food is not that of man; I do not destroy the lamb and the kid to glut my appetite; acorns and berries afford me sufficient nourishment. My companion will be of the same nature as myself, and will be content with the same fare. We shall make our bed of dried leaves; the sun will shine on us as on man, and will ripen our food. The picture I present to you is peaceful and human, and you must feel that you could deny it only in the wantonness of power and cruelty. Pitiless as you have been towards me, I now see compassion in your eyes; let me seize the favorable moment, and persuade you to promise what I so ardently desire."

"You propose," replied I, "to fly from the habitations of man, to dwell in those wilds where the beasts of the field will be your only companions.

How can you, who long for the love and sympathy of man, persevere in this exile? You will return, and again seek their kindness, and you will meet with their detestation; your evil passions will be renewed, and you will then have a companion to aid you in the task of destruction. This may not be: cease to argue the point, for I cannot consent."

"How inconstant are your feelings! but a moment ago you were moved by my representations, and why do you again harden yourself to my complaints? I swear to you, by the earth which I inhabit, and by you that made me, that, with the companion you bestow, I will quit the neighborhood of man, and dwell as it may chance in the most savage of places. My evil passions will have fled, for I shall meet with sympathy! my life will flow quietly away, and, in my dying moments, I shall not curse my maker."

His words had a strange effect upon me. I compassionated him, and sometimes felt a wish to console him; but when I looked upon him, when I saw the filthy mass that moved and talked, my heart sickened, and my feelings were altered to those of horror and hatred. I tried to stifle these sensations; I thought that, as I could not sympathize with him, I had no right to withhold from him the small portion of happiness which was yet in my power to bestow.

"You swear," I said, "to be harmless; but have you not already shown a degree of malice that should reasonably make me distrust you? May not even this be a feint that will increase your triumph by affording a wider scope for your revenge?"

"How is this? I must not be trifled with: and I demand an answer. If I have no ties and no affections, hatred and vice must be my portion; the love of another will destroy the cause of my crimes, and I shall become a thing of whose existence every one will be ignorant. My vices are the children of a forced solitude that I abhor; and my virtues will necessarily arise when I live in communion with an equal. I shall feel the affections of a sensitive being, and become linked to the chain of existence and events, from which I am now excluded."

I paused some time to reflect on all he had related, and the various arguments which he had employed. I thought of the promise of virtues which he had displayed on the opening of his existence, and the subsequent blight of all kindly feeling by the loathing and scorn which his protectors had manifested towards him. His power and threats were not omitted in my calculations: a creature who could exist in the ice-caves of the glaciers, and hide himself from pursuit among the ridges of inaccessible precipices, was a being possessing faculties it would be vain to cope with. After a long pause of reflection, I concluded that the justice due both to him and my fellow-creatures demanded of me that I should comply with his request. Turning to him, therefore, I said—

"I consent to your demand, on your solemn oath to quit Europe for ever, and every other place in the neighborhood of man, as soon as I shall deliver into your hands a female who will accompany you in your exile."

"I swear," he cried, "by the sun, and by the blue sky of Heaven, and by the fire of love that burns my heart, that if you grant my prayer, while they exist you shall never behold me again. Depart to your home, and commence your labors: I shall watch their progress with unutterable anxiety; and fear not but that when you are ready I shall appear."

Saying this, he suddenly quitted me, fearful, perhaps, of any change in my sentiments. I saw him descend the mountain with greater speed than the flight of an eagle, and quickly lost among the undulations of the sea of ice.

His tale had occupied the whole day; and the sun was upon the verge of the horizon when he departed. I knew that I ought to hasten my descent towards the valley, as I should soon be encompassed in darkness; but my heart was heavy, and my steps slow. The labor of winding among the little paths of the mountains, and fixing my feet firmly as I advanced, perplexed me, occupied as I was by the emotions which the occurrences of the day had produced. Night was far advanced when I came to the half-way resting-place, and seated myself beside the fountain. The stars shone at intervals, as the clouds passed from over them; the dark pines rose before me, and every here and there a broken tree lay on the ground: it was a scene of wonderful solemnity, and stirred strange thoughts within me. I wept bitterly; and clasping my hands in agony, I exclaimed, "Oh! stars, and clouds, and winds, ye are all about to mock me: if ye really pity me, crush sensation and memory; let me become as nought; but if not, depart, depart, and leave me in darkness."

These were wild and miserable thoughts; but I cannot describe to you how the eternal twinkling of the stars weighed upon me, and how I listened to every blast of wind as if it were a dull ugly siroc on its way to consume me.

Morning dawned before I arrived at the village of Chamounix; I took no rest, but returned immediately to Geneva. Even in my own heart I could give no expression to my sensations—they weighed on me with a mountain's weight, and their excess destroyed my agony beneath them. Thus I returned home, and entering the house, presented myself to the family. My haggard and wild appearance awoke intense alarm; but I answered no question, scarcely did I speak. I felt as if I were placed under a ban—as if I had no right to claim their sympathies—as if never more might I enjoy companionship with them. Yet even thus I loved them to adoration; and to save them, I resolved to dedicate myself to my most abhorred task. The prospect of such an occupation made every other circumstance of existence pass before me like a dream; and that thought only had to me the reality of life.

XVIII

Day after day, week after week, passed away on my return to Geneva; and I could not collect the courage to recommence my work. I feared the vengeance of the disappointed fiend, yet I was unable to overcome my repugnance to the task which was enjoined me. I found that I could not compose a female without again devoting several months to profound study and laborious disquisition. I had heard of some discoveries having been made by an English philosopher, the knowledge of which was material to my success, and I sometimes thought of obtaining my father's consent to visit England for this purpose; but I clung to every pretense of delay, and shrunk from taking the first step in an undertaking whose immediate necessity began to appear less absolute to me. A change indeed had taken place in me: my health, which had hitherto declined, was now much restored; and my spirits, when unchecked by the memory of my unhappy promise, rose proportionably. My father saw this change with pleasure, and he turned his thoughts towards the best method of eradicating the remains of my melancholy, which every now and then would return by fits, and with a devouring blackness overcast the approaching sunshine. At these moments I took refuge in the most perfect solitude. I passed whole days on the lake alone in a little boat, watching the clouds, and listening to the rippling of the waves, silent and listless. But the fresh air and bright sun seldom failed to restore me to some degree of composure; and, on my return, I met the salutations of my friends with a readier smile and a more cheerful heart.

It was after my return from one of these rambles, that my father, calling me aside, thus addressed me:—

"I am happy to remark, my dear son, that you have resumed your former pleasures, and seem to be returning to yourself. And yet you are still unhappy, and still avoid our society. For some time I was lost in conjecture as to the cause of this; but yesterday an idea struck me, and if it is well founded, I conjure you to avow it. Reserve on such a point would be not only useless, but draw down treble misery on us all."

I trembled violently at his exordium, and my father continued—

"I confess, my son, that I have always looked forward to your marriage with our dear Elizabeth as the tie of our domestic comfort, and the stay of my declining years. You were attached to each other from your earliest infancy; you studied together, and appeared, in dispositions and tastes, entirely suited to one another. But so blind is the experience of man that what I conceived to be the best assistants to my plan may have entirely destroyed it. You, perhaps, regard her as your sister, without any wish that she might become your wife. Nay, you may have met with another whom you may love; and, considering yourself as bound in honor to Elizabeth, this struggle may occasion the poignant misery which you appear to feel."

"My dear father, reassure yourself. I love my cousin tenderly and sincerely. I never saw any woman who excited, as Elizabeth does, my warmest admiration and affection. My future hopes and prospects are entirely bound up in the expectation of our union."

"The expression of your sentiments of this subject, my dear Victor, gives me more pleasure than I have for some time experienced. If you feel thus, we shall assuredly be happy, however present events may cast a gloom over us. But it is this gloom, which appears to have taken so strong a hold of your mind, that I wish to dissipate. Tell me, therefore, whether you object to an immediate solemnization of the marriage. We have been unfortunate, and recent events have drawn us from that every-day tranquility befitting my years and infirmities. You are younger; yet I do not suppose, possessed as you are of a competent fortune, that an early marriage would at all interfere with any future plans of honor and utility that you may have formed. Do not suppose, however, that I wish to dictate happiness to you, or that a delay on your part would cause me any serious uneasiness. Interpret my words with candor, and answer me, I conjure you, with confidence and sincerity."

I listened to my father in silence, and remained for some time inca-pable of offering any reply. I revolved rapidly in my mind a multitude of thoughts, and endeavored to arrive at some conclusion. Alas! to me the idea of an immediate union with my Elizabeth was one of horror and dismay. I was bound by a solemn promise, which I had not yet ful-filled, and dared not break; or, if I did, what manifold miseries might not impend over me and my devoted family! Could I enter into a festival with this deadly weight yet hanging round my neck, and bowing me to the ground. I must perform my engagement, and let the monster depart with his mate, before I allowed myself to enjoy the delight of an union from which I expected peace.

I remembered also the necessity imposed upon me of either journeying to England, or entering into a long correspondence with those philosophers of that country, whose knowledge and discoveries were of indispensable use to me in my present undertaking. The latter method of obtaining the desired intelligence was dilatory and unsatisfactory: besides, I had an insurmountable aversion to the idea of engaging myself in my loathsome task in my father's house, while in habits of familiar intercourse with those I loved. I knew that a thousand fearful accidents might occur, the slightest of which would disclose a tale to thrill all connected with me with horror. I was aware also that I should often lose all self-command, all capacity of hiding the harrowing sensations that would possess me during the progress of my unearthly occupation. I must absent myself from all I loved while thus employed. Once commenced, it would quickly be achieved, and I might be restored to my family in peace and happiness.

My promise fulfilled, the monster would depart for ever. Or (so my fond fancy imaged) some accident might meanwhile occur to destroy him, and put an end to my slavery for ever.

These feelings dictated my answer to my father. I expressed a wish to visit England; but, concealing the true reasons of this request, I clothed my desires under a guise which excited no suspicion, while I urged my desire with an earnestness that easily induced my father to comply. After so long a period of an absorbing melancholy, that resembled madness in its intensity and effects, he was glad to find that I was capable of taking pleasure in the idea of such a journey, and he hoped that change of scene and varied amusement would, before my return, have restored me entirely to myself.

The duration of my absence was left to my own choice; a few months, or at most a year, was the period contemplated. One paternal kind precaution he had taken to ensure my having a companion. Without previously communicating with me, he had, in concert with Elizabeth, arranged that Clerval should join me at Strasburgh. This interfered with the solitude I coveted for the prosecution of my task; yet at the commencement of my journey the presence of my friend could in no way be an impediment, and truly I rejoiced that thus I should be saved many hours of lonely, maddening reflection. Nay, Henry might stand between me and the intrusion of my foe. If I were alone, would he not at times force his abhorred presence on me, to remind me of my task, or to contemplate its progress?

To England, therefore, I was bound, and it was understood that my union with Elizabeth should take place immediately on my return. My father's age rendered him extremely averse to delay. For myself, there was one reward I promised myself from my detested toils—one consolation for my unparalleled sufferings; it was the prospect of that day when, enfranchised from my miserable slavery, I might claim Elizabeth, and forget the past in my union with her.

I now made arrangements for my journey; but one feeling haunted me, which filled me with fear and agitation. During my absence I should leave my friends unconscious of the existence of their enemy, and unprotected from his attacks, exasperated as he might be by my departure. But he had promised to follow me wherever I might go; and would he not accompany me to England? This imagination was dreadful in itself, but soothing, inasmuch as it supposed the safety of my friends. I was agonized with the idea of the possibility that the reverse of this might happen. But through the whole period during which I was the slave of my creature, I allowed myself to be governed by the impulses of the moment; and my present sensations strongly intimated that the fiend would follow me, and exempt my family from the danger of his machinations.

It was in the latter end of September that I again quitted my native country. My journey had been my own suggestion, and Elizabeth, therefore, acquiesced: but she was filled with disquiet at the idea of my suffering, away from her, the inroads of misery and grief. It had been her care which provided me a companion in Clerval—and yet a man is blind to a thousand minute circumstances, which call forth a woman's sedulous attention. She longed to bid me hasten my return,—a thousand conflicting emotions rendered her mute as she bade me a tearful silent farewell.

I threw myself into the carriage that was to convey me away, hardly knowing whither I was going, and careless of what was passing around. I remembered only, and it was with a bitter anguish that I reflected on it, to order that my chemical instruments should be packed to go with me. Filled with dreary imaginations, I passed through many beautiful and majestic scenes; but my eyes were fixed and unobserving. I could only think of the borne of my travels, and the work which was to occupy me whilst they endured.

After some days spent in listless indolence, during which I traversed many leagues, I arrived at Strasburgh, where I waited two days for Clerval. He came. Alas, how great was the contrast between us! He was alive to every new scene; joyful when he saw the beauties of the setting sun, and more happy when he beheld it rise, and recommence a new day. He pointed out to me the shifting colors of the landscape, and the appearances of the sky. "This is what it is to live," he cried, "now I enjoy existence! But you, my dear Frankenstein, wherefore are you desponding and sorrowful!" In truth, I was occupied by gloomy thoughts, and neither saw the descent of the evening star, nor the golden sunrise reflected in the Rhine.—And you, my friend, would be far more amused with the journal of Clerval, who observed the scenery with an eye of feeling and delight, than in listening to my reflections. I, a miserable wretch, haunted by a curse that shut up every avenue to enjoyment.

We had agreed to descend the Rhine in a boat from Strasburgh to Rotterdam, whence we might take shipping for London. During this voyage, we passed many willowy islands, and saw several beautiful towns. We stayed a day at Manheim, and, on the fifth from our departure from Strasburgh, arrived at Mayence. The course of the Rhine below Mayence becomes much more picturesque. The river descends rapidly, and winds between hills, not high, but steep, and of beautiful forms. We saw many ruined castles standing on the edges of precipices, surrounded by black woods, high and inaccessible. This part of the Rhine, indeed, presents a singularly variegated landscape. In one spot you view rugged hills, ruined castles overlooking tremendous precipices, with the dark Rhine rushing beneath; and, on the sudden turn of a promontory, flourishing vineyards, with green sloping banks, and a meandering river, and populous towns occupy the scene.

We traveled at the time of the vintage, and heard the song of the laborers, as we glided down the stream. Even I, depressed in mind, and my spirits continually agitated by gloomy feelings, even I was pleased. I lay at the bottom of the boat, and, as I gazed on the cloudless blue sky, I seemed to drink in a tranquility to which I had long been a stranger. And if these were my sensations, who can describe those of Henry? He felt as if he had been transported to Fairyland, and enjoyed a happiness seldom tasted by man. "I have seen," he said, "the most beautiful scenes of my own country; I have visited the lakes of Lucerne and Uri, where the snowy mountains descend almost perpendicularly to the water, casting black and impenetrable shades, which would cause a gloomy and mournful appearance, were it not for the most verdant islands that relieve the eye by their gay appearance; I have seen this lake agitated by a tempest, when the wind tore up whirlwinds of water, and gave you an idea of what the waterspout must be on the great ocean; and the waves dash with fury the base of the mountain, where the priest and his mistress were overwhelmed by an avalanche, and where their dying voices are still said to be heard amid the pauses of the nightly wind; I have seen the mountains of La Valais, and the Pays de Vaud: but this country, Victor, pleases me more than all those wonders. The mountains of Switzerland are more majestic and strange; but there is a charm in the banks of this divine river, that I never before saw equalled. Look at that castle which overhangs yon precipice; and that also on the island, almost concealed amongst the foliage of those lovely trees; and now that group of laborers coming from among their vines; and that village half hid in the recess of the mountain. Oh, surely, the spirit that inhabits and guards this place has a soul more in harmony with man than those who pile the glacier, or retire to the inaccessible peaks of the mountains of our own country."

Clerval! beloved friend! even now it delights me to record your words, and to dwell on the praise of which you are so eminently deserving. He was a being formed in the "very poetry of nature." His wild and enthusiastic imagination was chastened by the sensibility of his heart. His soul overflowed with ardent affections, and his friendship was of that devoted and wondrous nature that the worldly-minded teach us to look for only in the imagination. But even human sympathies were not sufficient to satisfy his eager mind. The scenery of external nature, which others regard only with admiration, he loved with ardor.—

> The sounding cataract
> Haunted him like a passion: the tall rock,
> The mountain, and the deep and gloomy wood,
> Their colors and their forms, were then to him
> An appetite; a feeling, and a love,
> That had no need of a remoter charm,
> By thought supplied, or any interest
> Unborrow'd from the eye.*

And where does he now exist? Is this gentle and lovely being lost for ever? Has this mind, so replete with ideas, imaginations fanciful and magnificent, which formed a world, whose existence depended on the life of its creator;—has the mind perished? Does it now only exist in my memory? No, it is not thus; your form so divinely wrought, and beaming

---

* Wordsworth's "Tintern Abbey."

with beauty, has decayed, but your spirit still visits and consoles your unhappy friend.

Pardon this gush of sorrow; these ineffectual words are but a slight tribute to the unexampled worth of Henry, but they soothe my heart, overflowing with the anguish which his remembrance creates. I will proceed with my tale.

Beyond Cologne we descended to the plains of Holland; and we resolved to post the remainder of our way; for the wind was contrary, and the stream of the river was too gentle to aid us.

Our journey here lost the interest arising from beautiful scenery; but we arrived in a few days at Rotterdam, whence we proceeded by sea to England. It was on a clear morning, in the latter days of December, that I first saw the white cliffs of Britain. The banks of the Thames presented a new scene; they were flat, but fertile, and almost every town was marked by the remembrance of some story. We saw Tilbury Fort, and remembered the Spanish armada; Gravesend, Woolwich, and Greenwich, places which I had heard of even in my country.

At length we saw the numerous steeples of London, St. Paul's towering above all, and the Tower famed in English history.

XIX

London was our present point of rest; we determined to remain several months in this wonderful and celebrated city. Clerval desired the intercourse of the men of genius and talent who flourished at this time; but this was with me a secondary object; I was principally occupied with the means of obtaining the information necessary for the completion of my promise, and quickly availed myself of the letters of introduction that I had brought with me, addressed to the most distinguished natural philosophers.

If this journey had taken place during my days of study and happiness, it would have afforded me inexpressible pleasure. But a blight had come over my existence, and I only visited these people for the sake of the information they might give me on the subject in which my interest was so terribly profound. Company was irksome to me; when alone, I could fill my mind with the sights of heaven and earth; the voice of Henry soothed me, and I could thus cheat myself into a transitory peace. But busy uninteresting joyous faces brought back despair to my heart. I saw an insurmountable barrier placed between me and my fellow-men; this barrier was sealed with the blood of William and Justine; and to reflect on the events connected with those names filled my soul with anguish.

But in Clerval I saw the image of my former self; he was inquisitive, and anxious to gain experience and instruction. The difference of manners which he observed was to him an inexhaustible source of instruction and amusement. He was also pursuing an object he had long had in view. His design was to visit India, in the belief that he had in his knowledge of its various languages, and in the views he had taken of its society, the means of materially assisting the progress of European colonization and trade. In Britain only could he further the execution of his plan. He was for ever busy; and the only check to his enjoyments was my sorrowful and dejected mind. I tried to conceal this as much as possible, that I might not debar him from the pleasures natural to one who was entering on a new scene of life, undisturbed by any care or bitter recollection. I often refused to accompany him, alleging another engagement, that I might remain alone. I now also began to collect the materials necessary for my new creation, and this was to me like the torture of single drops of water continually falling on the head. Every thought that was devoted to it was an extreme anguish, and every word that I spoke in allusion to it caused my lips to quiver, and my heart to palpitate.

After passing some months in London, we received a letter from a person in Scotland, who had formerly been our visitor at Geneva. He mentioned the beauties of his native country, and asked us if those were not sufficient allurements to induce us to prolong our journey as far north as Perth, where he resided. Clerval eagerly desired to accept this invitation; and I, although I abhorred society, wished to view again mountains and streams, and all the wondrous works with which Nature adorns her chosen dwelling-places.

We had arrived in England at the beginning of October, and it was now February. We accordingly determined to commence our journey towards the north at the expiration of another month. In this expedition we did not intend to follow the great road to Edinburgh, but to visit Windsor, Oxford, Matlock, and the Cumberland lakes, resolving to arrive at the completion of this tour about the end of July. I packed up my chemical instruments, and the materials I had collected, resolving to finish my labors in some obscure nook in the northern highlands of Scotland.

We quitted London on the 27th of March, and remained a few days at Windsor, rambling in its beautiful forest. This was a new scene to us mountaineers; the majestic oaks, the quantity of game, and the herds of stately deer, were all novelties to us.

From thence we proceeded to Oxford. As we entered this city, our minds were filled with the remembrance of the events that had been transacted there more than a century and a half before. It was here that Charles I had collected his forces. This city had remained faithful to him, after the whole nation had forsaken his cause to join the standard of parliament and liberty. The memory of that unfortunate king, and his companions, the amiable Falkland, the insolent Goring, his queen, and son, gave a peculiar interest to every part of the city, which they might be supposed to have inhabited. The spirit of elder days found a dwelling here, and we delighted to trace its footsteps. If these feelings had not found an imaginary gratification, the appearance of the city had yet in itself sufficient beauty to obtain our admiration. The colleges are ancient and picturesque; the streets are almost magnificent; and the lovely Isis, which flows beside it through meadows of exquisite verdure, is spread forth into a placid expanse of waters, which reflects its majestic assemblage of towers, and spires, and domes, embosomed among aged trees.

I enjoyed this scene; and yet my enjoyment was embittered both by the memory of the past, and the anticipation of the future. I was formed for peaceful happiness. During my youthful days discontent never visited my mind; and if I was ever overcome by *ennui*, the sight of what is beautiful in nature, or the study of what is excellent and sublime in the productions of man, could always interest my heart, and communicate elasticity to my spirits. But I am a blasted tree; the bolt has entered my soul; and I felt then that I should survive to exhibit what I shall soon cease to be—a miserable spectacle of wrecked humanity, pitiable to others, and intolerable to myself.

We passed a considerable period at Oxford, rambling among its environs, and endeavoring to identify every spot which might relate to the most animating epoch of English history. Our little voyages of discovery were often prolonged by the successive objects that presented themselves. We visited the tomb of the illustrious Hampden, and the field on which that patriot fell. For a moment my soul was elevated from its debasing and miserable fears, to contemplate the divine ideas of liberty and self-sacrifice, of which these sights were the monuments and the remembrancers. For an instant I dared to shake off my chains, and look around me with a free and lofty spirit; but the iron had eaten into my flesh, and I sank again, trembling and hopeless, into my miserable self.

We left Oxford with regret, and proceeded to Matlock, which was our next place of rest. The country in the neighborhood of this village resembled, to a greater degree, the scenery of Switzerland; but everything is on a lower scale, and the green hills want the crown of distant white Alps, which always attend on the piny mountains of my native country. We visited the wondrous cave, and the little cabinets of natural history, where the curiosities are disposed in the same manner as in the collections at Servox and Chamounix. The latter name made me tremble when pronounced by Henry; and I hastened to quit Matlock, with which that terrible scene was thus associated.

From Derby, still journeying northward, we passed two months in Cumberland and Westmoreland. I could now almost fancy myself among the Swiss mountains. The little patches of snow which yet lingered on the northern sides of the mountains, the lakes, and the dashing of the rocky streams, were all familiar and dear sights to me. Here also we made some acquaintances, who almost contrived to cheat me into happiness. The delight of Clerval was proportionably greater than mine; his mind expanded in the company of men of talent, and he found in his own nature greater capacities and resources than he could have imagined himself to have possessed while he associated with his inferiors. "I could pass my life here," said he to me; "and among these mountains I should scarcely regret Switzerland and the Rhine."

But he found that a traveler's life is one that includes much pain amidst its enjoyments. His feelings are for ever on the stretch; and when he begins to sink into repose, he finds himself obliged to quit that on which he rests in pleasure for something new, which again engages his attention, and which also he forsakes for other novelties.

We had scarcely visited the various lakes of Cumberland and Westmoreland, and conceived an affection for some of the inhabitants, when the period of our appointment with our Scotch friend approached, and we left them to travel on. For my own part I was not sorry. I had now neglected my promise for some time, and I feared the effects of the daemon's disappointment. He might remain in Switzerland, and wreak his vengeance on my relatives. This idea pursued me, and tormented me at every moment from which I might otherwise have snatched repose and peace. I waited for my letters with feverish impatience: if they were delayed, I was miserable, and overcome by a thousand fears; and when they arrived, and I saw the superscription of Elizabeth or my father, I hardly dared to read and ascertain my fate. Sometimes I thought that the fiend followed me, and might expedite my remissness by murdering my companion. When these thoughts possessed me, I would not quit Henry for a moment, but followed him as his shadow, to protect him from the fancied rage of his destroyer. I felt as if I had committed some great crime, the consciousness of which haunted me. I was guiltless, but I had indeed drawn down a horrible curse upon my head, as mortal as that of crime.

I visited Edinburgh with languid eyes and mind; and yet that city might have interested the most unfortunate being. Clerval did not like it so well as Oxford: for the antiquity of the latter city was more pleasing to him. But the beauty and regularity of the new town of Edinburgh, its romantic castle, and its environs, the most delightful in the world, Arthur's Seat, St. Bernard's Well, and the Pentland Hills, conpensated him for the change, and filled him with cheerfulness and admiration. But I was impatient to arrive at the termination of my journey.

We left Edinburgh in a week, passing through Coupar, St. Andrew's, and along the banks of the Tay, to Perth, where our friend expected us. But I was in no mood to laugh and talk with strangers, or enter into their feelings or plans with the good humor expected from a guest; and accordingly I told Clerval that I wished to make the tour of Scotland alone. "Do you," said I, "enjoy yourself, and let this be our rendezvous. I may be absent a month or two; but do not interfere with my motions, I entreat you: leave me to peace and solitude for a short time; and when I return, I hope it will be with a lighter heart, more congenial to your own temper."

Henry wished to dissuade me; but, seeing me bent on this plan, ceased to remonstrate. He entreated me to write often. "I had rather be with you," he said, "in your solitary rambles, than with these Scotch people, whom I do not know: hasten then, my dear friend, to return, that I may again feel myself somewhat at home, which I cannot do in your absence."

Having parted from my friend, I determined to visit some remote spot of Scotland, and finish my work in solitude. I did not doubt but that the monster followed me, and would discover himself to me when I should have finished, that he might receive his companion.

With this resolution I traversed the northern highlands, and fixed on one of the remotest of the Orkneys as the scene of my labors. It was a place fitted for such a work, being hardly more than a rock, whose high sides were continually beaten upon by the waves. The soil was barren, scarcely affording pasture for a few miserable cows, and oatmeal for its inhabitants, which consisted of five persons, whose gaunt and scraggy limbs gave tokens of their miserable fare. Vegetables and bread, when they indulged in such luxuries, and even fresh water, was to be procured from the main land, which was about five miles distant.

On the whole island there were but three miserable huts, and one of these was vacant when I arrived. This I hired. It contained but two rooms, and these exhibited all the squalidness of the most miserable penury. The thatch had fallen in, the walls were unplastered, and the door was off its hinges. I ordered it to be repaired, bought some furniture, and took possession; an incident which would, doubtless, have occasioned some surprise, had not all the senses of the cottagers been benumbed by want and squalid poverty. As it was, I lived ungazed at and unmolested, hardly thanked for the pittance of food and clothes which I gave; so much does suffering blunt even the coarsest sensations of men.

In this retreat I devoted the morning to labor; but in the evening, when the weather permitted, I walked on the stony beach of the sea, to listen to the waves as they roared and dashed at my feet. It was a monotonous yet ever-changing scene. I thought of Switzerland; it was far different from this desolate and appalling landscape. Its hills are covered with vines, and its cottages are scattered thickly in the plains. Its fair lakes reflect a blue and gentle sky; and, when troubled by the winds, their tumult is but as the play of a lively infant, when compared to the roarings of the giant ocean.

In this manner I distributed my occupations when I first arrived; but, as I proceeded in my labor, it became every day more horrible and irksome to me. Sometimes I could not prevail on myself to enter my laboratory for several days; and at other times I toiled day and night in order to complete my work. It was, indeed, a filthy process in which I was engaged. During my first experiment, a kind of enthusiastic frenzy had blinded me to the horror of my employment; my mind was intently fixed on the consummation of my labor, and my eyes were shut to the horror of my proceedings. But now I went to it in cold blood, and my heart often sickened at the work of my hands.

Thus situated, employed in the most detestable occupation, immersed in a solitude where nothing could for an instant call my attention from the actual scene in which I was engaged, my spirits became unequal; I grew restless and nervous. Every moment I feared to meet my persecutor. Sometimes I sat with my eyes fixed on the ground, fearing to raise them, lest they should encounter the object which I so much dreaded to behold. I feared to wander from the sight of my fellow-creatures, lest when alone he should come to claim his companion.

In the meantime I worked on, and my labor was already considerably advanced. I looked towards its completion with a tremulous and eager hope, which I dared not trust myself to question, but which was inter-mixed with obscure forebodings of evil, that made my heart sicken in my bosom.

XX

I sat one evening in my laboratory; the sun had set, and the moon was just rising from the sea; I had not sufficient light for my employment, and I remained idle, in a pause of consideration of whether I should leave my labor for the night, or hasten its conclusion by an unremitting attention to it. As I sat, a train of reflection occurred to me, which led me to consider the effects of what I was now doing. Three years before I was engaged in the same manner, and had created a fiend whose unparalleled barbarity had desolated my heart, and filled it for ever with the bitterest remorse. I was now about to form another being, of whose dispositions I was alike ignorant; she might become ten thousand times more malignant than her mate, and delight, for its own sake, in murder and wretchedness. He had sworn to quit the neighborhood of man, and hide himself in deserts; but she had not; and she, who in all probability was to become a thinking and reasoning animal, might refuse to comply with a compact made before her creation. They might even hate each other; the creature who already lived loathed his own deformity, and might he not conceive a greater abhorrence for it when it came before his eyes in the female form? She also might turn with disgust from him to the superior beauty of man; she might quit him, and he be again alone, exasperated by the fresh provocation of being deserted by one of his own species.

Even if they were to leave Europe, and inhabit the deserts of the new world, yet one of the first results of those sympathies for which the dæmon thirsted would be children, and a race of devils would be propagated upon the earth who might make the very existence of the species of man a condition precarious and full of terror. Had I right, for my own benefit, to inflict this curse upon everlasting generations? I had before been moved by the sophisms of the being I had created; I had been struck sense-less by his fiendish threats: but now, for the first time, the wickedness of my promise burst upon me; I shuddered to think that future ages might curse me as their pest, whose selfishness had not hesitated to buy its own peace at the price, perhaps, of the existence of the whole human race.

I trembled, and my heart failed within me; when, on looking up, I saw, by the light of the moon, the dæmon at the casement. A ghastly grin wrinkled his lips as he gazed on me, where I sat fulfilling the task which he held allotted to me. Yes, he had followed me in my travels; he had loi-tered in forests, hid himself in caves, or taken refuge in wide and desert heaths; and he now came to mark my progress, and claim the fulfillment of my promise.

As I looked on him, his countenance expressed the utmost extent of malice and treachery. I thought with a sensation of madness on my promise of creating another like to him, and trembling with passion, tore to pieces the thing on which I was engaged. The wretch saw me destroy the creature on whose future existence he depended for happiness, and, with a howl of devilish despair and revenge, withdrew.

I left the room, and, locking the door, made a solemn vow in my own heart never to resume my labors; and then, with trembling steps, I sought my own apartment. I was alone; none were near me to dissipate the gloom, and relieve me from the sickening oppression of the most terrible reveries.

Several hours passed, and I remained near my window gazing on the sea; it was almost motionless, for the winds were hushed, and all nature reposed under the eye of the quiet moon. A few fishing vessels alone specked the water, and now and then the gentle breeze wafted the sound of voices, as the fishermen called to one another. I felt the silence, although I was hardly conscious of its extreme profundity, until my ear was suddenly arrested by the paddling of oars near the shore, and a person landed close to my house.

In a few minutes after, I heard the creaking of my door, as if some one endeavored to open it softly. I trembled from head to foot; I felt a presentiment of who it was, and wished to rouse one of the peasants who dwelt in a cottage not far from mine; but I was overcome by the sensation of helplessness, so often felt in frightful dreams, when you in vain endeavor to fly from an impending danger, and was rooted to the spot.

Presently I heard the sound of footsteps along the passage; the door opened, and the wretch whom I dreaded appeared. Shutting the door, he approached me, and said, in a smothered voice—

"You have destroyed the work which you began; what is it that you intend? Do you dare to break your promise? I have endured toil and misery: I left Switzerland with you; I crept along the shores of the Rhine, among its willow islands, and over the summits of its hills. I have dwelt many months in the heaths of England, and among the deserts of Scotland. I have endured incalculable fatigue, and cold, and hunger; do you dare destroy my hopes?"

"Begone! I do break my promise; never will I create another like yourself, equal in deformity and wickedness."

"Slave, I before reasoned with you, but you have proved yourself unworthy of my condescension. Remember that I have power; you believe yourself miserable, but I can make you so wretched that the light of day will be hateful to you. You are my creator, but I am your master;—obey!"

"The hour of my irresolution is past, and the period of your power is arrived. Your threats cannot move me to do an act of wickedness; but they confirm me in a determination of not creating you a companion in vice. Shall I, in cool blood, set loose upon the earth a dæmon, whose delight is in death and wretchedness? Begone! I am firm, and your words will only exasperate my rage."

The monster saw my determination in my face, and gnashed his teeth in the impotence of anger. "Shall each man," cried he, "find a wife for his bosom, and each beast have his mate, and I be alone? I had feelings of affection, and they were requited by detestation and scorn. Man! you may hate; but beware! your hours will pass in dread and misery, and soon the bolt will fall which must ravish from you your happiness for ever. Are you to be happy while I grovel in the intensity of my wretchedness? You can blast my other passions; but revenge remains—revenge, henceforth dearer than light or food! I may die; but first you, my tyrant and tormentor, shall curse the sun that gazes on your misery. Beware; for I am fearless, and therefore powerful. I will watch with the wiliness of a snake, that I may sting with its venom. Man, you shall repent of the injuries you inflict."

"Devil, cease; and do not poison the air with these sounds of malice. I have declared my resolution to you, and I am no coward to bend beneath words. Leave me; I am inexorable."

"It is well. I go; but remember, I shall be with you on your wedding-night."

I started forward, and exclaimed, "Villain! before you sign my death-warrant, be sure that you are yourself safe."

I would have seized him; but he eluded me, and quitted the house with precipitation. In a few moments I saw him in his boat, which shot across the waters with an arrowy swiftness, and was soon lost amidst the waves.

All was again silent; but his words rung in my ears. I burned with rage to pursue the murderer of my peace and precipitate him into the ocean. I walked up and down my room hastily and perturbed, while my imagination conjured up a thousand images to torment and sting me. Why had I not followed him, and closed with him in mortal strife? But I had suffered him to depart, and he had directed his course towards the main land. I shuddered to think who might be the next victim sacrificed to his insatiate revenge. And then I thought again of his words—*"I will be with you on your wedding-night."* That then was the period fixed for the fulfillment of my destiny. In that hour I should die, and at once satisfy and extinguish his malice. The prospect did not move me to fear; yet when I thought of my beloved Elizabeth,—of her tears and endless sorrow, when she should find her lover so barbarously snatched from her,—tears, the first I had shed for many months, streamed from my eyes, and I resolved not to fall before my enemy without a bitter struggle.

The night passed away, and the sun rose from the ocean; my feelings became calmer, if it may be called calmness, when the violence of rage sinks into the depths of despair. I left the house, the horrid scene of the last night's contention, and walked on the beach of the sea, which I almost regarded as an insuperable barrier between me and my fellow-creatures; nay, a wish that such should prove the fact stole across me. I desired that I might pass my life on that barren rock, wearily, it is true, but uninterrupted by any sudden shock of misery. If I returned, it was to be sacrificed, or to see those whom I most loved die under the grasp of a daemon whom I had myself created.

I walked about the isle like a restless spectre, separated from all it loved, and miserable in the separation. When it became noon, and the sun rose higher, I lay down on the grass, and was overpowered by a deep sleep. I had been awake the whole of the preceding night, my nerves were agitated, and my eyes inflamed by watching and misery. The sleep into which I now sunk refreshed me; and when I awoke, I again felt as if I belonged to a race of human beings like myself, and I began to reflect upon what had passed with greater composure; yet still the words of the fiend rung in my ears like a death-knell, they appeared like a dream, yet distinct and oppressive as a reality.

The sun had far descended, and I still sat on the shore, satisfying my appetite, which had become ravenous, with an oaten cake, when I saw a fishing-boat land close to me, and one of the men brought me a packet; it contained letters from Geneva, and one from Clerval, entreating me to join him. He said that he was wearing away his time fruitlessly where he was; that letters from the friends he had formed in London desired his return to complete the negotiation they had entered into for his Indian enterprise. He could not any longer delay his departure; but as his journey to London might be followed, even sooner than he now conjectured, by his longer voyage, he entreated me to bestow as much of my society on him as I could spare. He besought me, therefore, to leave my solitary isle, and to meet him at Perth, that we might proceed southwards together. This letter in a degree recalled me to life, and I determined to quit my island at the expiration of two days.

Yet, before I departed, there was a task to perform, on which I shuddered to reflect: I must pack up my chemical instruments; and for that purpose I must enter the room which had been the scene of my odious work, and I must handle those utensils, the sight of which was sickening to me. The next morning, at daybreak, I summoned sufficient courage, and unlocked the door of my laboratory. The remains of the half-finished creature, whom I had destroyed, lay scattered on the floor, and I almost felt as if I had mangled the living flesh of a human being. I paused to collect myself, and then entered the chamber. With trembling hand I conveyed the instruments out of the room; but I reflected that I ought not to leave the relics of my work to excite the horror and suspicion of the peasants; and I accordingly put them into a basket, with a great quantity of stones, and, laying them up, determined to throw them into the sea that very night; and in the meantime I sat upon the beach, employed in cleaning and arranging my chemical apparatus.

Nothing could be more complete than the alteration that had taken place in my feelings since the night of the appearance of the dæmon. I had before regarded my promise with a gloomy despair, as a thing that, with whatever consequences, must be fulfilled; but I now felt as if a film had been taken from before my eyes, and that I, for the first time, saw clearly. The idea of renewing my labors did not for one instant occur to me; the threat I had heard weighed on my thoughts, but I did not reflect that a voluntary act of mine could avert it. I had resolved in my own mind, that to create another like the fiend I had first made would be an act of the basest and most atrocious selfishness; and I banished from my mind every thought that could lead to a different conclusion.

Between two and three in the morning the moon rose; and I then, putting my basket aboard a little skiff, sailed out about four miles from the shore. The scene was perfectly solitary: a few boats were returning towards land, but I sailed away from them. I felt as if I was about the commission of a dreadful crime, and avoided with shuddering anxiety any encounter with my fellow-creatures. At one time the moon, which had before been clear, was suddenly overspread by a thick cloud, and I took advantage of the moment of darkness, and cast my basket into the sea: I listened to the gurgling sound as it sunk, and then sailed away from the spot. The sky became clouded; but the air was pure, although chilled by the north-east breeze that was then rising. But it refreshed me, and filled me with such agreeable sensations, that I resolved to prolong my stay on the water; and, fixing the rudder in a direct position, stretched myself at the bottom of the boat. Clouds hid the moon, everything was obscure, and I heard only the sound of the boat, as its keel cut through the waves; the murmur lulled me, and in a short time I slept soundly.

I do not know how long I remained in this situation, but when I awoke I found that the sun had already mounted considerably. The wind was high, and the waves continually threatened the safety of my little skiff. I found that the wind was north-east, and must have driven me far from the coast from which I had embarked. I endeavored to change my course, but quickly found that, if I again made the attempt, the boat would be instantly filled with water. Thus situated, my only resource was to drive before the wind. I confess that I felt a few sensations of terror. I had no compass with me, and was so slenderly acquainted with the geography of this part of the world, that the sun was of little benefit to me. I might be driven into the wide Atlantic, and feel all the tortures of starvation, or be swallowed up in the immeasurable waters that roared and buffeted around me. I had already been out many hours, and felt the torment of a burning thirst, a prelude to my other sufferings. I looked on the heavens, which were covered by clouds that flew before the wind, only to be replaced by others: I looked upon the sea, it was to be my grave. "Fiend," I exclaimed, "your task is already fulfilled!" I thought of Elizabeth, of my father, and of Clerval; all left behind, on whom the monster might satisfy his sanguinary and merciless passions. This idea plunged me into a reverie, so despairing and frightful, that even now, when the scene is on the point of closing before me for ever, I shudder to reflect on it.

Some hours passed thus; but by degrees, as the sun declined towards the horizon, the wind died away into a gentle breeze, and the sea became free from breakers. But these gave place to a heavy swell: I felt sick, and hardly able to hold the rudder, when suddenly I saw a line of high land towards the south.

Almost spent, as I was, by fatigue, and the dreadful suspense I endured for several hours, this sudden certainty of life rushed like a flood of warm joy to my heart, and tears gushed from my eyes.

How mutable are our feelings, and how strange is that clinging love we have of life even in the excess of misery! I constructed another sail with a part of my dress, and eagerly steered my course towards the land. It had a wild and rocky appearance; but, as I approached nearer, I easily perceived the traces of cultivation. I saw vessels near the shore, and found myself suddenly transported back to the neighborhood of civilized man. I carefully traced the windings of the land, and hailed a steeple which I at length saw issuing from behind a small promontory. As I was in a state of extreme debility, I resolved to sail directly towards the town, as a place where I could most easily procure nourishment. Fortunately I had money with me. As I turned the promontory, I perceived a small neat town and a good harbor, which I entered, my heart bounding with joy at my unexpected escape.

As I was occupied in fixing the boat and arranging the mills, several people crowded towards the spot. They seemed much surprised at my appearance; but, instead of offering me any assistance, whispered together with gestures that at any other time might have produced in me a slight sensation of alarm. As it was, I merely remarked that they spoke English; and I therfore addressed them in that language: "My good friends," said I, "will you be so kind as to tell me the name of this town, and inform me where I am?"

"You will know that soon enough," replied a man with a hoarse voice. "May be you are come to a place that will not prove much to your taste; but you will not be consulted as to your quarters, I promise you."

I was exceedingly surprised on receiving so rude an answer from a stranger; and I was also disconcerted on perceiving the frowning and angry countenances of his companions. "Why do you answer me so roughly?" I replied; "surely it is not the custom of Englishmen to receive strangers so inhospitably."

"I do not know," said the man, "what the custom of the English may be; but it is the custom of the Irish to hate villains."

While this strange dialogue continued, I perceived the crowd rapidly increase. Their faces expressed a mixture of curiosity and anger, which annoyed, and in some degree alarmed me. I inquired the way to the inn; but no one replied. I then moved forward, and a murmuring sound arose from the crowd as they followed and surrounded me; when an illlooking man approaching, tapped me on the shoulder, and said, "Come, sir, you must follow me to Mr. Kirwin's to give an account of yourself."

"Who is Mr. Kirwin? Why am I to give an account of myself? Is not this a free country?"

"Ay, sir, free enough for honest folks. Mr. Kirwin is a magistrate; and you are to give an account of the death of a gentleman who was found murdered here last night."

This answer startled me; but I presently recovered myself. I was innocent; that could easily be proved: accordingly I followed my conductor in silence, and was led to one of the best houses in the town. I was ready to sink from fatigue and hunger; but, being surrounded by a crowd, I thought it politic to rouse all my strength, that no physical debility might be construed into apprehension or conscious guilt. Little did I then expect the calamity that was in a few moments to overwhelm me, and extinguish in horror and despair all fear of ignominy or death.

I must pause here; for it requires all my fortitude to recall the memory of the frightful events which I am about to relate, in proper detail, to my recollection.

XXI

I was soon introduced into the presence of the magistrate, an old benevolent man, with calm and mild manners. He looked upon me, however, with some degree of severity: and then, turning towards my conductors, he asked who appeared as witnesses on this occasion.

About half a dozen men came forward; and one being selected by the magistrate, he deposed that he had been out fishing the night before with his son and brother-in-law, Daniel Nugent, when, about ten o'clock, they observed a strong northerly blast rising, and they accordingly put in for port. It was a very dark night, as the moon had not yet risen; they did not land at the harbor, but, as they had been accustomed, at a creek about two miles below. He walked on first, carrying a part of the fishing tackle, and his companions followed him at some distance. As he was proceeding along the sands, he struck his foot against something, and fell at his length on the ground. His companions came up to assist him; and, by the light of their lantern, they found that he had fallen on the body of a man who was to all appearance dead. Their first supposition was that it was the corpse of some person who had been drowned, and was thrown on shore by the waves; but, on examination, they found that the clothes were not wet, and even that the body was not then cold. They instantly carried it to the cottage of an old woman near the spot, and endeavored, but in vain, to restore it to life. It appeared to be a handsome young man, about five and twenty years of age. He had apparently been strangled; for there was no sign of any violence, except the black mark of fingers on his neck.

The first part of this deposition did not in the least interest me; but when the mark of the fingers was mentioned, I remembered the murder of my brother, and felt myself extremely agitated; my limbs trembled, and a mist came over my eyes, which obliged me to lean on a chair for support. The magistrate observed me with a keen eye, and of course drew an unfavorable augury from my manner.

The son confirmed his father's account: but when Daniel Nugent was called, he swore positively that, just before the fall of his companion, he saw a boat, with a single man in it, at a short distance from the shore; and, as far as he could judge by the light of a few stars, it was the same boat in which I had just landed.

A woman deposed that she lived near the beach, and was standing at the door of her cottage, waiting for the return of the fishermen, about an hour before she heard of the discovery of the body, when she saw a boat, with only one man in it, push off from that part of the shore where the corpse was afterwards found.

Another woman confirmed the account of the fishermen having brought the body into her house; it was not cold. They put it into a bed, and rubbed it; and Daniel went to the town for an apothecary, but life was quite gone.

Several other men were examined concerning my landing; and they agreed that, with the strong north wind that had arisen during the night, it was very probable that I had beaten about for many hours, and had been obliged to return nearly to the same spot from which I had departed. Besides, they observed that it appeared that I had brought the body from another place, and it was likely that, as I did not appear to know the shore, I might have put into the harbor ignorant of the distance of the town—from the place where I had deposited the corpse.

Mr. Kerwin, on hearing this evidence, desired that I should be taken into the room where the body lay for interment, that it might be observed what effect the sight of it would produce upon me. This idea was probably suggested by the extreme agitation I had exhibited when the mode of the murder had been described. I was accordingly conducted, by the magistrate and several other persons, to the inn. I could not help being struck by the strange coincidences that had taken place during this eventful night; but knowing that I had been conversing with several persons in the island I had inhabited about the time that the body had been found, I was perfectly tranquil as to the consequences of the affair.

I entered the room where the corpse lay, and was led up to the coffin. How can I describe my sensations on beholding it? I feel yet parched with horror, nor can I reflect on that terrible moment without shuddering and agony. The examination, the presence of the magistrate and witnesses, passed like a dream from my memory, when I saw the lifeless form of Henry Clerval stretched before me. I gasped for breath; and, throwing myself on the body, I exclaimed, "Have my murderous machinations deprived you also, my dearest Henry, of life? Two I have already destroyed; other victims await their destiny: but you, Clerval, my friend, my benefactor—"

The human frame could no longer support the agonies that I endured, and I was carried out of the room in strong convulsions.

A fever succeeded to this. I lay for two months on the point of death: my ravings, as I afterwards heard, were frightful; I called myself the murderer of William, of Justine, and of Clerval. Sometimes I entreated my attendants to assist me in the destruction of the fiend by whom I was tormented; and at others I felt the fingers of the monster already grasping my neck, and screamed aloud with agony and terror. Fortunately, as I spoke my native language, Mr. Kirwin alone understood me; but my gestures and bitter cries were sufficient to affright the other witnesses.

Why did I not die? More miserable than man ever was before, why did I not sink into forgetfulness and rest? Death snatches away many blooming children, the only hopes of their doating parents: how many brides and youthful lovers have been one day in the bloom of health and hope, and the next a prey for worms and the decay of the tomb! Of what materials was I made, that I could thus resist so many shocks, which, like the turning of the wheel, continually renewed the torture?

But I was doomed to live; and, in two months, found myself as awaking from a dream, in a prison, stretched on a wretched bed, surrounded by gaolers, turnkeys, bolts, and all the miserable apparatus of a dungeon. It was morning, I remember, when I thus awoke to understanding: I had forgotten the particulars of what had happened, and only felt as if some great misfortune had suddenly overwhelmed me; but when I looked around, and saw the barred windows, and the squalidness of the room in which I was, all flashed across my memory, and I groaned bitterly.

This sound disturbed an old woman who was sleeping in a chair beside me. She was a hired nurse, the wife of one of the turnkeys, and her countenance expressed all those bad qualities which often characterize that class. The lines of her face were hard and rude, like that of persons accustomed to see without sympathizing in sights of misery. Her tone expressed her entire indifference; she addressed me in English, and the voice struck me as one that I had heard during my sufferings:—

"Are you better now, sir?" said she.

I replied in the same language, with a feeble voice, "I believe I am; but if it be all true, if indeed I did not dream, I am sorry that I am still alive to feel this misery and horror."

"For that matter," replied the old woman, "if you mean about the gentleman you murdered, I believe that it were better for you if you were dead, for I fancy it will go hard wth you! However, that's none of my business; I am sent to nurse you, and get you well; I do my duty with a safe conscience; it were well if everybody did the same."

I turned with loathing from the woman who could utter so unfeeling a speech to a person just saved, on the very edge of death; but I felt languid, and unable to reflect on all that had passed. The whole series of my life appeared to me as a dream; I sometimes doubted if indeed it were all true, for it never presented itself to my mind with the force of reality.

As the images that floated before me became more distinct, I grew feverish; a darkness pressed around me: no one was near me who soothed me with the gentle voice of love; no dear hand supported me. The physician came and prescribed medicines, and the old woman prepared them for me; but utter carelessness was visible in the first, and the expression of brutality was strongly marked in the visage of the second. Who could be interested in the fate of a murderer, but the hangman who would gain his fee?

These were my first reflections; but I soon learned that Mr. Kirwin had shown me extreme kindness. He had caused the best room in the prison to be prepared for me (wretched indeed was the best); and it was he who had provided a physician and a nurse. It is true, he seldom came to see me; for, although he ardently desired to relieve the sufferings of every human creature, he did not wish to be present at the agonies and miserable ravings of a murderer. He came, therefore, sometimes, to see that I was not neglected; but his visits were short, and with long intervals.

One day, while I was gradually recovering, I was seated in a chair, my eyes half open, and my cheeks livid like those in death. I was overcome by gloom and misery, and often reflected I had better seek death than desire to remain in a world which to me was replete with wretchedness. At one time I considered whether I should not declare myself guilty, and suffer the penalty of the law, less innocent than poor Justine had been. Such were my thoughts when the door of my apartment was opened and Mr. Kirwin entered. His countenance expressed sympathy and compassion; he drew a chair close to mine, and addressed me in French—

"I fear that this place is very shocking to you; can I do anything to make you more comfortable?"

"I thank you; but all that you mention is nothing to me: on the whole earth there is no comfort which I am capable of receiving."

"I know that the sympathy of a stranger can be but of little relief to one borne down as you are by so strange a misfortune. But you will, I hope, soon quit this melancholy abode; for doubtless, evidence can easily be brought to free you from the criminal charge."

"That is my least concern: I am, by a course of strange events, become the most miserable of mortals. Persecuted and tortured as I am and have been, can death be any evil to me?"

"Nothing indeed could be more unfortunate and agonizing than the strange chances that have lately occured. You were thrown, by some surprising accident, on this shore renowned for its hospitality, seized immediately, and charged with murder. The first sight that was presented to your eyes was the body of your friend, murdered in so unaccountable a manner, and placed, as it were, by some fiend across your path."

As Mr. Kirwin said this, notwithstanding the agitation I endured on this retrospect of my sufferings, I also felt considerable surprise at the knowledge he seemed to possess concerning me. I suppose some astonishment was exhibited in my countenance; for Mr. Kirwin hastened to say—

"Immediately upon your being taken ill, all the papers that were on your person were brought me, and I examined them that I might discover some trace by which I could send to your relations an account of your misfortune and illness. I found several letters, and, among others, one which I discovered from its commencement to be from your father. I instantly wrote to Geneva: nearly two months have elapsed since the departure of my letter.—But you are ill; even now you tremble: you are unfit for agitation of any kind."

"This suspense is a thousand times worse than the most horrible event: tell me what new scene of death has been acted, and whose murder I am now to lament?"

"Your family is perfectly well," said Mr. Kirwin, with gentleness; "and some one, a friend, is come to visit you."

I know not by what chain of thought the idea presented itself, but it instantly darted into my mind that the murderer had come to mock at my misery, and taunt me with the death of Clerval, as a new incitement for me to comply with his hellish desires. I put my hand before my eyes and cried out in agony—

"Oh! take him away! I cannot see him; for God's sake do not let him enter!"

Mr. Kirwin regarded me with a troubled countenance. He could not help regarding my exclamation as a presumption of my guilt, and said, in rather a severe tone—

"I should have thought, young man, that the presence of your father would have been welcome instead of inspiring such violent repugnance."

"My father!" cried I, while every feature and every muscle was relaxed from anguish to pleasure: "is my father indeed come? How kind, how very kind! But where is he, why does he not hasten to me?"

My change of manner surprised and pleased the magistrate; perhaps he thought that my former exclamation was a momentary return of delirium, and now he instantly resumed his former benevolence. He rose and quitted the room with my nurse, and in a moment my father entered it.

Nothing, at this moment, could have given me greater pleasure than the arrival of my father. I stretched out my hand to him and cried—

"Are you then safe—and Elizabeth—and Ernest?"

My father calmed me with assurances of their welfare, and endeavored, by dwelling on these subjects so interesting to my heart, to raise my desponding spirits; but he soon felt that a prison cannot be the abode of cheerfulness. "What a place is this that you inhabit, my son!" said he, looking mournfully at the barred windows and wretched appearance of the room. "You traveled to seek happiness, but a fatality seems to pursue you. And poor Clerval—"

The name of my unfortunate and murdered friend was an agitation too great to be endured in my weak state; I shed tears.

"Alas! yes, my father," replied I; "some destiny of the most horrible kind hangs over me, and I must live to fulfill it, or surely I should have died on the coffin of Henry."

We were not allowed to converse for any length of time, for the precarious state of my health rendered every precaution necessary that could ensure tranquility. Mr. Kirwin came in and insisted that my strength should not be exhausted by too much exertion. But the appearance of my father was to me like that of my good angel, and I gradually recovered my health.

As my sickness quitted me, I was absorbed by a gloomy and black melancholy that nothing could dissipate. The image of Clerval was for ever before me, ghastly and murdered. More than once the agitation into which these reflections threw me made my friends dread a dangerous relapse. Alas! why did they preserve so miserable and detested a life? It was surely that I might fulfill my destiny, which is now drawing to a close. Soon, oh! very soon, will death extinguish these throbbings, and relieve me from the mighty weight of anguish that bears me to the dust; and, in executing the award of justice, I shall also sink to rest. Then the appearance of death was distant although the wish was ever present to my thoughts; and I often sat for hours motionless and speechless, wishing for some mighty revolution that might bury me and my destroyer in its ruins.

The season of the assizes approached. I had already been three months in prison; and although I was still weak, and in continual danger of a relapse, I was obliged to travel nearly a hundred miles to the county-town where the court was held. Mr. Kirwin charged himself with every care of collecting witnesses and arranging my defense. I was spared the disgrace of appearing publicly as a criminal, as the case was not brought before the court that decides on life and death. The grand jury rejected the bill on its being proved that I was on the Orkney Islands at the hour the body of my friend was found; and a fortnight after my removal I was liberated from prison.

My father was enraptured on finding me freed from the vexations of a criminal charge, that I was again allowed to breathe the fresh atmosphere, and permitted to return to my native country. I did not participate in these feelings; for to me the walls of a dungeon or a palace were alike hateful. The cup of life was poisoned for ever; and although the sun shone upon me as upon the happy and gay of heart, I saw around me nothing but a dense and frightful darkness, penetrated by no light but the glimmer of two eyes that glared upon me. Sometimes they were the expressive eyes of Henry languishing in death, the dark orbs nearly covered by the lids, and the long black lashes that fringed them; sometimes it was the watery, clouded eyes of the monster as I first saw them in my chamber at Ingolstadt.

My father tried to awaken in me the feelings of affection. He talked of Geneva, which I should soon visit—of Elizabeth and Ernest; but these words only drew deep groans from me. Sometimes, indeed, I felt a wish for happiness; and thought, with melancholy delight, of my beloved cousin; or longed, with a devouring *maladie du pays*, to see once more the blue lake and rapid Rhone that had been so dear to me in early childhood: but my general state of feeling was a torpor in which a prison was as welcome a residence as the divinest scene in nature; and these fits were seldom interrupted but by paroxysms of anguish and despair. At these moments I often endeavored to put an end to the existence I loathed; and it required unceasing attendance and vigilance to restrain me from committing some dreadful act of violence.

Yet one duty remained to me, the recollection of which finally triumphed over my selfish despair. It was necessary that I should return without delay to Geneva, there to watch over the lives of those I so fondly loved; and to lie in wait for the murderer, that if any chance led me to the place of his concealment, or if he dared again to blast me by his presence, I might, with unfailing aim, put an end to the existence of the monstrous image which I had endued with the mockery of a soul still more monstrous. My father still desired to delay our departure, fearful that I could not sustain the fatigues of a journey: for I was a shattered wreck—the shadow of a human being. My strength was gone. I was a mere skeleton; and fever night and day preyed upon my wasted frame.

Still, as I urged our leaving Ireland with such inquietude and impatience, my father thought it best to yield. We took our passage on board a vessel bound for Havre-de-Grace, and sailed with a fair wind from the Irish shores. It was midnight. I lay on the deck looking at the stars and listening to the dashing of the waves. I hailed the darkness that shut Ireland from my sight; and my pulse beat with a feverish joy when I reflected that I should soon see Geneva. The past appeared to me in the light of a frightful dream; yet the vessel in which I was, the wind that blew me from the detested shore of Ireland, and the sea which surrounded me, told me too forcibly that I was deceived by no vision, and that Clerval, my friend and dearest companion, had fallen a victim to me and the monster of my creation. I repassed, in my memory, my whole life; my quiet happiness while residing with my family in Geneva, the death of my mother, and my departure for Ingolstadt. I remembered, shuddering, the mad enthusiasm that hurried me on to the creation of my hideous enemy, and I called to mind the night in which he first lived. I was unable to pursue the train of thought; a thousand feelings pressed upon me, and I wept bitterly.

Ever since my recovery from the fever I had been in the custom of taking every night a small quantity of laudanum; for it was by means of this drug only that I was enabled to gain the rest necessary for the preservation of life. Oppressed by the recollection of my various misfortunes, I now swallowed double my usual quantity and soon slept profoundly. But sleep did not afford me respite from thought and misery; my dreams presented a thousand objects that scared me. Towards morning I was possessed by a kind of nightmare; I felt the fiend's grasp in my neck, and could not free myself from it; groans and cries rung in my ears. My father, who was watching over me, perceiving my restlessness, awoke me; the dashing waves were around: the cloudy sky above; the fiend was not here: a sense of security, a feeling that a truce was established between the present hour and the irresistible, disastrous future, imparted to me a kind of calm forgetfulness, of which the human mind is by its structure peculiarly susceptible.

XXII

The voyage came to an end. We landed and proceeded to Paris. I soon found that I had overtaxed my strength, and that I must repose before I could continue my journey. My father's care and attentions were indefatigable; but he did not know the origin of my sufferings, and sought erroneous methods to remedy the incurable ill. He wished me to seek amusement in society. I abhorred the face of man. Oh, not abhorred! they were my brethren, my fellow-beings, and I felt attracted even to the most repulsive among them as to creatures of an angelic nature and celestial mechanism. But I felt that I had no right to share their intercourse. I had unchained an enemy among them, whose joy it was to shed their blood and to revel in their groans. How they would, each and all, abhor me, and hunt me from the world, did they know my unhallowed acts and the crimes which had their source in me!

My father yielded at length to my desire to avoid society, and strove by various arguments to banish my despair. Sometimes he thought that I felt deeply the degradation of being obliged to answer a charge of murder, and he endeavored to prove to me the futility of pride.

"Alas! my father," said I, "how little do you know me. Human beings, their feelings and passions, would indeed be degraded if such a wretch as I felt pride. Justine, poor unhappy Justine, was as innocent as I, and she suffered the same charge; she died for it; and I am the cause of this—I murdered her. William, Justine, and Henry—they all died by my hands."

My father had often, during my imprisonment, heard me make the same assertion; when I thus accused myself he sometimes seemed to desire an explanation, and at others he appeared to consider it as the offspring of delirium, and that, during my illness, some idea of this kind had presented itself to my imagination, the remembrance of which I preserved in my convalescence. I avoided explanation, and maintained a continual silence concerning the wretch I had created. I had a persuasion that I should be supposed mad; and this in itself would for ever have chained my tongue. But, besides, I could not bring myself to disclose a secret which would fill my hearer with consternation, and make fear and unnatural horror the inmates of his breast. I checked, therefore, my impatient thirst for sympathy, and was silent when I would have given the world to have confided the fatal secret. Yet still words like those I have recorded would burst uncontrollably from me. I could offer no explanation of them; but their truth in part relieved the burden of my mysterious woe.

Upon this occasion my father said, with an expression of unbounded wonder, "My dearest Victor, what infatuation is this? My dear son, I entreat you never to make such an assertion again."

"I am not mad," I cried energetically; "the sun and the heavens, who have viewed my operations, can bear witness of my truth. I am the assassin of those most innocent victims; they died by my machinations. A thousand times would I have shed my own blood, drop by drop, to have saved their lives; but I could not, my father, indeed I could not sacrifice the whole human race."

The conclusion of this speech convinced my father that my ideas were deranged, and he instantly changed the subject of our conversation and endeavored to alter the course of my thoughts. He wished as much as possible to obliterate the memory of the scenes that had taken place in Ireland, and never alluded to them, or suffered me to speak of my misfortunes.

As time passed away I became more calm: misery had her dwelling in my heart, but I no longer talked in the same incoherent manner of my own crimes; sufficient for me was the consciousness of them. By the utmost self-violence, I curbed the imperious voice of wretchedness, which sometimes desired to declare itself to the whole world; and my manners were calmer and more composed than they had ever been since my journey to the sea of ice.

A few days before we left Paris on our way to Switzerland, I received the following letter from Elizabeth:—

"MY DEAR FRIEND,—It gave me the greatest pleasure to receive a letter from my uncle dated at Paris; you are no longer at a formidable distance, and I may hope to see you in less than a fortnight. My poor cousin, how much you must have suffered! I expect to see you looking even more ill than when you quitted Geneva. This winter has been passed most miserably, tortured as I have been by anxious suspense; yet I hope to see peace in your countenance, and to find that your heart is not totally void of comfort and tranquility.

"Yet I fear that the same feelings now exist that made you so miserable a year ago, even perhaps augmented by time. I would not disturb you at this period when so many misfortunes weigh upon you; but a conversation that I had with my uncle previous to his departure renders some explanation necessary before we meet.

"Explanation! you may possibly say; what can Elizabeth have to explain? If you really say this, my questions are answered, and all my doubts satisfied. But you are distant from me, and it is possible that you may dread, and yet be pleased with this explanation; and, in a probability of this being the case, I dare not any longer postpone writing what, during your absence, I have often wished to express to you, but have never had the courage to begin.

"You well know, Victor, that our union had been the favorite plan of your parents ever since our infancy. We were told this when young, and taught to look forward to it as an event that would certainly take place. We were affectionate playfellows during childhood, and, I believe, dear and valued friends to one another as we grew older. But as brother and sister often entertain a lively affection towards each other without desiring a more intimate union, may not such also be our case? Tell me, dearest Victor. Answer me, I conjure you, by our mutual happiness, with simple truth—Do you not love another?

"You have traveled; you have spent several years of your life at Ingolstadt; and I confess to you, my friend, that when I saw you last autumn so unhappy, flying to solitude, from the society of every creature, I could not help supposing that you might regret our connection, and believe yourself bound in honor to fulfill the wishes of your parents although they opposed themselves to your inclinations. But this is false reasoning. I confess to you, my friend, that I love you, and that in my airy dreams of futurity you have been my constant friend and companion. But it is your happiness I desire as well as my own when I declare to you that our marriage would render me eternally miserable unless it were the dictate of your own free choice. Even now I weep to think that, borne down as you are by the cruelest misfortunes, you may stifle, by the word *honor*, all hope of that love and happiness which would alone restore you to yourself. I, who have so disinterested an affection for you, may increase your miseries tenfold by being an obstacle to your wishes. Ah! Victor, be assured that your cousin and playmate has too sincere a love for you not to be made miserable by this supposition. Be happy, my friend; and if you obey me in this one request, remain satisfied that nothing on earth will have the power to interrupt my tranquility.

"Do not let this letter disturb you; do not answer tomorrow, or the next day, or even until you come, if it will give you pain. My uncle will send me news of your health; and if I see but one smile on your lips when we meet, occasioned by this or any other exertion of mine, I shall need no other happiness.

ELIZABETH LAVENZA.

"GENEVA, *May 18th, 17—.*"

This letter revived in my memory what I had before forgotten, the threat of the fiend—"*I will be with you on your wedding-night!*" Such was my sentence, and on that night would the dæmon employ every art to destroy me, and tear me from the glimpse of happiness which promised partly to console my sufferings. On that night he had determined to consummate his crimes by my death. Well, be it so; a deadly struggle would then assuredly take place, in which if he were victorious I should be at peace, and his power over me be at an end. If he were vanquished I should be a free man. Alas! what freedom? such as the peasant enjoys when his family have been massacred before his eyes, his cottage burnt, his lands laid waste, and he is turned adrift, homeless, penniless, and alone, but free. Such would be my liberty except that in my Elizabeth I possessed a treasure; alas! balanced by those horrors of remorse and guilt which would pursue me until death.

Sweet and beloved Elizabeth! I read and re-read her letter and some softened feelings stole into my heart and dared to whisper paradisiacal dreams of love and joy; but the apple was already eaten, and the angel's arm bared to drive me from all hope. Yet I would die to make her happy. If the monster executed his threat, death was inevitable; yet, again, I considered whether my marriage would hasten my fate. My destruction might indeed arrive a few months sooner; but if my torturer should suspect that I postponed it influenced by his menaces he would surely find other, and perhaps more dreadful, means of revenge. He had vowed *to be with me on my wedding-night*, yet he did not consider that threat as binding him to peace in the meantime; for, as if to show me that he was not yet satiated with blood, he had murdered Clerval immediately after the enunciation of his threats. I resolved, therefore, that if my immediate union with my cousin would conduce either to hers or my father's happiness, my adversary's designs against my life should not retard it a single hour.

In this state of mind I wrote to Elizabeth. My letter was calm and affectionate. "I fear, my beloved girl," I said, "little happiness remains for us on earth; yet all that I may one day enjoy is centered in you. Chase away your idle fears; to you alone do I consecrate my life and my endeavors for contentment. I have one secret, Elizabeth, a dreadful one; when revealed to you it will chill your frame with horror, and then, far from being surprised at my misery, you will only wonder that I survive what I have endured. I will confide this tale of misery and terror to you the day after our marriage shall take place; for, my sweet cousin, there must be perfect confidence between us. But until then, I conjure you, do not mention or allude to it. This I most earnestly entreat, and I know you will comply."

In about a week after the arrival of Elizabeth's letter we returned to Geneva. The sweet girl welcomed me with warm affection; yet tears were in her eyes as she beheld my emaciated frame and feverish cheeks. I saw a change in her also. She was thinner and had lost much of that heavenly vivacity that had before charmed me; but her gentleness and soft looks of compassion made her a more fit companion for one blasted and miserable as I was.

The tranquility which I now enjoyed did not endure. Memory brought madness with it; and when I thought of what had passed a real insanity possessed me; sometimes I was furious and burnt with rage; sometimes low and despondent. I neither spoke nor looked at any one, but sat motionless, bewildered by the multitude of miseries that overcame me.

Elizabeth alone had the power to draw me from these fits; her gentle voice would soothe me when transported by passion, and inspire me with human feelings when sunk in torpor. She wept with me and for me. When reason returned she would remonstrate and endeavor to inspire me with resignation. Ah! it is well for the unfortunate to be resigned, but for the guilty there is no peace. The agonies of remorse poison the luxury there is otherwise sometimes found in indulging the excess of grief.

Soon after my arrival, my father spoke of my immediate marriage with Elizabeth. I remained silent.

"Have you, then, some other attachment?"

"None on earth. I love Elizabeth, and look forward to our union with delight. Let the day therefore be fixed; and on it I will consecrate myself, in life or death, to the happiness of my cousin."

"My dear Victor, do not speak thus. Heavy misfortunes have befallen us; but let us only cling closer to what remains, and transfer our love for those whom we have lost to those who yet live. Our circle will be small, but bound close by the ties of affection and mutual misfortune. And when time shall have softened your despair, new and dear objects of care will be born to replace those of whom we have been so cruelly deprived."

Such were the lessons of my father. But to me the remembrance of the threat returned: nor can you wonder that, omnipotent as the fiend had yet been in his deeds of blood, I should almost regard him as invincible, and that when he had pronounced the words, "I shall be with you on your wedding-night," I should regard the threatened fate as unavoidable. But death was no evil to me if the loss of Elizabeth were balanced with it; and I therefore, with a contented and even cheerful countenance, agreed with my father that, if my cousin would consent, the ceremony should take place in ten days, and thus put, as I imagined, the seal to my fate.

Great God! if for one instant I had thought what might be the hellish intention of my fiendish adversary, I would rather have banished myself for ever from my native country, and wandered a friendless outcast over the earth, than have consented to this miserable marriage. But, as if possessed of magic powers, the monster had blinded me to his real intentions; and when I thought that I had prepared only my own death, I hastened that of a far dearer victim.

As the period fixed for our marriage drew nearer, whether from cowardice or a prophetic feeling, I felt my heart sink within me. But I concealed my feelings by an appearance of hilarity, that brought smiles and joy to the countenance of my father, but hardly deceived the ever-watchful and nicer eye of Elizabeth. She looked forward to our union with placid contentment, not unmingled with a little fear, which past misfortunes had impressed, that what now appeared certain and tangible happiness might soon dissipate into an airy dream, and leave no trace but deep and everlasting regret.

Preparations were made for the event; congratulatory visits were received; and all wore a smiling appearance. I shut up, as well as I could, in my own heart the anxiety that preyed there, and entered with seeming earnestness into the plans of my father, although they might only serve as the decorations of my tragedy. Through my father's exertions, a part of the inheritance of Elizabeth had been restored to her by the Austrian government. A small possession on the shores of Como belonged to her. It was agreed that, immediately after our union, we should proceed to Villa Lavenza, and spend our first days of happiness beside the beautiful lake near which it stood.

In the meantime I took every precaution to defend my person in case the fiend should openly attack me. I carried pistols and a dagger constantly about me, and was ever on the watch to prevent artifice; and by these means gained a greater degree of tranquility. Indeed, as the period approached, the threat appeared more as a delusion, not to be regarded as worthy to disturb my peace, while the happiness I hoped for in my marriage wore a greater appearance of certainty as the day fixed for its solemnisation drew nearer and I heard it continually spoken of as an occurrence which no accident could possibly prevent.

Elizabeth seemed happy; my tranquil demeanor contributed greatly to calm her mind. But on the day that was to fulfill my wishes and my destiny she was melancholy, and a presentiment of evil pervaded her; and perhaps also she thought of the dreadful secret which I had promised to reveal to her on the following day. My father was in the meantime over-joyed, and, in the bustle of preparation, only recognized in the melancholy of his niece the diffidence of a bride.

After the ceremony was performed a large party assembled at my father's; but it was agreed that Elizabeth and I should commence our journey by water, sleeping that night at Evian, and continuing our voyage on the following day. The day was fair, the wind favorable; all smiled on our nuptial embarkation.

Those were the last moments of my life during which I enjoyed the feeling of happiness. We passed rapidly along: the sun was hot, but we were sheltered from its rays by a kind of canopy, while we enjoyed the beauty of the scene, sometimes on one side of the lake, where we saw Mont Salêve, the pleasant banks of Montalêgre, and at a distance, surmounting all, the beautiful Mont Blanc, and the assemblage of snowy mountains that in vain endeavor to emulate her; sometimes coasting the opposite banks, we saw the mighty Jura opposing its dark side to the ambition that would quit its native country, and an almost insurmountable barrier to the invader who should wish to enslave it.

I took the hand of Elizabeth: "You are sorrowful, my love. Ah! if you knew what I have suffered, and what I may yet endure, you would endeavor to let me taste the quiet and freedom from despair that this one day at least permits me to enjoy."

"Be happy, my dear Victor," replied Elizabeth; "there is, I hope, nothing to distress you; and be assured that if a lively joy is not painted in my face, my heart is contented. Something whispers to me not to depend too much on the prospect that is opened before us; but I will not listen to such a sinister voice. Observe how fast we move along, and how the clouds, which sometimes obscure and sometimes rise above the dome of Mont Blanc, render this scene of beauty still more interesting. Look also at the innumerable fish that are swimming in the clear water, where we can distinguish every pebble that lies at the bottom. What a divine day! how happy and serene all nature appears!"

Thus Elizabeth endeavored to divert her thoughts and mine from all reflection upon melancholy subjects. But her temper was fluctuating; joy for a few instants shone in her eyes, but it continually gave place to distraction and reverie.

The sun sunk lower in the heavens; we passed the river Drance, and observed its path through the chasms of the higher, and the glens of the lower hills. The Alps here come closer to the lake, and we approached the amphitheatre of mountains which forms its eastern boundary. The spire of Evian shone under the woods that surrounded it, and the range of mountain above mountain by which it was overhung.

The wind, which had hitherto carried us along with amazing rapidity, sunk at sunset to a light breeze; the soft air just ruffled the water, and caused a pleasant motion among the trees as we approached the shore, from which it wafted the most delightful scent of flowers and hay. The sun sunk beneath the horizon as we landed; and as I touched the shore, I felt those cares and fears revive which soon were to clasp me and cling to me for ever.

XXIII

It was eight o'clock when we landed; we walked for a short time on the shore enjoying the transitory light, and then retired to the inn and contemplated the lovely scene of waters, woods, and mountains, obscured in darkness, yet still displaying their black outlines.

The wind, which had fallen in the south, now rose with great violence in the west. The moon had reached her summit in the heavens and was beginning to descend; the clouds swept across it swifter than the flight of the vulture and dimmed her rays, while the lake reflected the scene of the busy heavens, rendered still busier by the restless waves that were beginning to rise. Suddenly a heavy storm of rain descended.

I had been calm during the day; but so soon as night obscured the shapes of objects, a thousand fears arose in my mind. I was anxious and watchful, while my right hand grasped a pistol which was hidden in my bosom; every sound terrified me; but I resolved that I would sell my life dearly, and not shrink from the conflict until my own life, or that of my adversary, was extinguished.

Elizabeth observed my agitation for some time in timid and fearful silence; but there was something in my glance which communicated terror to her, and trembling she asked, "What is it that agitates you, my dear Victor? What is it you fear?"

"Oh! peace, peace, my love," replied I; "this night and all will be safe: but this night is dreadful, very dreadful."

I passed an hour in this state of mind, when suddenly I reflected how fearful the combat which I momentarily expected would be to my wife, and I earnestly entreated her to retire, resolving not to join her until I had obtained some knowledge as to the situation of my enemy.

She left me, and I continued some time walking up and down the passages of the house, and inspecting every corner that might afford a retreat to my adversary. But I discovered no trace of him, and was beginning to conjecture that some fortunate chance had intervened to prevent the execution of his menaces, when suddenly I heard a shrill and dreadful scream. It came from the room into which Elizabeth had retired. As I heard it, the whole truth rushed into my mind, my arms dropped, the motion of every muscle and fibre was suspended; I could feel the blood trickling in my veins and tingling in the extremities of my limbs. This state lasted but for an instant; the scream was repeated, and I rushed into the room.

Great God! why did I not then expire! Why am I here to relate the destruction of the best hope and the purest creature of earth? She was there, lifeless and inanimate, thrown across the bed, her head hanging down, and her pale and distorted features half covered by her hair. Everywhere I turn I see the same figure—her bloodless arms and relaxed form flung by the murderer on its bridal bier. Could I behold this and live? Alas! life is obstinate and clings closest where it is most hated. For a moment only did I lose recollection; I fell senseless on the ground.

When I recovered, I found myself surrounded by the people of the inn; their countenances expressed a breathless terror: but the horror of others appeared only as a mockery, a shadow of the feelings that oppressed me. I escaped from them to the room where lay the body of Elizabeth, my love, my wife, so lately living, so dear, so worthy. She had been moved from the posture in which I had first beheld her; and now, as she lay, her head upon her arm, and a handkerchief thrown across her face and neck, I might have supposed her asleep. I rushed towards her, and embraced her with ardor; but the deadly languor and coldness of the limbs told me that what I now held in my arms had ceased to be the Elizabeth whom I had loved and cherished. The murderous mark of the fiend's grasp was on her neck, and the breath had ceased to issue from her lips.

While I still hung over her in the agony of despair, I happened to look up. The windows of the room had before been darkened, and I felt a kind of panic on seeing the pale yellow light of the moon illuminate the chamber. The shutters had been thrown back; and, with a sensation of horror not to be described, I saw at the open window a figure the most hideous and abhorred. A grin was on the face of the monster; he seemed to jeer as with his fiendish finger he pointed towards the corpse of my wife. I rushed towards the window and, drawing a pistol from my bosom, fired; but he eluded me, leaped from his station, and, running with the swiftness of lightning, plunged into the lake.

The report of the pistol brought a crowd into the room. I pointed to the spot where he had disappeared, and we followed the track with boats; nets were cast, but in vain. After passing several hours, we returned hopeless, most of my companions believing it to have been a form conjured up by my fancy. After having landed, they proceeded to search the country, parties going in different directions among the woods and vines.

I attempted to accompany them, and proceeded a short distance from the house; but my head whirled round, my steps were like those of a drunken man, I fell at last in a state of utter exhaustion; a film covered my eyes, and my skin was parched with the heat of fever. In this state I was carried back and placed on a bed, hardly conscious of what had happened; my eyes wandered round the room as if to seek something that I had lost.

After an interval I arose and, as if by instinct, crawled into the room where the corpse of my beloved lay. There were women weeping around—I hung over it, and joined my sad tears to theirs—all this time no distinct idea presented itself to my mind; but my thoughts rambled to various subjects, reflecting confusedly on my misfortunes and their cause. I was bewildered in a cloud of wonder and horror. The death of William, the execution of Justine, the murder of Clerval, and lastly of my wife; even at that moment I knew not that my only remaining friends were safe from the malignity of the fiend; my father even now might be writhing under his grasp, and Ernest might be dead at his feet. This idea made me shudder and recalled me to action. I started up and resolved to return to Geneva with all possible speed.

There were no horses to be procured, and I must return by the lake; but the wind was unfavorable and the rain fell in torrents. However, it was hardly morning, and I might reasonably hope to arrive by night. I hired men to row, and took an oar myself; for I had always experienced relief from mental torment in bodily exercise. But the overflowing misery I now felt, and the excess of agitation that I endured, rendered me incapable of any exertion. I threw down the oar, and leaning my head upon my hands gave way to every gloomy idea that arose. If I looked up, I saw the scenes which were familiar to me in my happier time, and which I had contemplated but the day before in the company of her who was now but a shadow and a recollection. Tears streamed from my eyes. The rain had ceased for a moment, and I saw the fish play in the waters as they had done a few hours before; they had then been observed by Elizabeth. Nothing is so painful to the human mind as a great and sudden change. The sun might shine or the clouds might lower: but nothing could appear to me as it had done the day before. A fiend had snatched from me every hope of future happiness: no creature had ever been so miserable as I was; so frightful an event is single in the history of man.

But why should I dwell upon the incidents that followed this last overwhelming event? Mine has been a tale of horrors; I have reached their *acme*, and what I must now relate can but be tedious to you. Know that, one by one, my friends were snatched away; I was left desolate. My own strength is exhausted; and I must tell, in a few words, what remains of my hideous narration.

I arrived at Geneva. My father and Ernest yet lived; but the former sunk under the tidings that I bore. I see him now, excellent and venerable old man! his eyes wandered in vacancy, for they had lost their charm and their delight—his Elizabeth, his more than daughter, whom he doted on with all that affection which a man feels, who in the decline of life, having few affections, clings more earnestly to those that remain. Cursed, cursed be the fiend that brought misery on his grey hairs, and doomed him to waste in wretchedness! He could not live under the horrors that were accumulated around him; the springs of existence suddenly gave way: he was unable to rise from his bed, and in a few days he died in my arms.

What then became of me? I know not; I lost sensation, and chains and darkness were the only objects that pressed upon me. Sometimes, indeed, I dreamt that I wandered in flowery meadows and pleasant vales with the friends of my youth; but I awoke, and found myself in a dungeon. Melancholy followed, but by degrees I gained a clear conception of my miseries and situation, and was then released from my prison. For they had called me mad; and during many months, as I understood, a solitary cell had been my habitation.

Liberty, however, had been an useless gift to me had I not, as I awakened to reason, at the same time awakened to revenge. As the memory of past misfortunes pressed upon me, I began to reflect on their cause—the monster whom I had created, the miserable dæmon whom I had sent abroad into the world for my destruction. I was possessed by a maddening rage when I thought of him, and desired and ardently prayed that I might have him within my grasp to wreak a great and signal revenge on his cursed head.

Nor did my hate long confine itself to useless wishes; I began to reflect on the best means of securing him; and for this purpose, about a month after my release, I repaired to a criminal judge in the town, and told him that I had an accusation to make; that I knew the destroyer of my family; and that I required him to exert his whole authority for the apprehension of the murderer.

The magistrate listened to me with attention and kindness:—"Be assured, sir," said he, "no pains or exertions on my part shall be spared to discover the villain."

"I thank you," replied I; "listen, therefore, to the deposition that I have to make. It is indeed a tale so strange that I should fear you would not credit it were there not something in truth which, however wonderful, forces conviction. The story is too connected to be mistaken for a dream, and I have no motive for falsehood." My manner, as I thus addressed him, was impressive but calm; I had formed in my own heart a resolution to pursue my destroyer to death; and this purpose quieted my agony, and for an interval reconciled me to life. I now related my history, briefly, but with firmness and precision, marking the dates with accuracy, and never deviating into invective or exclamation.

The magistrate appeared at first perfectly incredulous, but as I continued he became more attentive and interested; I saw him sometimes shudder with horror, at others a lively surprise, unmingled with disbelief, was painted on his countenance.

When I had concluded my narration, I said, "This is the being whom I accuse, and for whose seizure and punishment I call upon you to exert your whole power. It is your duty as a magistrate, and I believe and hope that your feelings as a man will not revolt from the execution of those functions on this occasion."

This address caused a considerable change in the physiognomy of my own auditor. He had heard my story with that half kind of belief that is given to a tale of spirits and supernatural events; but when he was called upon to act officially in consequence, the whole tide of his incredulity returned. He, however, answered mildly, "I would willingly afford you every aid in your pursuit; but the creature of whom you speak appears to have powers which would put all my exertions to defiance. Who can follow an animal which can traverse the sea of ice, and inhabit caves and dens where no man would venture to intrude? Besides, some months have elapsed since the commission of his crimes, and no one can conjecture to what place he has wandered, or what region he may now inhabit."

"I do not doubt that he hovers near the spot which I inhabit; and if he had indeed taken refuge in the Alps, he may be hunted like the chamois, and destroyed as a beast of prey. But I perceive your thoughts: you do not credit my narrative, and do not intend to pursue my enemy with the punishment which is his desert."

As I spoke, rage sparkled in my eyes; the magistrate was intimidated:— "You are mistaken," said he, "I will exert myself; and if it is in my power to seize the monster, be assured that he shall suffer punishment proportionate to his crimes. But I fear, from what you have yourself described to be his properties, that this will prove impracticable; and thus, while every proper measure is pursued, you should make up your mind to disappointment."

"That cannot be; but all that I can say will be of little avail. My revenge is of no moment to you; yet, while I allow it to be a vice, I confess that it is the devouring and only passion of my soul. My rage is unspeakable when I reflect that the murderer, whom I have turned loose upon society, still exists. You refuse my just demand: I have but one resource; and I devote myself, either in my life or death, to his destruction."

I trembled with excess of agitation as I said this; there was a frenzy in my manner and something, I doubt not, of that haughty fierceness which the martyrs of old are said to have possessed. But to a Genevan magistrate, whose mind was occupied by far other ideas than those of devotion and heroism, this elevation of mind had much the appearance of madness. He endeavored to soothe me as a nurse does a child, and reverted to my tale as the effects of delirium.

"Man," I cried, "how ignorant art thou in thy pride of wisdom! Cease; you know not what it is you say."

I broke from the house angry and disturbed, and retired to meditate on some other mode of action.

XXIV

My present situation was one in which all voluntary thought was swallowed up and lost. I was hurried away by fury; revenge alone endowed me with strength and composure; it molded my feelings, and allowed me to be calculating and calm, at periods when otherwise delirium or death would have been my portion.

My first resolution was to quit Geneva for ever; my country, which, when I was happy and beloved, was dear to me, now, in my adversity, became hateful. I provided myself with a sum of money, together with a few jewels which had belonged to my mother, and departed.

And now my wanderings began, which are to cease but with life. I have traversed a vast portion of the earth, and have endured all the hardships which travelers, in deserts and barbarous countries, are wont to meet. How I have lived I hardly know; many times have I stretched my failing limbs upon the sandy plain and prayed for death. But revenge kept me alive; I dared not die and leave my adversary in being.

When I quitted Geneva my first labor was to gain some clue by which I might trace the steps of my fiendish enemy. But my plan was unsettled; and I wandered many hours round the confines of the town, uncertain what path I should pursue. As night approached, I found myself at the entrance of the cemetery where William, Elizabeth, and my father reposed. I entered it and approached the tomb which marked their graves. Everything was silent, except the leaves of the trees, which were gently agitated by the wind; the night was nearly dark; and the scene would have been solemn and affecting even to an uninterested observer. The spirits of the departed seemed to flit around and to cast a shadow, which was felt but not seen, around the head of the mourner.

The deep grief which this scene had at first excited quickly gave way to rage and despair. They were dead, and I lived; their murderer also lived, and to destroy him I must drag out my weary existence. I knelt on the grass and kissed the earth, and with quivering lips exclaimed, "By the sacred earth on which I kneel, by the shades that wander near me, by the deep and eternal grief that I feel, I swear; and by thee, O Night, and the spirits that preside over thee, to pursue the dæmon who caused this misery until he or I shall perish in mortal conflict. For this purpose I will preserve my life: to execute this dear revenge will I again behold the sun and tread the green herbage of earth, which otherwise should vanish from my eyes for ever. And I call on you, spirits of the dead; and on you, wandering ministers of vengeance, to aid and conduct me in my work. Let the cursed and hellish monster drink deep of agony; let him feel the despair that now torments me."

I had begun my abjuration with solemnity and an awe which almost assured me that the shades of my murdered friends heard and approved my devotion; but the furies possessed me as I concluded, and rage choked my utterance.

I was answered through the stillness of night by a loud and fiendish laugh. It rung on my ears long and heavily; the mountains re-echoed it, and I felt as if all hell surrounded me with mockery and laughter. Surely in that moment I should have been possessed by frenzy, and have destroyed my miserable existence, but that my vow was heard and that I was reserved for vengeance. The laughter died away; when a well-known and abhorred voice, apparently close to my ear, addressed me in an audible whisper—"I am satisfied: miserable wretch! you have determined to live, and I am satisfied."

I darted towards the spot from which the sound proceeded; but the devil eluded my grasp. Suddenly the broad disk of the moon arose and shone full upon his ghastly and distorted shape as he fled with more than mortal speed.

I pursued him; and for many months this has been my task. Guided by a slight clue I followed the windings of the Rhone, but vainly. The blue Mediterranean appeared; and, by a strange chance, I saw the fiend enter by night and hide himself in a vessel bound for the Black Sea. I took my passage in the same ship; but he escaped, I know not how.

Amidst the wilds of Tartary and Russia, although he still evaded me, I have ever followed in his track. Sometimes the peasants, scared by this horrid apparition, informed me of his path; sometimes he himself, who feared that if I lost all trace of him I should despair and die, left some mark to guide me. The snows descended on my head, and I saw the print of his huge step on the white plain. To you first entering on life, to whom care is new and agony unknown, how can you understand what I have felt and still feel? Cold, want, and fatigue were the least pains which I was destined to endure; I was cursed by some devil, and carried about with me my eternal hell; yet still a spirit of good followed and directed my steps; and, when I most murmured, would suddenly extricate me from seemingly insurmountable difficulties. Sometimes, when nature, overcome by hunger, sunk under the exhaustion, a repast was prepared for me in the desert that restored and inspirited me. The fare was, indeed, coarse, such as the peasants of the country ate; but I will not doubt that it was set there by the spirits that I had invoked to aid me. Often, when all was dry, the heavens cloudless, and I was parched by thirst, a slight cloud would bedim the sky, shed the few drops that revived me, and vanish.

I followed, when I could, the courses of the rivers; but the dæmon generally avoided these, as it was here that the population of the country chiefly collected. In other places human beings were seldom seen; and I generally subsisted on the wild animals that crossed my path. I had money with me, and gained the friendship of the villagers by distributing it; or I brought with me some food that I had killed, which, after taking a small part, I always presented to those who had provided me with fire and utensils for cooking.

My life, as it passed thus, was indeed hateful to me, and it was during sleep alone that I could taste joy. O blessed sleep! often, when most miserable, I sank to repose, and my dreams lulled me even to rapture. The spirits that guarded me had provided these moments, or rather hours, of happiness, that I might retain strength to fulfill my pilgrimage. Deprived of this respite, I should have sunk under my hardships. During the day I was sustained and inspirited by the hope of night: for in sleep I saw my friends, my wife, and my beloved country; again I saw the benevolent countenance of my father, heard the silver tones of my Elizabeth's voice, and beheld Clerval enjoying health and youth. Often, when wearied by a toilsome march, I persuaded myself that I was dreaming until night should come, and that I should then enjoy reality in the arms of my dearest friends. What agonizing fondness did I feel for them! how did I cling to their dear forms, as sometimes they haunted even my waking hours, and persuade myself that they still lived! At such moments vengeance, that burned within me, died in my heart, and I pursued my path towards the destruction of the dæmon more as a task enjoined by heaven, as the mechanical impulse of some power of which I was unconscious, than as the ardent desire of my soul.

What his feelings were whom I pursued I cannot know. Sometimes, indeed, he left marks in writing on the barks of the trees, or cut in stone, that guided me and instigated my fury. "My reign is not yet over" (these words were legible in one of these inscriptions); "you live, and my power is complete. Follow me; I seek the everlasting ices of the north, where you will feel the misery of cold and frost to which I am impassive. You will find near this place, if you follow not too tardily, a dead hare; eat and be refreshed. Come on, my enemy; we have yet to wrestle for our lives; but many hard and miserable hours must you endure until that period shall arrive."

Scoffing devil! Again do I vow vengeance; again do I devote thee, miserable fiend, to torture and death. Never will I give up my search until he or I perish; and then with what ecstasy shall I join my Elizabeth and my departed friends, who even now prepare for me the reward of my tedious toil and horrible pilgrimage!

As I still pursued my journey to the northward, the snows thickened and the cold increased in a degree almost too severe to support. The peasants were shut up in their hovels, and only a few of the most hardy ventured forth to seize the animals whom starvation had forced from their hiding-places to seek for prey. The rivers were covered with ice and no fish could be procured; and thus I was cut off from my chief article of maintenance.

The triumph of my enemy increased with the difficulty of my labors. One inscription that he left was in these words:—"Prepare! your toils only begin: wrap yourself in furs and provide food; for we shall soon enter upon a journey where your sufferings will satisfy my everlasting hatred."

My courage and perseverance were invigorated by these scoffing words; I resolved not to fail in my purpose; and, calling on Heaven to support me, I continued with unabated fervor to traverse immense deserts until the ocean appeared at a distance and formed the utmost boundary of the horizon. Oh! how unlike it was to the blue seas of the south! Covered with ice, it was only to be distinguished from land by its superior wildness and ruggedness. The Greeks wept for joy when they beheld the Mediterranean from the hills of Asia, and hailed with rapture the boundary of their toils. I did not weep; but I knelt down and, with a full heart, thanked my guiding spirit for conducting me in safety to the place where I hoped, notwithstanding my adversary's gibe, to meet and grapple with him.

Some weeks before this period I had procured a sledge and dogs, and thus traversed the snows with inconceivable speed. I know not whether the fiend possessed the same advantages; but I found that, as before I had daily lost ground in the pursuit, I now gained on him: so much so that, when I first saw the ocean, he was but one day's journey in advance, and I hoped to intercept him before he should reach the beach. With new courage, therefore, I pressed on, and in two days arrived at a wretched hamlet on the sea-shore. I inquired of the inhabitants concerning the fiend, and gained accurate information. A gigantic monster, they said, had arrived the night before, armed with a gun and many pistols, putting to flight the inhabitants of a solitary cottage through fear of his terrific appearance. He had carried off their store of winter food, and placing it in a sledge, to draw which he had seized on a numerous drove of trained dogs, he had harnessed them, and the same night, to the joy of the horror-struck villagers, had pursued his journey across the sea in a direction that led to no land; and they conjectured that he must speedily be destroyed by the breaking of the ice or frozen by the eternal frosts.

On hearing this information, I suffered a temporary access of despair. He had escaped me; and I must commence a destructive and almost end-less journey across the mountainous ices of the ocean—amidst cold that few of the inhabitants could long endure, and which I, the native of a genial and sunny climate, could not hope to survive. Yet at the idea that the fiend should live and be triumphant, my rage and vengeance returned, and, like a mighty tide, overwhelmed every other feeling. After a slight repose, during which the spirits of the dead hovered round and instigated me to toil and revenge, I prepared for my journey.

I exchanged my land-sledge for one fashioned for the inequalities of the Frozen Ocean; and purchasing a plentiful stock of provisions, I departed from land.

I cannot guess how many days have passed since then; but I have endured misery which nothing but the eternal sentiment of a just retribu-tion burning within my heart could have enabled me to support. Immense and rugged mountains of ice often barred up my passage, and I often heard the thunder of the ground sea which threatened my destruction. But again the frost came and made the paths of the sea secure.

By the quantity of provision which I had consumed, I should guess that I had passed three weeks in this journey; and the continual protraction of hope, returning back upon the heart, often wrung bitter drops of despondency and grief from my eyes. Despair had indeed almost secured her prey, and I should soon have sunk beneath this misery. Once, after the poor animals that conveyed me had with incredible toil gained the summit of a sloping ice-mountain, and one, sinking under his fatigue, died, I viewed the expanse before me with anguish, when suddenly my eye caught a dark speck upon the dusky plain. I strained my sight to discover what it could be, and uttered a wild cry of ecstasy when I distinguished a sledge and the distorted proportions of a well-known form within. Oh! with what a burning gush did hope revisit my heart! warm tears filled my eyes, which I hastily wiped away that they might not intercept the view I had of the dæmon; but still my sight was dimmed by the burning drops until, giving way to the emotions that oppressed me, I wept aloud.

But this was not the time for delay: I disencumbered the dogs of their dead companion, gave them a plentiful portion of food; and, after an hour's rest, which was absolutely necessary, and yet which was bitterly irksome to me, I continued my route. The sledge was still visible; nor did I again lose sight of it except at the moments when for a short time some icerock concealed it with its intervening crags. I indeed perceptibly gained on it; and when, after nearly two days' journey, I beheld my enemy at no more than a mile distant, my heart bounded within me.

But now, when I appeared almost within grasp of my foe, my hopes were suddenly extinguished, and I lost all trace of him more utterly than I had ever done before. A ground sea was heard; the thunder of its progress, as the waters rolled and swelled beneath me, became every moment more ominous and terrific. I pressed on, but in vain. The wind arose; the sea roared; and, as with the mighty shock of an earthquake, it split and cracked with a tremendous and overwhelming sound. The work was soon finished: in a few minutes a tumultuous sea rolled between me and my enemy, and I was left drifting on a scattered piece of ice, that was continually lessening, and thus preparing for me a hideous death.

In this manner many appalling hours passed; several of my dogs died; and I myself was about to sink under the accumulation of distress when I saw your vessel riding at anchor, and holding forth to me hopes of succour and life. I had no conception that vessels ever came so far north, and was astounded at the sight. I quickly destroyed part of my sledge to construct oars; and by these means was enabled, with infinite fatigue, to move my ice-raft in the direction of your ship. I had determined, if you were going southward, still to trust myself to the mercy of the seas rather than abandon my purpose. I hoped to induce you to grant me a boat with which I could pursue my enemy. But your direction was northward. You took me on board when my vigor was exhausted, and I should soon have sunk under my multiplied hardships into a death which I still dread—for my task is unfulfilled.

Oh! when will my guiding spirit, in conducting me to the daemon, allow me the rest I so much desire; or must I die and he yet live? If I do, swear to me, Walton, that he shall not escape; that you will seek him and satisfy my vengeance in his death. And do I dare to ask of you to undertake my pilgrimage, to endure the hardships that I have undergone? No; I am not so selfish. Yet, when I am dead, if he should appear; if the ministers of vengeance should conduct him to you, swear that he shall not live—swear that he shall not triumph over my accumulated woes, and survive to add to the list of his dark crimes. He is eloquent and persuasive; and once his words had even power over my heart: but trust him not. His soul is as hellish as his form, full of treachery and fiendlike malice. Hear him not; call on the names of William, Justine, Clerval, Elizabeth, my father and of the wretched Victor, and thrust your sword into his heart. I will hover near and direct the steel aright.

WALTON, *in continuation*

August 26th, 17—

You have read this strange and terrific story, Margaret; and do you not feel your blood congeal with horror like that which even now curdles mine? Sometimes, seized with sudden agony, he could not continue his tale; at others, his voice broken, yet piercing, uttered with difficulty the words so replete with anguish. His fine and lovely eyes were now lighted up with indignation, now subdued to downcast sorrow, and quenched in infinite wretchedness. Sometimes he commanded his countenance and tones, and related the most horrible incidents with a tranquil voice, suppressing every mark of agitation; then, like a volcano bursting forth, his face would suddenly change to an expression of the wildest rage, as he shrieked out imprecations on his persecutor.

His tale is connected, and told with an appearance of the simplest truth; yet I own to you that the letters of Felix and Safie, which he showed me, and the apparition of the monster seen from our ship, brought to me a greater conviction of the truth of his narrative than his asseverations, however earnest and connected. Such a monster has then really existence! I cannot doubt it; yet I am lost in surprise and admiration. Sometimes I endeavored to gain from Frankenstein the particulars of his creature's formation: but on this point he was impenetrable.

"Are you mad, my friend?" said he; "or whither does your senseless curiosity lead you? Would you also create for yourself and the world a demoniacal enemy? Peace, peace! learn my miseries, and do not seek to increase your own."

Frankenstein discovered that I made notes concerning his history: he asked to see them, and then himself corrected and augmented them in many places; but principally in giving the life and spirit to the conversations he held with his enemy. "Since you have preserved my narration," said he, "I would not that a mutilated one should go down to posterity."

Thus has a week passed away, while I have listened to the strangest tale that ever imagination formed. My thoughts, and every feeling of my soul, have been drunk up by the interest for my guest, which this tale, and his own elevated and gentle manners, have created. I wish to soothe him; yet can I counsel one so infinitely miserable, so destitute of every hope of consolation, to live? Oh, no! the only joy that he can now know will be when he composes his shattered spirit to peace and death. Yet he enjoys one comfort, the offspring of solitude and delirium: he believes that, when in dreams he holds converse with his friends and derives from that communion consolation for his miseries or excitements to his vengeance, they are not the creations of his fancy, but the beings themselves who visit him from the regions of a remote world. This faith gives a solemnity to his reveries that render them to me almost as imposing and interesting as truth.

Our conversations are not always confined to his own history and misfortunes. On every point of general literature he displays unbounded

knowledge and a quick and piercing apprehension. His eloquence is forc-
ible and touching; nor can I hear him, when he relates a pathetic incident,
or endeavors to move the passions of pity or love, without tears. What a
glorious creature must he have been in the days of his prosperity when
he is thus noble and godlike in ruin! He seems to feel his own worth and
the greatness of his fall.

"When younger," said he, "I believed myself destined for some great
enterprise. My feelings are profound; but I possessed a coolness of
judgement that fitted me for illustrious achievements. This sentiment
of the worth of my nature supported me when others would have been
oppressed; for I deemed it criminal to throw away in useless grief those
talents that might be useful to my fellow-creatures. When I reflected on
the work I had completed, no less a one than the creation of a sensitive
and rational animal, I could not rank myself with the herd of common
projectors. But this thought, which supported me in the commencement
of my career, now serves only to plunge me lower in the dust. All my
speculations and hopes are as nothing; and, like the archangel who
aspired to omnipotence, I am chained in an eternal hell. My imagination was vivid, yet my powers of analysis and application were intense;
by the union of these qualities I conceived the idea and executed the
creation of a man. Even now I cannot recollect without passion my
reveries while the work was incomplete. I trod heaven in my thoughts,
now exulting in my powers, now burning with the idea of their effects.
From my infancy I was imbued with high hopes and a lofty ambition;
but how am I sunk! Oh! my friend, if you had known me as I once was
you would not recognize me in this state of degradation. Despondency
rarely visited my heart; a high destiny seemed to bear me on until I fell,
never, never again to rise."

Must I then lose this admirable being? I have longed for a friend; I
have sought one who would sympathize with and love me. Behold, on
these desert seas I have found such a one; but I fear I have gained him
only to know his value and lose him. I would reconcile him to life, but he
repulses the idea.

"I thank you, Walton," he said, "for your kind intentions towards so
miserable a wretch; but when you speak of new ties and fresh affections,

think you that any can replace those who are gone? Can any man be to me as Clerval was; or any woman another Elizabeth? Even where the affections are not strongly moved by any superior excellence, the companions of our childhood always possess a certain power over our minds which hardly any later friend can obtain. They know our infantine dispositions, which, however they may be afterwards modified, are never eradicated; and they can judge of our actions with more certain conclusions as to the integrity of our motives. A sister or a brother can never, unless indeed such symptoms have been shown early, suspect the other of fraud or false dealing, when another friend, however strongly he may be attached, may, in spite of himself, be contemplated with suspicion. But I enjoyed friends, dear not only through habit and association, but from their own merits; and wherever I am the soothing voice of my Elizabeth and the conversation of Clerval will be ever whispered in my ear. They are dead, and but one feeling in such a solitude can persuade me to preserve my life. If I were engaged in any high undertaking or design, fraught with extensive utility to my fellow-creatures, then could I live to fulfill it. But such is not my destiny; I must pursue and destroy the being to whom I gave existence; then my lot on earth will be fulfilled, and I may die."

September 2nd.

My beloved Sister,—I write to you encompassed by peril and ignorant whether I am ever doomed to see again dear England, and the dearer friends that inhabit it. I am surrounded by mountains of ice which admit of no escape and threaten every moment to crush my vessel. The brave fellows whom I have persuaded to be my companions look towards me for aid; but I have none to bestow. There is something terribly appalling in our situation, yet my courage and hopes do not desert me. Yet it is terrible to reflect that the lives of all these men are endangered through me. If we are lost, my mad schemes are the cause.

And what, Margaret, will be the state of your mind? You will not hear of my destruction, and you will anxiously await my return. Years will pass, and you will have visitings of despair, and yet be tortured by hope. Oh! my beloved sister, the sickening failing of your heart-felt expectations is, in prospect, more terrible to me than my own death. But you have a husband and lovely children; you may be happy: Heaven bless you and make you so!

My unfortunate guest regards me with the tenderest compassion. He endeavors to fill me with hope; and talks as if life were a possession which he valued. He reminds me how often the same accidents have happened to other navigators who have attempted this sea, and, in spite of myself, he fills me with cheerful auguries. Even the sailors feel the power of his eloquence: when he speaks they no longer despair; he rouses their energies and, while they hear his voice, they believe these vast mountains of ice are mole-hills which will vanish before the resolutions of man. These feelings are transitory; each day of expectation delayed fills them with fear, and I almost dread a mutiny caused by this despair.

September 5th.

A scene has just passed of such uncommon interest that although it is highly probable that these papers may never reach you, yet I cannot forbear recording it.

We are still surrounded by mountains of ice, still in imminent danger of being crushed in their conflict. The cold is excessive, and many of my unfortunate comrades have already found a grave amidst this scene of desolation. Frankenstein has daily declined in health: a feverish fire still glimmers in his eyes; but he is exhausted, and when suddenly roused to any exertion he speedily sinks again into apparent lifelessness.

I mentioned in my last letter the fears I entertained of a mutiny. This morning, as I sat watching the wan countenance of my friend—his eyes half closed, and his limbs hanging listlessly—I was roused by half a dozen of the sailors who demanded admission into the cabin. They entered, and their leader addressed me. He told me that he and his companions had been chosen by the other sailors to come in deputation to me, to make me a requisition which, in justice, I could not refuse. We were immured in ice and should probably never escape; but they feared that if, as was possible, the ice should dissipate, and a free passage be opened, I should be rash enough to continue my voyage and lead them into fresh dangers after they might happily have surmounted this. They insisted, therefore, that I should engage with a solemn promise that if the vessel should be freed I would instantly direct my course southward.

This speech troubled me. I had not despaired; nor had I yet conceived the idea of returning if set free. Yet could I, in justice, or even in possibility, refuse this demand? I hesitated before I answered; when Frankenstein, who had at first been silent, and, indeed, appeared hardly to have force enough to attend, now roused himself; his eyes sparkled, and his cheeks flushed with momentary vigor. Turning towards the men he said—

"What do you mean? What do you demand of your captain? Are you then so easily turned from your design? Did you not call this a glorious expedition? And wherefore was it glorious? Not because the way was smooth and placid as a southern sea, but because it was full of dangers and terror; because at every new incident your fortitude was to be called forth and your courage exhibited; because danger and death surrounded it, and these you were to brave and overcome. For this was it a glorious, for this was it an honorable undertaking. You were hereafter to be hailed as the benefactors of your species; your names adored as belonging to brave men who encountered death for honor and the benefit of mankind. And now, behold, with the first imagination of danger, or, if you will, the first mighty and terrific trial of your courage, you shrink away, and are content to be handed down as men who had not strength enough to endure cold and peril; and so, poor souls, they were chilly and returned to their warm firesides. Why that requires not this preparation; ye need not have come thus far, and dragged your captain to the shame of a defeat, merely to prove yourselves cowards. Oh! be men, or be more than men. Be steady to your purposes and firm as a rock. This ice is not made of such stuff as your hearts may be; it is mutable and cannot withstand you if you say that it shall not. Do not return to your families with the stigma of disgrace marked on your brows. Return as heroes who have fought and conquered, and who know not what it is to turn their backs on the foe."

He spoke this with a voice so modulated to the different feelings expressed in his speech, with an eye so full of lofty design and heroism, that can you wonder that these men were moved? They looked at one another and were unable to reply. I spoke; I told them to retire and consider of what had been said: that I would not lead them farther north if they strenuously desired the contrary; but that I hoped that, with reflection, their courage would return.

They retired, and I turned towards my friend; but he was sunk in languor and almost deprived of life.

How all this will terminate I know not; but I had rather die than return shamefully—my purpose unfulfilled. Yet I fear such will be my fate; the men, unsupported by ideas of glory and honor, can never willingly continue to endure their present hardships.

September 7th.

The die is cast; I have consented to return if we are not destroyed. Thus are my hopes blasted by cowardice and indecision; I come back ignorant and disappointed. It requires more philosophy than I possess to bear this injustice with patience.

September 12th.

It is past; I am returning to England. I have lost my hopes of utility and glory;—I have lost my friend. But I will endeavor to detail these bitter circumstances to you, my dear sister; and while I am wafted towards England, and towards you, I will not despond.

September 9th, the ice began to move, and roarings like thunder were heard at a distance as the islands split and cracked in every direction. We were in the most imminent peril; but, as we could only remain passive, my chief attention was occupied by my unfortunate guest, whose illness increased in such a degree that he was entirely confined to his bed. The ice cracked behind us, and was driven with force towards the north; a breeze sprung from the west, and on the 11th the passage towards the south became perfectly free. When the sailors saw this, and that their return to their native country was apparently assured, a shout of tumultuous joy broke from them, loud and long-continued. Frankenstein, who was dozing, awoke and asked the cause of the tumult. "They shout," I said, "because they will soon return to England."

"Do you then really return?"

"Alas! yes; I cannot withstand their demands. I cannot lead them unwillingly to danger, and I must return."

"Do so, if you will; but I will not. You may give up your purpose, but mine is assigned to me by Heaven, and I dare not. I am weak; but surely the spirits who assist my vengeance will endow me with sufficient strength." Saying this, he endeavored to spring from the bed, but the exertion was too great for him; he fell back and fainted.

It was long before he was restored; and I often thought that life was entirely extinct. At length he opened his eyes; he breathed with difficulty, and was unable to speak. The surgeon gave him a composing draught and ordered us to leave him undisturbed. In the meantime he told me that my friend had certainly not many hours to live.

His sentence was pronounced, and I could only grieve and be patient. I sat by his bed watching him; his eyes were closed, and I thought he slept; but presently he called to me in a feeble voice, and, bidding me come near, said—"Alas! the strength I relied on is gone; I feel that I shall soon die, and he, my enemy and persecutor, may still be in being. Think not, Walton, that in the last moments of my existence I feel that burning hatred and ardent desire of revenge I once expressed; but I feel myself justified in desiring the death of my adversary. During these last days I have been occupied in examining my past conduct; nor do I find it blamable. In a fit of enthusiastic madness I created a rational creature, and was bound towards him, to assure, as far as was in my power, his happiness and wellbeing. This was my duty; but there was another still paramount to that. My duties towards the beings of my own species had greater claims to my attention, because they included a greater proportion of happiness or misery. Urged by this view, I refused, and I did right in refusing, to create a companion for the first creature. He showed unparalleled malignity and selfishness, in evil: he destroyed my friends; he devoted to destruction beings who possessed exquisite sensations, happiness, and wisdom; nor do I know where this thirst for vengeance may end. Miserable himself, that he may render no other wretched he ought to die. The task of his destruction was mine, but I have failed. When actuated by selfish and vicious motives I asked you to undertake my unfinished work; and I renew this request now when I am only induced by reason and virtue.

"Yet I cannot ask you to renounce your country and friends to fulfill this task; and now that you are returning to England you will have little chance of meeting with him. But the consideration of these points, and the well balancing of what you may esteem your duties, I leave to you;

my judgement and ideas are already disturbed by the near approach of death. I dare not ask you to do what I think right, for I may still be misled by passion.

"That he should live to be an instrument of mischief disturbs me; in other respects, this hour, when I momentarily expect my release, is the only happy one which I have enjoyed for several years. The forms of the beloved dead flit before me and I hasten to their arms. Farewell, Walton! Seek happiness in tranquility and avoid ambition, even if it be only the apparently innocent one of distinguishing yourself in science and discoveries. Yet why do I say this? I have myself been blasted in these hopes, yet another may succeed."

His voice became fainter as he spoke; and at length, exhausted by his effort, he sunk into silence. About half an hour afterwards he attempted again to speak, but was unable; he pressed my hand feebly, and his eyes closed for ever, while the irradiation of a gentle smile passed away from his lips.

Margaret, what comment can I make on the untimely extinction of this glorious spirit? What can I say that will enable you to understand the depth of my sorrow? All that I should express would be inadequate and feeble. My tears flow; my mind is overshadowed by a cloud of disappointment. But I journey towards England, and I may there find consolation.

I am interrupted. What do these sounds portend? It is midnight; the breeze blows fairly, and the watch on deck scarcely stir. Again; there is a sound as of a human voice, but hoarser; it comes from the cabin where the remains of Frankenstein still lie. I must arise and examine. Good night, my sister.

Great God! what a scene has just taken place! I am yet dizzy with the remembrance of it. I hardly know whether I shall have the power to detail it; yet the tale which I have recorded would be incomplete without this final and wonderful catastrophe.

I entered the cabin where lay the remains of my ill-fated and admirable friend. Over him hung a form which I cannot find words to describe; gigantic in stature, yet uncouth and distorted in its proportions. As he hung over the coffin his face was concealed by long locks of ragged hair; but one vast hand was extended, in color and apparent texture like that of a mummy. When he heard the sound of my approach he ceased to utter exclamations of grief and horror and sprung towards the window. Never did I behold a vision so horrible as his face, of such loathsome yet appalling hideousness. I shut my eyes involuntarily and endeavored to recollect what were my duties with regard to this destroyer. I called on him to stay.

He paused, looking on me with wonder; and, again turning towards the lifeless form of his creator, he seemed to forget my presence, and every feature and gesture seemed instigated by the wildest rage of some uncontrollable passion.

"That is also my victim!" he exclaimed: "in his murder my crimes are consummated; the miserable series of my being is wound to its close! Oh, Frankenstein! generous and self-devoted being! what does it avail that I now ask thee to pardon me? I, who irretrievably destroyed thee by destroying all thou lovedst. Alas! he is cold, he cannot answer me."

His voice seemed suffocated; and my first impulses, which had suggested to me the duty of obeying the dying request of my friend, in destroying his enemy, were now suspended by a mixture of curiosity and compassion. I approached this tremendous being; I dared not again raise my eyes to his face, there was something so scaring and unearthly in his ugliness. I attempted to speak, but the words died away on my lips. The monster continued to utter wild and incoherent selfreproaches. At length I gathered resolution to address him in a pause of the tempest of his passion: "Your repentance," I said, "is now superfluous. If you had listened to the voice of conscience, and heeded the strings of remorse, before you had urged your diabolical vengeance to this extremity, Frankenstein would yet have lived."

"And do you dream?" said the dæmon; "do you think that I was then dead to agony and remorse?—he," he continued, pointing to the corpse, "he suffered not in the consummation of the deed—oh! not the ten-thousandth portion of the anguish that was mine during the lingering detail of its execution. A frightful selfishness hurried me on, while my heart was poisoned with remorse. Think you that the groans of Clerval were music to my ears? My heart was fashioned to be susceptible of love and sympathy; and when wrenched by misery to vice and hatred it did not endure the violence of the change without torture such as you cannot even imagine.

"After the murder of Clerval I returned to Switzerland heart-broken and overcome. I pitied Frankenstein; my pity amounted to horror: I abhorred myself. But when I discovered that he, the author at once of my existence and of its unspeakable torments, dared to hope for happiness; that while he accumulated wretchedness and despair upon me he sought his own enjoyment in feelings and passions from the indulgence of which I was for ever barred, then impotent envy and bitter indignation filled me with an insatiable thirst for vengeance. I recollected my threat and resolved that it should be accomplished. I knew that I was preparing for myself a deadly torture; but I was the slave, not the master, of an impulse which I detested, yet could not disobey. Yet when she died!—nay, then I was not miserable. I had cast off all feeling, subdued all anguish, to riot in the excess of my despair. Evil thenceforth became my good. Urged thus far, I had no choice but to adapt my nature to an element which I had willingly chosen. The completion of my demoniacal design became an insatiable passion. And now it is ended; there is my last victim!"

I was at first touched by the expressions of his misery; yet, when I called to mind what Frankenstein had said of his powers of eloquence and persuasion, and when I again cast my eyes on the lifeless form of my friend, indignation was rekindled within me. "Wretch!" I said, "it is well that you come here to whine over the desolation that you have made. You throw a torch into a pile of buildings; and when they are consumed you sit among the ruins and lament the fall. Hypocritical fiend! if he whom you mourn still lived, still would he be the object, again would he become the prey, of your accursed vengeance. It is not pity that you feel; you lament only because the victim of your malignity is withdrawn from your power."

"Oh, it is not thus—not thus," interrupted the being; "yet such must be the impression conveyed to you by what appears to be the purport of my actions. Yet I seek not a fellow-feeling in my misery. No sympathy may I ever find. When I first sought it, it was the love of virtue, the feelings of happiness and affection with which my whole being overflowed, that I wished to be participated. But now that virtue has become to me a shadow and that happiness and affection are turned into bitter and loathing despair, in what should I seek for sympathy? I am content to suffer alone while my sufferings shall endure: when I die, I am well satisfied that abhorrence and opprobrium should load my memory. Once my fancy was soothed with dreams of virtue, of fame, and of enjoyment. Once I falsely hoped to meet with beings who, pardoning my outward form, would love me for the excellent qualities which I was capable of unfolding. I was nourished with high thoughts of honor and devotion. But now crime has degraded me beneath the meanest animal. No guilt, no mischief, no malignity, no misery, can be found comparable to mine. When I run over the frightful catalogue of my sins, I cannot believe that I am the same creature whose thoughts were once filled with sublime and transcendent visions of the beauty and the majesty of goodness. But it is even so; the fallen angel becomes a malignant devil. Yet even that enemy of God and man had friends and associates in his desolation; I am alone.

"You, who call Frankenstein your friend, seem to have a knowledge of my crimes and his misfortunes. But in the detail which he gave you of them he could not sum up the hours and months of misery which I endured, wasting in impotent passions. For while I destroyed his hopes, I did not satisfy my own desires. They were for ever ardent and craving; still I desired love and fellowship, and I was still spurned. Was there no injustice in this? Am I to be thought the only criminal when all human kind sinned against me? Why do you not hate Felix who drove his friend from his door with contumely? Why do you not execrate the rustic who sought to destroy the savior of his child? Nay, these are virtuous and immaculate beings ! I, the miserable and the abandoned, am an abortion, to be spurned at, and kicked, and trampled on. Even now my blood boils at the recollection of this injustice.

"But it is true that I am a wretch. I have murdered the lovely and the helpless; I have strangled the innocent as they slept, and grasped to death his throat who never injured me or any other living thing. I have devoted my creator, the select specimen of all that is worthy of love and admiration among men, to misery; I have pursued him even to that irremediable ruin. There he lies, white and cold in death. You hate me; but your abhorrence cannot equal that with which I regard myself. I look on the hands which executed the deed; I think on the heart in which the imagination of it was conceived, and long for the moment when these hands will meet my eyes, when that imagination will haunt my thoughts no more.

"Fear not that I shall be the instrument of future mischief. My work is nearly complete. Neither yours nor any man's death is needed to consummate the series of my being, and accomplish that which must be done; but it requires my own. Do not think that I shall be slow to perform this sacrifice. I shall quit your vessel on the iceraft which brought me thither, and shall seek the most northern extremity of the globe; I shall collect my funeral pile and consume to ashes this miserable frame, that its remains may afford no light to any curious and unhallowed wretch who would create such another as I have been. I shall die. I shall no longer feel the agonies which now consume me, or be the prey of feelings unsatisfied, yet unquenched. He is dead who called me into being; and when I shall be no more the very remembrance of us both will speedily vanish. I shall no longer see the sun or stars, or feel the winds play on my cheeks. Light, feeling, and sense will pass away; and in this condition must I find my happiness. Some years ago, when the images which this world affords first opened upon me, when I felt the cheering warmth of summer, and heard the rustling of the leaves and the warbling of the birds, and these were all to me, I should have wept to die; now it is my only consolation. Polluted by crimes, and torn by the bitterest remorse, where can I find rest but in death?

"Farewell! I leave you, and in you the last of human kind whom these eyes will ever behold. Farewell, Frankenstein! If thou wert yet alive, and yet cherished a desire of revenge against me, it would be better satiated in my life than in my destruction. But it was not so; thou didst seek my extinction that I might not cause greater wretchedness; and if yet, in some mode unknown to me, thou hast not ceased to think and feel, thou wouldst not desire against me a vengeance greater than that which I feel. Blasted as thou wert, my agony was still superior to thine; for the bitter sting of remorse will not cease to rankle in my wounds until death shall close them for ever.

"But soon," he cried, with sad and solemn enthusiasm, "I shall die, and what I now feel be no longer felt. Soon these burning miseries will be extinct. I shall ascend my funeral pile triumphantly, and exult in the agony of the torturing flames. The light of that conflagration will fade away; my ashes will be swept into the sea by the winds. My spirit will sleep in peace; or if it thinks, it will not surely think thus. Farewell."

He sprung from the cabin-window, as he said this, upon the ice-raft which lay close to the vessel. He was soon borne away by the waves and lost in darkness and distance.

RAMSEY CAMPBELL
A New Life

⌒━⌒

Ramsey Campbell was born in Liverpool, where he still lives with his wife, Jenny. His first book, a collection of stories entitled The Inhabitant of the Lake and Less Welcome Tenants, *was published by August Derleth's legendary Arkham House imprint in 1964. He has published numerous novels, collections and anthologies ever since.*

The author recently celebrated fifty years in horror with the publication from PS Publishing of his novel, Think Yourself Lucky, *along with a volume of all the author's correspondence with Derleth, edited by S. T. Joshi. His most current novel is* Thirteen Days by Sunset Beach.

As one of the world's most respected authors of horror fiction, Ramsey Campbell has won multiple World Fantasy Awards, British Fantasy Awards and Bram Stoker Awards, and is a recipient of the World Horror Convention Grand Master Award, the Horror Writers Association Lifetime Achievement Award, the Howie Award of the H. P. Lovecraft Film Festival for Lifetime Achievement and the International Horror Guild's Living Legend Award. He is also President of the Society of Fantastic Films.

About the story that follows, the author explains: "'A New Life' was one of the last of my EC Comics–inspired pieces. It was written in 1976, the year when much of my energy was devoted to writing novels based on classic Universal horror films. These were published under the house name of Carl Dreadstone—my original suggestion had been Carl Thunstone, but Manly Wade Wellman understandably thought people might assume that pseudonym was his—though in England, to add to the confusion, some were credited instead to E. K. Leyton. I was hoping to reissue my Dreadstone books as an omnibus, but alas, this is not to be. I can at least take this opportunity to make it clear that I wrote only The Bride of Frankenstein, The Wolfman *and* Dracula's Daughter. *The other novels are nothing to do with me, and by now even Piers Dudgeon, the editor who commissioned the series, can't recall who wrote one of them, though* The Werewolf of London *and* The Creature from the Black Lagoon *were the work of Walter Harris."*

Already he was blind again. But he was sure that someone had been peering at him. The glimpse was vague as the memory of a dream: the bright quivering outline of a head, which had had darkness for a face. Perhaps it had been a dream which had wakened him.

Darkness lay on his eyes, thick as soil, heavy as sleep. It seemed eager to soothe his mind into drifting. He fought the shapeless flowing of his thoughts. He was near to panic, for he had no idea where he was.

He tried to calm himself. He must analyze his sensations, surely that would help him understand. But he found he could scarcely think. In the darkness, whose depth he had no means of gauging, his mind seemed to dissolve. He felt as though its edges were crumbling, as though nothingness were eating toward its core. He cried out wordlessly.

At least he had a body, then. He hadn't been able to feel it, and had dreaded that—the echo of his cry was hollow, but quickly muffled by walls quite close to him. The cry hadn't sounded at all like his voice.

If it wasn't his voice, then whose—he quashed that thought. His self-control was firmer now that some sense of his body had returned. He could feel his limbs, though faintly. They felt very weak; he couldn't move them. Clearly he hadn't yet recovered from his ordeal.

Yes, his ordeal. He was beginning to remember: being swept away and sucked down by the river, which had closed over his face with a hectic roar; the enormous weight of water that had thrust him down, into depths where his breath had burst out with a muffled agonized gurgling. After that, darkness—perhaps the darkness that surrounded him now. Had the river carried him here?

That was absurd. Someone must have rescued him and brought him here. But what place was it? Why would a rescuer leave him alone in total darkness, even when he cried out?

He controlled his gathering panic. He must be philosophical—after all, that was his vocation. Ah, he remembered that too; it comforted him. Perhaps, as he lay waiting for his strength, he could reflect on his beliefs. They would sustain him. But a twinge of fear convinced him that it might be wise to avoid such thoughts here. He subsided nervously, feeling as though the core of him were exposed and vulnerable. Chill sweat pricked his forehead in the close dark.

He must resign himself to his situation, until he knew more. He must be still, and await his strength. Sensation trickled slowly into his limbs. They seemed to form gradually about him: as though he were being reborn into a body. His mind flinched from that thought. For a moment, panic was very near.

He concentrated on sensation. His limbs felt enlarged, and cold as stone. As yet he couldn't tell whether these feelings were distorted by sickness. The threat of distortion troubled him; it meant he could be sure of nothing. It oppressed him, like the blinding darkness. He felt as though his brain and his nerves were drifting exposed in a void. Was he really blind?

How could near-drowning have blinded him? But while he scoffed at the idea, the darkness pressed close as a mask. What dark in the world could be so total? He remembered the face he had seemed to glimpse. That proved he could see—except that it was dim as a ghost of the mind, and perhaps had never been more than that.

The idea of being blind as well as enfeebled, in this unknown place, terrified him. With lips that seemed gigantically swollen, he cried out again, to bring the watcher back—if there had been one.

He heard his echoes blunder, dull and misshapen, against stone. Suddenly he was awash with panic. He struggled within his unresponsive body, as though he could snatch back the cry. He shouldn't have drawn attention to himself, he shouldn't have let the watcher know he was alive and helpless. All the fears which he had been trying to avoid insisted that his mind knew where he was.

For a while he could hear only the rapid unsteady labouring of his heart. It seemed to become confused with its own echo, to imprison him with a clutter of muffled thudding. Then he realized that some of the uneven sounds were approaching. Very slowly, someone was shuffling irregularly toward him through the dark.

He squeezed his eyelids tight, and tried to keep absolutely still. He had lain so in his childhood, when the night had surrounded him with demons come to carry him to Hell. That memory appalled him. As he tried to ignore it, it clung to his mind. But he had no time to ponder it, for the footsteps had dragged to a halt close to him.

Something scraped harshly, and light splashed over him. The light was orange; it flickered, plucking at his eyelids. He felt as though the torch, whose sputtering he could hear, were thrust close to his eyes; he could almost feel its heat snatching eagerly at him. He shrank within himself, bathed in fear. He tried to hold his eyes still amid the flickering. At last the light withdrew a little, and metal scraped the dark into place again. The watcher shuffled away, dwindling.

Blinded once more, he lay in his cell. From the echoing stone, and the scrape of the spy-hole, he knew that was where he was. How could he have been imprisoned for trying to save a girl from drowning? Or had the authorities taken the chance to arrest him for his unchristian beliefs, which the University's theologians and his old parish priest had condemned? He tried to outshout his thoughts: no, his situation here had nothing to do with his beliefs, nothing at all.

His mind wasn't hushed so easily. It was as though fragments of thought that had remained from before his ordeal were settling together, clarifying themselves. Soon he would remember everything: far too much. Because he could almost remember it now, he realized that he didn't know his name. His panic seemed to sweep him deeper into darkness, where there was no sound, and no time. It felt like the beginning of eternity.

Perhaps it was. Before he could understand that thought, and give way entirely to terror, he made himself try to move. He must at least escape his helplessness. It might be possible to overpower the watcher. Surely it might be.

He strained. His limbs felt too large, and separate from him—as though bloated and stiffened by drowning. Of course that wasn't why they felt unfamiliar. The reason was— He struggled to reach his body with his mind, more to distract himself than in any real hope. His thoughts waited patiently for recognition.

At last, with a sigh that shuddered out of him as though he were relinquishing his life, he slumped helpless. At once his thoughts rushed forward. His body was beyond his control because he was dead.

The thought was terrible because it explained so much. It crushed him, as though the darkness had become stone. His blindness had robbed his mind of all defenses. If he tried to think, his philosophy led him straight to his fears. He was a child alone in the dark.

The image of the river was too vivid to be false. He'd been walking by the Danube when the girl had fallen in. He and another man had plunged in, to rescue her. The other man had reached her. But nobody had saved him; a hidden current had dragged him away and down, down, far too deep to have survived. The memory dragged him down now, into the relentless darkness.

As he walked, he'd been preparing the next day's lecture. Pythagoras, Plato, Kant. Could that have anything to do with his plight? No, he told himself. Of course not. Nothing. But he dreaded finding out where he was.

That was contemptible. He would know sooner or later, he couldn't change that; he must resign himself. If only he didn't feel so helpless! Perhaps, if he began very gradually, he could gain control of his body; if he could move just one limb—

He made himself aware of his limbs. They felt swollen, but not painful. A chill had gathered on them, from the surrounding stone. His back felt like a slab; his mind must be confusing it with the stone on which he lay.

He concentrated on his right arm. It felt distant, cut off from him by enormous darkness. He grew aware of the fingers. He tried to feel their separateness, but they were pressed together like a single lump of flesh, in a kind of mitten. They were bound, as was his entire body. Panicking, he strained to raise his hand. But it lay inert as meat on a butcher's slab.

Again he was a child in the dark, but more alone: even time had deserted him. He remembered lying in the darkness of his childhood, praying never to lose his beliefs, because if you died unbelieving you were doomed to eternal torment. His worst and vaguest terror had always been that the torment would be appropriate to the victim.

He fought against the current of his terror. How could he give up without trying all his limbs? His mind groped about, as though in a cluttered dark room; he was surrounded by jumbled dead flesh, his own. At last his awareness grasped his left arm.

It lay parcelled in its bindings, resting lifeless on the stone. That was how a mummy's arm must feel. Somewhere in there were nerves and muscles, buried in the meat: dead and unresponsive. He forced his mind to reach out. He was panting. His teeth scraped together, with a creak of bone that filled his skull.

He must reach out, just a little further. He could do it. Just one finger. But his mind was diffused by the darkness; it felt as though it were floating shapelessly in the meat. His thought of ancient history had stimulated it into babbling Pythagoras, Plato, Kant, von Herder, Goethe. All of them had believed— His mind writhed, trying to dislodge the thoughts. His violent frustration clenched his fist within its bindings.

For a moment he thought he'd imagined it. But his fingers were still moving, eager to be free of their mitten. He managed to subdue his gasp of triumph before it could reach the walls. He rested, then he raised his arm. It groped upward in the dark, brushing the chill wall beside him. Soon he would unwrap himself, and then— His arm rose a few inches, then shuddered and fell, jarring all its nerves.

He was still weak, he mustn't expect too much, must give it time. It took several tries to convince him that he couldn't raise his arm higher, nor move any other part of his body. His arm refused to bend, to reach his bindings; it refused to recognize him. His mind was a stagnant pool in a lump of unrecognizable flesh. He could no longer doubt that he knew where he was.

They had devised their torments well: allowing him the illusion of triumph, the better to destroy all hope. Now came the torment of waiting helplessly, like a condemned man—except that the sufferings to which he was condemned would be eternal.

His childhood fears had told the truth. He should never have thought beyond them. For questioning his childhood faith, for believing that he would be reincarnated—the belief to which he had clung at the moment of his death, in the river—he had been condemned appropriately. To be reborn in an unfamiliar body, for unending torture: this was his hell.

They might keep him waiting for an eternity: that would be only a fraction of the time he had to suffer. They wanted his mind to fill with the tortures they were preparing, so that he could suffer them more fully. It did so. His helpless flesh could not even writhe. But he was sure they would make it feel.

His head throbbed with his pulse, as though all its flesh were pumping. Blood deafened his ears, like a close sea. Again it was a while before he could be sure that there were other sounds. The shuffling had returned, together with another set of footsteps, lighter and more purposeful. They were coming for him.

He sucked in his breath. He must stay absolutely still; they were waiting for him to betray himself. His teeth clenched, his lips trembled. Beyond the door, blurred sounds muttered. Though they resembled human voices, he was sure not all the distortions could be caused by the door. They must be discussing him. He tried to calm his face.

Metal slid, scraping. The torch peered in. Light danced on his eyelids, challenging him not to twitch. His breath swelled, harsh as stone in his lungs. At last a voice muttered, and the metal cut off the light. At once his breath roared out, appallingly loud.

Surely they couldn't have heard him, surely the sound of the spy-hole had muffled—But keys were scrabbling at the lock. His eyelids shook, his face worked uncontrollably; his treacherous mouth drooled. The door squealed open, and figures were standing silently close to him.

He must keep still. Eventually they would go away. He'd rest then, and try to free himself. But his face felt like a huge unfamiliar mask. It grimaced independent of his will. As it did so, one of the watchers hissed in triumph.

He had betrayed himself. There was no longer any reason to pretend, and his imaginings were worse than anything he might see. But when his eyes twitched open he groaned in terror. Beside the flames a stooped figure was peering down at him. One of its heads was covered with cloth.

The second figure must be a demon too, although it looked human: a thin young man with troubled eyes. His face stooped close, relentlessly staring. Then he stood up, shaking his head sadly.

That was surely not a demon's reaction. As the young man gestured the light closer, the man on the slab saw that the torchbearer had only one head after all, and a hunched back. The light showed that the bindings of his limbs were bandages.

They had rescued him, after all! His fears and his paralysis were only symptoms of his sickness! He raised his arm, until it fell back feebly. The young man glanced at it, but continued to test the other limbs, shaking his head. The man on the slab tried to speak to him. But the sound that poured from his lips contained no syllables, no shape at all.

"Useless. Stupid. A failure," the young man muttered, almost to himself. "To think that I had that mind in my hands. How could I have reduced it to this?"

The shuffling man asked him what should be done. The young man told him indifferently, dismally, not even glancing at the victim he condemned. They went out, locking the darkness behind them.

Long after their footsteps had faded the man lay on the slab, straining to move his arm an extra inch, trying to pronounce three syllables, to prove his intelligence when someone returned. Just three syllables, the name he had heard the hunched man call his master: Frank-en-stein.

R. CHETWYND-HAYES
The Creator

⚜

Ronald Chetwynd-Hayes (1919–2001) had a publishing career that lasted more than forty years. He produced thirteen novels, twenty-five collections of stories, and edited twenty-four anthologies. Valancourt Books has recently reissued his collections The Monster Club *and* Looking for Something to Suck: The Vampire Stories of R. Chetwynd-Hayes.

In 1989 both the Horror Writers of America and the British Fantasy Society presented him with Life Achievement Awards, and he was the Special Guest of Honor at the 1997 World Fantasy Convention in London. His stories have been adapted for film, television, radio and comic strips, and have been translated into numerous languages around the world.

About the story that follows, the self-effacing author revealed: "Honestly—I can do no more than gaze upon this early work with unstinted admiration (quoting Nöel Coward). It slid out from my fingers and typewriter with oiled ease. And how right it is that Charles Brownlow received his monster-making training in the butcher shop and petrol station. I have a very strong suspicion that many surgeons learn their business in the same source and possibly know little more, even less, than my later-day Frankenstein.

"It may interest readers to know that at the age of sixteen—having seen Son of Frankenstein *at the local cinema—I got as far as pickling a sheep's heart in my grandfather's workshop and distilled pure alcohol from methylated spirit. But I never got around to actually making a monster . . ."*

Charlie Brownlow had decided to create a monster.

Nothing elaborate, you understand. Nothing that required an expensive laboratory and masses of flashing lights and buzzing machinery. Neither was he all that keen to open graves at midnight, pinch madmen's brains, murder unsuspecting peasants for their hearts, or employ any other of the tricks that had eventually led to Baron Frankenstein's downfall.

In fact after an intensive course of study—to wit: watching all the midnight horror movies on television—he came to the conclusion that the misguided baron had been too ambitious by far. His creation was much too big. A hulking great brute that no one could control. No, he would make a nice little monster, that could be taken for a run at night and given a clip round the ear whenever it got obstreperous.

Now, unless you have ever set out to create a monster yourself, you can have no idea of the problems involved. Gathering the materials—without reverting to the baron's unethical line of conduct—was in itself a sleep-murdering prospect, and might never have been achieved if Charlie's grandad had not decided to float into eternity on a sea of undiluted whisky. The old boy had been ailing for some time, his liver and kidneys having thrown in the sponge after a long lifetime of abuse, and the entire family agreed that it was a happy release for all concerned.

Everyone filed into the front room to pay their final respects before the coffin lid was screwed down and stared at the shrivelled old face with varying degrees of regret. Aunt Matilda, for example, regretted that the old man had not seen his way clear to pass over years ago, so that she could have enjoyed her share of whatever was going before galloping inflation had set in. Uncle George regretted that the mean old basket hadn't repaid the fiver he borrowed three weeks before his death. Cousin Marion regretted not allowing the dirty old devil to pinch her bottom, which might have resulted in a substantial mention in the yet to be opened will. In fact everyone regretted some lapse or lost opportunity—except Charlie.

His regrets would come later—if he failed to steal the body before the coffin was planted in the churchyard.

It is not my intention to suggest that stealing one's grandfather from his coffin is a nice thing to do—but worse deeds have been performed in the name of science. Also I am of the opinion that enterprise should be encouraged no matter in what field it raises an enquiring head. It may be asked what were Charlie's qualifications for monster making? Well, he had some surgical experience, having worked in the local butcher's shop for the best part of a year, during which period he skinned innumerable rabbits, dismembered sheep, uncovered the murky secrets of ox hearts, liver and kidneys; was able to pinpoint the exact location of sirloin, rump, silverside, topside, shoulder, leg and stewing steak. Few surgeons know more—many far less.

Then—having so to speak completed his medical training—he entered the field of auto-dynamics. In other words he became for a short while a petrol pump attendant with engine messing-about-duties at the *Quick-In Quick-Out Garage*. There he was initiated into the mysteries of what takes place under a car bonnet; the dark secrets of carburetor misbehavior; the mind boggling consequences of seeping batteries; the soul-disturbing results of erring sparking plugs.

It does not take much imagination to realize that the marriage of these two professions must sooner or later give birth to something very unusual.

After the family had retired to its individual beds—with the exception of Uncle George who was sharing with Cousin Marion—Charlie crept downstairs, went out to his laboratory (the disused potting shed), armed himself with two coal sacks, the larger portions of a dismembered mangle and one screwdriver, then returned to the house and prepared to acquire his monster-making material.

Removing the screws did not present any great problem. Getting Grandad to leave his coffin was quite another matter. Charlie heaved, shook, punched, pulled—all to no avail, for it seemed as if the corpse was determined to retain its wooden overcoat and defeat the cause of science.

Finally Charlie solved the problem by upending the coffin and tipping Grandad out on to the hearth-rug, where he lay, looking like a squatter who has been forcibly evicted from a suburban house. Then the latter-day-Frankenstein arranged mangle parts in the coffin, padded them with coal sacks and screwed the lid back into place. There only remained the task of getting Grandad into the potting-shed-cum-laboratory, where he could be bedded down in a barrel of brine, and left to acquire the pickled quality of salt-beef.

He lifted the uncooperative body up over his right shoulder and staggered out into the passage.

The funeral was a great success.

The Reverend Masters said some very nice things about the deceased, even if they were rather embarrassing to someone who knew exactly what was being interred.

"You must not think," the worthy clergyman stated, "that my old friend is in this wooden box. Believe me, he has been removed to a place where the worm cannot consume, age cannot wither, corruption destroy. Friends, we are about to commit to earth that which is no longer of use; that which has done its duty nobly and well, in fact—if I may coin a phrase—has served its turn."

Charlie almost had a heart attack when they lowered the coffin into the grave, for he heard one pall bearer whisper to another, "'Ere, Harry, the old bugger's rolling about in there!" but fortunately the recipient of this alarming information merely shrugged and said, "Yeah—well the old 'uns do—don't they?"

Back in the house everyone sat down to a slap-up high-tea and generally gave the impression that having discharged an unpleasant, but necessary duty, they were now going to enjoy themselves. Uncle George helped himself to a very large whisky from the sideboard, then winked suggestively at Cousin Marion. Aunt Matilda gave Aunt Mildred a generous helping of sausage and mash, then instructed three-times-removed Cousin Jane to pour out the tea.

"You're not decorative, so you might as well be useful," she observed cheerfully. "Something hot inside us will help drive out the churchyard chill."

"Went off very nicely," Great-Aunt Lydia said, while spearing a boiled potato. "I thought the Reverend Masters gave a lovely sermon. I like that bit about dear Arthur not being in that coffin. It was so uplifting."

"Have a pickled onion," Aunt Matilda invited.

"I won't, dear, if you don't mind. They repeat."

For a while the only sound was that of rattling cutlery and Uncle George's occasional belch. Then twice-removed-and-on-the-wrong-side-of-the-family Cousin Daniel who had spent the previous night in the box room, remarked darkly:

"He's still here."

Charlie shuddered and Aunt Mildred snapped:

"What are you talking about? Who's still here?"

Cousin Daniel nodded slowly and gave the impression that he knew much, but was prepared to reveal little.

"Him. Grandad. I heard him wandering about last night."

All the ladies squealed with either real or affected terror and Cousin Marion fainted and had to be helped to the best bedroom by Uncle George. Great Aunt Lydia voiced her indignation.

"How dare you say such a thing! The very idea! Tain't respectful. Apart from the fact you've frightened everyone. Apologize at once."

Cousin Daniel nodded again. "I heard what I heard. He thudded, then thumped—then went staggering along the passage. Mark my words—he won't rest."

During the ensuing storm Charlie popped out to the ex-potting shed and piled a heap of sacks over the brine tub. Not before, however, he had taken a quick peep inside. Grandad's bald head was already assuming the appearance of tanned leather.

Aunt Matilda was entertaining her best friend Jennifer Grandlee to tea.

"Charlie has got himself a hobby," she said with a certain amount of satisfaction. "I must say it's a real treat for him to have an interest."

"Every man should have a hobby," Jennifer remarked with deep profundity. "What kind of interest is he taking, dear?"

Aunt Matilda giggled. "I don't know. He's so secretive and just won't let me into that old potting-shed. It's something to do with sawing."

"Woodwork," Jennifer nodded. "They have to saw when they do woodwork."

"And a fair amount of chopping," Aunt Matilda continued. "There again, I've heard a fair amount of hammering."

"Probably a bookcase," Miss Grandlee suggested. "Or maybe a nice bedside cabinet. Of course he may be going to surprise you with something unusual. Such as a night-commode."

Aunt Matilda frowned and gave the impression she was trying to think. "But why should he want a needle and thread? And twenty yards of copper wire?"

Jennifer shook her head. "I honestly don't know, dear. I'm sure they don't use a needle and thread in woodwork. At least I don't think so. But of course Charlie has always had a sort of inventive streak. Remember that time he soled and heeled his shoes with a bit of fried steak? I know they got a bit smelly after a bit—but you've got to admit it did show an original mind."

"Oh, he's original all right," Aunt Matilda agreed. "Ah, here he comes now."

Charlie entered the room and started when he saw the visitor. Dressed in mud-stained overalls, he looked as every genius should, but rarely does.

"Don't sit on the sofa in those muddy things," Aunt Matilda instructed. "Spread a newspaper over the cushion first. What have you been doing?"

"Getting rid of surplus requirements," Charlie answered thoughtlessly. "That is to say—I've been digging a hole."

"All part of your hobby?" Jennifer enquired with a certain coyness. "Matilda tells me you're making something in that shed of yours."

But Charlie was lost in a world where half-legs met rump, spare-ribs needed certain adjustments, liver required replacement, kidneys had lost their suet, lights had to be exchanged for a battery—and the entire thing was still too large.

"A smaller top and a rolling base," he muttered. "And arms—who the hell wants arms? A couple of cut-down crankshafts should do the trick. Excuse me."

And without further explanation he jumped to his feet and raced from the room. Aunt Matilda sighed. "Whatever it is he's making, he's certainly wrapped up in it."

"You know, dear," Jennifer said after a while, "I think I've got it. He's making a rolling chair with metal arms. It will be very useful if you want to move about without getting up."

Uncle George was so annoyed he choked on his third glass of whisky and expressed his righteous indignation by banging a clenched fist down on the chair arm.

"Why? That's what I want to know—why?"

"It's all this television," Aunt Matilda exclaimed. "Sets the young a bad example. What with *Z Cars* and that awful baldheaded man who will ruin his teeth with lollipops, it's a wonder we aren't all murdered in our beds."

"That goat was a good friend to me," Uncle George said with a sob in his voice.

"But it was dead," Aunt Matilda pointed out. "I mean to say it wasn't as though it was a up and around goat. It had passed over."

"That's no reason for someone to pinch its flipping head," Uncle George roared. "I left the corpse in the outhouse, laid out as tidy as you please. Then this morning when I took the wheelbarrow in, so as to transport it to its last resting place—no head! Some ghoulish bleeder has cut it off. Now tell me this—why should anyone want to nick a goat's head. Must be a nut case."

"Same as Alfie's go-cart," Cousin Jane said. "Some thieving hound pinched the castors off that. Had springs on them. Came off my mother's tea trolley. Poor little devil cried his heart up when he found it on its uppers. Well—he likes to chase the milkman down Parson's Hill. Boys will be boys, I always say."

"Like Charlie," Aunt Matilda said proudly. "He'll chase anything that moves."

"You spoil that boy," Uncle George growled. "Let him do what he likes and no regular job! He'll come to a bad end."

Aunt Matilda folded her arms and shook her head in shocked reproof. "You mind your business, George Brownlow. Isn't Charlie me own brother's boy and with no parents to speak off, his father having passed away and his mother run off with the Prue man? He's a good boy to me, bringing his dole money home regular as you please and not wasting it in the betting shops as some I could mention."

"But what's he doing with himself all day?" Uncle George demanded. "Mucking about in that shed—a 'ammering and a sawing and muttering to himself. If you ask me he's going round the bend."

"No one has asked you," Aunt Matilda retorted. "If you must know he's making something for me that's going to be a surprise. Something in the chair line, Jennifer thinks."

There might have been further argument if Cousin Jane had not pointed out that it was seven-thirty and time for *Coronation Street*. Midway through the performance Charlie entered and slid into the armchair where he sat staring with glazed eyes at the bright screen and occasionally incurring Uncle George's wrath by low, but disturbing muttering. His appearance was by now well in keeping with the popular concept of a genius; long hair, unshaven chin, wrinkled clothing and fingernails that were in mourning for their last close relationship with soap and water. But there was a certain air of fulfillment that only comes to a man who has found a tiny nugget of success in a ton of back breaking endeavor. Suddenly the television screen trembled and Annie Walker appeared to be in danger of decapitation by a bright flash. Charlie jumped to his feet and yelled, "Thunderstorm!" then dashed from the room.

Uncle George delivered his sincere and considered opinion.

"There's no getting away from it—he's gone up the wall. Slipped his braces. Next thing you know he'll stand on his head when the sun comes out."

Aunt Matilda waited until a mighty clap of thunder had done its worst—which meant sending Cousin Jane whimpering under the table—before saying quietly:

"Because the boy has brains that are a bit different to ordinary people's, that's no reason for suggesting he's crazy. Mark my words—Charlie is going to shock all of us one day."

"But what the hell is so special about a thunderstorm?" Uncle George demanded.

"I expect he revels in the doings of nature. Jane, come out from under that table this instant. If the house is struck you'll be no more safer there than anywhere else. I'll make a nice jug of cocoa . . ."

She was interrupted by another peal of thunder and a loud cry that began somewhere at the bottom of the garden and grew louder as it approached the house. When the back door cracked open the cry took on a higher pitch and assumed the semblance of drawn out words.

"I . . . I . . . v . . . e . . . d . . . o . . . n . . . e . . . i . . . t . . ."

Charlie exploded into the room. Sent the door crashing back against the wall, knocked an occasional table over, bumped into the sideboard, then pulled Aunt Matilda from her chair and danced the flustered old lady round the room, while still shouting at the top of his voice:

"I've done it! It's complete in every detail. And it moves. Moves . . ."

Aunt Matilda managed to pull herself free, then pushed her still prancing nephew into a chair. She patted her hair, made certain that her cameo broach was still in its rightful place, then said quietly:

"You really must control yourself, dear. But I'm very pleased that you have completed—whatever it was you were doing. I'm sure it will be very comfortable."

But Charlie obviously had not been listening, for he clasped shaking hands to his head and stamped his right foot three times on the carpet.

"I forgot what I came for. Can . . . can I have one of Grandad's woollen vests? I don't think there's any danger of it catching cold, but some joins ought to be hidden. Not that it's not beautiful—in an irregular sort of way—but I'm not very good with a needle and thread."

Aunt Matilda looked like a lady who has lost her way and is not certain if it is wise to go on any further.

"In the wardrobe, dear . . . upstairs . . ."

Charlie leapt to his feet and jumped over Cousin Jane who had decided it was now safe to come out from under the table, and ran from the room. The heavy thud of his feet could be heard ascending the stairs.

"A chair—you say?" Uncle George enquired gently.

"That's what I understood."

"A chair that wears a vest?"

"Well, he did say it was to hide the joins. Some sort of padding I expect."

Charlie was heard running down some of the stairs and falling down the remainder. The crash of an overturned bucket marked his journey through the kitchen. Uncle George climbed laboriously to his feet.

"I'm going to have a look," he announced.

"But it's to be a surprise."

"Then I'll surprise myself."

The two women were left staring at one another and when one moved the other flinched. The marble clock on the mantelpiece struck eight and the thunderstorm gave a final ominous rumble before retiring to the west.

"Shall I switch the telly off?" Cousin Jane enquired.

"Yes, dear. There's nothing much on now."

Presently they heard slowly approaching footsteps, which preluded Uncle George's entry into the room. He walked with a strange stiff gait, his face was very pale, and he lowered himself into a chair without speaking a word. There he sat staring intently at a framed portrait of Dirk Bogarde—for whom Aunt Matilda entertained a partiality—which hung on the opposite wall. The silence became extremely oppressive.

Cousin Jane was the first to crack.

"Well—what has he made?"

Uncle George, without removing his gaze from Mr. Bogarde, opened his mouth—and screamed. It was a very loud, very hoarse and very unnerving scream. Then silence again descended on to the room, until Aunt Matilda ventured her enquiry.

"George . . . George, is there anything wrong? Have you been drinking too much? I've always said that whisky on an empty stomach cannot be good for anyone."

As though this statement had triggered off an automatic impulse, Uncle George rose and walked sedately over to the sideboard, where he poured himself a very generous helping of whisky; drank it in one mighty gulp, put down the glass with elaborate care, then turned and screamed again.

After this second and much improved performance, he went back to his chair and continued his contemplation of Mr. Bogarde's classic features.

"I'm going home," Cousin Jane announced after an interval of deep thought. "And I'm going to lock all the doors and windows and not come near this house again."

"Perhaps he's got the delirious trimmings," Aunt Matilda suggested. "I mean to say there can't be anything in that old shed that could make him like this. Could there . . . ?"

"I'm not waiting to find out."

"But you haven't had your cocoa, dear."

"You can pour your cocoa where the monkey poured his ginger-beer. Anything that can make old George bellow like a demented banshee is something I don't want to see. If you want my advice you'll have that boy put away."

And she gathered up her knitting, two copies of *True Confessions*, a box of chocolates and an electric torch, then moved swiftly towards the door. Another scream from Uncle George and a glimpse of Charlie coming down the passage did much to improve the order of her going and the house shook when she slammed the front door.

Charlie did not appear to be at all put out by this sudden exit, but poked his head round the door-frame and asked, "May I have some butter please?"

"Never mind butter," Aunt Matilda replied, patting Uncle George's forehead with a handkerchief, "what have you done to your poor uncle? I don't know what's wrong with him. He keeps screaming and my nerves won't stand much more of it."

Charlie assumed a sullen expression and he stared defiantly at the floor. "He shouldn't have peeped. It was supposed to be a surprise. And he looked in through the window before I had a chance to cover Oscar with Grandad's woollen vest."

Aunt Matilda raised an eyebrow. "Oscar! That's a funny name for a chair."

Charlie stood on one leg and swung the other back and forth. "It's not a chair. I can't make a chair. If you must know it's a monster. Now you've made me spoil the surprise and I've a good mind not to show him to you."

"I'm sure, dear, if you've made a monster it's a very nice one," Aunt Matilda said calmly. "But that still doesn't explain why your uncle persists in staring at dear Mr. Bogarde and screaming. I remember my mother used to say my brother was a little monster, but I'm certain she never screamed."

"Can I have some butter?" Charlie repeated his former request. "The trolley wheels squeak."

"Very well. But don't take too much. It's now seventy pence a pound."

After about five minutes of having his forehead bathed with Eau de Cologne, Uncle George began to display signs of returning life. He examined every item of furniture in the room with mild interest, counted his fingers and seemed profoundly astonished to find they were all present, then turned to Aunt Matilda and whispered:

"It's got 'orns."

"Has it now? Well I'm sure they'll be very useful for something or the other. Would you like a nice cup of cocoa?"

"And long metal arms," Uncle George added thoughtfully.

"I wouldn't care for metal arms myself," Aunt Matilda admitted, "but I daresay they'd be better than nothing. Shall I make you a nice condensed-milk sandwich to eat with your cocoa?"

She shook her head reprovingly when Uncle George insisted on volunteering another piece of shocking information.

"And it's down to its 'ambones."

A retreat to the kitchen was clearly the only recourse, where Aunt Matilda made a jug of cocoa and coated thick slices of bread and butter with a generous layer of condensed milk. She seemed to remember that something sweet and hot was strongly recommended as a curative for anyone suffering from shock. While she was engaged in this act of mercy,

Charlie came in from the garden and after opening the kitchen door to its fullest extent, asked quietly:

"Do you mind if Oscar comes in? He wasn't happy in my laboratory."

Aunt Matilda scraped the lingering residue of condensed milk from the tin and spread it on a crust. "You know, dear, I never object to anyone you might invite home. So long as they are refined."

Without waiting for any further invitation Oscar glided into the kitchen.

I find difficulty in describing this product which symbolized the marriage between two widely divided trades. Butchery was of course responsible for Grandad's torso and the goat's head; while the motor industry must be given credit for the metal arms, the red flashing eyes and the sparking plugs which were embedded on either side of the Grandad/goat blended neck. Inner tubes aided by glue hid whatever needlework that had been necessary to unite crankshaft arms to Grandad's shoulders, while hands—complete with six fingers—had been fashioned from back-seat cushion springs. Remembering that compactness was of major importance, Charlie had sacrificed most of Grandad's legs, and he was—as Uncle George had most tactlessly stated—down to his hambones. Short thick stubs encased in inverted car wheel-hubs and held firmly in position by glutinous rubber solution. A pair of trolley castors—that might well have been liberated from Alfie's go-cart—were riveted on to the underside of the wheel-hubs and served as an excellent—even an improved—substitute for feet. A woollen vest mercifully concealed whatever liberties that had been taken with Grandad's torso.

Oscar—for such we must now designate this collection of bits and pieces—was not more than three foot six high and decidedly disconcerting in appearance to anyone who did not appreciate the unadorned work of genius. His communication apparatus also left a little to be desired.

The goat jaws opened, a sliver of rotary fan-blade glittered in the lamp-light and a high pitched oscillating sound gradually emerged into recognizable words.

"This is BBC Radio Four. For the next half an hour Professor Hughes will describe his journey along the Zambezi River . . ."

"Oh, blast it!" Charlie protested giving Oscar a hearty thump on the back. "There must be an overcharge between the radio valves and the loudspeaker. Wait a minute—I've installed an instrument panel under his shoulder-blades."

He pulled up the woollen vest, pushed what had formerly been a self-starter, adjusted a small plastic knob—and finally aimed a kick at the lower portion of Grandad's torso. This drastic action must have achieved some result for a bleating voice enquired:

"What the bl . . . eedin . . . g . . . h . . . ell is go . . . ing . . . on . . .?"

Charlie positively beamed with satisfaction.

"That must be coming from that portion of Grandad's brain I was able to plant in the goat's skull. You see I made a little sump . . ."

Contrary to her usual practice Aunt Matilda interrupted a man while he was speaking. Ever since Oscar's entrance she had stared, sighed, on occasion made small appreciative sounds, but had not attempted to contribute any observation of her own. Now she spoke quite sharply.

"Charlie, am I to understand that you have used a portion of your dear Grandad's remains to make this contraption?"

"Well—yes. You see materials were very hard to come by and Grandad was going to be wasted . . ."

"That's no excuse. Although I can understand your wish to be usefully employed, you still should not have laid rude hands on your Grandad. He wasn't yours to take. In a way he belonged to us all and certainly I—at least—should have been consulted."

Charlie hung his head. "Sorry, Auntie. I didn't think."

Aunt Matilda nodded. "That's the trouble with the young generation—they never think. Well, I've said all I'm going to say. The matter is now closed. Tell me about your invention. What can it do?"

They both watched Oscar circle the kitchen table, then roll smoothly towards the sitting-room, where Uncle George sat considering the mad possibility of becoming a tee-totaller. Charlie, like all true artists, had not thought of his creation in terms of sordid usefulness, because, so far as he could remember Baron Frankenstein's monster had not been expected to find gainful employment.

"Well," he said after a thoughtful silence, "I might be able to train it to do little jobs round the house. Fetch the letters from the doormat, punch holes in tins of condensed milk and things like that."

Aunt Matilda did not comment on these suggestions, but listened to the bleated words that came from the sitting-room.

"Wh . . . ere . . . the . . . bl . . . eeding . . . g . . . h . . . ell . . . is . . . me . . . l . . . e . . . gs?"

"What a pity you had to save that part of your grandad that used bad language," she murmured.

A loud—and by now familiar—scream rang out; only now it was much louder, more drawn out and was perhaps the cry of someone who had crossed the barrier of fear and walked in that black and white country where reality takes on the shape of mad fantasy. Then Uncle George came out of the sitting-room; moving with a speed that would have excited the envy of a much younger man who had not formed a close alliance with a whisky bottle. Oscar was not far behind. Rolling smoothly, eyes gleaming like car rear lights, head lowered, butter-lubricated trolley wheels turning silently; he gave the distinct impression that he was, at least for the time being, a very happy little monster.

Uncle George's scream as he was propelled out through the back door was most certainly his best effort to date; and Oscar, having perhaps decided that he had more than done his duty, rolled back to his creator and bleated two words.

"Bl . . . e . . . eeding . . . tw . . . i . . . t . . ."

"You must do something about this bad language," Aunt Matilda insisted. "It is really most unpleasant."

Now I am aware that a man-made monster is supposed to come to a bad end. Be roasted in a burning mill; dissolved in a lake of acid; or blow itself up by pulling a convenient handle which in some mysterious way ignites a ton of high explosives. From a purely moral point of view it would be nice if I could record that is what happened to Oscar, but truth—that monster whose face must never be hidden—forces me to confess that he is at this very moment alive and well.

Charlie recharges his battery once a week and has trained him to fetch the newspaper and letters from the doormat, punch holes in condensed milk tins with his horns, and give hell to anyone who turns up whenever Aunt Matilda is watching *Coronation Street*. But to be honest this doesn't happen very often, as visitors are the exception rather than the rule these days.

Uncle George has joined the Sons of Temperance and has twice appeared on television, where he caused much alarm and despondency among publicans by describing the terrifying effects of strong drink.

Charlie is now considering making a mate for Oscar, but of course is handicapped by the same old problem—the lack of materials. He keeps looking at Aunt Matilda with a speculative eye, but as the old lady appears to be good for at least another twenty years, it may be sometime before the world of science is shocked out of its complacency by the birth of a Do-it-yourself-done-by-themselves monster.

In the meanwhile, if you should have an old decrepit female relative to spare—drop me a line.

BASIL COPPER

Better Dead

Basil Copper (1924–2013) was born in London, and for thirty years he worked as a journalist and editor of a local newspaper before becoming a full-time writer in 1970.

His first story in the horror field, "The Spider," was published in 1964 in The Fifth Pan Book of Horror Stories, and since then, his short fiction has appeared in numerous anthologies, been extensively adapted for radio, and collected in Not After Nightfall, Here Be Daemons, From Evil's Pillow, And Afterward the Dark, Voices of Doom, When Footsteps Echo, Whispers in the Night, Cold Hand on My Shoulder and Knife in the Back.

One of the author's most reprinted stories, "Camera Obscura," was adapted for a 1971 episode of the anthology television series Rod Serling's Night Gallery.

Besides publishing two nonfiction studies of the vampire and werewolf legends, his other books include the novels The Great White Space, Necropolis, House of the Wolf *and* The Black Death. *He also wrote more than fifty hardboiled thrillers about Los Angeles private detective Mike Faraday, and continued the adventures of August Derleth's Holmes-like consulting detective Solar Pons in several volumes, including the novel* Solar Pons versus The Devil's Claw.

More recently, PS Publishing has produced the non-fiction study Basil Copper: A Life in Books, *and a massive two-volume set of* Darkness, Mist & Shadow: The Collected Macabre Tales of Basil Copper. *A restored version of Copper's 1976 novel* The Curse of the Fleers *appeared from the same imprint in 2012.*

The following story could be considered something of a companion piece to the author's classic tale about movie collecting, "Amber Print" . . .

I

Better dead!" said Robert exultantly as Boris pulled the lever.

The whole laboratory and watchtower exploded in dust and flames.

"Great!" said Robert, getting up to turn down the sound on the projector as the Universal end titles started coming up.

Joyce, who had just poked her head in at her husband's specially-built brick projection room, yawned, glancing at the hundreds of metal film cans that lined the interior of the thirty-foot-long auditorium, the metal shelving reflecting back the screen images in tiny flickering points of light. Normally Robert had the curtains drawn across his archive treasures but for some reason he had not bothered this evening. The room lights went on as the last foot of black trailer went through the machine.

"You must have seen *Bride of Frankenstein* a hundred times by now," Joyce said wearily.

Robert's eyes glowed.

"And I expect to see it another hundred times before the year's out. The classics never stale."

Joyce shook her head.

"Tea's ready. Is there any chance of you cutting the lawn tonight?"

Robert gave her an expression of mock regret.

"Doubtful. I have two more film parcels to open yet."

"I've had enough of the dead alive," his wife said, a steely undertone coming into her voice. "Film collecting will be the death of you."

Robert chuckled, his eyes vacantly fixed on two huge cardboard cartons on the bench near his canvas viewing chair.

"What a way to go!"

The outer door slamming cut off any further remarks he might have made, and with a slightly crestfallen expression he switched off the mains electricity and made his way back to the house. The couple ate their tea in silence, Joyce's eyes fixed smolderingly on his face. An attractive, dark-haired woman of thirty-six, she had to rein back the resentment within her at her husband's extravagant collecting habits, while she was forced to hold on to a boring secretarial job in order to help pay the bills.

Robert crumbled a piece of toast into his tea and ate it with satisfaction.

"I think *Night of the Living Dead* just turned up," he said at length. "We were looking forward to that one."

"You mean you were," his wife said pointedly.

She got up to clear her plate, the set of her shoulders indicating extreme displeasure.

She paused by the buffet, delicately cutting a slice of the cream gateau that they had started at lunch-time.

"I shan't be back until late this evening. I have a committee meeting and then I have some more typing to finish off at the office."

"Don't forget your key," said Robert absently, his mind still fixed on the parcels in his projection room at the bottom of the garden. He gazed fondly to where the roof showed through the top of the rose trellis outside the French windows. "I may be running stuff down there."

Joyce's eyes glinted with suppressed anger as she stood with the cake knife in one slim, well-manicured hand.

"Do you want any of this?" Robert shook his head.

"Just another cup of tea, if you'd be so kind."

There was an oppressive silence in the room as Joyce bent to pour, accentuated as the faint hum of a motor mower came faintly on the summer breeze.

"Incidentally," she said sourly, "Karloff never said, 'Better dead!' Even after all those viewings you can't remember the dialogue properly."

"Oh," said Robert.

He gave his wife a twisted smile. For the first time she realized how ugly and worn he was looking, even in his early forties.

"Well," he said eventually, with an air of quiet triumph. "If he didn't say it, he should have!"

Joyce turned her face away so that he should not see the expression on it. She put the teapot down on the metal stand with barely suppressed fury.

She left the room without saying goodbye. The phone rang as she was crossing the hall. She turned quickly, made sure the dining room door was firmly closed.

"Hullo, darling!"

The voice was unmistakable. She changed color, put her hand quickly over the receiver.

"How many times have I told you, Conrad. Don't ring here!"

"Why, is he home?"

She smiled tautly at the alarm in the other's voice.

"Don't worry; he's having tea in the dining room. See you tonight as arranged."

She put the phone down quickly as Robert's footsteps sounded over the parquet. She was putting on her light raincoat in front of the mirror when he opened the door.

"Just the office," she said, answering his unspoken question.

She smiled maliciously.

"Hope you're not too disappointed. It wasn't one of your film dealer friends."

She went out quickly, slamming the front door before he had time to reply.

II

Light exploded, splitting the darkness with dazzling incandescence. Joyce, nude, got out of bed, revelling in the fact that the dark, strongly-built young man next her was admiring her sinuous curves, softly explored by the bedside lamp. But she ignored the imploring look in his eyes, dressing quickly with the ease born of long practice in the dangerous game they were playing. She glanced at her wrist watch, noted it had only just turned ten P.M. There was plenty of time then.

"When will I see you?"

She shrugged.

"Soon, obviously. But we can't keep this pace up, Conrad. We're meeting too frequently."

"Nowhere near frequently enough for me!"

He rolled over quickly, reaching for her, as she sat crosslegged, one stocking half drawn on. But she skipped out of reach, laughing, and sat down on the bedside stool to finish dressing. He lay and watched her with the concentration she had often noticed; even when sated with sex men were never satisfied. As soon as the woman had dressed the mystery was there again, waiting to be revealed at the next encounter. She could not really understand the fascination, though she appreciated it in Conrad's case. She had never owned a man like him; the affair had begun two years earlier and he was a person of integrity, held to her by so many bonds of unswerving loyalty.

She deftly made up her mouth in the mirror, the ratchets of her mind clicking over hopelessly, as they had ever since the affair had begun. If there were only some way out that would make three people happy. If only Robert would find someone else. But that was not within his nature. He was so absorbed in his film collecting that he hardly noticed she was there; that being so, he would hardly turn his attention to another woman. And if he did not appreciate her attractions—and Conrad certainly did—things could go on as they were forever if she and Conrad did not make some attempt to solve the problem.

"I can't understand him," Conrad said, as though he could read her mind.

"Who?"

Naturally, turning back from the mirror, she knew what he meant.

The dark-haired man in the bed shrugged impatiently.

"Your husband, of course. With all that under his roof he just doesn't seem interested."

Joyce smiled bitterly.

"You should be grateful, darling. People hardly ever value what they possess."

Conrad gave her a twisted smile in return.

"Until they've lost it . . ."

The sentence seemed to hang heavily in the scented air of the bedroom.

Joyce bent swiftly and kissed him gently on the brow.

"We'll see in due course," she said in a low voice. "We have to be patient."

"I thought we had been. For two long years."

Joyce did not answer, her emotions suddenly overcoming her. She turned to the mirror, only the faint trembling of her fingers as she put on the lightweight raincoat betraying her inmost feelings.

"I'll ring you," she said through tight lips. "Please don't ring the house again. It's too dangerous.'

He did not answer and she went without a backward glance, letting herself out the back door into the secluded garden. It was a bright, starry night and she leaned against the wall, drinking in the fresh air until she had recovered herself. She drove home slowly, her mind still turning over useless prospects. It was still only a quarter to eleven when she got in. Lights burned in the dining room and the French windows were open to the lawn.

From the projection room at the end of the garden came the faint, tinny music. *Night of the Living Dead* was under way. She sat down at the end of the dining room table, her emotions overcoming her. Slowly her head fell forward and she put her hands up to her face as she rested her elbows on the cold oak surface. Salt tears trickled through her fingers as the raucous music went on.

III

"It's alive! It's alive!"

There was a sudden burst of laughter from the other end of the dining room. Joyce shrank inwardly. The guests round the long table wore blank faces. Only Robert and his friend John at the head were laughing inanely.

"For God's sake, Robert," said Joyce irritably. "Can't you leave it alone for even a few hours?"

The nearest guests looked startled at the vehemence of her tone and John and Robert resembled figures congealed in a photo-flash picture. Joyce forced a smile, aware that she had made a social gaffe. John's wife was setting next to her and she turned toward Isabel.

"I'm sorry about that, but this film collecting business is getting on my nerves."

The guests relaxed then, exchanging knowing smiles among themselves and Joyce was inwardly gratified to see that both John and Robert wore chastened looks.

Isabel nodded, fixing her husband with a warning glance.

"Don't I know it, dear. John and I have no conversation at all nowadays unless it's about films."

She paused.

"Or, it's 'Pass the salt!'"

"We must split them up when we have coffee," Joyce said. Isabel sighed.

"I've tried before," she said resignedly. "There's no stopping them once they get on that topic."

Joyce stabbed her silver fork into the remains of her dessert with an almost savage gesture.

"They're hardly ever off it."

The two women laughed uneasily and then Joyce was in command of herself again. A few minutes later, when she had ushered the last of the guests into the drawing room and she and Isabel had returned to the kitchen to make the coffee, they were silent, as though both were absorbed with weighty thoughts that they did not like to impart to the other.

That night, long after the guests had departed, Joyce was washing up in the kitchen, when she heard the back door slam. Robert had, of course, gone off with John somewhere, as soon as he could decently excuse himself. Now he had come in and, despite the lateness of the hour, had gone out to his projection room. A few minutes later, as she finished drying the glasses, she could hear raucous music coming from the end of the garden.

The nearest house to theirs was quite a long way off, so Robert had not bothered to completely sound-proof his private cinema.

Joyce paused; a sudden thought had come into her mind. Robert's acquisitions had risen to an alarming total in the past few months. Alarming in the sense that his "hobby," if it could be called that, must be costing him a great deal. Costing them a great deal, she suddenly realized. She stood, her lips pursed, her flat stomach against the draining board, the last glass poised in her hand. She caught a glimpse of herself in the mirror opposite. She looked absurdly like Joan Crawford in one of her Warner Brothers melodramas, she felt. Then she angrily dismissed the thought. She was catching Robert's disease. She crossed the kitchen and took the last trayful of clean glasses back into the dining room.

Then she went swiftly along the corridor to Robert's study. She switched on the green-shaded desk lamp, making sure that the thick curtains were already drawn across the windows. Robert always kept his chequebooks and stubs in the top righthand drawer. She went through them quickly, her breath coming faster as she noted the sums. She got out a sheet of paper and a pencil and started jotting down the figures. Anger was growing like a dull fire within her. He had spent several thousand pounds in the last two months alone! She fought back the feeling as she completed her calculations. And Robert sometimes grumbled that she was careless with the housekeeping money . . . When she had finished, she replaced everything as she had found it, switched off the lamp and went back to the dining room.

She put the sheet with the notations at the bottom of her handbag and then replaced all the glasses in the big antique glass-fronted corner cupboard. She had just finished when she heard Robert come in, locking and bolting the back door behind him. He looked in at the open dining room door, as though surprised to see her still working. He rubbed his hands with satisfaction.

"I think it all went very well, don't you?"

Joyce nodded.

"Yes, very well," she said slowly.

She kept her eyes fixed steadily on his face. It was as if she were seeing him clearly for the first time.

IV

It was hard work mowing the lawn. Joyce was perspiring and a savage resentment was building up. Robert had disappeared some hours earlier, but she had no doubt where he was and her eyes wandered to his cinema building on the far side of the garden. Another two parcels of film had arrived that morning and that had added to her anger. The two had spoken very briefly; long silences were becoming the norm within the marriage and Joyce was conscious that things had deteriorated to a dangerous degree over the past two years. This was one of the factors which had driven her into another man's arms; the utter indifference of her partner to her needs both as a woman and a human being.

Joyce put the mower away in the small shed just beyond the cinema, aware all the time of the faint music issuing into that corner of the garden. She ate lunch alone and when she went out again to continue her gardening activities she was only vaguely conscious of the fact that the shadowy figure of Robert had passed briefly across her field of vision, presumably on his way to the kitchen where she had left a cold salad lunch for him.

It was late afternoon and the shadows were lengthening on the ground before Joyce had finished her current projects in the garden and when she went back indoors to make herself a much-needed cup of coffee, there was no sign of Robert. She went through all the rooms in turn but he was not there. She made a quick, cautious call to Conrad confirming their next meeting, then returned to the garden, sitting on a teak bench in a small arbor to finish her coffee and biscuits. It was almost dark by this time and leaving the coffee tray on the bench she collected her spade, intending to take it back to the garden shed.

She paused by the entrance to Robert's private cinema. Strangely enough, he did not seem to be there. Or at least there was no sound of films being projected this evening. She bent to the door, listening intently. Unless he was showing silent films . . . She made up her mind. It was time they had a serious talk. They could not go on in this manner. She was inside the vestibule now. Robert had constructed a small lobby which featured glass cases containing film stills. Of very old films, of course; mainly from the twenties and thirties. There was an inner door leading to the cinema proper, with its archive material, constructed not only to muffle the sound when films were being projected, but to prevent light spill from the outside.

Very quietly Joyce opened the inner door and glanced through. Yes, there was a film showing, but it appeared to be silent. Then she saw it was one of the Frankenstein series. Odd that there was no sound. Unless Robert had it switched off for some reason. She could not see him for the moment as she had not yet adjusted to the light intensity in here. Her eyes were again directed to the screen; she suddenly felt dizzy and her heart had begun to thump uncontrollably. Was she ill or had she over-exerted herself in her gardening activities today?

Yes, it was the *Bride*. There was Elsa Lanchester in her incredible makeup as the Monster's mate and the hysterical Colin Clive facing the sardonic Ernest Thesiger, both men in their white surgeon's smocks. And here came Karloff himself, clumping clumsily into the laboratory. Or was it Karloff? The screen image seemed to be going out of focus, wavering and insubstantial as mist. Joyce's breath caught in her throat and she stared incredulously at the burning rectangle before her. It was impossible, but there was Robert's face up there on the screen with the other actors. Karloff's massive body and Robert's features! It was impossible but it was happening. And still the silent pantomime went on.

She must be ill. This could not be happening. She pressed the sharp point of her shoe against her right instep. There was pain, certainly, so she was wide awake and not dreaming. Instead she was enmeshed in a nightmare. She looked around desperately for the light switch, could not find it. Then her eyes were caught by something else. The reflected light from the screen was strobing across the floor and winking on the masses of film tins. Robert could not have drawn the curtains across them tonight, as he usually did, to avoid the reflections from the projector beam. Then thunderous music began, startling her so much that she almost fell.

The screen light was falling across Robert's figure now, hunched in a canvas chair at the back of the projection room, apparently intent on the drama being played out before him. Joyce took one step forward, then froze. It was not Robert; someone much taller and more massive, wearing a thick sheepskin coat. She screamed then as the reflected light from the projector made vivid bars across the flat skull and horrific features of Karloff's Monster. The light glinted on the neck bolts and the metal clip on the skull as the leering mouth was turned toward her. Joyce moved then, hardly realizing that scream after scream was still being wrenched from her throat. The paralysis left her. She still had the spade in her hand, having apparently carried it in, though she had not been conscious of having done so.

She went forward rapidly, raining blow after blow on the hideous form in the chair. The music from the screen speakers dinned in her ears as the film came to its climax. Sick and trembling, she at last found the light switch as the final leader of the film ran thrashing off the end of the spool. The noise went on until she pulled out the plug. The silence was thunderous as she turned to the crumpled form of the thing that had been watching the film. Rivers of blood, scarlet splashes on the spade she held in her hand. The face was almost unrecognizable. Joyce fell to her knees as she recognized the shattered remnants of the man who had once been Robert. She must have fainted then because her wrist watch showed that more than two hours had passed when she finally became aware of her surroundings.

Shaking uncontrollably, she dragged herself to her feet. No, it had not been a mirage, but terrible reality. Her brain was working again now. Somehow she forced herself to look at her handiwork. Could the whole ghastly error have been an optical illusion? That somehow the mirror at the back of the hall and the reflection off the hundreds of film cans might have transposed her husband's image on to that of the screen? While the visage of Karloff had been superimposed on to her husband's features? Impossible, surely. And yet the deed was done. Wild thoughts passed through her head. Her first impulse was to ring the police. But how could she explain? No one would believe her. It would mean years of prison at the least and the loss of all of her dreams of a shared future with Conrad. She forced herself into motion, her mind made up.

The keys were on the side of the projection stand where they always were. She went out, her course of action clear. She switched off the light, locked the door, then washed the spade carefully under the garden tap. Cold water would remove all traces of blood, she had read somewhere. Not hot. That could be fatal. When the spade was absolutely clean she dried it thoroughly with a piece of sacking and then thrust it into the earth several times before replacing it in the garden shed. This she locked also. The garden was extremely secluded, with very high hedges and it was a bright moonlit night.

Back in the house, she locked and bolted the front door and poured herself a stiff brandy in the dining room. Fortified, she returned to the garden, procured a big tarpaulin from the shed and then selected Robert's spade, which was much bigger than her own, and more suitable for the night's work. She had already locked the back door of the house and bolted the side gate so no one would disturb her and she had all night. The earth was very friable about eight feet from the hedge, in the spot she had chosen.

She and Robert had always planned to have a York stone terrace there. She would need to be careful. Fortunately, Robert had no living relatives but there would be questions, of course, from friends and neighbors. And after several weeks she would have to report his disappearance to the police. There would be problems, naturally, but they were not insurmountable. And in the course of time, when people's memories had faded, they would come to think that Robert had walked out after a row; or had found another woman. Both she and Conrad were still young and would be able to marry after the statutory period was over.

She breathed deeply as she walked toward the most remote part of the garden. The moon shone on serenely as she began to dig like a madwoman.

V

It was a bright, sunny morning when Joyce went down the front path to check the car. She was meeting Conrad in an hour and they would spend the next fortnight in the Cotswolds. She had told him that Robert was away on business, which frequently happened, and he had asked no questions. She had already telephoned the contractors about the work on the new terrace. She and Robert had often discussed establishing it there, so there was nothing untoward in the request. Especially as the builders already knew of their intentions.

The tarpaulin with its contents was a good eight feet down. Fortunately, the soil had been very easy to work, though it had taken her almost until dawn to accomplish the task. It would be several weeks before the earth would settle, but then the contractors would not arrive on the site until another month had passed, as they had a large number of commissions to fulfill. Joyce walked back to the house for a final check and then again toured the garden to see that everything was in order.

She noticed as she passed the spot where Robert lay that there was a slight mound of earth over the place. She tamped it down with one elegantly shod foot.

Her heart was light as she ran toward the front gate.

"Better dead!" she said.

NANCY KILPATRICK
Creature Comforts

~·~

Nancy Kilpatrick is the award-winning author of eighteen novels, more than two hundred short stories, six collections, one non-fiction book, and has edited thirteen anthologies. Her recent titles include the anthologies Danse Macabre: Close Encounters with the Reaper, Expiration Date *and* nEvermore! Tales of Murder, Mystery & the Macabre, *along with her collection of short fiction,* Vampyric Variations.

Her current work appears in Zombie Apoclaypse: Endgame!, Searchers After Horror, The Darke Phantastique, Blood Sisters: Vampire Stories by Women, The Madness of Cthulhu 2, Stone Skin Bestiary, Dreams from the Witch House: Female Voices of Lovecraftian Horror *and* Innsmouth Nightmares.

About the following story, the author explains: "It always seemed to me that Victor Frankenstein was so driven, he must have had several reasons for creating a monster. Also, the vampire has moved into the present, and I wanted to see how Frankenstein's creation would fare now. The creature likely was in his twenties, around Victor's age. He's described as tall, pale and scarred. Sounds like rock-star material to me . . ."

Only a year ago, plenty of club kids were calling the band *Monster* a bunch of British clones, cheap imitations of *Nine Inch Nails*. Until *Monster* flew the big ocean. Candy, though, had never seen them that way. She always knew *Monster* was brilliant, and Creature, their main man, a rock icon.

Tonight, from Dead Zone's small stage, the four bandboys pounded out heavy bass and garbled archaic lyrics from their latest CD. The sound that crunched through the amps and throbbed from the stack of oversized speakers said *Monster* was definitely headed for big time. Candy wasn't really listening, although her foot tapped automatically to all music. She was watching. Especially the lead.

Creature. Taller than tall. Lean. In his twenties. Long black hair, ear cuffs, trademark small-calibre bullet piercing his left ear lobe. Pasty skin, dead black lipstick, sexy eye makeup. Pale, wet-ice eyes that sliced right through you like chilled blades. Or at least that's how Candy felt whenever he glanced her way.

Fran leaned close, breathing hot, moist air into Candy's ear, and screamed above the music, "He's dangerously cooooool!"

Candy nodded, barely glancing at her friend. She couldn't take her eyes off Creature. She loved his scars.

This close to the stage she could see every one. They streaked his forehead, jaw and cheeks like red sutures, wounds from a battle. Tonight he wore black snake-skin pants, tight as flesh, matching kick-ass boots, and an open chain-mail vest. Signature black-skull bandana wrapped around his head. Under the strobe, criss-crossing red marks flashed over most of his exposed body.

Something about those warrior stripes turned her on. She wondered what it would be like to run the tip of her tongue slowly over them, up the pink mountains, and down into the redder valleys. Would the skin be hard and smooth like a regular scar? Would they open and bleed? They looked so fresh, it was like he'd had surgery yesterday—but the doctor wasn't too good with a needle and thread.

She'd followed the band for a year, since they'd arrived from London, through underground clubs, never missing a gig. And now that they had a home club, she was here every night. Those scars had been the first thing she'd noticed about Creature. And from that moment, she'd been hooked.

Monster cranked it for the last song. At the end, the drummer slammed the cymbals and snares mercilessly, while his foot stomped the bass pedal to death. Creature and the two other axe players ran riffs that broke the sound barrier for sheer volume and speed. She was so close to the speakers, the low notes throbbed through her body, and the blast of sound ruffled her hair.

They had never played so well. The room exploded. Candy's eardrums vibrated, driving her to her feet, screaming and shoving with the rest. Man, if *only* she wasn't so shy, she could *meet* him. Those scars made her sweat sex!

But a dozen groupies clung to the band like mold. Even before Creature jumped down from the stage, adoring hands of both genders grabbed his legs, fondled his crotch. Reached for his scars.

Taped music replaced live. "You have *got* to do it, and I mean now!" Fran yelled.

Candy sighed. Fran was right, but that didn't make it easy. Ground zero, nowhere to backstep to. If she didn't go in there and meet him now, she'd be crawling after him forever. And it didn't take a demon-brain to figure out that the competition was fierce.

She jammed her bag onto the seat, opened it, and pulled out a couple of things. "Watch me," she told Fran, then turned her back.

The mosh-pit at the foot of the stage was packed with drinkers and dancers and she pushed between sweat-streaked bodies towards the corridor that led to the dressing rooms.

She hurried down a dead-black hallway, another strobe flashing, stills from *Night of the Living Dead* glued to the walls. The taped music behind her became muted. The floor sloped downward. She felt hot; her black velvet dress buttoned from the throat to the ankles.

Before she saw them, she heard them: the groupies clustered outside the dressing rooms, stage hands moving equipment, security controlling it all. She'd been back here once before, but lost her nerve. This time, she headed right for the door she'd avoided last time.

"Brake, babe! Nobody drives into the Lab." In front of her loomed a big guy with tattooed biceps, things with wings that flapped when his muscles flexed. His bulk blocked a door with a clean star mark in the center where that symbol had been ripped off. Over it, in blood red, "The Laboratory" had been scrawled.

Man, what could she say? She wanted Creature's autograph? Lame. How the hell could she get past this guy? But being this close made her brave. Stick to the plan, she told herself. "I'm, like, here to interview Creature." She held up the notebook and pencil she'd brought along and waved them in his face. Stupid. Really stupid. He wouldn't fall for it.

"Right. And I'm here to fuck Madonna. Got any ID?"

She handed over the fake press pass Fran had created at the copy shop where she worked. Above her name, and next to the photo, it identified her as a writer with *Chaos*, one of the local entertainment mags.

"Creature don't do interviews. He don't talk to people."

"He'll talk to me," she said boldly. "Tell him I'm here."

He flicked the pass with his finger and gave her a hostile once-over. "Stay, baby sister." He rapped his knuckles on the door three times, then slipped inside.

What am I doing? Candy asked herself. Now's the time to run, before he gets back and bars me from the club. But she couldn't move, or maybe didn't want to. She might not get to meet Creature, but she just had to try.

The muscle came back without her press pass. She expected the worst and was boggled when he said, "Yeah, okay."

He stepped aside and held the door open about an inch. This guy's dumb, she thought, relieved. It made her braver. A little, anyway.

Heart jack-hammering, she pushed the door open.

It was like staring into night space. The room stank of wet rot. The air felt dry electric. She touched the brass knob and got a shock.

In seconds her eyes adjusted. Two black candles had been wedged between the wall and the makeup mirror like torches. Ahead, shuffling in his seat, a dim shape. Remember, nowhere to step back to, she reminded herself. Candy picked up her Doc Martens and moved into the dressing room.

Silence pierced as bad as the music that had so recently punched her eardrums.

"Sit." A raspy voice. No mistaking it. Creature.

Nervous, excited, she looked around. It was hard to see. A kind of cot in the corner, and the chair he sat on. She perched on the edge of the hard cot, facing him.

She'd never been this close to Creature. He sat at the makeup table with the candles behind him, the back of his head reflected in the glass, his front in shadow. Even sitting, he was bigger than she'd realized.

"I, uh . . ." she began, afraid to keep up the lie, but too scared to rely on the truth. "I *know* you don't do many interviews, but . . . You guys are great. *You're* great."

A kind of wheeze came out of him. He held up the press pass. "You are Elizabeth." His English accent was sexy.

"Candy." *That* sounded inane. "I mean, my real name's Elizabeth. Everybody calls me Candy."

Another sound. Maybe the word, "Appropriate"?

More nervous than ever, she fumbled with the pencil and notebook she'd brought with her, trying to look official, hoping to hell he wouldn't ask about the magazine she supposedly wrote for.

She tried to cover it by taking the initiative. "So, how long have you played music?"

"I began with the flute. Nearly two centuries ago."

"Right!" Candy giggled, but she was the only one laughing, so she stopped. "So, you're like, the real Frankenstein or something?" She'd heard this, the rumor in the clubs. What he'd said on MTV recently. His first interview. Great promo.

"No!"

The volume of his voice sliced down her backbone as if it were a scalpel cutting her open. Instinctively, she jumped to her feet.

"Sit. Elizabeth, please." His voice had dimmed to that fine rasp she found so appealing.

She sat, but glanced at the door.

"Victor Frankenstein was the man. I am his creation. Do you not recall his confession, as relayed to Robert Walton and recorded by Mary Shelley?"

What the hell was he talking about? "You mean the book? *Frankenstein?*" Another snort.

"Well, we read it in school," she said hesitantly. Half true. The class read it. She'd skimmed the abridged version. "I saw the movie," she said hopefully.

"He created me, and yet his account was a lie! I am not driven by malice! Oh, of one thing, yes, he quoted me true. Immortal though it has been my misfortune to be, am I not as sensitive as any human being? Do I not feel cold and heat, pain and pleasure? Does not the sun blind my eyes, and the darkness of night stir fear in my heart? Am I not like you, beautiful Elizabeth?"

Wow! Was Creature coming on to her? She couldn't believe her luck. Alone in his dressing room, with the sexiest guy in the world! Fran will die, she thought.

His pause made her remember why she was supposed to be here. She jotted down the last thing he'd said, about her being beautiful. She looked up. "So, uh, what's the real story?"

Creature stood. She was startled by his height. On stage he was enormous, but here, two feet away, he was a giant. He must be eight feet tall! His head skimmed the ceiling as he paced, his hands scraped his knees, although his body seemed to be in proportion. He moved in that lanky, jerky way of his, as though his joints ached, or his legs had been badly broken. The candle glow created shadows in the valleys of the scars that lined his face, chest and arms. Her mother caught Creature on that TV interview and labelled him ugly, but Candy saw the beauty of being wounded.

"He did it for *her*," he finally said.

"Her? Who?"

He paused to look down at Candy, candlelight making his black hair shimmer, and the stitch marks on his face resemble war paint. He was so big! It was as though a warrior god peered down at her. "Elizabeth, of course. He made me for Elizabeth."

She wasn't sure what he was getting at. Then it clicked. He was like these guys who talk as if they're Lestat. Creature was trying to tell her about himself, and "Frankenstein" worked for him. It was a symbol. Of course. All the lyrics of all of *Monster*'s songs had to do with being treated like a nonhuman. An outsider. They talked about being misunderstood and rejected.

Desperately she tried to remember details from the book. Even the different versions of the movie were vague. She couldn't recall anybody named Elizabeth. There was that other film, where the doctor made a female creature, with that great lightning bolt streaking up the sides of her hair. Maybe *she* was Elizabeth. Maybe not. Candy decided she'd better keep her mouth shut as much as possible.

"Say some more about it, okay?"

He had resumed pacing the small room, his steps heavy on the raw wood floor. His arms swung in a strange way, but it just made him more attractive to her eyes. He was different, not one of those pathetic clones on TV, pretty boys who spend all day flossing. Creature was flesh and blood. Human.

"He claimed to love her. Yet, can a man truly love a woman he cannot satisfy?" he said. "You see, Victor was impotent. The crude anatomical examinations of the day produced no physical cause. I would expect a diagnosis today would be the same. His problems lay in the realm of the mind. As you might put it, Victor Frankenstein felt inadequate. Inferior. Perhaps he feared women, or even despised them. Perhaps he despised all of humanity. In any event, he built a creature, me, one who would be what he was not."

"So, he wanted you to, like, be his stand-in with his girlfriend?"

"More. The lover of his soon-to-be bride."

Bits of the story of *Frankenstein* were catching up to her, but not enough that she could piece all this together. She started jotting down a few sentences, but then realized he wasn't really paying attention, so what was the point. She lay the notebook and pencil on the cot. "Look, that's crazy. I mean, she'd have to be crazy not to know it was somebody else in bed with her, right?"

Creature stopped. With one step he was at the cot, sitting next to her. His towering body was cool. Charged. He took her hand and Candy's heart thumped so hard she almost fainted. His nails were long and black, his scarred hand so large it engulfed hers. He was not just big, but strong. He made her feel protected. She looked into his moist eyes, taking in the gashes surrounding them, and breathed in intimacy.

"You so resemble her. More than in name. The same innocent blonde hair and blue eyes. The identical soft demeanor." His finger touched her cheek. A shock ran through her skin, all the way to her crotch. Suddenly, in the candlelight, a glint flashed through his eyes which she interpreted as torment. The moment she felt pity for him, he dropped his head and stared down at the floor.

Her heart reached out to him. She rubbed her palm over the chain mail vest covering his back. "Look, sometimes it helps to get it all out. I mean, this guy, Victor, he sounds like major corruption material. He used you. He was no friend."

Creature turned to her. His black lips twitched, as if they were struggling to smile but just couldn't cut it. "You are understanding, as was my Elizabeth. If only I had not loved her . . ."

Candy didn't like hearing about this old girlfriend, but maybe if he talked about it, he'd get over her. "So, how did she find out she was screwing the wrong guy?"

"On her wedding night. I am, as you have surely noticed, large even for this day. Then I was as another species, although my entire body is in proportion. Even in the darkness of the boudoir, she could not fail to detect a difference between the man with whom she had made her vows that morning, and the one who possessed her body and soul that warm Victorian night. And yet she was too sweet, too gentle to voice her concerns."

She didn't really want to hear the detail of their sex life. "Well, you must look different, too, right?"

"Alas, but no. Victor, as with all architects of abominations, had fashioned his creation in his own image. In my case, in every respect but stature. And, of course, these remnants of his inept hand."

Candy stared at the large scar running the length of his cheek. She wanted so much to touch it. To kiss it. To run her tongue along the red groove. Embarrassed, she looked away and said, "Wow! So she really didn't know for sure you weren't Victor until you two made it. 'Cause you were in the dark and all. Man, that's truly weird."

"Indeed."

"So what happened when she found out you weren't him?"

"At the moment our love was consummated, Elizabeth screamed. Frankenstein abandoned his voyeuristic pursuits and came upon us in a fit of jealous rage."

"He attacked you?"

"With all his might. In my haste to protect myself from his fatal blows, I fear that in the darkness and confusion the unthinkable occurred. Elizabeth was dead."

The silence was like dead air. Finally, Candy asked, "How?"

He raised his hands to his face and sobbed.

Candy jumped to her feet. She stood before him, her legs straddling his, cradling him to her breasts. He didn't have to go on. She remembered now, everything. How Elizabeth had been murdered on her wedding night. And the book said Creature strangled her! And it was really that sick bastard Frankenstein! Something just like that story had happened to Creature and he'd been suffering all alone ever since. Not only was his girlfriend dead, but he was blamed. And he was innocent! Maybe that's why the band moved to North America! He must be so lonely.

While he sobbed, while she held him, stroking the flaky skin down the back of his neck, his arms circled her hips and he clung to her as if she were a life raft. He cried "Elizabeth!" over and over, pulling Candy down onto his lap, and she hugged him tighter.

Candy felt her body locked in his firm grip, as if he could not get enough of her. As if he would never let her go. He needed her. She could be his new Elizabeth, the one who wouldn't die on him.

His hands slid up under her velvet skirt while hers automatically slipped down inside the chain mail vest and found the scars on his back, on his arms, his chest. The hot gouges in his skin seemed to pump and throb beneath her fingers, calling for her to cool and comfort them. To offer them release. Her flesh fit the wounds as though she had been made to heal him.

She traced the scars that lined his forehead, his cheeks, sliding into the connecting grooves, links in his flesh that now joined the two of them together. Their lips met.

As he entered her, she felt pain and tried to shift into a new position to ease it. "You're hurting me. Let up, huh?"

He gripped her tighter. Her hands tried to pry his from her waist. She shoved at his chest, and struggled to twist out of his embrace, but Creature was too strong, his need too great. She yelled as her fists pounded his shoulders. The pain became excruciating, but he had locked onto her as if they were chained together.

All the while his face hovered before her own, so large, so forlornly sexy, so hopelessly scarred. She reached out a quivering finger to stroke the gash running up his cheek, searching for connection. But if she reached him, it was not in the way she intended; he jammed her body down onto his.

Sharp, like a knife blade inside. He seemed to cut her in two. Candy screamed. Lightning exploded in her head.

One of his massive hands crawled up her body and encircled her throat in a stifling caress. She clawed at the steely grip, but it only made him squeeze harder. All the while tears seeped from his pale eyes. The scars in his cheeks and forehead rippled, and his face contorted. His black lips twisted; she did not want to believe he was smiling.

Candy gasped for air. For some reason it was important for her to choke out one final word. Saying it made it real. "Monster!" But it wasn't the band she had in mind.

ROBERT BLOCH
Mannikins of Horror

*Robert Bloch (1917–1994) was born in Chicago and later
moved to Los Angeles, California, where he worked as a
scriptwriter in movies and television. His interest in the pulp
magazine* Weird Tales *led to a correspondence with author
H. P. Lovecraft, who advised him to try his own hand at
writing fiction. The rest, as they say, is history.*

*Despite having published more than two dozen novels and
over four hundred short stories, he will always be identified
with his 1959 book* Psycho *and Alfred Hitchcock's subsequent film version. In 1993 he published his "Unauthorized
Autobiography,"* Once Around the Bloch.

*At the suggestion of producer Milton Subotsky, "Manni-
kins of Horror" formed the basis for the linking episode of*

the 1972 movie Asylum *(aka* House of Crazies), *which Bloch scripted from his own short stories. Patrick Magee starred as the insane Dr. Rutherford who experimented with creating life in miniature. Unfortunately, because of the low budget, the author's perfectly-formed homunculi were transformed on the screen into unconvincing mechanical toys!*

"I can only claim credit—or blame—for those portions of the film which were shot in accordance with my script," explained the writer. "Considering the handicaps and limitations under which they worked, the producers, director, cast and production people deserve full marks and I can only be grateful for their efforts."

Here's your opportunity to read the original story, with the author's imagination unrestricted by budget limitations . . .

I

Colin had been making the little clay figures for a long time before he noticed that they moved. He had been making them for years there in his room, using hundreds of pounds of clay, a little at a time.

The doctors thought he was crazy; Doctor Starr in particular, but then Doctor Starr was a quack and a fool. He couldn't understand why Colin didn't go into the workshop with the other men and weave baskets, or make rattan chairs. That was useful "occupational therapy," not foolishness like sitting around and modeling little clay figures year in and year out. Doctor Starr always talked like that, and sometimes Colin longed to smash his smug, fat face. "Doctor" indeed!

Colin knew what he was doing. He had been a doctor once: Doctor Edgar Colin, surgeon—and brain surgeon at that. He had been a renowned specialist, an authority, in the days when young Starr was a bungling, nervous intern. What irony! Now Colin was shut up in a madhouse, and Doctor Starr was his keeper. It was a grim joke. But mad though he was, Colin knew more about psychopathology than Starr would ever learn.

Colin had gone up with the Red Cross base at Ypres; he had come down miraculously unmangled, but his nerves were shot. For months after that final blinding flash of shells Colin had lain in a coma at the hospital, and when he had recovered they said he had *dementia praecox*. So they sent him here, to Starr.

Colin asked for clay the moment he was up and around. He wanted to work. The long, lean hands, skilled in delicate cranial surgery, had not lost their cunning—their cunning that was like a hunger for still more difficult tasks. Colin knew he would never operate again; he wasn't Doctor Colin any more, but a psychotic patient. Still he had to work. Knowing what he did about mental disorders, his mind was tortured by introspection unless he kept busy. Modeling was the way out.

As a surgeon he had often made casts, busts, anatomical figures copied from life to aid his work. It had been an engrossing hobby, and he knew the organs, even the complicated structure of the nervous system, quite perfectly. Now he worked in clay. He started out making ordinary little figures in his room. Tiny mannikins, five or six inches high, were molded accurately from memory. He discovered an immediate knack for sculpture, a natural talent to which his delicate fingers responded.

Starr had encouraged him at first. His coma ended, his stupor over, he had been revivified by this new-found interest. His early clay figures gained a great deal of attention and praise. His family sent him funds: he bought instruments for modeling. On the table in his room he soon placed all the tools of a sculptor. It was good to handle instruments again; not knives and scalpels, but things equally wonderful: things that cut and carved and reformed bodies. Bodies of clay, bodies of flesh—what did it matter?

It hadn't mattered at first, but then it did. Colin, after months of painstaking effort, grew dissatisfied. He toiled eight, ten, twelve hours a day, but he was not pleased—he threw away his finished figures, crumpled them into brown balls which he hurled to the floor with disgust. His work wasn't good enough.

The men and women looked like men and women in miniature. They had muscles, tendons, features, even epidermal layers and tiny hairs Colin placed on their small bodies. But what good was it? A fraud, a sham. Inside they were solid clay, nothing more—and that was wrong. Colin wanted to make complete miniature mortals, and for that he must study.

It was then that he had his first clash with Doctor Starr, when he asked for anatomy books. Starr laughed at him, but he managed to get permission.

So Colin learned to duplicate the bony structure of man, the organs, the quite intricate mass of arteries and veins. Finally, the terrific triumph of learning glands, nerve structure, nerve endings. It took years, during which Colin made and destroyed a thousand clay figures. He made clay skeletons, placed clay organs in tiny bodies. Delicate, precise work. Mad work, but it kept him from thinking. He got so he could duplicate the forms with his eyes closed. At last he assembled his knowledge, made clay skeletons and put the organs in them, then allowed for pinpricked nervous system, blood vessels, glandular organization, dermic structure, muscular tissue—everything.

And at last he started making brains. He learned every convolution of the cerebrum and cerebellum; every nerve ending, every wrinkle in the gray matter of the cortex. Study, study, disregard the laughter, disregard the thoughts, disregard the monotony of long years imprisoned; study, study make the perfect figures, be the greatest sculptor in the world, be the greatest surgeon in the world, be a creator.

Doctor Starr dropped in every so often and subtly tried to discourage such fanatical absorption. Colin wanted to laugh in his face. Starr was afraid this work was driving Colin madder than ever. Colin knew it was the one thing that kept him sane.

Because lately, when he wasn't working, Colin felt things happen to him. The shells seemed to explode in his head again, and they were doing things to his brain—making it come apart, unravel like a ball of twine. He was disorganizing. At times he seemed no longer a person but a thousand persons, and not one body, but a thousand distinct and separate structures, as in the clay men. He was not a unified human being, but a heart, a lung, a liver, a bloodstream, a hand, a leg, a head—all distinct, all growing more and more disassociated as time went on. His brain and body were no longer an entity. Everything within him was falling apart, leading a life of its own. Nerves no longer coordinated with blood. Arm didn't always follow leg. He recalled his medical training, the hints that each bodily organ lived an individual life.

Each cell was a unit, for that matter. When death came, you didn't die all at once. Some organs died before others, some cells went first. But it shouldn't happen in life. Yet it did. That shell shock, whatever it was, had resulted in a slow unraveling. And at night Colin would lie and toss, wondering how soon his body would fall apart—actually fall apart into twitching hands and throbbing heart and wheezing lungs; separated like the fragments torn from a spoiled clay doll.

He had to work to keep sane. Once or twice he tried to explain to Doctor Starr what was happening, to ask for special observation—not for his sake, but because perhaps science might learn something from data on his case. Starr had laughed, as usual. As long as Colin was healthy, exhibited no morbid or homicidal traits, he wouldn't interfere. Fool!

Colin worked. Now he was building bodies—real bodies. It took days to make one; days to finish a form complete with chiseled lips, delicate aural and optical structures correct, tiny fingers and toenails perfectly fitted. But it kept him going. It was fascinating to see a table full of little miniature men and women!

Doctor Starr didn't think so. One afternoon he came in and saw Colin bending over three little lumps of clay with his tiny knives, a book open before him.

"What are you doing there?" he asked.

"Making the brains for my men," Colin answered.

"Brains? Good God!"

Starr stooped. Yes, they *were* brains! Tiny, perfect reproductions of the human brain, perfect in every detail, built up layer on layer with unconnected nerve endings, blood vessels to attach them in craniums of clay!

"What—" Starr exclaimed.

"Don't interrupt. I'm putting in the thoughts," Colin said.

Thoughts? That was sheer madness, beyond madness. Starr stared aghast. Thoughts in brains for clay men?

Starr wanted to say something then. But Colin looked up and the afternoon sun streamed into his face so that Starr could see his eyes. And Starr crept out quietly under that stare; that stare which was almost—*godlike*.

The next day Colin noticed that the clay men moved.

II

"Frankenstein," Colin mumbled. "I am Frankenstein." His voice sank to a whisper. "I'm not like Frankenstein. I'm like God. Yes, like God."

He sank to his knees before the tabletop. The two little men and women nodded gravely at him. He could see thumbprints in their flesh, his thumbprints, where he'd smoothed out the skulls after inserting the brains. And yet they lived!

"Why not? Who knows anything about creation, about life? The human body, physiologically, is merely a mechanism adapted to react. Duplicate that mechanism *perfectly* and why won't it live? Life is electricity, perhaps. Well, so is thought. Put thought into perfect simulacra of humanity and they will live."

Colin whispered to himself, and the figures of clay looked up and nodded in eerie agreement.

"Besides, I'm running down. I'm losing my identity. Perhaps a part of my vital substance has been transferred, incorporated in these new bodies. My—my disease—that might account for it. But I can find out."

Yes, he could find out. If these figures were animated by Colin's life, then he could control their actions, just as he controlled the actions of his own body. He created them, gave them a part of his life. They *were* him.

He crouched there in the barred room, thinking, concentrating. And the figures moved. The two men moved up to the two women, grasped their arms, and danced a sedate minuet to a mentally-hummed tune; a grotesque dance of little clay dolls, a horrid mockery of life.

Colin closed his eyes, sank back trembling. It was true!

The effort of concentration had covered him with perspiration. He panted, exhausted. His own body felt weakened, drained. And why not? He had directed four minds at once, performed actions with four bodies. It was too much. But it was real.

"I'm God," he muttered. "God."

But what to do about it? He was a lunatic, shut away in an asylum. How to use his power?

"Must experiment, first," he said aloud.

"What?"

Doctor Starr had entered, unobserved. Colin cast a hasty glance at the table, found to his relief that the mannikins were motionless.

"I was just observing that I must experiment with my clay figures," he said, hastily.

The doctor arched his eyebrows. "Really? Well, you know, Colin, I've been thinking. Perhaps this work here isn't so good for you. You look peaked, tired. I'm inclined to think you're hurting yourself with all this; afraid hereafter I'll have to forbid your modeling work."

"Forbid it?"

Doctor Starr nodded.

"But you can't—just when I've—I mean, you can't! It's all I've got, all that keeps me going, alive. Without it I'll—"

"Sorry."

"You can't."

"I'm the doctor, Colin. Tomorrow we'll take away the clay. I'm giving you a chance to find yourself, man, to live again—"

Colin had never been violent until now. The doctor was surprised to find lunatic fingers clawing at his throat, digging for the jugular vein with surgically skilled fingers. He went over backward with a bang, and fought the madman until the aroused guards came and dragged Colin off. They tossed him on his bunk and the doctor left.

It was dark when Colin emerged from a world of hate. He lay alone. They had gone, the day had gone. Tomorrow they and the day would return, taking away his figures—his beloved figures. His *living* figures! Would they crumple them up and destroy them, destroy actual *life*? It was murder!

Colin sobbed bitterly, as he thought of his dreams. What he had meant to do with his power—why, there were no limits! He could have built dozens, hundreds of figures, learned to concentrate mentally until he could operate a horde of them at will. He would have created a little world of his own; a world of creatures subservient to him. Creatures for companionship, for his slaves. Fashioning different types of bodies, yes, and different types of brains. He might have reared a private little civilization.

And more. He might have created a race. A new race. A race that bred. A race that was developed to aid him. A hundred tiny figures, hands trained, teeth filed, could saw through his bars. A hundred tiny figures to attack the guards, to free him. Then out into the world with an army of clay: a tiny army, but one that could burrow deeply in the earth, travel hidden and unseen into high places. Perhaps, some day, a world of little clay men, trained by him. Men that didn't fight stupid wars to drive their fellows mad. Men without the brutal emotions of savages, the hungers and lusts of beasts. Wipe out flesh! Substitute godly clay!

But it was over. Perhaps he was mad, dreaming of these things. It was over. And one thing he knew: without the clay he would be madder still. Tonight he could feel it, feel his body slipping. His eyes, staring at the moonlight, didn't seem to be a part of his own form any longer. They were watching from the floor, or from over in the corner. His lips moved, but he didn't feel his face. His voice spoke, and it seemed to come from the ceiling rather than from his throat. He was crumpling himself, like a mangled clay figure.

The afternoon's excitement had done it. The great discovery, and then Starr's stupid decision. Starr! He'd caused all this. He was responsible. He'd drive him to madness, to a horrid, unnamed mentally-diseased state he was too blind to comprehend. Starr had sentenced him to death. If only he could sentence Starr!

Perhaps he could.

What was that? The thought came from far away—inside his head, outside his head. He couldn't place his thoughts any more—body going to pieces like this. What was it now?

Perhaps he could kill Starr.

How?

Find out Starr's plans, his ideas. How?

Send a clay man.

What?

Send a clay man. This afternoon you concentrated on bringing them to life. They live. Animate one. He'll creep under the door, walk down the hall, listen to Starr. If you animate the body, *you'll* hear Starr.

Thoughts buzzing so . . .

But how can I do that? Clay is clay. Clay feet would wear out long before they got down the hall and back. Clay ears—perfect though they may be—would shatter under the conveyance of actual sounds.

Think. Make the thoughts stop buzzing. There is a way . . .

Yes, there was a way! Colin gasped. His insanity, his doom, were his salvation! If his faculties were being disorganized, and he had the power of projecting himself into clay, why not project special faculties into the images? Project his hearing into the clay ears by concentration? Remodel clay feet until they were identical replicas of his own, then concentrate on walking. His body, his senses, were falling apart. Put them into clay!

He laughed as he lit the lamp, seized a tiny figure and began to recarve the feet. He kicked off his own shoes, studied carefully, looked at charts worked, laughed, worked—and it was done. Then he lay back on the bed in darkness, thinking.

The clay figure was climbing down from the table. It was sliding down the leg, reaching the floor. Colin felt his feet tingle with shock as they hit the floor. Yes! *His* feet.

The floor trembled, thundered. Of course. Tiny vibrations, unnoticed by humans, audible to clay ears. *His* ears.

Another part of him—Colin's actual eyes—saw the little creeping figure scuttle across the floor, saw it squeeze under the door. Then darkness, and Colin sweated on the bed, concentrating.

Clay Colin could not see. He had no eyes. But instinct, memory guided.

Colin walked in the giant world. The foot came out, the foot of Colossus. Colin edged closer to the woodwork as the trampling monster came down, crashing against the floor with monstrous vibrations.

Then Colin walked. He found the right door by instinct—the fourth door down. He crept under, stepped up a foot onto the carpet. At least, the grassy sward seemed a foot high. His feet ached as the cutting rug bit swordblades into his soles. From above, the thunder of voices. Great titans roared and bellowed a league in the air.

Doctor Starr and Professor Jerris. Jerris was all right; he had vision. But Starr . . .

Colin crouched under the mighty barrier of the armchair, crept up the mountainside to the great peaks of Starr's bony knees. He strained to distinguish words in the bellowing.

"This man Colin is done for, I tell you. Incipient breakdown. Tried to attack me this afternoon when I told him I was removing his clay dolls. You'd think they were live pets of his. Perhaps he thinks so."

Colin clung to the pants-cloth below the knees. Blind, he could not know if he would be spied; but he must cling close, high, to catch words in the tumult.

Jerris was speaking.

"Perhaps he thinks so. Perhaps they are. At any rate—what are you doing with a doll on your leg?"

Doll on your leg? Colin!

Colin on the bed in his room tried desperately to withdraw life; tried to withdraw hearing and sensation from the limbs of his clay self, but too late. There was an incredulous roar: something reached out and grasped him, and then there was an agonizing squeeze . . .

Colin sank back in bed, sank back into a world of red, swimming light.

III

Sun shone in Colin's face. He sat up. Had he dreamed?

"Dreamed?" he whispered.

He whispered again. "Dreamed?"

He couldn't hear. He was deaf.

His ears, his hearing faculty, had been focused on the clay figure, and it was destroyed last night when Starr crushed it. Now he was deaf!

The thought was insanity. Colin swung himself out of bed in panic, then toppled to the floor.

He couldn't walk!

The feet were on the clay figure, he'd willed it, and now it was crushed. He couldn't walk!

Disassociation of his faculties, his members. It was real, then! His ears, his legs, had in some mysterious way been lent vitally to that crushed clay man. Now he had lost them. Thank heaven he hadn't sent his eyes!

But it was horror to stare at the stumps where his legs had been; horror to feel in his ears for bony ridges no longer there. It was horror and it was hate. Starr had done this. Killed a man, crippled him.

Right then and there Colin planned it all. He had the power. He could animate his clay figures, and then give them a *special* life as well. By concentrating, utilizing his peculiar physical disintegration, he could put part of himself into clay. Very well, then. Starr would pay.

Colin stayed in bed. When Starr came in the afternoon, he did not rise. Starr mustn't see his legs, or realize that he could no longer hear. Starr was talking, perhaps about the clay figure he'd found last night, clinging to his leg; the clay figure he'd destroyed. Perhaps he spoke of destroying these clay figures that he now gathered up, together with the rest of the clay. Perhaps he asked after Colin's health: why he was in bed.

Colin feigned lethargy, the introspection of the schizoid. And Starr gathered up the rest of the clay and went away.

Then Colin smiled. He pulled out the tiny clay form from under the sheets; the one he'd hidden there. It was a perfect man, with unusually muscled arms, and very long fingernails. The teeth, too, were very good. But the figure was incomplete. It had no face.

Colin began to work, very fast there as the twilight gathered. He brought a mirror and as he worked on the figure he smiled at himself as though sharing a secret jest with someone—or something. Darkness fell, and still Colin worked from memory alone; worked delicately, skillfully, like an artist, like a creator, breathing life into clay. Life into clay . . .

IV

"I tell you the damned thing *was* alive!" Jerris shouted. He'd lost his temper at last, forgot his superior in office. "I saw it!"

Starr smiled.

"It was clay, and I crushed it," he answered. "Let's not argue any longer."

Jerris shrugged. Two hours of speculation. Tomorrow he'd see Colin himself, find out what the man was doing. He was a genius, even though mad. Starr was a fool. He'd evidently aggravated Colin to the point of physical illness, taking away his clay.

Jerris shrugged again. The clay—and last night, the memory of that tiny, perfectly formed figure clinging to Starr's pantsleg where nothing could have *stuck* for long. It had *clung*. And when Starr crushed it, there had been a framework of clay bones protruding, and viscera hung out, and it had writhed—or seemed to writhe, in the light.

"Stop shrugging and go to bed," Starr chuckled. It was a matter-of-fact chuckle, and Jerris heeded it. "Quit worrying about a nut. Colin's crazy, and from now on I'll treat him as such. Been patient long enough. Have to use force. And—I wouldn't talk about clay figures any longer if I were you."

The tone was a command. Jerris gave a final shrug of acquiescence and left the room.

Starr switched off the light and prepared to doze there at the night desk. Jerris knew his habits.

Jerris walked down the hall. Strange, how this business upset him! Seeing the clay figures this afternoon had really made him quite sick. The work was so perfect, so wonderfully accurate in miniature! And yet the forms were clay, just clay. They hadn't moved as Starr kneaded them in his fists. Clay ribs smashed in, and clay eyes popped from actual sockets and rolled over the tabletop—nauseous! And the little clay hairs, the shreds of clay skin so skillfully overlaid! A tiny dissection, this destruction. Colin, mad or sane, was a genius.

Jerris shrugged, this time to himself. What the devil! He blinked awake. And then he saw—it.

Like a rat. A little rat. A little rat scurrying down the hall, upright, on two legs instead of four. A little rat without fur, without a tail. A little rat that cast the perfect tiny shadow of—a *man*!

It had a face, and it looked up. Jerris almost fancied he saw its eyes *flash* at him. It was a little brown rat made of clay—no, it was a little clay man like those Colin made. A little clay man, running swiftly toward Starr's door, crawling under it. A perfect little clay man, alive!

Jerris gasped. He was crazy, like the rest, like Colin. And yet it had run into Starr's office, it was moving, it had eyes and a face and it was clay.

Jerris acted. He ran—not toward Starr's door, but down the hall to Colin's room. He felt for keys; he had them. It was a long moment before he fumbled at the lock and opened the door, another before he found the lights, and switched them on.

And it was a terribly long moment he spent staring at the thing on the bed—the thing with stumpy legs, lying sprawled back in a welter of sculpturing tools, with a mirror flat across its chest, staring up at a sleeping face that was not a face.

The moment *was* long. Screaming must have come from Starr's office for perhaps thirty seconds before Jerris heard it. Screaming turned into moans and still Jerris stared into the face that was not a face; the face that changed before his eyes, melting away, scratched away by invisible hands into a pulp.

It happened like that. Something wiped out the face of the man on the bed, tore the head from the neck. And the moaning rose from down the hall . . .

Jerris ran. He was the first to reach the office, by a good minute. He saw what he expected to see.

Starr lay back in his chair, throat flung to one side. The little clay man had done its job and Doctor Starr was quite dead. The tiny brown figure had dug perfectly-formed talons into the sleeping throat, and with surgical skill applied talons, and perhaps teeth, to the jugular at precisely the most fatal spot in the vein. Starr died before he could dislodge the diabolically clever image of a man, but his last wild clawing had torn away the face and head.

Jerris ripped the monstrous mannikin off and crushed it; crushed it to a brown pulp between his fingers before others arrived in the room.

Then he stooped down to the floor and picked up the torn head with the mangled face, the miniature, carefully-modeled face that grinned in triumph, grinned in death.

Jerris shrugged himself into a shiver as he crushed into bits the little clay face of Colin, the creator.

DANIEL FOX
El Sueño de la Razón

❦

Daniel Fox is a British writer who first went to Taiwan at the millennium and became obsessed with the culture, to the point of learning Mandarin and writing about the country in three different genres, most notably in his mythic Moshui trilogy of fantasy novels, Dragon in Chains, Jade Man's Skin *and* Hidden Cities.

Before this he had published a couple of dozen books and many hundreds of short stories under a clutch of other names. He has also written poetry and plays, and some of this work has won awards.

"I've always read Frankenstein *as a tragedy rather than a horror story,"* observes the author, *"more sad than terrible. The keystone of all tragedy, of course, is inevitability: it's the*

inherent necessity of disaster that appalls. Making a man is easy, compared to the challenge of making a place for such a man in a world peopled by the rest of us; and we know that, and we nod wisely and shake our heads in sorrow more than anger, and murmur that saviors should always be sought, never achieved.

"And as ever, the more we know, the more we seek to know. That's inevitable. Only bring us fire and the blastfurnace must follow. Time's coming when making a man or woman to prescription will be comparatively easy; and what can be done will be done. That's inherent. And by definition, what follows will simply be necessary . . ."

Reason is sleeping, in the village and the castle both.

Reason is sleeping: and up in the castle the doctor sharpens his bone-saw and tests the edge on his scalpels, polishes them brightly on the sleeve of his white coat. In the village below there are crutches and eye-patches, empty sleeves and absent organs; every torso has its scars. And the villagers watch the sky hopefully for signs of an incipient, a beneficent storm: and they bless the good and fruitful doctor, bless him and bless him . . .

Reason is sleeping: and in a world with too many children, here's a child that all the world can welcome.

Planned even to genetic level, every building-block examined and found good, he has Nobel prizes and Olympic golds in his near ancestry, beauty and vigor and health. His immaculate conception occurs under a microscope, under the eyes of the foremost specialists; his host-mother has passed every selection test they could devise, physical and psychological both. She spends all the months of her pregnancy in an exclusive nursing-home, constantly monitored, her exercise and diet rigorously controlled.

Brought forth by Caesarean at the optimum time, he is named—after long argument—Nathaniel; but that's disingenuous. No gift from any

God, he. They made him themselves, nor do they intend to share the praise. His host-mother is sewn up and sent away, much the richer and legally bound.

His foster-parents have been similarly chosen. Nothing overlooked, nothing left to chance: here are two people well paid to be perfect, nor will they fail in that. Conceived in glass vessels, Nathaniel will be raised also under glass, the epitomic hothouse child, encyclopedias in his cot and the total concentration of two adults through all his crucial years.

It'll be the best and most challenging life that money can buy, for the best lad that humankind can create . . .

Reason is sleeping: five hours a night were enough. Even here, even in this wretched company his discipline held good. He had come to bed with the others, he'd slept his regular time, and now he was awake again.

And had hours to fill before the six o'clock reveille; and while he wasn't bored, while he'd never understood how that was possible, still it wasn't easy to find a use for dead time in the darkness, too far from his books and computers, his TV and his radio.

All he had with him was his pocket chess, running on a program he'd written himself. *Start stupid, learn fast*: every game the computer played it got better, it learned from his victories and its own mistakes. So that's what he was doing now, he was tutoring his chess set, playing it game after game and letting it learn.

But he could still do that on autopilot, it wasn't smart enough yet to give him any kind of contest. As his fingers played, his mind moved on other pathways, considering the values of things. As of the softly glowing symbols in his lap, the knight and the bishop and the rook, each ascribed a value according to what it could achieve. And the queen, of course, strong and beautiful and by far the best of them, head and shoulders above the rest. Power and responsibility, the farsighted strategist with a fist of iron . . .

He teased White's queen into what seemed to him a ludicrously obvious trap, and took it with a pawn.

Not good enough, he thought sadly; and in honesty, he thought, she never would be. The fault lay with the piece, not the player. The most powerful piece on the board, yes—but still it wasn't enough if a pawn could bring her down, if stupidity could undo her. *Not good enough* was the doom of most things, was certainly his own.

Six o'clock, and a whistle blew; and Nathaniel was instantly out of his bunk and pulling on his tracksuit, neat and efficient and fast. Feet into running shoes, velcro fasteners and he was off. Five compulsory laps of the camp, about four miles in all: and if he was first out, he could run alone all the way so long as he remembered to hold himself back after the first mile, not to catch up with the stragglers. Alone was easier, alone was always easier.

So he ran, and he came in from running breathing easy, running down. Into the shower and a fast shampoo and he was finished, he was coming out as the others started to arrive.

Even amid their hot jostling bodies, he avoided their eyes. He was good at that, too. Programmed for it, by now. *Start stupid, learn fast.*

Not possible at breakfast, though, at communal tables with plates and dishes and jugs constantly passing, the day's teams to be selected and projects to be announced. Best he could manage here was to be quiet, amiable, inoffensive.

Not easy sitting next to Raoul, who had been frightened on the mast of the training ship over the weekend, who had needed Nathaniel's cool strength to help him down, who had refused to swim underneath the hull and cost their team points all along the line.

Or sitting opposite Charlotte who was national chess champion at fifteen, who was acclaimed the best player the nation had so far produced, who had lost three times to Nathaniel in one afternoon and wouldn't play him any more, saying that she couldn't understand his game, it was too deep for her, too different.

Or sitting at the same table or the next table or simply in the same hall as Peter and Annie and Josephine, Tarian and Michaela. Three weeks he'd been here, and in that time he'd upset or embarrassed or offended almost everyone he'd come into contact with. None of that was of his making, except that he couldn't lie and wouldn't dissemble. If a thing was so, he would say so; if not, again he would say. If a game was to be played, he would play it as best he could within the rules. If he was better or faster or stronger than the others, then he would win.

And he was better, faster, stronger, as he always had been: that was simply the way the world was. And the others resented it, some of them hated him for it; and that too was the way the world was, and always had been.

And it didn't matter how good he was, he still wasn't good enough. That was inherent in the piece. He'd been trained to command and trained to follow orders, but something was missing in him, something he lacked to make them love him.

And he only knew one way to find it, as he only knew one way to live: to be better, to try harder, to learn more and win by a greater margin. It was the constant theme of his childhood, playing on in his adolescence. *Not good enough, you must shine more brightly. So much potential, it must not be wasted; but only you can drive yourself to your limits. We can't reach that far. What you achieve is in your own hands now, all we can do is make opportunities.*

Drive he had in abundance, and motive too. The race is to the swift, and the battle to the strong; only winners got the glittering prizes. If he outreached even the ambitions held for him, if he could shine blazingly bright, surely then he'd earn more than a nod of satisfaction and a harder challenge next time round . . .

The camp leader was generally held to be a bastard. A softspoken, smiling man, he was softly and smilingly unbending even to his favorites, and pitiless on defaulters.

Today at breakfast he left them eating longer than usual, until appetites were sated; then a single stroke of his little bell, and those few who weren't already watching him turned as he rose to his feet, interest and apprehension mixing on their faces.

"Well," he said, "I think we've mollycoddled you long enough." And smiled, spread his hands disarmingly, paused a moment. Didn't seem at all perturbed that his little joke raised not a smile, broke no one's concentration. "You're all fit," he went on, "you're all intelligent and adaptable; you were demonstrably self-reliant and you already understood something of teamwork, or you would never have been accepted here. These last weeks, I hope we've underlined what you knew before, honed your bodies to a sharper edge and taught you a little more about yourselves and each other.

"Today, we really start to test you.

"From now on, it's for real. Special risks, special opportunities. You'll be divided into teams, and given various targets to achieve. For the next fortnight those teams will eat together, work together, sweat and suffer and weep together. Sleep together if you want to, but only if your leader thinks it's good for the team.

"Each team will have a leader, chosen by me: this is not a democracy. But here on in, there will be no supervision. You're on your own out there. Your safety will be entirely in your own hands; there will be no staff looking out for you, no one to step in and rescue if you're stupid.

"So don't be. We've had accidents every year, you must expect emergencies and disaster; and while we've never lost a camper yet, it's statistically certain to happen sometime. Every year that passes, the odds get worse. Remember this. The odds are *not* in your favor out there; so take every precaution you can think of, take care, don't be stupid.

"But don't fail, either. Don't be weak."

The team selection might not have been deliberately malicious, but Nathaniel thought that quite probably it was. The staff liked him no more than the other campers; they envied his future, he thought, his bright and burning future, and so sought to make his present as difficult as they were able.

Nothing new there. Sometimes he wondered when this supposed future would finally begin. Ten years ago, he'd been sure to have achieved it by sixteen; from here it seemed as far away as ever, a golden dream blocked off by a wall of days, dark days heaped one upon another.

But be it accident or design, Nathaniel found himself teamed with Raoul and with Charlotte, with Peter and Josephine, Tarian and Michaela. Almost his entire roll-call of the ill-disposed; and no, surely this couldn't be accidental. The staff watched them too closely to get it so very wrong.

Nor was Nathaniel appointed leader, though his record at the camp must have required that. *Best at everything but still not good enough, huh?* he thought ruefully, as the job went to Josephine.

Perhaps he maligned them, though. On his way back to the dormitory to pack—"just one bag, and bare essentials only. Remember, you've got to carry it; but remember, you can't come back for what you've forgotten or thought you wouldn't need"—he was taken aside by one of the climbing instructors, a man he liked better than most.

"Here," the man said, "I want you to carry this, in case of an emergency. Every team gets one; but don't tell your team leader, or anyone else."

"What is it?" The question was instinctive, but actually, taking the device and turning it over in his hands, Nathaniel knew already what it was. A small black sealed unit on a stiff cord, a light amulet of rubberized plastic, no marks on it, no distinguishing features—in the circumstances, there was really only one thing it could be.

"Panic button," the man said, a beat behind Nathaniel's mind. "We do have responsibilities. There'll be a helicopter standing by, never more than half an hour's flight away. Better if the team doesn't know that, though. A promise of rescue makes people careless."

"Why choose me?"

The man shrugged. "Because you won't tell the others. And you're better equipped than most, to decide what constitutes a genuine emergency. You won't panic, and you're not too proud to know when you do need help. Get out by yourselves if you can, of course; but call for us if you must. Whatever the leader says, we really don't want a fatality. Not good for business."

Nathaniel nodded. "How does the button work, then, just with a squeeze?"

"Squeeze and hold. There's a switch inside, but it needs constant pressure for a couple of seconds, or it won't activate. That's just a precaution against accidental knocks. Then it triggers an alarm here, which is constantly monitored; and after that it acts as a radio beacon for the helicopter. Wear it round your neck; there's an aerial inside the cord. Try not to get separated from your team, or you're the only one we'll find.

And just getting separated, getting lost does *not* count as an emergency. Understood?"

Nathaniel nodded, slipped the cord over his head and tucked the button inside his T-shirt.

Two hours later, with wet suits and waterproof packs, he and his team sat in a flat-bellied Zodiac being bumped across a hard and rising sea.

The shore was lost behind them, in a mist of spray and grey cloud. Shadows ahead and to either side resolved themselves as rocks or clusters of rock; occasionally the wind whipped a hole in the mist long enough for Nathaniel to think he could see a longer, bulkier shadow on the near skyline, the promise of an island. Certainly there ought to be islands. Orientation wasn't easy in this enveloping murk, but he knew how long since they left camp, he knew the direction roughly and the top speed of a Zodiac; after three weeks here he knew the coastline and the maps. Yes, there ought to be islands all around them.

And yes, sudden as a whale, there was an island dead ahead, the navigation reassuringly professional and precise.

Not much of an island, only a low silhouette with a softer outline than the rocks they'd passed already. Perhaps not a full-blown whale, then, perhaps only a calf; but every calf has a mother. He squinted to windward, thought perhaps he spotted her, though perhaps he only wanted to.

The man on the tiller edged the black craft through the surf, till Nathaniel felt its bottom scrape on rock. The air was drenched with spray here; he choked on salt, as the wind flung it against his teeth.

"Out you get, then," the man shouted. "Don't leave anything behind, I'm not coming back."

"What are we supposed to do?" Josephine demanded.

"Survive, and keep moving. That's all. Pick-up point is on Jamesay, forty-eight hours from now."

"How the hell do we get there?" They knew Jamesay; they'd circumnavigated her in the three-masted schooner last week. At the time, they'd thought they were only learning to sail a big vessel in a contrary wind.

Nathaniel consulted a sketch-map in his head. Jamesay must be twenty miles south of here, and five miles further out to sea.

The man shrugged, uninterested. "That's up to you. Out you get, now. Move it."

Bewildered, angry or uncertain, they were all none the less obedient by now. One by one they jumped out into almost a meter's depth of bitter water, feeling a steep-shelving stony shore below their feet. They hurried up out of the surf with packs clutched in their arms, then turned and stood in a tight group, unspeaking, to watch the Zodiac bounce away over the water.

The man on the tiller didn't wave, didn't call a farewell, didn't look back.

What now? was the question no one asked, a confession of weakness and a pointless waste of breath.

"There'll be something," Josephine said. "There must be something, they don't expect us to *swim* it. Split into two, we'll go opposite ways around the shore. Meet on the far side, and report."

So they did that, jogging for warmth and speed, as best they could on the treacherous ground. The two groups lost sight of each other fast in the haze, but the island was as small as Nathaniel had thought; they met up again fifteen minutes later.

"Nothing."

"Us neither. Not a thing."

So they climbed instead to the island's crown, and from there could just make out all of its shoreline; and no, there was no boat, nor anything to build with.

"Ideas?" Josephine looked around her team; and when no one else spoke, Nathaniel pointed out what seemed so obvious to him, what surely shouldn't have needed saying.

"The tide's high."

"How can you tell?"

"No high water mark. Where the surf's reaching now, that must be its limit."

"Okay. So the tide's in. So?"

"So if there's no boat and they're not expecting us to swim, we can walk off. Or scramble, anyway. Look," pointing, "there's a bigger island to the east there. It's hardly any distance, if we could see clearly. And the tidal fall is bound to be significant, in an environment like this. At low water, I bet we'll be able to make our way over, pretty much dryshod. You can see, those rocks almost make a causeway already, or the start of one . . ."

He was right, and they knew it; and they weren't grateful, but he hadn't expected that.

They sheltered in the driest crevice they could find, where the island was split down to bedrock. Six hours more or less to kill, before they tried the crossing; and Raoul produced a knife.

"We're a team," he said, "we depend on each other. We need to bond. A sign, a symbol would be helpful. What I feel, you all feel also."

And he laid the blade across the palm of his hand; but Josephine stopped him.

"No," she said. "I'll do it. I'll do it for all of you. I'm leader."

She took the knife from him, held his open hand firmly in hers and drew the blade deeply through the pad of flesh below his thumb. He flinched but didn't pull away, didn't take his eyes from hers.

"Good," she said. "You'll feel that. But it won't bleed for long in this cold, and the salt'll keep it clean. Who's next?"

One by one, they offered their hands to her knife, and their blood all mingled on her skin.

Nathaniel came last, thinking this foolish and unnecessary: why do the team damage, when it most needed all its strength? But it would be damaged more by his refusal; he kept his face neutral and held out his hand, already subvocalizing a mantra he had taught himself, a mental trick to suppress pain.

Josephine's hard fingers closed around his, she looked into his eyes, she smiled; and the blade stabbed down, and the point drove through all the flesh of his hand, grating against bone and almost shaking him out of his mantric flux.

Almost, but not quite. Pain's shout was lost in the murmuring of his mind; he held her gaze, and thought he saw more hurt in her than she would have seen in him.

He sat unmoving, until she jerked the knife free; then she held up her hand, and yes, she was bleeding too. The blade had gone all the way through his hand and into hers, as perhaps it had been meant to.

Correction: as certainly it had been meant to.

"If we harm each other," she said—making a virtue, making a lie of it, though not one meant to be believed, by him or anyone—"we also harm ourselves. We're a team, we're bonded now. The team has primacy. Let's remember that."

At the tide's turn, as Nathaniel had predicted, exposed rocks made a road from calf to mother, their small island to its far larger neighbor.

It was a hard road to follow, jumping from one sharp wet tooth of rock to the next, while vicious currents sucked at icegrey water only a little below their feet. But they helped each other: the brave encouraged the nervous or else abused them, whichever was more prolific of result; the strongest made the journey twice or three times, ferrying packs across and offering a hand to grip where it was most needed; and at last they might be soaked with spray and shivering, they might have torn their jeans and the skin on their hands to add more blood-loss to what they'd given already, but they were all safely over. Tumbled together on scant grass, they grinned exhaustedly at each other, punched the air and whooped with what little breath they had left.

No one grinned at Nathaniel, no one so much as glanced in his direction although he'd found the road for them and been both the first and the last across, though he'd carried more than anyone and had barely made it back with his final load, leaping from toehold to toehold on vanishing rocks as the waters rose more quickly than they'd guessed.

He nodded unsmilingly, wishing not to feel it, not to care; he rested for five minutes, and then he went to search along the shoreline.

Under a pegged tarpaulin, he found seven canoes with lifejackets, helmets and paddles.

There were rations there also, a collapsible stove and billycans, everything they needed. No tents, but the tarpaulin was large enough to shelter them all, stretched over a framework of paddles; weighted with rocks and lashed together, the canoes made a useful windbreak.

After they'd eaten they built a fire of driftwood, lighting it—Nathaniel's idea—with wood chips dried in a billy on the stove.

"No map," Tarian said. "They haven't given us a map. How're we going to find Jamesay?"

"Follow the islands down," Nathaniel said. "They're like a chain, all the way; if we stay on the landward side, we'll miss the worst of the weather and the high seas too. Then there's just a mile of open water, we go dead south and there's Jamesay."

"You knew," Charlotte accused him. "You knew what we'd be doing, that's how come you're so well sussed about it all."

"No," he said.

"You just happen to have memorized the charts, then, is that right?"

He shrugged. "I suppose, yes. I looked at them, on the schooner," which was quite enough; he'd learned them at a glance, and he'd never understood about forgetting. Once learned, a thing was with him always. "It's a trick, that's all. Useful, but not significant."

"Like you, then. Right?"

He just looked at her, looked at her frustrated anger and recognized it from their chess games earlier. Emotional maps were no different. Any kind of lesson, the same applied: once learned, never forgotten.

Alas, he thought, and turned his eyes to the fire, where bright flames burned green with salt.

Barely sheltered where he slept, farthest from the windbreak and least in touch, least belonging, he felt no constraint to stay with the team when he woke, when they were still close-huddled in sleep. He rolled out from under the canopy, got to his feet and walked down to the sea's fretful edge. The wind's bite was fierce through damp clothing, but he welcomed the cold of it, and the hard spray in his face.

Staring out at dark water in the hiss and crash of water breaking on rock, he neither saw nor heard her until she was there beside him, touching his arm for attention.

Josephine, of course. Team captain, prime mover: not a bad choice after all, given that any team with himself in charge would have been in a state of constant rebellion. *Start stupid, learn fast:* lessons in the psychology of leadership would never be enough for someone like him, and so he'd tell people if he could only make them listen. In case they meant to try again. *You got me wrong,* he'd tell them, *it doesn't work this way. Evolution's got muddied by democracy, you can't just overleap the majority any more. You'll have to be more careful next time, give the poor bastard some handle on normality or there'll be nothing to hang on to, first or last . . .*

"Remember," Josephine said, her voice tight with distaste, "what he said at breakfast, about sleeping with each other? If it was good for the team?"

"Yes," neutral as he could make it.

"Well, I've been thinking about it. I thought, anything that would make you a part of us, it had to be worth it . . . But it wouldn't work, would it?"

"No," he agreed, still neutral. Still separate. "It's too late for that."

"Yes." It had been too late for a long time now, since his first week in camp. Ever since he'd started stupid, measuring himself publicly against the others.

"You're—artificial," she said, seeking to explain it to herself. "*Built* to be better than us. That's what it is . . ."

"No. Doesn't matter how I happened, I'm as real as you are. No different."

"Better is different. State of the art, right? Real maybe, but—well, hell, humankind cannot bear very much reality. You know?"

"I know," he said, burdened by too much knowledge, far too much reality.

"Okay, then. Nothing changes, I guess."

"I guess not." Nothing ever changed, nor ever would.

He thought she nodded in the darkness, as though she'd caught the thought; and then she turned, back to her sleeping team. And stopped, and turned again, and said, "You know Goya?"

He smiled briefly, bitterly; and killed the smile before he spoke, so that she wouldn't hear it in his voice. "*El sueño de la razón produce monstruos,*" he said.

"Yeah. Right. Hang on to that." And then she was gone, and for once in his life he was uncertain, he was confused. *The sleep of reason begets monsters:* that was inarguable, it was a constant theme in his life. But he couldn't be sure if she'd meant it as an accusation, or an apology.

They set off at first light, with weary work ahead of them if they were to reach Jamesay today. They kept in the lee of the island chain, and swung their paddles in a constant rhythm; and here at least Nathaniel could fool some imagined observer if not himself, if none of the others. He could echo the rhythm precisely and imitate the power of their strokes, he could keep his place and seem no different.

At noon they broke for a meal and a rest in a sheltered bay, and he was again no part of what they were together; and then it was back to the water and aching muscles locked into relentless rhythm, and yes, dwelling on the pain in his hand, he could understand their need for bonding. It would be the only way for some of them to survive this. As usual, though, he understood without sharing. Keeping time was only a pretense. He'd have been better on his own, setting his own rhythms and timing his own rests.

But he stayed with the team, never striking to the front even when they needed that, when it was clear to him that they'd never reach Jamesay before darkfall unless they sprinted. Displace Josephine, he thought, and he was lost, they were all lost.

In fact, they reached open water with just enough light left to show them Jamesay's shadow on the horizon. They could camp again, there'd be time enough tomorrow to make the rendezvous; but camping meant going back, it was half a mile or more since they'd past any land they could beach on. And there'd be no food, no shelter there. They'd be expected to make Jamesay today; there were no allowances for failure.

Clustering together and shouting between canoes, they agreed to go on. Michaela had a compass, she'd take a bearing now and keep them straight. Besides, there were houses on the island, there'd be lights. One last push, they said, and they'd be done. Credit to the team, they thought, to travel by night at need.

Nathaniel took no part in that decision. His only suggestion was that they should call out their names in order as they paddled, so that none of them was separated in the dark.

The life-jackets had luminescent strips also, activated by contact with seawater; those helped to keep them in touch. It was as a group that they headed into the surge of open water, though Nathaniel held himself deliberately a little adrift of the pack, to see more clearly if tiredness or lack of concentration pulled any of the others off course.

And it was as a group, if not as a team, that they met disaster when it came.

Disaster was high and fast and fitting, evidence perhaps of some higher order, envious of its prerogatives: a freak wave aimed at a bunch of freaks, and Nathaniel only the freakiest among them.

No time, no anticipation. Only a sudden warning cry, shrill as a gannet's, and then the water abruptly rising contrary to the steady swell, and the canoes tipping and tumbling and the dark that closed over, cut them off and contained them, gave them cold and crushing weight and nothing to breathe or hope for . . .

Except that these kids didn't hope and didn't panic, they kicked. Training and good sense and life-jackets all dragged them upwards; and when Nathaniel broke surface, when he sucked in a lungful of good wet salty air at last, he looked around and saw figures gasping in the water all around him, amid the dark bobbing shapes of empty canoes.

Those were first priority, and didn't need discussing. Nathaniel struck out for the nearest, and took the nylon painter between his teeth to keep his hands free. Hearing a high whooping call he looked around, saw someone silhouetted briefly against the stars and waving; saw a general drift of his dim-lit companions in that direction and joined it.

It was Josephine, of course, calling them in. Counting lights, counting heads as he swam, Nathaniel counted seven eventually, though he wasn't certain until they were all gathered, all rising and falling together in the heavy swell. Seven meant the whole team, no one missing; but of those seven, only three had brought in their canoes.

Not enough. Lifting himself as high as he could on the one he towed, before it ducked and slithered out from under him, Nathaniel thought he could make out a couple more, slim shadows sliding further into the dark. He took the painter from his mouth and pressed it into the nearest hand he could grab, Raoul's; grunted, "Hold on to that, for God's sake," and plunged off after them, swimming hard for warmth and speed when he should be swimming slow for survival, preserving energy.

Behind him, Josephine's voice called sharply after, but he ignored it. If she couldn't see the need, he didn't have time to explain.

Hard to orient in this heaving, heavy darkness, with the horizon always shifting and tilting and his eyes stinging with wind-hurled water, though he swam head-high and always looking, trying to fix on the stars when he wasn't watching for canoes. Vampire cold sucked at his muscles, for all the heat he could make; without the wet suits, he thought, they might be dead in an hour. With them, with luck and intelligence, they could survive maybe three or four. Till morning, not. He'd doubted it before; he was certain now.

Intelligence they had, luck they could manufacture or achieve—as he did now, chasing the luck that hadn't lost these two canoes, fighting to conserve it.

As much stubborn as strong, bred in part for precisely a need such as this—and sent here, of course, to meet it—he caught up with the luck at last and brought it back, though towing two canoes with his teeth was far harder than one, and reaching the others again against the sea's tug was harder even than finding them.

"What's the point of that?" Josephine demanded when he did rejoin the group. "We had enough already to use as floats, we don't need one each . . ."

And they were doing that already, clinging two or three to a canoe, only kicking their legs sluggishly to keep the blood flowing; but he said, "No, we can do better. Look, with five we can make a frame, four in a square and one diagonal to hold it open. Lash them together with the painters. Then some of us at least can get right out of the water, the ones who need to rest most. We can take it in turns, spell each other . . ."

And again he was right, and they knew it. No one argued. And again they were none of them grateful, though he was maybe saving lives here; he saw resentment in their faces, clear as daylight. And knew that they saw it in each other, and suddenly this felt dangerous. Fire and flood, irresistible forces feeding, massing against him: he knew no way to meet them except to try harder, to be better still.

So it was Nathaniel who swam from canoe to canoe, upturning those that weren't already hull-up and drawing them together, numbed fingers fumbling with nylon rope to knot them into his vision, a raft-frame to support exhausted bodies.

And it was Nathaniel who helped the smallest, the coldest, the most tired aboard, and devised the most stable way for them to lie across the slippery hulls; Nathaniel who was last among the others to reach for a handhold, reaching to grip and cling and be buoyed up against the dragging depths.

Nathaniel who was the only one missing when the helicopter's searchlight finally found them, after twenty minutes' probing of dark waters.

Reason is sleeping: and of course everyone applauds the team's survival, offers comfort to their grief at a companion's loss, encourages the media stories about the boy genius who turned hero at the last and sacrificed himself in his great effort to save others.

And of course no one who was at the camp believes those stories. Reason is sleeping, yes, but not that deeply. Not dreaming in fantasies.

Rumors are mostly unspoken, as the team itself is not speaking of Nathaniel; but rumors spread none the less. People have pictures in their minds: dark water and determined faces, *he shan't be a hero and live, he shan't make us accessories to his triumph. Not again . . .*

Dark water and determined, desperate faces; *No room! No room!* and hands that thrust and punched, nails that clawed and pinched and gouged at flesh and eyes. Too many hands and too much hatred, those are the themes in people's private pictures in the camp.

But those too are dreams, perhaps, though dreaming close to true.

They found the panic button knotted at one of the canoeframe's corners, the button submerged but the aerial cord above the waterline. Tied there and squeezed and held it was, deliberately set off; and none of the team has mentioned it at all.

Nathaniel must have set it there, set it and left it and gone. And maybe the kids did as everyone secretly believes they did, maybe they drove him off; but what haunts the people who know about the button, what draws pictures in their minds is the other possibility.

Maybe, facing the team's active and relentless hostility, Nathaniel had faced in that moment a lifetime of the same, and made his own choice. *Start stupid, learn fast.* Cued by the throbbing in his hand, maybe, he'd maybe quietly tied the button where they needed it, and turned, and swum away.

Maybe it was they after all who were not good enough, the world which failed. That's the thought that haunts their waking dreams, those few who know. And no, they don't discuss it either.

Reason is sleeping, and their beautiful children never stay.

But in the castle, the doctor perseveres; and in the village they are not downcast. They forget the light that failed, and look still for the dawn. Next time, they tell themselves; next time, they tell each other.

And this time, next time, every time they queue to give what they can, and are glad to do it. The doctor honors them, by taking what they have. What they most prize, they give most freely; and what's new?

MANLY WADE WELLMAN
Pithecanthropus Rejectus

━━◆━━

Manly Wade Wellman (1903–1986) was born in Portuguese West Africa. He was one of the great pulp writers of the 1930s and '40s, with more than seventy-five books and over two hundred short stories to his credit. During his long and distinguished career he wrote in almost every genre, including biography, mystery, science fiction, fantasy, horror, juvenile and regional fiction.

He twice won the World Fantasy Award, and some of his best stories are collected in Who Fears the Devil? *(filmed in 1972),* Worse Things Waiting, Lonely Vigils, The Valley So Low *and Night Shade Books' five-volume* The Selected Stories of Manly Wade Wellman *series.*

"Pithecanthropus Rejectus" is generally considered to be one of the author's very best science fiction stories. However, it infuriated a young Lester del Rey, who read it at Christmas time, and was inspired to start writing science fiction to prove he could do much better. Thus was a memorable career launched.

My first memories seem to be those of the normal human child—nursery, toys, adults seriously making meaningless observations with charts, tape measures and scales. Well, rather more than average of that last item, the observations. My constant companion was a fat, blue-eyed baby that drooled and gurgled and barely crept upon the nursery linoleum, while I scurried easily hither and thither, scrambling up on tables and bedposts, and sometimes on the bureau. I felt sorry for him now and then. But he was amazingly happy and healthy, and gave no evidence of having the sudden fearful pains that struck me in head and jaw from time to time.

As I learned to speak and to comprehend, I found out the cause of those pains. I was told by the tall, smiling blond woman who taught me to call her "Mother." She explained that I had been born with no opening in the top of my skull so needed for bone and brain expansion—and that the man of the house—"Doctor"—had made such an opening, governing the growth of my cranium and later stopping the hole with a silver plate. My jaw, too, had been altered with silver, for when I was born it had been too shallow and narrow to give my tongue play. The building of a chin for me and the remodeling of several tongue-muscles had made it possible for me to speak. I learned before the baby did, by several months. I learned to say "Mother," "Doctor," to call the baby "Sidney" and myself "Congo." Later I could make my wants known although, as this writing shows and will show, I was never fluent.

Doctor used to come into the nursery and make notes by the hour, watching my every move and pricking up his ears at my every sound. He was a stout, high-shouldered man, with a strong, square beard. He acted grave—almost stern where I was involved. But with baby Sidney he played most tenderly. I used to feel hurt and would go to Mother for sympathy. She had enough for me and Sidney, too. She would pick me up and cuddle me and laugh—give me her cheek to kiss.

Once or twice Doctor scowled, and once I overheard him talking to Mother just beyond the nursery door. I understood pretty well even then, and since that time I have filled in details of the conversation.

"I tell you, I don't like it," he snapped. "Showering attentions on that creature."

She gave him a ready laugh. "Poor little Congo!"

"Congo's an ape, for all my surgery," he replied coldly. "Sidney is your son, and Sidney alone. The other is an experiment—like a shake-up of chemicals in a tube, or a grafting of twigs on a tree."

"Let me remind you," said Mother, still good-natured, "that when you brought him from the zoo, you said he must live here as a human child, on equal terms with Sidney. That, remember, was part of the experiment. And so are affection and companionship."

"Ah, the little beast!" Doctor almost snarled. "Sometimes I wish I hadn't begun these observations."

"But you have. You increased his brain powers and made it possible for him to speak. He's brighter than any human child his age."

"Apes mature quickly. He'll come to the peak of development and Sidney will forge ahead. That always happens in these experiments."

"These experiments have always been performed with ordinary ape-children before," said Mother. "With your operations you've given him something, at least, of human character. So give him something of human consideration as well."

"I'm like Prospero, going out of my way to lift up Caliban from the brute."

"Caliban meant well," Mother responded, reminding him of something I knew nothing about. "Meanwhile, I don't do things by halves, dear. As long as Congo remains in this house, he shall have kindness and help from me. And he shall look to me as his mother."

I heard and, in time, digested all of this. When I learned to read, during my third year, I got hold of some of Doctor's published articles about me and began to realize what everything meant.

Of course, I'd seen myself in mirrors hundreds of times and knew that I was dark, bow-legged and long-armed, with a face that grew out at an acute angle, and hair all over my body. Yet this had not set me very far apart, in my own mind, from the others. I was different from Sidney—but so was Mother, in appearance, size and behavior. I was closer to them—in speech and such things as table manners and self-reliance—than he. But now I learned and grew to appreciate the difference between me, on one side, and Sidney, Doctor and Mother on the other.

I had been born, I found, in an iron cage at the Bronx Zoo. My mother was a great ape, a Kulakamba, very close to human type in body, size and intelligence—not dwarfed like a common chimpanzee nor thickset and surly like a gorilla. Doctor, a great experimental anthropologist—words like those happen to be easy for me, since they were part of daily talk at Doctor's house—had decided to make observations on a baby ape and his own newborn child, rearing them side by side under identical conditions. I was the baby ape.

Incidentally, I have read in a book called *Trader Horn* that there are no Kulakambas, that they are only a fairy story. But there are—many and many of us, in the Central African forests.

I tell these things very glibly, as if I knew all about them. Doctor had written reams about the Kulakamba, and clippings of all he wrote were kept in the library. I had recourse to them as I grew older.

When I was four, Doctor led me into his big white laboratory. There he examined and measured my hands, grunting perplexedly into his beard.

"We'll have to operate," he said at last.

"Will we?" I quavered. I knew what the word meant.

He smiled, but not exactly cheerfully. "You'll have an anesthetic," he promised, as though it were a great favor. "I want to fix your hands. The thumbs don't oppose and it makes your grasp clumsy. Not human, Congo; not human."

I was frightened, but Mother came to comfort me and say that I would be better off in the long run. So, when Doctor commanded, I lay on the sheet-spread table and breathed hard into the cloth he put on my face. I went to sleep and dreamed of high, green trees and of people like myself who climbed and played there—building nests and eating nuts as big as my head. In my dream I tried to join them, but found myself held back, as if by a pane of glass. That made me shed tears—though some say that apes cannot shed tears—and thus weeping, I awoke. My hands had a dull soreness in them and were swathed in bandages to the elbows. After weeks, I could use them again and found that their calloused palms had been softened, the awkward little thumbs somehow lengthened and newly jointed. I grew so skillful with them that I could pick up a pin or tie a bow knot. This was in the winter time, and once or twice when I played on the porch I had terrible pains in brow and jaw. Doctor said that the cold made my silver plates hurt, and that I must never go outside without a warm cap and a muffler wrapped high.

"It's like a filling against the nerve of a tooth," he explained. At seven I was all about the house, helping Mother very deftly with her work. Now Doctor grew enthusiastic about me. He would lecture us all at the table—Sidney and I ate with him when there was no company—and said that his experiment, faulty in some ways, gave promise of great things along an unforeseen line.

"Congo was only a normal ape-cub," he would insist, "and he's developing in every possible way into a very respectable lower-class human being."

"He's by no means lower-class," Mother always argued at this point, but Doctor would plunge ahead.

"We could operate on his people wholesale, making wonderful, cheap labor available. Why, when Congo grows up he'll be as strong as six or eight men, and his keep is almost nothing."

He tested me at various occupations—gardening, carpentry and iron-working, at which last I seem to have done quite well—and one day he asked me what I would rather do than anything else.

I remembered the dream I had had when he operated on me—and many times since. "Best of all," I replied, "I would like to live in a tree, build a nest of leaves and branches—"

"Ugh!" he almost screamed in disgust. "And I thought you were becoming human!"

After that he renewed his demands that Mother treat me with less affection.

Sidney was going to school at this time. I remained at home with Doctor and Mother—we lived in a small New Jersey town—and confined most of my activities to the house and the shrub-grown back yard. Once I ran away after a little quarrel with Doctor, and frightened the entire neighborhood before I was brought back by a nervous policeman with a drawn revolver. Doctor punished me by confining me to my room for three days. During that lonely time I did a lot of thinking and set myself down as an outcast. I had been considered strange, fearful and altogether unbelonging, by human beings. My crooked body and hairy skin had betrayed me to enmity and capture.

At the age of ten I gained my full growth. I was five feet six inches tall and weighed as much as Doctor. My face, once pallid, had become quite black, with bearded jaws and bristly hair on the upper lip. I walked upright, without touching my knuckles to the ground as ordinary apes do, for I usually held some tool or book in my hands. By listening to Sidney as he studied aloud at night I got some smattering of schooling, and I built upon this by constant and serious reading of his discarded textbooks. I have been told that the average shut-in child is apt to do the same. On top of this, I read a great deal in Doctor's library, especially travel. But I disliked fiction.

"Why should I read it?" I asked Mother when she offered me a book about "Tom Sawyer." "It isn't true."

"It's interesting," she said.

"But if it's not true, it's a lie; and a lie is wicked."

She pointed out that novel-readers knew all the time that the books were not true. To that I made answer that novel-readers were fools. Doctor, joining the conversation, asked me why, then, I enjoyed my dreams.

"You say that you dream of great green forests," he reminded. "That's no more true than the books."

"If it is a good dream," I replied, "I am glad when I wake, because it made me happy. If it is a bad dream, I am glad because I escape by waking. Anyway, dreams happen and novels do not."

Doctor called it a *sophistication*, and let that conclude the argument.

I have said that I am no proper writer, and I have shown it by over-looking an important fact—the many visits of scientists. They came to observe and to discuss things with Doctor, and even with me. But one day some men appeared who were not scientists. They smoked long cigars and wore diamond rings and derby hats. Doctor had them in his study for an hour, and that night he talked long to Mother.

"Eighteen thousand dollars!" he kept saying. "Think of it!"

"You've never thought of money before," she said sadly.

"But eighteen th—my dear, it would be only the beginning. We'd do the experiment again, with two baby apes—two new little Congos for you to fuss over—"

"And the first Congo, my poor jungle foster son," mourned Mother. "He'd be miserable somewhere. How can you think of such a thing, dear? Didn't your grandfather fight to free slaves in his day?"

"Those were human slaves," replied Doctor. "Not animals. And Congo won't be miserable. His ape-instinct will enjoy the new life. It'll fairly glitter for him. And we need the money to live on and to experiment with."

That went on and on, and Mother cried. But Doctor had his way. In the morning the men with the cigars came back, and Doctor greeted them gayly. They gave him a cheque—a big one, for they wrote it very reverently. Then he called me.

"Congo," he said, "you're to go with these people. You've got a career now, my boy; you're in the show business."

I did not want to go, but I had to.

My adventures as a theatrical curiosity have been described in many newspapers all over the world, and I will mention them but briefly. First I was rehearsed to do feats of strength and finish the act with alleged comedy—a dialogue between myself and a man in clown costume. After that, a more successful turn was evolved for me, wherein I was on the stage alone. I performed on a trapeze and a bicycle, then told my life story and answered questions asked by the audiences. I worked in a motion picture, too, with a former swimming champion. I liked him on sight, as much as I liked any human being except Mother. He was always kind and under-standing, and did not hate me, even when we were given equal billing.

For a while many newspaper reporters thought I was a fake—a man dressed up in a fur suit—but that was easily disproven. A number of scientists came to visit me in the various cities I performed in, and literally millions of curious people. In my third year as a show-piece I went to Europe. I had to learn French and German, or enough to make myself understood on the stage, and got laughed at for my accent, which was not very good. Once or twice I was threatened, because I said something in the theatres about this political leader or that, but for the most part people were very friendly.

Finally, however, I got a bad cough. My owners were fearfully worried and called a doctor, who prescribed a sea voyage. Lots of publicity came of the announcement that I would sail south, to "visit my homeland of Africa."

Of course I had not been born in Africa, but in the Bronx Zoo; yet a thrill came into my heart when, draped in a long coat and leaning on the rail, we sighted the west coast just below the Equator.

That night, as the ship rode at anchor near some little port, I contrived to slip overside and into a barge full of packing cases. I rode with it to land and sneaked out upon the dock, through the shabby little town, and away up a little stream that led into a hot, green forest.

I tell it so briefly and calmly because that is the way the impulse came to me. I read somewhere about the lemmings, the little ratlike animals that go to the sea and drown themselves by the thousands. That is because they must. I doubt if they philosophize about it; they simply do it. Something like that dragged me ashore in Africa and up the watercourse.

I was as strange and awkward there as any human being would be for the first time. But I knew, somehow, that nature would provide the right things. In the morning I rested in a thicket of fruit trees. The fruit I did not know, but the birds had pecked at it, so I knew it was safe for eating. The flavor was strange but good. By the second day I was well beyond civilization. I slept that night in a tree, making a sort of nest there. It was clumsy work, but something beyond my experience seemed to guide my hands.

After more days, I found my people, the Kulakambas.

They were as they had been in the dream, swinging in treetops, playing and gathering food. Some of the younger ones scampered through the branches, shrilling joyfully over their game of tag. They talked, young and old—they had a language, with inflections and words and probably grammar. I could see a little village of nests, in the forks of the big trees; well-made shelters, with roofs over them. Those must have been quickly and easily made. Nothing troubled the Kulakambas. They lived without thought or worry for the next moment. When the next moment came they lived that, too.

I thought I would approach. I would make friends, learn their ways and their speech. Then I might teach them useful things, and in turn they would teach me games. Already the old dream was a reality and the civilization I had known was slipping away—like a garment that had fitted too loosely.

I approached and came into view. They saw, and began to chatter at me. I tried to imitate their sounds, and I failed.

Then they grew excited and climbed along in the trees above me. They began dropping branches and fruits and such things. I ran, and they followed, shrieking in a rage that had come upon them from nowhere and for no reason I could think of. They chased me all that day, until nightfall. A leopard frightened them then, and me as well.

I returned, after many days, to the town by the sea. My owners were there, and greeted me with loud abuse. I had cost them money and worry, important in the order named. One of them wanted to beat me with a whip. I reminded him that I could tear him apart like a roast chicken and there was no more talk of whipping me. I was kept shut up, however, until our ship came back and took us aboard.

Nevertheless, the adventure turned out well, so far as my owners were concerned. Reporters interviewed me when I got back to London. I told them the solemn truth about what I had done, and they made publicity marvels out of the apeman's return to the jungle.

I made a personal appearance with my picture, for it had come to England just at that time. A week or so later came a cable from America. Somebody was reviving the plays of William Shakespeare, and I was badly wanted for an important role. We sailed back, were interviewed by a battery of reporters on landing, and went to an uptown hotel. Once or twice before there had been trouble about my staying in hotels. Now I was known and publicized as a Shakespearean actor, and the management of the biggest and most sumptuous hotel was glad to have me for a guest.

At once my owners signed a contract for me to appear in *The Tempest*; the part given me to study was that of Caliban, a sort of monster who was presented as the uncouth, unwelcome villain. Part of the time he had to be wicked, and part of the time ridiculous. As I read of his fumblings and blunderings, I forgot my long-held dislike of fiction and fable. I remembered what Doctor and Mother had said about Caliban, and all at once I knew how the poor whelp of Sycorax felt.

The next day a visitor came. It was Doctor.

He was greyer than when I had seen him last, but healthy and happy and rich-looking. His beard was trimmed to a point instead of square, and he had white edging on his vest. He shook my hand and acted glad to see me.

"You're a real success, Congo," he said over and over again. "I told you that you'd be." We talked a while over this and that, and after a few minutes my owners left the room to do some business or other. Then Doctor leaned forward and patted my knee.

"I say, Congo," he grinned, "how would you like to have some brothers and sisters?"

I did not understand him, and I said so.

"Oh, perfectly simple," he made reply, crossing his legs. "There are going to be more like you."

"More Kulakambas?"

He nodded. "Yes. With brains to think with, and jaws to talk with. You've been a success, I'd say—profitable, fascinating. And my next experiment will be even better, more accurate. Then others—each a valuable property—each an advance in surgery and psychology over the last."

"Don't do it, Doctor," I said all at once.

"Don't do it?" he repeated sharply. "Why not?"

I tried to think of something compelling to reply, but nothing came to mind. I just said, "Don't do it, Doctor," as I had already.

He studied me a moment, with narrow eyes, then he snorted just as he had in the old days. "You're going to say it's cruel, I suppose," he sneered at me.

"That is right. It is cruel."

"Why, you—" He broke off without calling me anything, but I could feel his scorn, like a hot light upon me. "I suppose you know that if I hadn't done what I did to you, you'd be just a monkey scratching yourself."

I remembered the Kulakambas, happy and thoughtless in the wilderness.

He went on, "I gave you a mind and hands and speech, the three things that make up a man. Now you—"

"Yes," I interrupted again, for I remembered what I had been reading about Caliban. "Speech enough to curse you."

He uncrossed his legs. "A moment ago you were begging me not to do something."

"I'll beg again, Doctor," I pleaded, pushing my anger back into myself. "Don't butcher more beasts into—what I am."

He looked past me, and when he spoke it was not to me, but to himself. "I'll operate on five at first, ten the next year, and maybe get some assistants to do even more. In six or eight years there'll be a full hundred like you, or more advanced—"

"You mustn't," I said very firmly, and leaned forward in my turn.

He jumped up. "You forget yourself, Congo," he growled. "I'm not used to the word 'mustn't'—especially from a thing that owes me so much. And especially when I will lighten the labor of mankind."

"By laying mankind's labor on poor beasts."

"What are you going to do about it?" he flung out.

"I will prevent you," I promised.

He laughed. "You can't. All these gifts of yours mean nothing. You have a flexible tongue, a rational brain—but you're a beast by law and by nature. I," and he thumped his chest, "am a great scientist. You can't make a stand of any kind."

"I will prevent you," I said again, and I got up slowly.

He understood then, and yelled loudly. I heard an answering cry in the hall outside. He ran for the door, but I caught him. I remember how easily his neck broke in my hands. Just like a carrot.

277

The police came and got me, with guns and gas bombs and chains. I was taken to a jail and locked in the strongest cell, with iron bars all around. Outside some police officials and an attorney or two talked.

"He can't be tried for murder," said someone. "He's only an animal, and not subject to human laws."

"He was aware of what he did," argued a policeman. "He's as guilty as the devil."

"But we can hardly bring him into court," replied one of the attorneys. "Why, the newspapers would kid us clear out of the country—out of the legal profession."

They puzzled for a moment, all together. Then one of the police officers slapped his knee. "I've got it," he said, and they all looked at him hopefully.

"Why talk about trials?" demanded the inspired one. "If he can't be tried for killing that medic, neither can we be tried for killing him."

"Not if we do it painlessly," seconded someone.

They saw I was listening, and moved away and talked softly for a full quarter of an hour. Then they all nodded their heads as if agreeing on something. One police captain, fat and white-haired, came to the bars of my cell and looked through.

"Any last thing you'd like to have?" he asked me, not at all unkindly.

I asked for pen and ink and paper and time enough to write this.

JOHN BRUNNER
Tantamount to Murder

～✦～

*John Brunner (1934–1995) was one of Britain's most prolific
and influential science fiction writers. He won numerous
literary awards, including the Hugo Award, the British
Science Fiction Award (twice), the British Fantasy Award,
the French Prix Apollo and the Italian Cometa d'Argento
(twice).*

The author of such acclaimed science fiction novels as
Stand on Zanzibar, The Sheep Look Up, The Jagged Orbit
and The Shockwave Rider, *he also wrote mystery, fantasy
and thriller fiction.*

*The story that follows, which was written especially for
this book, blends a number of genres . . .*

n hour remained before sunset on this wet and windy autumn day, but in the sanctum of the Marquis de Vergonde it was always dark, and had been for more than seven years. The sole permitted luminance was shed on the portrait of Sibylle *née* Serrouiller, who had so briefly been his wife—*the* portrait, all there had been time for, though he had intended to commission one a year—before which, as on an altar, burned candles and sweet-smelling incense cones.

Few had laid eyes on it, but those who had might testify how beauty such as hers could snatch the breath.

Having re-dedicated himself to what had become his all absorbing purpose, the marquis withdrew and made ready to secure the room—its key being one of two that never left his belt, while the other had never been used save once and was destined to be used only once more, on his day of final triumph—before crossing the tiled floor of the *château*'s spacious albeit shabby entrance hall to the laboratory where he daily wrestled with the ultimate mystery of nature: the secret of life itself. His servant and confidant Jules (if the fellow had another name it had long been forgotten by all except himself) roused from the settle where he had been drowsing and started to draw back clumsy iron bolts.

At precisely which moment resounded from outside the noise of smashing glass. An instant later it was followed by a thunderous banging on the vast black oak front door.

But there were never any callers at this house.

Only intruders.

Lent arrogance by the brandy which was already empurpling his nose and cheeks despite his youth, Paul Serrouiller stared mockingly at his brother-in-law. How despicable he seemed! Unshaven, clad in garments fit only for a scarecrow, haggard as though he had not slept properly in years, and redolent of the chemicals wafting from the direction of the laboratory Jules had opened up and not had time to shut again—

Where had the lout vanished to, anyway, after admitting the newcomers? Why was he not bowing and scraping and offering to take this soaking Burberry and rain-dulled beaver hat, and the like outerwear from his companions? For an instant Paul's sense of triumph was diminished.

What, though, did a servant matter? The purpose of this visit was to be achieved at all costs, and those who had agreed to escort him hither stood to gain as surely as did he himself, so they would abet him in whatever he said or did. It was obvious that their first sight of the *château* had gone a long way toward convincing them that his wildest accusations against the marquis were likely to be borne out. Who but a madman would tolerate such conditions? The cobwebs that hung from the arched ceiling were as dense as tapestry!

Oh, Jules had probably fled in the sensible certainty that his employer was done for.

"You know me, brother-in-law!" he rasped. "Long though it be since we met! But you don't know my friends, who have come to put a term to your squandering of what rightly should be my inheritance! I present Maître Poltenaire, doctor of civil law; Monsieur Schaefer, his *huissier*; and last but very far from least, Dr. Michel Largot, the celebrated alienist from the Salpêtrière, who is accompanied by his trusted male nurse, Serge."

Eyes bleared from years of study by inadequate light and constant exposure to noxious fumes, the marquis sought and finally donned thick spectacles just in time to find his attention directed toward Serge, who towered over his employer massive as a treetrunk, his shaven head round and smooth as a cannonball.

"What—what do you want?" he husked.

"Justice!" rasped Paul. "And even sooner, a drink! There used to be a fine cellar here. I recall it from my sister's nuptials. Schaefer, try that room on the left—"

"No! No!" The marquis was almost babbling.

"You want to keep us out of there, do you?" sneered Paul. "I wonder why!" And with one swift stride planted his hand on the iron latch of the sanctum and flung wide the door the marquis had not had the chance to re-lock.

"*Faugh!*" he exclaimed as the draught of its opening disturbed more than a lustrum's worth of dust and made the candles gutter. "Serge, pull back these curtains!"

"No, no!" The marquis was battering at him with futile fists. "You have no right! This is my home, not yours!"

The lawyer gave a discreet cough.

"Begging your excellency's pardon, there is room for doubt on that score. If, as we have been advised, you have pretended for seven years that your wife, who is in fact dead, is still alive, in order to enjoy the estate she brought to your marriage for you to share, and I quote, 'during her lifetime, and afterward—'"

Until the majority of your eldest child, if any! The marquis knew all the conditions of his late father-in-law's will by heart, and all the threatening documents sent on his brother-in-law's behalf by corrupt and venial lawyers like this new one.

Oddly, though, the stern legal voice had faded between words. Drawn aside amid a downpour of dead moths and flies, the curtains of the nearest window had parted to let the fading daylight fall squarely on the image of Sibylle, glorious in her nineteen-year-old nudity from her curly blonde crown to her tiny soles.

"You see?" the marquis cried triumphantly. "She isn't dead! How can she be? Beauty such as hers can never die! It mustn't be allowed to!"

Panting, he caught at the arm of M. Poltenaire, gesturing to attract the attention of the alienist as well.

"I can show you all the references to my work on the longevity of the *Bufonidae*—the toad family, that is. I have hundreds of reports concerning the way they can survive being enclosed in dry mud or even rock, including many from Australia where they are especially abundant. We found an example right here on our estate, sealed up in a tree!"

Dr. Largot raised a pale-palmed hand.

"One moment, please. Are we to believe what your brother-in-law has told us? When his sister, your wife, died—"

"She isn't dead!"

"With respect—"

"Oh, forget the respect stuff!" Paul snarled. "The plain fact is, the man's crazy! And never mind the 'famous scientist' rubbish! He simply can't accept—"

"But I've proved my claim!" Behind his glasses the marquis was unashamedly weeping. "Having obtained her full permission, using the data I had garnered from my study of toads, at the very moment that the vital spark expired I perfused her system with the extracts my studies had convinced me would preserve her in a state of suspended animation." He was regaining his composure. Wiping his eyes with a large silk kerchief, he continued.

"All that remained was to exclude air. The compounds I had injected would preserve her indefinitely against dehydration and putrefaction, but until a cure could be found for her malady she must remain immobile, unthinking, unfeeling. So I put her mausoleum under a hermetic seal. Now if you will accompany me into my laboratory I can show you how much progress is being made towards a cure. I correspond with the most renowned physicians in this country, in Germany, England, America, even Russia where marvelous work is being carried on concerning the resuscitation of debilitated cell-lines . . . Is something wrong?"

"Mausoleum?" Paul scoffed. "That shack beside the driveway with her name scrawled over the door? Not even decently carved!"

"Why, you—!" But the marquis, mindful of his weakened state, let his fists fall at his sides. "I must admit," he muttered, "I deemed it preferable to spend my funds on research rather than—"

"Whose funds?" Paul rasped. And added to the lawyer, "Make a note of that! Not that it matters, apparently." He uttered a cynical chuckle.

"What—what do you mean?"

"Shouldn't have fitted a glass window to your outsize coffin, should you? Serge! Why haven't you found us anything to drink yet, you lazy bastard?"

The marquis's face turned literally grey, as though he had divined the import of Paul's words. In a strained voice Poltenaire said, "I must advise my client to refrain from any further statement on this subject—"

From outside came a clatter of horses' hooves. Bewildered, all save the marquis, they turned as the front door swung open to reveal Jules, followed by a scowling man in a wet cloak, and he in turn by another bearing a large leather portfolio.

"This is our distinguished neighbor Monsieur Vautrian," announced Jules. "He is a *juge d'instruction*, an examining magistrate. As Monsieur le Marquis took the precaution of advising me I should in such a case, when you marched in without a by-your-leave I betook myself to his house and swore out a complaint for trespass and false accusation."

"But—!" Paul stammered.

"No buts," Vautrian ordered. "Let's get this nonsense out of the way. Anton"—to his companion, clearly his own *huissier*, approximately bailiff or legal clerk—"there's the dining-room. We can sit round the table."

"Just a moment."

The marquis's voice was as dry as the rustle of a beetle's wingcases.

"Is it true that . . .?" He had to break off and swallow. "Is it true, Paul, that you—you broke the window of Sibylle's resting-place?"

"Hah!"—defiantly. "I didn't mean to. I just ran out of brandy on the way up your front steps, and what use is an empty bottle? I chucked it away, that's all."

The marquis's tone became dull, resigned. He said, "Jules?"

"Yes, sir."

"Did his bottle—? Don't bother to reply. I can tell from your face."

Vautrian said impatiently, "What's this about?"

"As well he knew it would, his action"—the marquis's words took on a tone like a great bell tolling for a funeral—"broke the seal ensuring my wife's chance to live again."

"Did you ever hear such nonsense?" roared Paul. "Still, at least he's finally admitting that she's dead. He has no more claim on my rightful inheritance!"

"Is that the way of it?" Vautrian demanded.

"Why, it must be!" Poltenaire supplied hastily. "It's all turned out exactly as Monsieur Serrouiller claimed. For seven years the marquis has been deranged by the loss of his wife. He has refused to admit she is dead. Even on his own terms, though . . . Doctor, do you wish to say something?"

The alienist was looking grave and sympathetic.

"Yes, the situation is indeed as we were warned. But one need not despair. There has been progress. Even in what appears an intractable case one may still hope for a remission."

"Be quiet!" snapped the marquis. "I have long feared that Paul, as full of greed and evil as his sister of goodness and beauty, would find a way to destroy my years of work. I was so close . . . Yet what does it matter?

Would Sibylle have wanted to return to a world where on his own admission her nearest blood relative had spent years trying to deprive her of her second lease of life?"

Largot said, "One is aware your reputation as a scientist—"

"Oh, I believe I've earned it. There are natural philosophers in ten countries who will say as much. But what boots it now? My life has lost all purpose . . . Speaking of purposes, I take it that it's yours to strip me of my estates and indeed my freedom, on the grounds that I am and have long been deranged. Very well. As I say, my life has lost all reason and all meaning. Do not, though, be so hardhearted as to deny me one last glimpse of my beloved."

The others exchanged glances. Paul broke the silence with a snort.

"Go if you wish! Take your neighbor with you! It will be fine to have a *juge d'instruction* certify how far your sickness has progressed! Take his *huissier* as well, if you like. The more witnesses the merrier! Meantime my friends and I can celebrate our victory. Serge—Schaefer—why the hell have you not found the brandy yet? Jules, show them where to look!"

The second, the third, glassful sufficed to put them all in a good humor again: the heir presumptive who had been fuming at the way his brother-in-law was spending what he felt to be his portion on a doomed and lunatic attempt to bring his wife back; the impoverished lawyer who stood to gain fees enough to live on for a year from the conclusion of this case, and his *huissier* who would be correspondingly better off; the alienist whose practice had formerly been lucrative but whose private asylum sorely lacked just such patients as a titled member of the Old Nobility would attract, for there were many old rich families looking for places to conceal the products of generations of inbreeding and over-indulgence, and his authorized bully Serge who was so skilled at cowing even nobles into doing as they were told . . . They were in the dining-room relaxing into laughter at the speed and completeness of their victory when there came a scream from the hallway. Before they could more than react, the room's door was flung wide by Jules. Headlong through the opening fell the marquis—it had been he who screamed, they realized—in a dead faint.

Scrambling to their feet in astonishment, they found themselves confronting Vautrian, his face like thunder.

"Your name Schaefer?" he barked.

"Ah—yes!"

"You're a certified *huissier*?"

"Yes!"

"I am a duly appointed *juge d'instruction*. I invoke your assistance in the name of the law."

Slowly, confusedly, lowering his third glass of brandy—except that it wasn't his third, not of the day, but more like his tenth or twelfth—Paul Serrouiller cancelled the joke he had planned to make concerning disposal of that nude painting of his sister to the Moulin Rouge where it would look perfect in the entrance *foyer*.

Vautrian did not have the air of a man inclined for jokes.

He continued, "You are Paul Serrouiller, brother of the late Marquise de Vergonde?"

"What the hell are you going on about?"

His face eloquent of something between disgust and terror, the magistrate drew a deep breath.

"I arrest you for the culpable homicide of your sister."

"What?" Paul overturned his glass in the act of trying to set it down. "Are you crazy? My sister has been dead for seven years!"

His brother-in-law the marquis roused, scrabbling at the dirty floor with equally dirty fingernails, apparently in search of his spectacles. Jules hastened to his side.

"I was so close to success," he whispered. "I was so much closer than I knew . . ."

Vautrian ignored the distraction, continuing to address Paul.

"Did you throw a brandy bottle at the tomb in which she was sealed up, thereby breaking its window and admitting air?"

"What?" Paul licked his lips, casting around for support. But his cronies had sensed something amiss and were withholding it.

"You had been told, had you not, that your sister stood a chance of being resuscitated if the seal could be maintained until a cure was found for her disease?"

"Who pays attention to that sort of rubbish?" Paul exclaimed hysterically. "My sister had been dead for seven years! How can you claim I killed her?"

The marquis moaned, still writhing on the floor.

"But she cannot have been dead for seven years," said the magistrate. Again he filled his lungs to maximum, as though afraid he might otherwise run out of oxygen.

"On entering the mausoleum, we found your sister not on her catafalque but on the floor, and in the dust around such marks as make it clear that she had risen, taken three clear steps, and collapsed."

Paul stared, mind bludgeoned into incredulity.

"Moreover . . . Anton?"

The bailiff had been keeping one hand behind his back. Now he revealed what was in it: a swatch of bright blonde hair.

Sibylle's hair.

"She can have had strength only for a moment. On contact with the full force of fresh air, all that was left of her—save those golden locks . . ."

He had to pause and swallow.

"Dissolved," grated Jules.

"But she had lived!" the marquis cried, striving to raise himself.

Vautrian nodded heavily. "Yes, long enough. Monsieur Serrouiller, I repeat my charge. You had been told that breaching the seal that protected your sister would be tantamount to murdering her—"

"But I didn't know she was alive!" shrieked Paul.

"You mean you didn't believe she was," corrected the magistrate. "That she was, however, has been proved."

"I—I . . ."

Wherever Paul looked, though, he read no pity in the others' eyes. It was as though they were all wordlessly concluding:

The marquis really had found out a way to raise the dead. This bastard insisted that he couldn't have because he wanted to get his hands on the money that was needed to perfect it.

To waste on brandy, more than like!

The marquis uttered a stifled groan, rolled on his back and lay still. Jules checked his wrist for a pulse. He found none.

"Now there truly is no chance of knowing what my master invented," he said in a gravelly voice, and crossed himself.

"Thanks to this greedy fool," Largot snapped, adding to Vautrian, "You need assistance in arresting him, monsieur? Serge!"

Expert hands clamped on Paul's windpipe, dispatching him to limp oblivion. Not before, however, he had heard:

"To cheat humanity of resurrection? Has there ever been a fouler traitor?"

Conscious or not, Paul would have had no answer.

GUY N. SMITH
Last Train

❧

Guy N. Smith was born and raised in the village of Hopwas in Staffordshire. His mother was a historical author, and she encouraged her son to write from an early age. He was first published at the age of twelve in a local newspaper.

While working as a bank manager, he wrote his first three novels—Werewolf by Moonlight, The Sucking Pit *and* Slime Beast—*but it was the publication in 1976 of* Night of the Crabs *that gave him his first bestseller. Six further titles in the series followed.*

In addition to the more than one hundred books he has written since 1974, the author also runs Black Hill Books, selling vintage and modern editions. The Guy N. Smith Fan Club was formed in 1992.

Jeremy was frightened. Very frightened. For a number of reasons.

The last time he'd been to the city was when he was twelve, he could not remember much about it except that his parents had been with him. He hadn't been anywhere without them since, except on those rare occasions when they let him go into town on the bus on his own, and then Mother was waiting at the bus stop for his return. Once he'd missed the bus home, come on the next one, and she'd been nearly hysterical. That was when he was sixteen; he was twenty now and nothing had changed much.

Jeremy was still paying the price for his misfortune in being the only child of farmers who had sheltered him from infancy to adolescence and beyond. His mother was turned forty when he was born; it had been a difficult birth, both mother and offspring only survived with a struggle. His father was sixteen years older than Jeremy's mother, and even now they did not trust their son to run the 100-acre spread on his own. Even the simplest chore had to be referred to them before it was attempted, and it was usually criticized heavily after its completion.

"You'm lucky, Jerry," his father repeatedly reminded him, spittle stringing from his toothless mouth, his chest wheezing beneath his old brown smock even though he had never smoked. "You could be livin' close to a town with all kinds o' things to lead you astray. Out here you'm safe, and after we've gone the place'll be your'n. That's the time to get married, when you've nobody to cook and clean for you. But you've got your mother, God willing for a number o' years to come, so you won't need a wife yet."

Jeremy had worked on the farm all his life, six days a week and chapel twice on Sundays, the routine never altered. The farm was situated down a rough track, two miles from the public road, and the only person, apart from his parents, whom Jeremy saw regularly was the postman. And mostly that was a distant glimpse of a red van.

Jeremy became a reluctant recluse. Taking sheep to market with the tractor and trailer on Fridays was no social excursion. Naturally, his father came along and the gathering in the stockyard was invariably that of an older generation. Jeremy became extremely lonely.

Bingo in the village hall was taboo to a true chapelman, his father was aghast that his son had even *thought* of going. The monthly dance was a waste of time and, anyway, how would Jeremy get home afterwards because there were no buses at that time of night and taxis were too expensive; another thing, a young man needed to be abed early if he was to be up and about at daylight the next morning.

Jeremy was young, his mother supported her husband's views; when the time came, and Jeremy needed a wife, *then* he could take himself along to a dance. Dances had their temptations, there was a rumor that young Milly Wain was pregnant and she was always hanging round the hall on dance nights, flirting with chaps. "We don't want you going getting no wench into trouble, Jeremy!"

The urge was strong, almost unbearable, with Jeremy. Had his mother's eyesight not been so poor she might have noticed stains on his bedsheets and lectured him on the evils that led to blindness. But she didn't, and at twenty his craving for a woman was almost unbearable.

It was at the cattle market that an exciting idea came to him. December heralded the annual Smithfield show in the city and there were some tickets on sale; the price included a return train fare and a night in a modest hotel. Whilst his father was busily engaged discussing the alarming drop in the price of lamb, Jeremy bought a ticket. Just one.

"What you bin and wasted your money on that for?" His mother stared in disbelief.

"Because I want to go," Jeremy held the ticket beyond her reach or else it would probably have been thrown on the woodstove. "It's educational. And, anyway, I haven't had a holiday since I was twelve when you took me to London. I'd like to go again."

"We was with you then," her lower lip was trembling. "London's no place for a boy on his own. Nor a woman. Nor nobody. It's full of drug addicts, muggers, murderers and . . ." But Jeremy went to London all the same. He walked to the village, caught the bus into town, boarded an inter-city bound for Euston. And eventually arrived in the metropolis.

He'd heard that whores lurked in side streets and shop doorways, that took your money and gave you dreadful diseases in return. But he'd risk anything just to experience that forbidden pleasure which his parents pretended never existed, switching to an alternative television channel if anything came on the screen which did not pass their censorship.

It was wrong, God would know what he'd done, but he'd pray for forgiveness in chapel every Sunday for the rest of his life, if necessary. He'd find a woman somewhere, give her every penny he'd brought with him if she would just let him do what he could not live without any longer. He didn't care if she was fat or thin, pretty or ugly, just so long as she let him have what he wanted.

He'd almost given up. He'd tramped the pavements until his feet were blistered inside his best Sunday shoes. His collar was turned up against the drizzle of a raw winter's night, he glanced furtively into every doorway and alley he passed. What did a whore look like? How did you approach one? He found himself hurrying on past dark shadows where only the glow of a cigarette revealed that somebody waited there.

Tired, dejected, lost, he started when a voice spoke to him from the darkness of a passageway between the tall buildings. "Cost you a tenner, love."

A month's pocket money for working on the farm, his board and lodgings were his wages, so Father said. Pocket money and nothing to spend it on except a new set of overalls. This time he meant to have full value for his money.

He could not see what she looked like in the stygian blackness of the alley, but he didn't care. She insisted on payment up front, then she leaned spread-legged against the wall, undid enough of her clothing as she deemed necessary.

That was when the most awful thing happened to Jeremy. Years of fantasizing about this mythical experience came to nothing, those arousements of a thousand lonely nights deserted him. Her annoyance at his impotence only served to further soften his intended prowess. Time was money, and time was running out for her.

Suddenly, she was gone, his ten pound note stuffed in the pocket of her frayed coat, leaving him to his despair and embarrassment.

It was then that Jeremy's terror began.

He slunk back out into the misty, deserted street, looked right and left. A couple hurried past but they scarcely glanced at him. Alien surroundings, he could not even remember in which direction he had come, where the tube station was where he had alighted in this notorious area.

The earlier traffic had thinned to a spasmodic trickle. An approaching car bore a neon sign with the word "taxi" on it. Just in time Jeremy checked his upraised arm; the only money he had was the loose change jingling in his pocket. In the city, his parents had advised him reluctantly, one didn't walk about with a wad of money in one's pocket. His neatly folded banknotes were hidden under the carpet back in his sparse hotel room. He had just enough for a single underground fare to . . .

To where? The names of streets, stations were foreign to him, easily forgotten. Approaching footsteps had him glancing behind him. Somebody was coming, they'd spotted him, they were stalking him. Stopping because he had stopped; walking again when he started off; quickly, trying to catch him up.

He ran. It might have been the echoes of his own footsteps on the pavement but it sounded like his pursuers were running, too. He turned left into a side street; they followed. Right, and left again. Another main thoroughfare. People stood on the opposite pavement, staring.

Everybody was hunting him.

They drove him one way, then another. Physically fit, Jeremy walked the Dingle at home daily, and then up to the top fields to check on the sheep, but the city concrete was sapping his strength. His calves ached, his broad chest heaved with the intake of polluted air. He almost gave up, stood and waited for them to come and take him.

And then he saw the blue and red circle that designated an underground station.

He found the strength to run again, stumbling down a flight of wide steps. Across a foyer, vaulting a ticket barrier. There were no uniformed attendants, the robots had taken over.

On down a steep escalator, looking fearfully behind him. There was nobody in sight, temporarily he had outdistanced those who sought to run him down. Pray God that there was a train imminent, its destination mattered not. Please God, let there be a train and forgive me for what I have done.

There was a train standing at the platform. A long line of cars waited, doors open, they appeared to be deserted. Jeremy ran along the platform, searching for one with late night travelers, company when he needed it most. Alone in a deserted carriage, he was trapped. *Mind the gap.*

The doors were starting to close. He hurled himself aboard, sprawled headlong as the train jerked forward, began to pick up speed.

The last train, he had made it with seconds to spare. He had escaped the clutches of those who sought to mug him and to do other unthinkable things to him.

It was only when the train was in the tunnel that Jeremy realized that he was not alone in the carriage. He clambered into a seat, glanced apprehensively at his fellow passengers. It was obvious that all three were traveling together.

The man sat opposite his female companions. His age was indeterminable, there was a distinct lack of care about his appearance, yet he had the bearing of one too preoccupied with important matters to be concerned with his personal appearance. His bald head was fringed with iron grey hair that stuck out, demanding a brush and comb. Bushy eyebrows and a hooked nose, the nostrils encrusted with dried mucus, gave him the appearance of a bird of prey.

A well worn, shiny overcoat was belted at the waist, the trousers were several inches too short, revealed odd socks that almost matched, had perhaps been selected carelessly from a clothes drawer without a second glance. The hallmark of one engrossed in his ambitions.

The two women were possibly in their mid-twenties and a similarity of features bespoke sisters, possibly even twins. The one was raven-haired, the other peroxide blonde, dressed in tight-fitting, two-piece suits that showed their slim figures to perfection. Their beauty was breathtaking to one who had come direct from the impatient gropings of a street slut. It was also . . . *frightening*.

Because of their lack of expression, the way their eyes saw without revealing their thoughts, the manner in which they sat stiffly, unnaturally. Almost a subservience to the one who leaned across and spoke to them in low, barely audible, gutteral tones, spittle dangling from his thin lips.

The blonde woman's arm moved jerkily, she handed something to the man. Perhaps she was an arthritic like Mother. Jeremy watched out of the corner of his eyes. Or maybe she had suffered some serious accident that had partially immobilized her. *Just as it had rendered her sister a semi-cripple.* Maybe they had both been in the same car accident.

Something changed hands, rustled. Jeremy recognized bank notes, tenners. The man was smoothing them out, folding them, unashamedly gloating over them as he transferred them to the pocket of his coat.

"Good, good!" The stranger grunted, tapped his pocket with long white fingers. "You have done well. Everything has worked."

The eyes beneath those heavy brows stole a glance at the newcomer to the journey. Jeremy cringed, his guts balled and his mouth went even drier than before. This man was undoubtedly a pimp. He had watched a television programme on prostitution late one night when he had stayed up during the lambing season. The other sent these women out to work on the streets, collected their earnings afterwards. He had probably shadowed them to ensure that they didn't cheat him, met up at a prearranged place afterwards. Now he was escorting them home; they probably lived in his brothel. They were his slaves.

Another sensation pervaded Jeremy. His pulses speeded up, his heart was pounding madly, and not just from his recent exertions. There was a familiar stirring in his lower regions. He became angry over his own failure to achieve an ambition that had plagued his nights of loneliness. Now his arousement had returned to taunt him when it was too late. For even if these women were whores, he had not the money to pay for their services.

All three of them were looking at him, the man from beneath hooded eyebrows, the females staring fixedly. Watching him as a hawk might have watched an unwary rabbit.

Jeremy shifted uneasily in his seat, he dropped his gaze, was embarrassed to see the protrusion behind his zip. They were all looking at it, they knew what was happening to him.

"Copulation is the strongest urge known to Mankind," the man spoke in a deep voice, he might have been addressing a gathering of students at a biology lecture. "Greater even than the will to survive. *Stronger than death*. I have proved it unequivocably!" Smug satisfaction, self pride, words that might once have been uttered by the great Darwin himself.

Female heads nodded, they reminded Jeremy of puppets at a Punch and Judy show, inanimate creatures that were solely dependent upon their master. Their lips parted, a leer rather than a smile. Only their eyes reflected their inner lust. His skin prickled as his earlier terror returned.

"*More!*" A whisper in unison from lips that suddenly were no longer beautiful. A noise, Jeremy thought at first it was made by the rushing of the train. It wasn't. *These sinister creatures of the night were panting.*

"Perhaps the gentleman will oblige," the strange man's head was thrust forward, he regarded Jeremy as though the other was some specimen to be examined with interest in the confines of a laboratory. "His powerful build reflects his stamina, his complexion is that of an outdoor man in the peak of health. A worthy male to test the results of a lifetime of labor, trials and disappointments. My dears, this is the ultimate test for you."

"*Please!*" Again they spoke in unison, edged forward on their seats, their features masks of lust and expectation, vibrating rather than trembling in anticipation of being granted their request; a faint rattling, it could have been the rushing train.

"Very well," the stranger turned, addressed himself directly to Jeremy now. "Perhaps, sir, you would care to indulge in some pleasure to satisfy my two . . . companions. Two for the price of one, if you understand me." He chuckled.

"I . . . I don't have any money, I'm afraid," Jeremy pressed himself back in his seat. In spite of his fear his arousement was only too evident. These women had a fatal attraction for him, they were no tarts selling their bodies in dark alleys. Terrifying, yet they were the realization of all his fantasies.

"*Please!*" It sounded like a well worn and scratched 78 rpm record. They had lifted themselves up, crouched as if to spring at their master's command.

"Very well. It is the gentleman's lucky night. *Go to him!*"

The rushing, swaying train hooted its signal for the unholy union to commence.

Jeremy cowered, stared in disbelief. The females were naked now but their beauty had become grotesque. *Perfectly formed yet their bodies were a scarred patchwork of stitching and surgical improvisation—hastily repaired tailor's dummies that had hidden beneath their clothing but were now revealed in their true awfulness. Arms and legs moved jerkily, wired and hinged, dead flesh reinforced with synthetic materials.*

The train swayed on a bend. The dark-haired one staggered, banged her head against a stanchion with a force that should have opened up an ugly wound, drawn blood. *She did not even appear to notice.*

Hands reached out for Jeremy, icy fingers tore at his clothing. He screamed, struggled, but their strength rendered him a child in their grasp. The breath from the mouths that vied for his own was fetid, their slobbering kisses muffled his cries of terror.

Behind them the stranger hovered, bent double, twisting this way and that in a voyeurism that transcended perversion. Grunting in time with their own expletives of carnal delight, urging them on. His eyes were aglow with crazed delight.

Jeremy was spent but their lust was inexhaustible. He screamed as sharp teeth bit into his neck, began to tear at his flesh.

"*No!*" The man's exultation turned instantly to anger, he grasped at their nakedness, tugged, lifted a foot up on to a seat as an added lever. "No, not *that!*"

One of them turned, pushed at him, sent him staggering backwards. Then her bloodied teeth returned to their mutilated victim.

Jeremy's vision blurred, the pain was unbearable. He jerked, writhed, struggled but they were too strong for him. Harsh gutteral laughter came from improvised lungs, their cries of pleasure squelched through mouthfuls of raw human flesh.

Consciousness was slipping from him. His head lolled to one side, afforded him a glimpse of the one who had perpetrated this atrocity. The man was slumped in a seat, holding his head as if he shared his victim's agony. Anguished moans, the eyes were closed in utter despair.

"As before," he shrieked against the background of the train's klaxon. "It is always the same. *Cannibalizm is the strongest urge, destroys everything that I have created!*"

The blood-streaked females reared up from their inert prey, turned upon each other with a ferocity that defied the instincts of human existence. One lust had been appeased, the other was insatiable.

Their master slumped, waited. In his hour of triumph he had lost all control. Whatever remained of a lifetime of experimenting would take him, too, this time.

PETER TREMAYNE
The Hound of Frankenstein

"Peter Tremayne" is the pseudonym of acclaimed Celtic scholar and historian Peter Berresford Ellis. Born in Coventry, England, of Irish descent on his father's side, he traveled widely in Ireland, studying its history, politics, language and mythology.

As "Tremayne," his many books include the horror novels Dracula Unborn *(aka* Bloodright*),* The Revenge of Dracula, The Ants, The Curse of Loch Ness, Zombie!, Snowbeast, Kiss of the Cobra *and* Trollnight.

He has edited the anthologies Masters of Terror: William Hope Hodgson *and* Irish Masters of Fantasy, *and he collaborated with the late Peter Haining on the 1997 nonfiction study* The Un-Dead: The Legend of Bram Stoker and

Dracula. *He has also written biographies of authors H. Rider Haggard, W. E. Johns, Talbot Mundy and E. Charles Vivian.*

In 1994 Tremayne published Absolution of Murder, *the first of his international best-selling murder mystery novels about seventh century Irish advocate Sister Fidelma, who uses the ancient Brehon Law system. It has since been followed by twenty-four further titles, the most recent being* The Second Death *(2015) and the forthcoming* Penance of the Damned *(2016).*

The Hound of Frankenstein *was the first Tremayne book ever to be published (by Mills & Boon, in August 1977). The setting of this story is Cornwall, a favorite area of Tremayne's and from where he devised his pseudonym. Tremayne (Cornish* tre = habitation, mayne/maen = *stone) is the name of a little hamlet just north of Penzance which, according to the author, is the site of the best Italian restaurant in Cornwall and the only reason why he chose this, a favorite watering hole, as his* nom-de-plume.

The short novel that follows introduces the reader to a fictional village named Bosbradoe on the wild north Cornwall coast beyond the desolate Bodmin Moor. Based on a combination of real places, Bosbradoe and its scenic tavern, The Morvren Arms *(morvren = mermaid), also feature in Tremayne's novels* The Vengeance of She *(1977) and* The Morgow Rises! *(1982), as well as in his short story* "The Hungry Grass."

I

A man was running across the dark moorland; running in terror of his life.

Dark storm clouds hurried westward across the night sky, across the pale orb of the moon. The clouds seemed to fly fast and thick as the wind whipped the topmost branches of the trees. Far down on the eastern horizon, lightning spat into the sky, and thunder reverberated the air. And the rain splattered heavily down in isolated showers.

In the distance the man could hear the low, mournful howl of a hound hunting its quarry.

He paused to rest a moment against the wet granite of a boulder; paused to try to catch his breath and ease the awful pain in his side.

He was an elderly man; his clothes had once been well tailored, but now they were torn and mud stained. Blood dripped from a great gash in his forehead and his hair was matted with dirt and rain water. His eyes stood wide and stark out of his pale, death-white face and his mouth hung open, half in fear and half in an attempt to regain his lost breath.

The mournful howl reached his ears again. This time it was close, very close.

The man turned, almost sobbing, and set off over the desolate night landscape.

He did not know where he was making for. All he knew was that he had to flee, to escape, to run.

A hill before him stood black and gaunt in silhouette. Atop the hill he could see the great stone monoliths of a former age and civilization. Large granite menhirs, standing as a memorial to the religion of the ancients. Unthinking, the man began to ascend the hill, gasping and sobbing in his terror, his heart beating wildly within him.

Gorse and thorn bushes tore at him, scratching his hands and face and tearing at his already tattered clothing. He did not heed them.

Scrambling, sometimes upright, sometimes on his hands and knees, the man forced his way to the top of the hill and into the moonlit stone circle.

He flung himself forward on a black menhir which had fallen on its side and now lay, altar-like, to one side of the circle.

For a while he tried to breathe deeply, to regulate the pattern of his gasping, shallow breaths. He tried to silence his rasping lungs and listen.

A low growl made him whirl round.

Never before, even in the most horrific nightmares of a delirious mind, had he envisaged such a beast as that which slunk forward into the pale moonlight and stood glaring malevolently at him from vicious red eyes.

It was a hound. No; a grotesque parody of a hound, large as a lion and black as jet. Its eyes gleamed with an unholy aura like glowing red coals.

Its great white fangs were bared, and its muzzle, hackles and dewlap were dripping with saliva which was tinged with blood.

As the man stood before it, frozen in terror, the great beast threw back its muzzle and gave up its low, mournful howl.

Then it sprang upon him, its mighty jaws snapping and tearing.

II

Along a darkened moorland road, a coach came clattering and swaying dangerously, pulled by four sturdy horses whose necks strained forward and hooves pounded in unison, urged by the harsh cries of their driver and the stinging crack of his whip about their flattened ears. Their eyes rolled in terror and there was a suspicion of white lather where their teeth ground against the metal bit of the harness.

Now and again, the roadway was lit starkly in black and white by flashing lightning, but for the most part, the coach plunged into darkness. Its two side lanterns were nothing more than thick candles placed in a storm glass, and cast little illumination to show the driver the way along the desolate road.

At intervals, the coach bucked and pitched and threatened to turn over, as the driver edged it too near the grassy embankment, or a stone caused the entire carriage to make a wild leap into the air.

"I swear the idiot will have us over before long," gasped the young man who constituted one of the two passengers in the coach. The other, a pale-faced girl, gave an involuntary cry as the coach gave a sudden lurch, and seemed to leave the roadway altogether.

"Sir, I pray you," she gasped. "Please ask the driver to slow his horses, for I fear that I shall faint if he maintains this speed much longer."

The young man leant forward in concern. He wished he had some light by which to observe his traveling companion. He had not seen her until he climbed into the mail coach, *The Bodmin Flyer*, at the coaching station in Bodmin, and she had sat in a shadowy corner of the coach, hardly speaking since then. If voices were anything to go by, she was surely young and pretty.

"Madam, I am a doctor. Doctor Brian Shaw at your service. Are you unwell?" His tone was solicitous.

The girl clung tightly to the passenger straps of the coach and replied in a soft, breathless voice.

"I was perfectly well, sir, when we left the town of Bodmin. But this man drives as if the furies of hell were at his heels, and I feel quite upset. So I pray you, sir, please ask him to slow the coach."

Brian Shaw stood up, balancing himself precariously, holding on to a passenger strap with one hand, and pushing open the flap in the roof of the coach through which driver and passengers could communicate.

"Hey, hey there! Driver! Slow down!" he called.

His voice seemed drowned by the clatter of the coach and the thunder of the horses' hooves on the stone of the roadway.

"Damn me," cursed the young man. "Is the fellow deaf or drunk?"

He banged agitatedly on the roof.

"Driver! D'you hear me? Slow down!"

Just then the coach careered around a corner, tipping over at an alarming angle before righting itself. The young man was thrown on to the floor and struck his head against the far door, stunning himself momentarily. The girl gave a low cry and, hanging on her strap with one hand, bent forward in the gloom. The young man was aware of the fragrance of her perfume.

"Are you all right, sir?"

Brian shook his head doubtfully.

"I believe so, madam. No thanks to the idiot of a driver. Ye gods! I believe the fellow is drunk. I'll put a stop to this."

The young girl suddenly raised a fist to her mouth and suppressed a cry of alarm, as the man opened one of the doors of the swaying coach and climbed on to the iron footrest outside.

"Have a care, sir!"

If the young man heard, he did not reply, but with teeth clenched, he hauled himself out, clutching the railings which protected the passengers' baggage on top of the coach. Then, placing a foot on the sill of one of the windows, he heaved himself on to the roof and lay panting for a second or two, spreadeagled among the baggage. Regaining his breath, he swung himself down on the driving box, by the side of the red faced driver.

The man gave an inarticulate cry, almost of terror, and raised his whip as if in protection.

Brian snatched it from his hand and grabbed at the reins which suddenly hung loose in the driver's nerveless fingers. It took him all his strength to haul back the four stout horses, and bring them shuddering to a halt, snorting and blowing, with sweat glistening on their dark bodies.

The driver sat huddled in his seat as if he had collapsed from the exertion of his drive.

Brian turned to him with a stern eye.

"What do you mean by this, man?" he demanded. "Are you trying to kill us all?"

The man muttered something which Brian could not understand, and reached into the folds of his greatcoat, brought forth a bottle, uncorked it and put it to his lips.

Brian snorted in disgust.

"I thought so. Drink. Well, I tell you, my man, I shall bring this to the attention of your employers. Do you realize that you have scared the young lady half to death? Do you realize that you have made her ill with your infernal driving?"

"Better to be ill, better to be alive to be ill, young sir," muttered the man, wiping his mouth with the back of a calloused hand. "There be some things worse."

Brian gave him a hard look. "What do you mean by that?"

"You be an upcountry man, sir. You be from beyond the Tamar, eh? Ah, I knows. Well, you be in Cornwall now, sir. Bodmin Moor, and it don't do to dawdle across the moor at night. There be many a strange thing loose on the moor at night."

The young man laughed.

"What superstitious nonsense is this, man? How much of that bottle have you had?"

"Scarcely a drop, young sir. Scarcely a drop. And it be no superstitious nonsense, that I tell 'ee. The road to Bosbradoe is a wild, desolate road, and it don't do to dawdle along it at night . . . especially this night of all nights in the year."

The driver shuddered.

"What do you mean—this night of all nights?" demanded Brian.

"Why, sir," said the man wonderingly. "It be the last day of October . . . have you forgotten what night this is? It be the Eve of All Saints, when evil marches across the world, when spirits and ghosts set out to wreak their vengeance on the living."

The driver rolled his eyes wildly and raised his bottle once again.

Brian grabbed it from him and threw it into the darkness and cursed the man for a drunken fool.

Just then, there seemed a pause in the storm, and it became quiet except for the soft patter of rain. And—it seemed as if the sound emanated from nearby—their ears were filled by the long, drawn-out baying of a hound. The sound was cut short by the flash of lightning and the crash of thunder.

The driver leant forward, and grasped the young man tightly by the sleeve.

"You hear it, sir? You hear it? 'Tis the hound of hell, sir. I tell 'ee. The hound of hell! Old Tregeagle's hound!"

Brian was surprised to note that the man was positively shaking with fright.

"Look, my man, if you paid more time to your driving, and less to your drinking, then the hound of hell, or where ever, would not bother you."

"Ah, ah," the driver rocked to and fro in his seat, his arms wrapped across his chest, "you upcountry people are alike; you mock things which you cannot understand. Look out there, sir . . . look!"

Brian's gaze followed the shaky finger of the driver into the darkness of the night which shrouded the moor from their sight. Now and again, a flash of lightning would light up the landscape, causing a vivid white to highlight the trees and what looked like precipitous mountains.

"I didn't know you had mountains in Cornwall?"

The driver spat.

"Ain't no mountains, young sir. They be hills . . . Rough Tor, Brown Willy . . . they ain't mountains. No, sir, beyond them . . . beyond them. There lies Dormazy Pool."

"Dormazy Pool?"

"Aye, a lake of black water near a mile around, sir. That's where old Jan Tregeagle is, God save us. That's where the hound of hell waits!"

Brian sighed his exasperation.

"Who is this Tregeagle?"

"He were steward to old Lord Robartes," said the moon faced driver in a hoarse whisper. "It were back in the days of Charles the Second. Jan Tregeagle were an evil man, vain and godless. They do say he sold his soul to the Devil. When Tregeagle died his spirit was claimed by the eternal furies, but in his life, old Jan had done one good deed, and because of that he was allowed to spend eternity trying to empty Dormazy Pool with a leaky limpet shell. Ah, but the Devil, he swore to claim old Tregeagle's soul for his own, and he still hunts him over the moor with his hell hound baying."

The man sunk back on his seat twitching in fear.

Again, in the night air, came the lonely baying of a hound.

"Hear it, young sir? Hear it?"

Brian laughed and pushed the reins and whip back at the man.

"Listen you," he said evenly. "I might be an upcountry man, but I am not to be taken in by such fanciful stories, entertaining as they might be. I am told you have a nice folklore down here in Cornwall but I tell you, I am, as yet, not over-impressed by it."

He eyed the man sternly.

"Furthermore, I am tired. And the young lady is not in the best of health, thanks to your driving. So, take these reins and drive your coach at a nice, steady trot. Steady, mind you. And, so help me, if you so much as canter your horses I shall come and whip you across the moor myself! Do I make myself clear, fellow? Now get on with you; we want to reach Bosbradoe before midnight."

The driver took the reins from him and sunk back muttering to himself.

Brian climbed down and re-entered the coach.

"Are you all right now, madam?" he enquired.

The young girl inclined her head.

"Thanks to your intervention, sir."

As the driver urged the horses slowly forward, the bay of the hound came again. This time it seemed nearer than before, and Brian leant out of the carriage window and peered curiously into the darkness.

For a moment he could have sworn he saw a shape in the gloom, a rather large shape slinking along the road behind the coach. But it was surely not a wild dog. It seemed far too large. Then a flash of lightning illuminated the road and Brian saw that it was empty. Either he was seeing things, or perhaps the lightning was playing tricks with the shadows.

III

As *The Bodmin Flyer* continued its journey along the stony moorland road, a wind sprang up fiercely from the south east, moaning across the undulating hills, around the jagged boulders and stone monoliths which dotted the moor. The same wind dispersed the low storm clouds and soon the brilliant white of the moon was shining down unimpeded. The eerie light dispelled the gloom in the interior of the coach and Brian Shaw observed, with a satisfied pleasure, that his estimation of his traveling companion had been right. She was, indeed, pretty.

Under the dark hood of her traveling cloak he could discern a pale, heart-shaped face with a straight nose and a delicate red mouth whose dimples suggested that it was a mouth used to smiling. She had big solemn-looking eyes, whose color, although it was difficult to tell in the moonlight, must surely be grey or green.

"Is your home at Bosbradoe?" enquired Brian in an attempt to end the silence that had fallen between them.

"I was born there and live there with my father." The girl answered and then, as if in afterthought, added: "My name is Helen Trevaskis."

A sensation of delight caught Brian.

"Trevaskis? Your father would not, by any chance, be Doctor Talbot Trevaskis?"

The girl arched her eyebrows in surprise.

"Indeed he is, sir. Why, then, do you know my father?"

"We have never met, but I am to be his new partner in his medical practice."

The girl bit her lip in bewilderment as she gazed at the handsome featured young man before her.

"I knew my father was going into partnership with a doctor . . . someone from London, but I thought it was some worthy and elderly gentleman who had known my father when he was a medical student."

Brian smilingly shook his head.

"My father, who is also a doctor, went to medical school with Doctor Trevaskis. But my father is now retired. When I qualified in medicine I spent some years at St. Luke's Hospital in London, but I was in need of experience in general practice in the provinces. My father accordingly wrote to Doctor Trevaskis asking him if he would take me on in partnership and, very kindly, Doctor Trevaskis agreed."

The girl gave Brian a swift, shy smile.

"Bosbradoe is not a town for a young and ambitious doctor, Doctor Shaw. There is little social life there. Indeed, it is a dull place."

"That I refuse to believe if you live there," exclaimed Brian fervently. The girl's cheeks reddened but the smile came readily to her lips.

"You will find it quiet after a great city like London, I'll warrant."

"Miss Trevaskis," said Brian adamantly. "My aim is to spend two years in general practice in the provinces in order to encounter and observe the illnesses of the rural populace. But with this experience behind me, my ambition is to return to London and join the staff of a hospital to enter into medical research."

They chattered on until *The Bodmin Flyer* turned from the moorland road, through dark forests of tall trees, and along an open stretch of highway that ran parallel to a cliff top. The salt smell of the sea came to their nostrils and the rhythmic roar and crash of the waves on the rocks below caught their ears.

"We are nearly there," announced the girl. And, indeed, within a few minutes the mail coach was clattering down a village street. The coach driver was tugging his horses to a standstill and crying out, unnecessarily: "Bosbradoe! Bosbradoe!"

Bosbradoe was a tiny village which stood atop a long stretch of rugged cliffs, some four hundred feet above sea level, on the north coast of Cornwall. From its cluster of thick-set stone cottages, a tiny path ran down to a small cove—a tiny haven amidst the forbidding granite cliffs of the coastline—where an old harbor had been built. Some fishermen's cottages clung defiantly to the slope of the path as it wound its perilous way down to the harbor. By its side, a stream plunged on its way, cascading down into the harbor waters.

The coachman had brought his team to a standstill outside the tavern, a low, rambling building, which was little different in design from the cottages, although it was, of course, much larger. A wooden sign, creaking on its hinges outside the door, displayed a picture of a mermaid while underneath this picture the word *morvoren* was painted in ancient lettering. Brian Shaw later learnt from the landlord that it was the Cornish word for mermaid, since the inn had been in existence when the old language was generally spoken from Land's End to the Tamar.

As Brian alighted from the coach and turned to help Helen Trevaskis down, he was aware of flickering lights and singing in the square. It seemed that the entire village was packed into this square, standing around two large bonfires which sent their sparky blaze up into the blue-black darkness of the night.

"What is happening?" asked Brian as the landlord lifted his trunk down from the roof of the coach.

"Why, bless you, sir, it's All Hallows' Eve! The village turns out to light bonfires and sing, to keep away the evil spirits. Tonight be the night that all manner of evil things come abroad and prey on the unwary."

Brian smiled indulgently and offered his arm to Helen Trevaskis as she climbed from the coach.

He noticed that the landlord's face had suddenly become pinched and worried as his eyes fell upon the young girl. The big man moved forward awkwardly and raised a crooked finger to his forehead.

"Why, Miss Helen . . . we weren't expecting you back from Bodmin until the end of the week."

Helen smiled.

"Hello, Noall. I have come back earlier, because things are so boring in Bodmin. Would you fetch my bag? It is the red leather one."

Noall, the innkeeper, half opened his mouth to say something, and then bit his lip and turned away to pick up the girl's bag. Brian sensed that there was something that he wanted to say to the girl; something that he did not know how to tell her. His gaze turned to Helen but she seemed blithely unaware.

"Will you be staying long, sir?" It was the innkeeper, come back with the girl's bag.

It was the girl who answered for him.

"Oh, Noall, this is Doctor Brian Shaw from London. He is my father's new partner, and he will be living with us."

The red faced landlord shot a suspicious glance at Brian and then nodded begrudgingly.

"Where is my father, Noall?" continued the girl. "I expected him to meet the coach, for I let him know I was returning early."

The man hung his head and moved his weight awkwardly from one foot to the other.

Helen frowned.

"What is it, Noall? Have you something to tell me?"

"Miss Helen . . ." the man began. He stopped and chewed his lip as if searching for the right words. "It's like this, Miss Helen . . . Doctor Trevaskis . . ."

"My father? Has anything happened to him?"

"He's gone missing. He's been missing for the past two days."

The girl went white, stumbled back and might have fallen had not Brian caught her arm in time.

Helen Trevaskis sat before the roaring fire in the Morvoren Inn and sipped at a glass of mulled wine.

"I'm much better now," she said with a ghost of a smile at the anxiously hovering Brian. The color had, indeed, returned to her pale cheeks and highlighted well the redness of her hair which was offset by the vivid blue of her eyes.

"You nearly fainted then," he said in accusation.

"I'm sorry, Miss Helen," said Noall, the landlord, remorsefully. "I tried to break it to you as gently as I knew how . . ."

"It's all right, Noall. But you must tell me what has happened."

Noall scratched an ear.

"Well, it were the day afore yesterday. The doctor, your father, set off on his rounds about midday. They tell me he were last seen walking along the cliff tops towards Breaca way, towards the foreigner's house. When the evening came and he did not return, Mrs. Trevithick came here to see if he were in here."

"And was a search made?" intervened Brian.

The red-faced man looked at the ground and shrugged.

"It be All Hallows' Eve, and you know the customs of folks here about. Why, fishermen do not even put to sea on such a day. It be unlucky to be found wandering too far from the village."

"But damn it, man," cried Brian, aghast, "the doctor might have had an accident and be lying somewhere hurt upon the moor."

"Then God help him," said the innkeeper.

Helen's face was pale with anger.

"Do I hear aright, Noall? Do I understand that the villagers have made no attempt to find my father?"

"Miss Helen, you were born and bred here . . . you know the beliefs and customs of us village folk . . . you know what it would mean if we wandered on the moor on a day like this?"

"I cannot believe you would leave a man to die on the moors," exclaimed Brian.

"If he be not dead already," snapped the innkeeper, then added to Helen: "Begging your pardon, Miss Helen. But 'twere best to face the facts."

Helen suppressed a sob that rose in her throat.

"I cannot believe folk here would let him die, Noall. My father has lived in Bosbradoe twenty-five years, he has brought many of the villagers into the world, nursed them when they were sick, saved their lives . . . and this, this is how they repay him!"

"Let me organize a search now," said Brian.

"No!"

They turned at the hoarse voice. It was a ruddy-complexioned man with a shock of white hair. He was dressed completely in black, and stood at the open door of the inn.

"I said 'no'," he repeated as he entered the inn and shut the door.

"And who are you, sir, who presumes to give orders?" demanded Brian.

"Brother Willie Carew, the leader of our community in Christ here, sir," he said. "It is for their immortal souls that I do fear. And that responsibility gives me the right to give orders. On no account will the people of this village stir abroad until tomorrow morning."

"So a man might be lying in desperate straits on the moor this night because you are too cowardly to save him?" sneered Brian.

The stocky man's eyes flashed.

"Cowardly? No. But we are good Christians, and fear the Devil and all his works. Today is the ancient feast of the dead, when the spirits of the dead visit their former homes, when it is dangerous to leave the confines of the village, because the dead prey on the living and, unless vigilance is maintained, will send a soul shrieking into hell. The people—as you see—build fires, lit from sunset to sunrise, to protect them from the devils who ride through the night seeking victims."

The man turned to Helen.

"I am truly sorry that your father is lost to us. He was a good man; a Christian man. God send we can help him on the morrow."

Helen turned her face away from him.

The stocky man shrugged and walked out.

Only then did the girl's shoulders shake in sobs.

Brian caught her by the arm.

"I'll go and see what I can find, if these cowards will point the way."

She tried to repress the sobs which racked her body and shook her head violently.

"You are a stranger here, Brian. What can you do alone at night, not knowing the treacherous countryside which surrounds us?"

It was the first time she had used his first name.

"But it will be better than sitting hopeless and useless," he insisted.

"No. It would be better to wait until dawn. Then maybe we'll be able to persuade the villagers to help us."

"Those cowards?" There was a sneer in Brian's voice.

"Perhaps it is understandable, Brian," she said sadly. "We Cornish are a strange and superstitious people. We live too near to nature, to the elements, the sea, the wind, the land. So we are superstitious. We have an old mythology, an ancient folklore and a religion which was old thousands of years before the birth of Christ. Perhaps we are not yet truly Christian, for all our high-sounding phrases. Therefore we do not open our hearts readily to people from across the Tamar, to the upcountry people, as we call them. Let us wait until tomorrow."

She held out a hand to Brian.

"Let us go to my father's house. I am well enough."

She let Brian conduct her from the inn, along the street filled with carousing villagers, dancing round their bonfires, to the Trevaskis house at the end of the village street. The door was opened at Brian's imperious knock by a wet-eyed matron who gave a cry when she saw Helen.

"Oh, Miss Helen! My lamb, my dear!" She threw her arms about the girl and swept her indoors.

It was then that Helen's control broke down and she sobbed unashamedly on Mrs. Trevithick's ample bosom. Clucking like a mother hen with its young, the housekeeper—for such was Mrs. Trevithick's position—conducted Helen to her bedroom above the stairs.

Brian made himself at ease before the log fire to await her return.

A nervous cough made him look up. A gaunt-looking man stood hesitantly by the door. One eyebrow seemed to twitch in agitation.

"Good evening, sir. I am Trevithick. My wife is the housekeeper here. I understand you escorted Miss Helen home, sir."

"Quite right, Trevithick," answered Brian. "I am Doctor Shaw, Doctor Trevaskis' new partner."

The man frowned.

"Oh? Yes, the doctor was expecting you."

"Good. I believe the arrangement was that I was to have a room in this house?"

"Aye, sir . . . er, doctor. My wife has made up a room all ready for you. It only needs airing."

"Good. And now, perhaps, you can give me some information about this disgraceful affair, of the disappearance of the doctor?"

"I fear he be dead already, doctor."

Brian's eyes narrowed.

"What do you mean by that, Trevithick?"

"The last time anyone saw the doctor, he were going along the cliff tops towards the foreigner's house."

"The foreigner?"

Noall had mentioned "the foreigner" in exactly the same tone of voice. Trevithick nodded.

"Strange things happen up there, they say."

"Strange things? Who says? And who is this foreigner?"

Trevithick's eyes flickered from side to side.

"The foreigner? He is . . ."

"Trevithick!"

The gaunt man jumped and turned guiltily, as his rotund wife came into the room.

"I was . . . I was . . ." he muttered.

"I know what you were about," answered his wife shortly.

"You still have the chores to do, Trevithick. Be about them."

The man gave an imperceptible sigh and left the room without another glance at Brian.

Mrs. Trevithick gave him a steely examination.

"And now, sir . . ."

There was a challenge in her voice.

"And now, Mrs. Trevithick, as I explained to your husband, I am Doctor Shaw, Doctor Trevaskis' new partner. I believe you are expecting me."

The woman bit her lip.

"I see."

She straightened her shoulders as if she had momentarily received some blow.

"Yes, Doctor Trevaskis was expecting you," she admitted. "If you would be so good, sir, as to follow me, I shall show you your room."

"How is Miss Trevaskis?"

"She will be the better for a good night's sleep, sir."

Taking a candle, she conducted Brian up the stairs to a small bedroom. It was cold, but the woman went to the fireplace, where a log fire was already laid, and within a few minutes a fine blaze was leaping into the hearth.

"I shall return shortly, sir, with warming pans for the bed. Will there be anything else?"

"You can tell me why everyone here seems so suspicious of me."

Mrs. Trevithick sniffed loudly.

"Suspicious, sir? You are in Cornwall now. We do not take readily to upcountry people and their ways. They have brought us nothing but harm. I cannot understand why Doctor Trevaskis did not employ a good Cornishman, before importing an upcountry man."

She swept from the room leaving Brian to ponder over the strangeness of his arrival in Bosbradoe.

IV

Brian was awake just before dawn the next morning; was washed, dressed and downstairs before anyone else was stirring in the house.

The street was empty and littered with the remains of the previous night's revelry.

Brian observed that on every cottage the shutters were closed and the door firmly shut. The only movement was a stray dog burrowing into a pile of rubbish left by the revellers. The ash from their bonfires still smoldered.

With a shrug, he returned to the Trevaskis house, passing the square-towered church and its vicarage. He had opened the gate, which led up the short path to the door, when a voice called: "Good morning."

He looked up to see an elderly man of medium height regarding him with bleary red eyes from the vicarage garden. His sombre clothing proclaimed him as a man of the cloth, and judging by his dishevelled appearance, the man had not been to bed since the night before.

"Good morning, mister . . .?" Brian returned his greeting.

"Pencarrow, sir. Simon Pencarrow. I am pastor of the flock of Christ in the village, sir."

Brian frowned.

"Forgive me, Mr. Pencarrow," said Brian, "but I thought a Brother Willie Carew was . . .?"

The parson interrupted him with a laugh.

"I am a vicar of the Anglican Church, sir, and that is my church." He flung an arm to the nearby church building. "But, sir, meet with a Cornishman and you will meet with a follower of John and Charles Wesley. The lower orders are Methodists, every man-jack of them. Why, I have only three souls in my entire Parish, sir. You are not a Methodist, are you?"

Brian introduced himself and the vicar extended a limp hand.

"You are welcome to my poor parish, sir. Welcome."

"Why does the church keep you here, Mr. Pencarrow, if you have no flock to preach to?" enquired Brian.

"Why? Oh, come to the house and have some wine with me. Too early? Surely not, sir? 'Take a little wine for thy stomach's sake'—it is in the Good Book. No? I cannot tempt you? Very well. What was I saying?"

"You were going to tell me, sir, why you stay here with no flock to preach to," answered Brian, smiling.

"Ah, indeed. Well, sir, I do not complain to my bishop, for you will see, sir, that this is a beautiful spot, and I do not want to see new pastures at my time of life. The quietness of the spot lets me indulge in my antiquarian studies."

"What of Doctor Trevaskis, sir?" He said bluntly. "Is it not time we started to organize a search?"

The vicar sighed and pulled out a silver flask from his pocket and swallowed a liberal draught.

Brian caught the unmistakable odor of rum and noted the thin, trembling hands.

"I doubt if you will get the village awake before midday, sir. They have drunk enough on which to launch a schooner."

"Then I must organize a search, Mr. Pencarrow. Will you join me?"

"Would that I could, sir. Would that I could. But I am none too young in years and am possessed of the gout. This little beverage," he gestured to his flask, "is the only thing that keeps it at bay, sir. I wish you luck, though. I wish you luck."

Brian scowled. That was all that was needed: a village full of superstitious fools and now an alcoholic parson. There must be some one in authority in the village, a squire perhaps, who could stir the people from their lethargy. He put the question to the Reverend Simon Pencarrow, who shook his head sadly.

"Squire? Alas no, sir. The last squire of Bosbradoe was Sir Hugh Trevanion who was killed in the European wars against the Corsican despot. His mansion is sold now, for he left no heirs. A sorry day for Bosbradoe when Sir Hugh died. A sorry day when the foreigner came here."

"Ah, yes," nodded Brian. "The foreigner. It was in the direction of his estate that Doctor Trevaskis was last seen heading. Perhaps I could go and talk with the man. He might know something further."

The parson shuddered and took another long drink from his flask.

"The foreigner, a queer man, sir. A queer man! Strange things have happened since the foreigner came here, sir. He bought Sir Hugh's mansion and from that day a black cloud descended on Bosbradoe. No, sir, I could not advise you to seek his help."

The old man turned abruptly and walked into his house, slamming his door.

Brian stood looking in surprise.

The sun was coming up in a bright blue autumn sky. There was scarce a cloud about and Brian was almost deafened by the loud cry of the gulls as they swept and whirled along the cliff tops. He walked round the house, and went into the garden which ended abruptly on the cliff tops. The view was spectacular and Brian had to catch his breath as the beauty of the landscape took him.

"Brian!"

He turned at the breathless voice.

Helen stood before him, her pale face was drawn and he could discern a faint red edging to her eyes.

"Brian, are the others out looking for father yet?"

Brian bit his lip. "No one is stirring yet."

She gave a small cry, half a sob and half a cry of anger.

He reached out and took her hand.

"Do not worry, Helen. I have been speaking to Mr. Pencarrow. But I think it would recompense me if I went to see this foreigner that people keep talking about. It would seem that the last time anyone saw your father was when he was walking in the direction of the man's estate."

"Yes. Yes," the girl nodded eagerly. "Noall did say that, didn't he?"

"Tell me, who is this foreigner?"

"A German, I think. A nobleman . . . a baron or something of the kind. My father visited him a few times, but I do not think anyone really knows his name. He bought Tymernans about ten years ago . . . that is the name of the great mansion which stands just beyond the ruins of Breaca Castle. It used to belong to Sir Hugh Trevanion, but he was killed at Waterloo."

"Tymernans," repeated Brian. "Just beyond the castle. I shall find it. Nothing else is known of this man? The people here do not seem to like him."

She shook her head.

"No. He lives as a recluse and discourages visitors. No one goes up there now."

"Does he visit the village at all?"

"Only twice in the last ten years, as I recall," replied the girl. "He has some kind of servant; a half-wit and very ugly-looking, whom he sends now and then for various provisions."

"Do not worry, Helen. I am sure we will find your father."

He went out into the street and started to climb the hilly incline towards the spot where the crumbling stone tower of Breaca Castle rose perilously into the air, against the azure sky.

The pathway wound up a rise towards a heavily wooded flat and Brian paused by a stone road marker to look about him. He could see no sign of a house which, he gathered, must be sheltered by the thick woods which grew down towards the cliff edge.

At the edge of the woods he noticed, as he drew nearer, a high stone wall which wavered unevenly from the direction of the cliff tops around its perimeter. In it were two large wrought iron gates, but the pathway to them was overgrown as if it had not been used in years. For a moment, Brian thought there must be some mistake and that there must be another roadway to the estate. But the rotting wood board beside the gates, hanging crazily from one nail, declared it to be "Tymernans." For a while, Brian hesitated and then, catching the top of the iron gate, he hauled himself up over the stone wall and dropped down the other side.

Once among the trees, he had an overpowering feeling of gloom. The tall trees blotted out the rising morning sun and the cloudless blue sky of late autumn. His nostrils were assailed by the dank smell of rotting vegetation. Not being a country-bred man, he did not miss the song of the birds or the other woodland noises, although he noted that the woods were strangely quiet.

It was fairly easy to follow the overgrown pathway, and only occasionally did a shrub or bush bar his progress, but he soon pushed past these. As he walked further and further along the path, he fell to wondering whether anyone could live in the house at all. Brian pushed on, the feeling of chill and gloom shrouding his spirit.

Then he heard a sound and stopped.

The sound was indistinctive. He could not place it. Perhaps it had been the snapping of a twig or the rustle of branches. Yet he felt a presence . . . it was difficult to describe. He felt someone or something watching him from the bushes.

He swung round but there was nothing there. The wood was quiet. The silence echoed like the silence of a tomb.

He rebuked himself for giving way to emotions created by the superstition of the villagers. Certainly, the dank chill of wood which surrounded Tymernans gave a haunted aspect to the place.

Then came a rustling and crashing through the undergrowth. The branches and leaves swayed this way and that along one side of the pathway he was treading, moving from behind him to the front.

He stopped still.

"Who's there?"

Only silence answered him.

He walked a few paces forward and hesitated.

A grotesque shape suddenly launched itself from the bushes and before he realized it, he had been knocked to the ground and felt steel-like bands constricting his throat.

V

For a moment Brian lay stunned under the gibbering thing that had leapt upon him. He raised his hands in a futile effort to prize loose the constricting bands from their strangle hold around his neck. He tried to open his eyes to see his assailant, but all he could glimpse was a straggling mass of dirty black hair. He hardly knew whether the form was human or animal. No sooner had he started to struggle, than he became aware of the futility of the task. The thing had muscles of steel, the strength of a dozen men.

He was on the verge of blacking out, when there came a merciful release. The bands at his throat relaxed and the form above him moved away. He lay gasping and became aware of a cracking noise and a man's harsh voice shouting in a foreign language.

Brian shook his head to clear it and raised himself on one elbow.

He beheld a tall man dressed in sombre black from his calf length riding boots to his high crowned hat. Under a long black cloak, the man wore a black suit and a black cravat. The only relief to this dark garb was the white of his face, a cadaverous face which seemed like the pale wax face of a corpse. Only the eyes were animated, and shone like burning coals from the fires of hell. The man held a whip in his right hand, which he now and then cracked at the cowering figure before him.

It was this figure that caused the breath to catch in Brian's throat.

The face was large, with a long bulbous nose atop a horseshoe-shaped mouth, open to display straggling teeth with breaches here and there, and protruding slightly over the lower lip and letting a trickle of saliva dribble on to the stubby fork-bearded chin. The eyes were terrible; under bushy black brows there was a small right eye, so small and closed that at first, one might think he was peering into an eyeless socket, until they caught the pinprick of malignancy shining brightly from a bloodshot surround. The right eye was misshapen by an enormous wart.

But if the face was horrible, the body was sickening.

The head bristled with hair, like the hair of a mad dog, while between the shoulders rose a humpy protrusion and a corresponding hump stuck from the chest. The arms were long and muscular, and hung downwards like the arms of an ape, but the rest of the body was of thighs and legs so bowed that Brian wondered if the creature could move on them at all.

The whip was raised yet again and the horrible apparition went scuttling into the undergrowth.

The tall man turned to Brian and he was surprised to see an expression of concern on the man's face.

"Are you hurt?" the English was stilted and heavily accented.

Brian raised a hand to his throat and massaged the tender area carefully. He coughed several times.

"I do not think so, sir. I would be the better for a glass of water, however."

The tall man bent down and raised him up.

"Lean on my arm, sir, and I'll bring you to my house."

"I'm most grateful, sir. Are you the German gentleman?"

"I am, by birth, a Genevese, a native of the Swiss Republic."

"And you are the owner of Tymernans?" persisted Brian.

"I am."

Brian was silent for a moment.

"By all that is holy," he burst out. "What, or who was that creature?"

"Merely a servant of mine."

"A servant?" said Brian in astonishment. "But he was so grotesque, so animal-like . . ."

"He is a creature of nature, endowed with life in the same way as you or I," replied the man. "He is misshapen, but if I did not give him employment, then he would be stoned to death by the miserable natives hereabouts."

His voice was full of a bitterness which startled Brian.

"But is he not dangerous and deserving of restraint?"

"Ah, because he attacked you? Would you say the same of a guard dog which attacked a man entering your property? My estate is forbidden to visitors and this Hugo knows. For all he knew, you might have meant me ill. Why should I restrain him when he is doing his duty by guarding his master? He is no more dangerous than the average guard dog. He will do what he is told and if he does it well, then he is rewarded. If he does it ill, then he is punished. This is his simple life. If you mean me no ill, then you need have no fear of Hugo."

They did not speak further until the tall man led Brian from the woods and across a wide ill-kept lawn which separated the woods from a large rambling house. It stood precariously, almost on the edge of the cliffs. Brian noticed that most of the windows were closed and shuttered and the house had the appearance of a deserted ruin.

The man beside him noticed his absorption in the condition of the building.

"I am a recluse, sir," he said by way of explanation. "A man of scientific pursuits who cannot afford to waste time in dabbling with the upkeep of a property. All I need is a quiet place to work, to be left alone. If I am left alone by people I, in turn, will leave them alone."

This last was said by way of accusation.

"I came to see you," said Brian. "To speak of the disappearance of Doctor Trevaskis."

The man shot him a quick, searching glance but said nothing.

He motioned Brian to follow him into a scullery and drew a glass of water from a pump.

"And now, sir?" he said when Brian had eased his throat sufficiently and returned the glass.

"I am Doctor Trevaskis' new partner, Doctor Brian Shaw."

The tall man bowed.

"I . . . I am the Baron Victor Frankenberg."

Brian detected a slight pause before the final syllable of the name. He explained about the disappearance of Doctor Trevaskis. The baron's face was an impassive mask.

"Perhaps you would accompany me into my library?" he said, suddenly turning and leading the way, without waiting for a response. Puzzled, Brian followed him across a musty hallway into a large, well-lit room which was clearly in constant use. Brian's eyes flickered around the shelves which contained many hundreds of books; books in many languages which, he was surprised to note, were mostly on natural philosophy and chemistry.

"A glass of claret?"

Brian shook his head.

He was about to press the baron as to whether he knew Doctor Trevaskis when a long eerie howl filled the room. It was the howl of a hound, similar to that which he had heard the previous night out on the moorland. But this time it seemed as if the hound was in the room itself.

The baron calmly replaced his half-emptied glass of claret.

"Forgive me, sir," he said, "an indulgence of mine. I keep a small hunting pack for whenever the urge takes me to follow the fox through my grounds. At the moment one of my best hounds lies ill."

There was a silence while the baron reached for a silver decanter and refilled his glass, sipping it slowly as if savoring the fragrance of every sip.

"I beg your pardon, sir. Of what were we speaking?"

322

"Doctor Trevaskis, sir."

"The doctor called by here a few times since I have been here. As a man of science with a degree of medical ability myself, I had no cause to consult him. I did, however, see him walking along the moorland path two days ago, but only from a distance."

The baron rose to his feet.

"Now, sir, there is no more I can suggest. I regret the disappearance of Doctor Trevaskis, but the countryside hereabouts is wild and often dangerous. Let us hope there is a happy solution to the disappearance, that he stayed with friends, or that he has lost his way and will return anon."

He led Brian to the door.

Brian hesitated and motioned with his head towards the woods.

"What of . . ." he paused.

The baron drew back his thin lips in a mirthless smile.

"Hugo? Do not worry about Hugo. He has learnt his lesson, like a good dog and will have learnt it well."

The baron gestured to the whip that stood by the door.

The heavy wooden door of the house was swung shut in Brian's face. For a moment he stood irresolutely and then began to follow the path back towards the iron gates.

He could not help but suppress a violent shiver as he thought of the grotesque beast lurking in the bushes, waiting ready to pounce, the hairy hands closing round his throat. But he strode grimly on, trying to keep his head firmly upright, letting only his eyes dart from side to side as he walked down the gloomy woodland path.

The feeling of being followed suddenly seized him, and he could swear he heard the rustle of the undergrowth and the sound of labored breathing.

He swung round and found the path had wound so far into the woods that he was out of sight of the house and any aid from the baron.

A bush suddenly trembled before him and he raised his hands to protect himself.

Brian stepped back in surprise as the bush swung back and a woman almost fell at his feet.

"Help me, *mein Herr*, help me!" she gasped.

Brian reached down and helped the woman from her knees. He could not discern her age; it could have been anything from thirty to fifty. She must have once been strikingly beautiful. Her face was well-formed, the eyes wide and blue and the mouth a rosebud of red. But the once flaxen hair was streaked prematurely with grey, and lines of worry crept in tiny crevices around her eyes and mouth. A strange deadness could be read in her eyes. They lacked any form of vitality.

"You must help me, *mein Herr*, you must!" she gasped again.

"Why, what is it, madam?" asked Brian in astonishment.

The woman cast a terrified glance over her shoulder and began talking in voluble German.

Brian interrupted her with a shrug.

"Alas, madam, I cannot understand your language. Can you speak in English?"

"He . . . the baron! Do not trust him, *mein Herr*. I heard you at the house. You must trust him not. He is evil, evil! Oh, God's curse on the day I married him!"

Brian started at her vehemence.

"You are the Baroness Frankenberg?"

The woman threw back her head and laughed obscenely.

"*Grüss Gott!* Frankenberg? Frankenberg?"

She went off into a peal of laughter so maniacal that Brian thought she must be possessed of some disorder.

The woman suddenly shot a look back along the pathway and lent closer to him.

"Trust not the baron," she said in her broken English. "He is an evil man. You must help me get away from him. His name is not . . ."

There was a movement in the undergrowth.

The woman turned pale and nearly fell forward. She turned with a cry of despair and vanished into the undergrowth.

Brian looked up in the direction in which she had been looking.

The grotesque features of the man-beast, Hugo, leered at him from the bushes.

He felt his heart skip a beat and race wildly. But the grotesque man made no movement towards him and so, his pulse drumming rapidly, he walked slowly down the path to the wrought iron gates, swiftly climbed over them and hastened down the pathway to the village. He did not pause or relax the tension in his body until he saw the first of the stone, whitewashed cottages of Bosbradoe appearing round a bend in the roadway.

Helen Trevaskis, still looking pale and drawn, was seated in the parlor of the house when Brian returned. She turned quickly as he entered and Brian saw the faint light of hope die in her eyes as she read the lack of news in his face. Briefly, he recited the events of the morning.

"So father was last seen going over the moor?" she summarized at the end of his recital.

He nodded.

"I have managed to get Mr. Trevithick and a few other men to ride along the moorland paths," she went on. "Perhaps they will discover something. Oh, but I wish I were a man! This sitting waiting is so destructive to my nature."

Brian reached out a sympathetic hand for hers and she let him take it unprotestingly.

"I am sure he will be found, Helen. I shall see if I can organize some men who know the area and will set off to look myself."

"You are kind, Brian. I do not know what I should do without your support."

He squeezed her hand again and stood up.

VI

It had been a tiring day for Brian Shaw. Many of the villagers, sheepishly recovering from their alarms of Hallowe'en, had accompanied Brian and the Reverend Simon Pencarrow in searching across the moor, but when, as dusk fell, no sign of the doctor was forthcoming, the search was called off, in spite of the desperate efforts of Helen to get the search continued by torchlight.

It was Brian who suggested that he take Helen to the Morvoren Inn and ask Noall to provide their meal. The atmosphere in the inn was not exactly a happy one, and most of the villagers sat in silence, studiously avoiding Helen's eye.

Noall seated them in an alcove and brought them hot roast beef and mulled wine. The meal was eaten in silence. Brian said little out of respect for Helen's feelings and Helen was oppressed by the weight of the thoughts which tumbled in her mind.

Suddenly the soft chatter in the inn died away altogether.

Brian and Helen looked up to see the inn door swinging open and the grotesque shape of Hugo, the baron's servant, shuffling in.

The creature stood a moment on the threshold, leering at the company with his twisted and misshapen eyes. Then he shuffled forward, his arms akimbo, towards the bar.

The villagers knew him, although Hugo was not a frequent visitor to the village. Now and again, if the need was vital, the baron would send him to the village to obtain certain provisions. The villagers avoided Hugo as they avoided the baron's estate.

The grotesque form stopped before the bar, behind which Noall was standing watching his approach with evident distaste.

A hairy arm slapped down some silver coins on to the counter.

The mouth opened and a series of inarticulate sounds came forth.

This drew a nervous laugh from the villagers.

The mouth twisted and turned. Then suddenly words formed, strained, twisted words but comprehensible nevertheless.

"Wine . . . master wants wine."

Noall looked at the creature in disgust as he swept up the coins and counted them.

"Wine is it? Why don't your master and you leave here? You ain't wanted."

The creature seemed to hang his head.

Brother Willie Carew, the preacher, called from his seat.

"That's telling him, Noall. We want no creatures of Satan in this god-fearing town!"

Noall laughed grimly.

"I'll give you wine. But you tell your master that we don't like his sort here."

A chorus of approval greeted this. "Get out, baboon!"

"Bandy legs!"

"Devil!"

With alcoholic courage, the villagers started to shout ribald remarks at the unfortunate creature who stood staring sullenly at them.

It was Tom Jenner, full of rum, who staggered up to the silent Hugo and prodded him with a fore-finger.

"I bet 'ee can dance on them fine legs of yourn, can't 'ee?" he said in a confidential tone, which brought a gust of laughter from the company.

Hugo scowled fiercely.

"Wine," he said, doggedly.

"What's 'ee say then, Tom?" demanded Evan Tregorran.

"'Ee says he wants wine."

Tom Jenner threw a coin on the counter.

"Give him wine, landlord," he ordered imperiously.

Noall hesitated.

"Don't you think you best leave him alone, Tom?"

"Give him wine."

A glass was placed in the creature's hands.

Hugo sniffed it suspiciously and then drained it.

"Wine . . . good," he said, after a moment's contemplation.

A shout of laughter went round the room.

"Now then," interrupted Tom Jenner, prodding the creature again. "Now then, let's see 'ee do a hornpipe or a jig on them fine legs of yourn."

The creature looked at him puzzled.

Tom Jenner took up a fiddle and started up a tune. "Go on," cried several people. "Dance, dance!"

"Don't 'ee know how to dance?" demanded Evan Tregorran.

He executed a few ungainly steps. The creature looked at him in surprise. Then he suddenly realized what these people wanted him to do. His mouth twisted into a grimace which was, for him, a smile.

He stumbled about on his short legs making weird sounds, the nearest sounds the creature possessed to laughter.

Faster and faster went Willie Carew's fiddle.

Faster and faster stumbled Hugo.

Suddenly the creature tripped and fell, landing in a wild heap at Brian's feet.

The creature lay moaning awhile amidst the shouts of laughter. Then he climbed to his feet, raising an arm to the table at which Helen and Brian were sitting, and using it as a lever to draw himself upright. Brian was surprised to notice that the arm was a well-shaped limb with a fine hand and long delicate fingers. Also on the arm was a strange tattoo mark, two whales supporting a mermaid who was playing some sort of pipe. And across the tattoo was a white line of livid flesh which Brian knew to be a scar. The arm surprised Brian because it was out of keeping with the rest of the creature's grotesque body. He instinctively looked at Hugo's other arm, and saw that it was as gross and misshapen as the rest of the body, hairy with thick, stubby fingers.

He was about to remark on it when the inn door opened with a shattering crash.

The tall cadaverous figure of the baron, clad from head to toe in black, stood surveying the interior of the inn in grim silence.

His cold eyes swept the room and fell, finally, on Hugo. The creature seemed to whimper and crouch grovelling before him.

"Hugo!" snapped the baron. *"Komm mit!"*

Like a whipped dog, the creature ambled across to the baron and squatted at his feet.

There was a deathly silence in the tavern room.

The baron walked across to the counter and picked up the two bottles of wine that Noall had drawn up for the pitiful creature.

"Mine, I think?"

The baron's voice was soft, almost sibilant.

"Yes, sir."

"Good. You would like Hugo to dance for you some more?"

The pale, cold eyes bore into the landlord. "It were just a bit of fun, sir. Just fun."

"Yes? Fun?"

There was an awkward pause.

"When I send my servant here in the future you will treat him with respect," the baron's voice was suddenly harsh. "If I hear of a man maltreating Hugo again, I will personally take my riding crop to that man, and his wife will have to live with a sight which will be infinitely worse than the face of Hugo. *Verstehen?*"

The baron twisted on his heel and, with Hugo gibbering and scrambling behind him, was gone into the black night.

In the silence that followed Brian turned to Helen and suddenly cried in surprise.

The girl lay in a swoon on her seat.

It took a little time to bring her, with the help of a sobered Tom Jenner, to her house and seat her before the fire in the parlor.

She gave a tiny rueful laugh as Brian lent over her and felt her pulse.

"I seem to be making a habit of fainting."

Brian waved away Mrs. Trevithick who stood armed with a jar of smelling salts.

"Just lie back and relax a bit, Helen. Don't worry."

But a fierce light blazed in her eyes.

She reached up and caught Brian's wrist in a grasp which was almost painful.

"Did you see that creature's arm?"

Brian nodded.

"The arm with the weird tattoo, you mean?"

Helen swallowed as if something was hurting her.

"Yes, yes. That was it."

"I thought it was strange for a creature like Hugo to indulge in tattoos," smiled Brian. "What of it?"

"Did you also see the scar?"

"Yes."

The girl placed the back of her hand to her mouth and gave a shuddering cry.

Brian bent forward in alarm.

"Helen, what is it?"

"Brian, that arm . . . that arm! It was my father's arm!"

Brian reached out and touched the girl's forehead.

It was not unduly hot. And her pulse, though a trifle rapid, gave no indication of temperature.

"Didn't you hear me?" the girl demanded. "I said, the arm was that of my father."

Brian bit his lip.

"I hear you, but I am not sure that I understand."

The girl gave a sigh of exasperation.

"I mean no more nor less than what I say. It is horrible! Horrible!"

"You mean your father has a similar tattoo mark?" enquired Brian wonderingly.

The girl banged a clenched fist on the table in agitation.

"The arm, the tattoo, the scar . . . they are just not similar. They are the same. They *are*!"

Brian picked up his medical bag and silently rummaged through the contents. He picked up a dark yellow bottle marked "Laudanum" and measured some drops into a glass. Then he rang the bell and instructed Mrs. Trevithick to bring some hot water and honey.

The girl watched him in silence.

"Look, Helen, it has been an upsetting day for you . . ." he began.

"You think I am insane?" snapped the girl.

"No, no," he said gently. "But what you say is impossible. Though the tattoo could be similar."

Mrs. Trevithick returned with a kettle of hot water. Brian motioned her out and mixed a small drink.

"This will help you to relax."

"But what of the creature? You still don't believe . . ."

He cut her short with a gesture.

"I believe you. But I want you to relax and get a good night's sleep. But certainly the matter needs investigation. You go upstairs to bed, and I will go and have a few words with the baron and see if we can clear up the mystery. The creature must have had the tattoo copied from somewhere."

The girl was about to protest again, but resignedly took the glass from Brian's hands.

When she had gone Brian poured himself a glass of rum and slumped into a chair.

Was she hallucinating? No, he had seen the arm for himself, and he remembered distinctly how, at the time, he felt that it was odd and did not seem to fit the creature's general grotesqueness. But the very idea . . . the creature with an arm similar to the doctor's—the *same* as the doctor's arm. Ridiculous!

He rang the bell and Mrs. Trevithick entered with her perpetual sniff.

"Did you want something, Doctor Shaw?"

"Indeed I did, Mrs. Trevithick," answered Brian. "You have worked for Doctor Trevaskis for many years. Did the doctor have any distinguishing marks on him?"

"What, sir?"

Mrs. Trevithick frowned.

"Did he have any marks that were different from other people, from which he might be identified. Marks, such as tattoos."

"Oh that!" The woman's mouth quirked in an attempt at a smile. "Yes. The doctor had a tattoo on his right arm. Now let's see . . . it was a mermaid, sitting atop two whales . . . sitting there playing a pipe or some such thing."

Brian felt a cold gnawing in his stomach.

"Oh, and there was a scar on the same arm. He fought a duel once, so they say, and some man cut his arm with a sword."

Brian sat in silence.

"Will that be all, sir?"

"What? Oh, yes. That's all, Mrs. Trevithick," he said waving her from the room.

Why had Hugo devised a similar tattoo to the doctor? Had he seen the marks and liked them so much that he got somebody to repeat the tattoo on his arm? But how had he managed to obtain a similar scar? It was surely not possible. And Helen; Helen said that the arm *was* her father's. But that was also impossible. How could someone else's arm be transferred and grafted to another human being? It would require a surgery so advanced that . . . no, he was mad even to contemplate the idea. Beside which, the doctor had been missing only two days, and even if such an operation were possible, the graft could not be made and healed within that time.

There was only one way to solve the mystery, for mystery it surely was. He must go up to Tymernans, the baron's house, and seek some explanation.

VII

The moon was lighting the landscape with an eerie luminescence when Brian Shaw made his way along the cliff path that led to the grim blackness of the forest which surrounded Tymernans. Storm clouds, low and heavy with rain, were scudding across the blackness of the sky, sometimes scraping across the face of the moon and hiding the myriad of stars that hung like silver pinpoints in the black void. A slight wind made the tall grasses rustle and the leaves on the evergreens blow this way and that. Its breath through the tall trees made an almost human moaning which rose and fell, fell and rose with monotonous persistence. Several times, as the light was blacked out by the clouds, Brian stumbled and cursed in the darkness.

As he drew near the wrought-iron gates, and began to climb over, the rain began to splatter down and he was thankful for his heavy traveling cloak.

An instinct drew him along the overgrown path and this time he kept all his senses atune to any threatened danger. He stopped several times and listened attentively, wondering whether the unseen eyes of Hugo were upon him.

Slowly he moved on until he stood on the edge of the grass lawn before that once splendid mansion.

The rain was blowing in torrents now, mingling with the salt spray whipped up from the sea. He could feel the nearness of the sea, hear the angry crash of its breakers on the rocks somewhere below the cliffs, feel its menace in the air. The trees afforded him some shelter, and he stood irresolutely under their protection, trying to find courage to sprint across to the house.

A blinding light suddenly caused thousands of shadows to be thrown this way and that and lit up the house like some bizarre nightmare scene, painting it in vivid blacks and whites.

There was but the merest second before the heavy crash of thunder followed the lightning stroke.

Then the lightning struck again. This time Brian, his heart pounding, was prepared for the blinding flash.

What made him start, however, was the fact that the lightning seemed to fork straight into the old mansion before him and the noise of its impact seemed like a thousand wailing banshees.

He raised a hand to shade his eyes from the rain and waited until a third and a fourth stroke caught at the roof of the house.

No, he was not mistaken. There, on the roof of a tower, the tallest part of the old building, was a weird contraption—a sort of disc-like affair made of some gleaming metal. It was to this that the lightning seemed attracted, striking again and again, and causing the metal to turn yellow, red, blue and then white. It was a strange contraption, and after the lightning and thunder had passed echoing out to sea, the weird disc continued to glow and continued to hum with strange noises.

What did it mean? It seemed as if the baron was trying to tame the very elements to whatever experiments he was conducting.

The strange disc Brian supposed was a means to conduct the energy of the lightning into some usable means for experimentation. It glowed red like an angry eye in the dark night, hissing as the rain spattered against its hot surface. Brian drew his cloak tightly around his shoulders and walked across the lawn to the door.

To his surprise he found that it stood open a fraction, and he gently pushed it wide. It swung with a groan from its rusty hinges and Brian stood on the threshold, peering down a dark, unlit corridor.

Somewhere, deep inside the house, he could hear a strange humming, almost like the panting whine of an animal in pain.

He decided to follow the noise of the humming. He walked to a small hall which had once been the servants' hall, for here he stopped to strike a light from his tinder box and saw a row of bells hanging from the walls. These bells would be connected to the various rooms from which the occupants of this once palatial residence could ring for their servants. In the dying light of the match he saw a stub of candle and struck another light to ignite it.

There were several doors leading off this hall, but one door was open a little and from behind it Brian could hear the hum which had become soft and rhythmic. He pushed it open and found the way led down a shallow flight of stairs to another somewhat tiny hall. Two doors led from this hall and from behind one came a strange eerie glow which seemed to rise and fall with the sound of the humming noise.

Gradually he pushed open the heavy iron-studded door. He stood at the top of a flight of stone steps which led down to what was obviously a cellar. A series of little arches gave a weird ornateness to the stairway.

Brian crept softly down them and halfway down he crouched and peered through an arch.

It was a sight which astounded him.

The great cellar—it was more of a cavern—was lit with several lanterns suspended by chains from an almost cathedral-like roof. But although the cellar was underground, Brian had the strange sense of a breeze and the tang of salt spray upon it. He let his eyes wander over the great cavern and could see on one side an answer to the puzzle.

On one side the walls opened out to a large cave mouth, which must stand directly on the cliff face, open to the sea.

In spite of the constant light of the many lanterns, a white brilliance seemed to dominate the cavern. It came from a great lamp which stood on top of a big metal box, prominent in a corner. From it, several wires ran both to the roof and which, Brian guessed, were probably connected to the strange disc which crowned the house. Other wires ran to various weird boxes on which were strange markers, valves and other instruments. To one side stood a chemical bench. And there were surgical cases, packed with instruments the like of which Brian, in all his medical career, had not seen before.

In another corner were several boxes and a table covered with a canvas sheet. Close by, were some wooden crates from which came a constant whining and whimpering and on peering closely Brian realized they were makeshift kennels and decided that they contained several dogs on which the baron was experimenting.

But it was the center of this great underground laboratory to which Brian turned his fullest attention.

There stood an operating table and beside it the baron, in surgeon's gown and mask. On the other side crouched Hugo. They were peering at something which lay inert on the bloodstained sheet.

It was the black form of a gigantic wolfhound.

"And now, Hugo." It was the voice of the baron, and it carried a triumphant note in it. "Now, Hugo, let us see the result of our work."

The baron bent over the dog and seemed to adjust something.

"Yes, yes, my friend, the stitches are in order."

The creature made some noise in its throat.

"Yes, Hugo. Now comes the moment." The baron removed some surgical instruments from the table and stood back. "Everything is ready except the very spark of life, but now . . ."

He moved towards the great box which was, Brian later discovered, a large generator, and made a rapid check of the dials and switches.

"It has stored sufficient electricity from the storm, my friend. So all we have to do now is pull the switch. Stand back!"

The noise from the machine rose to an ear-piercing whine, a whine so intense that Brian covered his ears with his hands and he noticed that Hugo had backed away into a corner with the kennelled dogs. The light on top of the machine glowed blinding white. Incredibly, Brian saw this whiteness race along some wires to the inert body on the table, saw the body of the animal jump with the shock of the current, fall back and jump again.

The baron snapped back the switch and the whine died back into the former rhythmic hum.

The baron ran forward to the dog and Brian saw him place a listening instrument against the animal's ribcage. For a while the baron leant over the animal, oblivious to any thing else. Then he flung the stethoscope from himself and there was a look of wild exultation on the man's face.

"*Wunderbar! Wunderbar!* I have succeeded. Once again, I have succeeded!"

Hugo came scuttling back to his master's side and peered at the animal.

"Look at him, Hugo. Look at him. I have given it life, I have breathed life into a hound. So my success of last week was not the merest fluke even though the first beast died. This one shall live. I knew what I could do once, I would do again. They . . ." there was a catch in his voice, "they broke my equipment before, tore up my notes, destroyed my experiments. But I knew that sooner or later I could repeat that experiment. Look, my Hugo, the hound lives . . . and I have given it life. Soon I will recreate man once again!"

Brian looked on in amazement as the cadaverous baron seemed to dance about the room.

The black shape on the table was stirring and had risen from its side and lay on its belly on the table, a grotesque head on top of its long body, a red gash of a tongue lolling over its gigantic fangs. Even from where he hid, the creature looked like some vicious nightmare to Brian.

"Come Hugo, let us get it in the cage. We don't want another accident such as happened to the previous creature. This will be my hound of hell . . . my enemies shall come to know his jaws in time."

The baron gave a short bray of laughter as his servant pushed forward a great box-like kennel and, carefully avoiding the snapping fangs of the awakening animal, managed to manhandle it into the box and slam shut the wire mesh door.

"Think of it, Hugo," rhapsodized the baron. "I have given it life. Next it will be my task to create a man . . . a beautiful man that will so expunge from the mind of mankind my past mistakes, that they will honor me as their god!"

Hugo made a snarling sound and tugged at the ecstatic baron's sleeve.

"Eh? What is it, Hugo? Oh, you. Yes, you."

The baron laughed at the slobbering face of his servant.

"Yes, yes. You will be next. I promised, did I not? I will recreate your body limb by limb. You will see, my friend. Did I not give you a nice arm in replacement for your misshapen one? Two days but with my technique it is exactly as your own. Soon you will not even see the scars where the arm joins your own body."

Hugo nodded happily and waved the arm in the air, gurgling like a new born child.

"Well, peace, Hugo. We will soon refit your other limbs until you stand as tall as I do. I shall change your face and your body, my ugly friend."

Suddenly Brian realized his danger. The baron and Hugo were walking towards the stairs. He turned and made to scramble up the cellar steps to the door. He was almost there when his foot slipped on the stone slabs and he fell, face down, slithering on his stomach on the cellar steps. Before he could move he felt his arms held in a vice-like grip.

He was turned, none too gently, to find the fiendish face of Hugo peering down at him.

Behind him the white face of the baron was gazing down in ironical amusement.

"Well, Hugo, it seems we have had an audience for our little medical experiment. An appreciative audience, I trust. Welcome, Doctor Shaw. Welcome to my humble laboratory."

VIII

Brian looked up at the white mask-like face of the baron. He sat with his back against a large packing case, his hands bound securely behind him and his ankles were also tied tightly. Hugo had gone and the baron was sitting on a stool looking down at his unfortunate prisoner. There was the trace of a smile on his thin, bloodless lips.

He pulled from his pocket a long, black cheroot, bit off the end and proceeded to light it.

"You cannot get away with this, baron," said Brian between clenched teeth.

"It is only fair to tell you that you will never leave here alive," said the baron in a conversational tone. "But as you are a man of medicine, a scientist like myself, you will appreciate my reasons, of which I shall tell you presently.

"My name, sir, is not Frankenberg. It is the Baron Victor Frankenstein."

The baron paused to see what effect it had on the young doctor.

The name meant nothing to Brian.

The baron smiled ruefully.

"Ah, vanity," he said quietly. "I thought the name was universal, a byword. But then, I forget you were a mere child at the time . . . when was it? 1816—ten years ago. A long time, eh?"

As Brian watched the baron's eyes glazed as he drifted off into his remembrances.

"My father was the Baron Alphonse Frankenstein of Geneva, and we were an old and rich family. I had what they called 'promise,' and when I was seventeen I had already graduated from the schools of Geneva and went on to the great university of Ingolstadt. There I studied under Krempe, that great professor of natural philosophy, and under Waldman, who taught that chemistry was but a branch of natural philosophy.

"I engaged in scientific pursuit so closely that I outstripped even my fellow students and teachers. For two years I studied so hard that I did not even return to Geneva to visit my family, spending my holidays in my laboratory, wresting nature's secrets from her unwilling grasp.

"Ah, my young friend, the phenomena which had peculiarly attracted my attention was the structure of the human frame and, indeed, any animal which was endowed with life. Whence, I often asked, did the principle of life proceed? A bold question, and one which has ever been considered a great mystery. But I, Victor Frankenstein, dared to grasp the nettle."

He paused. There was a wild exultation in his eyes. His pale face had become animated with a strange light.

Brian felt a growing revulsion.

The man was obviously mad; but there was, in his madness, a ghastly genius which both repelled and attracted the young doctor. The immorality of what the man was saying shocked him, while its scientific importance took his breath away.

The baron had resumed his speech.

"It needed the life spark, as I called it, to animate the body once it was carefully prepared for life. Where would I find that life spark? Ah! From the elements themselves! I wrested the life force out of nature herself—learnt how to harness nature's electricity, the lightning flash, to my will.

"At a time when men were still playing with the electric arc, while Seebeck was using copper and bismuth to discover simple electric current generated by thermocouple, I, Victor Frankenstein, was wresting that life force from the fount of power itself.

"So astonishing a power was placed into my hands, that I hesitated a long time concerning the manner in which I should employ it. Finally, I decided that I would create a being such as myself.

"It was a dreary November night, I recall, that I beheld the accomplishment of my toils. I collected my instruments around me and infused the spark of being into the lifeless form I had created. It was already one in the morning; the rain pattered dismally against the panes, and my candle was nearly burnt out, when, by the glimmer of the half extinguished light,

I saw the dull yellow eyes of the creature open: it breathed hard, and a convulsive motion agitated its limbs.

"My toils of two years, in which I had worked for the sole purpose of infusing life into an inanimate body, and which had deprived me of rest and health, were over.

"But the people did not understand. They attacked my creation and they attacked me. They drove me and that creature into the bleak Arctic wastes, where it perished. But I was picked up by an English ship, and in my despair I related my story to one Robert Walton. He was horrified, disgusted, even as he wrote my story down and which he afterwards published through his friendship with Mary Shelley, the wife of the English poet. He thought me dead when he published the story, for he recounted how, in my despair, I leapt from the ship on to an iceberg and was borne off into the darkness of the Arctic night, never to be seen again."

The baron sat back and laughed wildly.

"Poor fool, poor fool! I leapt on to the iceberg because I knew two things. First, that this stupid moralist would give me in charge to the police when we docked and that they would send me back to Geneva to stand trial for the murders committed by my poor creature while defending his life from the madness of the people. Second, I had seen a ship astern of us which I knew would have to pass by that iceberg. I was only half an hour on the ice before I was taken off by an American brigantine which landed me in Plymouth. From there, I sent for my wife, and she came bearing the remnants of my fortune, which was still large enough to make me secure from prying eyes."

The baron stood up smiling.

"And so, my friend, I have spent the last ten years in this godforsaken land, continuing my researches, trying to find out where I had gone wrong before. For I will admit that my first creation was not perfect." His eyes flashed. "No, no! I made a mistake somewhere, for it turned out to be a mindless monster, whereas my creation was to have been the perfect man, a beautiful man. But I shall succeed eventually, do you hear me?"

His voice rose to an hysterical note.

He swayed for a few minutes and then gathered his self-control again.

He threw down the butt of his cheroot on to the floor.

"And now, my friend, I will leave you to your contemplation. Tomorrow I shall start work on poor Hugo. I promised him a beautiful body."

He chuckled.

"It is not a creation of life, but by it I can improve my grafting techniques and make his twisted form into a body fit enough to aid me in my greater experiments. Thanks to your help," the baron twisted his mouth into an evil grin, "and the help of the so stupid Doctor Trevaskis, who tried to interfere with my work, Hugo shall soon have a fine young body."

He twisted on his heel and was gone.

For several seconds Brian lay still, chewing his lips and lying to fight down the feelings of panic which assailed his nerves.

It was the breeze, with the salt sea taste, sweeping in through the open cave entrance, which jerked his mind to the thought of escape. He cast his eyes wildly about the cavern seeking some means of severing his bonds. There was none.

Then his eyes fell on the butt of the baron's cheroot. A faint whisp of smoke still curled from it.

Brian rolled over on his stomach, and slowly inched his way towards it, turning his back, stretched out his bound wrists towards it, feeling for it with his finger tips. He burnt his hands three times before he had managed to maneuver the red tip of the butt against one of the cords which bound him.

The smoldering rope hurt his wrists and hands. It became almost unbearable, but Brian set his teeth tightly and kept the cheroot pressed firmly in place.

With a jerk, Brian felt the strand go slack and it was but the work of a few minutes more gradually to unloosen his bonds, and finally free his wrists.

Quickly Brian untied his feet and stood up. For a few seconds he crouched in agony as the blood surged to his feet, causing excruciating cramps in his lower limbs. He stood unsteadily, and peered around, seeking a weapon by which to defend himself if either Hugo or the baron returned. Most of the surgical instruments had been cleared away and locked in various cabinets which surrounded the cavern.

He walked across to the cabinets and tugged vainly at the doors.

Perhaps, he thought, there might be something which would help him, a crowbar or like implement, lying among the various boxes which were shrouded by a great canvas sheet at the back of a pile of packing cases. The cases were near the kennels in which the baron had placed his experimental dogs. For the most part these dogs seemed under the influence of some kind of drug. They looked at Brian with unseeing eyes, although one noticed his approach and whimpered pitifully.

A vicious snarl closer at hand made him jump and he turned to see the great wolfhound on which the baron had operated, glaring at him from crazed bloodshot eyes. Its fighting fangs were displayed, and the great jaws snapped convulsively.

He carefully skirted the box and hoped the great beast would not start barking and so attract attention.

He began to poke about among the cases. Surely there was an iron bar or hatchet among them? Perhaps under the canvas? He drew back the covering, which revealed a series of fairly sizeable glass tanks containing bubbling liquids. But it was the sight of the contents of those tanks which brought Brian's heart into his throat, and the nausea to well within him.

In the first tank was a severed head. The head floated in the liquid, supported by wires along which a faint current was still flowing, causing the horrid eyelids to flicker open and shut, revealing wide, staring, dead eyes. The face had been that of an elderly man, a kindly face, now frozen white in death. The mouth was open and the tongue lolling. The greying hair was plastered over the forehead. It was a head that looked strangely familiar.

It took a while for Brian to bring his horrified gaze back and examine it carefully. He knew now that he was looking at the severed head of Doctor Talbot Trevaskis.

Weapon or no, he decided to try to escape from this morgue of a house, back to the village and seek someone in authority to whom he could tell his fantastic story.

He climbed slowly to the cellar door. The great iron handle gave, and Brian inwardly cursed the noisy squeaking of the rusty hinges as he swung the door open.

The hallway outside was in darkness, but there was just enough light to make out the stairs which led up to the servants' hall.

Holding his breath, Brian climbed the stairs and stood for a second behind the door.

The house was quiet.

Stealthily he stole down the corridor, keeping carefully to the shadows of the walls. He reached the door and opened it, and was out into a bright moonlit night. The storm clouds had been swept far out to sea, and the rain had ceased. It had left the lawn between the house and the trees carpeted with a silver sheen where the silvery moonlight was reflected against the rain-sodden grass.

Brian was halfway across the lawn when he heard a cry. Without pausing in his stride he darted a swift look over his shoulder and saw the figure of Hugo looking in his direction from the corner of the house. Then Brian was among the trees and racing through the undergrowth towards the stone wall of the estate.

A sound caused him to stop dead and froze his very heart.

From the direction of the house came the solitary howl of a hound. No sooner had it died away than came a series of yelpings and barkings. It was the sound of a hunting pack, turned loose upon its quarry.

A cold sweat began to pour from Brian as he realized that the baron had unleashed his hounds. He began to run forward blindly, uncaring as he stumbled into bushes, as branches snapped across his body and scratched at his face. The single thought in his mind was to reach the stone wall, and to this end he bent his will, jumping across muddy ditches, pushing aside restricting branches, not noticing the pricking of the gorse and the thorns which tore into the flesh of his arms and legs.

Brian began to run as he had never run before, his heart pounding madly. Sweat began to flow from his forehead, trickling into his eyes, almost blinding him. His mouth hung open and his breath came in harsh, painful gasps.

He could feel the muscles in his legs growing weaker and weaker at the exertion.

Some part of his mind registered the yappings and barkings of the dog pack as they came on behind him. He could hear them pushing through the undergrowth in his wake. Closer still and closer they came.

He could run no more.

He stumbled against the trunk of a tree and rested there, his heart thundering against his rib cage, an excruciating pain in his side.

A hound, fleeter than the rest, raced into the clearing before him, saw him and gave an excited yelp. The beast paused not a second but sprang for the man. Exerting some hidden strength, Brian stepped back and swung his foot at the animal, the toe of his boot caught it in the throat as it started its spring and there was a snap. The animal fell back without a sound, its head strangely twisted to one side.

But the others were closing in.

He turned and stumbled on. His legs were like jelly. He could go little farther. It was hopeless.

Almost weeping in frustration, he stumbled against another tree. He tried to marshal what remained of his resources, but it was useless. A kind of lethargy of despair overcame him. What was the use of struggling on? They would get him in the end. Better to have done with it all now.

A hand grasped his arm.

He turned, his heart beating twice as rapidly.

It was the woman who called herself the baroness.

"*Komm, komm mit!*" she cried in agitation.

"No good. No good. I'm done. Done, I tell you!"

She seized his arm and began to drag him.

"Down there," she jerked her head towards a stream. Brian allowed himself to be dragged forward, the woman half pushed, half pulled him towards the stream. Then they splashed along it until they came to some great overhanging embankment which jutted out, forming an almost cave-like hollow.

Brian found himself pushing through an iron-framed doorway in which he could see no door.

He could hear the splashing of the dogs as they drew nearer.

Then his energy deserted him. With a shuddering sigh he fell down in the tiny passageway and gave himself up for lost.

The dogs, fangs barred, had almost reached the doorway when the woman reached forward. There was a cranking of a chain, and suddenly, an old iron portcullis slid from an unseen slot, barring the entrance, and leaving the hounds angry and puzzled, snapping through its bars.

"We must not wait here to be found by Hugo, *mein Herr*," whispered the baroness urgently. "We must go on."

Brian raised his eyes and saw the hounds barking and yapping on the far side of the iron bars. He muttered a prayer of thanks. It seemed to give him new strength, and he raised himself up, half supported by the woman.

They passed several winding tunnels, and came through several iron-shod doors, which the baroness carefully secured behind them. Their route lay through a maze of waterlogged passageways.

"Where are we going?" gasped Brian.

"Ahead is a small room, where I often hide when he . . . the baron . . . is in a bad mood. These tunnels are part of an ancient tin mine, and the tunnels come up under the house itself. They lead into the cavern where the baron has his laboratory. From there, through the mouth of the cave which leads on to the cliff face, one can climb down and make one's way along the edge of the cliffs to the cove below Bosbradoe. Care must be taken along the rocks which lay directly beneath the cliffs."

Brian was incapable of further speech and allowed himself to be led through the subterranean maze until, finally, they came to a little cave-like room.

"It is my sanctum," said the baroness as she helped Brian on to the bed. "I often hide here."

She let him lay for a while, breathing deeply, until his wind came back and the pain was gone from his side. Then she handed him some water. It was cool, and refreshed him greatly.

"You are his wife . . . Baroness Frankenstein?" he asked at length.

The woman nodded unhappily.

"Ah, *mein Herr*, did I not tell you he was evil?"

"How long have you been married to him, madam?"

"Just before he had to flee from Geneva, with the curse of the people upon him, and the evil thing which he had created. I was young then . . . young and beautiful." She paused in reflection then continued. "I feel I have lived several lifetimes in these last few years. When I married Victor he was handsome, rich, and people said he was going to be a great scientist. Alas, they did not know what evil experiments he was conducting.

"Can you believe that I loved Victor, despite all that? I thought he had made a tragic mistake, that the people had been unfair to him.

"So it was that, when I heard from him, telling that he had escaped, that his creature was dead and that he wanted to start a new life in England, I took what money remained to us and came running, running to his side.

"We bought this house here, in Cornwall, and soon after, Victor began his experiments. It was then that I discovered that Victor, unbalanced by the awfulness of what he had done, had become mad, totally mad. There were no excuses I could make for him. He somehow believed he was God; that he could create life. But what a terrible path he trod to achieve his ends!"

She placed her hands over her face and sobbed loudly.

"The greatest evil he did was to Hugo."

"Hugo?" asked Brian puzzled.

"Yes, Hugo." It took some moments before the baroness would continue. "Hugo was a young man. A student of science at the Sorbonne in Paris, who was intrigued with the experiments Victor had performed at Ingolstadt. He wanted, like Victor, to find the source of life. Over the years the young man traced Victor, until he finally arrived here some five years ago. He was a young man of twenty-two, handsome, tall, aristocratic."

Brian's face shone with amazement.

"Hugo?"

The woman smiled softly.

"You don't believe it? That the grotesque creature you see now was once a handsome young man?"

"It is not possible," breathed Brian.

"Indeed, it is so. Victor welcomed him into the house. Hugo was a kind and sympathetic man. So sympathetic that it was natural for me, in my lonely despair and anguish, to turn to that young gallant. We fell in love, Hugo and I, and made our plans accordingly. But I didn't realize that, although he loved me, he loved his scientific ambition more. And that ambition was to discover Victor's secret of life. We could have escaped; we delayed and Victor grew suspicious and finally discovered us."

Again the baroness broke out in sobs.

"One night Victor enticed Hugo into his laboratory. I heard Hugo screaming. I tried to enter but the doors were locked. I never saw the Hugo I knew again."

Not for the first time, Brian had to fight down the feeling of horror, as the implications of what the baroness said grew clear in his mind.

The baroness was nodding.

"Yes, with his infernal skill, Victor recreated Hugo . . . recreated him as the awful monster you see today, in order to punish us both for our infidelity. In that recreation he also destroyed Hugo's mind."

"My God!" ejaculated the young man.

The baroness seized his hand.

"We must escape! You must help me escape! Victor must be punished for his evil, his blasphemy!"

Brian looked into the pain-stricken eyes of the woman and nodded.

"Don't worry. We shall get away this night."

"We shall have to go down the cliff face."

"It will be all right," assured Brian. "I have even climbed mountains before now."

"You will help me?"

"I will. But tell me. Why is the baron—after what he did to Hugo—now rebuilding," he paused over the right word, "rebuilding his body?"

"I think it is because he needs Hugo to assist him in his experiments. He knows that Hugo's mind is gone, his very memory of me. Hugo is merely an animal. But a clever one. So Victor has decided to give him better limbs by which to carry out the terrible tasks that Victor demands of him."

Brian stood up.

"We must go now."

"I have been ready these past ten years."

"You have not tried to escape on your own?"

"Escape to whom, *mein Herr*? Who would believe me? Victor would merely say that I am his poor deranged wife. They would send me back or, worse, lock me into an asylum."

The baroness led the way from the small room, along the maze of passageways, and up several stone steps, pausing before a rotting wooden door. She listened intently before swinging it open.

Brian followed her into the great cavern-like cellar.

"This way, young *Herr*," she called softly.

Brian followed her across to the cave entrance. Four hundred feet below, he could make out the pale rocks and the white foam where the sea crashed against them. To the left, the grey granite cliffs obscured his vision of the coast line, but to the right he could see them curving away towards a little cove, above which the lights of Bosbradoe twinkled invitingly.

At first glance, the cliffs seemed to fall precipitously, but when he looked closely he could see a series of jutting stones by which a careful climber might begin to make his way down for the first hundred feet. After that he would have to consider his route.

"I will go first," he said, "then you must follow me. Keep close, and I will direct you as to where you must place your feet. Do not move from one hold to the next until you are sure that you have made yourself secure with your other limbs."

The woman nodded.

Carefully Brian levered himself over the edge of the cave entrance and stood balancing precariously on the first foothold.

He was glancing down to find a firmer foothold when he heard the baroness scream.

At the foot of the cellar steps stood Baron Victor Frankenstein, and at his side the deformed and twisted figure of Hugo.

IX

The baron's thin lips twisted into a sneer. His cruel, pale eyes flitted from Brian to his terrified wife. She stood trembling from head to foot, the back of her hand covering her twitching mouth.

"And this is how you repay me, my dutiful wife?" said the baron sarcastically. "Ah, ah! What am I to do with you?"

"Victor . . ." she began, a hopelessness in her voice.

"Victor!" mimicked the baron. "I could have made you great, Elizabeth. Sometime, the world will acknowledge me for my genius; glory and riches undreamed of will be mine when the world knows that God has no prerogative for the creation of man, and that I," he thumped his chest and raised his voice, "I, Victor Frankenstein, can create life too."

Tears stood in the baroness' eyes.

"Victor, you are ill . . . ill," she wailed.

"Ill? Ill, am I? You, who with your puny mind, cannot comprehend the sublety of my brain? And so, not understanding, you call me ill?"

Brian stood balanced over the lip of the cave mouth, his mind racing. If he attempted to continue downwards, he would have to leave the baroness to whatever fate awaited her. Also, it would not take a moment for the creature, Hugo, to follow and send him crashing to his death on the rocks below.

But what was the alternative? To return and admit defeat?

No, he thought grimly, he must escape. He must take his chance and bring help to rescue the baroness.

The baron had turned towards him.

"I see, Doctor Shaw, that you have made a companion in distress of my poor, deluded wife? Is it not so?"

He paused but Brian made no reply.

"My wife seems to have developed a fondness for handsome young men of science. Ah, but I too was once a handsome young man of science! You and she were running away together, eh? Perhaps to start some new life beyond my reach?"

Brian shook his head dumbly.

The man was clearly insane.

"Well," chuckled the baron grimly, "others have tried that before now, is it not so, my Hugo? Is it not so, my ugly one? *Schweinhund!*"

Hugo, hearing his name, nodded his large head up and down and let forth a gibbering cry.

The baron raised his head and laughed.

"Yes, Hugo. You were once a fine young man of science, only you cannot remember now. You once tried to entice my wife away from her duties . . . just like this young man. Well, he, too, shall learn the wrath of Frankenstein!"

Brian's eyes flickered downward to the night-shrouded cliff. The path for the first hundred feet or so was easy. Perhaps he could reach the beach before Hugo could overtake him. He must try.

The baroness looked towards Brian, and it was as if she read his thoughts.

"You must fly, young *Herr*! Fly for your life! Do not worry about me. I shall try to prevent a pursuit. Fly, for the love of your mother!"

With a sob she turned and grabbed an iron lantern holder, a tripod affair which she brandished before her as a defensive weapon, throwing back her shoulders in defiance.

"Put that down!" the baron snarled.

"No, Victor. Once I loved you . . . I should have tried to stop your mad designs years ago. Now perhaps it is too late, but I owe a duty to God and to the people you have made suffer by your evil."

The baron's lips curled back over his teeth.

"You will obey me or perish!"

"No, Victor!"

"Then perish!"

He turned to Hugo with a gesture.

Without further ado, Brian began to make his hasty descent from outhanging rock to outhanging rock.

As his head disappeared beneath the ledge, the baroness sighed and lifted up her iron lantern holder.

Hugo was looking at her in puzzlement. One tiny glinting eye shone at her in the gloom. He raised a massive, hairy hand and scratched his head as if trying to conjure up some long forgotten memory.

"Destroy them!" shrieked the baron. "Go, *Schwein*, destroy!"

The baroness gave a deep sob and, shutting her eyes, raised her weapon and brought it down with a sickening thud on the head of the creature crying: "Hugo, Hugo! Oh my God! I'm sorry, I'm sorry!"

The creature staggered from the blow but did not fall. He blinked his one bizarre eye and made a weird whimpering sound.

The baroness opened her eyes wide in horror and took a step back.

Hugo gave a grunt and moved forward with deceptive speed. A hairy arm shot out and twisted the metal from the woman's hands as if she were possessed only of the strength of a baby. The creature sent the weapon clattering into a far corner of the cavern.

"Kill! Kill! Kill!" screamed the baron, beside himself with rage.

For a moment the woman and creature stood there, eyes locked.

"Hugo!" whispered the woman.

The creature drew the muscles of its face together in an attempt to frown.

Again some thought played at the back of his mind, some small thought, like a match struck in the midnight darkness of some great cathedral; struck to be immediately extinguished.

The creature shuffled forward, hands raised to grasp the baroness' slender throat. Fear lent her the strength of many. She beat and clawed at the man-thing with her puny fists. Fought and scratched, until the creature began to whimper in pain. The two figures, locked in an embrace which would only end in death, stood swaying in the mouth of the cave.

Biting, kicking, scratching, punching, the baroness fought for her frail life, in the arms of the thing which had once been her lover. They swayed to and fro, to and fro. Then the baroness' hand scratched down into the creature's good eye. With a howl, still not releasing his hold, Hugo stumbled forward.

Over the edge of the cave mouth the two figures became locked in death's embrace. The creature made no sound as he fell and only the baroness' shrill cry marked their passage downwards.

Pausing for breath on a ledge some hundred feet below, Brian saw their bodies hurtle by, heard the sickening thud as they reached the rocks below, and then . . . then the silence, broken only by the faint roar of the surf.

He looked up in the gloom.

Above him, in the entrance of the cave, he could see a pale face peering downwards.

The harsh tones of the baron came faintly to his ears.

"Are you there, Doctor Shaw? You are, I know it. Well, do not think that yours is the victory. I shall win yet, you shall see. I am Frankenstein! I am master over all creatures, for I can give them life . . . or death! I shall win yet. You shall see."

The face vanished into the darkness.

Brian paused breathing deeply. Then he began his descent again.

Here the cliff was difficult, and almost devoid of any holds by which he could make a safe descent. Once he looked down and caught sight of the surf far, far below him and felt his center of gravity momentarily displace itself and a sickening feeling of giddiness rose within him. The terror of the open space gripped him as he felt the attractive power of the abyss.

For several seconds he clung, sweating, to the granite rock face.

Then slowly, foot by foot, he continued downwards. On the vertical face, as he went down, he found several irregularities of formation which facilitated his descent.

Every twenty-five feet, or his rough estimation of that distance, he paused to regain his strength.

His clothes were saturated with his own sweat and his legs, tired by the support of his body against the vertical cliff, felt like jelly and several times gave way to an uncontrollable shaking.

It felt like hours before he neared the bottom.

The pounding of his heart was overshadowed by the roar and pounding of the surf on the rocks below him. His clothes were now swamped by another dampness . . . that of the salt sea spray. He looked down anxiously for a moment and saw, to his great relief, that the tide was out, leaving a wide space of rocks along the cliff foot and out towards the cove at Bosbradoe.

He paused again before commencing the final descent. His whole body was shaking from exertion.

He put out a foot for the next hold, and suddenly the trembling in his calf muscles caused the leg to crumple as he placed his weight upon it. With a cry he fell, hitting the sandy shingle of the beach and then—it seemed to him—that he was falling further, further into a black, bottomless pool.

He recovered consciousness almost immediately and, in the pale moonlight, realized that he had fallen a matter of twelve feet. He breathed a prayer of gratitude, and began to examine his limbs to ensure that he had not broken or fractured any bones.

It seemed hours before he arrived, wet, sticky and uncomfortable, and climbing up on to the quay, made his way through the deserted village to the house of the late Doctor Trevaskis. As he climbed along the path, by the side of the house, a coach suddenly spun round the bend. A small black coach, almost hearse-like, drawn by two jet black horses. The momentary impression of the tall coachman, sitting atop the box, was strangely familiar to Brian. The coach vanished speedily around a bend of the road, out of the village.

A shocked looking Mrs. Trevithick opened to his repeated knockings.

"Lord, Doctor Shaw! We wondered where you'd got to. Why, sir, you be all covered in sea and grime and . . . land sakes, sir . . . there be blood on you. Be you hurt?"

Brian shook his head dumbly.

"Just get me some hot water, Mrs. Trevithick, a change of clothing . . . oh, and some rum, by God. The rum first. Oh," he called to her retreating form, "and send your husband to me immediately."

Trevithick came in while he was downing his second glass of rum.

"Run and fetch Mr. Pencarrow."

Pencarrow arrived as Brian was dressing after a brief, but refreshing wash.

"Thank God, Pencarrow, that you are here. I have a horrific tale to tell you . . ." he suddenly looked puzzled. "Where is Miss Trevaskis? Surely she can't have slept through my arrival. I have made noise enough to waken the dead."

Mrs. Trevithick sniffed.

"She was tired and that stuff you gave her made her sleep fine."

"Oh yes, I'd forgotten the laudanum. Well, she must be roused, I'm afraid, Mrs. Trevithick."

Unwillingly, Mrs. Trevithick went to fetch her.

In a moment she had returned, her face pale, her eyes wide. She clutched a piece of paper in her hand.

Brian shot one look at her, and leapt towards the stairs.

Helen's bedroom was empty. The bedclothes on her small four-poster were flung back as if a struggle had taken place. Of Helen there was no sign.

Mrs. Trevithick was sobbing as he came back down the stairs.

"I found . . . I found this on her pillow, sir," she cried and pressed the paper into his hand.

Brian took it. The message was curt.

A hostage for your good behavior. Frankenstein.

"It is not possible," gasped a white-faced Pencarrow when Brian had finished his narrative. The old parson was visibly shaken. He reached forward with a trembling hand and poured himself a glass of rum.

Brian watched him in silence.

"I have heard of this Frankenstein before, of course. Yes, yes. I recall now that there was some scandal in Switzerland and that the tale was told by a Mrs. Mary Shelley. But Frankenstein, alive? And here? It is so fantastic."

"Fantastic or not, Mr. Pencarrow," said Brian grimly, "it is the truth. Doctor Trevaskis was killed by him, and now two more bodies lie beneath the cliffs on which Tymernans stands."

The old man gave him a searching look.

"What do you suggest we do, my boy?"

"Ring your church bells to rally the village, arm the villagers and let us attack the house," cried Brian.

The old man shook his head sorrowfully.

"The baron says he has taken the girl as a hostage for your good conduct. What do you think he will do if he hears the alarm bells, and sees the people storming his house?"

"Then what must we do?" demanded Brian, desperation sounding in his voice.

The vicar raised a finger to his lips, and began to nibble at a nail in his concentration.

"Do you have any weapons?" enquired the parson.

Brian shook his head.

"I am a doctor, sir."

"Hold here then, doctor, for I have some firearms next door which may be of assistance to us."

He was back within a few minutes carrying a rusty saber.

"Here," he wheezed with his exertion. "Take the sword. I am not much of a hand with knives."

Brian gave a rueful smile.

"I am more at ease with a surgical knife than this mortician's piece."

As they left the house, they encountered Mrs. Trevithick in the hall.

Tears welled into her eyes.

"God send you rescue her, for I have nursed Miss Helen ever since she were a bairn in arms. Good luck, sir. Good luck."

Brian patted her hand silently and followed Pencarrow from the house.

They made their way up to the cliff tops without incident. There was a hint of light in the eastern sky, and Brian realized that dawn must be just below the eastern horizon, although the sky above Bosbradoe was like pitch.

He paused at the entrance to the estate, by the wrought-iron gates, and could clearly see where these had been torn back to admit the coach in which the baron had abducted Helen. The gates were now back in place, chained and locked once more.

Brian raised a finger to his lips and spoke in a low voice to Pencarrow.

"We must go silently from here. I fear he will be expecting us and have some defences ready."

The old man nodded.

Together they climbed the old stone wall and dropped noiselessly down on the other side into the dark woodland.

Brian led the way, keeping well clear of the overgrown pathway he had used on his previous visits. The two men, encumbered by their weapons, pushed through the heavy undergrowth towards the house.

The two men came through the woods to the moonlit lawn. It seemed to Brian that he knew every inch of the lawn, so many times had he crossed it during the past day.

Surprisingly the door of the house stood open.

As they entered they heard a scream from somewhere within the building.

"Miss Helen!" cried Pencarrow.

Brian plunged down the black passageway calling over his shoulder:

"Quick! To the cellar!"

The two men raced to the servants' hall, and the vicar, panting, followed the young doctor down the stairs to the secondary hall and through the iron-studded door to the great cavern which was the baron's laboratory.

They halted at the head of the stairs, which wound through the ornate arches to the cavern floor. Their hearts came to their mouths as they beheld the figure of Helen strapped on to the surgical table in the center of the cavern with the baron standing over her, a gleaming knife in his raised hand.

X

The baron's head came up with a jerk, and his pale cold eyes glared at the intruders with a rage that Brian had never before seen in a man.

Mercifully, Helen lay unconscious.

For a while, various emotions fought for control on the dead white face of the baron, and then the face seemed to form into the pale mask that was habitual to the man. The thin lips drew back, displaying his teeth.

A surge of maniacal laughter shook the man's frame.

Brian stepped forward.

"Back!" the word was a scream. The knife wavered in the air. "Back, or she dies now!"

Brian let his hands fall to his side, still holding the saber in one hand.

"What now, Frankenstein?" asked Pencarrow softly.

The baron chuckled.

"Frankenstein! You say that august name with a sneer, my friend. One day the world will resound to that name. Frankenstein, the greatest scientist the world had known. On your knees, on your knees, dogs, because you are in the presence of a god!"

Pencarrow bit his lip.

"He is totally insane," he whispered. "There's no reasoning with him."

The young doctor nodded.

"Can you see any way to rush him before he can reach Helen?"

"No, we must not risk her life."

The baron regarded them suspiciously.

"What are you whispering about?"

Brian shook his head.

"Nothing. But what are you doing? Why are you holding Miss Trevaskis as a prisoner?"

An evil grin spread over the baron's features.

"So, young friend. So, you think to take away Miss Trevaskis from me also? As you took away my wife? I tell you, Hugo . . ."

Brian glanced quickly at Pencarrow, who shrugged.

"My name is not Hugo. Hugo is dead. Didn't you punish him enough?"

A puzzled frown passed across the baron's brow.

"Hugo dead?"

"Yes," said Brian. A plan began to develop in his mind. If he could distract the baron's attention long enough, he and Pencarrow could reach Helen and perhaps stand between her and the baron's knife.

"Hugo is not dead! You are Hugo!" screamed the baron. "But . . . but you've changed, Hugo. You look as you used to look, before I . . . before I operated on you. How did you do it? Do you know the secret?"

"I am not Hugo," insisted Brian. "Hugo lies dead at the bottom of the cliffs . . . there!"

He threw out a hand towards the cave mouth.

The baron followed the pointing finger and Brian seized the opportunity to make another step forward.

Frankenstein glanced back with a look of suspicion on his face.

"I cannot be deceived," he said slowly. "You must know that, Hugo."

"I am not Hugo," persisted Brian. "Hugo lies there. See for yourself."

The baron drew himself up.

"I cannot be deceived," he intoned again.

"You have only to look for yourself. Look at the bottom of the cliffs."

Hesitantly, the baron walked towards the cave mouth.

"Now!" cried Brian.

The two men raced down the steps even as the baron gave a cry of rage and sprang back, knife upraised, towards the girl. Pencarrow, with a speed surprising for one so advanced in years, reached the surgical table first and swung a clenched fist at the baron's upraised hand.

There was a dull smack and the knife went flying across the floor.

The baron gave a sharp cry of pain, and clutching his wrist, turned after the flying weapon.

Within a second, Brian was by the table and had unstrapped Helen, and was carrying the unconscious girl to the foot of the stairs. The girl was clearly drugged and he could smell the gaseous anaesthetic which had rendered her unconscious. He laid her unconscious form at the bottom of the stairs and turned back to aid Pencarrow.

"What shall we do with him?" asked the parson, jerking a hand towards the baron, who was scrabbling furiously among the packing cases, searching for his knife.

The two men moved towards the baron. He saw them coming and drew back with a snarl.

The long, drawn out howl of a hound echoed through the cavern.

In an instant the baron's eyes blazed with an unholy light. He reached forward and snapped off the catch of one of the great wooden packing cases.

From its gloom the great wolfhound, the terrifying creation of Frankenstein, bounded forth.

Pencarrow, who was standing before Brian, gave a cry of horror and amazement. He threw up his arms before his face as the beast bounded towards him. Even Brian, who had seen the beast before, could not help the terror which gripped his heart as the massive black dog came into the light of the lanterns. It was a hound, a jet black animal, such as no mortal could conceive. Fire seemed to flash from its eyes, which were red glowing coals. Its great white fangs were bare, and its muzzle, hackles and dewlap were dripping with saliva, tinged red with blood from the fresh meat which the baron had fed it.

As it came forward it gave vent to a vicious snarl and let out a hideous howling, paralyzing Pencarrow and Brian to the spot.

The frightful creature reached Pencarrow. The old parson fell like a ninepin beneath the leap of the great brute, whose gaunt and savage frame was surely as large as that of a lion.

Even in his terror, the old man reached out his hands to fend off those death-dealing jaws, to ward away those small, deep-set, cruel eyes which seemed ringed with red fire. Several times, the jaws snapped within fractions of an inch from Pencarrow's throat.

Brian, recovering from his paralysis, ran forward, the saber in his hand. But his attempts to stab the animal were thwarted by the fierce struggle of the man and beast as they rolled across the floor. At the same time Brian was distracted by the fact that the baron, taking advantage of the struggle, was seeking to escape from the cavern.

The struggle between Frankenstein's evil creation and the old parson was unequal. There was only one way it could end. A shrill cry of pain rose from the old man as the massive jaws of the beast suddenly fastened on his throat. The hound stood over his prey growling victoriously as its great canine teeth sunk deeper and deeper.

A feeble hand was flung out by the old man in an instinctive attempt to close upon some weapon. In that last moment before death, the hand found the knife of the baron, closed upon it and found a new surge of strength. The hand was upraised and struck once, twice and once again into the neck of the beast.

The great jaws opened to emit a harsh howl of agony. Old Pencarrow never heard that sound for he fell back, his neck bloody and twisted.

For a moment, the beast stood over the body of the parson, its massive head between its shoulders, panting and growling. Then the hound raised its head and its tiny fiery eyes met Brian's horrified gaze. He saw the great muscles and thews of its hindlegs gather together for a spring, saw the great jaws open to display its evil bloodstained molars, saw the animal spring forward.

But before the beast had reached him, the animal dropped prone upon the floor. It was dead. The blows struck by Pencarrow in his death agony had severed several arteries, and only the uncanny power of the animal had kept it upon its feet for so long.

For a moment Brian stood shuddering at the carcass of the dead beast.

Then a sound caused him to look up.

The baron, eyes ablaze, came towards him. From somewhere, the man had procured a sword. A transfiguration had taken place. The crouching maniacal look had vanished and once again Brian viewed the calm, detached man who seemed to have perfect control of himself and his emotions. There was a faint smile on his thin lips and his face had once more drawn into a mask.

He drew himself up before Brian and brought his sword to the salute.

"Well, well, my young friend. You have wrecked my household and destroyed my great creations. Is it not so? For this you must pay, *hein?*"

He tested his blade with a whip-like motion, hissing it through the air. Brian could see in his movements that he was no stranger to the sword.

The baron smiled.

"You observe that I have some knowledge of the weapon, young *Herr?* I was the best swordsman at Ingolstadt, perhaps in all Switzerland. I trust you know the rudiments of the weapon, because I am going to play with you before I kill you . . . *Schweinhund!*"

The baron suddenly launched himself at Brian, his silver blade slashing and sweeping. Brian, who had little knowledge of the sword, raised his old rusty weapon in an attempt to ward off the blows. The click and slither of steel upon steel, and the stamp of the baron's feet, were interspersed by the harsh breathing of the two combatants.

Brian only just side-stepped as the blade flickered beneath his arm. It was a miracle it had not found his breast.

Like a flickering light the baron's blade caused Brian to dance and twist and it came with a sickening certainty in his mind that, at any time, the baron could have cut him down. He was, as he had said, merely playing with him, driving him further and further across the cavern floor towards—with a desperate glance behind him Brian saw the danger—the mouth of the cave, towards the four hundred foot sheer drop to the rocks.

Frankenstein saw his look of fear with a smile of satisfaction.

Brian made a desperate attempt to stop his backward passage, slashing at the baron.

The sword flashed in the baron's hand, and to his horror Brian felt a tug and found his sword whistling out of his hand across the cavern floor.

Frankenstein's sword point twinkled wickedly before his eyes.

"Alas, young friend, no *coup de gráce* for you. Behind you is your exit to a better life."

Step by step, the baron forced Brian backwards.

He heard Helen's terrified scream as she regained consciousness and in trying to turn in her direction he slipped and fell. He found himself lying half on, and half off, the edge of the cave mouth. It seemed an eternity since he had lain there, with the baroness resolutely defending his escape; an eternity, although it could have only been a matter of hours.

The baron raised his blade.

"And so . . ." he said, and kicked his foot at Brian's hands as they clung desperately to the rocky floor.

With a crash the cellar door was flung back, and a mass of villagers began to spill down the steps into the cavern. Many of them carried pikes, scythes and burning torches.

"Kill the monster!"

"There he is!"

"Destroy the evil beast!"

"Burn him!"

The baron turned in rage at the angry gaggle of their voices.

"So," was all he said.

Brian felt the strength giving out in his hands. He looked up at the baron. The man had dropped his sword and then, calmly, he stepped past Brian into space.

Brian did not hear the body fall to the rocks below. His mind was too full of expending his last energies to prevent himself from falling. But soon, willing hands were lifting him up.

Hands helped him from the cavern, where angry villagers were smashing and destroying equipment, cases and other paraphernalia. Someone had put a torch to the mess, and flames were hungrily licking at the walls.

Outside on the lawn, he was reunited with Helen. For a long while he held her in his arms, under the approving eye of Trevithick.

Suddenly there came a great roaring sound.

"'Tis the floors of the house collapsing into the cellar," explained Trevithick.

Brian and Helen turned and made their way back to the village. Dense black smoke belched into the early morning light, rising from the pyre of Frankenstein's evil laboratory.

It was a crisp autumn morning. *The Bodmin Flyer* was making its weekly run from Bosbradoe to Camelford and then across the moor to Bodmin. The coach was full. There were six first class passengers within and five more, who could afford only a second class fare, seated on top of the coach with the driver.

The coachman, muffled in an overcoat against the chill of the morning air, flicked his whip continuously to keep his four great bays at a steady trot along the bleak moorland road. In the distance, Brown Willy and Rough Tor rose high on the horizon with a distinct and dramatic force, although they were only thirteen hundred feet in height.

Autumn presented a splendid scene on the moor. The fronds of bracken and the leaves of the trees had turned yellow, brown and russet, and the heather blooms had already faded and fallen. A few late blackberries added to the color of the roadside, nestling along the grey stone walls. Across the brown and green of the moor, the arcs of hills, the texture and fabric of the granite rocks, the grass and heather made strange contrasts. And here and there, in criss-cross patterns, the swift rush of the autumn waters, small brooks flowing with swift vigor and full throated voice, washed into the muddy sediment of stately pushing rivers.

Inside the bouncing coach, Doctor Brian Shaw was smiling happily at Miss Helen Trevaskis.

They were oblivious to the disapproving stares of the other occupants of the coach, a fat lawyer on his way to the Quarter Sessions at Bodmin; an elderly parson and his prim, hook-nosed wife; and a rough country squire in riding boots who was insisting on polluting the air with his pipe.

Brian reached forward and grasped the girl's hand.

"You've made the right decision?" he asked anxiously.

Helen placed her hand on his and gave an answering smile which told him what he wanted to know. He sat back with a sigh of happiness.

"Things will be fine from now on, Helen. I assure you. We'll be in London by the end of the week, and I am sure my appointment with the hospital will be open for me. We can get married and . . ."

Helen nodded happily.

"Things will be all right now."

"But what of . . ." she hesitated. ". . . of him? The baron? Why was his body not found?"

"I wouldn't worry about it, Helen," said Brian reassuringly. "The baron is dead. I saw him go to his death myself. He stepped past me out of the cave mouth and it is four hundred feet down to those rocks. What remained of his body must have been washed out to sea. It took a long time before we discovered the remains of the poor baroness and Hugo."

Helen nodded meditatively.

"In a way, since you told me their story, I feel very sorry for the baroness and Hugo. Think of the torture they must have gone through. How could the baron have been so inhuman?"

Brian shook his head.

"He was clearly insane. If a man sets himself up as a god, then he does become inhuman. But the story is ended now. We will hear no more of Frankenstein."

Helen squeezed his hand.

"No, there is so much else to look forward to now."

On the top of the coach, the five second class passengers sat in less comfort than their traveling companions below. They were tossed about to the swaying rhythm of the coach and had to cling on to whatever hold they could, to prevent themselves from being precipitated on to the road.

Most of them were grumbling, in the fashion of country people, as the chill autumn wind whipped their ruddy cheeks and made their eyes smart.

Now and again the sun would shine thinly down from a blue sky in which long, straggly white clouds blurred its warmth.

One second class passenger rode a little apart from the others, sitting silently by the side of the coachman who had long since given up trying to make conversation with the man. Privately, the coachman had estimated him to be an undertaker or a mortician. He was clad from head to toe in black, with a muffler and hat almost obscuring his deathly white, cadaverous face.

He sat with his eyes staring straight ahead along the roadway, his thin mouth set firmly.

Only now and then would the mouth twitch in a parody of a smile as his mind plotted some vengeance against the people who had destroyed his life's work, his great creations. And already his mind was forming a new creation, a creation which would be the perfect man.

GRAHAM MASTERTON

𝔐other of 𝔍nvention

━━◆━━

Graham Masterton was born in Edinburgh, the son of a Sutherland army officer and grandson of an eccentric scientist (who was apparently the first man to keep bees in central London and was also the inventor of "day-glo").

After working as a journalist, he became the editor of Mayfair *and* Penthouse *magazines which led to the publication of his first book,* Your Erotic Fantasies. *This was followed by other how-to sex books, including the bestseller* How to Drive Your Man Wild in Bed.

He made his debut as a horror novelist in 1975 with The Manitou *(filmed in 1978)—he has followed it with around a hundred horror novels and stories, many of which have been adapted for television and graphic novels.*

Masterton was the first Western horror novelist to be published in Poland, and he is a frequent visitor to that country.

"'Mother of Invention' is set around that part of Middlesex where my grandparents lived when I was young," explains the author. "It was inspired by all the perfumed evening-gowned ladies who used to come in to kiss me goodnight. They were glassy-eyed and over made-up and walked disjointedly, and I always thought they were rather ghoulish. It was only when I grew older that I realized that their disjointedness was the result of too many gin-and-tonics."

He left her sitting on the sun-blurred veranda under the cherry blossoms, which showered down softly all around her like the confetti on her wedding day all those years ago.

She was seventy-five now: her hair shone white, her neck was withered, her eyes were the color of rainwashed irises. But she still dressed elegantly, the way that David always remembered her, with pearl necklaces and silk dresses, and although she was old she was still very beautiful.

David could remember his father dancing around the dining room with her, and saying that she was the Queen of Warsaw, the most stunning woman that Poland had ever produced, from a nation which was renowned for its stunning women.

"There is no woman to equal your mother: there never will be," his father had said, on his eighty-first birthday, as they walked slowly together beside the Thames, at the foot of the steep hill which led up to Cliveden. Dragonflies had darted over the dazzling water; oarsmen had shouted and a girl had screamed with glee. Three days later, his father died, quite peacefully, in his sleep.

David's tan suede shoes crunched across the gravel. Bonny was already waiting for him in his decrepit blue open-topped MG, applying a violently-pink shade of lipstick in the rearview mirror. Bonny was his second wife, and eleven years younger than he was—blonde, still child-faced, funny— and totally different from Anne, his first wife, who had been brunette and very serious and *lank*, somehow. His mother still didn't approve of Bonny. She rarely said anything, but he could tell that she thought her thoroughly ill-behaved for taking a loving husband away from his family. As far as his mother was concerned, marriages were made in heaven, even if they often descended into hell.

"Your father would have had some very strong words to say to you, David," she had told him, staring at him resentfully, unblinking, her head tilted to one side, her fingers fiddling with her diamond engagement ring and her wedding band. "Your father said that a man should always stay faithful to one woman, and one woman only."

"Father loved you, mother. That was easy for him to say. I didn't love Anne at all."

"Then why did you marry her and give her children and make the poor girl's life an absolute misery?"

David still didn't really know the answer to that. He and Anne had met at college and somehow they had just got married. The same thing had happened to dozens of his friends. Twenty years later they were sitting in mortgaged houses in the suburbs staring out of the window and wondering what happened to all those laughing, golden-legged girls they *should* have married.

What he did know, however, was that he loved Bonny in a way that he had never loved Anne. With Bonny, he could understand for the very first time what it was that his father had seen in his mother. A captivating look about her that was almost angelic; an overwhelming femininity; a softness of skin; a shining of hair. He could sit and watch her for hours sometimes, as she sat at her drawing board, painting wallpaper designs. He could have watched her for a living, if only it had paid a salary.

"How was she?" asked Bonny, as David eased himself into the car. He was a tall man, very English-looking in his rusty-colored sweater and his fawn twill trousers. He had inherited his mother's deep-set Polish eyes and her dead-straight hair, but his Englishness was established beyond doubt by the same long, handsome face as his father, and his insistence on driving the tiniest of sports cars, even though he was six feet, two inches tall.

"She was fine," he said, as he started up the engine. "She wanted to know where you were."

"Hoping I'd left you forever, I suppose?"

He swung the car in a wide semi-circle, and headed off down the long avenue of pollarded lime trees which gave The Limes Retirement Home its name.

"She doesn't want to break us up, not anymore," said David. "She can see how happy I am."

"Perhaps that's the problem. Perhaps she thinks that the longer you and I stay together, the less chance there's going to be of you going back to Anne."

"I wouldn't go back to Anne for all the Linda McCartney meat-free foods in her freezer." He checked his watch, the Jaeger-le-Coultre that had once belonged to his father. "Talking of food, we'd better get moving. Remember we promised to drop in to see Aunt Rosemary for tea on the way back."

"How could I ever forget?"

"Oh, come on, Bonny, I know she's odd, but she's been part of the family for years."

"So long as she doesn't start dribbling, I don't mind."

"Don't be unkind."

They reached the gates of the nursing home, and turned east, toward the motorway, and London. The late afternoon sun flickered through the trees, so that they looked as if they were driving through a Charlie Chaplin movie.

"Does your Aunt Rosemary ever visit your mother?" asked Bonny.

David shook his head. "Aunt Rosemary isn't my real aunt. She was more like my father's personal assistant—receptionist, general factotum, secretary—although I never saw her doing any secretarial work. I don't know who she is, exactly. She came to stay with us when I was about twelve or thirteen and after that she never left . . . not until father died, anyway. Then she and mother had some kind of falling out."

"Your mother isn't exactly the forgiving kind, is she?"

They drove for a while in silence, then David said, "Do you know what she showed me today?"

"You mean apart from her continuing disapproval?"

David ignored that remark. He said, "She showed me an old photograph of her whole family—her grandfather, her grandmother, her mother and her father and her three brothers and her, all standing outside the Wilanow Palace in Warsaw. They were all very good-looking, as far as I can see."

"When was this photograph taken?"

"I think it was about 1924 . . . mother would have been five or six, that's all. But it gave me an idea for her birthday present. I thought I might see if I could trace her life back to when she was born . . . I know father had hundreds of photographs and letters and stuff. I could make her a kind of *This Is Your Life* book."

"Won't it take an awful lot of work? You've still got that thesis to finish for the Wellcome Foundation."

He shook his head. "The whole attic is crammed to the rafters with photograph albums and diaries. Father kept them all in immaculate order. He was that kind of man. Very neat, very precise. A perfectionist. Well . . . he'd have to be."

"Where did he meet your mother?"

"In Warsaw, in 1937. Didn't I tell you? He went to Poland to assist the great Magnus Stothard when Sir Magnus was called to operate on Count Szponder, to remove a tumor on his spine. Unsuccessfully, I'm afraid. My mother came with her family to one of the dinners the Szponder family gave in Sir Magnus's honor . . . this was *before* the operation, I might add. My mother wasn't an aristocrat, but her father was very respectable . . . something in shipping, I think. In those days, my mother's name was Katya Ardonna Galowska. She always used to tell me that she wore a grey silk dress with lace on the collar, and sang a song called *The Little Song-Thrush*. Apparently my father sat staring at her with his mouth open. He invited her to spend a holiday in Cheltenham, which she did, in the following spring. Of course things started looking rather threatening in Poland, so she stayed in England, and she and my father were married, and that was that."

"Did your mother never see her family again?"

"No," replied David. "Her brothers joined the Polish Resistance and nobody ever found out what happened to them. Her father and mother were denounced as Jews by one of her father's business partners, and were sent to Birkenau."

They were joining the M4 now, and he had to adjust his rearview mirror because Bonny had altered it when she was putting on her lipstick. A huge truck blared its horn at them, and David had to swerve back into the feeder lane as it came bellowing past.

"You're taking your life into your hands," said Bonny. Then, as they rejoined the motorway, and picked up speed, "Do you remember that programme, *Your Life In Their Hands?* That surgery thing, where they showed people having operations?"

"Of course I do. Father was on one of them, doing a liver transplant."

"Really? I didn't know that."

David nodded proudly. "They called him the Tailor of Gloucester, because his suturing was always so incredibly neat. He said the trouble with today's surgeons is that their mummies never taught them to sew. He always used to sew on his own buttons and take up his own trouser-cuffs. I think he would have embroidered his patients if he ever had half a chance."

David's hand was resting on the gear-shift, and Bonny laid her hand on top of it. "It's strange to think that if some old Polish count hadn't had a tumor on his spine, and if Hitler hadn't invaded Poland, we wouldn't be together now."

Aunt Rosemary lived in a small bungalow in New Malden, on an uninspiring street that was straddled by giant pylons. Her front garden was covered in concrete, which had been scored with a crazy-paving pattern, and a concrete birdbath stood in the center of it, with a headless concrete robin perched on the rim. The hedge was tangled with last autumn's leaves and crisp-bags.

David rang and Aunt Rosemary slowly heaved her way to the door. When she opened it up, they could smell lavender furniture polish and liniment, and the sourness of unchanged flower vase water.

Aunt Rosemary was in her mid-seventies. She was almost handsome, but she walked with a terrible crablike limp, and all of her movements were haphazard and uncoordinated. She had told David that she suffered from chronic arthritis, made worse by the treatment that doctors had given her in Paris in the 1920s. In those days, the latest thing was to inject the joints of arthritis sufferers with gold, a technique that was not only ruinously expensive but permanently crippling.

"David, you came," she said, her lower lip sloping in a parody of a smile. "Will you have time for some tea?"

"We'd love to," said David. "Wouldn't we, Bonny?"

"Oh yes," Bonny agreed. "We'd love to."

They sat in the small gloomy sitting room drinking weak PG Tips and eating rock cakes with cherries in them. Aunt Rosemary had to keep a handkerchief gripped in her hand in case cake crumbs poured out of the side of her mouth.

Bonny tried to look at something else. The clock on the mantelpiece, the china figurines of racehorses, the goldfish flapping in its murky bowl.

Before they left, David went to the toilet. Bonny and Aunt Rosemary sat in silence for a while. Then Bonny said, "I was asking David earlier why you never go to visit his mother."

"Oh," said Aunt Rosemary, dabbing her mouth. "Well, she and I were very close at one time. But she was the kind who always took and never gave. A very selfish woman, in ways that you wouldn't understand."

"I see," said Bonny, uncomfortably.

Aunt Rosemary laid a distorted hand on hers. "No, dear. I don't really think that you do."

David spent almost the entire weekend up in the attic. Fortunately, Bonny didn't mind too much, because she had a wallpaper design to finish for Sanderson's, a new range based on the 19th-century fabric designs of Arthur Mackmurdo, all curling leaves and flowers in the arts and crafts style. The attic was airless and rather too warm, but it was well-lit, with a dormer window looking out over the lawns, and a cushioned window seat where David could sit and sort through some of his father's old documents and photograph albums.

The albums smelled like musty old clothes and unopened closets: the very essence of yesterday. They contained scores of pictures of smiling young medical students in the 1920s, and people in boaters and striped summer blazers having picnics. His father had been photographed with lots of pretty girls, but after March 1938, he was only ever photographed with one girl—Katya Ardonna Galowska—and even though she was his own mother, David could clearly see why his father had adored her so much.

Their wedding day—April 12, 1941. His mother had worn a smart titled Robin Hood hat and a short dress with a bolero top. His father had worn a tight double-breasted suit, and spats. Yes, *spats*! They looked as glamorous as film stars, the pair of them; like Laurence Olivier and Vivien Leigh, and their eyes had that odd, unfocused brightness of the truly happy. The truly happy look only inward, dazzled by their own delight.

David in his mother's arms, the day after he was born. There was a larger print of his photograph in the drawing room downstairs, in a silver frame. David when he was eleven months old, sleeping in his mother's arm. Her face was limned by the sunlight that shone through the leaded-glass window, her wispy curls shone like traveler's joy. Her eyes were slightly hooded, as if she were dreaming, or thinking of another land. She was so magnetically beautiful that David found it almost impossible to turn the page—and when he did, he had to turn back again, just for another look.

The date on the photograph was August 12, 1948.

He kept on leafing through the album. There he was, at the age of two, his first visit to the circus. His first Kiddi-Kar. Oddly, though, no sign of his mother—not until January 1951, when she was pictured next to a frozen pond somewhere, wrapped up in furs, her face barely visible.

She appeared fairly consistently until September 1951. She was standing at the end of Sea View pier on the Isle of Wight (a pier that was later blown down in a storm). She was wearing a wide-brimmed hat and a calf-length floral dress, and white strappy shoes. Her face was hardly visible in the shadow of her hat, but she seemed to be laughing.

Then again, his mother seemed to disappear. There were no photographs of her until November 1952, when she had attended Lolly Bassett's wedding at Caxton Hall, in London. She wore a grey suit with a pleated skirt. She looked extremely thin, almost emaciated. Her face was still beautiful but slightly *lumpy* in a way, as if she were recovering from a beating, or hadn't slept well.

Throughout the first five photograph albums that he looked at, David discovered seven material gaps in his mother's appearance . . . almost as if she had taken seven extended vacations throughout his early childhood. When he came to think about it, she *had* been away now and again, but he had always been so well looked after by Iris, his nanny (his father's maiden sister), and then by Aunt Rosemary, that it had never really occurred to him until now how extended those absences must have been. He remembered that his mother had been ill a great deal, in those days, and that she had been obliged to stay in her bedroom for weeks on end, with the curtains tightly drawn. He remembered tiptoeing into her bedroom to kiss her goodnight, and scarcely being able to find her in the darkness. He remembered touching her soft, soft face, and feeling her soft, soft hair; and smelling her perfume and something else, some strong, penetrating smell, like antiseptic.

But then, in 1957, she had reappeared, as strong and as beautiful as ever before, and the sun had shone in every room, and his father had laughed, and he had thought sometimes that he must have the best parents that any boy could wish for.

There was a sixth album, bound in black leather, but it was fastened with a lock, and he couldn't find the key. He made a mental note to himself to look through his father's desk.

He turned back to the photograph of his mother in 1948, and laid the flat of his hand on it, as if he could somehow absorb some understanding of what had happened through the nitrates on the paper.

All through his early life, it seemed as if his mother had come and gone, come and gone, like the sunlight on a cloudy afternoon.

He parked outside Northwood Nursing Home and spent some time wrestling the MG's waterproof cover into place, because it looked like rain.

Inside, he found the registrar's office down at the end of a long linoleum-floored corridor, which echoed and smelled of wax polish. The registrar was a tired-looking woman in a lilac cardigan who noisily clicked extra strong mints around her teeth, making little sucking noises. She made it more than obvious that David's request was extremely tiresome, and that she could have been doing something much more important instead (such as making Nescafe).

David waited while she leafed through the record book, making a performance of turning each page.

"Yes . . . here we are. July 3, 1947. Mrs. Katerina Geoffries. Blood group O. Medical history, measles, chicken pox, mild scarlatina. Live male birth—I presume that's you?—weighing 7lbs 4ozs."

David peered over the desk. "There's another note there, in red ink."

"That's because somebody has checked her medical record at a later date."

"I see. Why would anybody want to do that?"

"Well, in this case, because of her accident."

"Accident? What accident?"

The registrar stared at him very oddly, her eyes magnified by her spectacles. "You are who you say you are?" she asked him.

"Of course. Why shouldn't I be?"

The registrar closed the book with an emphatic slap. "It just strikes me as rather peculiar that you don't know about your mother's accident."

David pulled out his wallet, and showed the registrar his driving license and a letter from the Borough Council. "I'm David Geoffries. Mrs. Katya Geoffries is my mother. Look . . . here's a photograph of us together. I don't know why she never told me about her accident. Perhaps she didn't think that it was very important."

"I would say that it was extremely important—at least as far as your mother was concerned."

"But why?"

The registrar opened the book again, and turned it around so that David could read what was written in red ink. "Senior med. reg. from Middlesex Hosp. inquired blood grp & med. history urgent 2 a.m. 14/09/48 (unable contact GP). Mrs. G. seriously crushed in car accident."

Underneath, in black ink, in another hand: "Mrs. Geoffries deceased 15/09/48."

David looked up. He felt as if he had been breathing in nitrous oxide at the dentist—light-headed and echoey and detached from everything around him. "This must be a mistake," he heard himself saying. "She's still alive, and perfectly well, and living at The Limes. I saw her only yesterday."

"Well, if that's the case, I'm very pleased," said the registrar, making a loud rattle with her mint. "Now, if you can excuse me—"

David nodded, and stood up. He left the Nursing Home and stood on the steps outside, while the rain began to spot the red-asphalt driveway, and the wind began to rise.

He found a copy of the death certificate at Somerset House. Mrs. Katerina Ardonna Geoffries had died on September 15, 1948, in the Middlesex Hospital, cause of death multiple internal injuries. His mother had been killed and here was the proof.

He visited the offices of the *Uxbridge Gazette* and leafed through amber-colored back-issues in the morgue. There it was: in the issue dated September 18, complete with a photograph. A few minutes after midnight, a Triumph Roadster had run through a red traffic light at Greenford, and collided with a lorry carrying railway lines. David recognized the car at once. He had seen it in several photographs at home. It hadn't occurred to him that it had failed to reappear after September 1948.

His mother was dead. His mother had died when he was only a year old. He had never known her, never talked to her, never played with her.

So who was the woman in The Limes? And why had she pretended for all of these years that *she* was his mother?

He went back home. Bonny had made him a devastatingly hot chili-con-carne, one of his favorites, but he found that he could only pick at it.

"What's the matter?" she asked him. "You're so pale! You look as if you need a blood transfusion."

"My mother's dead," he said; and then he told her whole story.

They left their supper and sat on the sofa with glasses of wine and talked about it. Bonny said, "What I can't understand is why your father never told you. I mean, it wouldn't have upset you, would it? You wouldn't have remembered her."

"It wasn't just me he didn't tell. He didn't tell *anybody*. He called her Katya and he told everybody how they had met in Poland before the war . . . he used to call her the Queen of Warsaw. Why would he have done that, if it wasn't her at all?"

They pored over the photograph albums again. "These later pictures," said Bonny, "they certainly *look* like your mother. She's got the same hair, the same eyes, the same profile."

"No . . . here's a difference," said David. "Look . . . in this picture of her holding me when I was eleven months old, look at her earlobes. They're very small. But look at *this* picture taken in 1951. There's no doubt about it, she's got different ears."

Bonny went to her easel and came back with her magnifying glass. They scrutinized the woman's hands, her feet, her shoulders. "There . . . she has three moles on her shoulder in this picture, but not in this one."

At last, with the bottle of wine almost empty, they sat back and looked at each other in bewilderment.

"It's the same woman, yet it isn't the same woman. She keeps changing, very subtly, from year to year."

"My father was a brilliant surgeon. Maybe he was giving her cosmetic surgery."

"To make her earlobes bigger? To give her moles where she didn't have moles before?"

David shook his head. "I don't know . . . I can't understand it at all."

"Then perhaps we'd better ask the only person who really knows . . . your mother, or whoever she is."

She sat with her face half in shadow. "I am Katya Ardonna," she said. "I always have been Katya Ardonna, and I will remain Katya Ardonna until the day I die."

"But what about the accident?" David insisted. "I've seen my mother's death certificate."

"I *am* your mother."

He went through the photograph albums again and again, searching for clues. He had almost given up when he found a photograph of his mother at Kempton Park racecourse in 1953, arm in arm with a smiling brunette. The caption read, *Katya & Georgina, lucky day at the races!!*

Clearly visible on her friend Georgina's shoulder were three moles.

Georgina's father sat by the window, staring sightlessly out at the traffic on the Kingston Bypass through his grimy net curtains. He wore a frayed grey cardigan. A resentful tortoiseshell cat sat in his lap and gave David an unblinking death stare.

"Georgina went out on New Year's Eve, 1953, and that was the last anybody ever saw of her. The police were very good about it, they did their best, but there were no clues to go on, not one. I can see her face like it was yesterday. She turned around and said, 'Happy New Year, Dad!' I can hear it now. But after that night, I never had one happy new year, not one."

David said to his mother, "Tell me about Georgina."

"Georgina?"

"Georgina Philips, she was a friend of yours. One of your best friends."

"Why on earth do you want to know about her? She went missing, disappeared."

David said, "I think I've found out where she is. Or at least, I think I know where part of her is. Her arm?"

His mother stared at him. "My God," she said. "After all these years . . . I never thought that anybody would ever find out."

She stood in the center of her room, wearing nothing but her pale peach dressing gown. Bonny stood in the corner, right in the corner, fearful but fascinated. David stood close to his mother.

"He worshipped me, that was the trouble. He thought I was a goddess, that I wasn't real. And he was so possessive. He wouldn't let me talk to other men. He was always telephoning me to make sure where I was. In the end, I began to feel that I was trapped, that I was suffocating. I had too much whisky to drink and I went for a drive.

"I don't remember the accident. All I remember is waking up in your father's clinic. I was terribly crushed, the lorry had driven right over my pelvis. You were right, of course, I *was* dead. But your father took possession of my body, and took me to Pinner.

"You probably didn't know very much about your father's work with electrical galvanization. He had found a way of stimulating life into dead tissue by injecting it with negatively charged minerals and then inducing a massive positive shock. He had perfected it in wartime for the War Office . . . and of course they had been only too happy to supply him with dead soldiers to experiment on. The first man he brought back to life was a Naval petty officer who had drowned in the Atlantic. The man's memory was badly impaired, but later your father found a way of preventing that from happening by using amino acids."

She paused, and then continued, "I was killed in that accident, all those years ago, and I should have stayed dead. But your father revived me. Not only that, he rebuilt me, so that I was almost as perfect as I had been when he first met me.

"My legs were crushed beyond repair . . . he gave me new legs. My body was pulped . . . he gave me a new body. New heart, lungs, liver, pelvis, pancreas . . . new arms, new ribs, new breasts."

She dropped the shoulder of her dressing gown. "There," she said, "look at my back."

David could barely see the scar that his father's surgery had left on his mother's back. The faintest of silvery lines, where Georgina's arm had been sewn onto somebody else's shoulder.

"How much of you is really you?" he asked her, hoarsely. "How much of you is Katya Ardonna?"

"Over the years," his mother said, "your father used six different women, restoring me piece by piece to what I once was."

"And you let him do it? You let him murder six women so that he could use their body parts, just for you?"

"Your father was beyond my control. Your father was beyond anybody's control. He was a great surgeon, but he was obsessed."

"I still can't believe you allowed him to do it."

His mother lifted her dressing gown again. "I suffered years of agony, David . . . years when I was scarcely conscious from one month to the next. It was like living in a dream, or a nightmare. Somethings I used to wonder if I was actually dead."

"But how did he get away with it, killing all of those women? How did he get rid of the bodies?"

From around her neck, Katya Ardonna took a small silver key. "You've seen that black leather album in the attic? The one that's locked? Well, this key will open it. This key will let you know everything that you'll ever want to know, and more."

They looked through the album in silence. It was a complete photographic record of his father's surgical reconstruction of his mother's shattered body as brightly-colored as a sex magazine. Page by page, year after year, they could follow his progress as he painstakingly put her back together again. The surgical techniques were extraordinary—even involving a rudimentary kind of micro-surgery, to reconnect nerve fibers and tiny blood capillaries.

First of all, they saw how David's father had sewn new limbs onto his mother's shattered body—then replaced her ribcage and her lungs and all of her internal organs.

After years of meticulous surgery, she had emerged as perfect as she was today. The same beautiful woman that his father had met in Poland in 1937—almost flawless, finely proportioned, and scarcely scarred at all.

She smiled from the album like the Queen of Warsaw.

But the photographs told a darker story, too. Stage by horrifying stage, they showed what David's father had done with the limbs and the organs that had been surplus to his needs. He hadn't wrapped them up in newspaper, or burned them, or buried them, or dissolved them in acid. He had painstakingly sutured them together, muscle to muscle, nerve to nerve. Every photograph was a grisly landscape of veins and membranes and bloody flesh. Glutinous chasms opened up; glutinous chasms were closed. Blood welled scarlet over thin connective tissues; blood was drained away.

Neither of them had ever seen the human body opened up like this. It was a monstrous garden of grisly vegetables: livers shining like aubergines, intestines heaped like cauliflower curds, lungs as big as crumpled pumpkins.

Out of this riot of skin and bone and offal, out of all of these rejects, David's scrupulous father had been able to create another woman. Of course, she wasn't as beautiful as Katya Ardonna . . . he had pillaged the best parts from six women's bodies to restore Katya Ardonna's beauty, the way he had remembered it to be.

But this other woman had been presentable enough, under the circumstances. And she had given him the opportunity to practice his suturing skills, and some of his new ideas on connecting nerve-fibers.

And she had *lived* just as Katya Ardonna had lived—six murder victims tangled into one living woman.

The last few photographs in the album showed the woman's toes being sewn on, and the skin being closed over her open leg incisions.

The very last picture showed the day that the bandages had come off this new woman's face. She was bruised and stunned, and her eyes were out of focus. But with a sickening, surging sensation of pity and disgust, they saw the desperate, lopsided face of David's Aunt Rosemary.

ADRIAN COLE
The Frankenstein Legacy

—⁘—

Adrian Cole was born in Devon, where he still lives. He is the author of more than twenty-five novels and numerous short stories, writing in several genres, including science fiction, fantasy, sword and sorcery and horror.

His first books were published in the 1970s—The Dream Lords trilogy—and he went on to write, among others, the Omaran Saga and the Star Requiem series, as well as writing two young adult novels, Moorstones *and* The Sleep of Giants.

More recent books have included the Voidal trilogy, which collects all the original short stories from the 1970s and '80s and adds new material to complete the saga; the novels Night of the Heroes *and* The Shadow Academy, *and* the Lovecraftian short story collection Nick Nightmare *Investigates, featuring the occult detective of the title.*

"*My first memory of Frankenstein and his bizarre creation goes back to when I was a boy of seven," recalls the author, "living at the time in Malaya, my father having been in the Army. Our house backed on to a rubber plantation, itself an ideal environment into which to let loose a fermenting imagination. The tropical afternoons were sweltering, a time to be in the shade, and my mother regularly took me to the local cinemas—not, I hasten to add, to see Frankenstein movies!—or we talked about books we had read or movies we had seen and loved.*

"*I do recall quite vividly her telling me the plot of the Boris Karloff movie, which had left a lasting impression on her, as her description of it then left on me. She had transposed the tremendous impact of Karloff's performance, which had wowed the movie world, on to my inner eye: ironically it had not filled me with terror, but rather with fascination, certainly pity. Since then, Frankenstein's creature has always been one of my favorites—at school I was notorious for doodling a kind of* Mad *magazine version of it in my jotters and other less acceptable places. And of course, I became an avid fan of the movies, which I still watch over and over again.*

"'*The Frankenstein Legacy' posed a problem for me— how to explain Victor Frankenstein's survival and that of his creation? In Mary Shelley's novel, the scientist clearly dies, the Monster determined to self-destruct. But then it struck me that we only have Robert Walton's word for that, don't we? And he was a man with a quest, a desire for glory, blessed of remarkable determination and resiliance. Could he really have resisted an opportunity such as Victor Frankenstein presented? Was he such a fine chap as his letters to his sister imply? Those letters . . . I wonder . . .*"

I

A fierce wind drove landward from the Atlantic, a predatory elemental force, almost sentient in its fury. In its screaming wake line upon line of breakers smashed on rocky shores, spume and rain mingling, lashing the cliffs. The cauldron of the skies mirrored the churning grey maelstrom, thick black clouds pulsing and fomenting, ripped through with bolts of light. Beyond the rim of the cliffs, a single cottage seemed to crouch down in a fold of moorland out of the storm's anger, the rain clawing at it, tearing loose slates from the roof, dragging down a length of guttering that tumbled across the adjacent fields and was gone in the blink of an eye.

Inside the cottage, mind closed to the hysteria of the night, Staverton slumped in a high backed chair, reading through one of the numerous volumes that lined the wall of his small living room. A coal fire smoldered in the grate: he would retire to bed soon, though it was relatively early. Too wild a night to go out to the shed for more logs. When he had been a young man, he would have revelled in a night such as this, but now, at fifty, he felt the cold too easily, and his bones ached at the very thought of a stiff breeze. But it was the price he paid for isolation, for severance from the world he had once inhabited.

He jerked as the thought was given substance by a sudden pounding on the front door. Far too rhythmic to be the wind. And it demanded to be answered. His light was on; it would have been seen.

Cursing, he went to the door and slid back the long bolt, easing the door inward. A blast of freezing air cuffed at him and as he lifted his arm to protect himself, he saw figures beyond. Three dishevelled youths confronted him. Beyond them, on a knoll by the cliff edge, he caught a glimpse of another, hunched over against the tempest but positioned like a sentinel.

He had no time to study it: his visitors were inside, the door banged shut and bolted anew against the storm.

"Doctor Staverton?" said the first of them. He was in his early twenties, his near-shaven head bare, his eyes sunken and dark-ringed. Clothes poor, jacket and faded trousers baggy and creased, shirt stained, buttons missing. The two other youths could have been his brothers, equally as shabby. Didn't they call them travelers?

"Not doctor. I was a surgeon. And I'm retired," said Staverton.

"We know," said the youth, half smiling. His teeth were bad, his mouth cruel.

"I don't have anything worth stealing—"

"We're not here to do the place over. It's you we want. Better sit down."

Staverton had no alternative. He dropped back into his chair. The spokesman sat awkwardly in the chair opposite him as if it were alien to him; the others stayed by the door, watching vacantly.

"I'm Turner. You don't know me," said the youth. His face gleamed with the rain and Staverton saw now that his jacket was sodden, though the youth didn't seem bothered, hardly noticing the fire.

"Who sent you?" said Staverton uneasily.

"Not who you think. Not Walton."

In spite of himself, Staverton gasped. "What do you know about him?"

"You worked for him, at the Institute. For years." Turner's eyes were tiny, but they fixed on Staverton's face, the youth's gaze irresistible, frightening.

"It was a long time ago—"

"It's taken my boss years to track you down. After you left the Institute, you really did go to earth, Doctor."

"Look, I've nothing worth having, worth knowing."

"My boss doesn't think so."

"Who is he? Not the police?"

Turner's face creased in a semblance of a grin. "No chance. You'll meet my boss soon enough. Then you'll know him. He'll make it worth your while. And you won't get hurt. He needs you."

"Has—Walton—got anything to do with this?"

Turner snorted. "Oh, yes. Indeed he has."

"I won't go back to him, not now—"

"Sounds to me like you hate him."

Staverton pulled his jacket tighter about him. "He's despicable. Treats people like dirt. Uses them and discards them."

"You should know, eh?" Turner leaned forward, a hellish gleam in those tiny eyes. "You don't know half of it. Want to?"

Staverton shuddered. "No. I'm glad to be out of there now. I'd outlasted my usefulness. God, it's such a relief to be free of him."

"It's time you knew the truth about him."

Staverton shook his head. "No. All I want is to be left alone."

"Tough. My boss needs your help. He said to tell you everything about Walton. Then you'd help."

Staverton looked up, then across at the other two youths. They were slouched against the door, seeming to drowse. "I don't have much choice."

"Hear me out, then choose," said Turner.

Staverton again felt the onset of coldness creeping in the air. It molded ominous shapes from his past, but he nodded. There was an inevitability in all this that part of him had always dreaded.

II

"Did Robert Walton ever talk about his first partner, Victor Frankenstein?" Turner began.

Staverton pondered the name, but murmured a negative.

"Frankenstein was, among other things, a brilliant surgeon. He lived in the eighteenth century. We don't know when he died."

Staverton frowned. "But you said he was a partner of Walton's. That's not possible—"

"Walton is not what he seems. You know he's a surgeon, well, sort of. But Frankenstein was the master. His genius is what Walton wanted, what he stole.

"Two hundred years ago, this woman, Margaret Saville, got a series of letters from her brother, who was an explorer, gone on a voyage to the Arctic. This brother, also called Robert Walton, said how he happened across a couple of weird people in the ice wastes. One of them was Victor Frankenstein. Exhausted, near enough dead, Frankenstein told Walton how he had created a living being built from cadavers and body parts, alive for a second time. This Monster, as Frankenstein called it, created havoc, went berserk, killing in a rage against mankind. It ran off to the Arctic wilderness, with its creator chasing it.

"In his letters to his sister, Walton said how Frankenstein died on board his ship, and how the Monster went right on to the north, meaning to set itself alight on a funeral pyre. As far as anyone knew, both Victor Frankenstein and his creation ended up dead in the frozen wastes." Turner looked meaningfully at Staverton. "That was what Walton put in his letters."

"And this Walton was related to the Robert Walton I knew?"

Turner snorted. "They're the same. The last letter to Margaret Saville was a cover up. Frankenstein didn't die on Walton's ship. Walton kept him going, brought him back to England. He was wealthy and had a lot of rich contacts. Victor Frankenstein was kept like a prisoner, though he didn't realize. And Walton fed on him like a vampire sucking the juice out of its prey. All that knowledge!"

"This is preposterous!" Staverton began to protest, but already his doubts were uncoiling, coaxed out of him.

"Life," said Turner. "Immortality. Mankind's dream since he could first walk. Frankenstein had created it. Walton wanted to do it. And he wanted much more. He wanted it for himself.

"Modern surgeons transplant vital organs every day, and medical science leaps forward. But Frankenstein was the greatest medical genius that ever lived. He went further than any modern surgeon. He thought Walton was his friend and he believed that his Monster had perished. Walton gave him a fresh sense of purpose, new hope. Goaded on by him, Frankenstein started his work again. Not to create another Monster. This time he wanted to step up. Who knows better than you, Doctor, his speciality, his obsession? He wanted to transplant the human brain."

Staverton made to speak, but something held him back.

"Walton learned, made himself into a surgeon, though he could never hope to match Frankenstein's brilliance. There were errors, trials, successes. In the end, the big test. Walton wanted to live forever. Frankenstein transplanted his brain into the body of a younger man. The operation was a perfect success. Walton had his wish."

Staverton's blood was coagulating, his hands pressed to his face. He would have poured derision on this, but he knew, God help him, he knew that somehow this answered so many questions about the man he had worked for.

"How many times since then has Robert Walton transferred himself into a younger body?" said Turner scathingly. "Who knows? How soon was Victor Frankenstein made redundant, eh? You can bet his body is buried somewhere well out of the way, or his ashes are long since scattered."

"Robert Walton, alive for over two hundred years," muttered Staverton.

"You know enough about him and his work to understand, Doctor. You, of all people, know it's the truth. Your own speciality was the brain."

Staverton looked at his hands.

Turner smiled coldly. "Steady as a rock. My boss will be very pleased. You better get ready."

Staverton shivered: resistance was not an option.

III

They traveled in an old van, Staverton in the front, Turner driving. The youth had insisted on leaving immediately. Staverton had no alternative: they allowed him to bring an overnight bag, a few clothes. Turner hardly spoke now, and as the vehicle ground its way through the night and endless storm, Staverton mulled over his own past, his dealings with Robert Walton.

As a surgeon himself, he had known about the Waltonian Institute, as everyone in his profession had. Walton was a reputable surgeon, but had apparently also inherited vast sums of money through family connections that went way back. The word was that his grandfather had set up the Institute, a private research center specializing in neurosurgery and more recently, genetic engineering. There had been a degree of opposition to the Institute's methods and somewhat secretive programs, but Walton was well connected in the political world. There were more than a few stories about the Institute's successes in the field of plastic surgery. Parliamentary perks.

Walton had a network that spread throughout Europe: the Institute was able to seduce many of the most gifted surgeons, neurologists and geneticists, even if only for a brief stay. Staverton had been one of them, lured into the fortress-like Institute by the opportunities that its funds promised, funds that were simply not available to him elsewhere. For five years he had worked inside the place, its slave, oblivious to the outside world, reveling, yes reveling in the possibilities. But—to *transplant* a brain—was that really what Walton had achieved? Staverton's own work had been in repair, adjustment, precision tuning of the brain. Moving a human brain from one body to another remained a fantasy.

After five years, Staverton had suddenly been summoned by Walton, his contract terminated. There had never been a proper explanation: at thirty-eight he still had his clarity of eye, his deftness of touch, all the artistry his science demanded of him. But the Institute, it seemed, wanted a change. Perhaps he knew too much, or was in danger of questioning what it did. He had become critical of some of its methods, its insensitivities.

He would have been horrified by his dismissal, but Walton had paid him a ridiculously generous sum, a "pension," so that when he had left he felt a kind of disappointment rather than anger. The bitterness accrued later as he tried to return to his work in the outside world. Walton, for it must have been him, had made sure no one would employ him. The network was very effective. The money was no compensation at first, but gradually he used it to ease his disillusionment. But as an ex-Waltonian, he found himself ostracized. He thought at first it was professional jealousy, but gradually understood that it was the hand of Robert Walton. How many other former staff had been cast out, each of them knowing no more than a fragment of the Institute's truths? He had traced some of them, but none of them would discuss the Institute. Their fear clung to them like a shroud.

Staverton's anger welled up anew as he recalled the wasted years, the frustration. He evaded sleep, eyes fixed on the road ahead, his vision blurred by rain, the greys of dawn.

"You want food?" said Turner suddenly, his own eyes lidded, though his control of the old van was tight, mechanical. "We'll eat soon," he said, answering his own question. "Then rest for the day. This evening you'll meet my boss."

Outside, the wind fisted the van, but the wheels clung to the road, its purpose fixed, inexorable.

IV

They did as Turner said. Staverton eventually succumbed to sleep, the van parked up a side road, somewhere in the country where the lane had hedges high enough to conceal it from prying eyes. Staverton somehow felt furtive. He told himself it was fear of Walton, the network of power webbed about the man.

By late afternoon, when Staverton woke, the storm had abated, leaving a dripping landscape, fields churned, threaded with miniature lakes. Turner drove on, still the silent automaton.

Staverton recognized the countryside: they were very close to the Institute. Soon the van would be swallowed up by the vastness of forest that surrounded the place, locked it away. Twenty miles from Greater London, though it may as well have been the Moon.

Staverton finished a stale sandwich and swigged the last of his tea from a cheap thermos they had bought on the journey. Turner brought the van to a halt, the shadows outside gathering. Staverton peered into the gloom, and recognized the high, black railings of a long fence that parallelled the road opposite the forest.

"We get out here," said Turner bluntly.

Outside the van, Staverton felt a renewed chill. He clutched his suitcase and glanced uncomfortably at the wrought iron gates before him. He knew the place: a familiar landmark to staff at the Institute. An old cemetery, closed now in favor of a new crematorium in its pristine grounds and gardens adjacent to the Institute, partly funded by its generous master.

Turner's henchmen watched the road while he, to Staverton's surprise, tugged out a large key from his pocket and unlocked the huge padlock on the chains of the gate. He motioned Staverton within. Moments later, with the gates again locked, they were all inside the graveyard. Overgrown and neglected, the graves and their various headstones disappeared into the dusk on every side. Huge, Gothic crosses jutted intimidatingly, tiny headstones poked up from choking grass, an occasional shrub or tree dotted the scene.

Turner walked down the central path, the gravel crunching faintly, though even it could not hold back the weed army.

"Why are we here?" said Staverton at last. Behind him, Turner's henchmen seemed like gaolers, alert for any break that Staverton might make. "The Institute is—"

"He's here," said Turner simply.

They turned down a side path and threaded through a maze of them. "He likes the night, and the privacy," said Turner. "You don't have to be afraid."

Staverton nodded, but all he could see ahead of him now was his own pain, his own torment.

Turner pointed to a solid building, partly hidden in a mass of matted brambles. A mausoleum, squat and somber, its twin pillars symbols of a distant age, dead as its tenants.

"In there."

Staverton no longer had a choice. Haltingly he stumbled through the open portal, surprised to find a guttering light within. Turner wrestled with a thick wooden door, shutting out the twilight, his henchmen with it. He led Staverton farther into the building, coming to a stairway that led downward to its rotting vaults. Light seeped up from below, another brand, mark of another time.

Turner nodded and Staverton went hesitantly down. Stone arches curved to support a ceiling, pillars forming narrow columns. A few blocks of solid stone lined the walls, their lids bearing sculpted forms, daubed now in the orange glow of the torches.

At the far end of the catacomb, Staverton could make out a hunched figure, broad in the shoulder, its back to him as it sat crouched over something, a book, perhaps. Turner went towards the figure cautiously, feet gently slapping the stone floor. It lifted its immense head, turning.

Staverton realized that this was Turner's master, the leader of the youths. As the man turned, Staverton felt his heart jar and he had to reach for a pillar to steady himself, thinking his knees would betray him.

The face was horrifically ugly, a pale, wasted grey; the skin looked dried, rotten, the flesh of a mummy, and the eyes were black, windows on an emptiness that was chilling. Wisps of hair straggled, shoulder length, tangled and dry. It was the head and face of a corpse, garishly animated and it moved with an almost mechanical uncertainty. When the creature, for such Staverton took it to be, spoke, the voice was doubly unnerving, for it was not in the least coarse, either in tone or manner. It was cultured, deep and rich, completely out of keeping, as if another spoke through the ghoulish body.

"You are Daniel Staverton," it said. It had not risen, but even hunched in its makeshift chair it was huge, its square shoulders almost on a level with Staverton's.

"Yes," Staverton breathed.

"You are terrified of my appearance. All your kind are. I have lived with that for a long time. But if you do as I tell you, you have no need to fear me."

"But . . . who are you?" murmured Staverton.

"Turner told you about Victor Frankenstein? I am his creation, his demon."

V

The creature spoke then of its tormented life, the chase across the ice floes of the Arctic, the flight to the Pole.

"I passed Robert Walton's ship among the bergs. Frankenstein paused in his mad pursuit of me, doubtless exhausted. Walton took him aboard, nurtured him for days. I spied on them both. The fury of the elements is nothing to me, who was forged with primal fire. Ice or fire, it is all one to me." The terrible eyes seemed to reinforce the statement. "They were not aware of me. I could see that Frankenstein's pursuit of me was over, whether he lived or died. So I quit them, intent on reaching the heartlands, offering myself up in a funereal sacrifice. Ah, but life, no matter how twisted, no matter how much a parody, does not render itself up so easily. When the moment came, self-destruction, even for one so hideous as I, was no less repulsive to me than it would be to you. The elements could not destroy me.

"I wandered those vast wastes with nothing but my memories for company. My bitterness, my disgust, my self-repugnance dogged me like wolves, always snapping at me, but never tearing me down. Year after year it went on, until they tired, those emotional scavengers, skulking away, toothless and contemptible. All faded but my hate.

"And I came back."

"For him?"

"Yes. Fate had tied us as surely as the birth cord ties a babe to its mother. I had had none, but I was secured to Frankenstein by his very act of creation."

"You found him—"

"No. By the time I had unravelled the details of his life after he returned from the Arctic, a task of considerable years, he was no more. I assume he was a victim of Robert Walton's perfidy. Certainly he is dead. But Robert Walton lives on. Like me, he cheats death, safe in his disguise, for who would believe the truth about him?"

Staverton shook his head. "Medical science would mock such an idea, unless—" He gazed uneasily at the creature before him.

"Unless I came forward? Yes, I could undo him with the truth. But I have lived in darkness since my return. I have made the graveyard my home, the secret places of your world, the crawling dark. And my companions are the denizens of that sub-world. The dregs of humanity, spurned by it as I have been: they understand me and serve me well. Time is meaningless to me, as it is to Robert Walton. But I am ready for him now, ready for the reckoning."

Staverton winced at the raw pain in the words, as though the creature had fashioned the agonies of its entire life into a weapon of retribution. "But what is my part in this? I have had nothing to do with Walton for years."

"You, too, have sought seclusion. You live alone, without relatives or friends, shut away in a barren land, forgotten by the world that knew you. You are a ghost, Daniel Staverton, a shadow person. No one notices what you do. But your arts are not lost to you."

"I don't know—"

"I need them. Do not deny me. How can you? You would see the fall of Robert Walton as I would."

Staverton could not deny it. His emotions had become dulled over the years. But Walton could rekindle hatred, anger.

"Walton once wrote to his sister that I had gone to my funeral pyre, that I would exult in its agony. But I am not destroyed by words, any more than I am destroyed by actions. As he will learn."

VI

It was only after Staverton had left the presence of the cadaverous being in the vault that the true horror of its nature struck him. Above in the mausoleum, he felt an onrush of dread, a need to get outside into the air. Night greeted him; he sagged against a headstone, watched by the ever-present Turner and his seedy trio of companions.

"He's real," Turner said. "Hate made him, keeps him alive. Nothing stronger than hate, Doctor. Fear makes you weak. Hate makes you strong. You want to remember that."

Staverton nodded. He clung to his own hate now. Either that or terror would undo him.

Later, deep into the night, they left the cemetery in the van and soon the forest enclosed them, the silence as intense as the darkness. Turner knew the way: everything from now on had been planned with the precision of a surgeon's work.

A high wall loomed up beside the road, the boundary of the Waltonian Institute, topped with barbed wire. Too many people had too much to gain from the Institute for the law of the land to be adhered to: the wire was electrified. Turner swerved off the narrow road to where another vehicle was parked under the wall. A huge figure clambered out of it, and Staverton realized just how enormous, how monstrous, this creature truly was.

"You'll find everything you need inside," said the creature, handing Staverton a leather bag, which was oddly heavy. The creature turned and watched silently as Turner's minions slid together two sections of ladder and propped it up against the wall. When they had secured it, the creature climbed woodenly up to the top of the wall.

"The current—" began Staverton, but Turner's face was a mocking grimace.

"Just get ready to move fast, Doctor."

Staverton's trepidation turned to shock as the creature reached the barbed wire and gripped it with both hands. Electric current sizzled, the air snapping with brilliant light, smoke billowing in the glow. But the creature merely tore the wires apart, impervious to pain, the horrible scorching of its flesh. Using inexorable strength, it ripped away wire and stanchions alike, creating a sizeable gap through which it disappeared.

"Move!" snarled Turner, and Staverton clambered upwards, barely able to hang on to the black bag. At the top, the smell of cooked flesh was nauseating, but he forced himself over the wall. The drop on the other side was eased by a tall mass of shrubbery and undergrowth which eased his fall. Turner and the others were beside him in moments, the ladder recovered and hidden away.

"They'll know we're here," said Turner. "But it don't matter."

His master towered over them. "In the forest, there will be dogs, and worse things. Keep together, especially you, Staverton."

Staverton turned away from its charred hands and as he did so he felt another surge of horror: Turner and his men pulled from their jackets long machetes.

The group had not moved far through the labyrinth of trees when the sound of baying came to them. There could be no escaping the hunt and within moments the first of the huge black beasts came crashing through the bracken. The creature met it with a blur of movement, its arm striking the neck of the hound before it could sink its teeth into flesh, and the sound of snapping bone was loud in the night. The hound catapulted sideways, dead before it thudded into the earth.

Others tore into the men, but they used their wide-bladed weapons with devastating effect. Staverton crouched down, clutching the bag as if it could hide him, while around him the hounds snarled, blades gleamed, and blood ran. There must have been a dozen in the pack. A few minutes later none were left alive. One of the men had taken a bad wound on his arm where teeth had torn the flesh open, but his companions bound it up with a ripped section of jacket, stemming the flow of blood.

They moved on through the forest, and for now it was again silent, though Staverton was certain that their movements were being watched. Closed-circuit television maybe.

It was a two-mile hike to the buildings of the Institute, and although they heard more baying in the distance, there were as yet no more attacks by the hounds. In the shrubbery beside the gravel car park at the front of the Institute, they squatted down and watched.

"You know this place," said the creature to Staverton. "What is the least difficult way to enter it?"

"We'll never get in," muttered Staverton. "The dogs are one thing, but they have armed guards, a small army of them. Look." To illustrate his point, he indicated a group of men who had appeared from around a corner of the massive building: uniformed, carrying weapons of some kind, they fanned out. Lights above stabbed at the forest, search beams, and the party among the trees ducked down. The Institute was crawling with the guards.

Staverton could see the creature's ghoulish features twisting with frustration. "I was foolish to imagine that Walton would protect himself any less thoroughly."

"There's one possible way in," Staverton told him. "About a mile on the other side of the Institute, at the back of the gardens, there's an old orangery. In the buildings around it there's a way down to some cellars that were dug when part of the Institute was a monastery. They lead under it, though I've never been down there."

"Take us there," the creature grunted.

VII

They goaded Staverton through the undergrowth, weaving like escaped criminals as the lights stabbed out into the forest. But the guards, scores of them now, remained on the gravel paths surrounding the house, not eager to be drawn out into the vast woodland, secure in the knowledge that no one could get past them. Gradually Staverton and his bizarre companions moved back into the forest's thick shadows, the sounds of the hounds receding. Twice they were found by the hounds, but these were despatched as swiftly and as decisively as the others had been.

The orangery was as Staverton had remembered it, the lawns before it immaculate, the shrubs neatly maintained. It took him a while to locate the outbuildings; Turner and the others felt it was safe enough now to use their flashlights. In one of the musty rooms a rotting door revealed stone steps.

"I'm sure this is it," said Staverton. At the foot of the steps there was another wooden door, heavily padlocked. The creature wrenched the lock off and shouldered the door inward. Beyond was a low corridor, cut from the naked rock. They all had to stoop down to follow the passageway. Staverton had been right: it wormed its way under the earth for about a mile, gradually sloping downwards as it went. At its far end yet another door barred the way.

The creature put its ear to it and listened. "Do you know what is beyond?" it asked Staverton.

"Either cellars or possibly laboratories. There were places we were not allowed to visit. We knew some of them were far below the Institute. God knows what Walton got up to."

"Guarded?"

"Above, perhaps. But not down here. Hardly anyone would know this area exists."

The creature nodded, bent almost double by the confines of the tunnel. It used its damaged hands to tear at the door as though pain were totally unknown to it. The wood protested; dust trickled down from above. But the door began to splinter. A thick plank dragged loose and it was all the creature needed: in moments it had forced the door off its massive hinges, wrenching it aside in another dust cloud.

It shone its torch inward and up a short corridor. At its end was a grille, rusting and ancient. Again the creature used its incalculable strength to rip it aside like a curtain. Beyond was a chamber, unexpectedly cavernous, a vaulted catacomb, its many pillars a stone forest in the bowels of the earth.

The party emerged from the tunnel, Staverton's nerves attuned to the slightest sound: there were a number of them and he stifled a moan of terror. An uneven slithering came from the right, a muted croaking from the left, and other uneasy sounds echoed softly from all around. Something stirred in Staverton's memory, images of long buried myths about the Institute's remote history, its forgotten, shameful past. Once they had been no more than stories, jokes among the staff. But here they were real, rising up to defend their grim domain.

VIII

In the crossbeams of the torches, the shapes reared abruptly and Staverton lurched back, appalled. The creature and its henchmen were prepared to defend themselves, unmoved by the nature of the things that loomed out of the shadows. These things were human, but there was something drastically wrong with all of them, as though they were unfinished, the victims of a defective genetic process. They moaned at the intrusive beams of light, which were far more effective than any weapon, cutting at them, substantial as razors. Scores of the creatures thronged the chamber, some chained, straining against the locks that impeded their movements.

Again Staverton gasped as he realized they had not gathered to attack. They wanted something, reaching out with claws, talons, and in some cases snake-like arms.

"Food," said Turner, his own grim features twisted into a rictus of revulsion. "They want food."

In the eerie torch glow, Staverton saw the profile of the Monster, caught an almost frightening look of pity in those sunken eyes. It alone understood the suffering of the beastmen in this hellish dungeon. It turned to Staverton, pity turning to a vast anger.

"Did you know of this?"

Staverton shook his head as the torch beams dazzled him. But the light must have vindicated his own shock. "The experiments of a lifetime, of several lifetimes!" he murmured. "The by-products of Walton's evil work. Why in God's name has he preserved them!"

The creature turned away and went amongst the throng, invulnerable. It began tearing at chains, ripping them out of the walls, tossing them aside, releasing as many of the monstrous creatures as it could. Turner urged Staverton to follow in his master's wake. It was clear now that they would not be attacked.

"What will happen to them?" Staverton called to the creature.

"Let them find their way out into the forest."

"But they'll—" die, Staverton thought, but did not say. Yes, better to die out there than be preserved here in this hole. That's what the creature wants. Let them die avenging themselves, taking as many of their tormentors with them as they could.

The creature had crossed the chamber. Several hunched figures dogged its footsteps, as if it had spoken silent commands to them. Like zombies, flesh-bloated, grey as putty, their dead eyes fixed on it, like hounds awaiting fresh commands.

Again Turner prodded Staverton forward, the other henchmen close behind them. Already the mass of shapes was thinning: they had found the exit, choking it with their exodus as if they could smell the night air a mile beyond.

The creature forced open another door; there was a modern stairway beyond. Turner killed the lights, using only a single torch to guide the party up into the Institute. There were no guards here: none had been thought necessary. The creature's new followers remained deathly silent, and in a brief flicker of light, Staverton saw why: they had no mouths. It was too dark to see what alternative Walton's warped science had given them.

The creature motioned Staverton to the head of the party. "You should know your way from here. Find Robert Walton."

There was no point arguing. Staverton did as bidden, knowing that they were now inside the main block of the Institute. Walton was just as likely to be here as anywhere else. On a carpeted landing several flights up, they came across an armed guard.

Turner despatched one of his henchmen to deal with him, and he blended with the wall, creeping forward until it was too late for the guard to prevent himself from being caught in a steely grip. Turner's henchman dragged the guard back to the others.

"Where's Walton?" Staverton demanded nervously.

The guard's eyes bulged with terror as he saw Staverton's ghastly companions. He had no choice but to furnish them with what they wanted. "He's not far. In one of the main halls. But—"

Staverton fought down his nausea as the creature choked the life from the guard in one brief, terrible squeeze of its charred hands, dropping the corpse like a rag doll.

They wove along a few more corridors until Staverton recognized the doors to the hall that the guard had referred to. One was slightly ajar. Voices came from beyond, the sound of an argument.

The creature's massive head lifted, eyes filled with an icy hatred. "It's him. Walton is in there." It swung around to the zombies it had brought up from the bowels of the Institute and although it said nothing, its eyes must have conveyed something to them, some dread command. As one they plodded forward, knocking aside the twin doors and entering the hall beyond.

Staverton heard the gasps, then the deafening blast of guns being discharged. He dropped to his knees, crawling to a wall and trying to melt into it, his terror sweeping over him in a wave. Someone came rushing out, only to be felled by the creature's flailing fist. Other people, surgeons possibly, as well as guards, tried to get out of the room where all hell had broken loose, but the creature and its henchmen dealt with them with the deadly efficiency of commandos.

Eventually Staverton felt himself dragged to his feet, still clutching his black bag, face streaked with tears. He was bundled into the tall room beyond. The mayhem was over, but the place was like a battlefield, bodies strewn among the shattered furniture. Four of the zombies had been cut down and lay twitching amongst their victims. The other two merely stood like robots that had been switched off.

At the heart of the chaos, the creature confronted the only other survivor, gripping his shirt and swinging him round. Staverton found himself looking into the terror-stricken eyes of his former employer.

"I know you," Robert Walton gasped. "You—"

Anger welled up in Staverton. Anger at the loss of everything he had once wanted to be, anger at his rejection, and anger now at Walton's ultimate cruelty. It sluiced away all other emotions. "I was one of the best you had, Walton."

The creature's grip on Walton's shoulder tightened. "If he did not know that then," it said, "he soon will. Open your bag. It is time to begin the real work."

IX

Robert Walton looked out of the tall window, studying the group of men below as they got into their black vehicles and began to leave the Institute. His eyes were cold, unemotional. Satisfied that the procession of cars would soon be swallowed by the forest, carrying back to Westminster its lackeys with their glib report, he turned. His movements were a little stiff, as if he were recovering from a minor accident. Those cold eyes met the uneasy gaze of Staverton.

"It must be nearly time," said Walton in his deep, cultured voice. "My dear fellow, you must be exhausted. Such a demanding operation. But you can have all the rest you want soon."

Staverton drew himself together with an effort. He looked as if he'd been without sleep for days, his face grey, his eyes shrunken.

"Come along," said Walton suddenly. "Let us have done with this wretched business."

Outside on the landing, two armed guards stiffened, but Walton spoke to them softly, reassuringly: order had been restored, chaos explained, glossed over. Then he motioned Staverton to follow him.

They went down into the heart of the Institute. There were no guards here, but at the foot of an old staircase, the door was securely locked. Walton took out a thick key and undid the padlock, gesturing Staverton within. The latter went forward resignedly.

The chamber was lit by a number of dangling bulbs. Almost empty now, devoid of the frightful creatures that had until recently inhabited it, it boasted a single occupant, stretched out on a slab, a mock-tomb. A white sheet covered the being from the neck down.

Walton leaned over the face and its eyes flickered open. "Ah, we have chosen the perfect moment to come to you."

The being on the slab, huge, misshapen, skin like putty, hair matted and straggling, tried to sit up, but failed.

"It will be a while yet before you are able to move," said Walton. "But you will learn."

Staverton watched grimly: it was like seeing a child playing with a damaged spider.

"I must congratulate you, Staverton," said Walton. "Your workmanship is superb. Unique in fact. I am sure our friend would agree. Tell me, how was my first performance?"

The eyes in the creature stared up at him, fear mingled with loathing.

"Immaculate," muttered Staverton. "None of them realized. None of them will ever know. You have become Robert Walton. You have his coldness, his cynicism, his lack of compassion. You have mastered that far more quickly than you have mastered your new body."

Walton looked down at the prone figure. "Yes, it won't be easy to forget the constraints of that monstrous shape. But you, Robert Walton that was," he added, leaning closer to the eyes that bored into his, "You have a lifetime to learn how to manipulate it. Many lifetimes. Yes, so many lifetimes. Eternity, no less. It is what you always desired."

DENNIS ETCHISON

The Dead Line

⌐—◆—⌐

Dennis Etchison is a three-time winner of both the British Fantasy and World Fantasy Awards. Many of his short stories may be found in the collections The Dark Country, Red Dreams, The Blood Kiss, The Death Artist, Talking In the Dark, Fine Cuts *and* Got To Kill Them All & Other Stories.

He is also the author of the novels Darkside, Shadowman, California Gothic, Double Edge, The Fog, Halloween II, Halloween III *and* Videodrome, *and editor of the anthologies* Cutting Edge, Masters of Darkness I–III, MetaHorror, The Museum of Horrors *and (with Ramsey Campbell and Jack Dann)* Gathering the Bones.

Etchison has written extensively for film, television and radio, including scripts for John Carpenter, Dario Argento,

The Twilight Zone Radio Dramas, Fangoria Magazine's Dread Time Stories *and* Christopher Lee's Mystery Theater. *He is a former two-term president of the Horror Writers Association (HWA).*

His latest books are It Only Comes Out At Night and Other Stories, *a career retrospective from Centipede Press, and* A Little Black Book of Horror Stories *from Borderlands Press.*

When it comes to the classic tale that follows, it is easy to understand Ramsey Campbell's opinion that "Dennis Etchison is the finest writer of short stories now working in the field." It also happens to be an opinion that I wholeheartedly agree with . . .

I

This morning I put ground glass in my wife's eyes. She didn't mind. She didn't make a sound. She never does.

I took an empty bottle from the table. I wrapped it in a towel and swung it, smashing it gently against the side of her bed. When the glass shattered it made a faint, very faint sound like wind chimes in a thick fog. No one noticed, of course, least of all Karen. Then I placed it under my shoe and stepped down hard, rocking my weight back and forth until I felt fine sand underfoot. I knelt and picked up a few sharp grains on the end of my finger, rose and dropped them onto her corneas. First one, then the other. She doesn't blink, you know. It was easy.

Then I had to leave. I saw the technicians coming. But already it was too late; the damage had been done. I don't know if they found the mess under the bed. I suppose someone will. The janitors or the orderlies, perhaps. But it won't matter to them, I'm sure.

I slipped outside the glass observation wall as the technicians descended the lines, adjusting respirators, reading printouts and making notations on their pocket recorders. I remember that I thought then of clean, college-trained farmers combing rows of crops, checking the condition of the coming harvest, turning down a cover here, patting a loose mound there, touching the beds with a horticulturist's fussiness, ready to prune wherever necessary for the demands of the marketplace. They may not have seen me at all. And what if they had? What was I but a concerned husband come to pay his respects to a loved one? I might have been lectured about the risk of bringing unwanted germs into the area, though they must know how unlikely that is with the high-intensity UV lights and sonic purifiers and other sanitary precautions. I did make a point of passing near the Children's Communicable Diseases Ward on my way there, however; one always hopes.

Then, standing alone behind the windows, isolated and empty as an expectant father waiting for his flesh and blood to be delivered at last into his own hands, I had the sudden, unshakable feeling that I was being watched.

By whom?

The technicians were still intent on their readouts.

Another visitor? It was unlikely; hardly anyone else bothers to observe. A guilty few still do stop by during the lonely hours, seeking silent expiation from a friend, relative or lover, or merely to satisfy some morbid curiosity; the most recently-acquired neomorts usually receive dutiful visitations at the beginning, but invariably the newly-grieved are so overwhelmed by the impersonalness of the procedure that they soon learn to stay away to preserve their own sanity.

I kept careful track of the progress of the white coats on the other side of the windows, ready to move on at the first sign of undue concern over my wife's bed.

And it was then that I saw her face shining behind my own in the pane. She was alert and standing for the first time since the stroke, nearly eighteen months ago. I gripped the handrail until my nails were white, staring in disbelief at Karen's transparent reflection.

I turned. And shrank back against the wall. The cold sweat must have been on my face, because she reached out shakily and pressed my hand.

"Can I get you anything?"

Her hair was beautiful again, not the stringy, matted mass I had come to know. Her makeup was freshly applied, her lips dark at the edges and parted just so, opening on a warm, pink interior, her teeth no longer discolored but once more a luminous bone-white. And her eyes. They were perfect.

I lunged for her.

She sidestepped gracefully and supported my arm. I looked closely at her face as I allowed her to hold me a moment longer. There was nothing wrong with that, was there?

"Are you all right?" she said.

She was so much like Karen I had to stop the backs of my fingers from stroking the soft, wispy down at her temple, as they had done so many, many times. She had always liked that. And so, I remembered, had I; it was so long ago I had almost forgotten.

"Sorry," I managed. I adjusted my clothing, smoothing my hair down from the laminar airflow around the beds. "I'm not feeling well."

"I understand."

Did she?

"My name is Emily Richterhausen," she said.

I straightened and introduced myself. If she had seen me inside the restricted area she said nothing. But she couldn't have been here that long. I would have noticed her.

"A relative?" she asked.

"My wife."

"Has . . . has she been here long?"

"Yes. I'm sorry. If you'll excuse me—"

"Are you sure you're all right?" She moved in front of me. "I could get you a cup of coffee, you know, from the machines. We could both have one. Or some water."

It was obvious that she wanted to talk. She needed it. Perhaps I did, too. I realized that I needed to explain myself, to pass off my presence before she could guess my plan.

"Do you come here often, Emily?" It was a foolish question. I knew I hadn't seen her before.

"It's my husband," she said.

"I see."

"Oh, he's not one of . . . them. Not yet. He's in Intensive Care." The lovely face began to change. "A coma. It's been weeks. They say he may regain consciousness. One of the doctors said that. How long can it go on, do you know?"

I walked with her to a bench in the waiting area.

"An accident?" I said.

"A heart attack. He was driving to work. The car crossed the divider. It was awful." She fumbled for a handkerchief. I gave her mine. "They say it was a miracle he survived at all. You should have seen the car. No, you shouldn't have. No one should have. A miracle."

"Well," I told her, trying to sound comforting, "as I understand it, there is no 'usual' in comatose cases. It can go on indefinitely, as long as brain death hasn't occurred. Until then there's always hope. I saw a news item the other day about a young man who woke up after four years. He asked if he had missed his homework assignment. You've probably heard—"

"Brain death," she repeated, mouthing the words uneasily. I saw her shudder.

"That's the latest Supreme Court ruling. Even then," I went on quickly, "there's still hope. You remember that girl in New Jersey? She's still alive. She may pull out of it at any time," I lied. "And there are others like her. A great many, in fact. Why—"

"There *is* hope, isn't there?"

"I'm sure of it," I said, as kindly as possible.

"But then," she said, "supposing . . . What is it that actually happens, afterwards? How does it work? Oh, I know about the Maintenance and Cultivation Act. The doctor explained everything at the beginning, just in case." She glanced back toward the Neomort Ward and took a deep, uncertain breath. She didn't really want to know, not now. "It looks so nice and clean, doesn't it? They can still be of great service to society. The kidneys, the eyes, even the heart. It's a wonderful thing. Isn't it?"

"It's remarkable," I agreed. "Your husband, had he signed the papers?"

"No. He kept putting it off. William never liked to dwell on such matters. He didn't believe in courting disaster. Now I only wish I had forced him to talk about it, while there was still time."

"I'm sure it won't come to that," I said immediately. I couldn't bear the sight of her crying. "You'll see. The odds are very much on your side."

We sat side by side in silence as an orderly wheeled a stainless-steel cleaning cart off the elevator and headed past us to the observation area. I could not help but notice the special scent of her skin. Spring flowers.

It was so unlike the hospital, the antisepticised cloud that hangs over everything until it has settled into the very pores of the skin. I studied her discreetly: the tiny, exquisite whorls of her ear, the blood pulsing rapidly and naturally beneath her healthy skin. Somewhere an electronic air ionizer was whirring, and a muffled bell began to chime in a distant hallway.

"Forgive me," she said. "I shouldn't have gone on like that. But tell me about your wife." She faced me. "Isn't it strange?" We were inches apart. "It's so reassuring to talk to someone else who understands. I don't think the doctors really know how it is for us, for those who wait."

"They can't," I said.

"I'm a good listener, really I am. William always said that."

"My—my wife signed the Universal Donor Release two years ago," I began reluctantly, "the last time she renewed her driver's license." Good until her next birthday, I thought. As simple as that. Too simple. Karen, how could you have known? How could *I*? I should have. I should have found out. I should have stopped your hand. "She's here now. She's been here since last year. Her electroencephalogram was certified almost immediately."

"It must be a comfort to you," she said, "to know that she didn't suffer."

"Yes."

"You know, this is the first time I've been on this particular floor. What is it they call it?" She was rattling on, perhaps to distract herself.

"The Bioemporium."

"Yes, that's it. I guess I wanted to see what it would be like, just in case. For my William." She tried bravely to smile. "Do you visit her often?"

"As often as possible."

"I'm sure that must mean a great deal."

To whom? I thought, but let it pass.

"Don't worry," I said. "Your husband will recover. He'll be fine. You'll see."

Our legs were touching. It had been so long since I had felt contact with sentient flesh. I thought of asking her for that cup of coffee now, or something more, in the cafeteria. Or a drink.

"I try to believe that," she said. "It's the only thing that keeps me going. None of this seems real, does it?"

She forced the delicate corners of her mouth up into a full smile.

"I really should be going now. I could get something for him, couldn't I? You know, in the gift shop downstairs? I'm told they have a very lovely store right here in the building. And then I'll be able to give it to him during visiting hours. When he wakes up."

"That's a good idea," I said.

She said decisively, "I don't think I'll be coming to this floor again."

"Good luck," I told her. "But first, if you'd like, Emily, I thought—"

"What was . . . what is your wife's name? If you don't mind my asking?"

"Karen," I said. Karen. What was I thinking? Can you forgive me? You can do that, can't you, sweetheart?

"That's such a pretty name," she said.

"Thank you."

She stood. I did not try to delay her. There are some things that must be set to rest first, before one can go on. You helped remind me of that, didn't you, Karen? I nearly forgot. But you wouldn't let me.

"I suppose we won't be running into each other again," she said. Her eyes were almost cheerful.

"No."

"Would you . . . could you do me one small favor?"

I looked at her.

"What do you think I should get him? He has so many nice things. But you're a man. What would you like to have, if you were in the hospital? God forbid," she added, smiling warmly.

I sat there. I couldn't speak. I should have told her the truth then. But I couldn't. It would have seemed cruel, and that is not part of my nature.

What do you get, I wondered, for a man who has nothing?

II

I awaken.

The phone is silent.

I go to the medicine cabinet, swallow another fistful of L-tryptophan tablets and settle back down restlessly, hoping for a long and mercifully dreamless nap.

Soon, all too soon and not soon enough, I fall into a deep and troubled sleep.

I awaken to find myself trapped in an airtight box.

I pound on the lid, kicking until my toes are broken and my elbows are torn and bleeding. I reach into my pocket for my lighter, an antique Zippo, thumb the flint. In the sudden flare I am able to read an engraved plate set into the satin. Twenty-five-year guarantee, it says in fancy script. I scream. My throat tears. The lighter catches the white folds and tongues of flame lick my face, spreading rapidly down my squirming body. I inhale fire.

The lid swings open.

Two attendants in white are bending over me, squirting out the flames with a water hose. One of them chuckles.

Wonder how that happened? he says.

Spontaneous combustion? says his partner.

That would make our job a hell of a lot easier, says the other. He coils the hose and I see through burned-away eyelids that it is attached to a sink at the head of a stainless-steel table. The table has grooves running along the sides and a drainage hole at one end.

I scream again, but no sound comes out.

They turn away.

I struggle up out of the coffin. There is no pain. How can that be? I claw at my clothing, baring my seared flesh.

See? I cry. I'm alive!

They do not hear.

I rip at my chest with smoldering hands, the peeled skin rolling up under my fingernails. See the blood in my veins? I shout. I'm not one of them!

Do we have to do this one over? asks the attendant. It's only a cremation. Who'll know?

I see the eviscerated remains of others glistening in the sink, in the jars and plastic bags. I grab a scalpel. I slash at my arm. I cut through the smoking cloth of my shirt, laying open fresh incisions with white lips, slicing deeper into muscle and bone.

See? Do I not bleed?

They won't listen.

I stagger from the embalming chamber, gouging my sides as I bump other caskets which topple, spilling their pale contents onto the mortuary floor.

My body is steaming as I stumble out into the cold, grey dawn.

Where can I go? What is left for me? There must be a place. There must be—

A bell chimes, and I awaken.

Frantically I locate the telephone.

A woman. Her voice is relieved but shaking as she calls my name.

"Thank God you're home," she says. "I know it's late. But I didn't know who else to call. I'm terribly sorry to bother you. Do you remember me?"

No luck this time. When? I wonder. How much longer?

"You can hear me," I say to her.

"What?" She makes an effort to mask her hysteria, but I hear her cover the mouthpiece and sob. "We must have a bad connection. I'll hang up."

"No. Please." I sit forward, rubbing invisible cobwebs from my face. "Of course I remember you. Hello, Mrs. Richterhausen." What time is it? I wonder. "I'm glad you called. How did you know the number?"

"I asked Directory Information. I couldn't forget your name. You were so kind. I have to talk to someone first, before I go back to the hospital."

It's time for her, then. She must face it now; it cannot be put off, not anymore.

"How is your husband?"

"It's my husband," she says, not listening. Her voice breaks up momentarily under electrical interference. The signal re-forms, but we are still separated by a grid, as if in an electronic confessional. "At twelve-thirty tonight his, what is it, now?" She bites her lips but cannot control her voice. "His EEG. It . . . stopped. That's what they say. A straight line. There's nothing there. They say it's non-reversible. How can that be?" she asks desperately.

I wait.

"They want you to sign, don't they, Emily?"

"Yes." Her voice is tortured as she says, "It's a good, thing, isn't it? You said so yourself, this afternoon. You know about these things. Your wife . . ."

411

"We're not talking about my wife now, are we?"

"But they say it's right. The doctor said that."

"What is, Emily?"

"The life-support," she says pathetically. "The Maintenance." She still does not know what she is saying. "My husband can be of great value to medical science. Not all the usable organs can be taken at once. They may not be matched up with recipients for some time. That's why the Maintenance is so important. It's safer, more efficient than storage. Isn't that so?"

"Don't think of it as 'life-support,' Emily. Don't fool yourself. There is no longer any life to be supported."

"But he's not dead!"

"No."

"Then his body must be kept alive . . ."

"Not alive, either," I say. "Your husband is now—and will continue to be—neither alive nor dead. Do you understand that?"

It is too much. She breaks down. "H-how can I decide? I can't tell them to pull the plug. How could I do that to him?"

"Isn't there a decision involved in *not* pulling the plug?"

"But it's for the good of mankind, that's what they say. For people not yet born. Isn't that true? Help me," she says imploringly. "You're a good man. I need to be sure that he won't suffer. Do you think he would want it this way? It was what your wife wanted, wasn't it? At least this way you're able to visit, to go on seeing her. That's important to you, isn't it?"

"He won't feel a thing, if that's what you're asking. He doesn't now, and he never will. Not ever again."

"Then it's all right?"

I wait.

"She's at peace, isn't she, despite everything? It all seems so ghastly, somehow. I don't know what to do. Help me, please . . ."

"Emily," I say with great difficulty. But it must be done. "Do you understand what will happen to your husband if you authorize the Maintenance?"

She does not answer.

"Only this. Listen: this is how it begins. First he will be connected to an IBM cell separator, to keep track of leucocytes, platelets, red cells, antigens that can't be stored. He will be used around the clock to manufacture an endless red tide for transfusions—"

"But transfusions save lives!"

"Not just transfusions, Emily. His veins will be a battleground for viruses, for pneumonia, hepatitis, leukemia, live cancers. And then his body will be drained off, like a stuck pig's, and a new supply of experimental toxins pumped in, so that he can go on producing anti-toxins for them. Listen to me. He will begin to decay inside, Emily. He will be riddled with disease, tumors, parasites. He will stink with fever. His heart will deform, his brain fester with tubercles, his body cavities run with infection. His hair will fall, his skin yellow, his teeth splinter and rot. In the name of science, Emily, in the name of their beloved research."

I pause.

"That is, if he's one of the lucky ones."

"But the transplants . . ."

"Yes, that's right! You are so right, Emily. If not the blood, then the transplants. They will take him organ by organ, cell by cell. And it will take years. As long as the machines can keep the lungs and heart moving. And finally, after they've taken his eyes, his kidneys and the rest, it will be time for his nerve tissue, his lymph nodes, his testes. They will drill out his bone marrow, and when there is no more of that left it will be time to remove his stomach and intestines, as soon as they learn how to transplant those parts, too. And they will. Believe me, they will."

"No, please . . ."

"And when he's been thoroughly, efficiently gutted—or when his body has eaten itself from the inside out—when there is nothing left but a res-pirated sac bathed from within by its own excrement, do you know what they will do then? *Do you?* Then they will begin to strip the skin from his limbs, from his skull, a few millimeters at a time, for grafting and re-grafting, until—"

"Stop!"

"Take him, Emily! Take your William out of there now, tonight, before the technicians can get their bloody hands on him! Sign nothing! Take him home. Take him away and bury him forever. Do that much for him.

And for yourself. Let him rest. Give him that one last, most precious gift. Grant him his final peace. You can do that much, can't you? *Can't you?*"

From far away, across miles of the city, I hear the phone drop and then clack dully into place. But only after I have heard another sound, one that I pray I will never hear again.

Godspeed, Emily, I think, weeping. *Godspeed.*

I resume my vigil.

I try to awaken, and cannot.

III

There is a machine outside my door. It eats people, chews them up and spits out only what it can't use. It wants to get me, I know it does, but I'm not going to let it.

The call I have been waiting for will never come.

I'm sure of it now. The doctor, or his nurse or secretary or dialling machine, will never announce that they are done at last, that the procedure is no longer cost-effective, that her remains will be released for burial or cremation. Not yesterday, not today, not ever.

I have cut her arteries with stolen scalpels. I have dug with an ice pick deep into her brain, hoping to sever her motor centers. I have probed for her ganglia and nerve cords. I have pierced her eardrums. I have inserted needles, trying to puncture her heart and lungs. I have hidden caustics in the folds of her throat. I have ruined her eyes. But it's no use. It will never be enough.

They will never be done with her.

When I go to the hospital today she will not be there. She will already have been given to the interns for their spinal taps and arterio grams, for surgical practice on a cadaver that is neither alive nor dead. She will belong to the meat cutters, to the first-year med students with their dull knives and stained cross sections . . .

But I know what I will do.

I will search the floors and labs and secret doors of the wing, and when I find her I will steal her silently away; I will give her safe passage. I can do that much, can't I? I will take her to a place where even they can't reach, beyond the boundaries that separate the living from the dead. I will carry her over the threshold and into that realm, wherever it may be.

And there I will stay with her, to be there with her, to take refuge with her among the dead. I will tear at my body and my corruption until we are one in soft asylum. And there I will remain, living with death for whatever may be left of eternity.

Wish me Godspeed.

LISA MORTON
Poppi's Monster

—⚬—

Lisa Morton lives in North Hollywood, California. She is a screenwriter, author of nonfiction books, award-winning prose writer and Halloween expert whose work was described by the American Library Association's Readers' Advisory Guide to Horror as "consistently dark, unsettling, and frightening."

Her feature film credits include the cult favorite Meet the Hollowheads, *the vampire film* Blood Angels *and the mutant shark thriller* Blue Demon.

She is a four-time recipient of the Bram Stoker Award for horror writing, and her 2012 release, Trick or Treat?: A History of Halloween, *won the Grand Prize at the Halloween Book Festival.*

Her most recent books include the novels Zombie Apocalypse! Washington Deceased *and* Netherworld, *and the novellas* The Devil's Birthday *and* By Insanity of Reason *(with John R. Little).*

Poppi had hurt her bad this time, worse than usual. She'd known it would be bad as soon as he'd walked in the door.

It was after 10:00 P.M., he was late and her babysitter Heather from down the street had left at seven.

She was sprawled in front of the blaring TV, last working on an *Aladdin* coloring book she'd bought with lunch money she had secretly saved. She hadn't seen the movie, of course, but she liked to look at the bright printed scenes on the cover and the line drawings inside and pretend that she had. With her box of 64 Crayon colors, she could make the movie within the drawings look the way it did in her imagination. She liked the pictures in her head because they were all hers, Poppi couldn't touch them.

When he'd come in he was muttering under his breath. He immediately crossed to the television set and lowered the volume to an inaudible level.

"Christ almighty, Stacey, you always have to blast the goddamn TV? Last thing I need is some complaint from the neighbors."

As he turned, his foot kicked the box of Crayons, and they flew in a multihued arc across the room. "Aw, what is this . . . ?"

Poppi picked up the coloring book, glanced at it once and then shook it in her face. "Stacey, how many times do I have to tell you, you're too old for this nonsense. You're ten years old, too old to play with this little-kid bullshit."

Stacey heard her Crayons crack under his shoes. Vermilion, Burnt Sienna, Cornflower Blue, three broken colors she'd never use again.

She knew Poppi was right, though—ten-year-olds weren't supposed to play with coloring books, or Fisher-Price Farm Sets, or stuffed animals. The other kids in her class at school already had favorite bands, they could win video games and had posters up in their rooms of handsome TV stars. Not Stacey. She knew they thought she was weird or stupid; one teacher had used the word "remedial." That had been when Poppi had taped a funnel into her mouth and forcefed her a bad-tasting vitamin mash he said would make her smarter.

Tonight, though, she knew it wouldn't be that. He was already halfway out of his clothes, the heavy genuine leather belt tugging loose from the loops in his expensive slacks. She didn't understand what he was saying, something about a boy in the office today who had screamed and bitten him. He showed her a tiny red mark on one finger. Stacey didn't understand; the marks he left on her once or twice a month were a lot worse than that.

He told her to go into her room and lay on her stomach on her bed. She didn't fight or try to escape; she knew that would just make it worse. She went into her room and grabbed Baloo her stuffed bear. If she held onto Baloo very tightly it helped a little bit. Not much, but a little bit.

Poppi had his belt off and held it in both hands when he lumbered in. He reached up under her little skirt, flipped it up and tugged her tights and panties down. She didn't realize she was biting Baloo's ear. The leather whistled, and she tried not to cry out or jerk—sometimes that just made it worse. All she could do was let the tears squirt out silently and hope Poppi was tired tonight.

When it was over, he took her by the wrist and put her in the closet. She heard the latch he'd installed click into place, then he left the room and she was alone at last.

What Poppi didn't know was that she liked being in the closet. Her friends were there, Babar the Elephant and Pluto in his fuzzy orange fur. The tiny Watchman TV her Auntie Gina had given her last year was there. She even kept pillows and an old blanket in there; when she pushed her shoes aside it was really pretty comfortable. Or would have been if it hadn't hurt so much to just lay down.

She snuggled her animals close to her and turned on the TV. It was tuned to a station that started showing cartoons at five in the morning, but Stacey didn't really care what was on. The tinny voices and moving pictures lulled her, made her feel a little less lonely.

After a while she dozed off. When she awoke she was hot all over, her bottom an excruciating fire. She tried to find a comfortable position, and ended up on her side with her face only inches from the screen. There was a man on it, he was talking in front of some curtains, he had on a funny suit and a funnier accent. Then the man finished talking and words came on, but Stacey wasn't a very good reader. She didn't care what they said anyway. There were eyes spinning behind the words . . .

Stacey was sick, she knew what a fever was and that she had one. She remembered when Mommi had been alive, the way she'd lay a hand on Stacey's forehead when she was sick, and could tell just by that how sick Stacey was. She remembered one time when she'd had a very bad flu with a very high fever, Mommi had gone into the bathtub with her and held her in the cool water, rocking her until the temperature had gone down . . .

Stacey awoke from the dream of her mother and found herself face to face with the dream on the TV. There was a man who looked like her Poppi, a man with dark hair and sunken eyes and thin lips. The man and his friend, who was bent all crooked and walked with a little cane, were cutting somebody down from a wooden bar. The man who looked like Poppi said the body was broken and useless.

Stacey couldn't really sleep, but her eyes would close until the pain forced them open again. The next time she saw the man he was wearing the same kind of white coat Poppi wore at his work. He was showing the man with the funny accent how he had sewn a hand onto an arm it wasn't born onto. Somehow Stacey understood that the man who looked like Poppi had built this other man—Monster, they called it—from all kinds of different parts. The Monster was scary-looking, but it was afraid of being burned, of being whipped, of being chained up, of getting a shot. Stacey understood all those things.

She even understood when a little girl—who wasn't much younger than she was—used flowers to ask the Monster to throw her into a lake.

Stacey did fall asleep after that, relieved to know she wasn't alone.

Poppi let her out in the morning, of course. She went to school dressed as always in heavy sweaters, skirt and tights, although it was nearly eighty degrees. She thought of the lovely blue swimming pool in their next-door neighbor's backyard and knew she'd never be able to use it. If Stacey's mode of dress was ever questioned, there was a standard response: her father was a pediatrician and said she suffered from a neurological disorder.

That covered a lot of the questions. Why Stacey often fell asleep in class, why she sometimes seemed to ache too much to participate in recess, why she had trouble concentrating or relating or remembering. There was also, of course, the story of how Stacey's mother had died of cancer six years ago, and her father had raised her alone since.

In fact, many felt sorry for Stacey's father, that a young pediatrician with such obvious concern for children should be left alone to care for such a dull-witted and sickly girl.

That night Poppi got home early enough to send the sitter off and fix dinner for them. He made Stacey a ghastly-smelling soup and told her to eat it while it was hot.

She could see the steam curling off it, but she picked up a spoon and ladled some of the stuff in. It burned her tongue and the roof of her mouth, but Poppi insisted it was good for her. He made her eat it all while it was still steaming.

After that she did the dishes, then went to her room, where she laid on the bed snuggling Baloo. Her mind drifted through images from the movie that had played last night on her TV. She floated with them, forgetting the burning in her mouth for a while.

Poppi is dressed in his white coat, but his office is bigger, darker, made of rocks. There's lots of equipment she doesn't understand lining the walls, some of it spitting sparks like 4th of July fireworks. Poppi is hunched over a worktable, his back to her, his hands moving rhythmically. The viewpoint moves around him until Stacey can see plainly what he's doing.

There's a figure on the table before him, a human figure but one that's unfinished, lacking. It has arms but no hands, legs but no feet, head but no face. Stacey sees a needle and thread in Poppi's fingers and realizes he's sewing, like Mommi used to when Stacey tore buttons off or ripped holes in her pants.

Stacey gets close enough to see what he's sewing. He's working on the mouth, which gapes like a blank black hole. There's a lump of dead grey flesh in his left hand, one end dark with stitches, while his right moves up and down, up and down.

He's sewing a tongue in.

The Monster is begun.

The next day Stacey's own tongue is badly blistered. Poppi has treated the welts on her backside and they feel better, but the tongue causes her to be even more closemouthed than usual. Finally Miss Washington, of all people, who works in the cafeteria, sees the tongue and asks her what happened.

Stacey doesn't want to answer, but the image of Poppi with needle and thread rears up before her vision. Unable to stop, she blurts it out.

"Poppi made me eat something hot."

Miss Washington, who has never spoken to Stacey before, knows only her face, not her name, asks who Poppi is.

"My daddy," Stacey says thickly.

Miss Washington, who runs the cash register, hesitates a long while. Then she says softly to Stacey, "Next time you say no, you hear?"

Stacey hurriedly gives Miss Washington her money and flees. She can't even taste the lunch, can only feel.

A week later Poppi comes home with a bitter smell of beer clinging to him. Stacey is writing a letter to an imaginary penpal, carefully penning the words and laboring over the spelling; the letter is about Poppi. Poppi finds it, reads the first sentence, and tells Stacey if she likes those words so much she can eat them. Poppi tears the page into strips and forces them into Stacey's mouth, holding it closed until she has no choice but to swallow. She is made to consume the entire page that way, then sent to bed with no other dinner.

That night Stacey sees Poppi at work again. His creation is more fully formed—there are the beginnings of features on the face now. Poppi has cut it up the middle, and he's lowering in something that looks like a shimmery blue grey balloon full of jelly, with tubes dangling from either end. As she watches, he connects the tubes to those already within the Monster, then begins to sew it shut.

The thing has guts now.

Stacey is in the middle of fourth period the next day when she vomits. She's sent home immediately; the other students are dismissed on an extra recess while the janitor cleans the mess up. He's dipping his mop back in to the bucket when something catches his eye, and he leans over. There in the bile is a half-chewed scrap of paper with the crayoned words "then Poppi made" plainly visible.

He considers informing the teacher, then shrugs and goes about his work.

Nearly a month passes without major incident. Stacey is beginning to think Poppi may have given up his Monster when he comes home early actually crying. It would have been Mommi's birthday today, and Poppi stares at a framed picture of her while he drinks from a bottle of sour liquor. He's talking but to no one at all, about how he could have saved Mommi from the cancer if he'd been a real doctor instead of a pediatrician. When he sees Stacey looking at him he lunges at her; she unthinkingly puts out her hands to ward him off. Poppi takes her small hands in his and rubs them roughly along his unshaven jaw while he sobs. Finally he releases Stacey, lost in his grief. She flees to her room. Although there's no physical pain this time, the remembrance of Poppi's skin under her fingertips is as bad in its own way.

She watches as Poppi attaches the hands. She sees he's been hard at work—the figure looks almost human now, beneath the bandages. She knows it'll be over soon.

The Monster is almost done.

They're working on an art project at school the following afternoon when Stacey's teacher, Mr. Torres, notices that Stacey is not applying her brush to paper but to her own arms. He takes Stacey into the back to talk to her about the strange red marks she has meticulously painted on each wrist. Stacey tells him that's how Poppi makes sure the hands will stay on. Mr. Torres looks around to make sure the other students are occupied, then he takes Stacey outside and sits with her on the steps.

"Stacey," he asks carefully, "does Poppi ever do things to hurt you?"

Stacey, who has never been asked this question before and so doesn't know how to answer, just shrugs.

"Would it be alright if we let the school nurse look you over, Stacey?"

Again, Stacey shrugs. Mr. Torres gives her a hall pass and sends her to the nurse, but Stacey never makes it. She gets halfway there, then is seized by an inexplicable panic. Her heart groans in her throat; she feels like she's going to wet her panties. She runs for home as fast as she can and buries herself in her closet, clutching Baloo and Babar and Pluto to her tightly.

Stacey's own birthday is two weeks later. Poppi buys her a new "eleventh-birthday celebration" dress and takes her out to a fancy restaurant, where Poppi has so much to drink even the waiter in his little short jacket and bowtie questions him. Poppi brushes the polite enquiry off with a wave of his credit card; when he giggles as the man walks off, Stacey actually joins him. Poppi even gives her a little drink of his wine—"now that she's getting to be such a big girl"—and Stacey feels a surge of affection for Poppi, forgetting the Monster for the moment.

On the ride home Poppi stops by a liquor store and tells Stacey she can have anything she wants from the ice-cream case. She takes a pineapple Push-Up, Poppi gets himself a bottle, and they laugh all the way home about the messy yellow sherbet oozing out of the paper tube.

In the house Poppi takes a long gulp from his bottle, then sees how Stacey has stained her chin and part of the new dress with sherbet. She expects him to become angry, she tenses in anticipation . . . Instead he smiles sweetly and takes her into the kitchen. He wets a paper towel, gently wipes off her chin, then starts on the dress. The dress is beautiful crushed velvet, though, and he tells Stacey he doesn't want to ruin it, so she'd better take it off. He helps her, right there in the kitchen; she crosses her arms to cover her cold chest.

Poppi asks her what she's trying to hide—hasn't he seen her before? She wants to giggle, wants to think this is another birthday game, but the look in Poppi's eyes tells her this is something else. He pulls her arms away from her chest and begins to stroke her there. Stacey tries to pull away, and Poppi does become angry now. He asks her if she loves her Poppi. She doesn't answer.

He asks her again . . . only now he's pushing her down over the table, and Stacey smells his hot breath curling around her ear.

Electricity is coursing through the Monster now, a primal force brought by Poppi. The equipment shrieks and flashes, the Monster under the bandages jerks and spasms . . . then the storm is over and the table is lowered.

A beat, a silent hesitation—then fingers begin to unflex slowly and curl out, the great chest begins to heave, gulping in the first new breaths of air. Poppi undoes the restraining straps and steps back to survey his work proudly.

It lives.

Poppi has staggered off to his room to fall into a drunken slumber, leaving the misshapen wreck that was his daughter on the kitchen floor. She lays there until almost dawn, too terrified and pained to move. She can taste blood in her mouth, feel it running hot between her legs; one eye is swollen nearly shut and something aches in her chest.

When she begins to drag herself out of the kitchen, it's not to her room but out the back door. She nearly rolls down the three small steps to the grass lawn, then continues to pull herself towards the gap in the fence between her yard and the neighbor's. The sun is up now, but Stacey doesn't feel its heat, not when she has so much of her own.

She crawls through the space between the wooden planks, ignoring a splinter that digs into her arm. She can see the great blue expanse just ahead of her now, the calm waters inviting her. At last she's on the tile rimming the pool. She lets herself collapse there, her goal reached. Only her hand still moves, grasping at a nearby rose bush. The thorns tear her fingers, but she comes away with petals to scatter on the water, like tiny boats.

She hears the giant footsteps, and knows he's coming, coming at last. He will see the petals and know what she's asking; then, because they understand each other's pain, he will help. She sees a shadow on the other side of the fence, and her heart skips a beat. The shadow pauses before the gap, then continues on around to the side-by-side gates. The gate in her backyard opens, then the gate in this yard opens . . .

And the Monster is there.

Stacey smiles in welcome, and throws another rose petal. The Monster staggers forward; Stacey sees he's returning her smile. He kneels by her; as Stacey looks into his death-glazed eyes, she sees only kindness. He reaches for her, and she feels herself cradled in those giant's hands.

Then the water is covering her, a soothing blanket, like when Mommi rocked her in that tub so long ago . . .

And through the clear water she looks up and sees Poppi.

She opens her mouth in shock; water rushes in. She lets it fill her, and is surprised there's no pain or fear. Just floating, a delicious blue floating where no one can touch her and she's finally safe.

The gentle Monster is waiting for her on the other side.

KARL EDWARD WAGNER

𝕬𝖓𝖉𝖊𝖗𝖙𝖔𝖜

❦

Karl Edward Wagner (1945–1994) died at the ridiculously young age of forty-eight years old. He is remembered today as the insightful editor of fifteen volumes of The Year's Best Horror Stories series from DAW Books (1980–1994) and as an author of superior horror and fantasy fiction.

While still attending medical school, Wagner set about creating his own character, Kane, the Mystic Swordsman. After the first book in the series, Darkness Weaves with Many Shades, *was published in 1970, Wagner relinquished his chance to become a doctor and turned to writing full-time.* Death Angel's Shadow, *a collection of three original Kane novellas, was followed by the novels* Bloodstone *and* Dark Crusade, *and the collections* Night Winds *and* The Book of Kane. *These books were later reissued in the omnibus volumes* Gods in Darkness *and* Midnight Sun *from Night Shade Books.*

His horror fiction appeared in a variety of magazines and anthologies, and was collected in In a Lonely Place, Why Not You and I?, Author's Choice Monthly Issue 2: Unthreatened by the Morning Light *and the posthumous* Exorcisms and Ecstasies. *More recently, all the author's weird and supernatural fiction has been collected together in two volumes by Centipede Press, and the imprint is republishing all his Kane books in new, illustrated editions.*

Wagner admitted that the following story was probably his favorite of the Kane series, and he explained that "the structure of 'Undertow' was based on Alain Resnais' film Last Year at Marienbad *(1962), in which a deliberate distortion of linear time creates a nightmarish sense of shattered reality.*

"When I first saw this film as a college student, the projectionist at the campus theatre ran two reels out of sequence. No one in the audience noticed."

PROLOGUE

Ƨhe was brought in not long past dark," wheezed the custodian, scuttling crab-like along the rows of silent, shrouded slabs. "The city guard found her, carried her in. Sounds like the one you're asking about."

He paused beside one of the waist-high stone tables and lifted its filthy sheet. A girl's contorted face turned sightlessly upward—painted and rouged, a ghastly strumpet's mask against the pallor of her skin. Clots of congealed blood hung like a necklace of dark rubies along the gash across her throat.

The cloaked man shook his head curtly within the shadow of his hood, and the moon-faced custodian let the sheet drop back.

428

"Not the one I was thinking of," he murmured apologetically. "It gets confusing sometimes, you know, what with so many, and them coming and going all the while." Sniffling in the cool air, he pushed his rotund bulk between the narrow aisles, careful to avoid the stained and filthy shrouds. Looming over his guide, the cloaked figure followed in silence.

Low-flamed lamps cast dismal light across the necrotorium of Carsultyal. Smoldering braziers spewed fitful, heavy fumed clouds of clinging incense that merged with the darkness and the stones and the decay—its cloying sweetness more nauseating than the stench of death it embraced. Through the thick gloom echoed the monotonous drip-dripdrip of melting ice, at times chorused suggestively by some heavier splash. The municipal morgue was crowded tonight—as always. Only a few of its hundred or more slate beds stood dark and bare; the others all displayed anonymous shapes bulging beneath blotched sheets—some protruding at curious angles, as if these restless dead struggled to burst free of the coarse folds. Night now hung over Carsultyal, but within this windowless subterranean chamber it was always night. In shadow pierced only by the sickly flame of funereal lamps, the nameless dead of Carsultyal lay unmourned—waited the required interval of time for someone to claim them, else to be carted off to some unmarked communal grave beyond the city walls.

"Here, I believe," announced the custodian. "Yes. I'll just get a lamp."

"Show me," demanded a voice from within the hood.

The portly official glanced at the other uneasily. There was an aura of power, of blighted majesty about the cloaked figure that boded ill in arrogant Carsultyal, whose clustered, starreaching towers were whispered to be overawed by cellars whose depths plunged farther still. "Light's poor back here," he protested, drawing back the tattered shroud.

The visitor cursed low in his throat—an inhuman sound touched less by grief than feral rage.

The face that stared at them with too wide eyes had been beautiful in life; in death it was purpled, bloated, contorted in pain. Dark blood stained the tip of her protruding tongue, and her neck seemed bent at an unnatural angle. A gown of light-colored silk was stained and disordered. She lay supine, hands clenched into tight fists at her side.

"The city guard found her?" repeated the visitor in a harsh voice.

"Yes, just after nightfall. In the park overlooking the harbor. She was hanging from a branch—there in the grove with all the white flowers every spring. Must have just happened—said her body was warm as life, though there's a chill to the sea breeze tonight. Looks like she done it herself—climbed out on the branch, tied the noose, and jumped off. Wonder why they do it—her as pretty a young thing as I've seen brought in, and took well care of, too."

The stranger stood in rigid silence, staring at the strangled girl.

"Will you come back in the morning to claim her, or do you want to wait upstairs?" suggested the custodian.

"I'll take her now."

The plump attendant fingered the gold coin his visitor had tossed him a short time before. His lips tightened in calculation. Often there appeared at the necrotorium those who wished to remove bodies clandestinely for strange and secret reasons—a circumstance which made lucrative this disagreeable office. "Can't allow that," he argued. "There's laws and forms—you shouldn't even be here at this hour. They'll be wanting their questions answered. And there's fees . . ."

With a snarl of inexpressible fury, the stranger turned on him. The sudden movement flung back his hood.

The caretaker for the first time saw his visitor's eyes. He had breath for a short bleat of terror, before the dirk he did not see smashed through his heart.

Workers the next day, puzzling over the custodian's disappearance, were shocked to discover, on examining the night's new tenants for the necrotorium, that he had not disappeared after all.

I
SEEKERS IN THE NIGHT

There—he heard the sound again.

Mavrsal left off his disgruntled contemplation of the near-empty wine bottle and stealthily came to his feet. The captain of the *Tuab* was alone in his cabin, and the hour was late. For hours the only sounds close at hand had been the slap of waves on the barnacled hull, the creak of cordage, and the dull thud of the caravel's aged timbers against the quay. Then had come a soft footfall, a muffled fumbling among the deck gear outside his half-open door. Too loud for rats—a thief, then?

Grimly Mavrsal unsheathed his heavy cutlass and caught up a lantern. He catfooted onto the deck, reflecting bitterly over his worthless crew. From cook to first mate, they had deserted his ship a few days before, angered over wages months unpaid. An unseasonable squall had forced them to jettison most of their cargo of copper ingots, and the *Tuab* had limped into the harbor of Carsultyal with shredded sails, a cracked mainmast, a dozen new leaks from wrenched timbers, and the rest of her worn fittings in no better shape. Instead of the expected wealth, the decimated cargo had brought in barely enough capital to cover the expense of refitting. Mavrsal argued that until refitted, the *Tuab* was unseaworthy, and that once repairs were complete, another cargo could be found (somehow), and *then* wages long in arrears could be paid—with a bonus for patient loyalty. The crew cared neither for his logic nor his promises and defected amidst stormy threats.

Had one of them returned to carry out . . .? Mavrsal hunched his thick shoulders truculently and hefted the cutlass. The master of the *Tuab* had never run from a brawl, much less a sneak thief or slinking assassin.

Night skies of autumn were bright over Carsultyal, making the lantern almost unneeded. Mavrsal surveyed the soft shadows of the caravel's deck, his brown eyes narrowed and alert beneath shaggy brows. But he heard the low sobbing almost at once, so there was no need to prowl about the deck.

He strode quickly to the mound of torn sail and rigging at the far rail. "All right, come out of that!" he rumbled, beckoning with the tip of his blade to the half-seen figure crouched against the rail. The sobbing choked into silence. Mavrsal prodded the canvas with an impatient boot. "Out of there, damn it!" he repeated.

The canvas gave a wriggle and a pair of sandaled feet backed out, followed by bare legs and rounded hips that strained against the bunched fabric of her gown. Mavrsal pursed his lips thoughtfully as the girl emerged and stood before him. There were no tears in the eyes that met his gaze. The aristocratic face was defiant, although the flared nostrils and tightly pressed lips hinted that her defiance was a mask. Nervous fingers smoothed the silken gown and adjusted her cloak of dark brown wool.

"Inside." Mavrsal gestured with his cutlass to the lighted cabin.

"I wasn't doing anything," she protested.

"Looking for something to steal."

"I'm not a thief."

"We'll talk inside." He nudged her forward, and sullenly she complied. Following her through the door, Mavrsal locked it behind him and replaced the lantern. Returning the cutlass to its scabbard, he dropped back into his chair and contemplated his discovery.

"I'm no thief," she repeated, fidgeting with the fastenings of her cloak.

No, he decided, she probably wasn't—not that there was much aboard a decrepit caravel like the *Tuab* to attract a thief. But why had she crept aboard? She was a harlot, he assumed—what other business drew a girl of her beauty alone into the night of Carsultyal's waterfront? And she *was* beautiful, he noted with growing surprise. A tangle of loosely bound red hair fell over her shoulders and framed a face whose pale-skinned classic beauty was enhanced rather than flawed by a dust of freckles across her thin-bridged nose. Eyes of startling green gazed at him with a defiance that seemed somehow haunted. She was tall, willowy. Before she settled the dark cloak about her shoulders, he had noted the high, conical breasts and softly rounded figure beneath the clinging gown of green silk. An emerald of good quality graced her hand, and about her neck she wore a wide collar of dark leather and red silk from which glinted a larger emerald.

No, thought Mavrsal—again revising his judgement—she was too lovely, her garments too costly, for the quality of street tart who plied these waters. His bewilderment deepened. "Why were you on board, then?" he demanded in a manner less abrupt.

Her eyes darted about the cabin. "I don't know," she returned.

Mavrsal grunted in vexation. "Were you trying to stow away?"

She responded with a small shrug. "I suppose so."

The sea captain gave a snort and drew his stocky frame erect. "Then you're a damn fool—or must think I'm one! Stow away on a battered old warrior like the *Tuab*, when there's plainly no cargo to put to sea, and any

432

eye can see the damn ship's being refitted! Why, that ring you're wearing would book passage to any port you'd care to see, and on a first-class vessel! And to wander these streets at this hour! Well, maybe that's your business, and maybe you aren't careful of your trade, but there's scum along these waterfront dives that would slit a wench's throat as soon as pay her! Vaul! I've been in port three days and four nights, and already I've heard talk of enough depraved murders of pretty girls like you to—"

"Will you stop it!" she hissed in a tight voice. Slumping into the cabin's one other chair, she propped her elbows onto the rough table and jammed her fists against her forehead. Russet tresses tumbled over her face like a veil, so that Mavrsal could not read the emotions etched there. In the hollow of the cloak's parted folds, her breasts trembled with the quick pounding of her heart.

Sighing, he drained the last of the wine into his mug and pushed the pewter vessel toward the girl. There was another bottle in his cupboard; rising, he drew it out along with another cup. She was carefully sipping from the proffered mug when he resumed his place.

"Look, what's your name?" he asked her.

She paused so tensely before replying, "Dessylyn."

The name meant nothing to Mavrsal, although as the tension waxed and receded from her bearing, he understood that she had been concerned that her name would bring recognition.

Mavrsal smoothed his close-trimmed brown beard. There was a rough-and-ready toughness about his face that belied the fact that he had not quite reached thirty years, and women liked to tell him his rugged features were handsome. His left ear—badly scarred in a tavern brawl—gave him some concern, but it lay hidden beneath the unruly mass of his hair. "Well, Dessylyn," he grinned. "My name's Mavrsal, and this is my ship. And if you're worried about finding a place, you can spend the night here."

There was dread in her face. "I can't."

Mavrsal frowned, thinking he had been snubbed, and started to make an angry retort.

"I dare not . . . stay here too long," Dessylyn interposed, fear glowing in her eyes.

Mavrsal made an exasperated grimace. "Girl, you sneaked aboard my ship like a thief, but I'm inclined to forget your trespassing. Now, my cabin's cozy, girls tell me I'm a pleasant companion, and I'm generous with my coin. So why wander off into the night, where in the first filthy alley some pox-ridden drunk is going to take for free what I'm willing to pay for?"

"You don't understand!"

"Very plainly I don't." He watched her fidget with the pewter mug for a moment, then added pointedly, "Besides, you can hide here."

"By the gods! I wish I could!" she cried out. "If only I *could* hide from him!"

Brows knit in puzzlement, Mavrsal listened to the strangled sobs that rose muffled through the tousled auburn mane. He had not expected so unsettling a response to his probe. Thinking that every effort to penetrate the mystery surrounding Dessylyn only left him further in the dark, he measured out another portion of wine—and wondered if he should apologize for something.

"I suppose that's why I did it," she was mumbling. "I was able to slip away for a short while. So I walked along the shore, and I saw all the ships poised for flight along the harbor, and I thought how wonderful to be free like that! To step on board some strange ship, and to sail into the night to some unknown land—where *he* could never find me! *To be free!* Oh, I knew I could never escape him like that, but still when I walked by your ship, I wanted to try! I thought I could go through the motions—pretend I was escaping him!

"Only I know there's no escape from Kane!"

"Kane!" Mavrsal breathed a curse. Anger toward the girl's tormentor that had started to flare within him abruptly shuddered under the chill blast of fear.

Kane! Even to a stranger in Carsultyal, greatest city of mankind's dawn, that name evoked the specter of terror. A thousand tales were whispered of Kane; even in this city of sorcery, where the lost knowledge of prehuman Earth had been recovered to forge man's stolen civilization, Kane was a figure of awe and mystery. Despite uncounted tales of strange and disturbing nature, almost nothing was known for certain of the man save that for generations his tower had brooded over Carsultyal. There he followed the secret paths along which his dark genius led him, and the hand of Kane was rarely seen (though it was often felt) in the affairs of Carsultyal. Brother sorcerers and masters of powers temporal alike spoke his name with dread, and those who dared to make him an enemy seldom were given long to repent their audacity.

"Are you Kane's woman?" he blurted out.

Her voice was bitter. "So Kane would have it. His mistress. His possession. Once, though, I was my own woman—before I was fool enough to let Kane draw me into his web!"

"Can't you leave him—leave this city?"

"You don't know the power Kane commands! Who would risk his anger to help me?"

Mavrsal squared his shoulders. "I owe no allegiance to Kane, nor to his minions in Carsultyal. This ship may be weathered and leaky, but she's mine, and I sail her where I please. If you're set on—"

Fear twisted her face. "Don't!" she gasped. "Don't even hint this to me! You can't realize what power Kane—"

"What was that!"

Mavrsal tensed. From the night sounded the soft buffeting of great leathery wings. Claws scraped against the timbers of the deck outside. Suddenly the lantern flames seemed to shrink and waver; shadow fell deep within the cabin.

"He's missed me!" Dessylyn moaned. "He's sent it to bring me back!"

His belly cold, Mavrsal drew his cutlass and turned stiffly toward the door. The lamp flames were no more than a dying blue gleam. Beyond the door a shuffling weight caused a loosened plank to groan dully.

"No! Please!" she cried in desperation. "There's nothing you can do! Stay back from the door!"

Mavrsal snarled, his face reflecting the rage and terror that gripped him. Dessylyn pulled at his arm to draw him back.

He had locked the cabin door; a heavy iron bolt secured the stout timbers. Now an unseen hand was drawing the bolt aside. Silently, slowly, the iron bar turned and crept back along its mounting brackets. The lock snapped open. With nightmarish suddenness, the door swung wide.

Darkness hung in the passageway. Burning eyes regarded them. Advanced.

Dessylyn screamed hopelessly. Numb with terror, Mavrsal clumsily swung his blade toward the glowing eyes. Blackness reached out, hurled him with irresistible strength across the cabin. Pain burst across his consciousness, and then was only the darkness.

II
"NEVER, DESSYLYN"

She shuddered and drew the fur cloak tighter about her thin shoulders. *Would there ever again be a time when she wouldn't feel this remorseless cold?*

Kane, his cruel face haggard in the glow of the brazier, stood hunched over the crimson alembic. *How red the coals made his hair and beard; how sinister was the blue flame of his eyes . . .* He craned intently forward to trap the last few drops of the phosphorescent elixir in a chalice of ruby crystal.

He had labored sleepless hours over the glowing liquid, she knew. Hours precious to her because these were hours of freedom—a time when she might escape his loathed attention. Her lips pressed a tight, bloodless line. The abominable formulae from which he prepared the elixir! Dessylyn thought again of the mutilated corpse of the young girl Kane had directed his servant to carry off. Again a spasm slid across her lithe form.

"Why won't you let me go?" she heard herself ask dully for the . . . *how many times had she asked that?*

"I'll not let you go, Dessylyn," Kane replied in a tired voice. "You know that."

"Someday I'll leave you."

"No, Dessylyn. You'll never leave me."

"Someday."

"Never, Dessylyn."

"Why, Kane?"

With painful care, he allowed a few drops of an amber liqueur to fall into the glowing chalice. Blue flame hovered over its surface.

"Why?"

"Because I love you, Dessylyn."

A bitter sob, parody of laughter, shook her throat. "You love me." She enclosed a hopeless scream in those slow, grinding syllables.

"Kane, can I ever make you understand how utterly I loathe you?"

"Perhaps. But I love you, Dessylyn."

The sobbing laugh returned.

Glancing at her in concern, Kane carefully extended the chalice toward her. "Drink this. Quickly—before the nimbus dies."

She looked at him through eyes dark with horror. "Another bitter draught of some foul drug to bind me to you?"

"Whatever you wish to call it."

"I won't drink it."

"Yes, Dessylyn, you will drink it."

His killer's eyes held her with bonds of eternal ice. Mechanically she accepted the crimson chalice, let its phosphorescent liquor pass between her lips, seep down her throat.

Kane sighed and took the empty goblet from her listless grip. His massive frame seemed to shudder from fatigue, and he passed a broad hand across his eyes. Blood rimmed their dark hollows.

"I'll leave you, Kane."

The sea wind gusted through the tower window and swirled the long red hair about his haunted face.

"Never, Dessylyn."

III

AT THE INN OF THE BLUE WINDOW

He called himself Dragar . . .

Had the girl not walked past him seconds before, he probably would not have interfered when he heard her scream. Or perhaps he would have. A stranger to Carsultyal, nonetheless the barbarian youth had passed time enough in mankind's lesser cities to be wary of cries for help in the night and to think twice before plunging into dark alleys to join in an unseen struggle. But there was a certain pride in the chivalric ideals of his heritage, along with a confidence in the hard muscle of his sword arm and in the strange blade he carried.

Thinking of the lithe, white limbs he had glimpsed—the patrician beauty of the face that coolly returned his curious stare as she came toward him—Dragar unsheathed the heavy blade at his hip and dashed back along the street he had just entered.

There was moonlight enough to see, although the alley was well removed from the nearest flaring streetlamp. Cloak torn away, her gown ripped from her shoulders, the girl writhed in the grasp of two thugs. A third tough, warned by the rush of the barbarian's boots, angrily spun to face him, sword streaking for the youth's belly.

Dragar laughed and flung the lighter blade aside with a powerful blow of his sword. Scarcely seeming to pause in his attack, he gashed his assailant's arm with a upward swing, and as the other's blade faltered, he split the thug's skull. One of the two who held the girl lunged forward, but Dragar sidestepped his rush, and with a sudden thrust sent his sword ripping into the man's chest. The remaining assailant shoved the girl against the barbarian's legs, whirled, and fled down the alley.

Ignoring the fugitive, Dragar helped the stunned girl to her feet. Terror yet twisted her face, as she distractedly arranged the torn bodice of her silken gown. Livid scratches streaked the pale skin of her breasts, and a bruise was swelling out her lip. Dragar caught up her fallen cloak and draped it over her shoulders.

"Thank you," she breathed in a shaky whisper, speaking at last.

"My pleasure," he rumbled. "Killing rats is good exercise. Are you all right, though?"

She nodded, then clutched his arm for support.

"The hell you are! There's a tavern close by, girl. Come—I've silver enough for a brandy to put the fire back in your heart."

She looked as if she might refuse, were her knees steadier. In a daze, the girl let him half-carry her into the Inn of the Blue Window. There he led her to an unoccupied booth and called for brandy.

"What's your name?" he asked, after she had tasted the heady liquor.

"Dessylyn."

He framed her name with silent lips to feel its sound. "I'm called Dragar," he told her. "My home lies among the mountains far south of here, though it's been a few years since last I hunted with my clansmen. Wanderlust drew me away, and since then I've followed this banner or another's—sometimes just the shadow of my own flapping cloak. Then, after hearing tales enough to dull my ears, I decided to see for myself if Carsultyal is the wonder men boast her to be. You a stranger here as woll?"

She shook her head. When the color returned to her cheeks, her face seemed less aloof.

"Thought you might be. Else you'd know better than to wander the streets of Carsultyal after nightfall. Must be something important for you to take the risk."

The lift of her shoulders was casual, though her face remained guarded. "No errand . . . but it was important to me."

Dragar's look was questioning.

"I wanted to . . . oh, just to be alone, to get away for a while. Lose myself, maybe—I don't know. I didn't think anyone would dare touch me if they knew who I was."

"Your fame must be held somewhat less in awe among these gutter rats than you imagined," offered Dragar wryly.

"All men fear the name of Kane!" Dessylyn shot back bitterly.

"Kane!" The name exploded from his lips in amazement. *What had this girl to do . . . ?* But Dragar looked again at her sophisticated beauty, her luxurious attire, and understanding dawned. Angrily he became aware that the tavern uproar had become subdued on the echo of his outburst. Several faces had turned to him, their expressions uneasy, calculating.

The barbarian clapped a hand to his swordhilt. "Here's a man who doesn't fear a name!" he announced. "I've heard something of Carsultyal's most dreaded sorcerer, but his name means less than a fart to me! There's steel in this sword that can slice through the best your world-famed master smiths can forge, and it thrives on the gore of magicians. I call the blade Wizard's Bane, and there are souls in Hell who will swear that its naming is no boast!"

Dessylyn stared at him in sudden fascination.

And what came after, Dessylyn?

I . . . I'm not sure . . . My mind—I was in a state of shock, I suppose. I remember holding his head for what seemed like forever. And then I remember sponging off the blood with water from the wooden lavabo, and the water was so cold and so red, so red. I must have put on my clothes . . . Yes, and I remember the city and walking and all those faces . . . All those faces . . . they stared at me, some of them. Stared and looked away, stared and looked compassionate, stared and looked curious, stared and made awful suggestions . . . And some just ignored me, didn't see me at all. I can't think which faces were the most cruel . . . I walked, walked so long . . . I remember the pain . . . I remember my tears, and the pain when there were no more tears . . . I remember . . . My mind was dazed . . . My memory . . . I can't remember . . .

IV
A SHIP WILL SAIL . . .

He looked up from his work and saw her standing there on the quay—watching him, her face a strange play of intensity and indecision. Mavrsal grunted in surprise and straightened from his carpentry. She might have been a phantom, so silently had she crept upon him.

"I had to see if . . . if you were all right," Dessylyn told him with an uncertain smile.

"I am—aside from a crack on my skull," Mavrsal answered, eyeing her dubiously.

By the dawnlight he had crawled from beneath the overturned furnishings of his cabin. Blood matted his thick hair at the back of his skull, and his head throbbed with a deafening ache, so that he had sat dumbly for a long while, trying to recollect the events of the night. *Something* had come through the door, had hurled him aside like a spurned doll. And the girl had vanished—carried off by the demon? Her warning had been for him; for herself she evidenced not fear, only resigned despair.

Or had some of his men returned to carry out their threats? Had too much wine, the blow on his head . . . ? But no, Mavrsal knew better. His assailants would have robbed him, made certain of his death—had any human agency attacked him. She had called herself a sorcerer's mistress, and it had been sorcery that spread its black wings over his caravel. Now the girl had returned, and Mavrsal's greeting was tempered by his aware-ness of the danger which shadowed her presence.

Dessylyn must have known his thoughts. She backed away, as if to turn and go.

"Wait!" he called suddenly.

"I don't want to endanger you any further."

Mavrsal's quick temper responded. "Danger! Kane can bugger with his demons in Hell, for all I care! My skull was too thick for his creature to split, and if he wants to try his hand in person, I'm here to offer him the chance!"

There was gladness in her wide eyes as Dessylyn stepped toward him. "His necromancies have exhausted him," she assured the other. "Kane will sleep for hours yet."

Mavrsal handed her over the rail with rough gallantry. "Then perhaps you'll join me in my cabin. It's grown too dark for carpentry, and I'd like to talk with you. After last night, I think I deserve to have some questions answered, anyway."

He struck fire to a lamp and turned to find her balanced at the edge of a chair, watching him nervously. "What sort of questions?" she asked in an uneasy tone.

"Why?"

"Why what?"

Mavrsal made a vague gesture. "Why everything. Why did you get involved with this sorcerer? Why does he hold to you, if you hate him so? Why can't you leave him?"

She gave him a sad smile that left him feeling naive. "Kane is . . . a fascinating man; there is a certain magnetism about him. And I won't

441

deny the attraction his tremendous power and wealth held for me. Does it matter? It's enough to say that there was a time when we met and I fell under Kane's spell. It may be that I loved him once—but I've since hated too long and too deeply to remember.

"But Kane continues to love me in his way. *Love!* His is the love of a miser for his hoard, the love of a connoisseur for some exquisitely wrought carving, the love a spider feels for its imprisoned prey! I'm his treasure, his possession—and what concern are the feelings of a lifeless object to its owner? Would the curious circumstance that his prized statue might hate him lessen the pleasure its owner derives from its possession?

"And leave him?" Her voice broke. "By the gods, don't you think I've tried?"

His thoughts in a turmoil, Mavrsal studied the girl's haunted face. "But why accept defeat? Past failure doesn't mean you can't try again. If you're free to roam the streets of Carsultyal at night, your feet can take you farther still. I see no chain clamped to that collar you wear."

"Not all chains are visible."

"So I've heard, though I've never believed it. A weak will can imagine its own fetters."

"Kane won't let me leave him."

"Kane's power doesn't reach a tenth so far as he believes."

"There are men who would dispute that, if the dead cared to share the wisdom that came to them too late."

Challenge glinted in the girl's green eyes as they held his. Mavrsal felt the spell of her beauty, and his manhood answered. "A ship sails where its master wills it—may the winds and the tides and perils of the sea be damned!"

Her face craned closer. Tendrils of her auburn hair touched his arm. "There is courage in your words. But you know little of Kane's power."

He laughed recklessly. "Let's say I'm not cowed by his name."

From the belt of her gown, Dessylyn unfastened a small scrip. She tossed the leather pouch toward him.

Catching it, Mavrsal untied the braided thong and dumped its contents onto his palm. His hand shook. Gleaming gemstones tumbled a tiny rainbow, clattered onto the cabin table. In his hand lay a fortune in roughcut diamonds, emeralds, other precious stones.

Through their multihued reflections his face framed a question.

"I think there is enough to repair your ship, to pay her crew . . ." She paused; brighter flamed the challenge in her eyes. "Perhaps to buy my passage to a distant port—if you dare!"

The captain of the *Tuab* swore. "I meant what I said, girl! Give me another few days to refit her, and I'll sail you to lands where no man has ever heard the name of Kane!"

"Later you may change your mind," Dessylyn warned.

She rose from her chair. Mavrsal thought she meant to leave, but then he saw that her fingers had loosened other fastenings at her belt. His breath caught as the silken gown began to slip from her shoulders.

"I won't change my mind," he promised, understanding why Kane might go to any extreme to keep Dessylyn with him.

V

WIZARD'S BANE

"Your skin is like the purest honey," proclaimed Dragar ardently. "By the gods, I swear you even taste like honey!"

Dessylyn squirmed in pleasure and hugged the barbarian's shaggy blond head to her breasts. After a moment she sighed and languorously pulled from his embrace. Sitting up, she brushed her slim fingers through the tousled auburn wave that cascaded over her bare shoulders and back, clung in damp curls to her flushed skin.

Dragar's calloused hand imprisoned her slender wrist as she sought to rise from the rumpled bed. "Don't prance away like a contrite virgin, girl. Your rider has dismounted but for a moment's rest—then he's ready to gallop through the palace gates another time or more, before the sun drops beneath the sea."

"Pretty, but I have to go," she protested. "Kane may grow suspicious . . ."

"Bugger Kane!" cursed Dragar, pulling the girl back against him. His thick arms locked about her, and their lips crushed savagely. Cupped over a small breast, his hand felt the pounding of her heart, and the youth laughed and tilted back her feverish face. "Now tell me you prefer Kane's effete pawings to a man's embrace!"

A frown drifted like a sudden thunderhead. "You underestimate Kane. He's no soft-fleshed weakling."

The youth snarled in jealousy. "A foul sorcerer who's skulked in his tower no one knows how long! He'll have dust for blood, and dry rot in his bones! But go to him if you prefer his toothless kisses and withered loins!"

"No, dearest! Yours are the arms I love to lie within!" Dessylyn cried, entwining herself about him and soothing his anger with kisses. "It's just that I'm frightened for you. Kane isn't a withered greybeard. Except for the madness in his eyes, you would think Kane a hardened warrior in his prime. And you've more than his sorcery to fear. I've seen Kane kill with his sword—he's a deadly fighter!"

Dragar snorted and stretched his brawny frame. "No warrior hides behind a magician's robes. He's but a name—an ogre's name to frighten children into obedience. Well, I don't fear his name, nor do I fear his magic, and my blade has drunk the blood of better swordsmen than your black-hearted tyrant ever was!"

"By the gods!" whispered Dessylyn, burrowing against his thick shoulder. "Why did fate throw me into Kane's web instead of into your arms!"

"Fate is what man wills it. If you wish it, you are my woman now."

"But Kane . . . !"

The barbarian leaped to his feet and glowered down at her. "Enough snivelling about Kane, girl! Do you love me or not?"

"Dragar, beloved, you know I love you! Haven't these past days . . ."

"These past days have been filled with woeful whimperings about Kane, and my belly grows sick from hearing it! Forget Kane! I'm taking you from him, Dessylyn! For all her glorious legend and over-mighty towers, Carsultyal is a stinking pesthole like every other city I've known. Well, I'll waste no more days here.

"I'll ride from Carsultyal tomorrow, or take passage on a ship, perhaps. Go to some less stagnant land, where a bold man and a strong blade can win wealth and adventure! You're going with me."

"Can you mean it, Dragar?"

"If you think I lie, then stay behind."

"Kane will follow."

"Then he'll lose his life along with his love!" sneered Dragar.

With confident hands, he slid from its scabbard his great sword of silver-blue metal. "See this blade," he hissed, flourishing its massive length easily. "I call it Wizard's Bane, and there's reason to the name. Look at the blade. It's steel, but not steel such as your secretive smiths forge in their dragonbreath furnaces. See the symbols carved into the forte. This blade has power! It was forged long ago by a master smith who used the glowing heart of a fallen star for his ore, who set runes of protection into the finished sword. Who wields Wizard's Bane need not fear magic, for sorcery can have no power over him. My sword can cleave through the hellish flesh of demons. It can ward off a sorcerer's enchantments and skewer his evil heart!

"Let Kane send his demons to find us! My blade will shield us from his spells, and I'll send his minions howling in fear back to his dread tower! Let him creep from his lair if he dares! I'll feed him bits of his liver and laugh in his face while he dies!"

Dessylyn's eyes brimmed with adoration. "You can do it, Dragar! You're strong enough to take me from Kane! No man has your courage, beloved!"

The youth laughed and twisted her hair, "No man? What do you know of men? Did you think these spineless city-bred fops, who tremble at the shadow of a senile cuckold, were men? Think no more of slinking back to Kane's tower before your keeper misses you. Tonight, girl, I'm going to show you how a *man* loves his woman!"

> But why will you insist it's impossible to leave Kane?
> I know.
> How can you know? You're too fearful of him to try.
> I know.
> But how can you say that?
> Because I know.
> Perhaps this bondage is only in your mind, Dessylyn.
> But I know Kane won't let me leave him.
> So certain—is it because you've tried to escape him?

Have you tried, Dessylyn?
Tried with another's help—and failed, Dessylyn?
Can't you be honest with me, Dessylyn?
And now you'll turn away from me in fear!
Then there was another man?
It's impossible to escape him—and now you'll abandon me!
Tell me, Dessylyn. How can I trust you if you won't trust me?
On your word, then. There was another man . . .

VI

NIGHT AND FOG

Night returned to Carsultyal and spread its misty cloak over narrow alleys and brooding towers alike. The voice of the street broke from its strident daylight cacophony to a muted rumble of night. As the stars grew brighter through the sea mists, the streets grew silent, except for fitful snorts and growls like a hound uneasy in his sleep. Then the lights that glimmered through the shadow began to slip away, so stealthily that their departure went unnoticed. One only knew that the darkness, the fog, the silence now ruled the city unchallenged. And night, closer here than elsewhere in the cities of mankind, had returned to Carsultyal.

They lay close in each other's arms—sated, but too restless for sleep. Few were their words, so that they listened to the beating of their hearts, pressed so close together as to make one sound. Fog thrust tendrils through chinks in the bolted shutters, brought with it the chill breath of the sea, lost cries of ships anchored in the night.

Then Dessylyn hissed like a cat and dug her nails so deep into Dragar's arm that rivulets of crimson made an armlet about the corded muscle. Straining his senses against the night, the barbarian dropped his hand to the hilt of the unsheathed sword that lay beside their bed. The blade glinted blue—more so than the wan lamplight would seem to reflect.

From the night outside . . . Was it a sudden wind that rattled the window shutters, buffeted the streamers of fog into swirling eddies? A sound . . . Was that the flap of vast leathery wings?

Fear hung like a clinging web over the inn, and the silence about them was so desolate that theirs might have been the last two hearts to beat in all of haunted Carsultyal.

From the roof suddenly there came a slithering metallic scrape upon the slate tiles.

Wizard's Bane pulsed with a corposant of blue witch-fire. Shadows stark and unreal cringed away from the lambent blade.

Against the thick shutters sounded a creaking groan of hideous pressure. Oaken planks sagged inward. Holding fast, the iron bolts trembled, then abruptly smoldered into sullen rubrous heat. Mist poured past the buckling timbers, bearing with it a smell not of any sea known to man.

Brighter pulsed the scintillant glare of the sword. A nimbus of blue flame rippled out from the blade and encircled the crouching youth and his terrified companion. Rippling blue radiance, spreading across the room, struck the groaning shutters.

A burst of incandescence spat from the glowing iron bolts. Through the night beyond tore a silent snarl—an unearthly shriek felt rather than heard—a spitting bestial cry of pain and baffled rage.

The shutters sprang back with a grunting sigh as the pressure against them suddenly relented. Again the night shuddered with the buffet of tremendous wings. The ghost of sound dwindled. The black tide of fear ebbed and shrank back from the inn.

Dragar laughed and brandished his sword. Eyes still dazzled, Dessylyn stared in fascination at the blade, now suffused with a sheen no more preternatural than any finely burnished steel. It might all have been a frightened dream, she thought, knowing well that it had not been.

"It looks like your keeper's sorcery is something less than all powerful!" scoffed the barbarian. "Now Kane will know that his spells and coward's tricks are powerless against Wizard's Bane. No doubt your ancient spell-caster is cowering under his cold bed, scared spitless that these gutless city folk will some day find courage enough to call his bluff! And against that, he's probably safe."

"You don't know Kane," moaned Dessylyn.

With gentle roughness, Dragar cuffed the grim-faced girl. "Still frightened by a legend? And after you've seen his magic defeated by the star-blade! You've lived within the shadow of this decadent city too long, girl. In a few hours we'll have light, and then I'll take you out into the real world—where men haven't sold their souls to the ghosts of elder races!"

But her fears did not dissolve under the barbarian's warm confidence. For a timeless period of darkness Dessylyn clung to him, her heart restlessly drumming, shuddering at each fragment of sound that pierced the night and fog.

And through the darkened streets echoed the clop-clop of hooves.

Far away, their sound so faint it might have been imagined. Closer now, the fog-muffled fall of ironshod hooves on paving bricks. Drawing ever closer, a hollow, rhythmic knell that grew deafening in the absolute stillness. Clop-Clop Clop-Clop Clop-Clop CLOP-CLOP CLOP-CLOP. Approaching the inn unhurriedly. Inexorably approaching the mist-shrouded inn.

"What is it?" he asked her, as she started upright in terror.

"I know that sound. It's a black, black stallion, with eyes that burn like living coals and hooves that ring like iron!"

Dragar snorted.

"Ah! And I know his rider!"

CLOP-CLOP CLOP-CLOP. Hoofbeats rolled and gobbled across the courtyard of the Inn of the Blue Window. Echoes rattled against the shutters . . . *Could no one else hear their chill thunder?*

CLOP-CLOP *CLOP*. The unseen horse stamped and halted outside the inn's door. Harness jingled. *Why were there no voices?*

From deep within the chambers below echoed the dull chink of the bolt and bars falling away, clattering to the floor. A harsh creak as the outer door swung open. *Where was the innkeeper?*

Footfalls sounded on the stairs—the soft scuff of boot leather on worn planks. Someone entered the hallway beyond their door; strode confidently toward their room.

Dessylyn's face was a stark mask of terror. Knuckles jammed against her teeth to dam a rising scream were stained red with drawn blood. Dread-haunted eyes were fixed upon the door opposite.

Slipping into a fighting crouch, Dragar spared a glance for the bared blade in his taut grasp. No nimbus of flame hovered about the sword, only the deadly gleam of honed steel, reflected in the unnaturally subdued lamplight.

Footsteps halted in front of their door. It seemed he could hear the sound of breathing from beyond the threshold.

A heavy fist smote the door. Once. A single summons. A single challenge.

With an urgent gesture, Dessylyn signed Dragar to remain silent.

"Who dares . . . !" he growled in a ragged voice.

A powerful blow exploded against the stout timber. Latch and bolt erupted from their setting in a shower of splinters and wrenched metal. All but torn from its hinges, the door was hurled open, slammed resoundingly against the wall.

"*Kane!*" screamed Dessylyn.

The massive figure strode through the doorway, feral grace in the movements of his powerful, square-torsoed frame. A heavy sword was balanced with seeming negligence in his left hand, but there was no uncertainty in the lethal fury that blazed in his eyes.

"Good evening," sneered Kane through a mirthless smile.

Startled despite Dessylyn's warning, Dragar's practiced eye swiftly sized up his opponent. So the sorcerer's magic had preserved the prime of his years after all . . . At about six feet Kane stood several inches shorter than the towering barbarian, but the enormous bands of muscle that surged beneath leather vest and trousers made his weight somewhat greater. Long arms and the powerful roll of his shoulders signalled a swordsman of considerable reach and strength, although the youth doubted if Kane could match his speed. A slim leather band with a black opal tied back his shoulder-length red hair, and the face beneath the close-trimmed beard was brutal, with a savagery that made his demeanor less lordly than arrogant. And his blue eyes burned with the brand of killer.

"Come looking for your woman, sorcerer?" grated Dragar, watching the other's blade. "We thought you'd stay hidden in your tower, after I frightened off your slinking servants!"

Kane's eyes narrowed. "So that's . . . Wizard's Bane, I believe you call it. I see the legends didn't lie when they spoke of the blade's protective powers. I shouldn't have spoken of it to Dessylyn, I suppose, when I learned that an enchanted sword had been brought into Carsultyal. But then, its possession will compensate in some part for the difficulties you've caused me."

"Kill him, Dragar, my love! Don't listen to his lies!" Dessylyn cried.

"What do you mean?" rumbled the youth, who had missed Kane's inference.

The warrior wizard chuckled drily. "Can't you guess, you romantic oaf? Don't you understand that a clever woman has used you? Of course not—the chivalrous barbarian thought he was defending a helpless girl. Pity I let Laroc die after persuading him to tell me of her game. He might have told you how innocent his mistress—"

"Dragar! Kill him! He only means to take you off guard!"

"To be sure! Kill me, Dragar—if you can! That was her plan, you know. Through my . . . sources . . . I learned of this formidable blade you carry and made mention of it to Dessylyn. But Dessylyn, it seems, has grown bored with my caresses. She paid a servant, the unlamented Laroc, to stage an apparent rape, trusting that a certain lout would rush in to save her. Well plotted, don't you think? Now poor Dessylyn has a bold defender whose magic blade can protect her against Kane's evil spells. I wonder, Dessylyn—did you only mean to go away with this thickheaded dolt, or did you plan to goad me into this personal combat, hoping I'd be slain and the wealth of my tower would be yours?"

"Dragar! He's lying to you!" moaned the girl despairingly.

"Because if it was the latter, then I'm afraid your plotting wasn't as intelligent as you believed," concluded Kane mockingly.

"Dragar!" came the tortured choke.

The barbarian, emotions a fiery chaos, risked an agonized glance at her contorted face.

Kane lunged.

Off guard, Dragar's lightning recovery deflected Kane's blade at the last possible instant, so that he took a shallow gash across his side instead of the steel through his ribs. "Damn you!" he cursed.

"But I am!" laughed Kane, parrying the youth's flashing counterattack with ease. His speed was uncanny, and the awesome power of his thick shoulders drove his blade with deadly force.

Lightning seemed to flash with the ringing thunder of their blades. Rune-stamped star-metal hammered against the finest steel of Carsultyal's far-famed forges, and their clangor seemed the cries of two warring demons—harsh, strident with pain and rage.

Sweat shone on Dragar's naked body, and his breath spat foam through his clenched teeth. A few times only had he crossed blades with an opponent his equal in strength, and then the youth's superior speed had carried the victory. Now, as in some impossible nightmare, he faced a skilled and cunning swordsman whose speed was at least his equal—and whose strength seemed somewhat greater. After his initial attack had been deftly turned away, Dragar's swordplay became less reckless, less confident. Grimly he set about wearing down his opponent's endurance, reasoning that the sorcerer's physical conditioning could not equal that of a hardened mercenary.

In all the world there was no sound but their ringing blades, the desperate rush of their bodies, the hoarse gusts of their breath. Everywhere time stood frozen, save for the deadly fury of their duel, as they leaped and lunged about the baretimbered room.

Dragar caught a thin slash across his left arm from a blow he did not remember deflecting. Kane's lefthanded attack was dangerously unfamiliar to him, and only his desperate parries had saved him from worse. Uneasily he realized that Kane's sword arm did not falter as the minutes dragged past and that more and more he was being confined to the defensive. Wizard's Bane grew ragged with notches from the Carsultyal blade, and its hilt was slippery with sweat. Kane's heavier sword was similarly scarred from their relentless slash, parry, thrust.

Then as Kane deflected Dragar's powerful stroke, the youth made a quick thrust with the turning blade—enough so that its tip gashed diagonally across Kane's brow, severing his headband. A shallow cut, but blood flowed freely, matted the clinging strands of his unbound hair. Kane gave back, flung the blood and loose hair from his eyes.

And Dragar lunged. Too quick for Kane to parry fully, his blade gored a furrow the length of the sorcerer's left forearm. Kane's long sword faltered. Instantly the barbarian hammered at his guard.

The sword left Kane's grip as it clumsily threw back the star-blade. For a fraction of a second it turned free in mid air. Dragar exulted that he had at last torn the blade from Kane's grasp—as he raised his arm for a killing stroke.

But Kane's right hand caught up the spinning blade with practiced surety. Wielding the sword with skill scarcely inferior to his natural sword arm, Kane parried Dragar's flashing blow. Then, before the startled barbarian could recover, Kane's sword smashed through Dragar's ribs.

The force of the blow hurled the stricken youth back against the bed. Wizard's Bane dropped from nerveless fingers and skidded across the wide oaken planks.

From Dessylyn's throat came a cry of inexpressible pain. She rushed to him and cradled Dragar's head against her lap. Desperately she pressed ineffectual fingers against the pulsing wound in his chest. "Please, Kane!" she sobbed. "Spare him!"

Kane glanced through burning eyes at the youth's ruined chest and laughed. "I give him to you, Dessylyn," he told her insolently. "And I'll await you in my tower—unless, of course, you young lovers still plan on running off together."

Blood trailing from his arm—and darker blood from his sword—he stalked from the room and into the night mists.

"Dragar! Dragar!" Dessylyn moaned, kissing his haggard face and blood-foamed lips. "Please don't die, beloved! Onthe, don't let him die!"

Tears fell from her eyes to his as she pressed her face against his pallid visage. "You didn't believe him, did you, Dragar? What if I did engineer our meeting, dearest! Still I love you! It's true that I love you! I'll always love you, Dragar!"

He looked at her through glazing eyes.

"Bitch!" he spat, and died.

How many times, Dessylyn?
How many times will you play this game?

(But this was the first!)
The first? Are you sure, Dessylyn?
(I swear it! . . . How can I be sure?)
And how many after? How many circles, Dessylyn?
(Circles? Why this darkness in my mind?)
How many times, Dessylyn, have you played at Lorelei?
How many are those who have known your summoning eye?
How many are those who have heard your siren cry, Dessylyn?
How many souls have swum out to you, Dessylyn?
And perished by the shadows that hide below,
And are drawn down to Hell by the undertow?
How many times, Dessylyn?
(I can't remember . . .)

VII
"HE'LL HAVE TO DIE . . ."

"You know he'll have to die."

Dessylyn shook her head. "It's too dangerous."

"Clearly it's far more dangerous to let him live," Mavrsal pointed out grimly. "From what you've told me, Kane will never permit you to leave him—and this isn't like trying to get away from some jealous lord. A sorcerer's tentacles reach farther than those of the fabled Oraycha. What good is it to escape Carsultyal, only to have Kane's magic strike at us later? Even on the high sea his shadow can follow us."

"But we might escape him," murmured Dessylyn. "The oceans are limitless, and the waves carry no trail."

"A wizard of Kane's power will have ways to follow us."

"It's still too dangerous. I'm not even sure Kane *can* be killed!" Dessylyn's fingers toyed anxiously with the emerald at her throat; her lips were tightly pressed.

Angrily Mavrsal watched her fingers twist the wide silk and leather collar. Fine ladies might consider the fashion stylish here in Carsultyal, but it annoyed him that she wore the ornament even in bed. "You'll never be free of Kane's slave collar," he growled, voicing his thought, "until that devil is dead."

"I know," breathed the girl softly, more than fear shining in her green eyes.

"Yours is the hand that can kill him," he continued. Her lips moved, but no sound issued.

Soft harbor sounds whispered through the night as the *Tuab* gently rocked with the waves. Against the quay, her timbers creaked and groaned, thudded against the buffers of waste hemp cordage. Distantly, her watch paced the deck; low conversation, dimly heard, marked the presence of other crewmen—not yet in their hammocks, despite a hard day's work. In the captain's cabin a lamp swung slowly with the vessel's roll, playing soft shadows back and forth against the objects within. Snug and sheltered from the sea mists, the atmosphere was almost cozy—could the cabin only have been secure against a darker phantom that haunted the night.

"Kane claims to love you," Mavrsal persisted shrewdly. "He won't accept your hatred of him. In other words, he'll unconsciously lower his guard with you. He'll let you stand at his back and never suspect that your hand might drive a dagger through his ribs."

"It's true," she acknowledged in a strange voice.

Marvsal held her shoulders and turned her face to his. "I can't see why you haven't tried this before. Was it fear?"

"Yes. I'm terrified of Kane."

"Or was it something else? Do you still feel some secret love for him, Dessylyn?"

She did not reply immediately. "I don't know."

He swore and took her chin in his hand. The collar, with its symbol of Kane's mastery, enraged him—so that he roughly tore it from her throat. Her fingers flew to the bared flesh.

Again he cursed. "Did Kane do that to you?" She nodded, her eyes wide with intense emotion.

"He treats you as a slave, and you haven't the spirit to rebel—or even to hate him for what he does to you!"

"That's not true! I hate Kane!"

"Then show some courage! What can the devil do to you that's any worse than your present lot?"

"I just don't want you to die, too!"

The captain laughed grimly. "If you'd remain his slave to spare my life, then you're worth dying for! But the only death will be Kane's—if we lay our plans well. Will you try, Dessylyn? Will you rebel against this tyrant—win freedom for yourself, and love for us both?"

"I'll try, Mavrsal," she promised, unable to avoid his eyes. "But I can't do it alone."

"Nor would any man ask you to. Can I get into Kane's tower?"

"An army couldn't assail that tower if Kane wished to defend it."

"So I've heard. But can *I* get inside? Kane must have a secret entrance to his lair."

She bit her fist. "I know of one. Perhaps you could enter without his knowing it."

"I can if you can warn me of any hidden guardians or pitfalls," he told her with more confidence than he felt. "And I'll want to try this when he won't be as vigilant as normal. Since there seem to be regular periods when you can slip away from the tower, I see no reason why I can't steal inside under the same circumstances."

Dessylyn nodded, her face showing less fear now. "When he's deep into his necromancies, Kane is oblivious to all else. He's begun again with some of his black spells—he'll be so occupied until tomorrow night, when he'll force me to partake of his dark ritual."

Mavrsal flushed with outrage. "Then that will be his last journey into the demonlands—until we send him down to Hell forever! Repairs are all but complete. If I push the men and rush reprovisioning, the *Tuab* can sail with the tide of another dawn. Tomorrow night it will be, then, Dessylyn. While Kane is exhausted and preoccupied with his black sorcery, I'll slip into his tower.

"Be with him then. If he sees me before I can strike, wait until he turns to meet my attack—then strike with this!" And he drew a slender dirk from a sheath fixed beneath the head of his bunk.

As if hypnotized by his words, by the shining sliver of steel, Dessylyn turned the dagger about in her hands, again and again, staring at the flash of light on its keen edge. "I'll try. By Onthe, I'll try to do as you say!"

"He'll have to die," Mavrsal assured her. "You know he'll have to die."

VIII
DRINK A FINAL CUP . . .

Spread out far below lay Carsultyal, fog swirling through her wide brick streets and crooked filthy alleys, hovering over squalid tenements and palatial manors—although her arrogant towers pierced its veil and reared toward the stars in lordly grandeur. Born of two elements, air and water, the mist swirled and drifted, sought to strangle a third element, fire, but could do no more than dim with tears its thousand glowing eyes. Patches of murky yellow in the roiling fog, the lights of Carsultyal gained the illusion of movement, so that one might be uncertain at any one moment whether he gazed down into the mist-hung city or upward toward the cloud-buried stars.

"Your mood is strange tonight, Dessylyn," Kane observed, meticulously adjusting the fire beneath the tertiary alembic.

She moved away from the tower window. "Is it strange to you, Kane? I marvel that you notice. I've told you countless times that this necromancy disgusts me, but always before have my sentiments meant nothing to you."

"Your sentiments mean a great deal to me, Dessylyn. But as for demanding your attendance here, I only do what I must."

"Like that!" she hissed in loathing, and pointed to the young girl's mutilated corpse.

Wearily Kane followed her gesture. Pain etching his brow, he made a sign and barked a stream of harsh syllables. A shadow crossed the open window and fell over the vivisected corpse. When it withdrew, the tortured form had vanished, and a muffled slap of wings faded into the darkness.

"Why do you think to hide your depraved crimes from my sight, Kane? Do you think I'll forget? Do you think I don't know the evil that goes into compounding this diabolical drug you force me to drink?"

Kane frowned and stared into the haze of phosphorescent vapor which swirled within the cucurbit. "Are you carrying iron, Dessylyn? There's assymetry to the nimbus. I've told you not to bring iron within the influence of this generation."

The dagger was an unearthly chill against the flesh of her thigh. "Your mind is going, Kane. I wear only these rings."

456

He ignored her to lift the cap and hurriedly pour in a measure of dark, semi-congealed fluid. The alembic hissed and shivered, seemed to burst with light within its crimson crystal walls. A drop of phosphorescence took substance near the receiver. Kane quickly shifted the chalice to catch the droplet as it plunged.

"Why do you force me to drink this, Kane? Aren't these chains of fear that hold me to you bondage enough?"

His uncanny stare fixed her, and while it might have been the alchemical flames that made it seem so, she was astonished to see the fatigue, the pain that lined his face. It was as if the untold centuries whose touch Kane had eluded had at last stolen upon him. His hair billowed wildly, his face was shadowed and sunken, and his skin seemed imparted with the sick hue of the phosphorescent vapors.

"Why must you play this game, Dessylyn? Does it please you to see to what limits I go to hold you to me?"

"All that would please me, Kane, is to be free of you."

"You loved me once. You will love me again."

"Because you command it? You're a fool if you believe so. I hate you, Kane. I'll hate you for the rest of my life. Kill me now, or keep me here till I'm ancient and withered. I'll still die hating you."

He sighed and turned from her. His words were breathed into the flame. "You'll stay with me because I love you, and your beauty will not fade, Dessylyn. In time you may understand. Did you ever wonder at the loneliness of immortality? Have you ever wondered what must be the thoughts of a man cursed to wander through the centuries? A man doomed to a desolate, unending existence—feared and hated wherever men speak his name. A man who can never know peace, whose shadow leaves ruin wherever he passes. A man who has learned that every triumph is fleeting, that every joy is transient. All that he seeks to possess is stolen away from him by the years. His empires will fall, his songs will be forgotten, his loves will turn to dust. Only the emptiness of eternity will remain with him, a laughing skeleton cloaked in memories to haunt his days and nights.

"For such a man as this, for such a curse as this—is it so terrible that he dares to use his dark wisdom to hold something which he loves? If a hundred bright flowers must wither and die in his hand, is it evil that he hopes to keep one, just *one*, blossom for longer than the brief instant that Time had intended? Even if the flower hated being torn from the soil, would it make him wish to preserve its beauty any less?"

But Dessylyn was not listening to Kane. The billow of a tapestry, where no wind had blown, caught her vision. Could Kane hear the almost silent rasp of hidden hinges? No, he was lost in one of his maddened fits of brooding.

She tried to force her pounding heart to pulse less thunderously, her quick breath to cease its frantic rush. She could see where Mavrsal stood, frozen in the shadow of the tapestry. It seemed impossible that he might creep closer without Kane's unnatural keenness sensing his presence. The hidden dirk burned her thigh as if it were sheathed in her flesh. Carefully she edged around to Kane's side, thinking to expose his back to Mavrsal.

"But I see the elixir is ready," announced Kane, breaking out of his mood. Administering a few amber drops to the fluid, he carefully lifted the chalice of glowing liquor.

"Here, drink this quickly," he ordered, extending the vessel.

"I won't drink your poisoned drugs again."

"Drink it, Dessylyn." His eyes held hers.

As in a recurrent nightmare—*and there were other nightmares*—Dessylyn accepted the goblet. She raised it to her lips, felt the bitter liquor touch her tongue.

A knife whirled across the chamber. Struck from her languid fingers, the crystal goblet smashed into a thousand glowing shards against the stones.

"No!" shouted Kane in a demonic tone. "No! *No!*" He stared at the pool of dying phosphoresence in stunned horror.

Leaping from concealment, Mavrsal flung himself toward Kane—hoping to bury his cutlass in his enemy's heart before the sorcerer recovered. He had not reckoned on Kane's uncanny reflexes.

The anguished despair Kane displayed burst into inhuman rage at the instant he spun to meet his hidden assailant. Weaponless, he lunged for the sea captain. Mavrsal swung his blade in a natural downward slash, abandoning finesse in the face of an unarmed opponent.

With blurring speed, Kane stepped under the blow and caught the other's descending wrist with his left hand. Mavrsal heard a scream escape his lips as his arm was jammed to a halt in mid swing—as Kane's powerful left hand closed about his wrist and shattered the bones beneath the crushed flesh. The cutlass sailed unheeded across the stones.

His face twisted in bestial fury, Kane grappled with the sea captain. Mavrsal, an experienced fighter at rough and tumble, found himself tossed about like a frail child. Kane's other hand circled its long fingers about his throat, choking off his breath. Desperately he sought to break Kane's hold, beat at him with his mangled wrist, as Kane with savage laughter carried him back against the wall, holding him by his neck like a broken puppet.

Red fog wavered in his vision—pain was roaring in his ears . . . Kane was slowly strangling him, killing him deliberately, taunting him for his helplessness.

Then he was falling.

Kane gasped and arched his back inward as Dessylyn drove her dagger into his shoulder. Blood splashed her sweat-slippery fist. As Kane twisted away from her blow, the thin blade lodged in the scapula and snapped at the hilt.

Dessylyn screamed as his backhand blow hurled her to the stones. Frantically she scrambled to Mavrsal's side, where he lay sprawled on the floor—stunned, but still conscious.

Kane cursed and fell back against his worktable, over-turning an alembic that burst like a rotted gourd. *"Dessylyn!"* he groaned in disbelief. Blood welled from his shoulder, spread across his slumped figure. His left shoulder was crippled, but his deadliness was that of a wounded tiger. "Dessylyn!"

"What did you expect?" she snarled, trying to pull Mavrsal to his feet.

A heavy flapping sound flung foggy gusts through the window. Kane cried out something in an inhuman tongue.

"If you kill Mavrsal, better kill me this time as well!" cried Dessylyn, clinging to the sea captain as he dazedly rose to his knees.

He cast a calculating eye toward the fallen sword. Too far.

"Leave her alone, sorcerer!" rasped Mavrsal. "She's guilty of no crime but that of hating you and loving me! Kill me now and be done, but you'll never change her spirit!"

"And I suppose you love her, too," said Kane in a tortured voice. "You fool. Do you know how many others I've killed—other fools who thought they would save Dessylyn from the sorcerer's evil embrace? It's a game she often plays. Ever since the first fool . . . only a game. It amuses her to taunt me with her infidelities, with her schemes to leave with another man. Since it amuses her, I indulge her. But she doesn't love you."

"Then why did she bury my steel in your back?" Despair made Mavrsal reckless. "She hates you, sorcerer—and she loves me! Keep your lies to console you in your madness! Your sorcery can't alter Dessylyn's feelings toward you—nor can it alter the truth you're forced to see! So kill me and be damned—you can't escape the reality of your pitiful clutching for something you'll never hold!"

Kane's voice was strange, and his face was a mirror of tormented despair. "Get out of my sight!" he rasped. "Get out of here, both of you!

"Dessylyn, I give you your freedom. Mavrsal, I give you Dessylyn's love. Take your bounty, and go from Carsultyal! I trust you'll have little cause to thank me!"

As they stumbled for the secret door, Mavrsal ripped the emerald-set collar from Dessylyn's neck and flung it at Kane's slumping figure. "Keep your slave collar!" he growled. "It's enough that you leave her with your scars about her throat!"

"You fool," said Kane in a low voice.

"How far are we from Carsultyal?" whispered Dessylyn.

"Several leagues—we've barely gotten underway," Mavrsal told the shivering girl beside him.

"I'm frightened."

"Hush. You're done with Kane and all his sorcery. Soon it will be dawn, and soon we'll be far beyond Carsultyal and all the evil you've known there."

"Hold me tighter then, my love. I feel so cold."

"The sea wind is cold, but it's clean," he told her. "It's carrying us together to a new life."

"I'm frightened."

"Hold me closer, then."

"I seem to remember now . . ."

But the exhausted sea captain had fallen asleep. A deep sleep—the last unblighted slumber he would ever know.

For at dawn he awoke in the embrace of a corpse—the moldering corpse of a long-dead girl, who had hanged herself in despair over the death of her barbarian lover.

ROBERTA LANNES

A Complete Woman

⊷——⊶

Roberta Lannes has been publishing in the science fiction, dark fantasy and horror genres since 1985, and a selection of her short fiction can be found in the collection The Mirror of Night. *Her work has been translated into fourteen languages, while South African film-maker Aryan Kaganof's 1994 movie* Ten Monologues from the Lives of the Serial Killers *includes an adaptation of her acclaimed short story "Goodbye, Dark Love."*

As an artist, her artwork has appeared in Cemetery Dance *magazine, and her photography in* JPG Magazine. *She designs CD covers, app splash screens and website graphics, and she recently collaborated with author Christopher Conlon as the illustrator for his epic zombie poem* When

463

They Came Back, *contributing more than fifty photographs to the project.*

She lives just outside Los Angeles, in the Santa Clarita Valley, with her husband, British poet, journalist and classical music critic Mark Sealey.

As the author explains, "It was during a heated argument over the origin of homosexual behavior and lifestyle that 'A Complete Woman' first crept into my consciousness. Long ago, in my naïvete, I believed being gay was solely a result of conditioning, environment, opportunity, and preference. When challenged about the genesis of preference, I fell back on the psychological terms of 'modeling' and 'reaction-formation.' I was summarily blasted for relying on an inexact science. I realized then, I didn't know enough.

"Disgruntled, I went home and read. An article on genetic predestination theories, touted loudly by gay activist groups and their spokespeople, put things in perspective for me. Sexual preference is predominately determined on a cellular level, in our chromosomes.

"This story was written for those idiots who still believe that all gays and transsexuals have a choice."

I am blind and mute. I have not yet been given arms or legs, and I miss wiggling my toes when I wake up. There's so much I miss, but to think of running my fingers through my hair, or watching a sunset, is to make worse my pain. And after all, I chose this path.

The day nurse arrives at six in the morning, she tells me. I have no way to judge time except by what I hear. And I know well how words can fool. At night, the doctor's sister sits with me. She says she's an insomniac, that to sit and read as I sleep is a joy. I don't believe that, but then doubting the veracity of what these women tell me is the only sport I have sometimes. I am at this point, essentially, not much more than a mind.

The morning rituals revolve around bathing me, feeding me, and removing anything I've evacuated during the night. One of my two day nurses puts classical music on the radio. I smile and make approving moans. Of the two, she is my favorite.

My bath is alternately soothing and painful. The tubes that snake from my shoulders and hips are cleaned, as are the unique dressings of synthetic skin, the areas around them scrubbed of my dead skin and anti-bacterial salves are massaged in. This portion of the bath is agonizing, and only my anguished groans communicate that. If it is too painful, I'm given opiates.

When I'm doped, I cannot enjoy the best part. The one nurse, my favorite, moves her hand, with the soft soapy cloth, over my new nipples, down to the tender hungry flesh between what will be my legs. She knows the pleasure it brings me and lingers at her chore. I believe the great spasms that contort my face and torso in climax bring *her* pleasure. I can hear her breath go ragged in its rhythm.

After the morning ministrations, I am left to the darkness. The music plays softly without much distraction so that I can dream about the future and lament my past. Until the doctor arrives.

The doctor. Ah. His face remains clear in my mind, as do his pianist's hands, tall rangy body and wavy brown hair. Though I did not choose to do this because he was handsome, brilliant, and eloquent, these things made my decision easier. I can recall the evening he came to me. And our every word.

Cancer had robbed me of my breasts and lymph nodes, and I was in chemotherapy. I had a gloomy prognosis and no hair. The doctor came in just after visiting hours. There was no one to visit me, my having reached the age of seventy-eight and successfully maintained a reclusive existence as a writer and researcher. So when two strangers in street clothing approached my bed, I was addled and nearly shouted for the nurse.

The older man spoke. "Please, Miss Craig, I am a doctor." His voice was deep, timbre soothing.

I was my usual harsh and uninviting self. "What is it?"

He watched me cross my wizened arms over my sexless chest.

"I am an admirer of your work. I'm quite fascinated by the lives of renaissance artists, particularly musicians, and your books have a wonderfully gossipy tone to them."

"Well, a man of taste and questionable ethical standards. You like your history presented with a bit of sensationalism and sometimes slanderous speculation." He grinned at that. I remember feeling sad at that moment, dismayed that I hadn't the form nor visage to attract such a man any longer. A man who shared my greatest obsession, as well.

"I hope you won't be upset, but I took the liberty of going over your chart. I'm not an oncologist, but it seems you let things metastasize a bit too long."

"Yes, well, I'm paying for that gaff now, aren't I?"

"Yes, unfortunately. I'd like to offer you some hope, though."

As I struggled to sit up, he reached over to the position controls and raised the head of the bed for me. I cocked an eyebrow, scrutinizing him.

"What makes you think you can give me something a whole phalanx of physicians hasn't been able to do?"

"Your prognosis is poor, your age notwithstanding. But I have given others the potential for a new life. I'd like to give that to you, as well." He nodded to the young man beside him. I squinted, my glasses misplaced somewhere in this unfamiliar place, but saw nothing extraordinary.

"What is it, magic spells? Youth serum? More surgery?"

"I'm not offering you a panacea, Miss Craig. Without getting into serious medical jargon, I'd characterize it as a full brain transplant into a viable alternative head and body system." He waited for my response, his manner guarded.

Had someone told me of this possibility before my cancer, I don't know what I would have thought, but as I lay weakened, old and depressed, in a bed I might never get out of again, I considered it. After laughing heartily.

He was surprised by my laughter. I believe he expected me to be horrified or amazed. I don't know why I laughed, but it felt marvelous.

"This is really quite serious, Miss Craig. I chose you for so many reasons, one of them your sense of pragmatism."

He seemed so young, vulnerable, and self-righteously indignant just then, I simply fell in love with him. "My dear doctor . . ."

"Dr. Chernofsky . . . Kenneth."

"Dr. Chernofsky, it's obvious you completely believe in what you're doing, but I don't think you've ever been in my position before. It's not every day one is approached with such a fantastic offer."

"Yes, it *is* fantastic. Rare and marvelous. But so are *you*. Minds like yours are so extraordinary, they shouldn't be allowed to pass into oblivion. And think of it. I can compose the kind of body you want. I am Leonardo da Vinci and Michelangelo when it comes to surgery." He put his arm around the young man and moved him closer. "I brought along one of my completed works."

I looked the young man over more studiously. "Then you've done this ghoulish surgery before?"

"Yes, but you should know it isn't sanctioned by any medical board or school in the United States."

"It's illegal?"

"Not illegal in the sense that it's been outlawed. It's just not *done*. But it will be when I can establish the basis for its acceptance. Simon, the others, and hopefully you, will help me there."

I turned to an example of the last chance I was going to have. "Young man, tell me, is it painful?" The pain I'd already endured seemed to be fading as I considered this radical move.

He smirked. "I wish I could tell you otherwise, but it was very painful. Tranquilizers and pain killers were given to relieve the symptoms, with much success. And I must admit, now, this long after the surgeries, it was worth it."

I turned to the doctor. "Hooray for modern chemistry. How long does this Frankensteinian feat take?"

His shoulders tensed ever so slightly. A touchy area, I assumed. He looked at the young man.

"Simon took almost a year to be complete."

"A year? I don't understand." I was growing wearier by the minute.

"When I began my experimental work, professionally I was reattaching severed limbs; bone to bone, muscle to muscle, artery to artery, and reconnecting things, like detached eyes to optic nerves. My expertise is lauded here." He had a copy of a medical journal. I dismissed it. "Gradually, I learned plastic surgery techniques to make the reattachments almost invisible. The brain attachment was highly experimental for two years, until I perfected it. Even then, it required doing the entire assembly work limb by limb to a torso and head. A long and tedious process."

"Pardon my silly question, but wouldn't it save time just to put a brain in a head that's already attached to an entire body?"

"That's not a silly question at all. Of course it would expedite things. But as yet, I haven't stooped to finding an Igor to slip into graveyards or hang out at accident scenes. I am donated bodies and parts of bodies through private hospitals all over the world. I have never been sent an entire body in the condition of health and appearance I require. That *you* would find worthy."

"I suppose if I were to go through with the pain and gore, I would want it to be worth my while. So there's no getting around the bit-by-bit procedure?"

He shrugged as he shook his head. "As portions come in of the quality I need, I use them."

"What if I die before you find a great head?" I chuckled.

"That's not going to happen. You see, I have the perfect head and torso right now. You must decide within the next few hours."

"*Hours?*" I was suddenly filled with adrenaline and rest was far from my options.

"She's perfect. Came to me this afternoon. Her brain is dead, essentially, so I've got the remainder of her body on life support. I don't want any deterioration, so I need to operate soon."

I began to ask myself questions I couldn't imagine anyone asking themselves, except in some piece of fiction. If I had the chance to live another fifty years, would I take it? Could I exist in another person's body? Would I be able to do all the things I do now, and more? Would it be worth it, ultimately?

And was I really going to die as soon as I guessed, if I did nothing? I know my troubled face showed my confusion.

"Simon, talk to Miss Allison Neary Craig." By way of introduction, he went on. "Simon Le Fevre. My latest completed man."

My jaw dropped. "The novelist? He's *dead*."

"Yes, he was. He uses another name now."

I was incredulous. "He was ninety years old when he died of pneumonia. I know. I read the paper." I pulled the young man closer, looking him over.

"I took him before he died. I won't bore you with the details."

My mind was truly reeling now. I'd read all of Le Fevre's works. Powerful novels of profound conflicts of spirit. He'd even written one about Julius II, the Pope who was one of the renaissance's primary artistic supporters. A flawless work. And I'd been lying there all that time right beside him.

The young man was not older than nineteen, average in stature and pleasant in appearance, but not the colorful character I'd known of before. If this man had the mind of Simon Le Fevre, with another lifetime, he could create such great works! The doctor reflected my amazed delight.

"Simon, meet Allison Neary Craig."

He held my hands. I was enthralled. "I don't believe this." I shook my bald head.

"Well, it's my pleasure. I am a fan of yours. Your articles for *Art and Antiquities* are paradigms. You inspired me to write *The Pope*. I doubt if you recall, but I sent you a letter just before it came out."

"It *is* you. You're alive."

"I am, because of Kenneth's work. Look." He began showing me barely visible seams at his wrists, another at one shoulder. I marveled at the precision.

"Do you have much pain now?"

Simon put his hand to his cheek. "The immune-suppression drugs give me headaches, other side effects, and I feel creaky sometimes, but it's nothing compared to old age. Besides, it keeps getting better."

"Well, that's encouraging. I hope you're still writing."

"I am. I use a pseudonym, though. The ghost of Simon Le Fevre wouldn't work. Now, I am Jean Luc Forchaud."

"You just published a novel . . . *Eagle's Nest*! I have it at home." I stared at the boy who was once ninety. Who was now ninety-three. How I wanted what he had. To be beautiful, young and have the energy to write all day or night. A future.

"I don't know if you'll decide to have Kenneth do your work, but if you do, I'd like for us to keep in touch. I still admire *your* work."

"I've made my decision. I want this, Dr. Chernofsky. I want your work . . . and your company." I grinned like a girl at the two men. "To be young again."

"To forever . . ." The doctor proposed a mock toast.

I was removed from the hospital clandestinely, leaving the appearance that I left on my own. The next day, my body was found in a motel room, my head ravaged by the blast of a shotgun that was found in my hands. The dead woman, whose head my brain would soon inhabit, gave her brains for splattering on the wall. My suicide note was short and sweet.

Three weeks later, the swelling of the medulla oblongata went down and my coma lifted. I awoke to darkness and the sound of the doctor's voice. The first thing he did for me was read my obituaries, the newspaper articles about me, and the accolades from lay people to scholars. Then he explained the damaged optic nerves, and the temporary condition of my larynx. All within his abilities to mend, he said. I would just have to be patient.

I have been as I am for nearly two months. The doctor told me in his last visit, yesterday, that an arm was due in from Germany, the tissue match assured. I know having one arm will allow me to scratch my nose, feel my hair, get some sense of my world through touch. But I was warned that the nerves take months to regenerate. Every step required my endurance. My grace.

His footsteps. I know them as well as my new heartbeat.

"Your arm has arrived. It is beautiful. All that I was told. Greta will prep you, and we'll do the surgery in a few minutes."

I long to tell him I'm frightened—that the pain will be unbearable—that it won't work, that I will still be unable to touch the world. I try to make a sound that will convey that, but it comes out a whimper. He strokes my head, lovingly.

"It will be all right. And while I am operating on the arm, I will do the last of the repairs on the optic nerves. We may get eyes very soon."

He reassures me, as if he knows how I struggle to be stoical. But I am terrified. The doctor tells me what I want to hear, but I don't dare allow myself to be fooled.

As they wheel me into the operating room, I can smell the antiseptic atmosphere, the metal and tile. It's cooler and is devoid of human scents. I hear feet covered in booties shooshing over the tile floor. Voices dulled by the bunting of face masks. The clinking and tiny thudding of instruments being transferred onto metal trays. And my mind wanders to the last time Kenneth spoke to me of personal things. It had just been two days ago.

Before I drift into drugged oblivion, I imagine him over me. "Allison, I was thinking this morning at breakfast what it will be like when you're whole, and we can wake up together." He stroked my hair. "I can't help my fantasies. I remember the old woman I met in the hospital, but she was a shell. And I fell in love with the woman who was trapped in that diseased body. Now you're about to become an enchantingly beautiful woman, with the soul of an artist and one of the greatest minds of this century. I wonder if you think of it, too. What a powerful couple we could be."

I moved my head against his hand, hoping the gesture spoke the thrill hundreds of words might otherwise communicate. He touched my lips with his fingertips, then his lips. I kissed him with a strange mouth. He tasted of marzipan and lemon water.

"I'm so frustrated not to hear your voice, the words I want so much to hear. It won't be long before the reconstruction can be done. And then . . . then we can share our dreams together.

"I still don't know if you knew . . . that when I came to your hospital room, I had planned the moment for years. I'd seen you on news magazine shows and in that short film documentary by Ronald Knapp. I read everything you've ever written, and everything written about you. I knew your life. I knew you. I had only to meet you to love you. Even as a hairless old woman, your spirit shone through.

"If you could see the face you wear now, the gentle beauty of it, you would know I didn't choose a shell for you that would be garishly gorgeous or supremely pretty. But that I wanted a face that reflected the intelligent beauty I fell in love with.

"If I'm wrong and presumptuous, and there wasn't a spark of something between us for you, I want you to believe that this wasn't just a selfish act on my part. As with Simon, I wanted genius to live on. I was fortunate that Simon also wanted to be a friend. And I will be even more fortunate if you will consider me for . . . a mate."

Yes. Yes, I shouted in my mind. Of course I would. To have been found by someone so absolutely right for me when I was about to lose everything.

I'd lived alone for so many years, unhappy with the mediocrity of men, their interests so carnal and banal. On occasion I suffered their company, longing for one to become what I dreamed. They disappointed me often through no fault of their own. Some I pitied. But Kenneth was all I imagined a mate could be. Caring, but not doting. Attentive, yet independent. Sexy, yet not base. Handsome, and brilliant. Talented, but not compulsively so. And ultimately, he adored my *mind*.

Yes, I'd be his mate.

The pain precedes any other sense awareness. My shoulders feel like jack hammers have splintered them to shreds. I moan and I feel the cool touch of my favorite nurse.

"Miss Craig. I'm going to start a drip of morphine for you. Just enough to dull the pain, but not put you out. Doctor needs you cogent."

I murmur assent.

"I've been staring at your new hands. I've always wanted long nail beds and large moons. And your arms are really exquisite."

Hands? He's given me two arms and surprised me! Of course. It's like him. I grin drunkenly, as I feel the gauzy veil of the opiate.

"Oh, no. I've given it away. Don't tell. Please."

I can't tell. I wouldn't anyway. Greta's been so good to me. So very good.

"I hear him. Act surprised."

His footsteps are quick, light. He's been notified I am awake. He hurries to me, a concerned lover. How lucky I am!

"Allison, you're awake." I felt the movement of my IV, the sound of his fingers tapping the drip gauge. "Ah, Greta's started a bit of morphine for you. Do your shoulders hurt?"

I nod dramatically, but I'm probably wobbling my head instead, inebriated with the drug.

"Surprised? Did you think I would give you two different arms? A writer with mismatched hands? A travesty. For what I did to Simon, I still can't forgive myself." I hear his pen on paper on a metal chart. He brushes my hair off my forehead. He told me it's golden blonde. "You might like knowing the arms came from a eighteen year old ballerina. Imagine the sylph-like gestures they've performed. Imagine perfect arms and hands.

They're yours, now." His lips brush mine. His cheek presses against my cheek. I feel moisture. A tear?

How I want to reach out and hold him, but all I know is the pain where the tubes used to be. In time, as he's often said. In time.

I drift in and out of consciousness. The numbness extends to my brain, sometimes. The day becomes night, the night day. I know only the touch of my Kenneth, and Greta.

It must be night. His sister, Sonia, is sitting beside me, reading. I hear her whispering the words, sometimes. She never touches me, even if I cry out in pain. Then, she calls the doctor. I know only her voice and the sound of pages turning.

Suddenly, a deep guttural moan comes from me, unbidden. I am shocked by the sound. I try to make a word with it and hear myself say, "Help."

She drops her book and runs from the room. She leaves the door open, I know, because I feel the cooler air of the hallway. Then I hear her strained voice on the telephone.

"Yes, dammit, she *spoke* . . . Plainly . . . 'Help'."

Whoever she speaks to is flustered or excited by her news. Her tone is apologetic, careful, but indignant. Confused.

"All right. Of course. Immediately." She hangs up.

She rushes in, then slows as she nears my bed. It amazes me how stupid people think the blind are. As if blindness affects all the senses and the mind.

"I've called Kenneth. He'll be here shortly. I woke him."

I struggle with words. "I can talk." My voice is shrill and strained. The larynx is probably still damaged somewhat, the promised surgery not yet performed.

"Yes, you can." Under her feigned cheer, she's upset.

I wait until he arrives to speak again. He rushes in but doesn't slow. His lips are all over me, my face, neck.

"Sonia tells me you speak. Say only one thing. My name. Please."

I grin as he cradles my face in his hands. I feel beautiful in this moment.

"Kennnnettth."

"Ah! Rest the vocal chords now. I don't want to strain them. I can hardly believe this. Spontaneous regeneration!"

I nod, smiling. I'll do anything you ask. Tomorrow, I'll tell you I love you.

Just as I am dozing off to sleep again, the excitement of the event worn off, I hear them outside, in the hall. The door is almost completely closed, so their voices are not distinct.

"She *sounds* like her." Sonia is sarcastic.

"With the work I plan on doing on the larynx, she will sound like Allison. I will never listen to that woman's keening voice again in this lifetime. Or have those eyes staring at me with such . . . derision."

"Kenny, I know you think this is going to turn out ideally, but things are already turning ugly."

"Sonia, don't get negative with me." It isn't what Kenneth says that disturbs me, but the tone. As if he is saying, "I'll kill you if you say one more thing," and meaning it.

Sonia is silent. I hear her returning, sitting down, grabbing her book. Her breathing is shallow. She's afraid. I feel her hand, briefly, on my shoulder. Now, I am afraid.

There is no sleep for me. I make scenarios in my waking dream state, full of morphine. In all of them, I am the victim. Kenneth is no longer the benevolent, loving craftsman, but a butcher, out to eradicate the traces of someone who still haunts him.

Greta comes to relieve Sonia. I wait until she is washing me, then use my new voice.

"Greta."

"What did you say?" She hasn't been told I speak.

"I'm scared."

"Oh, my god." She begins again in a whisper. "Does he know you can talk?"

I nod. "Do you know who I am?"

"Allison Neary Craig. I actually read one of your books, and I'm not a reader. I'm an action person, got to see it, hear it. You know."

"I'm not someone else the doctor knew from before?"

"You know who you are, don't you?" She sounds frightened now.

"I'm who you say I am. But my body. Face. The doctor heard my voice and told his sister he would never listen to my voice again as long as he lived. That he's going to fix it."

"I don't know." Did she? I wondered. "You're very beautiful to me, but you . . . you know how I feel about . . ."

I'm learning. "I'm afraid he knows this body and face. Or that he took the eyes and larynx because they remind him of someone."

"Miss Allison." She cups my chin. "I won't let him hurt you."

We both hear the doctor's footsteps in the hallway and are quiet. She pulls away, begins readying my bath.

"How are you this morning?" He takes the light blanket covering me down, exposing my nakedness to his eyes.

"I hurt." I make my voice gravelly, low.

"After your bath, I'll double your drip and ease the pain. I have incredible news. Legs. I was faxed a photograph of them. I'm waiting on tissue matching, but I'm fairly certain they'll be yours. And they're long ones." I can hear the delight in his voice. He is truly happy. It softens my doubts.

"Fine." I grunt it out. "Then I'll dance for you."

He laughs coolly. "Be patient." I feel his fingertips tracing my areolas, making my nipples rigid. His hands move over my breasts, appreciating their curves. His fingers move downward. Suddenly, I worry for Greta. Seeing. Being hurt.

She makes a noise at the sink. "We're ready for our bath."

Kenneth's hand retreats. His voice is breathy. "Back in fifteen minutes."

As Greta washes my arms, I swear I feel something. She is washing me too quickly.

"Please, Greta. Take your time."

"I'm afraid now, too."

I wanted to quiet her fears, but instead I let her hurry my bath. There are no words that could take away her feelings. I share her concern too strongly. When she is done, she hems and haws, then apologizes. I ask her not to, though I am not satisfied by the lack of her touch. She sighs, and leaves.

Kenneth returns, adjusts my drip. "Sweet dreams, my love." And I disappear.

The fog lifts with molasses' speed. I hear the doctor speaking to a strange woman. A nurse. I smell the operating room, hear the hollowness of it.

"They're lovely legs. I imagine the dancer who lost them will miss them, if she survived."

"They didn't tell her they were amputating them?"

"Her abdomen was nearly crushed in the accident and she's been unconscious since they brought her in. How is she to know her legs came out of it unscathed?"

"You're a devil, Dr. Chernofsky. If I ever need this kind of work, I'll know who to come to."

"Debbie, you'll never need this kind of work."

She giggles, nervously, but the flirtation is over. I try to turn my head. There are bandages on my throat. I can't swallow. Or breath through my nose, mouth. I hear machines squealing.

"Herb! She's coming out of it. Bring her down. Now!" I disappear again.

Greta is bathing me as I wake. She is sniffling. I wonder if she has a cold. I try to speak, but my throat is closed. I think I will suffocate, but there is a tube in my throat sucking air into my lungs. I buck.

"Miss Allison. Please. Be still. He's done something to your larynx. You'll be breathing through a tube until the swelling goes down. There's been a lot of trauma to your body the past few weeks. Don't let yourself be stressed. I'm taking care of you. *Really.*" Her voice told me someone was near, listening. I relaxed under her touch. "That's my girl. You've got a lot of healing to do."

I can't even moan in pain. Kenneth comes in, distracted.

"I have two emergency surgeries this afternoon. I can't sit with you. Damn. Greta will be here. I'm turning up the drip." Again, I am no longer in the world.

My hips and shoulders are on fire when I wake and my supply of painkiller is depleted. My throat feels as though I am a cat with a hairball stuck there. I feel tingling in my hands, like the time I almost lost a few fingers to frostbite. How they felt as they came back to life. I wait for Greta to notice. She's become so close to me, it's as if she is me, acutely aware of any pain or pleasure I experience. No one comes.

For the first time, I try to cry. Try because I feel no tears, just the aching in my eye sockets and in my heart.

Then she comes.

"Here." I hear her changing my bag of chemical bliss. She adjusts it, and I gently begin the feather-light drift into painlessness. "I'm so sorry I took so long. I had the opportunity to sneak into his office. I thought I'd get a look at your records, but there's nothing unusual. I found other women's files in yours, but Simon has others in his file, too. Let me think . . . one's name is Lydia, another Chantal, and the last, her name is Carol." She clucks her tongue. "How I wish you could respond. I'm not sure what you'd want me to make of it."

I lazily rock my head. I may not be moving at all. It could be the rolling motion of the medication. I feel constantly at sea.

"I'll be off on Saturday. I'm going to my nephew's second birthday party. I don't want anything to happen to you. If anyone thought we were suspicious . . ." Her hands smooth my hair. "I'll save you a piece of cake."

I would not be eating it soon.

I begin to get feeling in my right arm, first. I manage to put my thumb and forefinger together. Kenneth is overjoyed, as usual. I keep waiting for him to remove the tube in my throat and let me speak. I know the swelling there has gone down. Yet, he continues the monologues, reassuring me that eyes are coming soon. I take to reverie when he does this now, not wanting to believe the words, and unable not to if I hear them.

I recall a visit of Simon's, nearly a year after I arrived in the doctor's clinic. He came in with Kenneth, but stayed on after Kenneth hurried off to do an emergency surgery.

"Kenneth has told me about your progress. I can see how wonderful you look."

I gestured clumsily with my new hands. Greta had taught me sign language. And I had a large pad of paper and kindergarten pencil to write out blindly what I wished to say.

"I don't understand."

I was sitting up by then, and grabbed the pencil and paper Greta had left on my nightstand. I wrote, "I wish I could see how wonderful *you* look. Eyes forthcoming."

"Oh, I hope so. Kenneth's told me he reconstructed your vocal chords. When's he going to take the tube out of you?"

I wrote, "Ask him. It's long overdue. Seems like months."

"That couldn't be right. I will ask. I see you have Greta. She was my nurse, too. The best. I couldn't have made it without her. She seems especially fond of you."

Scribbling quickly, "I agree. My angel of mercy."

"I can't quite read that. Oh, well, I know she's great."

He went on about his new book, but there was no more talk of my surgeries or Kenneth. Greta came in an hour later from lunch and they talked beside me. His affection for her touched me.

And Kenneth continues to reassure me.

It's now fourteen months since I arrived. Kenneth took the tube out last month. I will speak in days, he tells me. And eyes are on their way! I already speak, but I keep it from him, selfishly.

I listen to him tell me he loves me, but I don't believe him. A small part of me longs to, still. He exercises my legs with me when he visits, sometimes touching me, exciting me. He says we will make love soon. When I have eyes. I want no one to touch me that way but Greta, now. I don't understand it, but it is so.

There is a hunger in me that has been walled off all these months, too, and as I get feeling in my arms and legs, the hunger returns. I crave to write again. To read.

The eyes arrive. Green, Greta tells me. Kenneth warns me the nerves have been kept in optimal condition, but it is the trickiest of surgeries. If he can reattach my brain, he can do anything, I think.

This time when I wake, the darkness is wrapped in true gauze. I feel the bandages and, though I've been told not to move a muscle in my eyes, I can't resist turning them toward the sound of Greta when she comes in. The pain is bearable. I tell her I want the first thing I see to be her face.

She holds me. I can smell her breath, sweet with cloves and honey from her tea.

"I want that. But I'm afraid. I know what you look like. You've never seen me."

"How could I love you less when I've seen you? Why would I? If Kenneth could fall in love with me at seventy-eight, and I with you, sight unseen, anything is possible."

"That's what I fear. Oh, never mind me. I've grown too close, feel everything too much, for both of us. You know, as a nurse, we're taught not to get too close. *This* is the danger."

"Why didn't you stop it earlier? You could have."

"I've thought of that. Considered how different we are. I knew about your past—that you loved men. Made myself take time off, fought the feelings. But there is something that happens when our skins meet. It's like our electricity runs at the same wattage and we create a current that runs all through us. As if we make something bigger together, than we do on our own. It's definitely not something in my mind. I've always had a stubbornness there that could put an end to something, if I chose to. Not this. No way."

I chuckle. "I understand completely. Whatever this is, it's at a level I can't impose my control over. So, you see? You have no reason to fear."

Her voice is not as strong as her words. "You're right."

That night, I am lying awake, still bandaged, as Sonia reads in her whisper. I hear her get up and go into the hall. There she meets with someone whose voice is not familiar to me. They speak softly to avoid being heard, but my hearing is still acute. I listen hard.

"Well, he's almost done it." Sonia speaks conspiratorially.

"Talk about a total cure. It took a dying heterosexual scholar's brain to do it, but there's nothing left of Carol. All he has to do is train that voice."

"She'll need months of physical therapy for her legs. God, Reed, what if he's actually remade her? Her body, anyway. He got rid of the arms that pushed him away, the legs that were going to walk her distant from him, and replaced them. To his taste, I might add. He's always admired dancers. Something about the musculature. But he wanted Carol's head and torso. Where was he ever going to find anything better? That kind of beauty is too rare. She did have beautiful breasts. And that's the irony. This Craig person was dying of breast cancer. Had them both lopped off before Kenny saved her."

"Ironic, but divine providence. If Carol hadn't died like that . . . shit, he's been so much calmer, saner, since then. He just couldn't handle finding out she was just using him to get pregnant. And then she was going to leave him for her female lover? I thought he'd lose it *permanently*."

"Oh, come on Reed. How would you handle it if your wife left you for another woman?"

"It would never happen."

"Kenneth thought the same thing. Male vanity." She snorts. "It wasn't him, though. He doesn't understand that. And now he has to let it go."

"If he's ever going to make it with the new Carol."

"Allison. Her name is Allison. You'd better remember."

The rest of the conversation blurs. Every suspicion is confirmed. When Sonia returns, I roll over, as if asleep.

The bandages come off today. Each time the doctor removes the bandages to change them, I see a little. Only light really. I am happy for that. I've managed to keep my new voice to myself, except from Greta. I want to speak to Kenneth when I can see. There's so much I need to tell him, and I want to see his reaction.

Kenneth comes to unveil my eyes. I hear other nurses and the voice of Reed. Greta squeezes my hand quickly, then lets go, as Kenneth speaks to the assembled group.

"My Allison sits, she eats and writes and soon she will dance. Today, she sees. I wanted you all here to witness my first complete woman. Some of you know my brother, Reed, the neuro-surgeon. He's in town especially for the occasion." Then he turns to me. "Allison, my brother, Reed. Reed, Allison."

"I'm happy to finally meet you." His hand touches mine.

I nod. Kenneth removes the bandages without drama. I look about. There are jellyfish in vaseline with pale haloes around them. I blink until I think I see the doorway beyond the shapes.

"What do you see?" Kenneth plucks adhesive residue from my forehead. I know he expects me to reach for my pad and scrawl my blind scrawl.

I speak. "Shapes. Blurred shapes." My voice is uncannily like my own. It's not Carol's any longer.

A giddy laugh escapes from Kenneth. "You can talk. Ah. This is more than I'd hoped. Everyone, Allison can talk!" There is uncomfortable applause. They can see the look of shock on his face.

Reed takes an eye examination tool and shines a light in my eyes. "Retinal response is fine. Pupils dilate. You did a great job, little brother. I applaud you once again. Allison, you are a miracle." He lifts my hand limply, then drops it.

"I'm tired. I'm sorry I don't have the energy for a party."

Kenneth shoos everyone out, including Greta. I see her vaguely, small, dark.

"Can you see me?" Kenneth waves his hand before my face.

"You are the great Dr. Chernofsky, I presume?"

"Oh, Allison." His mouth falls on mine. Our kiss is nothing compared to mine with Greta. I wonder, as his tongue finds mine, if my attraction to Greta is a product of Carol's cells, the matter of her being, or if I've never acknowledged my feelings for my own sex. It doesn't make any difference. I can't be Kenneth's fantasy any longer. Mine, for him, is gone.

"I want to take you on a cruise. The Greek Isles. That would be perfect. What do you think?"

"Kenneth, I want to get back to my writing. One step at a time."

He looks mildly disappointed. "Listen to you. So impatient when you first arrived, and now you're the picture of calm." He pats my hand. "Whenever, Allison. We have a long life ahead."

I try to smile, but it comes off feigned. He frowns slightly, though I can't really see, yet. "Am I being too pushy?"

"It's that, and I need to find myself. My new self. You've given me this new body. And a new life. I want to learn what that means."

Desperation creeps into his voice. "I have a feeling I'm losing you. I can't lose you." He turns away, then back. "I won't." That tone again. The one he'd used with Sonia. "I'll kill you if . . ."

I try to sound steady, but I am frightened. "Kenneth. You're moving too fast, again."

He nods, mollified slightly. "I'll let you rest."

"Thank you." I squeeze his hand. He seems grateful for that. As he leaves, I close my eyes. I feel deeply sad.

Greta shuts the door behind her and rushes to me. I still can't see her clearly, but her lips are real on mine and her arms around me are sanctuary.

"I love you." I say the words that have been lying in wait all these months.

She holds me at arm's length, studying my face, waiting. Slowly, my eyes clear, but only for a moment. She's familiar in a way. A face I've known. Older, lined. Like my own a year ago. I've fallen in love with someone old. When I learn to use my hands as she uses hers, and have the delicate sense of touch I've yet to develop, I won't be feeling youthful skin beneath them. And I won't have a lifetime with her. Not *my* lifetime.

I pray my disappointment doesn't show. I think myself shallow and the sadness returns. If I had known, I don't know if I would have loved differently. If I could have. How little control we have over nature, even if, like Kenneth, we play God.

I open my arms to her. Her face nestles in my neck. I feel her tears, and too, for the first time, my own.

DAVID J. SCHOW
Last Call for the Sons of Shock

⚬━⧫━⚬

David J. Schow's short stories have been regularly selected for more than twenty-five volumes of Year's Best anthologies across three decades and have been awarded the World Fantasy Award and the ultra-rare Dimension Award from Twilight Zone *magazine, plus he won a 2002 International Horror Guild Award for his collection of* Fangoria *columns,* Wild Hairs.

His novels include The Kill Riff, The Shaft, Rock Breaks Scissors Cut, Bullets of Rain, Gun Work, Hunt Among the Killers of Men *(part of Hard Case Crime's Gabriel Hunt series),* Internecine, Upgunned *and* The Big Crush. *His short stories are collected in* Seeing Red, Lost Angels, Black Leather Required, Crypt Orchids, Eye, Zombie Jam *and* Havoc Swims Jaded.

He is the author of the exhaustively detailed Outer Limits Companion *and has written extensively for movies* (Leatherface: Texas Chainsaw Massacre III, The Crow) *and television* (Tales from the Crypt, Perversions of Science, The Hunger, Masters of Horror). *When a legendary movie poster artist asked him to write text for his next book of images, the result was* The Art of Drew Struzan.

You can see him talking and moving around on documentaries and DVDs for everything from Creature from the Black Lagoon, Incubus *and* The Shawshank Redemption *to* Scream and Scream Again *(a BBC4 special about the horror film boom of the 1980s available on YouTube),* Never Sleep Again, Beast Wishes *and* The Psycho Legacy.

"John Betancourt dared me to write a Frankenstein story for his anthology The Ultimate Frankenstein," *explains the author. "I told him it was a dopey idea. Twenty-four hours later I had the bare bones of 'Last Call for the Sons of Shock,' my smartass attempt to confuse John as to which of his three Ultimate anthologies* (Frankenstein, Dracula, Werewolf) *was the most suitable, thinking he'd give up and put the story in all three volumes.*

"Ultimately (pun intended), the story emerged as a thematic bookend to a previous story of mine, 'Monster Movies.' Craig Spector, John Skipp and I read it during a lecture gig at Vassar, among other places, with Craig reading the Dracula lines and John doing the Wolf Man. You had to be there . . ."

Blank Frank notches down the Cramps, keeping an eye on the blue LED bars of the equalizer. He likes the light. "Creature from the Black Leather Lagoon" calms.

The club is called Un/Dead. The sound system is from the guts of the old Tropicana, LA's altar of mud wrestling, foxy boxing and the cock-tease unto physical pain. Its specs are for metal, loud, lots of it.

The punch of the subwoofers is a lot like getting jabbed in the sternum by a big velvet piston.

Blank Frank likes the power. Whenever he thinks of getting physical, he thinks of the Vise Grip.

He perches a case of Stoli on one big shoulder and tucks another of Beam under his arm. After this he is done replenishing the bar. To survive the weekend crush, you've gotta arm. Blank Frank can lug a five-case stack without using a dolly. He has to duck to clear the lintel. The passage back to the phones and bathroom is tricked out to resemble a bank vault door, with tumblers and cranks. It is up past six-six. Not enough for Blank Frank, who still has to stoop.

Two hours till doors open.

Blank Frank enjoys his quiet time. He has not forgotten the date. He grins at the movie poster framed next to the backbar register. He scored it at a Hollywood memorabilia shop for an obscene price even though he got a professional discount. He had it mounted on foamcore to flatten the creases. He does not permit dust to accrete on the glass. The poster is duotone, with lurid lettering. His first feature film. Every so often some Un/Dead patron with cash to burn will make an exorbitant offer to buy it. Blank Frank always says no with a smile . . . and usually spots a drink on the house for those who ask.

He nudges the volume back up for Bauhaus, doing "Bela Lugosi's Dead," extended mix.

The staff sticks to coffee and iced tea. Blank Frank prefers a non-alcoholic concoction of his own devising, which he has christened a Blind Hermit. He rustles up one, now, in a chromium blender, one hand idly on his plasma globe. Michelle gave it to him about four years back, when they first became affordably popular. Touch the exterior and the purple veins of electricity follow your fingertips. Knobs permit you to fiddle with density and amplitude, letting you master the power, feel like Tesla showing off.

Blank Frank likes the writhing electricity.

By now he carries many tattoos. But the one on the back of his left hand—the hand toying with the globe—is his favorite: a stylized planet Earth, with a tiny propellored aircraft circling it. It is old enough that the cobalt-colored dermal ink has begun to blur.

Blank Frank has been utterly bald for three decades. A tiny wisp of hair issues from his occipital. He keeps it in a neat braid, clipped to six inches. It is dead white. Sometimes, when he drinks, the braid darkens briefly. He doesn't know why.

Michelle used to be a stripper, before management got busted, the club got sold and Un/Dead was born of the ashes. She likes being a waitress and she likes Blank Frank. She calls him "big guy." Half the regulars think Blank Frank and Michelle have something steamy going. They don't. But the fantasy detours them around a lot of potential problems, especially on weekend nights. Blank Frank has learned that people often need fantasies to *seem* superficially true, whether they really are or not.

Blank Frank dusts. If only the bikers could see him now, being dainty and attentive. Puttering.

Blank Frank rarely has to play bouncer whenever some booze-fueled trouble sets to brewing inside Un/Dead. Mostly, he just strolls up behind the perp and waits for him or her to turn around and apologize. Blank Frank's muscle duties generally consist of just *looming*.

If not, he thinks with a smile, there's always the Vise Grip.

The video monitor shows a Red Top taxicab parking outside the employee entrance. Blank Frank is pleased. This arrival coincides exactly with his finish-up on the bartop, which now gleams like onyx. He taps up the slide pot controlling the mike volume on the door's security system. There will come three knocks.

Blank Frank likes all this gadgetry. Cameras and shotgun mikes, amps and strobes and strong, clean alternating current to web it all in concert with maestro surety. Blank Frank loves the switches and toggles and running lights. But most of all, he loves the power.

Tap-tap-tap. Precisely. Always three knocks.

"Good," he says to himself, drawing out the vowel. As he hastens to the door, the song ends and the club fills with the empowered hiss of electrified dead air.

Out by limo. In by cab. One of those eternally bedamned scheduling glitches.

The Count overtips the cabbie because his habit is to deal only in round sums. He never takes . . . change. The Count has never paid taxes. He has cleared forty-three million large in the past year, most of it safely banked in bullion, out-of-country, after overhead and laundering.

The Count raps smartly with his umbrella on the service door of Un/Dead. Blank Frank never makes him knock twice.

It is a pleasure to see Blank Frank's face overloading the tiny security window, his huge form filling the threshold. The Count enjoys Blank Frank despite his limitations when it comes to social intercourse. It is relaxing to appreciate Blank Frank's conditionless loyalty, the innate tidal pull of honor and raw justice that seems programmed into the big fellow. Soothing, it is, to sit and drink and chat lightweight chat with him, in the autopilot way normals told their normal acquaintances where they'd gone and what they'd done since their last visit. Venomless niceties.

None of the buildings in Los Angeles has been standing as long as the Count and Blank Frank have been alive.

Alive. Now there's a word that begs a few new comprehensive, enumerated definitions in the dictionary. Scholars could quibble, but the Count and Blank Frank and Larry were definitely alive. As in "living"— *especially* Larry. Robots, zombies and the walking dead in general could never get misty about such traditions as this threesome's annual conclaves at Un/Dead.

The Count's face is mappy, the wrinkles in his flesh ricepaper fine. Not creases of age, but tributaries of usage, like the creeks and streams of palmistry. His pallor, as always, tends toward blue. He wears dark shades with faceted, lozenge-shaped lenses of apache tear; mineral crystal stained bloody-black. Behind them, his eyes, bright blue like a husky's. He forever maintains his hair wet and backswept, what Larry has called his "renegade opera conductor coif." Dramatic threads of pure cobalt-black streak backward from the snowwhite crown and temples. His lips are as thin and bloodless as two slices of smoked liver. His diet does not render him robustly sanguine; it merely sustains him, these days. It bores him.

Before Blank Frank can get the door open, the Count fires up a hand-rolled cigarette of coca paste and drags the milky smoke deep. It mingles with the dope already loitering in his metabolism and perks him up.

The cab hisses away into the wet night. Rain on the way.

Blank Frank is holding the door for him, grandly, playing butler.

The Count's brow is overcast. "Have you forgotten so soon, my friend?" Only a ghost of his old, marble-mouthed, middle-Euro accent lingers. It is a trait that the Count has fought for long years to master, and he is justly proud that he is intelligible. Occasionally, someone asks if he is from Canada.

Blank Frank pulls the exaggerated face of a child committing a big boo-boo. "Oops, sorry." He clears his throat. "Will you come in?"

Equally theatrically, the Count nods and walks several thousand worth of Armani double-breasted into the cool, dim retreat of the bar. It is *nicer* when you're invited, anyway.

"Larry?" says the Count.

"Not yet," says Blank Frank. "You know Larry—tardy is his twin. There's real time and Larry time. Celebrities *expect* you to expect them to be late." He points toward the backbar clock, as if that explains everything.

The Count can see perfectly in the dark, even with his murky glasses. As he strips them, Blank Frank notices the silver crucifix dangling from his left earlobe upside-down.

"You into metal?"

"I like the ornamentation," says the Count. "I was never too big on jewelry; greedy people try to dig you up and steal it if they know you're wearing it; just ask Larry. The sort of people who would come to thieve from the dead in the middle of the night are not the class one would choose for friendly diversion."

Blank Frank conducts the Count to three highback Victorian chairs he has dragged in from the lounge and positioned around a cocktail table. The grouping is directly beneath a pinlight spot, intentionally theatrical.

"Impressive." The Count's gaze flickers toward the bar. Blank Frank is way ahead of him.

The Count sits, continuing: "I once knew a woman who was beleaguered by a devastating allergy to cats. And this was a person who felt some deep emotional communion with that species. Then one day, poof!

She no longer sneezed; her eyes no longer watered. She could stop taking medications that made her drowsy. She had forced herself to be around cats so much that her body chemistry adapted. The allergy receded." He fingers the silver cross hanging from his ear, a double threat, once upon a time. "I wear this as a reminder of how the body can triumph. Better living through chemistry."

"It was the same with me and fire." Blank Frank hands over a very potent mixed drink called a Gangbang. The Count sips, then presses his eyelids contentedly shut. Like a cat. The drink must be industrial strength. Controlled substances are the Count's lifeblood.

Blank Frank watches as the Count sucks out another long, deep, soul-drowning draught. "You know Larry's going to ask again, whether you're still doing . . . what you're doing."

"I brook no apologia or excuses." Nevertheless, Blank Frank sees him straighten in his chair, almost defensively. "I could say that you provide the same service in this place." With an outswept hand, he indicates the bar. If nothing else remains recognizable, the Count's gesticulations remain grandiose: physical exclamation points.

"It's legal. Food. Drink. Some smoke."

"Oh, yes, there's the rub." The Count pinches the bridge of his nose. He consumes commercial decongestants ceaselessly. Blank Frank expects him to pop a few pills, but instead the Count lays out a scoop of toot inside his mandarin pinky fingernail, which is lacquered ebony, elongated, a talon. Capacious. Blank Frank knows from experience that the hair and nails continue growing long after death. The Count inhales the equivalent of a pretty good dinner at Spago. Capuccino included.

"There is no place in the world I have not lived," says the Count. "Even the Arctic. The Australian outback. The Kenyan sedge. Siberia. I walk unharmed through fire-fight zones, through sectors of strife. You learn so much when you observe people at war. I've survived holocausts, conflagration, even a low-yield one-megaton test, once, just to see if I could do it. Sue me; I was high. But wherever I venture, whatever phylum of human beings I encounter, they all have one thing in common."

"The red stuff." Blank Frank half-jests; he dislikes it when the mood grows too grim.

"No. It is their need to be narcotized." The Count will not be swerved. "With television. Sex. Coffee. Power. Fast cars and sado-games. Emotional encumbrances. More than anything else, with *chemicals*. All drugs are like instant coffee. The fast purchase of a feeling. You *buy* the feeling, instead of earning it. You want to relax, go up or go down, get strong or get stupid? You simply swallow or snort or inject, and the world changes because of you. The most lucrative commercial enterprises are those with the most undeniable core simplicity; just look at prostitution. Blood, bodies, armaments, position—all commodities. Human beings want so *much* out of life."

The Count smiles, sips. He knows that the end of life is only the beginning. Today is the first day of the rest of your death.

"I do apologize, my old friend, for coming on so aggressively. I've rationalized my calling, you see, to the point where it is a speech of lists; I make my case with demographics. Rarely do I find anyone who cares to suffer the speech."

"You've been rehearsing." Blank Frank recognizes the bold streak the Count gets in his voice when declaiming. Blank Frank has himself been jammed with so many hypos in the past few centuries that he has run out of free veins. He has sampled the Count's root-canal quality coke; it made him irritable and sneezy. The only drugs that still seem to work on him unfailingly are extremely powerful sedatives in large, near-toxic dosages. And those never last long. "Tell me. The drugs. Do they have any effect on *you*?"

He sees the Count pondering how much honesty is too much. Then the tiny, knowing smile flits past again, a wraith between old comrades.

"I employ various palliatives. I'll tell you the absolute truth: mostly it is an affectation, something to occupy my hands. Human habits—vices, for that matter—go a long way toward putting my customers at ease when I am closing negotiations."

"Now you're thinking like a merchant," says Blank Frank. "No royalty left in you?"

"A figurehead gig." The Count frowns. "Over whom, my good friend, would I hold illimitable dominion? Rock stars. Thrill junkies. Corporate monsters. No percentage in flaunting your lineage there. No. I occupy my time much as a fashion designer does. I concentrate on next season's line. I brought cocaine out of its Vin Mariani limbo and helped repopularize it in the Eighties. Then crank, then crack, then ice. Designer dope. You've heard of Ecstasy. You haven't heard of Chrome yet. Or Amp. But you will."

Suddenly a loud booming rattles the big main door, as though the entire DEA is hazarding a spot raid. Blank Frank and the Count are both twisted around in surprise. Blank Frank catches a glimpse of the enormous Browning Hi-Power holstered in the Count's left armpit.

It's probably just for the image, Blank Frank reminds himself.

The commotion sounds as though some absolute lunatic is kicking the door and baying at the moon. Blank Frank hurries over, his pulse relaxing as his pace quickens.

It has to be Larry.

"Gah-DAMN it's peachy to see ya, ya big dead dimwit!" Larry is a foot shorter than Blank Frank. Nonetheless, he bounds in, pounces, and suffocates his amigo in a big wolfy bear hug.

Larry is almost too much to take in with a single pair of eyes.

His skintight red Spandex tights are festooned with spangles and fringe that snake, at knee level, into golden cowboy boots. Glittering spurs on the boots. An embossed belt buckle the size of the grille on a Rolls. Larry is into ornaments, including a feathered earring with a skull of sterling, about a hundred metalzoid bracelets, and a three-finger rap ring of slush-cast 24K that spells out *AWOO*. His massive, pumped chest fairly bursts from a bright silver Daytona racing jacket, snapped at the waist but not zippered, so the world can see his collarless muscle tee in neon scarlet, featuring his caricature in yellow. Fiery letters on the shirt scream about THE REAL WOLF MAN. Larry is wearing his Ray-Bans at night and jingles a lot whenever he walks.

"Where's ole Bat Man? Yo! I *see* you skulking in the dark!" Larry whacks Blank Frank on the biceps, then lopes to catch the Count. With the Count, it is always a normal handshake—dry, firm, businesslike. "Off thy bunnage, fang-dude; the party has *arriiiived*!!"

"Nothing like having a real celebrity in our midst," says Blank Frank. "But jeez—what the hell is this *'Real'* Wolf Man crap?"

Larry grimaces as if from a gas pain, showing teeth. "A slight little ole matter of copyrights, trademarks, eminent domain . . . and some fuck-stick who *registered* himself with the World Wrestling Federation as 'The Wolfman.' Turns out to be a guy I bit, my ownself, a couple of decades ago. So I have to be 'The Real.' We did a tag-team thing, last Wrestlemania. But we can't think of a good team name."

"Runts of the Litter," opines the Count. Droll.

"Hellpups," says Blank Frank.

"Fuck ya both extremely much." Larry grins his trademark grin. Still showing teeth. He snaps off his shades and scans Un/ Dead. "What's to quaff in this pit? Hell, what *town* is this, anywho?"

"On tour?" Blank Frank plays host.

"Yep. Gotta kick Jake the Snake's ass in Atlanta next Friday. Gonna strangle him with Damien, if the python'll put up with it. Wouldn't want to hurt him for real but might have ole Jake pissing blood for a day, if you know what I mean."

Blank Frank grins; he knows what Larry means. He makes a fist with his left hand, then squeezes his left wrist tightly with his right hand. "Vise Grip him."

Larry is the inventor of the Vise Grip, second only to the Sleeper Hold in wrestling infamy. The Vise Grip has done Blank Frank a few favors with rowdies in the past. Larry owns the move, and is entitled to wax proud.

"I mean pissing *pure* blood!" Larry enthuses.

"Ecch," says the Count. "Please."

"Sorry, oh cloakless one. Hey! Remember that brewery, made about three commercials with the Beer Wolf before *that* campaign croaked and ate dirt? That was me!"

Blank Frank hoists his Blind Hermit. "Here's to the Beer Wolf, then. Long may he howl."

"*Prost,*" says the Count.

"Fuckin A." Larry downs his entire mugfull of draft in one slam-dunk. He belches, wipes foam from his mouth and lets go with a lupine *yee-hah.*

The Count dabs his lips with a cocktail napkin.

Blank Frank watches Larry do his thing and a stiff chaser of memory quenches his brain. That snout, the bicuspids and those beady, ball-bearing eyes will always give Larry away. His eyebrows ran together; that was supposed to be a classic clue in the good old days. Otherwise, Larry was not so hirsute. In human form, at least. The hair on his forearms was very fine tan down. Pumping iron and beating up people for a living has bulked out his shoulders. He usually wears his shirts open-necked. T-shirts, he tears the throats out. He is all piston-muscles and zero flab. He is able to squeeze a full beer can in one fist and pop the top with a gunshot bang. His hands are callused and wily. The pentagram on his right palm is barely visible. It has faded, like Blank Frank's tattoo.

"Cool," Larry says of the Count's crucifix.

"Aren't *you* wearing a touch as well?" The Count points at Larry's skull earring. "Or is it the light?"

Larry's fingers touch the silver. "Yeah. Guilty. Guess we haven't had to fret that movieland spunk for quite a piece, now."

"I had fun." Blank Frank exhibits his tat. "It was good."

"*Goood*," Larry and the Count say together, funning their friend.

All three envision the tiny plane in growly flight, circling a black and white world, forever.

"How long have you *had* that?" Larry is already on his second mug, foaming at the mouth.

Blank Frank's pupils widen, filling with his skin illustration. He does not remember.

"At least forty years ago," says the Count. "They'd changed the logo by the time he'd committed to getting the tattoo."

"Maybe that was why I did it." Blank Frank is still a bit lost. He touches the tattoo as though it will lead to a swirl dissolve and an expository flashback.

"Hey, we *saved* that fuckin' studio from bankruptcy." Larry bristles. "Us and A&C."

"They were shown the door, too." To this day, the Count is understandably piqued about the copyright snafu involving the use of his image. He sees his face everywhere, and does not rate compensation. This abrades his business instinct for the jugular. He understands too well why there must be a Real Wolf Man. "Bud and Lou and you and me and the big guy all went out with the dishwater of the Second World War."

"*I* was at Lou's funeral," says Larry. "You were lurking in the Carpathians." He turned to Blank Frank. "And *you* didn't even know about it."

"I loved Lou," says Blank Frank. "Did I ever tell you the story of how I popped him by accident on the set of—"

"*Yes.*" The Count and Larry speak in unison. This breaks the tension of remembrance tainted by the unfeeling court intrigue of studios. Recall the people, not the things.

Blank Frank tries to remember some of the others. He returns to the bar to rinse his glass. The plasma globe zizzes and snaps calmly, a man-made tempest inside clear glass.

"I heard ole Ace got himself a job at the Museum of Natural History." Larry refers to Ace Bandage; he has nicknames like this for everybody.

"The Prince," the Count corrects, "still guards the Princess. She's on display in the Egyptology section. The Prince cut a deal with museum security. He prowls the graveyard shift; guards the bone rooms. They've got him on a synthetic of tana leaves. It calmed him down. Like methadone."

"A night watchman gig," says Larry, obviously thinking of the low pay scale. But what in hell would the Prince need human coin for, anyway? "Hard to picture."

"Try looking in a mirror, yourself," says the Count.

Larry blows a raspberry. "Jealous."

It is very easy for Blank Frank to visualize the Prince, gliding through the silent, cavernous corridors in the wee hours. The museum is, after all, just one giant tomb.

Larry is fairly certain ole Fish Face—another nickname—escaped from a mad scientist in San Francisco and butterfly-stroked south, probably to wind up in bayou country. He and Larry had shared a solid mammal-to-amphibian simpatico. He and Larry had been the most physically violent of the old crew. Larry still entertained the notion of talking his scaly pal into doing a bout for pay-per-view. He has never been able to work out the logistics of a steel fishtank match, however.

"Griffin?" says the Count.

"Who can say?" Blank Frank shrugs. "He could be standing right here and we wouldn't know it unless he started singing 'Nuts in May.'"

"He was a misanthrope," says Larry. "His crazy kid, too. That's what using drugs will get you."

This last is a veiled stab at the Count's calling. The Count expects this from Larry, and stays venomless. The last thing he wants this evening is a conflict over the morality of substance use.

"I dream, sometimes, of those days," says Blank Frank. "Then I see the films again. The dreams are literalized. It's scary."

"Before *this* century," says the Count, "I never had to worry that anyone would stockpile my past." Of the three, he is the most paranoid where personal privacy is concerned.

"You're a romantic." Larry will only toss an accusation like this in special company. "It was important to a lot of people that we *be* monsters. You can't deny what's nailed down there in black and white. There was a time when the world *needed* monsters like that."

They each considered their current occupations, and found that they did indeed still fit into the world.

"Nobody's gonna pester you now," Larry presses on. "Don't bother to revise your past—today, your past is public record, and waiting to contradict you. We did our jobs. How many people become mythologically legendary for just doing their jobs?"

"Mythologically legendary?" mimicks the Count. "You'll grow hair on your hands from using all those big words."

"Bite this." Larry offers the unilateral peace symbol.

"No, thank you; I've already dined. But I have brought something for you. For both of you."

Blank Frank and Larry both notice the Count is now speaking as though a big Mitchell camera is grinding away, somewhere just beyond the grasp of sight. He produces a small pair of wrapped gifts, and hands them over.

Larry wastes no time ripping into his. "Weighs a ton."

Nestled in styro popcorn is a wolf's head—savage, streamlined, snarling. The gracile canine neck is socketed.

"It's from the walking stick," says the Count. "All that was left."

"No kidding." Larry's voice grows small for the first time this evening. The wolf's head seems to gain weight in his grasp. Two beats of his powerful heart later, his eyes seem a bit wet.

Blank Frank's gift is much smaller and lighter.

"You were a conundrum," says the Count. He enjoys playing emcee. "So many choices, yet never easy to buy for. Some soil from Transylvania? Water from Loch Ness? A chunk of some appropriate ruined castle?"

What Blank Frank unwraps is a ring. Old gold, worn smooth of its subtler filigree. A small ruby set in the grip of a talon. He holds it to the light.

"As nearly as I could discover, that ring once belonged to a man named Ernst Volmer Klumpf."

"Whoa," says Larry. Weird name.

Blank Frank puzzles it. He holds it toward the Count, like a lens.

"Klumpf died a long time ago," says the Count. "Died and was buried. Then he was disinterred. Then a few of his choicer parts were recycled by a skillful surgeon of our mutual acquaintance."

Blank Frank stops looking so blank.

"In fact, part of Ernst Volmer Klumpf is still walking around today . . . tending bar for his friends, among other things."

The new expression on Blank Frank's face pleases the Count. The ring just barely squeezes onto the big guy's left pinky—his smallest finger.

Larry, to avoid choking up, decides to make noise. Showing off, he vaults the bartop and draws his own refill. "This calls for a toast." He hoists his beer high, slopping the head. "To dead friends. Meaning us."

The Count pops several capsules from an ornate tin and washes them down with the last of his Gangbang. Blank Frank murders his Blind Hermit.

"Don't even think of the bill," says Blank Frank, who knows of the Count's habit of paying for everything. The Count smiles and nods graciously. In his mind, the critical thing is to keep the tab straight. Blank Frank pats the Count on the shoulder, hale and brotherly, since Larry is out of reach. The Count dislikes physical contact but permits this because it is, after all, Blank Frank.

"Shit man, we could make our own comeback sequel, with all the talent in this room," Larry says. "Maybe hook up with some of those new guys. Do a monster rally."

It could happen. They all look significantly at each other. A brief stink of guilt, of culpability, like a sneaky fart in a dimly lit chamber.

Make that dimly-lit *torture dungeon*, thinks Blank Frank, who never forgets the importance of staying in character.

Blank Frank thinks about sequels. About how studios had once jerked their marionette strings, compelling them to come lurching back for more, again and again, adding monsters when the brew ran weak, until they had all been bled dry of revenue potential and dumped at a bus stop to commence the long deathwatch that had made them nostalgia.

It was like living death, in its way.

And these gatherings, year upon year, had become sequels in their own right.

The realization is depressing. It sort of breaks the back of the evening for Blank Frank. He stands friendly and remains as chatty as he ever gets. But the emotion has soured.

Larry chugs so much that he has grown a touch bombed. The Count's chemicals intermix and buzz; he seems to sink into the depths of his coat, his chin ever-closer to the butt of the gun he carries. Larry drinks deep, then howls. The Count plugs one ear with a finger on his free hand. "I wish he wouldn't *do* that," he says in a proscenium-arch *sotto voce* that indicates his annoyance is mostly token.

When Larry tries to hurdle the bar again, moving exaggeratedly as he almost always does, he manages to plant his big wrestler's elbow right into the glass on Blank Frank's framed movie poster. It dents inward with a sharp crack, cobwebbing into a snap puzzle of fracture curves. Larry swears, instantly chagrined. Then, lamely, he offers to pay for the damage.

The Count, not unexpectedly, counter-offers to buy the poster, now that it's damaged.

Blank Frank shakes his massive square head at both of his friends. So many years, among them. "It's just glass. I can replace it. It wouldn't be the first time."

The thought that he has done this before depresses him further. He sees the reflection of his face, divided into staggered components in the broken glass, and past that, the lurid illustration. Him then. Him now.

Blank Frank touches his face as though it is someone else's.

His fingernails have always been black. Now they are merely fashionable.

Larry remains embarrassed about the accidental damage and the Count begins spot-checking his Rolex every five minutes or so, as though he is pressing the envelope on an urgent appointment. Something has spoiled the whole mood of their reunion, and Blank Frank is angry that he can't quite pinpoint the cause. When he is angry, his temper froths quickly. The Count is the first to rise. Decorum is all. Larry tries one more time to apologize. Blank Frank stays cordial, but is overpowered by the sudden strong need to get them the hell out of Un/Dead.

The Count bows stiffly. His limo manifests precisely on schedule. Larry gives Blank Frank a hug. His arms can reach all the way round.

"*Au revoir,*" says the Count.

"Stay dangerous," says Larry.

Blank Frank closes and locks the service door. He monitors, via the tiny security window, the silent, gliding departure of the Count's limousine, the fading of Larry's spangles into the night.

Still half an hour till opening. The action at Un/Dead doesn't really crank until midnight anyway, so there's very little chance that some bystander will get hurt.

Blank Frank bumps up the volume and taps his club foot. A eulogy with a beat. He loves Larry and the Count in his massive, broad, uncompromisingly loyal way, and hopes they will understand his actions. He hopes that his two closest friends are perceptive enough, in the years to come, to know that he is not crazy.

Not crazy, and certainly not a monster.

While the music plays, he fetches two economy-sized plastic bottles of lantern kerosene, which he ploshes liberally around the bar, saturating the old wood trim. Arsonists call such flammable liquids "accelerator."

In the scripts, it was always an overturned lantern, or a flung torch from a mob of villagers, that touched off the conclusive inferno. Mansions, mad labs, even stone fortresses burned and blew up, eliminating monster menaces until they were needed again.

Dark threads snake through the tiny warrior braid at the back of Blank Frank's skull. All those Blind Hermits.

The purple electricity arcs toward his finger and trails it loyally. He unplugs the plasma globe and cradles it beneath one giant forearm. The movie poster, he leaves hanging in its smashed frame.

He snaps the sulphur match with one black thumbnail. Ignition craters and blackens the head, eating it with a sharp hiss. Un/Dead's PA throbs with the bass line of "D.O.A." Phosphorus tangs the unmoving air. The match fires orange to yellow to a steady blue. The flamepoint reflects from Blank Frank's large black pupils. He can see himself, as if by candlelight, fragmented by broken picture glass. The past. In his grasp is the plasma globe, unblemished, pristine, awaiting a new charge. The future.

He recalls all of his past experiences with fire. He drops the match into the thin pool of accelerator glistening on the bartop. The flame grows quietly.

Good.

Light springs up, hard white, behind him as he exits and locks the door. The night is cool, near foggy. Condensation mists the plasma globe as he strolls away, pausing beneath a streetlamp to appreciate the ring on his little finger. He doesn't need to eat or sleep. He'll miss Michelle and the rest of the Un/ Dead folks. But he is not like them; he has all the time he'll ever need, and friends who will be around forever.

Blank Frank likes the power.

BRIAN MOONEY

Chandira

Brian Mooney has been contributing short stories to maga-
zines and anthologies for more than forty years, although he
has never been prolific.

His first short story, "The Arabian Bottle," appeared in
the London Mystery Selection *in 1971. Since then his fiction*
has appeared in such anthologies and magazines as The 21st
Pan Book of Horror Stories, Dark Voices 5, The Anthology of
Fantasy & the Supernatural, The Mammoth Book of Wolf
Men, Shadows Over Innsmouth, Dark Detectives, Final
Shadows, Fantasy Tales, Kadath *and* Dark Horizons.

"'Chandira' was another of those lucky tales which
appeared to me almost as written," reveals the author. "My
thinking on the tale started backwards with the two points

that most Frankenstein-type creations are things of pathos rather than horror, and so many horror films I've seen end with fire.

"I then got the idea of sati, *which may be acceptable amongst some Asian communities, but which is anathema to the Western mind. Next I saw the circumstance in which* sati *might be acceptable to a Westerner. My narrator had to be a European to see the ritual as alien, he had to be in a position of power, and he had to be young and independent enough not to be bound by inflexibility or the imposed rule of a senior.*

"Hence a young District Officer in the days of the British Raj, born in India so that he had a better understanding of the culture . . ."

I am an old man now and daily I think more and more about death. I think about death and then I recall certain events towards the end of the last century and I start to become frightened.

I am an old man, winter's damp chills gnaw at my bones and rack my joints and I curse the miserable climate of my supposed home land. Most evenings, even during the more clement months, I sit by a roaring fire and sip from a glass of fine malt whisky which helps to ease the aches. And sometimes the fire and the whisky evaporate my terror of death.

But I wasn't always so cold. Most of my life, save for when I was sent away to school, was spent under the torrid Indian sun which leathered my skin and thinned my blood. Nor did I always have a fear of dying. That didn't start until I was all of twenty years of age.

I was born near Poona, where my father was a district officer, and I grew up speaking Marati and Gujarati, dialects to which I was to add in later years. It therefore seemed the proper thing for me to enter the service when I became a man. Certainly India was more home to me than the bleak moors of my ancestors, and my return to the sub-continent as a very junior official was a great joy.

It was much the done thing in those long-ago days of the Raj to send young men like myself to remote stations. It was a way of testing our mettle, to see if we were fit for India and for eventual promotion to the higher grades. I often smirked when I heard the subalterns of the British Army complain of their hard lot. Most of them had only to worry about a suitable mount for the next bout of pig-sticking, or whether they could find a partner for the mess ball, or how to keep their rough and ready subordinates sane. At the age of twenty, I was controller, protector, adviser, tax-collector, administrator, magistrate, mediator, father-figure, all things to all men.

Sometimes now, more and more rarely, I go up to town to spend a day or two at my club. My fellow members like occasionally to hear tales of India from me and some of the younger ones josh me gently, asking about the rope trick and similar myths.

Forget the rope trick, for it is just that, a myth. I have seen fakirs perform strange acts, although these have been feats of physical endurance rather than supernatural demonstrations.

But I did once know a rishi—a holy man—whose powers far transcended such cheap displays. My recollections of that man are what scare me when I think of death. What I discovered of his capabilities impressed and terrified me to such an extent that I have never before told any person of them, mainly because I believed that I would be thought quite mad.

However, sixty years and more after the event, I don't much care what anyone thinks of me.

My sub-district covered perhaps two or three hundred square miles and contained a number of different villages. My supervisor, Barr-Taylor, was an older district officer who would call upon me once every two or three weeks to receive my reports, discuss problems, advise me where necessary, sometimes accompany me on visits around the territory. Most of the time I was left to my own devices, my sole aide being a fiercely dignified old Baluchi Pathan named Mushtaq Khan.

It was during one of Barr-Taylor's visits that I first heard of the rishi. My senior had decided to stay the night, probably to satisfy himself that I was adept at the social graces, district officers at times having to entertain passing dignitaries.

We were sitting on the veranda before dinner, sipping at our gins-and-tonic, listening to a multitude of night-noises and chatting about things in general.

We had been discussing my program of visits and Barr-Taylor said, "Tell me, Rowan, have you been out to Katachari yet?"

Katachari was one of the nearest villages to my HQ but I had not yet visited the place. I had chosen rather to go to the farthest communities first, believing that those nearby would know of me through the local gossip and could attend me more readily if my help was needed.

I explained this to Barr-Taylor who said, "Take my tip, see the place as soon as possible. The local zamindar's name is Gokul. Give him my compliments when you meet, we're old friends. But it's not really Gokul I want you to meet. There's a rishi in the village, fellow called Aditya."

He offered a cheroot and we lit up, blowing clouds of noxious smoke at the ferocious mosquitoes which were just starting their evening forays.

"Very interesting man, Aditya," my senior continued. "He turned up in Katachari a few years ago, told the locals that it was his destiny to die there. As you'd expect, they were deeply honored, welcomed him, built a small home for him and his wife, they've looked after him ever since. Of course, there is an element of quid pro quo, the rishi being expected to pray for the village, intercede with the deities, comfort the sick and the old, that sort of thing.

"You were born in India, Rowan, so I'm not trying to teach you things you don't know. I'd guess you're thinking there's nothing very unusual about this, it's a common enough occurrence. But Aditya is different. He claims to be over two hundred years old, says that his extraordinary willpower has kept him alive. Now I'm not saying that I believe this, but he's assuredly very well on in years and he speaks of certain events as if he was an eyewitness, describes them very convincingly. There does seem to be an inexplicable power about the man. I've been in the service for thirty-odd years now, and Aditya manages to make me feel like a callow youth."

Barr-Taylor pulled a face and drew deeply on his cigar. "There's something else," he admitted, "I have to confess that although he has given me no reason, there is something about Aditya that frightens me."

He stabbed a skinny forefinger at me for emphasis. "Don't delay, Rowan, go to Katachari as soon as you can. This is your district, and if there are likely to be any problems, then you should be aware of them."

Barr-Taylor raised his head and sniffed. "Is that korma I can smell? Let's go and see what Mushtaq Khan's got for dinner, shall we?"

I'm not saying that at that time I accepted all of what Barr-Taylor had told me. Hindu holy men, both rishis and saddhus, are commonplace in India, as are Buddhist monks. Some are itinerant, some tend to stay in one place, but all are reliant on the charity of others, and that charity is usually generous. However, the district officer had whetted my curiosity more than a little.

So at the earliest opportunity, I rode out to visit Katachari. As always, Mushtaq Khan accompanied me, alert that I should not come to harm. When first appointed to my district, I had protested to the old warrior that I would be perfectly safe in my travels, that I was sure the people would respect me.

"That may well be, Rowan-sahib," Mushtaq Khan had growled, "I doubt not that your God and mine will watch over you. And yet it will do no harm for you to be seen in my company. The sight of a Pathan is an excellent way of reinforcing respect among these unbelievers."

I had to admit he was right. When he rode high in the saddle, moustaches bristling, vicious curved dagger at his belt, and long Martini-Henry rifle balanced before him, he was fully capable of reinforcing my own respect. I felt that together we could have seen off the worst band of dacoits.

The way to Katachari led through forest, at times quite dense, in other places thinning out so that the path before us was dappled emerald and bronze and saffron by filtered sunlight. It was cooler here beneath the leafy canopy and the air was heady with fragrances of bright flowers and ripening fruits and the mulch of decaying vegetation. Above us flittered jewel-like birds, their cries tolling to their mates, while monkeys squabbled amongst themselves and scolded us when we passed.

Our conversation tended to be one-sided. Mushtaq Khan talked and I listened. While ostensibly his superior, I had the sense to know that I could learn much from the old man and I'm sure that everything he said to me was intended to impart some lesson. I wasn't his first sprog and I sometimes marvelled at his limitless patience.

We were probably about three-quarters of the way to Katachari when I began to catch glimpses of what looked like a stone building farther back among the trees.

"What's that?" I asked Mushtaq Khan, pointing towards the structure.

"An ancient Hindu temple, sahib," the Pathan told me. "It was left to the jungle many years ago, long, long before the coming of the sahibs."

"I'd like to take a look," I said. Mushtaq shrugged and tugged at the reins, guiding his horse to follow mine.

At one time, lord knows how many centuries previously, the temple must have stood within a considerable clearing, but now the forest had inexorably reclaimed its own. The grey, weathered stone was gripped by tangles of twisted, verdant branches and crawling vines, and bright blossoms hung from plants which had set themselves and taken life in the crumbling mortar between the gigantic blocks.

As is common with Hindu temples, the edifice was lavishly decorated with row upon row of sculpted figures depicting scenes from their mythology. Gods and warriors struggled, locked in combat until the stones finally crumbled. Nautch girls and courtesans and temple maidens allured, their time-weary enticements frozen and eroding.

Several rows of statuary at the friezes were brazenly erotic and I think I flushed, torn by the conflicting pressures of a young man's lusts and the restrictions of the society in which I was raised.

The focal point, above what probably had been the main entrance to the temple, was a carving much larger than all of the others. I believed it to be of Prithivi, the Hindu earthgoddess, the goddess of fertility. She smiled gently down upon me, her arms extended in welcome. By chance, nature had adorned the goddess with gorgeous hibiscus flowers, lending almost an illusion of fruitfulness.

I think more than anything I was struck by a great sense of peace in this place. And then, almost lost in myself, I was disturbed by a grumpy snort. I turned, to catch a slight frown on the face of the elderly Pathan. I had momentarily overlooked the Moslem disapproval of what they consider idolatry.

I covered by taking out my watch and glancing at the time.

"Yes, very interesting, Mushtaq Khan," I said, "but I really think that we'd better hurry on to Katachari."

I still sometimes wonder if the glint in his eye then had been approval or amusement at the transparency of the young sahib.

We reached the village about half-an-hour later, the forest thinning and clearing as we passed the huts of harijans—the Untouchables—and then those of the poorer farmers. We turned onto a wider road and our route became more busy. Men stooped under the weight of bundles, drivers of ox-carts, women in butterfly colors bearing laundry to the river, elders sitting in the shade, all called out greetings to us as we rode by them. Children began to tag onto us. The closer into the village we came, the longer became our train of frolicking urchins, happily ignoring Mushtaq Khan's admonitions to respect the sahib's dignity.

We guided our horses towards the village square and I was assailed by the odors of dust and frying spices and cattle dung and all those other wonderful smells of India.

A small group of men awaited, their manner respectful. When we had dismounted, one of them came forward, making namaste. "At last, Rowan-Sahib, I am honored to welcome you to Katachari. I am Gokul, the headman and landlord."

I returned Gokul's greetings and conveyed the good wishes of Barr-Taylor. I was quickly introduced to the others, a mixed group of men who comprised the village council. Within minutes all were seated and drinking hot, sweet tea as we discussed matters important to the village and the region. Three men sat slightly apart: two Brahmins whose caste disallowed close contact with non-Hindus, and Mushtaq Khan, guided more by his warrior alertness than by his distaste for infidels.

Then without warning, my hosts fell silent and slowly the councilmen rose to their feet, bowing their heads as they did so. Behind me, I heard an old and dry voice saying, "Enough of such mundane matters, Gokul, I am sure Rowan-sahib hears them daily and to whom is farming of any interest save another farmer? Anyway, I believe the sahib was advised to make this journey to meet me."

I, too, rose and turned to face the speaker. When I looked at him, I felt a breathless shock as if I had suddenly been plunged into an ice-cold bath. Aditya was small in stature and, in common with most holy men, very thin. He was clad in a white robe, and long white hair and beard cascaded down his body. But it was the deeply-shadowed, hypnotic eyes and the sense of sheer power emanating in waves from the man which held and enthralled.

Instinctively, I lowered my head, placing my palms together and making namaste to the holy man. I surprised myself in doing this, for protocol was that I should have been greeted first. Even greater was my surprise when I saw, from the corner of my eye, Mushtaq Khan also bowing and making salaam.

The rishi placed his hands over mine. "Come, my son, we will go to my home and talk." He turned and I followed without further bidding. Again I was astounded at the reaction of Mushtaq Khan who, instead of following at his usual discreet distance, resumed his seat and took up his tea.

The rishi's home was small and simple, as would have been expected. I had to stoop to pass through the low portal into the single room, poorly illuminated by lighted wicks floating in dishes of oil. The air was thick with the sweetness of the many smoldering incense sticks balanced in ornate brass holders which were scattered about the floor. And there was another underlying odor that I could not identify. Perhaps it was the smell of old age.

I could see at a glance that the place was sparsely furnished. Two single charpoys were positioned at opposite sides of the room, each furnished with a light blanket. There was a low table and several stools, while at the rear was a small stove and a number of clay cooking pots. There were niches in the mud walls which held statuettes of deities.

As we entered, a woman came silently to her feet and stood with her eyes cast down. Like Aditya, she was clothed entirely in white, but her garb was not the usual sari. Instead, she wore a burkha, the all-enveloping garb worn by most Moslem women. A veil was drawn across her face. Only her eyes, hands and feet were visible.

"Welcome to my home, Rowan-sahib," said the rishi, "this is Chandira, my wife." Turning to the woman, he added, "Bring chai for our guest, Chandira."

As the woman moved to the stove to make her preparations, the rishi gestured me to a stool before taking up the lotus position on one of the charpoys. He closed his eyes, apparently as a signal that until the niceties were observed we should refrain from conversation.

I took the opportunity to study the man. He was certainly unlike other holy men I had experienced. Not counting the Brahmin priests, there are two kinds of Hindu holy men: the rishis, who may marry if they wish, and the saddhus, the celibates.

If most people have a mental picture of Hindu holy men, it will probably be of the saddhus. They are the itinerants, the ones who travel naked or near naked, their bodies covered in ashes and dust. Many of them mortify the flesh as an offering to their pantheon of gods. But even the rishis will often maltreat themselves to demonstrate spirituality.

Aditya was clean, and to the casual glance seemed quite normal other than for his ascetic spareness. He was old, but more than two hundred? I doubted it.

I was startled from reverie by the woman's sudden appearance at my side as she set down tea and a dish of fruit slices. My senses were overwhelmed by the richly musky perfume with which she seemed to have dowsed herself. While not in itself unpleasant, the scent was cloying. I did not look at her too closely as I thanked her, being sensible of how easily I could give offense. I did notice rather beautiful eyes and elegant hands. Then she moved back to a corner and squatted mute on the earthen floor.

Aditya's eyes snapped open and seemed to penetrate my own. Then it was as if they filmed over and he gestured an invitation to the refreshments.

I sipped at the tea, which relaxed me a little and could not restrain my curiosity. "Your wife, Aditya-Sahib, is she a Moslem?" Such mixed marriages were not common, but neither were they unknown.

"A Moslem?" He glanced over at the woman. "No, she is not a Moslem." He smiled. "You have no wife, Rowan-sahib." It was not a question.

"No, sir." The rishi continued to stare at me and I felt somehow that I had to explain. "It's not our custom for a young man making his way in the world to marry. We believe that his career comes first."

"How very strange." Aditya selected a slice of orange and nibbled on it. "Young men of your race are placed in positions of great importance, of great responsibility, so that you may satisfy the urges of the mind, and yet at this time of your possibly greatest potency, you are expected to ignore the more natural urges of flesh. Tell me, Rowan-sahib, do you not find yourself frustrated by the unanswered cry of your loins? Do you not find yourself longing for the soft, naked body of a loving and compliant woman to comfort you in the long hours of the night?"

I thought again of those erotic carvings on the Prithivi temple in the forest and felt my face grow hot. I was thankful for the poor light in the rishi's home, thankful that my embarrassment was not visible to him. "Excuse me, Rishi-sahib, it is not our way to discuss such matters," I prevaricated, wishing that he would let the matter drop.

The holy man laughed, a crackling, raspy noise which was not too pleasant. "Such a young race, such children," he mused. "Now I have been married very many times, for is it not the natural way of life? Certain of my wives were more precious to me than others. Let me tell you of my favorites, let me tell you of the erotic pleasure that each one had to offer a man."

He raised his cup, slurping noisily at his tea. "Kumud had fair looks, great beauty. Her face was a perfect oval, with flesh like that of a fresh peach bearing traces of morning dew. Her eyes held the promise of heaven and her yoni fulfilled that promise.

"Radhika was the daughter of a Kashmiri Brahmin, with light skin, little darker than that of a sahib. Hers was the body which most delighted my senses. From neck to upper thighs she was perfect, with breasts . . . I think your own holy book is most eloquent when it likens the loved one's breasts to young roes feeding among the lilies. Her body hair was plucked, in the fashion of the ancient nobility, so that but a slim arrow showed the way to paradise and such a paradise, sahib, such a paradise."

Quite frankly, I didn't know where to put myself, hearing this talk which seemed to me to be so appallingly candid. I glanced frantically towards the woman, Chandira. The rishi correctly interpreted my hint, but his only reaction was to repeat that arid laugh. "Do not fret that my wife is shocked, Rowan-sahib. Is she not an Indian woman? Talk of sensual pleasures is not anathema to us.

"Now, where was I? Ah, my favorite wives. The loveliest, longest limbs were those of Shamin and Phoolan. Shamin's arms could draw a man close so it was as if being was melting into being. And Phoolan's legs were strong, like pythons, clasping a man to her as he entered, relaxing not until the course was run for both."

The rishi's eyes held me, and his smile seemed to mock my innocence. Selecting another piece of fruit, he continued, "Harpal was blind, and from an early age she had been trained in the art of massage. Her hands and feet were beautiful, well cared for, strong and delicate. They could coax from a man's well more than he believed himself to contain, so that his essence was as a perpetual fountain.

"These, then, Rowan-sahib, were the most-favored of my many wives." He thrust his head forward, one eyebrow raised sardonically, as if to ask my opinion of his marital history.

Compelled to say something, if only as a necessity to disguise my discomfiture, I asked, "How can a man have had so many wives in one lifetime?"

Yet again, the laugh, which was beginning to make me shiver. "One lifetime? How old do you think I am, young man?"

I hesitated, and Aditya snapped, "Then Barr-Taylor has already told you, and yet neither of you believe."

"How did you know what Barr-Taylor-sahib told me?" I demanded.

"I have powers beyond the extent of your reasoning. As you sat on your veranda, smoking and drinking, he told you that I am more than two hundred years old. This is true, sahib. Indeed, I am very much more than that. I was blessed with an inexorable will, a gift from the gods which has enabled me to defy death."

Aditya changed tack suddenly, his tone becoming less intense, more gentle. "Rowan-sahib, for me the two most powerful forces are those of sex and death, and thus far I have been in total control of both. Despite my great age, I am proud that Chandira and myself still enjoy frequent and vigorous couplings."

He gestured around the room. "Look about you, young sahib, look at the gods I keep in my dwelling. There is Prithivi, and yonder sits Yama, King of the dead. Here is Kama, controller of our desires, and there and there, Shiva and Kali, the Destroyers.

"But even I cannot defer death forever." The rishi smiled ruefully, "Which is why I have settled in this village, for it is my fate to end my days here."

Aditya stood abruptly. "Come with me, Rowan-sahib. I will give you a demonstration of my power over death." He had exited before I realized it.

At the doorway, I turned to thank the rishi's wife for her hospitality. My words were awkward for I was still shaken by Aditya's frankness in front of the woman.

After the inner gloom, the sunlight dazzled and the rishi took my arm to guide me. As we walked, he murmured, "There will be a service you can perform for me, sahib."

"Of course, if I can. What is it?"

"You will know when the time comes," he replied. "Ah, I think this will do."

He had led me to the far edge of the village and I became aware of a disgusting stink nearby.

Stepping a few yards into the fringes of the jungle, Aditya kicked aside some heavy grasses to reveal the rotting corpse of a pi-dog. A great cloud of flies arose and with them the smothering stench of death and corruption. The body had an oddly collapsed look about it and I noticed a long trail of ants coming and going from the anal region. Ribs were laid bare and shreds of ripped innards exposed where some small scavenger had been burrowing. The sockets were empty, the eyes no doubt pecked away by crows.

"I think you will agree that this dog is dead, Rowan-sahib?"

"Disgustingly so," I said, holding my handkerchief to my nose and mouth, trying to refrain from gagging.

"Then please, stand back a few yards and observe what happens."

I moved back as requested and carefully watched the rishi. He became motionless and his eyes rolled back until only the whites showed. It was hideously still, for even the normal forest cacophony had quieted. Then I heard a curious grunting noise and my attention was drawn towards the pi-dog.

The dead creature was lurching to its feet, its movements stiff and feeble, like those of a badly-strung puppet. Having gained a precarious standing position, it turned and began to stagger towards me, remnant of tail wagging half-heartedly. A swollen, blackened tongue, partly gnawed by something, lolled from the side of its mouth, and the blind holes gazed into my face. Deep in the sockets, I could see writhing nests of maggots and . . .

. . . And I think it was then that I yelled like a banshee and ran. I was in a blue funk and I'm not ashamed to admit to it.

I ran back through the village square, where Mushtaq Khan still sat with the leaders, dashed to my horse and galloped away. I was to find later that the poor creature was badly marked where I had spurred it so savagely, something I had never done to a horse before.

The Pathan caught up with me about a mile or so down the road, catching at my reins and pulling my horse to a halt. "What is it, sahib, what ails you?"

"The holy man . . . he . . ." I shook my head. "I cannot tell you, Mushtaq Khan. He . . . showed me something. It's enough of a burden for me. I just want to forget, and I never want to see the rishi again."

"Come, sahib, come with me. Let us go to a place of peace." And probably against all of his instincts, the old Pathan led me to that temple in the jungle where I stayed for a long time, staring at the welcoming goddess and trying to find some mental peace.

Life went on. I wrote Barr-Taylor a brief report of my visit to Katachari, mentioning that Aditya had welcomed me into his home. I omitted all reference to the rishi's conversation and nothing would have compelled me to mention the dead dog.

I immersed myself in work, went up country to visit other places, did anything I could to forget that dreadful experience. For a few weeks I had intermittent nightmares, usually involving dead animals, then they faded away. Gradually, as I overcame my horror, I persuaded myself of something that I should have thought of in the first instance. I became convinced that the rishi had somehow drugged or hypnotized me.

I was in my office one evening, smoking a cigar and sipping at a glass of lime juice as I struggled to balance my monthly accounts. It was stiflingly hot and the lazy flapping of the punkah did little to stir the air. I could not be bothered to urge greater efforts from the young lad paid a few annas to perform this menial task. He was probably as jaded by the heat as I was.

I stood up to stretch and to ease the aching muscles around my neck and shoulders, when I became aware of something out of the corner of my eye. I turned and found myself staring at the rishi, although how he had entered the room so quietly I have no notion. His palms were together in namaste, his eyes were closed, and there was a slight smile on his face. Then as I was about to greet him, somewhat irascibly, he faded from sight and I was faced by nothing more than a cornerful of shadows.

"*Sweet Jesus!*" The sweat on my body turned to ice as I lurched across the room to the drinks cabinet. Then came my next shock. As I fumbled with the top of the whisky bottle, I heard a scratching noise outside, on the other side from the veranda. Almost without thinking, I snatched my Webley pistol from the drawer where I kept it and threw back the shutters.

Staring in at me was the startled face of Yasim, an elderly harijan employed to tend the grounds around my bungalow. I snatched breath in sheer relief.

"Yasim! What are you doing out there? Why lurk about like a sneak thief? You must know that if you wish to see me you need only knock at the door. What is it you want, man?"

My visitor shook his head urgently and raised a finger to his lips. "I should not be here, Rowan-sahib, for there is great danger for me. I am come to tell you of a rumor that is rife in the district. They say that the rishi, Aditya, is very near to death. It may even be that he is gone now."

I cannot say that I was greatly disturbed by this news. The mention of the holy man's name brought back that scene of horror at the forest's edge, and my instinct was that the sooner he died the better.

Then I remembered the rishi's words. "There will be a service you can perform for me . . . you will know what it is when the time comes." The apparition, vision, hallucination, whatever it was that I had just experienced. Had this been some kind of telepathy? Had this been the rishi's way of calling on my services?

"I must go to Katachari, then," I said. "Aditya-sahib will wish me to attend the funeral rites, to represent the Raj."

There was a frightened look in the gardener's eyes. "Sahib, if ever asked, I will deny having told you this, such is the peril. I have to tell you the same rumors whisper that the holy man's wife intends to become *sati.*"

Sati. The word chilled me. I knew of it—who born and raised in India did not? Which well-read person or seasoned traveler did not shudder at the hideous and alien concept? Which district officer in the land did not pray that he would never encounter it?

Sati. A Sanskrit word. Literally, it means a virtuous woman. In practice, it means the self-immolation of a Hindu widow on her husband's funeral pyre for, it is held, why would a virtuous woman wish to survive her husband? And it need not always be *self*-immolation, for it had been known for reluctant widows to be bound and cast into the flames.

The practice had been outlawed some sixty or seventy years previously, but it was tacitly accepted that it continued in remoter places. Now it was to happen in Katachari and it was my duty to stop it.

Early in the morning I arose before anyone else and sneaked out of the bungalow. I saddled my horse and led the beast a good distance away before I mounted and began to ride.

I reached Katachari as the villagers were stirring. Plumes of smoke from early morning fires formed thin columns in the air and I could smell naan-bread baking and tea brewing. I had heard the sounds of chatter among families and neighbors but these fell silent as I rode into the square. I saw a boy running to Gokul's home and moments later the zamindar was scurrying towards me, a small crowd at his heels.

"Rowan-sahib!" His voice sounded anxious. "What are you doing here? And so early in the day?"

"Katachari is part of my district, is it not?" I demanded haughtily. "Surely I have the right to visit when I wish?"

Gokul lowered his eyes and muttered, "Yes, sahib."

"Anyway, I have heard that the rishi is unwell and I have come to pay my respects."

Gokul sighed. "Then I regret that the Rowan-sahib has made a wasted journey, for the holy man died several hours ago. The funeral is to be held at dawn tomorrow. There will be no need for you to stay now, sahib."

"I am sad to hear this," I lied. "I must then, of course, pay my respects to the rishi's widow."

"That would be most unseemly."

I stared hard at the man. "I don't see why," I told him. "In my country, it is an obligation to condole with a widowed person. I am a representative of the Queen-Empress, and it is her respects which I bear. Surely there is nothing wrong with that, Gokul-sahib?"

Gokul looked around frantically at his cronies, but it seemed that none wished to give him support.

"Anyway," I added, bending the truth somewhat, "it was the rishi's own wish that I do him the service of seeing that all is well with his widow. He told me this himself when we met. You would not wish to go against Aditya's own will."

The zamindar gave in with bad grace and led me to Aditya's hut. Chandira was waiting at the doorway, as if she was expecting me. She was still wearing the burkha and veil. As I neared, she made namaste and said, "You are welcome, Rowan-sahib, please enter our home."

Gokul made as if to wait at the entrance but I stared hard at him until, with obvious bad grace, he made off. Waiting only to ensure that he had truly gone, I accepted Chandira's invitation.

It seemed that even more incense sticks were being burned within the dwelling, and that Chandira had used rather more of her heady perfume than previously. This was understandable, though, for beneath the richness of the scents I caught a faint whiff of death.

I looked around for Chandira and saw that she had taken up position at the far side of the room by the small stove upon which flickered a small fire.

Aditya's white-clad corpse lay on his charpoy, arms resting by the sides, a garland of variegated flowers about the neck. I stepped over and gazed down. The rishi's flesh had assumed a greyish pallor, while the eyelids and cheeks were already beginning to fall in. I studied the lines and folds on that dead face and suddenly I had an inkling that Aditya's claims for greatly advanced age might well be true.

I turned to Chandira, deciding that this was not the time for the customary florid overtures. I was blunt. "I hear gossip that you wish to become *sati.*"

The woman inclined her covered head a little. "Not gossip but truth, Rowan-sahib," she told me.

I sighed heavily and sat down on one of the stools. "Why do this thing?"

"It is what I wish for, more than anything in the world."

I made a contemptuous gesture at Aditya's still form. "You mean it's what he wished for."

"No, it is *my* wish, my desire even." Chandira shook her head. *"He* died without even having expressed an opinion about it. If it was a matter of *his* wish, and I was able, I might well defy it, for he has used me ill and I have good reason to detest him."

"You know that *sati* is outlawed," I said. "And that it is my duty to prevent your death."

"Perhaps I can persuade the sahib that I should be allowed to do this thing." Chandira lowered her veil, showing to me a face of sublime beauty, a face which could have been that of a temple statue given life. Dark and fascinating eyes were lined with kohl and rich, full lips were painted scarlet. I felt breath tightening in my chest.

She took away the covering from her head and then started to loosen her gown.

I found myself torn between a well of longing and a flame of indignation. Chandira was about to offer me the use of her body now in exchange for her right to die tomorrow.

The lonely young man in me wanted to leap up and clasp her in my arms. The well-trained bureaucrat suppressed the young man.

"Stop this now, Chandira!" I snapped. "My duty is clear and I will not let you seduce me from it!"

She paused, and then she laughed. It was a sad, empty noise which made me feel immensely foolish and pompous.

"Be at ease, Rowan-sahib," she told me. "I have no intention of offering you love, or even the sham of love. But I must show you, so that you understand."

Moments later the burkha fell about her feet and she stood there naked. Something in her tone of voice had chilled me, and now I was able to gaze at her without desire.

Chandira's form was graceful, alluring, but in that dim light it seemed somehow to be disproportionate. There also appeared to be some disparity

517

in the flesh tints, and many parts of her body—her neck, for instance, and at the joints—were encircled by weird, bangle-like tattoos. She walked towards me, until just inches separated us.

She offered her right hand and against my will I took it in one of mine. Her palm was silken soft and surprisingly cool. With her free hand she indicated the marking about her wrist.

"Look closely, sahib."

I did so, then I rose quickly to my feet and gripped the woman by the arms. She stood passive as I examined the other tattoos.

But those were no tattoos. They were broad bands of stitches, hundreds of fine, close, delicate sutures layered over faint, long-healed scars.

I heard again Aditya's voice, a mocking remembrance. "Kumud had fair looks . . . Radhika's was the body which most delighted my senses . . . Shamin's arms . . . Phoolan's legs . . . Harpal's hands and feet . . ."

I dropped my hands from Chandira and stepped back, hoping that my sudden horror was ill-founded. "It's not possible . . . ," I muttered.

A tear spilled from the corner of an eye, slipping its sad course down the woman's cheek. "No, it is not possible . . . but it is true. Chandira is the name he gave to this . . . creation . . . He could not bring himself to let his favorites rest in peace and so he used the best attributes of each to give life to . . . Chandira."

I slumped back onto the stool. It was either that or perhaps faint. "But how . . . ," I floundered.

"He told both of you, you and Barr-Taylor-sahib, of his willpower, of how he could conquer death. Over the years, he told many sahibs. None believed him. He frightened you with a demonstration, but no doubt you thought that he had mesmerized you.

"After the death of each favorite, his willpower held the . . . essentials . . . from corruption. He held them over the years until he had sufficient to join as one and breathe life into her. Such was his power that I live now, even beyond his own death. But that willpower is slowly waning."

She held out her hand again, this time placing it delicately beneath my nostrils. At first there was only the musk of her perfume, and then I noticed that beneath the exotic fragrance was another aroma, the slightest hint of decay. The suggestion of death in the hut did not come from Aditya's remains alone.

I got up and walked from Chandira's home without another word. Gokul was waiting by my horse. He asked me something but I don't know what it was. I made some sort of non-committal comment and rode from the village.

When I reached that half-hidden jungle temple, I reined in and clambered down from the horse. I had some thought that perhaps Prithivi could help solve my dilemma. My old school chaplain would have been shocked. Army chaplains in barracks all over India would be shocked. And Mushtaq Khan, if he knew, would throw a blue fit. But, I reasoned, this was a Hindu matter, and a Hindu goddess was better qualified than God or Jesus or Allah to help.

I stepped through the trees and came to where the goddess sat. Something was different here now. The petals woven about Prathivi had faded and withered, like a dotard's skin, and as I gazed a great insect crawled from one of the stony nostrils, weaving about in parody of a blindly feasting grave-worm.

I was up early again the next day. This time, as I stepped from the bungalow, strapping on my Webley in its large holster, Mushtaq Khan was waiting for me.

"Where are you going this time, sahib?"

"I must go to Katachari on urgent business," I told him. "There will be no need for you to come."

"If you hope to stop the *sati* single-handed, Rowan-sahib, then you are a very foolish young man," the Pathan told me. He folded his arms across his chest and glowered at me. "Allah knows that these Hindus are little better than sheep, but when their beliefs are interfered with they are very dangerous sheep.

"And you, Rowan-sahib, are stubborn, as stubborn as any young warrior from my own hills. If I were your father, I would be concerned. Concerned and . . . proud. I will not be able to sway you from your duty, so do not try to sway me from mine. Come, sahib, our horses are saddled and ready."

Katachari was quiet and deserted when we reached it, the only life to be seen or heard; a few pi-dogs, some poultry searching the dust for tit-bits, the odd raucous crow.

Mushtaq Khan pointed beyond the village. "The burning ground is about a mile that way," he said. We rode on.

A little way on we began to hear a low, rhythmic drone. Although not yet fully audible, it was a sound filled with foreboding. The farther we rode, the louder the drone became, until at last it was clear. It was the chanting of many voices, a repetitious, hypnotic, *"Ram-ram . . . ram-ram . . . ram-ram . . ."*

At length we came upon the thickly-clustered chanting crowd. There were many more than belonged to Katachari: people must have traveled from great distances around to attend the cremation. From our vantage point on horseback, we could see clearly over their heads.

The funeral pyre—a platform of interwoven sticks and branches soaked in ghee—was about head height, roughly the same length, and perhaps four feet wide. The corpse, blanketed with great masses of flowers, rested on the top, and Chandira knelt at its head, hands clasped before her. She had discarded the burkha for a plain white sari. The area was filled with the combined stenches of decomposition and ghee.

We dismounted and approached slowly. Some of the mourners at the back of the crowd had seen us and glared threateningly.

I unstrapped my pistol and handed it to Mushtaq Khan. "Wait for me here," I instructed.

"They'll tear you to pieces, sahib!" he protested.

"Wait for me," I repeated. I clasped the old man's shoulders. "It will be all right."

"Very well, sahib." His hawk's eyes glared and his tone was grudging. He laid one hand upon his dagger and brandished my pistol with the other. "But let one of those unbelievers raise a hand against you and they'll find what it means to have the Pathans fall upon them," he growled. "If we die, we die together giving a good account."

I pushed my way into the crowd which parted before me. I think it was bravado that carried me through, that and their astonishment at my foolhardiness. I reached the pyre where the Brahmin priests were chanting their prayers. Gokul stood to one side clutching a burning faggot of wood. As I reached them, the prayers turned to cries of outrage.

I held out a hand. "Give me the torch, Gokul-sahib," I ordered.

"Go!" he hissed. "Go now you foolish young man, we have no wish to harm you."

"Give me the torch!" I repeated, filling my voice with as much quiet savageness as I could muster.

The zamindar did so, reluctantly. The crowd fell silent, waiting, I believe, for the command to rend me.

I turned to look at the woman on the pyre. Her face was older, much older, than before and I detected livid streaks of subcutaneous mortification. Her cheek bones had become prominent, the flesh below them concave, and her eyes, now lackluster, were already sinking back.

"Namaste, Chandira," I greeted her.

She bowed a little. "Namaste, Rowan-sahib." Her voice was but a dry croak.

"Your husband once told me that I was to perform a service for him. I am here to give that service."

Stepping forward, I thrust the torch deep into the tinder of the funeral pyre and leapt back as the mound of wood and ghee ignited with a roar.

I like to believe that I saw a look of gratitude and peace pass over Chandira's withering face before the purifying flames engulfed her.

STEPHEN VOLK

Celebrity Frankenstein

⚬⟞⟐⟝⚬

Stephen Volk is best known as the creator of the multi-award-winning drama series Afterlife *and the notorious 1992 TV "Hallowe'en hoax"* Ghostwatch *which jammed the switchboards at the BBC, terrified the nation, and even caused questions to be raised in Parliament.*

He cowrote the recent feature film The Awakening *starring Rebecca Hall and Dominic West, and his other screenplay credits include Ken Russell's Frankenstein-themed* Gothic *starring Gabriel Byrne and Natasha Richardson, and* The Guardian, *directed by William Friedkin. He also scripted the TV series* Afterlife *(2005–06) and* Midwinter of the Spirit *(2015), and won a British Film Academy Award for his short film* The Deadness of Dad *starring Rhys Ifans.*

His first collection of short stories, Dark Corners, *appeared in 2006, and his short fiction has previously been selected for* Year's Best Fantasy and Horror, Best New Horror *and* Best British Mysteries. *He is the author of the stand-alone novellas* Vardøger *and* Whitstable, *the latter published to coincide with the Peter Cushing centenary. A finalist for the Bram Stoker Award and the Shirley Jackson Award, his second collection,* Monsters in the Heart, *won the British Fantasy Award in 2014.*

As Volk explains: "Often I've heard the observation that pop stars these days are mere commodities, manufactured to the specifications of an industry hungry to create something or someone, thrust them in the limelight, then drop them just as quickly. People talk of 'Svengalis' and 'puppet-masters,' but I thought of Dr. Frankenstein's rejection of his creature and the parallels struck me as delicious fun to play with. Even if the fun ends in tragedy.

*"The title was a given. Almost every TV show, here in Britain anyway, has 'Celebrity' in the title (*Celebrity Bitchslap News *possibly taking the prize for the most inane and depressing of the bunch).*

"Unnecessary to point out, probably, is that my inspiration came from the tabloids, the talent shows, the stars forever in the limelight, as well as Mary Shelley—who certainly knew a thing or two about fame in her lifetime, but to my knowledge never had her own chat show."

I n my mind the gap was non-existent between falling asleep and waking up, but of course weeks had gone by. Obviously. There were many procedures to be done and one had to be recovered from, and stabilized, groggily, still under, before the next began. I had no idea of the doctors taking over in shifts, or working in tandem, to achieve the program-makers' aims. I was out of it. Meanwhile the video footage of the surgery circled the world. Screen grabs jumping from cell to cell. I learned later that at the moment the titles began running on the final segment of the Results show, we'd already had the highest ratings the network had ever had. *Any* network ever had. This was history, if I but knew it. If I was awake. Then I *was* awake . . .

Salvator's eyes took a while to focus. Some filmy bits floated in the general opaqueness like rats' tails which troubled me for a few seconds. That and a certain lack of pain which came from being pumped with 100%-proof Christ-knows-what anaesthetic and various other chemicals swashed together in a cocktail to keep me stable. The *new* me, that is. If you could call it "me" at all.

I raised a hand to examine it front and back. It was Murphy's hand, unmistakably. I'd know that blunt-ended thumb and slightly twisted pinkie anywhere. The tan ended at the stitches where it was attached to Vince Pybus's tattooed arm. I revolved it slightly, feeling the pull in my forearm muscles—not that they were mine at all. Except they were. There was the tremendous urge to yell something obscene, but I remembered being counselled not to do that on live TV for legal and other reasons, not least being the show might get instantly pulled. But the word "Fuck" seemed appropriate, given a new entity had been given life, of a sort, with no actual "fucking" involved. As befits suitable family entertainment. Primetime.

Anticipating my thoughts, some guardian angel out of my field of vision put an oxygen mask over my mouth—whose mouth? I felt a coldness not on my lips but on Finbar's, wider and more feminine than mine, a Jim Morrison pout—and I drank the air greedily: it stopped the feeling of nausea that was rising up from my guts. Or somebody's, anyway.

I raised my other hand and it was trembling. It also happened to be African-American, muscled and smooth. My man Anthony's. I flattened its palm and ran it over my chest, hairless, Hispanic, down to the hard, defined muscles of Rico's stomach. Maybe alarmingly, I didn't have to stifle a scream but a laugh. And almost as if it wanted to drown me out in case I did, up came the Toccata and Fugue, blasting loud enough to make the walls of Jericho crumble, and my hospital table tilted up, thirty, forty-five degrees, and shielding my eyes with Anthony's hand from the army of studio lights, I blinked, trying to make out the sea of the audience beyond.

"Are you ready for the mirror?" said a voice.

It was Doctor Bob and I saw him now, brown eyes twinkling above the paper mask, curly hair neatly tucked under the lime green medical cap. I nodded. As I had to. It was in my contract, after all.

I looked at Moritz's face as the reflection looked back. Long, lean, pale—not un-handsome, but not Moritz either. Finbar's lips, fat and engorged, maybe enhanced a little cosmetically while we were all under, gave him a sensuality the real Moritz lacked. Moritz, who lay somewhere backstage with his face removed, waiting for a donor. Next to armless Vince and armless Anthony, a fond tear in their eyes no doubt to see a part of them taken away and made famous. I saw, below a brow irrigated with a railway-track of stitches where the skull had been lifted off like a lid and my brain had been put in, Salvator's darkly Spanish eyes gazing back at me like no eyes in any mirror in Oblong, Illinois. Blind Salvator, now, who was sitting backstage, whose grandfather had been blind also, but had only eked a rotten existence as a beggar on the streets of Valladolid. Yet here was Salvator his eyeless grandson, rich and American, and about be richer still from the story he now had to tell, and sell. Salvator could see nothing now—true, but he had seen a future, at least.

"Wow," I said.

Doctor Bob and the other Judges were standing and applauding in front of me now, wearing their surgical scrubs and rubber gloves. Doctor Jude's cut by some fashion house in Rodeo Drive, her hair stacked high and shining. The gloves made a shrill, popping sound. Doctor Bob's facemask hung half off from one ear. I was still in a haze but I think they each said their bit praising us.

"I always believed in you guys."

"You're the real deal. That was fantastic."

"You know what's great about you? You never complained and you never moaned in this whole process."

It was the Host speaking next. Hand on my shoulder. Sharp charcoal suit, sharp white grin: "Great comments from the Doctors. What do you think of that? Say something to the audience."

With Alfry Linquist's voice, I said: "Awesome."

Soon the clip was on YouTube. Highest number of hits ever.

I got out of the hospital bed and they handed me a microphone. I sang the single that was released that Christmas and went straight to number one: "Idolized." One of the biggest downloads ever. Global.

As soon as I could record it, my first album came out. Producer worked with Frank Zappa (not that I was real sure who Frank Zappa was). *Born Winner*, it was called. The Doctors decided that. Guess they decided way before I recorded it. Like they decided everything, Doctor Bob and his team, the Judges. Went triple platinum. Grammys. Mercury. You name it. *Rolling Stone* interview. Jets to London. Private jets courtesy of Doctor Bob. Tokyo. Sydney. Wherever. Madness. But good madness.

(The other madness, that came later.)

I wish I could've been me out there watching me become famous. Because from where I sat there wasn't time to see it at all. Grab a burger and Pepsi, then on to the next gig. I was loving it. So people told me. So I believed.

Big appearance was I guested on the next Emmy awards, telecast across the nation, giving out a Best Actress (Comedy or Musical) to Natalie Portman, my Justin Bieber fringe covering my scars. The dancers gyrated round me, Voodoo-like. I spoke and the tuxedos listened. I sung alongside Miley Cyrus and got a standing ovation of the most sparkling people in entertainment. Face jobs and chin tucks and jewelery that could pay off the debt of a small African country.

It was weird to have a voice. Somebody else's voice, literally that voice box in your throat not being the one you were born with. Strange to have a talent, a gift, a kind of wish come true that you carry round in your body and it's your fortune now. Alfry was my voice but I guess I carried him. Without my brain and my thoughts he couldn't have gotten to the top. Without Anthony and Vince's big old arms and Allan Jake Wells's legs and Rico's perfect abs, without any one of those things neither one of us could've made it. But, this way, we all did.

The Judges gave us a name and it was complete and to say we were happy was an understatement. I just knew Anthony wanted to get those biceps pumped right up fit to explode and I could feel Rico's insides just churning with a mixture of nerves and excitement, and I said, *Okay buddies, this is here, this is now, this is us and this is me. No going back.* And I could feel every cell of them saying it with me.

And every night after performing I counted the scars on my wrists and shoulders and round my thighs and ankles and neck and said, "Doctor Bob, thank you so much for this opportunity. I won't let you down."

But all dreams got to end, right?

Bigtime.

I appeared on talk shows. Pretty soon got a talk show myself. Letterman eat your heart out. Guests like Lady Gaga. George Michael. (Outrageous.) Robert Downey, Jr. (Phenomenal. Wore a zipper on his head to get a laugh. Gripped my hand like a kindred spirit.) Title sequence, black hand, white hand, fingers adjusting the tie, cheesy grin on Finbar's Jagger lips. Salvator's eyes swing to camera. The cowboy-gun finger going bang.

All this while Doctor Bob and his people looked after me, told me what to sign, what to do, where to show up, which camera to smile at, which covers to appear on, which stories to take to court. Which journalists to spill my heart to. Rico's heart. And I did. I did what I was told. Doctor Bob was like a father to me. No question. He created me. How could I say no?

There were girlfriends. Sure there were girlfriends. How could there not be? I was unique. Everybody wanted to meet me, see me, touch me, and some wanted more of me. Sometimes I'd oblige. Sometimes obliging wasn't enough.

That money-grabbing crackpot named Justine, housemaid in some Best Western I'd never stayed at, hit me with a rape allegation, but truth is I never remembered ever meeting her. It was pretty clear she was a fantasist. We buried her.

Like I say there was a downside, but a hell of an upside. Most times I thought it was the best thing I ever did, kissing my old body goodbye. Didn't even shed a tear when the rest of me in that coffin went into the incinerator, empty in the head. Just felt Doctor Bob's hand squeezing Vince Pybus's shoulder and thought about the camera hovering in my face and the dailies next morning.

But the peasants were always chasing me. The peanut-heads. The flash of their Nikons like flaming torches they held aloft, blinding me, big time. I had nowhere to hide and sometimes I felt chained to my office up on the

99th Floor on the Avenue of the Stars. Felt like a $1,000-a-night-dungeon in a castle, the Plasma screen my window to the outside world. Doctors checking me, adjusting my medication so that I could go out on the new circuit of night clubs, appear on the new primetime primary-colored couch answering the same boring questions I'd answered a hundred thousand times before.

Sometimes I growled. Sometimes I grunted. Sometimes I plucked a sliver of flesh from my knee and said, "I'll deal with you later." And the audience howled like I was Leno, but they didn't know how bad the pain was in my skull. It was hot under the lights and sometimes it felt like it was baking me.

"We can fix that," the Doctors said, Doctor Jude with her legs and Doctor Bob with his nut-brown eyes. And they did that. They kept fixing it. They kept fixing me, right through my second album and third, right through to the *Best of* and double-download Christmas duets.

The problem was rejection. Balancing the drug cocktail—a whole Santa Claus list of them—so that my constituent body parts didn't rebel against each other. That was the problem. The new pharmaceuticals did it, thanks to up-to-the-minute research, thanks to a scientific breakthrough. All sorts of medical miracles were now possible. The show couldn't have gotten the green light without them. As Doctor Bob said, "It was all about taking rejection. All about coming back fighting."

I told my story in a book. Ghostwriter did a good job. I liked it when I read it. (The part I read, anyway.) Especially the part about Mom. Though Dad wasn't that happy. Tried to stop publication, till the check changed his mind. I did say some parts weren't true, but Doctor Bob said it didn't matter as long as it sold, and it did sell, by the millions. My face grinned out from every bookstore in the country. Scars almost healed on my forehead. Just a line like I wore a hat and the rim cut in, with little pin-pricks each side. Signing with Murphy's hand till my fingers went numb. Offering the veins of my arm for Doctor Jude to shoot me up, keep me going, stop me falling apart. I wondered if anybody had told her she was beautiful, and I guess they had. "You nailed it. You've got your mojo back. I'm so proud of you—not just as a performer but as a human being," she said as she took out the syringe.

On to the next job. Getting e-mails from loons saying it was all against nature and my soul was doomed to Hell. Well, doomed to Hell felt pretty damn good back then, all in all. Except for the headaches.

But pretty soon it wasn't just the headaches I had to worry about.

One day they held a meeting at Doctor Bob's offices and told me that, "in spite of the medical advancements," the new penis hadn't taken. *Necrotis* was the word they used. Bad match. I asked them if they were sure it wasn't because of over-use. They said no, this was a biomedical matter. "We have to cut Mick Donner off, replace him with someone new." So I had to go under again and this time had a johnson from a guy in psychiatric care named Cody Bertwhistle. Denver guy, and a fan. Wrote me a letter. Longhand. Told me it was an honor.

I don't know why, and there's no direct correlation, but from the time Mike Donner's got replaced by Cosmic Cody's, things went on the slide.

Maybe it was chemicals. Maybe the chemicals were different. They say we're nothing but robots made up of chemicals, we human beings, don't they? Well if a tiny tweak here or a tad there can send us crawlin'-the-wall crazy, what does it mean if you get several gallons of the stuff pumped into you? Where are you then?

These thoughts, I'll be honest, they just preyed on me. Ate me up, more and more. Maybe that's the cause of what happened later. Maybe I'm just looking for something to blame. I don't know. Probably I am.

Maybe Doctor Bob knows. Doctor Bob knows everything.

After all, before me made us, he made himself. Out of nothing, into the most powerful man in television. A god who stepped down from Mount Olympus after the opening credits with the light show behind him like *Close Encounters* on acid.

I remember standing under the beating sun with four other guys next to a sparkling swimming pool lined with palm trees outside this huge mansion in Malibu. Servants, girls, models, gave us giant fruit drinks with straws and thin Egyptian-looking dogs ran around the lawns biting at the water jerking from the sprinklers. And Kenny started clapping before I'd seen Doctor Bob in his open-neck Hawaiian shirt walking across the grass towards us, then we all clapped and whooped like a bunch of apes. Poor Devon hyperventilated and had to be given oxygen. I'd felt strangely calm. The whole thing was strangely unreal, like it wasn't really happening, or it was happening to somebody other than me. I couldn't believe that person who was on TV, on that small monitor I was looking at as it replayed, *was* me. Maybe I was already becoming somebody else, even then. We toasted with champagne and he wished us all luck, and I don't know if it was the champagne or the warmth of the Los Angeles evening, or the smell of gasoline and wealth and the sound of insects and police sirens in the air, but I felt excitement and happiness more than I ever had in my life before, and I didn't want it to end.

We were buddies, that was a fact. Through the entire competition he was less of a mentor, more of a friend, Doctor Bob. Then, once I'd won, well, our friendship went stratospheric. And I was grateful for it. Then.

We played golf together. He paid for me to train for my pilot's license. Took me up into the clouds. Every week we had lunch at The Ivy. Hello Troy. Hello Alex. Hello Sting. Hello Elton. Hello Harrison. Hello Amy. Still at Sony? He wanted me on display. I was his shop window. I knew that. Sure I knew that. But I always thought he was watching me. If I took too long to chew my food. If I scratched the side of my neck. It started to bug me. If I squinted across the room, or stammered over my words I felt he was mentally ringing it up. Cutting his chicken breast like a surgeon, he'd say, "You are okay?" I'd say, "Of course I'm okay. I'm great. I'm perfect." And he'd stare at me really hard, saying, "I know you're perfect, but are you okay?" One day I said, "You know what? Fuck your Chardonnay."

That was the day I took that fateful walk in the Griffith Park, up by the observatory. Just wanted to be on my own—not that I could be on my own any more, there being at least half-a-dozen of us in this body, now, that I knew of. Didn't want to even *contemplate* if they'd stuck in a few more organs I didn't know about. The semi-healed scars itched under my Rolex so I took it off and dropped it in a garbage can beside the path. Walked on, hands deep in the pants pockets of my Armani suit.

You know what I'm gonna tell you, but I swear to God I didn't do anything wrong. I wouldn't do that to my Mom, I just wouldn't. She raised me with certain values and I still got those values. Other people can believe what they want to believe.

She was making daisy chains.

This little bit of a thing, I'm talking about. Three, maybe four. Just sitting there beside the lake. I watched her plucking them from the grass and casting them into the water, just getting so much enjoyment from the simple joy of it, so I knelt down with her and did it too. Just wanting a tiny bit of that joy she had. And we spoke a little bit. She was nice. She said she wanted to put her toes in the water but she was afraid because her Mom said not to go near the water, she might drown. I said, "You won't drown. I'll look after you." She said, "Will you?" I said, "Sure." So that's how come there's this photograph of me lifting her over the rail. I was dangling her down so she could dip her feet in the water, that's all. They made it look crazy, like I was *hurling* her, but I wasn't. The front pages all screamed—*People, Us, National Enquirer*—he's gone too far, he's out of control, he's lost it. Wacko. I hadn't lost it. She wasn't in *danger.* We were just goofing around. And who took the shot anyway? Her Mom? Her Dad? What kind of *abuse* is that, anyway?

Parents! Jesus! After a fast buck, plastering their kid all over the tabloids? They're the freaks, not me. And that poor girl. That's what made her start crying. Her Mom and Dad, shouting and calling her away from me. "Honey! Honey! Get away from the man! Honey!" And I'm like . . .

Doctor Bob went ballistic. Brought me in to the Inner Sanctum, Beverly Hills, and ripped me a new one. (Which he could have done literally, given his medical expertise.) I just growled. I snarled. He looked frightened. I said, "See those chains over there?" pointing to his wall of platinum discs, "I'm not in your chains anymore." He shouted as I left, "You're nothing without me!" I turned to him and said, "You know what? I'm everything. You're the one who's nothing. Because if you aren't, why do you need me?" As the elevator doors closed I heard him say, "Fucking genius. Fucking moron."

I could do it without him. I knew I could.

But after Griffith Park, it wasn't easy to get representation. I still got by. Put my name to a series of novels. Thrillers. Sorta semi-sci-fi, I believe. Not read them. Celebrity endorsements. Sports and nutritional products. Failing brands. Except I was a failing brand too, they soon realized.

Then this lowlife cable network pitched me a reality series, à la *The Osbornes*, where a camera crew follow me around day in, day out.

Twenty-four seven. Pitched up in my Mulholland Drive home for three months. But the paycheck was good. Number one, I still needed my medication which was legal but expensive, and two, I reckoned I could re-launch my music career off the back of the publicity. So it was a done deal. Found a lawyer on Melrose that James Franco used. The producers sat on my couch fidgeting like junkies, these cheese straws in shades, saying they wanted to call it *American Monster*. I was like, "Whatever." The lights in my own home were too bright for me now, and I had to wear shades too. I'd have these ideas on a weekly basis, like my eyes were out of balance and I'd think a top-up from a hypo would get me back on the highway. It did. Periodically.

More and more I needed those boosts from the needle to keep me level, or make me think I was keeping level. Meanwhile the ideas wouldn't go away. I didn't know if the bright lights were inside or outside my skull. The bright lights are what everybody aspires to, right? The bright lights of Hollywood or Broadway, but when you can't get them out of your head even when you're sleeping they're a nightmare. And rats go crazy, don't they, if you deprive them of sleep? Except the drugs made you feel you didn't need sleep.

One of these ideas was there were germs around me and the germs I might catch would affect my immune system and inhibit the anti-rejection drugs. I was really convinced of this. I took to wearing a paper mask, just like the one Doctor Bob wore when he took my brain out and put it in another person's skull. Wore it to the mall. To the supermarket. To the ball game.

Then I guess I reached a real low patch. The reality show crashed and my new management bailed. Guess it wasn't the cash cow they were expecting. Clerval always was a ruthless scumbag, even as agents go, feet on his desk, giving a masturbatory mime as he schmoozes his other client on the phone, dining out on his asshole stories of Jodie and Mel.

Some reason I also got the idea that germs resided in my hair, and I shaved that off to the scalp. Felt safer that way. Safer with my paper mask and bald head, and the briefcase full of phials and pills, added to now with some that were off-prescription. Marvelous what you can find on the Internet, hey?

Didn't much notice the cameras anymore, trailing me to the parking lot or to the gym, jumping out from bushes, walking backwards in front of me down the sidewalk or pressed to the driver's window of my Hummer. Didn't care. I guess somewhere deep down I thought the photographs and photographers meant somebody wanted to see me. Someone wanted me to exist, so it was worth existing, for them. How wrong can you be?

It felt like it was all over. It felt like I was alone.

Then one day I got a call from Doctor Bob. No secretary. No gatekeeper. Just him. He said, "Listen, don't hang up on me. You know I'm good for you, you know we made it together and if I made some mistakes, I'm sorry. Let's move on." I reckoned it took a lot for him to pick up the phone, so the least I could do was listen. "I'm going in to the network to pitch a follow-up series. And if they don't clap till their hands bleed I'll eat this telephone. It's the same but different: what every network wants to hear. Hot females in front of the camera this time, and you know what, I'm not going to even *attempt* to sell it to them. The pitch is going to be just one word. We're going to walk in and sit down, and we're going to say: *Bride*."

I said: "We?"

He said, "I want you in on this. You're on the judges' panel."

And that's what happened. Contract signed, everything. It was my baby. My comeback. It meant everything to me. I went back to the fold. Doctor Jude kissed my cheek. I *did* have my juju. I *had* nailed it. I *was* fantastic, as a performer and as a human being . . .

Overnight, I was booked on *The Tonight Show*. I was back up there. I was going on to announce *Bride*. They wanted Doctor Bob to sit beside me on the couch but he said, "No, son. You do it. You'll be fine." And I was fine. I thought I was fine. But when the applause hit me and the lights hit me too I got a little high. I was back on the mountain-top. I wanted to sing—not sing, run, run a million miles. And I loved Doctor Bob so much, I said it. I wasn't ashamed of it. I said it again. I shouted it. I jumped up and down on the couch saying "I'm in love! I'm in love!" because that's what it felt like, all over again.

And, though it hit the headlines, I thought, what's the big deal? And, when my security pass didn't work at the rehearsal studio, I thought, what the hell? But when Doctor Bob didn't return my calls, then I knew something was turning to shit. Then I got a text from the producer saying my services were no longer required: there was a cancellation clause and they were invoking it. I was out.

I thought: Screw Doctor Bob.

Screw *Bride*.

I did commercials, appearances, while the series ran and the ratings climbed. If the first series knocked it out of the park, series two sent it stratospheric. I tried not to watch it but it was everywhere like a virus, magazine covers, newspapers. I kept to myself. I sunk low. I shaved my head again. I wore my mask. I took my meds.

Sleepless, I wandered Hollywood Boulevard amongst the hookers of both sexes. They looked in better shape than I did. Scored near Grauman's Chinese. Did hopscotch on the handprints in the cement. Watched the stretches sail by to fame and fortune. Watched pimps at their toil. Sometimes someone wanted to shake my black hand, other times wanted to shake my white.

In McDonald's I picked up a discarded *Enquirer* and saw what I didn't want to see: photographs of Doctor Bob leaving The Ivy with the winner of *Bride* on his arm. Lissom. Tanned. Augmented. A conglomerate of cheerleader from Wichita, swimmer from Oregon and pole-dancer from Yale. There she was, grinning for the cameras with her California dentition, just like I used to do.

Yes, I sent him texts. The texts that they showed in court: I admit that. Yes, I said I was going to destroy him. Yes, I said I was more powerful than him now and he knew it. In many ways I wanted him to suffer. I hated him, pure and simple.

But I didn't kill her. I swear on my mother's life.

Yes, she came to my house. Obviously, because that's where they found the body. But she came there, drunk and high, saying she wanted to reason with me and persuade me to mend broken bridges with Doctor Bob. When the prosecution claimed I abducted her, that I drugged her, that was all made up. She came to me doped up and in no fit state to drive home. I told her to use the bedroom, drive home with a clear head in the morning. It was raining, too, and I wasn't sure this girl—any of her—would know where to find the switch for the windshield wipers. Her pole-dancer arms were flailing all flaky and I saw the scars on her wrists and on the taut, fat-free swimmer muscles of her shoulders.

I put two calls in to Doctor Bob but they went to "message" so I hung up. She had two blocked numbers on her phone and my guess is she called someone to come pick her up while I was out.

I had an appointment with a supplier because my anti-rejection drugs were low. Maybe I shouldn't have left her but I did. Fact is, when the police found my fingerprints all over the carving knife—of course they did, it was in my house. From my kitchen. Anyway, *their* fingerprints were all over the damn thing too.

I didn't break the law. Not even in that slow-mo car chase along the interstate where I kept under the speed limit and so did they.

I know I was found not guilty, but a good portion of the American people still believed I killed her. Thirty-two wounds in her body. Had to be some kind of . . . not human being. And I am. I know I am.

But the public didn't like it that way. They blamed American justice. Blamed money. Yes, I came out free, but was I free? Really free? No way. I was acquitted, but everyone watching the whole thing on TV thought it was justice bought by expensive lawyers and I was guilty as sin. They near as hell wanted to strap me to the chair right there and then, but there wasn't a damn thing they could do about it.

God bless America.

I had to sell my place on Mulholland Drive. Live out of hotel rooms. Pretty soon I was a cartoon on *South Park*. A cheap joke on Jon Stewart. Couldn't get into The Ivy any more. Looked in at Doctor Bob, eating alone.

Now, where am I?

Plenty of new pitches to sell. Trouble is, I can't even get in the room. Maybe it's true that the saddest thing in Hollywood is not knowing your time is over.

Now the personal appearances are in bars and strip joints smelling of semen and liquor. Not too unlike the anaesthetic, back in the day. I ask in Alfry's voice if this signed photo, book, album is for them. They say, no, it's for their mother. And that's the killer. Nobody wants to say the autograph of the person who used to be something is for them.

Night, I flip channels endlessly on the TV set in some motel, the cocktail in my veins making me heavy-lidded but nothing less than alert. If I see a clip of me I write it in my notebook. Radio stations, the same. Any of my songs, I chase them for royalties. I'm human. Everybody wants a piece of me, but I'm not giving myself away any more. Not for free, anyway.

I look in the bathroom mirror and I see flab. Scrawn. Bone. Disease. Wrinkles. Puckers. Flaps. I'm wasting away. I'm a grey blob. What they didn't say when they build you is that you die like everybody else. Only quicker. Six times quicker. The techniques weren't registered and peer-reviewed, turns out. Nobody looked into the long-term effects of the anti-rejection regime. That's why I've been eating like a horse and my body keeps nothing in but the toxins. When I was passing through Mississippi and collapsed at the wheel, the intern at the hospital said the protein was killing me, the fat, cholesterol, all of it. My body was like a chemical plant making poison. I said, "What? Cut the munchies?" He said, "No more munchies. No more midnight snacks. One more ham-burger will kill you."

I'm a nineteen-year-old concoction, hurting like hell. Each part of me wants the other part of it back. It's not a spiritual or mental longing, it's a physical longing and it's pain and it's with me every sleepless second of the goddamned day.

My only crime was, I wanted to be somebody.

Trouble is, I was six people.

At least six, in fact.

To be honest, I lost count after the second penis.

Maybe you can hear the music in the background, in the next room. They're playing "Teenage Lobotomy" by the Ramones on the tinny radio beside my king-size bed.

While I'm here, sitting on toilet pan, coughing up blood.

Truthful? I'd be writing this the old-fashioned way, paper and pen, except Murph's fingers are feeling like sausages and I'm getting those flashes again in the corner of Salvator's left eye right now. They're like fireworks. Hell, they're like the fourth of July. That's why I'm talking into this recorder. The one Doctor Bob gave me, way back. The one I needed for interviews, he explained. "They record you, but you record them. You have a record of what you say. They get it wrong, sue their ass." Doctor Bob was full of good advice, till it all went wrong, which is why I guess I'm sitting here, wanting to set it all down, from the beginning. Like it was. Not like folks say it was. Not like the lies they're saying about me out there.

Half-an-hour ago I rang for a take-out and a mixed-race kid in a hoodie rang the doorbell, gave me a box with a triple bacon cheeseburger and large fries in it. Gave him a fifty. Figured, what the heck?

I've got it in my hand now, the hamburger, Anthony's fingers and Vince's fingers sinking into the bun, the grease dripping onto the bathroom floor between my feet, feet I don't recognize and never did. The smell of the processed cheese and beef thick and stagnant and lovely in its appalling richness—a big fat murderer. The intern was right. One more bite will *kill* me. I know it. The drugs were too much. The side-effects, I mean. Like steroids shrink your manhood, this shrinks me. The dairy, the fat. And nobody gave me a twelve-step. Nobody took me in.

I texted Doctor Bob just before I started talking into this thing. He'll be the first to know. He'll come here and he'll find me. Which is how it should be. There's a completeness to that I think he'll understand. For all that came between us, and boy, a lot did, I think we understood each other, deep down.

That's why I know, absolutely, this is what I have to do.

Whether he listens to this story—whether anybody presses "Play" and listens, is up to them. Whether they care. Whether anybody cares, any more.

All I know is, I'm taking a big mouthful. God, that tastes good . . . A great big mouthful, and I taste that meaty flavor on my tongue, and that juice sliding down my throat . . . And the crunch of the iceberg lettuce and the tang of the pickle and the sweetness of the tomato . . . God, oh God . . . And, you know what?

I'm loving it.

KIM NEWMAN
Completist Heaven

❦

Kim Newman is a novelist, critic and broadcaster. His fiction includes The Night Mayor, Bad Dreams, Jago, *the Anno Dracula novels and stories,* The Quorum, The Original Dr. Shade and Other Stories, Life's Lottery, Back in the USSA *(with Eugene Byrne) and* The Man from the Diogenes Club, *all under his own name, and* The Vampire Genevieve *and* Orgy of the Blood Parasites *as "Jack Yeovil."*

His nonfiction books include Ghastly Beyond Belief *(with Neil Gaiman),* Horror: 100 Best Books *and* Horror: Another 100 Best Books *(both with Stephen Jones),* Wild West Movies, The BFI Companion to Horror, Millennium Movies *and* BFI Classics *studies of* Cat People, Doctor Who *and* Quatermass and the Pit.

He is a contributing editor to Sight & Sound *and* Empire *magazines (supplying the latter's popular "Video Dungeon" column), has written and broadcast widely on a range of topics, and scripted radio and television documentaries.*

Newman's stories "Week Woman" and "Ubermensch" were adapted into episodes of the TV series The Hunger, *and the latter tale was also turned into an Australian short film in 2009. Following his Radio 4 play* Cry Babies, *he wrote an episode ("Phish Phood") for BBC Radio 7's series* The Man in Black, *and he was a main contributor to the stage plays* The Hallowe'en Sessions *and* The Ghost Train Doesn't Stop Here Anymore. *He has also directed and written a tiny film,* Missing Girl.

The author's most recent books include expanded reissues of his acclaimed Anno Dracula series, including the long-awaited fourth volume Anno Dracula 1976–1991: Johnny Alucard; *the Professor Moriarty novel* The Hound of the d'Urbervilles, *and the stand-alone novel* An English Ghost Story *(all from Titan Books), along with a much-enlarged edition of* Nightmare Movies *(from Bloomsbury).*

With Maura McHugh he scripted the comic book miniseries Witchfinder: The Mysteries of Unland *for Dark Horse Comics. Illustrated by Tyler Crook, it is a spin-off from Mike Mignola's Hellboy series. His most recent novel is* The Secrets of Drearecliff Grange *(2015). Forthcoming fiction includes the novel* Angels of Music.

As Newman explains: "I was inspired to write 'Completist Heaven' by the sad case of a friend who ruined his mind and health noting movie trivia for a series of reference books.

"Personally, I kicked the biscuit habit years ago. But it really annoys me when American magazines refer to a film which doesn't exist called The Cat People, *and I have twice looked at my DVD of* Cat People *to make sure they're wrong . . ."*

I'm plumbing additional channels, homing on signals from as far away as Hilversum and Macao. With each twiddle, the dish outside revolves like Jodrell Bank stock footage from the *Quatermass* serials. Lightning crackles above the garden, approximating a Karloff-Lugosi mad lab insert shot from the 1930s.

Unimaginable images and sounds are pulled down from the skies. With the new reflectors, this satellite system can not only haul in everything being broadcast but anything that has ever been broadcast. Shows listed as lost or wiped are beaming out to Alpha Centauri; now, those signals can be brought unscrambled back to Earth.

This is my creation. Fueled by coffee bags and custard creams, I have substantially made the system myself, like Rex Reason assembling the Interocitor in *This Island Earth*. It was an interesting technical exercise, jacking in all the signal boosters and calibrating the dish to the minutest fraction. My redundancy money was well spent, despite what Ciaran said when she left for the last time.

I admit it's true: I could spend the rest of my life eating biscuits and watching repeats on television. There is so much to see, so much to discover . . .

Just tuning the first channels, I come across a Patrick Troughton *Doctor Who* which does not officially survive, and a stumbling, live Sherlock Holmes from the late 1940s. If anyone on Mars or Skaro makes television programs, this dish will pick them up. To be honest, there is no need ever to leave the house except for groceries. Everything ever hurled out over the airwaves, on film or videotape, will turn up eventually. The full listings edition of *What's On TV* looks like a telephone directory.

This is Completist Heaven.

Whoever assigns frequencies has a sense of humor, though it often takes minutes to get the joke. *Channel* 5 is a perfume infomercial. Chanel No. 5. Channels 18 to 30 are *vérité* footage of drunken Brits being obnoxious on holiday in Greece, with "The Birdy Song" on a tape-loop soundtrack. Channel 69 is Danish porno. Channel 86 is *Get Smart* reruns. Maxwell Smart was Agent 86. I clock a Martin Kosleck cameo in a vampire episode and make a mental note to list it on Kosleck's file card. Channel 101 is disgusting true-life *mondo* horror, rats and bugs and atrocity and burial alive; in a minute, I remember that in *Nineteen Eighty-Four*, Room 101 is where you face the most frightening thing in the world.

What does that leave for Channel 1984?

Channel 666 is either a director's cut of *The Omen* or a Satanic televangelist. In the thousands, most of the channels are date-tied: Channel 1066 is a historical drama in unsubtitled Norman French; Channel 1492 is a collage of Columbus movies with Jim Dale being tortured by Marlon Brando; Channel 1776 is that *Bilko* episode set during the Revolutionary War. Channel 1789 is a miniseries about the French Revolution: Jane Seymour goes nobly to the guillotine while Morgan Fairchild knits furiously in the first row. It's not in Maltin, Scheuer or Halliwell, so it must be new. I don't count miniseries as movies, so I don't have to watch further, though I'm sure that's Reggie Nalder dropping the blade.

I hit Channel 1818. Dyanne Thorne, a couple of melons down the front of her SS major's uniform, tortures someone in black and white. A girl in a torn peasant blouse squeals unconvincingly as a rat eats cold lasagna off her exposed tummy. I figure this is a print of *Ilsa, She-Wolf of the SS* that I've never seen. I get out the file card for the film and my notes make no mention of a rat torture quite like this. This is the sort of revelation I pay the monthly fee for: it is quite possible no one has ever seen this version of the movie before. I take up my red ball pentel, and prepare to jot down any information. The store of human knowledge must always be added to.

The crowning moment of my life was when my letter in *Video Watchdog* finally corrected all previous misinformation and established, beyond a shadow of a doubt, the correct German running time of *Lycanthropus*, aka *Werewolf in a Girls' Dormitory* or *I Married a Werewolf*. Ciaran was especially cutting about that. Many people don't understand, but without accuracy all scholarship is meaningless and the least we can do is lay down the parameters of what we are talking about. Now my mission in life is to force all periodicals and reference books to list *Matthew Hopkins, Witchfinder General* (the title as it appears on the screen) under *M* for *Matthew* rather than *W* for *Witchfinder*. Ignorant souls, starting with the film's distributors, have been committing this error since 1968. Heathens who list the Michael Reeves movie under *C* for *The Conqueror Worm* are, of course, beneath contempt and not worth considering.

The *Ilsa* movies are in color, so I fine-fiddle the knobs. Snow crackles across the image as the victim screams. No color appears. Ilsa gets out her nipple clamps, sneering in a bad accent, "Vellcome to SS Experiment Kemp Sex!" The camera pulls back, and on the next slab over from the abused girl lies the unmistakable bulk of a flat-headed, clumpy-booted, electrodes-on-the-neck, Universal-copyright Pierce-Karloff-Strange Frankenstein Monster.

Puzzled and intrigued, I gnaw on a chocolate-coated ginger snap.

An ident crawl along the bottom of the picture identifies the film: Channel 1818 Feature Presentation *Frankenstein Meets the She-Wolf of the SS*.

Obviously, this must be some new retitling of a familiar movie. If the color came on, I could identify it. More twiddling is to no avail.

I dig out Weldon's *Psychotronic Enclyclopedia*, Glut's *The Frankenstein Catalog* and Jones' *The Illustrated Frankenstein Movie Guide*. *Frankenstein Meets the She-Wolf of the SS* does not make these standard reference tools. I venture further: consulting Lee's sadly-outdated *Reference Guide to the Fantastic Film*, Willis's three-volume *Horror and Science Fiction Films*, my bound collection of Joe Bob's *We Are the Weird* newsletter, some back issues of *Shock Xpress*, and such variably reliable sources as the Phantom's *Ultimate Video Guide* and the mysterious *Hoffmann's Guide to SF, Horror and Fantasy Movies*. No one lists a Frankenstein-Ilsa crossover. This is exciting, a discovery. I feel a thrill in my water, pull out a fresh file card, and write down the title. I curse myself for having missed the credits.

To celebrate, I hold a cheddar thin in my mouth and suck gently, until saliva seeps through the biscuit and dissolves it entirely. With my tongue, I work the paste bit by bit into my gullet. The sensation is exquisite.

Officially, there are only three Ilsa movies (*Ilsa, She-Wolf of the SS, Ilsa, Harem Keeper of the Oil Sheiks, Ilsa, Tigress of Siberia*) but Jesus Franco's *Greta, Hause Ohne Männer* aka *Wanda the Wicked Warden* or *Greta the Torturer*, with Thorne in the title role of Greta-Wanda, is sometimes spuriously roped into the series. Could this be a hither-to-undiscovered entry in the Ilsa series, or some apocryphal adventure of a lookalike Greta, Gerta, Irma, Helga, Erika or Monika? The sync is just off, but I'm sure this is shot in English, not dubbed. A heel-clicking subordinate salutes and snaps "Heil Hitler, Major Ilsa" establishing this as indeed part of the Isla canon. The black and white bothers me still. Is this a flashback within a color film? That would be a bit artsy for Ilsa.

The Nazi Bitch Queen is in an office, ranting. It's definitely Dyanne Thorne (once seen, those melons are unmistakable) and from the relative lack of lines on her face, the movie has to be from the mid-1970s. Oddly, it looks good in black and white: less like a bad dupe which has lost color than a film lit for monochrome. The shadows gathering in the office as night falls make the scene look better than the cheesy images I remember from other Ilsa movies. Not James Wong Howe good, but at least George Robinson good.

I look through Glut and Jones, trying to find a Thorne credit in a '70s Frankenstein movie. Of course, just because a film is called *Frankenstein Meets the She-Wolf of the SS* doesn't mean it's a Frankenstein movie. *Frankenstein's Bloody Terror* is a werewolf movie and several Japanese giant monster films have Frankenstein forced into their titles for German release, since Frankenstein is a generic term for monster in Germany. This must have been retitled since Glut came out, since he lists non-Frankenstein Frankenstein titles. With the proliferation of fly-by-night cable and video, some movies have multiple titles into double figures. I need three file cards just to list the alternate titles of *Horror of the Blood Monsters* or *No profanar el sueño de los muertos*. However, that Monster, noted in occasional cutaways, leads me to identify this tentatively as a genuine Frankenstein movie as well as an unknown Ilsa.

As the film plays on, I eat several bourbons, almost whole, chewing them like dog biscuits.

Something is definitely strange about *Frankenstein Meets the She-Wolf of the SS*. I'm convinced it was shot in black and white. Ilsa strides through what looks like the Universal Studios Middle European village (built for *All Quiet on the Western Front*, it shows up in all their monster movies) accompanied by pudgy SS extras. Wherever she stands in the shot, her mammoth breasts seem to be the center of the frame.

544

The plot involves Ilsa establishing a Nazi experiment camp in a ruined castle. Cringing villagers avoid Ilsa's goose-stepping buddies. The village is called Visaria. I guess it's supposed to be in Czechoslovakia or Poland. It's hard to tell, because it seems more like generic Eastern Europe than a real country. The burgomeister wears *Lederhosen* and an alpine hat with a peacock feather.

Visaria.

I flip back in Glut and Jones, trying to track down a niggling memory. I am right. Visaria is the name of the village in the later Universal horror films: 1940s monster rallies like *Frankenstein Meets the Wolf Man* and *House of Dracula*. Whoever wrote *Frankenstein Meets the She-Wolf of the SS* must be a monster trivia junkie. I assume Forry Ackerman will get a cameo, and the Ken Strickfaden lab equipment will be dusted off. That suggests the *auteur* touch of Al Adamson, who always liked to borrow leftover props from the Universals for atrocities like *Dracula vs. Frankenstein*. This looks too good to be an Adamson (no acid trip, no Russ Tamblyn, no bikers) but I feel I'm getting this movie pinned down. Maybe it's from about the same vintage as *Blackenstein*, the one with the Karloff-style monster sporting a flat afro.

I write: 1972 to 1975? American. Stars Dyanne Thorne (as Ilsa). The tortured girl looked like Uschi Digart.

Then Lionel Atwill shows up as a police inspector with a prosthetic arm and an eagle-crested cap, with Dwight Frye and Skelton Knaggs as the most cringing of cringing villagers. They are from the '40s, like the sets and the photography, and I'm lost.

Bourbon biscuit crumbs turn to ashes in my mouth.

Even if—and it's inconceivable—I'm wrong and the leading woman isn't Dyanne Thorne but a lookalike, then the scene with the rat and the nipple clamps could never have been shot in the '40s. Even for the private delectation of Lionel Atwill's houseguests. Ilsa doesn't have the lipsticky, marcelled look of the women in '40s horror films. Her hippie eye make-up and butch haircut are '70s to the bleached-blonde roots.

I swallow and am forced to assume this is a *Dead Men Don't Wear Plaid* gimmick, mixing footage from different films. Perhaps it has been overdubbed with wisecracks by *Saturday Night Live* regulars. I listen to the dialogue as Ilsa dresses down Inspector Atwill, and can't catch any deliberate camp. One-shots of Ilsa and Atwill alternate and I try to see inconsistencies in the backgrounds. The match is good.

Then Ilsa peels off her elbow-length black leather glove and slaps Atwill across the face with it. Thorne's Ilsa, from the '70s, is *in the same shot* with Atwill's Inspector, from the '40s, and their physical interaction is too complicated to be faked. Ilsa rips apart Atwill's many-buttoned uniform, yanking off his artificial arm, and squats on him, hip-thrusting against the stump that sticks out of his shoulder. Thorne's orgasmic moaning is as unconvincing as ever but Atwill looks as though he's getting something out of the scene. Unsatisfied, Ilsa gets up and rearranges her SS skirt, then has Atwill summarily executed. Black blood squirts out of his burst eye. The ketchupy '70s gore looks nastier, more convincing in hand-me-down '40s expressionist black and white.

The telephone rings and the answering machine cuts in. It's Ciaran, complaining about maintenance. She jabbers on, an uncertain edge to her voice, and I concentrate on important things.

This is definitely a crossover movie. I fervently wish I had seen it from the beginning so I could tell whether the title card was original or spliced in. Actually, trying to track this one down is pointless. Whatever it's really called, it's impossible.

It's the usual Ilsa story but the supporting characters are from the Universal monster series. Major Ilsa is the last granddaughter of the original Henry Frankenstein and the castle is her ancestral home. That would make her the character played by Ilona Massey in *Frankenstein Meets the Wolf Man*. Dyanne Thorne is even wearing an Ilona Massey beauty mark, which shifts alarmingly around her mouth from scene to scene with typical Ilsa continuity. She is supposed to be working on the creation of a race of super-Nazis for Hitler, but spends more time having weird sex and torturing people than contributing to the war effort.

To help her out around the laboratory, where Glenn Strange lies supine on the table, Ilsa drags Dr. Pretorius, Ernest Thesiger's swish mad scientist from *Bride of Frankenstein*, and Ygor, Bela Lugosi's broken-necked gypsy from *Son . . .* and *Ghost of Frankenstein*, out of their concentration camps. Pretorius keeps adjusting his pink triangle to set off his lab coat and Ygor leers gruesomely at Ilsa, tongue dangling a foot or so out of his mouth.

The sex scenes are near hardcore, but extremely silly. Ilsa needs a man who can sustain an erection for a whole night and most of the next morning if she is to achieve full satisfaction. She thinks she is in luck when virile Larry Talbot tears off his clothes as the full moon rises. In an unprecedented shot, yak hair swarms around the Wolf Man's crotch. Jack Pierce must really have given Lon Chaney, Jr., a hard time with that lap dissolve. Ilsa and the Wolf Man go at it all over the castle, with ridiculous grunting and gasping and Franz Waxman's Wedding Bells score from *Bride of Frankenstein*, but there's big disappointment at dawn as the moon goes down and the werewolf turns back into dumb old flabby Larry-Lon. Ilsa yells abuse at the befuddled and limp American, and batters him to death with a silver cane.

After this, Ilsa is so crabby she shoves the burgomeister's irritating daughter into the sulphur pits below the castle. As the little girl goes under, we cut to Ygor-Bela snickering over a lamp positioned under his chin to make him look scary.

In theory, Universal's creature features have contemporary settings. *Dracula* and *The Wolf Man* clearly establish 1931 and 1941 for the dates of the action, so their sequels must take place in the years of their production. *Ghost of Frankenstein* (1941), *Frankenstein Meets the Wolf Man* (1943), *House of Frankenstein* (1944) and *House of Dracula* (1945), the Visaria movies, are all set in an unspecified Eastern Europe of torch-bearing peasant mobs, gypsy musicians and saluting policemen. Though Atwill in *Son of Frankenstein* complains that he missed out on the First World War because the monster tore his arm off when he was a boy, no one ever mentions the then-current War. In its crazed way, *Frankenstein Meets the She-Wolf of the SS* is more "realistic." The War, as reflected in the Nazi pornos of the 1970s, has leaked into the enclosed world of Universal horror.

I mix Kettle Chips and Jaffa cakes, washing them down with Appletiser.

Predictably, at sunset, a distinguished visitor arrives at the castle, nattily-dressed in top hat, white tie and tails, peering hypnotically over his long nose. John Carradine announces himself as Baron Latos. As Ilsa escorts him to her boudoir, Carradine's floor-length cloak sweeps into a wing shape. An animated bat lands on Ilsa's breasts and writhes, pushing her back onto a canopied four-poster bed. Reverting to human form, Dracula nuzzles his moustache between Ilsa's thighs. The Count unbuttons his immaculate trouser fly to uncurl a white length of vampire manhood and pleasures Ilsa all through the night. The end, though, is inevitable. At sunrise, Dracula turns to ashes on top of an unsatisfied and infuriated Ilsa.

A sunburst of realization: Channel 1818 isn't showing movies that were made, but movies that can be *imagined*.

Appletiser blurts out of my nose at the conceptual breakthrough.

The ending is guessable: Dr. Pretorius charges the Monster and he gets up off his slab in time to be the insatiable stud Ilsa has looked for throughout the picture. Glenn Strange, naked but for asphalt-spreader's boots, pounds away at Ilsa's tender parts for what seems like hours as revolting partisan peasants burn down the castle around their ears. The Monster's tool is in proportion with the rest of him, scarred with collodion applications. As Ilsa finally comes like a skyrocket, burning beams fall on the bed and an end title flickers.

As usual on cheapo movie channels, the film fades before the end credits so there's no chance of noting down the copyright date. I howl in frustration and throw away the file card. With no concrete information, I might just as well not have watched the film.

In anger, I batter the cushions of my sofa. Then, I'm drawn back to the television. Over a frozen frame of Boris Karloff as the Monster in a Beatle Wig, Channel 1818 announces the rest of the evening's movie program.

King Kong Meets Frankenstein. Willis O'Brien's dream project.

The Marx Brothers Meet the Monsters. Through the bungling of Igolini (Chico), Professor Wolf J. Frankenstein (Groucho) puts the Monster's brain into Harpo's skull. Margaret Dumont is Dracula's Daughter.

House of the Wolf Man. A 1946 Universal, directed by Jean Yarbrough. Otto Kruger and Rondo Hatton tamper with the brains of Lon Chaney, Bela Lugosi and Glenn Strange.

Dr. Orloff, Sex Slave of Frankenstein. Directed by Jesus Franco, with Howard Vernon and Dennis Price, plus hardcore spliced in a decade after Price's death.

548

Frankenstein Meets the Space Monster: The Director's Cut. The three-hour extended version, with additional beach party numbers.

My bladder is uncomfortably full but I can't get up to pee lest I miss anything irreplaceable. Channel 1818 is a treasure trove. If I keep watching, I'll be able to note down credits. I'll be the true source of information. Weldon, Glut and Jones will have to beg me for credits. My interpretations will be definitive. Hardy's *Aurum Encyclopedia: Horror* will have to be junked entirely. The history of horror is written on shifting sands.

Then come trailers: Peter Cushing sewing new legs onto disco queen Caroline Munro in Hammer's *Frankenstein AD 1971*; an hour-long print of the 1910 Edison *Frankenstein*; Baron Rossano Brazzi singing "Some Lightning-Blasted Evening" in Rodgers and Hammerstein's *Frankenstein!*; Peter Cushing and Boris Karloff in the same laboratory; W.C. Fields as the Blind Hermit, sneering "never work with children or hunchbacked assistants"; James Whale's 1931 *Frankenstein*, with Leslie Howard as the doctor, Bette Davis as Elizabeth and a still-living Lon Chaney, all staring eyes and glittering teeth, as the monster; John Wayne and a cavalry troop tracking the Monster through Monument Valley in John Ford's *Fort Frankenstein*; a restored 1915 *Life Without Soul*, with Percy Darrell Standing; *Frankenstein 1980* in 3-D, with a better script; James Dean and Whit Bissell in *I Was a Teenage Frankenstein*.

1818 was the year in which Mary Shelley published *Frankenstein; or, the Modern Prometheus.* This is the Frankenstein Channel.

My bladder lets go, but I don't mind. I can't make it to the kitchen without looking away from the screen, so I'll have to improvise food. As always, I have enough munchies to keep me going. Sleep, I can do without. I have my vocation.

My wrist aches from writing down titles and credits. I have responsibilities.

David Cronenberg's *Frankenstein*. Dario Argento's *Frankenstein*. Ingmar Bergman's *Frankenstein*. Woody Allen's *Frankenstein*. Martin Scorsese's *Frankenstein*. Walerian Borowczyk's *Frankenstein*. Jerry Warren's *Frankenstine*. Akira Kurosawa's *Furankenshutain*. Ernest Hemingway's *Frank Stein*. Troma's *Frankenslime*. William Castle's *Shankenstein*. Jim Wynorski's *Wankenstein*. Wayne Newton's *Dankenshane*. Odorama's *Rankenstein*.

I watch, reference books strewn around the floor, all useless, all out-dated. On and on, monsters and mad doctors, hunchbacks and mobs, blind men and murdered girls, ice floes and laboratories.

Channel ident 1818 flickers. I fight pangs in my stomach and eat the crummy paper which was wrapped around my last pack of digestive biscuits. Sammy Davis, Jr., slicks hair across his flat-head in a Rat Packenstein picture, as Dino and Frank Sinatra fix up the electrodes.

I recognize the strange smell as my own. There are enough crumbs behind the cushions of the sofa to sustain life. I pick them out like a grooming gorilla and crack them between my teeth.

Badly-dressed black musicians rob the graves of blues singers in the endless *Funkenstein* series. Ridley Scott directs a run of *Bankenstein* ads for Barclays, with Sting applying for a small business loan to get his monster wired. Jane Fonda works the scars out of her thighs in the *Flankenstein* video.

I am transfixed. I would look away, but there is a chance I might miss something. I'm dreaming the electronic dream, consuming imaginary images made celluloid.

Brides, sons, ghosts, curses, revenges, evils, horrors, brains, dogs, bloods, castles, daughters, houses, ladies, brothers, ledgers, lodgers, hands, returns, tales, torments, infernos, worlds, experiments, horror chambers . . . of Frankenstein.

I hit the exhaustion wall and burn through it. My life functions are at such a low level that I can continue indefinitely. I'm plugged into Channel 1818. It's my duty to stay the course.

Abbott and Costello, Martin and Lewis, Redford and Newman, Astaire and Rogers, Mickey and Donald, Tango and Cash, Rowan and Martin, Bonnie and Clyde, Frankie and Annette, Hinge and Brackett, Batman and Robin, Salt and Pepa, Titch and Quackers, Amos and Andy, Gladstone and Disraeli, Morecambe and Wise, Block and Tackle . . . Meet Frankenstein.

I can barely move, but my eyes are open.

Credits roll, too fast to jot down. These films exist for one showing and are lost. Each frame is unique, impossible to recreate. I daren't even leave the room to get a pack of blank videotapes. It is down to me. I must watch and I must remember. My mind is the screen on which these Frankensteins perform.

The Frankenstein Monster is played by . . . Bela Lugosi (in 1931), Christopher Lee (in 1964), Lane Chandler, Harvey Keitel, Sonny Bono, Bernard Bresslaw, Meryl Streep, Bruce Lee, Neville Brand, John Gielgud, Ice-T, Rock Hudson, Traci Lords.

The experience is priceless. A red sun rises outside, and I draw the curtains.

"Now I know what it feels like to be a God," croaks Edward G. Robinson.

I will stay with the channel.

"We belong dead," intones Don Knotts.

I will watch.

"To a new world of Gods and monsters," toasts Daffy Duck.

PAUL McAULEY
The Temptation of Dr. Stein

⚬═⚬

Paul McAuley was born in Stroud, Gloucestershire. A former research biologist at Oxford University and UCLA, and a former lecturer at St. Andrews University, he became a full-time writer in 1996. McAuley sold a story to the SF Digest *when he was just nineteen, but the magazine folded before it could appear, and his first published story appeared in* Asimov's Science Fiction *in 1984.*

With his debut novel, Four Hundred Billion Stars *(1988), he became the first British writer to win the Philip K. Dick Memorial Award and he established his reputation as one of the best young science fiction writers in the field by winning the John W. Campbell Memorial Award in 1995.*

His other novels include Secret Harmonies *(aka* Of the Fall*)*, Eternal Light, Red Dust, Pasquale's Angel *(winner of the Sidewise Award for Best Long Form Alternate History fiction), the Arthur C. Clarke Award–winning* Fairyland, Child of the River, Ancients of Days, Shrine of Stars, Ship of Fools, The Secret of Life, Whole Wide World, White Devils, Mind's Eye, Players, Cowboy Angels, Evening's Empires, Something Coming Through *and* Into Everywhere.

The author's short fiction is collected in The King of the Hill and Other Stories, The Invisible Country, Little Machines *and* A Very British History.

"The Temptation of Dr. Stein" was written especially for this volume and won the British Fantasy Award for Best Short Story in 1995. It is set in the same alternate history as the author's novel Pasquale's Angel, *in which the inventions of the Great Engineer, Leonardo da Vinci, have made Florence into a world power.*

The novel features a cameo by a certain Dr. Pretorious (a character played by the great English eccentric Ernest Thesiger in the 1935 movie Bride of Frankenstein*), and this story concerns his activities in Venice, some ten years earlier . . .*

D r. Stein prided himself on being a rational man. When, in the months following his arrival in Venice, it became his habit to spend his free time wandering the city, he could not admit that it was because he believed that his daughter might still live, and that he might see her amongst the cosmopolitan throng. For he harbored the small, secret hope that when *Landsknechts* had pillaged the houses of the Jews of Lodz, perhaps his daughter had not been carried off to be despoiled and murdered, but had been forced to become a servant of some Prussian family. It was no more impossible that she had been brought here, for the Council of Ten had hired many *Landsknechts* to defend the city and the *terraferma* hinterlands of its empire.

Dr. Stein's wife would no longer talk to him about it. Indeed, they hardly talked about anything these days. She had pleaded that the memory of their daughter should be laid to rest in a week of mourning, just as if they had interred her body. They were living in rooms rented from the cousin of Dr. Stein's wife, a banker called Abraham Soncino, and Dr. Stein was convinced that she had been put up to this by the women of Soncino's family. Who knew what the women talked about, when locked in the bathhouse overnight after they had been purified of their menses? No good, Dr. Stein was certain. Even Soncino, a genial, uxorious man, had urged that Dr. Stein mourn his daughter. Soncino had said that his family would bring the requisite food to begin the mourning; after a week all the community would commiserate with Dr. Stein and his wife before the main Sabbath service, and with God's help this terrible wound would be healed. It had taken all of Dr. Stein's powers to refuse this generous offer courteously. Soncino was a good man, but this was none of his business.

As winter came on, driven out by his wife's silent recriminations, or so he told himself, Dr. Stein walked the crowded streets almost every afternoon. Sometimes he was accompanied by an English captain of the Night Guard, Henry Gorrall, to whom Dr. Stein had become an unofficial assistant, helping identify the cause of death of one or another of the bodies found floating in the backwaters of the city.

There had been more murders than usual that summer, and several well-bred young women had disappeared. Dr. Stein had been urged to help Gorrall by the Elders of the *Beth Din*; already there were rumors that the Jews were murdering Christian virgins and using their blood to animate a Golem. It was good that a Jew—moreover, a Jew who worked at the city hospital, and taught new surgical techniques at the school of medicine—was involved in attempting to solve this mystery.

Besides, Dr. Stein enjoyed Gorrall's company. He was sympathetic to Gorrall's belief that everything, no matter how unlikely, had at base a rational explanation. Gorrall was a humanist, and did not mind being seen in the company of a man who must wear a yellow star on his coat. On their walks through the city, they often talked on the new philosophies of nature compounded in the university of Florence's Great Engineer, Leonardo da Vinci, quite oblivious to the brawling bustle all around them.

Ships from twenty nations crowded the quay in the long shadow of the Campanile, and their sailors washed through the streets. Hawkers cried their wares from flotillas of small boats that rocked on the wakes of barges or galleys. Gondoliers shouted vivid curses as skiffs crossing from one side of the Grand Canal to the other got in the way of their long, swift craft. Sometimes a screw-driven Florentine ship made its way up the Grand Canal, its Hero's engine laying a trail of black smoke, and everyone stopped to watch this marvel. Bankers in fur coats and tall felt hats conducted the business of the world in the piazza before San Gia-cometto, amid the rattle of the new clockwork abacuses and the subdued murmur of transactions.

Gorrall, a bluff muscular man with a bristling black beard and a habit of spitting sideways and often, because of the chaw of tobacco he habitually chewed, seemed to know most of the bankers by name, and most of the merchants, too—the silk and cloth-of-gold mercers and sellers of fustian and velvet along the Mercerie, the druggists, goldsmiths and silversmiths, the makers of white wax, the ironmongers, coopers and perfumers who had stalls and shops in the crowded little streets off the Rialto. He knew the names of many of the yellow-scarfed prostitutes, too, although Dr. Stein wasn't surprised at this, since he had first met Gorrall when the captain had come to the hospital for mercury treatment of his syphilis. Gorrall even knew, or pretended to know, the names of the cats which stalked between the feet of the crowds or lazed on cold stone in the brittle winter sunshine, the true rulers of Venice.

It was outside the cabinet of one of the perfumers of the Mercerie that Dr. Stein for a moment thought he saw his daughter. A grey-haired man was standing in the doorway of the shop, shouting at a younger man who was backing away and shouting that there was no blame that could be fixed to his name.

"You are his friend!"

"Sir, I did not know what it was he wrote, and I do not know and I do not care why your daughter cries so!"

The young man had his hand on his long knife, and Gorrall pushed through the gathering crowd and told both men to calm down. The wronged father dashed inside and came out again, dragging a girl of about fourteen, with the same long black hair, the same white, high forehead, as Dr. Stein's daughter.

"Hannah," Dr. Stein said helplessly, but then she turned, and it was not her. Not his daughter. The girl was crying, and clasped a sheet of paper to her bosom—wronged by a suitor, Dr. Stein supposed, and Gorrall said that it was precisely that. The young man had run off to sea, something so common these days that the Council of Ten had decreed that convicted criminals might be used on the galleys of the navy because of the shortage of free oarsman. Soon the whole city might be scattered between Corfu and Crete, or even farther, now that Florence had destroyed the fleet of Cortés, and opened the American shore.

Dr. Stein did not tell his wife what he had seen. He sat in the kitchen long into the evening, and was still there, warmed by the embers of the fire and reading in Leonardo's *Treatise on the Replication of Motion* by the poor light of a tallow candle, when the knock at the door came. It was just after midnight. Dr. Stein picked up the candle and went out, and saw his wife standing in the door to the bedroom.

"Don't answer it," she said. With one hand she clutched her shift to her throat; with the other she held a candle. Her long black hair was down to her shoulders.

"This isn't Lodz, Belita," Dr. Stein said, perhaps with unnecessary sharpness. "Go back to bed. I will deal with this."

"There are plenty of Prussians here, even so. One spat at me the other day. Abraham says that they blame us for the bodysnatching, and it's the doctors they'll come for first."

The knocking started again. Husband and wife both looked at the door. "It may be a patient," Dr. Stein said, and pulled back the bolts.

The rooms were on the ground floor of a rambling house that faced onto a narrow canal. An icy wind was blowing along the canal, and it blew out Dr. Stein's candle when he opened the heavy door. Two city guards stood there, flanking their captain, Henry Gorrall.

"There's been a body found," Gorrall said in his blunt, direct manner. "A woman we both saw this very day, as it happens. You'll come along and tell me if it's murder."

The woman's body had been found floating in the Rio di Noale. "An hour later," Gorrall said, as they were rowed through the dark city, "and the tide would have turned and taken her out to sea, and neither you or I would have to chill our bones."

It was a cold night indeed, just after St. Agnes Eve. An insistent wind off the land blew a dusting of snow above the roofs and prickly spires of Venice. Fresh ice crackled as the gondola broke through it, and larger pieces knocked against its planking. The few lights showing in the facades of the *palazzos* that lined the Grand Canal seemed bleary and dim. Dr. Stein wrapped his ragged loden cloak around himself and asked, "Do you think it murder?"

Gorrall spat into the black, icy water. "She died for love. That part is easy, as we witnessed the quarrel this very afternoon. She wasn't in the water long, and still reeks of booze. Drank to get her courage up, jumped. But we have to be sure. It could be a bungled kidnapping, or some cruel sport gone from bad to worse. There are too many soldiers with nothing to do but patrol the defenses and wait for a posting in Cyprus."

The drowned girl had been laid out on the pavement by the canal, and covered with a blanket. Even at this late hour, a small crowd had gathered, and when a guard twitched the blanket aside at Dr. Stein's request, some of the watchers gasped.

It was the girl he had seen that afternoon, the perfumer's daughter. The soaked dress which clung to her body was white against the wet flags of the pavement. Her long black hair twisted in ropes about her face. There was a little froth at her mouth, and blue touched her lips. Dead, there was nothing about her that reminded Dr. Stein of his daughter.

Dr. Stein felt the skin move over the bones of her hand, pressed one of her fingernails, closed her eyelids with thumb and forefinger. Tenderly, he covered her with the blanket again. "She's been dead less than an hour," he told Gorrall. "There's no sign of a struggle, and from the flux at her mouth I'd say it's clear she drowned."

"Killed herself most likely, unless someone pushed her in. The usual reason, I'd guess, which is why her boyfriend ran off to sea. Care to make a wager?"

"We both know her story. I can find out if she was with child, but not here."

Gorrall smiled. "I forget that you people don't bet."

"On the contrary. But in this case I fear you're right."

Gorrall ordered his men to take the body to the city hospital. As they lifted it into the gondola, he said to Dr. Stein, "She drank to get courage, then gave herself to the water. Not in this little canal. Suicides favor places where their last sight is a view, often of a place they love. We'll search the bridge at the Rialto—it is the only bridge crossing the Grand Canal, and the tide is running from that direction—but all the world crosses there, and if we're not quick, some beggar will have carried away her bottle and any note she may have left. Come on, Doctor. We need to find out how she died before her parents turn up and start asking questions. I must have something to tell them, or they will go out looking for revenge."

If the girl had jumped from the Rialto bridge, she had left no note there—or it had been stolen, as Gorrall had predicted. Gorrall and Dr. Stein hurried on to the city hospital, but the body had not arrived. An hour later, a patrol found the gondola tied up in a backwater. One guard was dead from a single swordcut to his neck. The other was stunned, and remembered nothing. The drowned girl was gone.

Gorrall was furious, and sent out every man he had to look for the bodysnatchers. They had balls to attack two guards of the night watch, he said, but when he had finished with them they'd sing falsetto under the lash on the galleys. Nothing came of his enquiries. The weather turned colder, and an outbreak of pleurisy meant that Dr. Stein had much work in the hospital. He thought no more about it until a week later, when Gorrall came to see him.

"She's alive," Gorrall said. "I've seen her."

"A girl like her, perhaps." For a moment, Dr. Stein saw his daughter, running towards him, arms widespread. He said, "I don't make mistakes. There was no pulse, her lungs were congested with fluid, and she was as cold as the stones on which she lay."

Gorrall spat. "She's walking around dead, then. Do you remember what she looked like?"

"Vividly."

"She was the daughter of a perfumer, one Filippo Rompiasi. A member of the Great Council, although of the two thousand five hundred who have that honor, I'd say he has about the least influence. A noble family so long fallen on hard times that they have had to learn a trade." Gorrall had little time for the numerous aristocracy of Venice, who, in his opinion, spent more time scheming to obtain support from the Republic than playing their part in governing it. "Still," he said, scratching at his beard, "it'll look very bad that the daughter of a patrician family walks around after having been pronounced dead by the doctor in charge of her case."

"I don't recall being paid," Dr. Stein said.

Gorrall spat again. "Would I pay someone who can't tell the quick from the dead? Come and prove me wrong and I'll pay you from my own pocket. With a distinguished surgeon as witness, I can draw up a docket to end this matter."

The girl was under the spell of a mountebank who called himself Dr. Pretorious, although Gorrall was certain that it wasn't the man's real name. "He was thrown out of Padua last year for practicing medicine without a license, and was in jail in Milan before that. I've had my eye on him since he came ashore on a Prussian coal barge this summer. He vanished a month ago, and I thought he'd become some other city's problem. Instead, he went to ground. Now he proclaims this girl to be a miraculous example of a new kind of treatment."

There were many mountebanks in Venice. Every morning and afternoon there were five or six stages erected in the Piazza San Marco for their performances and convoluted orations, in which they praised the virtues of their peculiar instruments, powders, elixirs and other concoctions. Venice tolerated these madmen, in Dr. Stein's opinion, because the miasma of the nearby marshes befuddled the minds of her citizens, who besides were the most vain people he had ever met, eager to believe any promise of enhanced beauty and longer life.

Unlike the other mountebanks, Dr. Pretorious was holding a secret court. He had rented a disused wine store at the edge of the Prussian *Fondaco*, a quarter of Venice where ships were packed tightly in the narrow canals and every other building was a merchant's warehouse. Even walking beside a captain of the city guard, Dr. Stein was deeply uneasy there, feeling that all eyes were drawn to the yellow star he must by law wear, pinned to the breast of his surcoat. There had been an attack on the synagogue just the other day, and pigshit had been smeared on the mezuzah fixed to the doorpost of a prominent Jewish banker. Sooner or later, if the bodysnatchers were not caught, a mob would sack the houses of the wealthiest Jews on the excuse of searching out and destroying the fabled Golem which existed nowhere but in their inflamed imaginations.

Along with some fifty others, mostly rich old women and their servants, Gorrall and Dr. Stein crossed a high arched bridge over a dark, silently running canal, and, after paying a ruffian a soldi each for the privilege, entered through a gate into a courtyard lit by smoky torches. Once the ruffian had closed and locked the gate, two figures appeared at a tall open door that was framed with swags of red cloth.

One was a man dressed all in black, with a mop of white hair. Behind him a woman in white lay half-submerged in a kind of tub packed full of broken ice. Her head was bowed, and her face hidden by a fall of black hair. Gorrall nudged Dr. Stein and said that this was the girl.

"She looks dead to me. Anyone who could sit in a tub of ice and not burst to bits through shivering must be dead."

"Let's watch and see," Gorrall said, and lit a foul-smelling cigarillo.

The white-haired man, Dr. Pretorious, welcomed his audience, and began a long rambling speech. Dr. Stein paid only a little attention, being more interested in the speaker. Dr. Pretorious was a gaunt, bird-like man with a clever, lined face and dark eyes under shaggy brows which knitted together when he made a point. He had a habit of stabbing a finger at his audience, of shrugging and laughing immodestly at his own boasts. He did not, Dr. Stein was convinced, much believe his speech, a curious failing for a mountebank.

Dr. Pretorious had the honor, it appeared, of introducing the true Bride of the Sea, one recently dead but now animated by an ancient Egyptian science. There was much on the long quest he had made in search of the secret of this ancient science, and the dangers he had faced in bringing it here, and in perfecting it. He assured his audience that as it had conquered death, the science he had perfected would also conquer old age, for was that not the slow victory of death over life? He snapped his fingers, and, as the tub seemed to slide forward of its own accord into the torchlight, invited his audience to see for themselves that this Bride of the Sea was not alive.

Strands of kelp had been woven into the drowned girl's thick black hair. Necklaces layered at her breast were of seashells of the kind that anyone could pick from the beach at the mouth of the lagoon.

Dr. Pretorious pointed to Dr. Stein, called him out. "I see we have here a physician. I recognize you, sir. I know the good work that you do at the Pietà, and the wonderful new surgical techniques you have brought to the city. As a man of science, would you do me the honor of certifying that this poor girl is at present not living?"

"Go on," Gorrall said, and Dr. Stein stepped forward, feeling both foolish and eager.

"Please, your opinion," Dr. Pretorious said with an ingratiating bow. He added, *sotto voce*, "This is a true marvel, Doctor. Believe in me." He held a little mirror before the girl's red lips, asked Dr. Stein if he saw any evidence of breath.

Dr. Stein was aware of an intense sweet, cloying odor: a mixture of brandy and attar of roses. He said, "I see none."

"Louder, for the good people here." Dr. Stein repeated his answer.

"A good answer. Now, hold her wrist. Does her heart beat?"

The girl's hand was as cold as the ice from which Dr. Pretorious lifted it. If there was a pulse, it was so slow that Dr. Stein was not allowed enough time to find it. He was dismissed, and Dr. Pretorious held up the girl's arm by the wrist, and with a grimace of effort pushed a long nail though her hand.

"You see," he said with indecent excitement, giving the wrist a little shake so that the pierced hand flopped to and fro. "You see! No blood! No blood! Eh? What living person could endure such a cruel mutilation?"

He seemed excited by his demonstration. He dashed inside the doorway, and brought forward a curious device, a glass bowl inverted on a stalk of glass almost as tall as he, with a band of red silk twisted inside the bowl and around a spindle at the bottom of the stalk. He began to work a treadle, and the band of silk spun around and around.

"A moment," Dr. Pretorious said, as the crowd began to murmur. He glared at them from beneath his shaggy eyebrows as his foot pumped the treadle. "A moment, if you please. The apparatus must receive a sufficient charge."

He sounded flustered and out of breath. Any mountebank worth his salt would have had a naked boy painted in gilt with cherub wings to work the treadle, Dr. Stein reflected, and a drumroll besides. Yet the curious amateurism of this performance was more compelling than the polished theatricality of the mountebanks of the Piazza San Marco.

Gold threads trailed from the top of the glass bowl to a big glass jar half-filled with water and sealed with a cork. At last, Dr. Pretorious finished working the treadle, sketched a bow to the audience—his face shiny with sweat—and used a stave to sweep the gold threads from the top of the glass bowl onto the girl's face.

There was a faint snap, as of an old glass broken underfoot at a wedding. The girl's eyes opened and she looked about her, seeming dazed and confused.

"She lives, but only for a few precious minutes," Dr. Pretorious said. "Speak to me, my darling. You are a willing bride to the sea, perhaps?"

Gorrall whispered to Dr. Stein, "That's definitely the girl who drowned herself?" and Dr. Stein nodded. Gorrall drew out a long silver whistle and blew on it, three quick blasts. At once, a full squad of men-at-arms swarmed over the high walls. Some of the old women in the audience started to scream. The ruffian in charge of the gate charged at Gorrall, who drew a repeating pistol with a notched wheel over its stock. He shot three times, the wheel ratchetting around as it delivered fresh charges of powder and shot to the chamber. The ruffian was thrown onto his back, already dead as the noise of the shots echoed in the courtyard. Gorrall turned and levelled the pistol at the red-cloaked doorway, but it was on fire, and Dr. Pretorious and the dead girl in her tub of ice were gone.

Gorrall and his troops put out the fire and ransacked the empty wine store. It was Dr. Stein who found the only clue, a single broken seashell by a hatch that, when lifted, showed black water a few *braccia* below, a passage that Gorrall soon determined led out into the canal.

Dr. Stein could not forget the dead girl, the icy touch of her skin, her sudden start into life, the confusion in her eyes. Gorrall thought that she only seemed alive, that her body had been preserved perhaps by tanning, that the shine in her eyes was glycerin, the bloom on her lips pigment of the kind the apothecaries made of powdered beetles.

"The audience wanted to believe it would see a living woman, and the flickering candles would make her seem to move. You'll be a witness, I hope."

"I touched her," Dr. Stein said. "She was not preserved. The process hardens the skin."

"We keep meat by packing it in snow, in winter," Gorrall said. "Also, I have heard that there are magicians in the far Indies who can fall into so deep a trance that they do not need to breathe."

"We know she is not from the Indies. I would ask why so much fuss was made of the apparatus. It was so clumsy that it seemed to me to be real."

"I'll find him," Gorrall said, "and we will have answers to all these questions."

But when Dr. Stein saw Gorrall two days later, and asked about his enquiries into the Pretorious affair, the English captain shook his head and said, "I have been told not to pursue the matter. It seems the girl's father wrote too many begging letters to the Great Council, and he has no friends there. Further than that, I'm not allowed to say." Gorrall spat and said with sudden bitterness, "You can work here twenty-five years, Stein, and perhaps they'll make you a citizen, but they will never make you privy to their secrets."

"Someone in power believes Dr. Pretorious's claims, then."

"I wish I could say. Do you believe him?"

"Of course not."

But it was not true, and Dr. Stein immediately made his own enquiries. He wanted to know the truth, and not, he told himself, because he had mistaken the girl for his daughter. His interest was that of a doctor, for if death could be reversed, then surely that was the greatest gift a doctor could possess. He was not thinking of his daughter at all.

His enquiries were first made amongst his colleagues at the city hospital, and then in the guild hospitals and the new hospital of the Arsenal.

Only the director of the last was willing to say anything, and warned Dr. Stein that the man he was seeking had powerful allies.

"So I have heard," Dr. Stein said. He added recklessly, "I wish I knew who they were."

The director was a pompous man, placed in his position through politics rather than merit. Dr. Stein could see that he was tempted to divulge what he knew, but in the end he merely said, "Knowledge is a dangerous thing. If you would know anything, start from a low rather than a high place. Don't overreach yourself, Doctor."

Dr. Stein bridled at this, but said nothing. He sat up through the night, thinking the matter over. This was a city of secrets, and he was a stranger, and a Jew from Prussia to boot. His actions could easily be mistaken for those of a spy, and he was not sure that Gorrall could help him if he was accused. Gorrall's precipitous attempt to arrest Dr. Pretorious had not endeared him to his superiors, after all.

Yet Dr. Stein could not get the drowned girl's face from his mind, the way she had given a little start and her eyes had opened under the tangle of gold threads. Tormented by fantasies in which he found his daughter's grave and raised her up, he paced the kitchen, and in the small hours of the night it came to him that the director of the Arsenal hospital had spoken the truth even if he had not known it.

In the morning, Dr. Stein set out again, saying nothing to his wife of what he was doing. He had realized that Dr. Pretorious must need simples and other necessaries for his trade, and now he went from apothecary to apothecary with the mountebank's description. Dr. Stein found his man late in the afternoon, in a mean little shop in a *calle* that led off a square dominated by the brightly painted façade of the new church of Santa Maria di Miracoli.

The apothecary was a young man with a handsome face but small, greedy eyes. He peered at Dr. Stein from beneath a fringe of greasy black hair, and denied knowing Dr. Pretorious with such vehemence that Dr. Stein did not doubt he was lying.

A soldi soon loosened his tongue. He admitted that he might have such a customer as Dr. Stein described, and Dr. Stein asked at once, "Does he buy alum and oil?"

The apothecary expressed surprise. "He is a physician, not a tanner."

"Of course," Dr. Stein said, hope rising in him. A second soldi bought Dr. Stein the privilege of delivering the mountebank's latest order, a jar of sulphuric acid nested in a straw cradle.

The directions given by the apothecary led Dr. Stein through an intricate maze of *calles* and squares, ending in a courtyard no bigger than a closet, with tall buildings soaring on either side, and no way out but the narrow passage by which he had entered. Dr. Stein knew he was lost, but before he could turn to begin to retrace his steps, someone seized him from behind. An arm clamped across his throat. He struggled and dropped the jar of acid, which by great good luck, and the straw padding, did not break. Then he was on his back, looking up at a patch of grey sky which seemed to rush away from him at great speed, dwindling to a speck no bigger than a star.

Dr. Stein was woken by the solemn tolling of the curfew bells. He was lying on a moldering bed in a room muffled by dusty tapestries and lit by a tall tallow candle. His throat hurt and his head ached. There was a tender swelling above his right ear, but he had no double vision or dizziness. Whoever had hit him had known what they were about.

The door was locked, and the windows were closed by wooden shutters nailed tightly shut. Dr. Stein was prying at the shutters when the door was unlocked and an old man came in. He was a shrivelled gnome in a velvet tunic and doublet more suited to a young gallant. His creviced face was drenched with powder, and there were hectic spots of rouge on his sunken cheeks.

"My master will talk with you," this ridiculous creature said.

Dr. Stein asked where he was, and the old man said that it was his master's house. "Once it was mine, but I gave it to him. It was his fee."

"Ah. You were sick, and he cured you."

"I was cured of life. He killed me and brought me back, so that I will live forever in the life beyond death. He's a great man."

"What's your name?"

The old man laughed. He had only one tooth in his head, and that a blackened stump. "I've yet to be christened in this new life. Come with me."

They mounted a wide marble stair that wound through the middle of what must be a great *palazzo*. Two stories below was a floor tiled black and white like a chessboard; they climbed past two more floors to the top.

The long room had once been a library, but the shelves of the dark bays set off the main passage were empty now; only the chains which had secured the books were left. It was lit by a scattering of candles whose restless flames cast a confusion of flickering light that hid more than it revealed. One bay was penned off with a hurdle, and a pig moved in the shadows there. Dr. Stein had enough of a glimpse of it to see that there was something on the pig's back, but it was too dark to be sure quite what it was. Then something the size of a mouse scuttled straight in front of him—Dr. Stein saw with a shock that it ran on its hind legs, with a stumbling, crooked gait.

"One of my children," Dr. Pretorious said.

He was seated at a plain table scattered with books and papers. Bits of glassware and jars of acids and salts cluttered the shelves that rose behind him. The drowned girl sat beside him in a highbacked chair. Her head was held up by a leather band around her forehead; her eyes were closed and seemed bruised and sunken. Behind the chair was the same apparatus that Dr. Stein had seen used in the wine store. The smell of attar of roses was very strong.

Dr. Stein said, "It was only a mouse, or a small rat."

"You believe what you must, Doctor," Dr. Pretorious said, "but I hope to open your eyes to the wonders I have performed." He told the old man, "Fetch food."

The old man started to complain that he wanted to stay, and Dr. Pretorious immediately jumped up in a sudden fit of anger and threw a pot of ink at his servant. The old man sputtered, smearing the black ink across his powdered face, and at once Dr. Pretorious burst into laughter. "You're a poor book," he said. "Fetch our guest meat and wine. It's the least I can do," he told Dr. Stein. "Did you come here of your own will, by the way?"

"I suppose the apothecary told you that I asked for you. That is, if he was an apothecary."

Dr. Pretorious said, with a quick smile, "You wanted to see the girl, I suppose, and here she is. I saw the tender look you gave her, before we were interrupted, and see that same look again."

"I knew nothing of my colleague's plans."

Dr. Pretorious made a steeple with his hands, touched the tip of the steeple to his bloodless lips. His fingers were long and white, and seemed to have an extra joint in them. He said, "Don't hope he'll find you."

"I'm not afraid. You brought me here because you wanted me here."

"But you should be afraid. I have power of life and death here."

"The old man said you gave him life everlasting."

Dr. Pretorious said carelessly, "Oh, so he believes. Perhaps that's enough."

"Did he die? Did you bring him back to life?"

Dr. Pretorious said, "That depends what you mean by life. The trick is not raising the dead, but making sure that death does not reclaim them."

Dr. Stein had seen a panther two days after he had arrived in Venice, brought from the Friendly Isles along with a great number of parrots. So starved that the bones of its shoulders and pelvis were clearly visible under its sleek black pelt, the panther ceaselessly padded back and forth inside its little cage, its eyes like green lamps. It had been driven mad by the voyage, and Dr. Stein thought that Dr. Pretorious was as mad as that panther, his sensibility quite lost on the long voyage into the unknown regions which he claimed to have conquered. In truth, they had conquered him.

"I have kept her on ice for much of the time," Dr. Pretorious said. "Even so, she is beginning to deteriorate." He twitched the hem of the girl's gown, and Dr. Stein saw on her right foot a black mark as big as his hand, like a sunken bruise. Despite the attar of roses, the reek of gangrene was suddenly overpowering.

He said, "The girl is dead. I saw it for myself, when she was pulled from the canal. No wonder she rots."

"It depends what you mean by death. Have you ever seen fish in a pond, under ice? They can become so sluggish that they no longer move, yet they live, and when warmed will move again. I was once in Gotland. In winter, the nights last all day, and your breath freezes in your beard. A man was found alive after two days lying in a drift of snow. He had drunk too much, and had passed out; the liquor had saved him from freezing to death, although he lost his ears and his fingers and toes. She was dead when she was pulled from the icy water, but she had drunk enough to prevent death from placing an irreversible claim on her body. I returned her to life. Would you like to see how it is done?"

"Master?"

It was the old man. With cringing deference, he offered a tray bearing a tarnished silver wine decanter, a plate of beef, heavily salted and greenish at the edges, and a loaf of black bread.

Dr. Pretorious was on him in an instant. The food and wine flew into the air, Dr. Pretorious lifted the old man by his neck, dropped him to the floor. "We are busy," he said, quite calmly.

Dr. Stein started to help the old man to gather the food together. Dr. Pretorious aimed a kick at the old man, who scuttled away on all fours.

Dr. Pretorious said impatiently, "No need for that. I shall show you, Doctor, that she lives."

The glass bowl sang under his long fingernails; he smoothed the belt of frayed red silk with tender care. He looked sidelong at Dr. Stein and said, "There is a tribe in the far south of Egypt who have been metalworkers for three thousand years. They apply a fine coat of silver to ornaments of base metal by immersing the ornaments in a solution of nitrate of silver and connecting them to tanks containing plates of lead and zinc in salt water. Split by the two metals, the opposing essences of the salt water flow in different directions, and when they join in the ornaments draw the silver from solution. I have experimented with that process, and will experiment more, but even when I substitute salt water with acid, the flow of essences is as yet too weak for my purpose. This—" he rapped the glass bowl, which rang like a bell—"is based on a toy that their children played with, harnessing that same essence to give each other little frights. I have greatly enlarged it, and developed a way of storing the essence it generates. For this essence lives within us, too, and is sympathetic to the flow from this apparatus. By its passage through the glass the silk generates that essence, which is stored here, in this jar. Look closely if you will. It is only ordinary glass, and ordinary water, sealed by a cork, but it contains the essence of life."

"What do you want of me?"

"I have done much alone. But, Doctor, we can do so much more together. Your reputation is great."

"I have the good fortune to be allowed to teach the physicians here some of the techniques I learned in Prussia. But no surgeon would operate on a corpse."

"You are too modest. I have heard the stories of the man of clay your people can make to defend themselves. I know it is based on truth. Clay cannot live, even if bathed in blood, but a champion buried in the clay of the earth might be made to live again, might he not?"

Dr. Stein understood that the mountebank believed his own legerdemain. He said, "I see that you have great need of money. A man of learning would only sell books in the most desperate circumstances, but all the books in this library have gone. Perhaps your sponsors are disappointed, and do not pay what they have promised, but it is no business of mine."

Dr. Pretorious said sharply, "The fancies in those books were a thousand years old. I have no need of them. And it might be said that you owe me money. Interruption of my little demonstration cost me at least twenty ducats, for there were at least that many dowagers eager to taste the revitalizing essence of life. So I think that you are obliged to help me, eh? Now watch, and wonder."

Dr. Pretorious began to work the treadles of his apparatus. The sound of his labored breathing and the soft tearing sound made by the silk belt as it revolved around and around filled the long room. At last, Dr. Pretorious twitched the gold wires from the top of the glass bowl so that they fell across the girl's face. In the dim light, Dr. Stein saw the snap of a fat blue flame that for a moment jumped amongst the ends of the wires. The girl's whole body shuddered. Her eyes opened.

"A marvel!" Dr. Pretorious said, panting from his exercise. "Each day she dies. Each night I bring her to life."

The girl looked around at his voice. The pupils of her eyes were of different sizes. Dr. Pretorious slapped her face until a faint bloom appeared on her cheeks.

"You see! She lives! Ask her a question. Anything. She has returned from death, and there is more in her head than in yours or mine. Ask!"

"I have nothing to ask," Dr. Stein said.

"She knows the future. Tell him about the future," he hissed into the girl's ear.

The girl's mouth worked. Her chest heaved as if she was pumping up something inside herself, then she said in a low whisper, "It is the Jews that will be blamed."

Dr. Stein said, "That's always been true."

"But that's why you're here, isn't it?"

Dr. Stein met Dr. Pretorious's black gaze. "How many have you killed, in your studies?"

"Oh, most of them were already dead. They gave themselves for science, just as in the ancient days young girls were sacrificed for the pagan gods."

"Those days are gone."

"Greater days are to come. You will help. I know you will. Let me show you how we will save her. You will save her, won't you?"

The girl's head was beside Dr. Pretorious's. They were both looking at Dr. Stein. The girl's lips moved, mumbling over two words. A cold mantle crept across Dr. Stein's skin. He had picked up a knife when he had stooped to help the old man, and now, if he could, he had a use for it.

Dr. Pretorious led Dr. Stein to the pen where the pig snuffled in its straw. He held up a candle, and Dr. Stein saw clearly, for an instant, the hand on the pig's back. Then the creature bolted into shadow.

It was a human hand, severed at the wrist, poking out of the pink skin of the pig's back as if from a sleeve. It looked alive, the nails suffused, the skin as pink as the pig's skin.

"They don't last long," Dr. Pretorious said. He seemed pleased by Dr. Stein's shock. "Either the pig dies, or the limb begins to rot. There is some incompatibility between the two kinds of blood. I have tried giving pigs human blood before the operation, but they die even more quickly. Perhaps with your help I can perfect the process. I will perform the operation on the girl, replace her rotten foot with a healthy one. I will not have her imperfect. I will do better. I will improve her, piece by piece. I will make her a true Bride of the Sea, a wonder that all the world will worship. Will you help me, Doctor? It is difficult to get bodies. Your friend is causing me a great deal of nuisance . . . but you can bring me bodies, why, almost every day. So many die in winter. A piece here, a piece there. I do not need the whole corpse. What could be simpler?"

He jumped back as Dr. Stein grabbed his arm, but Dr. Stein was quicker, and knocked the candle into the pen. The straw was aflame in an instant, and the pig charged out as soon as Dr. Stein pulled back the hurdle. It barged at Dr. Pretorious as if it remembered the torments he had inflicted upon it, and knocked him down. The hand flopped to and fro on its back, as if waving.

The girl could have been asleep, but her eyes opened as soon as Dr. Stein touched her cold brow. She tried to speak, but she had very little strength now, and Dr. Stein had to lay his head on her cold breast to hear her mumble the two words she had mouthed to him earlier.

"Kill me."

Behind them, the fire had taken hold in the shelving and floor, casting a lurid light down the length of the room. Dr. Pretorious ran to and fro, pursued by the pig. He was trying to capture the scampering mice-things which had been driven from their hiding places by the fire, but even with their staggering bipedal gait they were faster than he was. The old man ran into the room, and Dr. Pretorious shouted, "Help me, you fool!"

But the old man ran past him, ran through the wall of flames that now divided the room, and jumped onto Dr. Stein as he bent over the drowned girl. He was as weak as a child, but when Dr. Stein tried to push him away he bit into Dr. Stein's wrist and the knife fell to the floor. They reeled backwards and knocked over a jar of acid. Instantly, acrid white fumes rose up as the acid burnt into the wood floor. The old man rolled on the floor, beating at his smoking, acid-drenched costume.

Dr. Stein found the knife and drew its sharp point down the length of the blue veins of the drowned girl's forearms. The blood flowed surprisingly quickly. Dr. Stein stroked the girl's hair, and her eyes focused on his. For a moment it seemed as if she might say something, but with the heat of the fire beating at his back he could not stay any longer.

Dr. Stein knocked out a shutter with a bench, hauled himself onto the window-ledge. As he had hoped, there was black water directly below: like all *palazzos*, this one rose straight up from the Grand Canal. Smoke rolled around him. He heard Dr. Pretorious shout at him and he let himself go, and gave himself to air, and then water.

Dr. Pretorious was caught at dawn the next day, as he tried to leave the city in a hired skiff. The fire set by Dr. Stein had burnt out the top floor of the *palazzo*, no more, but the old man had died there. He had been the last in the line of a patrician family that had fallen on hard times: the *palazzo* and an entry in the *Libro d'Oro* was all that was left of their wealth and fame.

Henry Gorrall told Dr. Stein that no mention need be made of his part in this tragedy. "Let the dead lay as they will. There's no need to disturb them with fantastic stories."

"Yes," Dr. Stein said, "the dead should stay dead."

He was lying in his own bed, recovering from a rheumatic fever brought about by the cold waters into which he had plunged on his escape. Winter sunlight pried at the shutters of the white bedroom, streaked the fresh rushes on the floor.

"It seems that Pretorious does have friends," Gorrall said. "There won't be a trial and an execution, much as he deserves both. He's going straight to the galleys, and no doubt after a little while he will contrive, with some help, to escape. That's the way of things here. His name wasn't really Pretorious, of course. I doubt if we'll ever know where he came from. Unless he told you something of himself."

Outside the bedroom there was a clamor of voices as Dr. Stein's wife welcomed in Abraham Soncino and his family, and the omelettes and other egg dishes they had brought to begin the week of mourning.

Dr. Stein said, "Pretorious claimed that he was in Egypt, before he came here."

"Yes, but what adventurer was not, after the Florentines conquered it and let it go? Besides, I understand that he stole the apparatus not from any savage tribe, but from the Great Engineer of Florence himself. What else did he say? I'd know all, not for the official report, but my peace of mind."

"There aren't always answers to mysteries," Dr. Stein told his friend. The dead should stay dead. Yes. He knew now that his daughter had died. He had released her memory when he had released the poor girl that Dr. Pretorious had called back from the dead. Tears stood in his eyes, and Gorrall clumsily tried to comfort him, mistaking them for tears of grief.

For Ernest Thesiger, *in memoriam.*

MICHAEL MARSHALL SMITH
To Receive Is Better

—◦—

*Michael Marshall Smith is a novelist and screenwriter. Under this name he has published eighty short stories and three novels—*Only Forward, Spares *and* One of Us—*winning the Philip K. Dick, International Horror Guild and August Derleth awards, along with the Prix Bob Morane in France; he has been awarded the British Fantasy Award for Best Short Fiction four times, more than any other author.*

Writing as "Michael Marshall," he has also published seven international best-selling thrillers, including The Straw Men, The Intruders—*recently made into a TV mini-series by BBC America—and* Killer Move. *His most recent novel is* We Are Here.

The author believes that the story which follows speaks for itself, but adds: "The image of the blue tunnels is one I dreamed about ten years ago, and I'm glad it's finally found somewhere to rest."

I'd like to be going by car, but of course I don't know how to drive, and it would probably scare the shit out of me. A car would be much better, for lots of reasons. For a start, there's too many people out here. There's *so many* people. Wherever you turn there's more of them, looking tired, and rumpled, but whole. That's the strange thing. Everybody is whole.

A car would also be quicker. Sooner or later they're going to track me down, and I've got somewhere to go before they do. The public transport system sucks, incidentally. Long periods of being crowded into subway cars that smell, interspersed with long waits for another line, and I don't have a lot of time. It's intimidating too. People stare. They just look and look, and they don't know the danger they're in. Because in a minute one of them is going to look just one second too long, and I'm going to pull his fucking face off, which will do neither of us any good.

So instead I turn and look out the window. There's nothing to see, because we're in a tunnel, and I have to shut my eye to stop myself from screaming. The subway car is like another tunnel, a tunnel with windows, and I feel like I've been buried far too deep. I grew up in tunnels, ones that had no windows. The people who made them didn't even bother to pretend that there was something to look out on, something to look for. Because there wasn't. Nothing's coming up, nothing that isn't going to involve some fucker coming at you with a knife. So they don't pretend. I'll say that for them, at least: they don't taunt you with false hopes.

Manny did, in a way, which is why I feel complicated about him. On the one hand, he was the best thing that ever happened to us. But look at it another way, and maybe we'd have been better off without him. I'm being unreasonable. Without Manny, the whole thing would have been worse, thirty years of utter fucking pointlessness. I wouldn't have known, of course, but I do now: and I'm glad it wasn't that way. Without Manny

I wouldn't be where I am now. Standing in a subway car, running out of time.

People are giving me a wide berth, which I guess isn't so surprising. Partly it'll be my face, and my leg. People don't like that kind of thing. But probably it's mainly me. I know the way I am, can feel the fury I radiate. It's not a nice way to be, I know that, but then my life has not been nice. Maybe you should try it, and see how calm you stay.

The other reason I feel weird towards Manny is I don't know why he did it. Why he helped us. Sue 2 says it doesn't matter, but I think it does. If it was just an experiment, a hobby, then I think that makes a difference. I think I would have liked him less. As it happens, I don't think it was. I think it was probably just humanity, whatever the fuck that is. I think if it was an experiment, then what happened an hour ago would have panned out differently. For a start, he probably wouldn't be dead.

If everything's gone okay, then Sue 2 will be nearly where she's going by now, much closer than me. That's a habit I'm going to have to break, for a start. It's Sue now, just Sue. No numeral. And I'm just plain old Jack, or I will be if I get where I am going.

The first thing I can remember, the earliest glimpse of life, is the color blue. I know now what I was seeing, but at the time I didn't know anything different, and I thought that blue was the only color there was. A soft, hazy blue, a blue that had a soft hum in it and was always the same clammy temperature.

I have to get out of this subway very soon. I've taken an hour of it, and that's about as far as I can go. It's very noisy in here too, not a hum but a horrendous clattering. This is not the way I want to spend what may be the only time I have. People keep surging around me, and they've all got places to go. For the first time in my life, I'm surrounded by people who've actually got somewhere to go.

And the tunnel is the wrong color. Blue is the color of tunnels. I can't understand a tunnel unless it's blue. I spent the first four years of my life, as far as I can work out, in one of them. If it weren't for Manny, I'd be in one still. When he came to work at the Farm I could tell he was different straight away. I don't know how: I couldn't even think then, let alone speak. Maybe it was just he behaved differently when he was near us to the way the previous keeper had. I found out a lot later that Manny's wife had died having a dead baby, so maybe that was it.

What he did was take some of us, and let us live outside the tunnels. At first it was just a few, and then about half of the entire stock of spares. Some of the others never took to the world outside the tunnels, such as it was. They'd just come out every now and then, moving hopelessly around, mouths opening and shutting, and they always looked kind of blue somehow, as if the tunnel light had seeped into their skin. There were a few who never came out of the tunnels at all, but that was mainly because they'd been used too much already. Three years old and no arms. Tell me that's fucking reasonable.

Manny let us have the run of the facility, and sometimes let us go outside. He had to be careful, because there was a road a little too close to one side of the farm. People would have noticed a group of naked people stumbling around in the grass, and of course we were naked, because *they didn't give us any fucking clothes.* Right to the end we didn't have any clothes, and for years I thought it was always raining on the outside, because that's the only time he'd let us out.

I'm wearing one of Manny's suits now, and Sue's got some blue jeans and a shirt. The pants itch like hell, but I feel like a prince. Princes used to live in castles and fight monsters and sometimes they'd marry princesses and live happy ever after. I know about princes because I've been told.

Manny told us stuff, taught us. He tried to, anyway. With most of us it was too late. With *me* it was too late, probably. I can't write, and I can't read. I know there's big gaps in my head. Every now and then I can follow something through, and the way that makes me feel makes me realize that most of the time it doesn't happen. Things fall between the tracks. I can talk quite well, though. I was always one of Manny's favorites, and he used to talk to me a lot. I learnt from him. Part of what makes me so fucking angry is that I think I could have been clever. Manny said so. Sue says so. But it's too late now. It's far too fucking late.

I was ten when they first came for me. Manny got a phone call and suddenly he was in a panic. There were spares spread all over the facility and he had to run round, herding us all up. He got us into the tunnels just in time and we just sat in there, wondering what was going on.

In a while Manny came to the tunnel I was in, and he had this other guy with him who was big and nasty. They walked down the tunnel, the big guy kicking people out of the way. Everyone knew enough not to say anything: Manny had told us about that. Some of the people who never came out of the tunnels were crawling and shambling around, banging off the walls like they do, and the big guy just shoved them out of the way. They fell over like lumps of meat and then kept moving, making noises with their mouths.

Eventually Manny got to where I was and pointed me out. His hand was shaking and his face looked strange, like he was trying not to cry. The big guy grabbed me by the arm and took me out of the tunnel. He dragged me down to the operating room, where there were two more guys in white clothes and they put me on the table in there and cut off two of my fingers.

That's why I can't write. I'm right-handed, and they cut off my fucking fingers. Then they put a needle into my hand with see-through thread and sewed it up like they were in a hurry, and the big man took me back to the tunnel, opened the door and shoved me in. I didn't say anything. I didn't say anything the whole time.

Later Manny came and found me, and I shrank away from him, because I thought they were going to do something else. But he put his arms round me and I could tell the difference, and so I let him take me out into the main room. He put me in a chair and washed my hand which was all bloody, and then he sprayed it with some stuff that made it hurt a little less. Then he told me. He explained where I was, and why.

I was a spare, and I lived on a Farm. When people with money got pregnant, Manny said, doctors took a cell from the foetus and cloned another baby, so it had exactly the same cells as the baby that was going to be born. They grew the second baby until it could breath, and then they sent it to a Farm.

The spares live on the Farm until something happens to the proper baby. If the proper baby damages a part of itself, then the doctors come to the farm and cut a bit off the spare and sew it onto the real baby, because it's easier that way because of cell rejection and stuff that I don't really understand. They sew the spare baby up again and push it back into the tunnels and the spare sits there until the real baby does something else to itself. And when it does, the doctors come back again.

Manny told me, and I told the others, and so we knew.

We were very, very lucky, and we knew it. There are Farms dotted all over the place, and every one but ours was full of blue people that just crawled up and down the tunnels, sheets of paper with nothing written on them. Manny said that some keepers made extra money by letting real people in at night. Sometimes the real people would just drink beer and laugh at the spares, and sometimes they would fuck them. Nobody knows, and nobody cares. There's no point teaching spares, no point giving them a life. All that's going to happen is they're going to get whittled down.

On the other hand, maybe they have it easier. Because once you know how things stand, it becomes very difficult to take it. You just sit around, and wait, like all the others, but you *know* what you're waiting for. And you know who's to blame.

Like my brother Jack, for example. Jamming two fingers in a door when he was ten was only the start of it. When he was eighteen he rolled his expensive car and smashed up the bones in his leg. That's another of the reasons I don't want to be on this fucking subway: people notice when something like that's missing. Just like they notice that the left side of my face is raw, where they took a graft off when some woman threw scalding water at him. He's got most of my stomach, too. Stupid fucker ate too much spicy food, drank too much wine. Don't know what those kind of things are like, of course: but they can't have been that nice. They can't have been nice enough. And then last year he went to some party, got drunk, got into a fight and lost his right eye. And so, of course, I lost mine.

It's a laugh being in a Farm. It's a real riot. People stump around, dripping fluids, clapping hands with no fingers together and shitting into colostomy bags. I don't know what was worse: the ones who knew what was going on and felt hate like a cancer, or those who just ricocheted slowly round the tunnels like grubs. Sometimes the tunnel people would stay still for days, sometimes they would move around. There was no telling what they'd do, because there was no one inside their heads. That's what Manny did for us, in fact, for Sue and Jenny and me: he put people inside our heads. Sometimes we used to sit around and talk about the real people, imagine what they were doing, what it would be like to be them instead of us. Manny said that wasn't good for us, but we did it anyway. Even spares should be allowed to dream.

It could have gone on like that forever, or until the real people started to get old and fall apart. The end comes quickly then, I'm told. There's a limit to what you can cut off. Or at least there's supposed to be: but when you've seen blind spares with no arms and legs wriggling in dark corners, you wonder.

But then this afternoon the phone went, and we all dutifully stood up and limped into the tunnel. I went with Sue 2, and we sat next to each other. Manny used to say we loved each other, but how the fuck do I know. I feel happier when she's around, that's all I know. She doesn't have any teeth and her left arm's gone and they've taken both of her ovaries, but I like her. She makes me laugh.

Eventually Manny came in with the usual kind of heavy guy and I saw that this time Manny looked worse than ever. He took a long time walking around, until the guy with him started shouting, and then in the end he found Jenny 2, and pointed at her.

Jenny 2 was one of Manny's favorites. Her and Sue and me, we were the ones he could talk to. The man took Jenny out and Manny watched him go. When the door was shut he sat down and started to cry.

The real Jenny was in a hotel fire. All her skin was gone. Jenny 2 wasn't going to be coming back.

We sat with Manny, and waited, and then suddenly he stood up. He grabbed Sue by the hand and told me to follow and he took us to his quarters and gave me the clothes I'm wearing now. He gave us some money, and told us where to go. I think somehow he knew what was going to happen. Either that, or he just couldn't take it any more.

We'd hardly got our clothes on when all hell broke loose. We hid when the men came to find Manny, and we heard what happened.

Jenny 2 had spoken. They don't use drugs or anaesthetic, except when the shock of the operation will actually kill the spare. Obviously. Why bother? Jenny 2 was in a terminal operation, so she was awake. When the guy stood over her, smiling as he was about to take the first slice out of her face, she couldn't help herself, and I don't blame her.

"Please," she said. "Please don't."

Three words. It isn't much. It isn't so fucking much. But it was enough. She shouldn't have been able to say anything at all.

Manny got in the way as they tried to open the tunnels and so they shot him and went in anyway. We ran then, so I don't know what they did. I shouldn't think they killed them, because most had lots of parts left. Cut out bits of their brain, probably, to make sure they were all tunnel people.

We ran, and we walked and we finally made the city. I said goodbye to Sue at the subway, because she was going home on foot. I've got further to go, and they'll be looking for us, so we had to split up. We knew it made sense, and I don't know about love, but I'd lose both of my hands to have her with me now.

Time's running out for both of us, but I don't care. Manny got addresses for us, so we know where to go. Sue thinks we'll be able to take their places. I don't, but I couldn't tell her. We would give ourselves away too soon, because we just don't know enough. We wouldn't have a chance. It was always just a dream, really, something to talk about.

But one thing I am going to do. I'm going to meet him. I'm going to find Jack's house, and walk up to his door, and I'm going to look at him face to face.

And before they come and find me, I'm going to take a few things back.

DAVID CASE

The Dead End

∘━━━∘

David Case was born in upstate New York in 1937. Since the early 1960s he has lived in London, as well as spending time in Greece and Spain.

His acclaimed first collection The Cell: Three Tales of Horror *appeared in 1969, and it was followed by the novels* Fengriffen: A Chilling Tale, Wolf Tracks *and* The Third Grave, *the latter published by the legendary Arkham House imprint.*

A regular contributor to the Pan Book of Horror Stories *series during the early 1970s, the author's collections of macabre short stories include* Brotherly Love and Other Tales of Trust and Knowledge *from Pumpkin Books, and* Pelican Cay and Other Disquieting Tales *from PS Publishing, the*

*latter taking its title from Case's World Fantasy Award–
nominated zombie novella.*

*More recently, Centipede Press has produced a major
retrospective of the author's work in its Masters of the Weird
Tale series, edited by S. T. Joshi, and Valacourt Books is
issuing new collections of David Case's work.*

His story "Fengriffin" was filmed by Amicus in 1973 as
—And Now the Screaming Starts! *starring Peter Cushing,
while his classic werewolf thriller "The Hunter" was adapted
into the 1974 TV movie* Scream of the Wolf.

*The author has always believed that the short novel which
follows has been unjustly neglected. He's absolutely right,
and I am delighted to rectify that oversight by reprinting it
here . . .*

I

The waiter splashed a little wine in my glass and waited for me to
taste it. Across the table, Susan was studiously avoiding my gaze.
She was looking out of the leaded window at the blur of motorcars
moving past in Marsham Street. The waiter stood, blank faced and
discreet. This was a place where we had often been very happy, but
we weren't happy now. I nodded and the waiter filled our glasses and
moved away.

"Susan . . ."

She finally looked at me.

"I'm sorry."

Susan shrugged. She was very hurt and I was very sad. It is a sad thing
to tell the woman you love that you aren't going to marry her, and I suppose I could have chosen a better place than this restaurant, but somehow
I felt I needed a familiar place, where we could be alone but have other
people surrounding us. A cowardly attitude, of course, and yet it had
taken great courage to break the engagement. I wanted nothing more in
the world than to marry Susan, and now it was impossible.

"I've been expecting it, Arthur. It wasn't really such a shock."

"Susan."

"I could tell, you know. It's been different. You've been different. Ever since you returned from South America, I've been expecting this. I expect you met someone else there . . ."

"No. Please believe that."

She gave a bitter little smile across the table.

"I love you, Susan. As much as ever. More. Now that I realize how much I'm losing, I want you more than ever."

"Arthur, you haven't even made love to me since you came back. How can I believe you?"

"I can't, Susan."

"Then tell me why."

I shook my head.

"You owe me that much, Arthur. At least that much. Some explanation. Whatever it is, I'll understand. If there's someone else, if you're tired of me, if you simply want your freedom, I'll understand. There'll be no bitterness. But you can't simply break it off like this, without even telling me why. It's inhuman."

And perhaps she would have understood. Susan, of all people, might have understood. But it was too horrible and I couldn't bring myself to tell her. I couldn't tell anyone. I didn't even tell the doctor who examined me what he was supposed to be looking for. It was a terrible secret, and I had to bear it alone.

"Susan, I can't tell you."

She looked towards the window again. The leaded panes distorted the outside world. I thought she was going to cry, then, but she didn't. Her lip trembled. Waiters moved efficiently past our table, and the other customers wined and dined and pursued their individual lives, while I sat there alone. Susan was there, but I was alone.

"If only you hadn't gone," she whispered.

Yes. If only I hadn't gone. If only a man could relive the past and undo what had been done. But I had gone, and I looked down at the wine shimmering in my glass and recalled how it had happened; recalled those monstrous things which had been, and could never be undone . . .

It is hard to believe that it was only two months since the director of the museum called me to his office on a grim London afternoon. I was excited and expectant about his summons, as I followed the echo of hollow footsteps through those hoary corridors to his office. I was well aware that Jeffries, the head of the anthropology department, planned to retire at the end of the year, and had hopes of being promoted to his position. I can recall the conflicting thoughts that bounded in my head, wondering if I wasn't too young to expect such promotion, counterbalancing this by mentally listing the well-received work I'd done since I'd been there, remembering that many of my views were opposed to the director's, but knowing him as a man who respected genuine disagreement and sought out subalterns who did not hesitate to put forth their own theories, and also, perhaps mainly, thinking how delighted Susan would be if I could tell her I'd been promoted and that we could change and hasten our plans in accordance with my new position. Susan wanted children, but was prepared to wait a few years until we could afford them; she wanted a house in the country but had agreed to move into my flat in town. Perhaps, now, we would not have to wait for these things. Visions of happiness and success danced in my head that afternoon, as they do when a man is young and hopeful.

I was only thirty-one years old that day, although I'm old now.

It was two months ago.

Doctor Smyth looked the part of a museum director, the template from which all men in that position should have been cut. He wore an ancient and immaculate double-breasted suit crossed with a gold watch chain, and reposed like a boulder behind a massive desk in his leather-bound den.

"Ah, Brookes. Sit down."

I sat and waited. It was difficult to feel so confident now that I faced him. He filled a blackened pipe carefully, pressing the tobacco down with his wide thumb.

"Those reports I sent on to you the other day," he said. He paused to touch a match to the tobacco, and I watched it uncurl in the flame. I was disappointed. I'd hoped this meeting would be far more momentous than that. A haze of smoke began to drift between us.

"You've studied them?"

"Yes, sir."

"What's your opinion?"

I was mildly surprised. I'd been surprised when he sent them to me. They were the sort of thing one usually takes with a grain of salt, various unsubstantiated reports from Tierra del Fuego concerning a strange creature that had been seen in the mountains; a creature that appeared vaguely manlike, but behaved like an animal. It was reported to be responsible for destroying a few sheep and frightening a few people. The museum receives a good many reports of this nature, usually either a hoax or desire for publicity or over-stimulated imagination. True, there had been several different accounts of this creature with no apparent connexion between the men who claimed to have seen it, but I thought myself too much a man of science to place much faith in rumors of this sort.

And yet Smyth seemed interested.

"Well, I don't really know. Some sort of primate, perhaps. If there is anything."

"Too large for a monkey."

"If it weren't South America, I'd think possibly an ape . . ."

"But it is South America, isn't it?"

I said nothing.

"You mentioned a primate. It isn't a monkey, and it can't very well be an ape. What does that leave?"

"Man, of course."

"Yes," he said.

He regarded me through the smoke.

I said: "Of course, the Indians in that area are very primitive. Possibly the most primitive men alive today. Darwin was certainly fascinated by them, running naked in that climate and eating raw mussels. This creature might well be a man, some hermit perhaps, or an aboriginal who has managed to avoid contact with civilization."

"And more power to him," Smyth said.

"I should think that's the answer."

"I doubt it, somehow."

"I don't see . . ."

"Several aboriginals have been known to have seen this creature. Surely they would have recognized him as a man like themselves."

"Perhaps. But there's certainly no proof to suggest it is something less than a man. I'd rate the plausibility of anything else well behind the Abominable Snowman, and you know my views on that."

Smyth smiled rather tolerantly. I had done some research on the Yeti which had been well received, but my conclusions had been strictly negative. Smyth was inclined to admit the possibility of such creatures, however.

"I thought much the same way, at first," he said.

"At first?"

"I've given it considerable thought. I was particularly impressed by the story that half-breed fellow told in Ushuaia. What was his name?"

"Gregorio?"

"Yes, that's the one. Hardly the sort of thing a man would imagine without some basis in truth, I should think. In fact, I sent a wire to a fellow I know there. Man named Gardiner. Used to be a manager with Explotadora, when the company was really big. Retired now, but he figured he was too old to start a new life in England and he stayed there. Splendid fellow, knows everyone. Helped us considerably the last time we had a field team out there. Anyway, he replied, and according to him this Gregorio is a fairly reliable sort. That got me wondering if there mightn't be more to this than I'd supposed. And then, there's another angle . . ."

His pipe had faltered. He spent several moments and several matches lighting it again.

"What do you know of Hubert Hodson?" he asked.

"Hodson? Is he still alive?"

"Hodson is several years younger than I," Smyth said, amused. "Yes, he's still very much alive."

"He was before my time. Not highly regarded these days, a bit outdated. I've read him, of course. A renegade with curious theories and an adamant attitude, but a first-class scientist. Some of his ideas caused quite a stir some twenty years ago."

Smyth nodded. He seemed pleased that I knew about Hodson.

"I'm rather vague on his work, actually. He specialized in the genetics of evolution, I believe. Not really my line."

"He specialized in many things. Spread himself too thin, perhaps. But he was a brilliant man." Smyth's eyes narrowed, he was recalling the past. "Hodson put forth many theories. Some nonsense, some perhaps not. He believed that the vocal cords were the predominant element in man's evolution, for instance—maintained that any animal, given man's power of communication, would in time have developed man's straight spine, man's thumb, even man's brain. That man's mind was no more than a by-product of assembled experience and thought unnecessary to development. A theory of enormous possibilities, of course, but Hodson, being the man he is, threw it down like a gauntlet, as a challenge to man's superior powers of reasoning. He presented it as though he preferred to cause consternation and opposition, rather than seeking acceptance.

"It was much the same with his mutation theory, when he claimed that evolution was not a gradual process, but moved in sudden forward spurts at various points in time, and that the time was different and dependent upon the place. Nothing wrong with these ideas, certainly, but his manner of presentation was such that the most harmless concepts would raise a hue and cry. I can remember him standing at the rostrum, pointing at the assembly with an accusing finger, his hair all wild, his eyes excited, shouting, 'Look at you! You think that you are the end product of evolution? I tell you, but for a freak Oligocene mutation, you would be no more than our distant cousins, the shrews. Do you think that you and I share a common ancestor? We share a common mutation, no more. And I, personally, find it regrettable.' You can imagine the reaction among the learned audience. Hodson merely smiled and said, 'Perhaps I chose my words rashly. Perhaps your relation to the shrews is not so distant after all.' Yes, I can remember that day clearly, and I must admit I was more amused than outraged."

Smyth smiled slightly around his pipe.

"The final insult to man came when he claimed all evolution had been through the female line. If I remember correctly, he stated that the male was no more than a catalyst, that man, being weaker, succumbed to these irregular mutations and in turn was merely the agent that caused the female to progress or change, was only necessary to inspire the female to evolve, so to speak. Men, even men of science, were hardly prepared to countenance that, naturally. Hodson was venomously attacked, both scientifically and emotionally, and, strangely enough, the attacks seemed to trouble him this time. He'd always delighted in the furore before, but this time he went into seclusion and finally disappeared entirely."

"You seem to know a great deal about him, sir," I said, "considering he's rather obscure."

"I respected him."

"But how does this tie in with the reports from South America?"

"Hodson is there. That is where he went when he left the country twenty-odd years ago, and he's been there ever since. That's why you've heard nothing from him for the last generation. But God knows what he's doing there. He's published nothing, made no statements at all, and that's very unlike Hodson. He was always a man to make a statement simply for shock value, whether he really believed it or not."

"Perhaps he's retired."

"Not Hubert."

"And you believe that his presence is connected with those reports?"

"I have no idea. I just wonder. You see, no one knows exactly where he is—I don't expect anyone has tried to find out, actually—but he's located somewhere in the Chilean part of Tierra del Fuego, in the south-western section."

"And that's where the reports have come from," I said.

"Exactly. It just makes me wonder a bit."

We both pondered for a few minutes while he lighted his pipe again. Then I thought I saw a flaw.

"But if he's been there for twenty years . . . these reports have all been within the last six months. I don't see how that would tie in."

"Don't you?"

I didn't. He puffed away for a while.

"This creature which may, or may not, have been seen. It was as large as a man. Therefore, we may assume it to be full grown. Say, twenty years old, perhaps?"

"I see. You believe—I mean to say, you recognize the possibility—that Hodson may have heard something about this creature twenty years ago, and went to investigate. That he has been looking for it all this time."

"Or found it."

"Surely he wouldn't keep something of that enormity secret?"

"Hodson is a strange man. He resented the attacks that were mounted against his ideas. He might well be waiting until he has a complete documentation, beyond refutation—a life's work, all neatly tied up and proven. Perhaps he found this creature. Or creatures. We may safely assume that, if it exists, it had parents. Possibly siblings, as well. I think it more likely that Hodson would have discovered the parents and studied the offspring, or the whole tribe. Lived with them, even. That's the sort of thing he'd do."

"It seems—well, far-fetched, sir."

"Yes, it does, doesn't it? A science fiction idea. What did they used to call it? The missing link?" He chuckled. "The common ancestor is more accurate, I suppose."

"But you can't really believe that a creature like that could be alive now?"

"I admit it is most unlikely. But then, so was the coelacanth, before it was discovered alive."

"But that was in the sea. God knows what may exist there. We may never know. But on land, if a creature like that existed, it would have been discovered before now."

"It's a wild, barren place, Tierra del Fuego. Rough terrain and a sparse population. I say only that it is possible."

"You realize that the Indians of Tierra del Fuego are prehistoric, so to speak?" I said.

"Certainly."

"And yet you feel there is a chance this creature might be something other than one of them?"

"A possibility."

"And still a man?"

Smyth gestured with his pipe.

"Let us say, of the genus homo but not of the species sapiens."

591

I was astounded. I couldn't believe that Smyth was serious. I said, with what I thought admirable understatement, "It seems most unlikely."

Smyth looked almost embarrassed. When he spoke, it was as though he was offering an explanation. He said, "I mentioned that I have great respect for Hodson. And a great curiosity. He's not a man to forsake his science, and he's spent the last twenty odd years doing something on that island. That in itself is interesting. Hodson was primarily a laboratory man. He had little time for field work and believed that to be the proper task for men with less imagination and intelligence—believed that lesser men should gather the data for men of his own calibre to interpret. And then, quite suddenly, he disappers into the wilds. There has to be a reason, something to which he was willing to dedicate the rest of his life. And Hodson placed the highest possible value on his life, in the sense of what he could accomplish while he lived. It may have nothing whatsoever to do with these reports. Quite likely it doesn't. But whatever he is doing is definitely of interest. Whatever he has accomplished in twenty years is bound to be fascinating, whether it is right or wrong. I've often considered sending someone to locate him, but always put it off. Now seems the perfect time to kill two birds with one stone. Or, perhaps, the same bird."

I nodded, but I was in no way convinced.

"I expect you think I'm grasping at a straw," Smyth said, noticing my hesitation. "I knew Hodson. Not well, not as a friend, but I knew him. You'd have to know him to understand how I feel. I was one of the last people he spoke with before he vanished, and I've always remembered that conversation. He was exuberant and excited and confident. He told me that he was working on something new, something very big. He even admitted that the results might disprove some of his earlier theories, which was very impressive, coming from a man who had never in his life admitted he might be mistaken. And he said that this time no one would be able to scoff or doubt or disagree, because when he was finished he would have more than a theory—he would have concrete proof."

Smyth tapped the ash from his pipe. He seemed tired now.

"You've never been to South America, have you?" he asked.

"No."

"Would you like to?"

"Very much."

"I think I'd like to send you there."

Smyth opened a drawer and began thumbing through some papers. There were handwritten notes in the margins. He said, "The place to start will be Ushuaia. I'll wire Gardiner to expect you, he should be helpful. You can spend a few days there checking on the reports in person. Then try to locate Hodson. Gardiner might know where he is. He'll certainly know where he buys his supplies, so you should be able to work back from there."

"Are you sure he gets his supplies from Ushuaia?"

"He must. There's nowhere else anywhere near there."

Everything seemed to be moving very fast suddenly.

"Now, I'd better arrange a hotel for you," Smyth said, turning a sheet to read the margin. "The Albatross or the Gran Parque? Neither has hot water nor central heating, but a dedicated scientist shouldn't mind that."

I tossed a mental coin.

"The Albatross."

"How soon will you be able to leave?"

"Whenever you like."

"Tomorrow?"

I believe I blinked.

"If that's convenient," Smyth said.

"Yes, all right," I said, wondering what Susan would think about it with no time to get used to the idea.

"Fine," Smyth said, and the interview was over. I was amazed and skeptical, but if Smyth had respect for Hodson, I had respect for Smyth. And the prospect of field work is always exciting.

I rose to leave.

"Oh, Brookes?"

"Sir?"

I was at the door and turned. He was filling another pipe.

"You know that Jeffries is retiring at the end of the year?"

"I'd heard as much, sir."

"Yes. That's all," he said.

Then I was very excited.

Tierra del Fuego.

Delighted as I was at Smyth's open hint of promotion, I think I was even more excited about the opportunity to visit that fascinating archipelago. I suppose that every anthropologist since Darwin has been fascinated by the opportunities existing there to study primitive man. Separated from the South American mainland by the Straits of Magellan and divided between Argentina and Chile, Tierra del Fuego consists of the large island, five smaller islands, numerous islets, peninsulas, channels, bays and sounds crouched beneath the low clouds and fierce winds where the Andes stagger down, stumbling across the straits and limping out to fall, at Cape Horn, into the mists at the end of the world. There was little there to attract civilization, 27,500 square miles of rugged wilds with sheep, lumbering and fishing, a recent discovery of poor oil in the plains to the north-east—and the fascination of Stone Age man.

They were there when Magellan discovered the land in 1520, and named it the land of fire because of the signal fires that smoldered along the windy coast, a group of human beings that time and evolution had overlooked, leading their natural and prehistoric lives. And they are still there, diminished by contact with civilization and unable to cope with the fingertips of the modern world that have managed to grope even to this forsaken place, reduced to living in wretched hovels on the outskirts of the towns. There are few left. These creatures who could face the wind and snow without clothing could not face the advance of time.

But surely not all had succumbed. And this, I felt, would prove the answer to the rumors of a wild creature, that it would be an aborigine who had refused to give up his dignity and forsake his wild freedom, and still ran savage and naked through those mountains and canyons. It was a far more feasible solution than Smyth had put forward, and no little opportunity for study in its own right. I believed that was what Hodson had been doing all these years, but that Smyth, never a skeptic, was so overpowered by the force of this man that his imagination had run wild; that he could have believed anything in relation to Hodson.

Or was Smyth, perhaps, testing me in some fashion? Could he be inviting me to draw my own conclusions as the future head of my department?

It was an intriguing thought, and I was quite willing to stand the examination. I needed no unfounded rumors or vague speculation, the opportunities of Tierra del Fuego were enough in themselves.

I had only one reservation. What was Susan going to think of this immediate and prolonged parting? I knew that she would put forth no objections, she was not the sort of woman who would interfere with a man's work, but I knew she would be disappointed and disturbed at our separation. I wasn't happy at the thought of being away from her either, of course, but this feeling was tempered by my excitement. It is always harder for the one who stays behind.

We had never been apart before. We'd met some six months before and become engaged within a fortnight—one of those rare and remarkable meetings of mind and body that seem destined to be, a perfect agreement in all things and a blissful contentment when we were together. We were old enough to know that this was what we wanted, and all we wanted, with no doubts whatsoever about our future. I knew Susan would understand the necessity for the separation, and had no qualms about telling her; I worried only that she would be saddened.

Susan was preparing dinner at her place that evening. She had a small flat in South Kensington where she practiced her culinary arts several times a week, not as the way to her man's heart, which she already had, but through a splendidly old-fashioned idea of being an ideal wife. I was still in an excited mood as I walked to her place through the late afternoon, scarcely noticing the steady drizzle as a discomfort, although possessed of a feeling that all my senses were alert, that I was aware of everything in the slightest detail. The sky was darkening and the street lamps had come on, pale and haloed. The traffic was heavy but strangely silent. Pedestrians hurried home from their work, collars up and heads lowered. They all seemed very dismal and drab to me, creatures of humdrum habit who could not but envy my life and future, my woman and my work, had they known. I would have liked to stop some passing stranger and tell him of my success, show him a photograph of Susan, not through vanity as much as a feeling of gratitude. It was the first time I could remember wanting to tell someone about myself. I had few friends and most of my acquaintances were professional, and had never felt the need before. But then, I had never felt this happy anticipation. I quickened my pace, anxious to be with Susan.

I had a key to her flat and let myself in at the front door, walked up the two flights to her floor and entered. The flat was warm and comfortable, the gramophone was playing a record of baroque harp and recorder and I could hear Susan manipulating utensils in the tiny kitchen. I stood in the doorway for a moment, appreciating the way Susan had decorated the room, with great care and taste and little expense, and feeling the contentment that always filled me when I was there. I realized then just how much I was going to long for Susan while I was away.

Susan heard the door close and came into the room. She was wearing a simple black dress of which I was exceptionally fond and her hair fell to her shoulders with all the tones and shades of a forest fire. She smiled as she crossed the room and we kissed. Then she must have seen something in my expression, because her forehead arched in query.

"You look thoughtful, darling."

"I was thinking."

"Oh?"

I moved to the couch. She didn't press her question.

"Dinner in fifteen minutes," she said. "Sherry?"

"Fine."

She poured the sherry from a cut-glass decanter and handed me a glass, then sat beside me on the couch, curling her long legs under her. I sipped the drink and the record ended and rejected. The Hebrides Overture began to play.

"What about?" she asked then.

"Two things, really. I was talking with Smyth today. He made a point of mentioning that Jeffries is retiring."

"But that's wonderful, Arthur."

"Oh, it's nothing definite. I mean, he didn't tell me I was in line for the position or anything."

"But he must have implied it."

"Yes, I suppose so."

"Oh, darling, I'm so pleased." She kissed me lightly. "I know you'd hoped for it. We should celebrate."

I smiled, not too cheerfully.

"Is anything wrong?"

"No, not really."

"You hardly seem elated."

"Well, there's another thing."

"Good?"

"In a way. It's just that—well, I don't know what you'll think about it."

She looked at me over the rim of her glass. Her eyes were green and lovely. She was very beautiful.

"Tell me," she said.

"I have to go to South America."

She blinked.

"Oh, not to live or anything. Just a field trip for the museum. A wonderful opportunity, really, except it will mean being away from you for a while."

"Did you expect me to object?"

"I knew better than that."

"How long will you be gone?"

I wasn't at all sure. I said, "Two or three months, I suppose."

"I'll miss you very much, darling. When will you have to leave?"

"Tomorrow."

"So sudden? But why?"

"Well, it's an idea Smyth has. I don't agree with him, but either way it's a marvelous opportunity. And my promotion might well rest on what I do there."

Susan pondered for a moment, then smiled. It was all right. She understood, as I'd known she would, and conflicting emotions struggled for only that moment before yielding to logic rare in a woman.

"I'm happy for you, darling. Really I am."

"It won't be long."

"You're very excited about it, aren't you?"

"Yes. It's a splendid opportunity. Except for being away from you."

She dismissed that with a gesture. "Tell me about it."

I talked for a while, telling her about Tierra del Fuego, Hubert Hodson, the recent reports and my own ideas about them. Susan listened, interested because it interested me, and getting used to the idea of our separation, balancing it with the advantages that would follow my potential promotion. Presently we had dinner with candlelight and wine, and Susan was as lively and cheerful as ever. I loved her very much. I could already feel the pain of parting, the emotional tone of our last evening together and a touch of the thrill that would come when we were together again on my return.

We took our brandy out to the little terrace that ran around the side of the building and stood hand in hand at the railing, looking out across the dark canyons of the city. The lights of the West London Air Terminal loomed garish and gaudy above the rooftops. They reminded me of my flight, making the prospect more concrete and immediate, and perhaps they did the same for Susan. She became solemn, holding my hand tightly.

"God, I'll miss you so much," she said.

"Me too."

"No longer than you have to, darling?"

"No longer."

"I'll be awfully lonely."

"So will I."

She looked at me then, feigning a frown of deep concern.

"Not lonely enough to seek solace in the arms of another woman, I trust," she said. But she said it as a joke, to dispel the tension. Susan knew I wanted no one but her, and never would. I'd never imagined a time when I would place a woman ahead of my work, but if she had asked me not to go, I would have remained with her.

Ah, why didn't she?

II

I refilled my glass.

Susan hadn't touched her wine. I recalled how happy we'd been the night before I'd left, and the contrast made our sorrow worse. If it could possibly be worse. The waiter looked towards our table to see if we wanted anything and looked quickly away. A man dining alone across the room glanced appreciatively at Susan, admiring her long legs and amber hair, then lowered his gaze as I looked at him. Susan would have no trouble finding a new man whenever she wanted, and this bitter knowledge sent a chill down my backbone, all the colder because I knew she wanted no one but me, and because I could never marry her. My hand trembled with the weight of the bottle and my heart trembled with the weight of despair.

Susan looked up through her lashes, a glance that would have been flirtatious had her eyes not been dull with grief.

"What happened in Tierra del Fuego, Arthur?" she asked, pleading for an answer, a reason which might make her sorrow less through understanding.

I shook my head.

I couldn't tell her.

But I remembered . . .

I flew from Buenos Aires to Ushuaia.

In the footsteps of Darwin, the modern speed seemed wrong and disappointing. Darwin had been there on HMS *Beagle* from 1826 to 1836, exploring the channel on which Ushuaia was situated. It was called, appropriately enough, the Beagle Channel. But I flew in from Buenos Aires in five hours, seated next to a middle-aged American tourist and disturbed by the thought that there could be nothing left for discovery in a town with an airport and the beginnings of a tourist trade.

The tourist wanted to talk, and nothing short of direct impoliteness would have silenced him.

"Going to Ushuaia?" he asked.

I nodded.

"Me too."

That seemed obvious enough, since that was where the aeroplane was headed.

"Name's Jones. Clyde Jones."

He had a big, healthy face clamped around a huge cigar.

"Brookes."

Jones extended a wide hand. He wore a ruby ring on his little finger and an expensive camera on a sling around his neck. His grip was very firm. I suppose he was a pleasant enough fellow.

"You a Limey? I'm a Yank."

He hesitated, as though wondering if this required another handshake.

"You a tourist? I am. Travel a lot, you know. Since my wife died I traveled all over. Been in your country. Been all over Europe. Spent two months there last summer, saw it all. Except the communist parts, of course. I wouldn't want to go there and give them any foreign exchange."

"Quite right," I said.

"Did you know this Ushuaia is one of the southernmost communities in the world? I want to see this Ushuaia. Don't know why. 'Cause it's there, I guess. Like mountain climbers, hah? Ha ha."

I looked out the window. The flat tableland and glacial lakes of the north were behind, and the terrain was beginning to rise in rugged humps and twisting rivers, glimpsed through clouds as heavy and low as the smoke from Jones's cigar. It was exciting land, but I was depressed. Jones did not seem interested. I suppose he saw nothing that was not framed in his camera's lens. He chatted away amicably, and I was seized with a feeling that I had been born too late, that nothing new remained to be discovered, and that all one could do now was study the past.

And no man has ever been more wrong.

Everything seemed much brighter after we landed.

The airport was on the edge of the town, and Jones shared a taxi with me. He was staying at the Albatross, too. The taxi was a huge American model, as modern as a missile, but somehow this didn't trouble me, now that I was in contact with the land. It was as if the motorcar were out of time and place, not that the land had changed. Jones may have felt something of this anachronism, as well, for he became quiet and almost apprehensive, perhaps sensing that he didn't belong here, that the soul of this place had not yet been sucked into the tourists' cameras. I looked from the window and became excited once more as we jolted through the streets.

Ushuaia looked like a Swiss mountain village set on a Norwegian fiord. Sharp-spined wooden chalets leaned on the steep hills and a glacier mounted the hill behind, impressive and impassive. Farther to the west the high peaks of Darwin and Larmeinto rose into the low clouds. The taxi slowed suddenly, throwing me forwards on the seat. We had braked behind a man on horseback, sitting slumped in his poncho. The horse moved sedately up the middle of the road. The driver sounded the horn and the rider, if anything, slumped more and carried on at his own pace. The driver cursed, revving the monstrous engine in helpless frustration and moving his hands in wide gesticulation. I was pleased.

The taxi stopped at the Albatross and we got out. The wind was dipping and swirling through the streets. It was late afternoon. Jones insisted on paying the fare and waved away my protest, saying I could stand him a drink later. He was shivering in his Brooks Brothers suit. We had to carry our own bags in to the desk while we registered, and I walked up to my room while Jones looked about for a page boy or a lift. I was gratified for the chance to be alone, and pleased with my room. It was primitive and satisfying, although I don't suppose Jones was too happy about such accommodation.

I washed and shaved with cold water and went to the window to look out. It would soon be dark, and I thought it too late to call on Gardiner that afternoon. This didn't displease me. I was far more anxious to pursue my own wanderings than Smyth's theory, and although I was certainly anxious to meet Hodson it was more because he was an eminent and interesting theorist in my own field than because he might provide a link in the implausible chain of Smyth's reasoning. I decided to spend what remained of the daylight in roaming about the town, getting the mood of Ushuaia as a fulcrum towards understanding the land.

I hoisted my suitcase to the bed and opened it, found a warmer coat and put it on, put a notepad and pencil in the pocket and left the room. I had to pass the entrance to the bar on the way out, and glanced in. Jones was already there, chatting in familiar tones with the barman. He didn't notice me. It was cold and damp in the street and the vortex of wind had straightened and came more steadily from the south. I turned my collar up and lighted a cigarette in the shelter of the building, then walked out to the street. The wind fanned the cigarette until it burned like a fuse, bouncing sparks as I turned my head.

I had a street map of the town, but didn't use it. I had no particular destination but walked in the general direction of the port, down steep streets lined with the trading companies that supplied the whole area, facing that powerful wind. Motorcars and horsecarts shared the streets with an assorted population of many nationalities and many backgrounds: English, Spanish, Yugoslavian, Italian, German—the racial mixture that invariably gathers at a frontier, colonialists and conquistadors, sailors and settlers, farmers and shepherds, the leftover dregs of the gold rush and the seepage from the oil fields in the north, men who had come to seek and men who had come where they would not be sought—and, of course, the few tourists looking disgruntled and uncomfortable and wondering what had possessed them to come here. This was a rich lode indeed for a social anthropologist, but that was not my field, and I had only a mild interest in observing the men who had come here. I wanted the men who had been here long before anyone came, and there were only a few natives in the town. They had been drawn towards this outpost of civilization but had not been integrated into its core; they had stopped and clustered at the outskirts.

Standing on the quay, I looked into the hard water of the Beagle Channel and the deserted islands in the mist beyond. The water ran in jagged lines of black and white, and a solitary hawk circled effortlessly in the air currents above. A man, almost invisible inside an ancient leather coat, led a loaded llama straight towards me, forcing me back from the water. He didn't notice me, although the beast turned a curious eye as he lumbered past.

I turned back up the incline. My heavy coat was proof against the cold, but the wind slid through the fabric and cascaded my hair over my brow. The sensation was not unpleasant, and I felt no urge to return to the hotel yet. I turned in the opposite direction and climbed away from the center of the town.

Night was deepening the sky beneath the darkened clouds when I found myself at the end of the modern world—the outskirts of Ushuaia. I had a very concrete sense of standing at a barrier. Behind me electric and neon blanketed the town, the light confined within the limits. This was the point to which civilization had penetrated, although it lay in a thin veneer within the boundaries, its roots shallow and precarious, a transplant that had not yet taken a firm hold. Before me the land broke upwards and away, jagged and barren and dotted with clusters of sheet-metal shacks painted in the brightest tones, oranges and yellows and reds. The thin chimneys rattled bravely in the wind, and the smoke lay in thin, flat ribbons. Kerosene lamps cast futile pastel light in the doorways, and a few shadowed figures moved.

This, then, was where the natives lived. This was where they had been drawn, and then halted, those who had surrendered. And beyond this fringe, perhaps, were those who had refused to yield to the magnet of time.

I walked slowly back to the hotel, and slept well.

III

I awoke early in the sharp cold. The window framed a rectangle of bright and brittle light blocked on the opposite wall. I dressed quickly and went to the window, expecting to see the sun, but the light was filtered through a tissue of cloud, diffused throughout the sky. It left the streets strangely without shadow or contrast, and made the day seem even colder than it was. I put an extra sweater on before going down to the breakfast room. No one else was there yet. A fire had been lighted but hadn't yet taken the chill from the room, and I didn't dawdle over my coffee. I wanted to send a wire to Susan to let her know I had arrived safely, and then I had to contact Gardiner. I was just leaving when Jones came in, looking haggard and bleary. He smiled perfunctorily.

"You tried that pisco yet?" he asked.

I didn't know what pisco was.

"The local booze. Grape alcohol. Gives a man a wicked hangover, I'll tell you."

He shook his head and sank into a chair. He was calling for black coffee as I left. I wondered if he'd ever managed to get out of the hotel bar the night before. And yet, in his fashion, he would learn things about this town that I would never know.

I walked to the telegraph office and sent the wire to Susan, lighted my first cigarette of the day and started back toward the hotel. Three hawks were perched, evenly spaced, on the telegraph wires, and I wondered, whimsically, if they would be aware of my message darting beneath their talons. A taxi had pulled up at the hotel to let a passenger out, and I asked the driver if he knew where Gardiner lived. He did, and I got in the back seat, smoking and looking out of the windows. We drove out past the ancient Indian cemetery on the crisp morning road, with crackling tires and white exhaust, on a day that made me feel very much alive.

Gardiner's big house was stuck against the glacier in twodimensional silhouette. I walked up from the road and Gardiner opened the door before I had knocked. He wore a red wool dressing gown and held a gin and tonic.

"You must be Brookes."

I nodded.

"Smyth wired me to expect you. Thought you'd be here last night."

"I got in rather late."

He stepped back and let me in. He hadn't shaved yet, and had vaguely waved the gin in lieu of a handshake. We went into a large room curiously devoid of furnishings. A beautifully engraved shotgun hung on the wall and there was a sheepskin rug by the fire.

"I hope I'm no trouble," I said.

"Not at all. Glad to help if I can. Glad to have some company. Gin or brandy?"

"It's rather early."

"Nonsense."

He gave me gin and we sat by the fire.

"Smyth said you've been very helpful to us in the past," I said.

"I'm no scientist, but I expect I know as much about this place as anyone. Been here thirty-odd years. Not much to do here now. A little shooting and a lot of drinking. Used to be different in the old days, before the land reforms whittled the company away." He shook his head, not necessarily in disapproval. "But that won't interest you."

"Well, I'm more interested in the natives."

"Of course." He looked thoughtful, shaking his head again. "There were three tribes when the white man came here. The Alacalufs, the Yahgans, and the Onas." I knew all this, but was content to listen. "They were absolutely prehistoric, stark naked savages. Probably very happy, too. They didn't understand the white man and they didn't trust him. Good judges. They were even rash enough to steal a few of the white man's sheep, and the white man shot a few of them, of course. Did them a little harm. But then the enlightened white men came. The missionaries. They came burning with the fever of reform and saw these unfortunate lambs of God running about naked and indecent and, in the fashion of their kind, gave them blankets for warmth and modesty. The blankets hadn't been disinfected, so they also gave them plague. Killed off all the Onas and most of the others. But, oh well, we couldn't have them trotting about naked, could we?"

Gardiner sighed and poured another gin.

"Will you stay here?" he asked.

"I'm already at the hotel."

"Ah." I think he would have welcomed a guest. "Well, how can I help you, then?"

I told him about the rumors and reports, and what Smyth thought possible. Gardiner nodded. He'd heard them himself, of course.

"Would you think there was anything in it?" I asked.

"There must be something. All rumors have some basis in fact. But I doubt if it's anything very interesting. Nothing like Smyth suggests. I've never seen or heard of anything like that before, and if something did exist it surely would have been discovered before. Left some evidence of its existence, at least."

"That's what I thought."

"I should think perhaps a wild dog, or possibly a man—maybe even an escapee from the penal colony, living wild."

"That would account for the dead sheep. But what about this man who claims to have seen it? The one Smyth queried you about?"

"Gregorio. Yes. Of course, when I answered Smyth's wire, I didn't know what he was interested in Gregorio for. I thought he might be contemplating using him for a guide perhaps, and he's reliable enough for that sort of thing. But as far as his account of this strange creature—" he paused, as if giving it every consideration. "Well, I suppose he did see something that frightened the hell out of him, but I'm sure it wasn't what he thought it was. He's a superstitious, imaginative sort of fellow, and he certainly hasn't tried to capitalize on the story so I expect we can discount the possibility that he made it up. He hasn't said anything about it for some time."

"I'd like to talk to him."

"No harm in that."

"Do you know where I might find him?"

"Yes. He lives in a shack just west of town. Scrapes out a living as a freelance farmer and tourist guide, now that they have started to come." Gardiner shuddered at the idea of tourists. "Speaks English well enough. I shouldn't offer him much money, though, or he's liable to feel he owes you a good story and embellish it."

"Anyone else I should see?"

"You might have a chat with MacPherson. He has a small farm near here. Had a few sheep destroyed. He'll be more accurate than Gregorio."

MacPherson was one of the names I remembered from the reports Smyth had received.

"Where will I find him?"

"He's in town right now, matter of fact."

"That will be convenient. Where?"

Gardiner was pouring another drink.

"Where else?" he said, smiling. "At the bar of the Gran Parque. I'll drive you in and introduce you, if you like."

Gardiner drove an ancient Packard with considerable panache. I asked him about Hodson as we rumbled ponderously into town.

"Hodson? Haven't seen him in years."

"Smyth seemed certain he was still here."

"Oh, he's here. But he never comes into Ushuaia."

"Any idea where he lives?"

"Not really. He's an unsociable type." Gardiner seemed scornful of such behavior. "He's out in the mountains somewhere. Graham might know more about it. He runs a trading company and I think Hodson gets his supplies there. But he never comes in himself."

"If you'll introduce me to Graham—"

"Certainly," Gardiner said, concentrating on the road with both hands on the wheel. He wore string-backed driving gloves and a flat tweed cap. We came over a sharp rise and there was a horse and rider blocking the road, slowly moving towards us. We seemed to be moving frightfully fast. I started to shout a warning but Gardiner was already moving, shifting down with a fluid sweep of the lever and letting the engine howl. He didn't bother with brakes or horn, and scarcely turned the steering wheel. The rider hauled the horse around in a rearing sidestep and the animal's flank flashed by my window. Remembering the taxi driver's difficulty, I decided that Gardiner must have a considerable reputation.

"Certainly I shall," he said.

The trading company was on our way and we pulled up in front. The old Packard ran considerably better than it stopped. It rocked to a halt like a weary steeplechaser refusing a jump. Gardiner led the way into a large building cluttered haphazardly with a catholic selection of goods and supplies. Graham was a dusty little man behind a dusty wooden counter, and when Gardiner introduced us, he said, "Baa."

I expect I looked startled.

"Local greeting," Gardiner said. "Has something to do with sheep, I assume."

"That's right," Graham said. "Baa."

"Baa," I said.

"Brookes is trying to get in touch with Hodson. Does he still trade with you?"

"That's right."

"Do you know where he lives?" I asked.

"Nope. Never see him. Haven't seen Hodson in three or four years."

"How does he have his supplies delivered?"

"He doesn't. Sends a man to fetch them."

"Well, do you know anyone who could take me to him?"

Graham scratched his head.

"Can't think of anyone off hand. Funny. I guess the best thing would be to wait for the man who fetches his supplies."

"That would do. If I could speak to him the next time he comes here."

"Can't speak to him."

"Oh?"

"Can't speak. He's a mute."

I felt rather frustrated. Gardiner was grinning. He asked, "Does he come frequently?"

"Yeah. Has to, pretty much. See, Hodson's camp or whatever it is, is up in the mountains. Probably over on the Chilean side. There aren't any roads up there, so he has to take the things on pack horses. Can't take very much stuff on horseback, so he has to come in every few weeks. Should be coming in any day now, matter of fact."

"Could you let me know when he does?"

"Guess so."

"I'm at the Albatross."

"Yep."

"I'll be glad to—"

"Not necessary," he said, foreseeing the offer of money. "If you need any supplies yourself, buy 'em here."

That was something I hadn't thought of. "What will I need to reach Hodson's?"

"Hard to say, since I don't know where it is. You'll need a horse and pack. I can get something ready for you, if you want. Have it waiting when Hodson's man arrives."

"That will be fine."

I wasn't sure how fine it would be. I hadn't been on a horse for years, but some obscure pride rose up in a dubious battle against the urge to ask him to find me a docile animal. The pride won. I suppose I was already being affected by contact with these self-sufficient frontiersmen.

We went back to the car.

"It's a rather rough trek up those hills," Gardiner said, as he started the engine. He let it idle for a moment. Perhaps he'd seen my doubts mirrored in my expression. "I suppose you can handle a horse all right?"

"I've ridden," I said. "Not for some time."

"Best to let the horse pick his own way. Good, sure-footed animals here."

"Well, the worst I can do is fall off."

Gardiner looked horrified.

"A gentleman never falls off," he said. "He is thrown."

He was chuckling happily as we drove off.

MacPherson wasn't in the Gran Parque.

This distressed Gardiner, who hated to have people behave out of character, and hated to have his predictions proven wrong. We found him in the next bar down the street, however, so it wasn't too unjustifiable. MacPherson was classically sandy haired, proving that truth has less regard for triteness than literary convention. He was standing at the bar, talking with a villainous-looking man with a drooping moustache and splendidly hand-tooled boots.

Gardiner drew me to the bar at the far end.

"He's talking business. We'll wait here until he's finished."

"What a remarkable looking fellow."

"Mac?"

"The other one. Looks like a Mexican bandit."

Gardiner grinned. "He is rather traditional, isn't he? A Yugoslav. Free zone trader."

"What would that be?"

"A smuggler. Works from here up to Rio Grande through the Gortbaldi Pass. Quite a bit of that goes on. This fellow is very respected in his line, I understand. Not that I would have any dealings with him, of course." Gardiner looked amused. The Spanish barman came over, running a rag along the bar, and Gardiner ordered gin and tonics, after checking his wristwatch to make sure it wasn't yet time to switch to the afternoon whiskies. I expect he lived by a rigid code in such matters. The barman set the drinks down and wiped his hands on the same rag he'd wiped the bar with.

Gardiner said, "Cheers," and took a large swallow.

I was unaccustomed to drinking this much, and certainly not this early in the day, and sipped cautiously. Gardiner drank fast. I could see that Clyde Jones, in many ways, would fit into this society much more readily than I; that my first impression had been hasty and ungracious and single-minded. But I resisted the temptation to drink more quickly.

Presently the Yugoslav departed, walking very tall and proud with his spurs clanking, and we moved down the bar. Gardiner introduced us and

I bought MacPherson a drink. He drank Scotch, but I expect his code was more accountable to nationality than chronometry.

"Lived here long?" I asked.

"Too long," MacPherson said. Then he shrugged. "Still, it's not a bad life. It's all right."

"Brookes is interested in this thing that's been killing your sheep," Gardiner said.

"Oh?"

"Came all the way from London to investigate it."

"I don't suppose there are many natural predators here, are there?" I asked.

"Ah, there's the odd fox and the hawks and such. Never been anything like this before, though."

"It's a curious business, from what I've heard."

"It is that."

"What do you make of it?"

He considered for a few moments and a few swallows of Scotch, the skin on his brow like furrowed leather. "Well, it's not serious, really. Not enough damage been done to do me any financial harm. I guess I lost half a dozen sheep all told. But it's the way they were killed that bothers me."

"How was that?"

"Well, they were torn apart. Mutilated. Throats torn out and skulls crushed. Never saw anything quite like it. Whatever did it is not only powerful but vicious. And the strangest part is that my dogs seem helpless."

Gardiner signalled for another round of drinks, and MacPherson seemed to be thinking deeply while the barman brought them.

"Have you tried to find it?"

"Of course. I almost had it once. That was the strangest part of all. It was a month or so ago and I was sort of keeping an eye out for it. Had my gun with me, and four good dogs. Well, we found a sheep that had just been killed. Couldn't have been dead more than a few minutes. Torn to pieces. I put the dogs on to it and they started howling and growling and sniffing about, then they got the scent and took off after the thing. The land's rocky and I couldn't see a trail myself, but the dogs had it sure enough. I followed them and they tracked it a few hundred yards in to a ravine. I thought I had it then for sure. But when I was coming up behind, the dogs suddenly stopped dead and for no reason I could see, the whole pack started yelping and came running back with their tails between their legs. Made the hair stiffen on my neck, I'll tell you that. They came back so fast they almost knocked me down, and they all crowded around my legs, whimpering. Gave me a funny sensation, that. I kicked 'em and beat 'em but damned if I could make them go into that ravine. Even when I went up to the edge myself, they wouldn't follow. I looked around a little, walked along the edge for a little way, but it was rocky wasteland with heavy undergrowth all along the bottom and I had no chance of finding it without the dogs. But I was sure that it was in there, waiting."

He paused. He looked a little shaken.

"Matter of fact, I was scared to go in after it."

MacPherson didn't look the type to be afraid of much.

"Any trouble recently?" I asked.

"Oh, it's still there all right. Whatever the hell it is. I've tried setting traps for it and poisoned one of the carcasses, but it did no good. Cunning brute. I got the idea, you know the feeling, that it was watching me all the while I was putting the traps out."

"Could it be a wild dog or something of the sort?"

"I doubt that. No dog could have put the fear into my pack that way. And no dog could've crushed those sheep's skulls that way, either. No dog I ever saw."

"A man?"

"Maybe. I thought of that. Used to have a few sheep carried off by the Indians. But they always stole them to eat. This thing just mangles them and leaves them where they died. Maybe eats a mouthful or two, the carcasses are so shredded I can't really tell. But no more than that."

"Few animals kill purely for pleasure," I said. "Wolverine, leopard maybe . . . and man, of course."

"If it's a man, it's a madman."

MacPherson bought a round. I had a glass in my hand and two waiting on the bar now, and felt that I'd soon be in no condition to pursue any investigations.

"Would it be possible for me to stay at your place if I find it necessary to look for this thing?" I asked.

"Surely. I don't know if you can find it, but I'll give you every help I can. I'll have to take you out, though. You'd never find my place on your own. It's in the mountains west of here and there are no roads and only crude maps. I'm not even sure if I'm in Chile or Argentina."

"I have some other things to do first," I said. "I may not have to take advantage of your hospitality."

"I hope you get the bastard. What gun are you using?" It took me a moment to comprehend that.

"I didn't come to shoot it," I said.

MacPherson blinked.

"Then what the hell are you going to do?"

"That depends on what it turns out to be."

MacPherson snorted. Then he looked serious. He said: "Well, it's none of my business, but if you're going to look for this thing, you'd better take a gun with you."

"Surely it wouldn't attack a man?"

MacPherson shrugged.

"You haven't seen those sheep, son. I have. Believe me, you better take a gun."

The way he said it was quite impressive.

It was past noon now, and Gardiner had switched to Scotch. MacPherson approved. We had not had lunch, and Gardiner and MacPherson both seemed content to spend the afternoon at the bar. I'd had more than enough to drink, and the barman brought me a coffee with the next round. A few more customers wandered in and stood at the bar, talking and drinking. I noticed them vaguely, my thoughts on what MacPherson had told me. It was virtually the same story that I'd read in the reports, but hearing it in person, and seeing the man who told it, was far more effective than reading it in the grey safety of London. I was far less sceptical, and ready to believe a great deal more. Perhaps the alcohol had stimulated my imagination; it had certainly fired my impatience to get to the bottom of the mystery. I was convinced now that something very strange indeed was roaming those all but inaccessible mountains, and much too excited to waste any more time in that bar.

"Would this be a good time to see Gregorio?" I asked.

"Good as any," Gardiner said.

"If you could direct me—"

"I'll drive you there. It's not far."

He looked a shade disappointed at the prospect of leaving the bar.

"That's not necessary. Actually, I could use some air to clear my head. I'll walk."

"Are you sure?"

"Absolutely. It'll give me an opportunity to look around a bit more, too. I couldn't see much at the speed you drive."

Gardiner laughed. He was possibly a certain degree in his cups by this time. MacPherson seemed absolutely impervious to intoxication. I took my note pad out to write down the address, but Gardiner laughed more at this, and when he'd given me the directions, I saw why. They were accurate but somewhat unusual. Gregorio lived in the third orange shack on the western approach to town. There was a grey horse in a tin shed beside the shack. The shed was green and the horse was gelded. It was surely a more exact method of location than street names and postal districts, as any stranger who has asked directions in London will know.

I finished my coffee.

"One last drink before you leave?" Gardiner asked.

"Not now, thanks. Will you be here?"

"Undoubtedly."

I turned to leave and Jones came walking down the bar. He was wearing a purple sports shirt and smiling. His hangover seemed to have been effectively reduced by drowning.

"Hello there, Brookes. Have a drink?"

"I can't just now. I have some business to attend to."

He looked disappointed. He had a very American friendliness, and was probably lonely. I introduced him to Gardiner and MacPherson and he shook hands eagerly.

"You fellas live here? Quite a place, this."

Jones bought drinks and merged easily into the group. I felt obliged to wait for a few minutes and not leave him with strangers, but it proved unnecessary. He was perfectly suited to the situation. When I left, Gardiner was telling him how the Explotadora company used to virtually rule the territory and give the governor his orders, and Jones was agreeing that government by private enterprise was vastly superior to Democrats and communism.

I walked out beyond the town.

The wind was stronger here, without the shelter of the sturdy buildings of the town. A *pasajero* rode past me, leading a pack horse burdened with all his possessions and trailed by a pack of mangy mongrels. There were shacks on both sides of the road, hideously bright and clattering metallically. Indians sat huddled in the doorways and on the crooked steps. Men of ancient leather and twisted cord, their eyes turned listlessly after me, not really interested but simply following a motion, the same way that they watched a ragged newspaper tumble before the wind; sullen and listless and uncomprehending, perhaps sensing their lives were changed and unnatural, but not recognizing their defeat. A few sheep grazed behind the shacks, facing away from the wind with splendid unconcern, placid and eternal, and forming perhaps the only bridge between the present and the past.

Gregorio was sitting on a gnarled log beside his door, smoking a handmade pipe. God knows what he was smoking in it. He wore a poncho with a hood roughly sewn on and shadowing his eyes. His hands were strangely delicate, despite the horny calluses, the fingers long and mobile. He peered at me suspiciously. He'd had enough experience of civilization to be wary, unlike the Indians who had watched me walk past.

"Are you Gregorio?" I asked.

The head nodded under the hood.

"You speak English?"

He nodded again.

I squatted down beside him.

"My name is Brookes. I'd like to speak with you for a few moments if you can spare the time."

There was no reaction.

"I'll gladly pay you for your time."

He nodded again I began to wonder if he actually did speak English.

"It's about the creature you claim . . . the creature that you saw in the mountains."

Gregorio rustled within the poncho and the hood fell back from his head. He had hair like black wire and a face like a Cornish farmhouse, somber, grey and grim. But his eyes were bright with intelligence and perhaps something else—perhaps it was fear.

"*Bestia hombre,*" he said. His voice rasped. I felt certain then, looking into his face, that this man was not faking or pretending. He had seen something and that something was very terrible indeed.

I took a small bank note from my pocket and offered it to him. He took it without looking at it, with a vestige of pride long vanquished by necessity. He held it crumpled in his palm.

"Tell me what you saw." He hesitated. "Is that enough?"

He motioned with the hand holding the note, a scornful gesture. "It is enough," he said. His English was surprisingly clear, with a faint North American intonation. "It is not a good memory, Señor." He puffed on his pipe, his lean cheeks sinking inwards. I felt he was gathering more than his thoughts, and waited anxiously.

"When I tell them, they do not believe me," he said, turning his eyes toward the town. "They laugh. They think I see things that are not there."

"I believe you."

His eyes shifted back to me.

"I've come all the way from London to speak with you, and to find what you saw."

"You will look for this thing?" he said, incredulously. He couldn't believe that anyone would voluntarily seek the creature he had seen—or thought he'd seen. A curious mixture of disbelief and respect moved his expression.

"Yes. And I will find it, if you help me."

"Help you?"

"Tell me all you can remember."

"I will tell you, yes."

"When was it that you saw this thing?"

"It was some weeks ago." He shrugged. "I have no calendar."

"You were in the mountains?"

He nodded and looked westward. The land rose steadily away from us and the clouds seemed to tilt down to meet the far mountains. Gregorio stared into the distance. And, without looking at me, he began to speak. His voice moved musically over the foreign English words, but it was music without gaiety, a tragic overture introducing his somber theme.

"I was looking for work on the sheep ranches. I had the horse and two dogs." He stabbed the stem of his pipe toward the green tin shack. "That is the horse. The dogs—" he hesitated, his face still turned away from me, and I saw the cords knot in his neck. "The dogs were running after me. They were happy to be away from this town, in the mountains. They were good dogs. One especially, a dog of great courage and strength. El Rojo he was called. His breeding one does not know, but his loyalty was firm. He was mine many years, although I had been offered much money for him." He paused again. His hands were restless. Then he seemed to shrug, although his shoulders did not actually move.

"We rode on a narrow trail through trees. The trees there lean and turn because of the great wind. The wind was very loud then, and the horse made great noise on the rock. It was becoming night. I do not know what hour, I have no clock. But it was time that I make camp, and I looked for a place. I went from the trail and was among dark trees. And then there was no noise. It was like a storm about to break, that silence. But there was no storm, the sky was clear. It was something else. I knew it was not good. The dogs also knew. The little dog cried and El Rojo had stiff hair over his neck. I felt the horse tremble between my knees. All up my legs I feel this, and the eyes are white, the nostrils wide. I kicked at the horse with my heels, but it did not walk."

Gregorio turned to face me then. His face was terrible. He was reliving those moments vividly, and perhaps this was how his face had appeared then. He seemed scarcely aware of me, his eyes turned on the past.

"Then I heard the sound of this thing. It was a snarl. Not like a dog. A warning, perhaps a challenge. I am not sure what it was. I turned to the sound and then I saw it. It was in a thicket, but I saw it plainly. I looked at it, and it looked at me. We regarded one another. I was unable to move and my throat would not work. My backbone was of ice.

"It was not tall. It bent forwards with long arms. Its chest was huge and shoulders heavy. There was much thick hair, and where there was not hair the skin was dark. For some time we do nothing, and it made the sound again. The hindquarters raise, as if it is stiffening its tail. But it has no tail. Something was beneath it. A sheep, I think. It was woolly and red with blood, and this thing was red at the mouth. Blood dropped heavily from the teeth. But they were teeth. They were not fangs of a beast, they were teeth. And the eyes are on me all this time. It has the eyes of a man . . ."

He was staring into my eyes as he said this. His pipe had burned out, but his teeth were clamped on the stem. I didn't move, afraid to break the memory that held him, and the belief that gripped me.

"I wished to run from this thing, but the horse was filled with fear. It would not run. And I, too, am frozen. Only El Rojo has sufficient courage. He feared nothing, that dog. He moved toward the thing. The other dog was not so brave. It ran. The movement makes the horse able to run, also, and he followed after the dog. The horse ran faster than he could run. Faster than I think any horse can run. I am a horseman. All my life I have ridden horses, and I knew this horse well. But Señor, I could no more stop this horse than stop the wind. And I did not want to."

He was aware of me again, and I thought the story was finished. But he lowered his face and spoke again, more softly.

"But I looked back," he said. "I could not look away from this thing. I saw the dog make a circle on stiff legs. The dog is snarling with bare fangs, and then the thing moved to the dog. The dog was not fast enough. Or the thing is too fast. They are together on the ground then, and I could see no more. But I can hear what happens. I can hear the cry of the dog, the sound of pain and death. It is loud, then it is not so loud, and when I can hear the dog no longer I hear the sound of this thing. It is not like before. It is more terrible. It is the worst sound a man has ever heard. There was nothing I could do. I could not stop the horse for a long ways, and when finally I did I was trembling more than the horse. I thought of the dog. I loved that dog. But I did not go back."

Gregorio lapsed into silence. He seemed sad and exhausted. The note was still clasped in his hand. I waited for several moments before he raised his head.

"That is what happened," he said.

"Do you have any idea what it was?"

He shrugged.

"Could it have been some animal? Some animal you have never seen before?"

"It was a man."

"It was dark you said . . ."

"The light was sufficient."

"A man then. An Indian?"

He shook his head patiently.

"A man and a beast," he said.

"A beast-man. A man like no man ever was."

A man like no man ever was? Or is?

I left him then. I said that I might wish to talk with him again and he shrugged. He was filling his pipe again, and when I looked back from the road he was slumped on the log exactly as he'd been when I came. I was profoundly affected by his tale. I believed him. He might have been mistaken, but he had not deceived me. He had seen something much too terrible to be imagined, and the emotions of his memory were far too genuine to be feigned. Somewhere in those trackless and forsaken wastes, a creature existed. I did not know what it was, but I knew that I had to find it.

I thought of MacPherson's advice.

I did not like the idea of carrying a gun, but I decided that I should. There was another idea that I liked considerably less . . .

IV

I spent the next three days in Ushuaia.

It gave me the opportunity to observe these primitive people, as I'd wanted, but my interest in this pursuit had greatly waned. I regarded it now as something that had been done by others before me, interesting enough but hardly a challenge, compared to the possibilities of a new discovery. The tales I had heard from Gregorio and, to a lesser extent, MacPherson, had inflamed my imagination. I had never been a man to draw easy conclusions from incomplete data, and yet the same idea that had seemed absurd when Smyth presented it to me in his quiet, dark office, and the same statements I had passed over lightly in the objective reports that reached the museum, took on a new reality now, just as the clouded sky cast a new light over this land.

I was consumed by an impetuous urge to proceed with my investigations, and frustrated by the need to wait. But the first essential was still to locate Hodson. That was why Smyth had sent me, and it would have been foolish to follow another line of research until I'd seen him, and settled my mind one way or the other on that account. And it seemed there was no way to find Hodson until his man arrived for supplies.

I went to Graham's every morning to inquire, and be disappointed. Graham had prepared a knapsack and saddlebags for me, and arranged with the stables down the street to have a horse ready to be hired at any time. The knapsack contained a portable stove and foodstuffs in light-weight plastic containers, along with other articles which surprised me, but which Graham thought might possibly prove handy if not essential in traversing that rugged land: a small hatchet, a folding knife, several lengths of rope and cord—things of potential value in survival, rather than in comfort. There was also a sleeping bag and groundsheet. It hadn't occurred to me that I might be spending a night in the open, and I was grateful for Graham's foresight, although not so pleased by several tales he told me of men who had been lost in the mountains. With his guidance, I purchased a suitable outfit of clothing for the trek, heavy whip-cord trousers, wool plaid shirt, quilted windbreaker with hood attached, and sturdy, treble-soled boots equally suited to riding and walking over broken land. I felt a certain satisfaction in being so well prepared which somewhat mollified my impatience.

In the meanwhile, I spent the days walking miles into the country on all sides. I wore my new clothing, getting accustomed to the freedom of this new manner of dress at the same time as I felt myself becoming acquainted with the land. I made no particular effort at observation, and made no entries in my notebook. Whatever I learned was simply absorbed without conscious effort, coming through the senses while my mind turned over manifold plans and possibilities. I didn't attempt to restrict my thoughts to what I knew, or could be proved. It was out of character for me, but I was out of the world I knew, and anxious to enter the world of which Gregorio had spoken.

There were aspects of his story that fascinated me, that had the solid ring of truth, fantastic as that truth might be. These were not the things that seemed to have affected Gregorio most, however. He had seemed most impressed by the creature's eyes, but I passed this over. Many animals have eyes that seem almost human in their intelligence, often the most loathsome creatures, rats and moray eels for instance. Gregorio could easily have been misled in this. But he claimed it had teeth, not fangs, and referred to its foreward or upper limbs as arms, not the legs he would have attributed to most animals—small points he had not pressed unduly, but which convinced me. And, more than anything else, there was the action he'd described—the raising of a non-existent tail. I have often wondered why mankind emotionally resents the tail that his forebears carried; why that is so frequently the point chosen when a man without knowledge scorns the process of evolution. For the same reason that he portrays the devil with a tail, perhaps? A feeling of superiority for the misguided reason that man has lost a useful and functional part of his anatomy. Surely a man like Gregorio would have given a tail to a figment of his imagination, or added one to a trick of light upon a superstitious nature. The tail is an integral part of bestial evil, and it seemed reasonable to assume that he would have. But he hadn't. The thing had no tail, and moved as if it had.

My mind danced back through the aeons, obscuring fact with fancy and the present with the past, jamming two dimensions into one space, in my readiness to believe almost anything. I built fantasies of unbeliev-able intricacy and detail, and was content not to hinder the construction of this fragile architecture of the imagination. And, in this structure, there was the cornerstone of truth. For somewhere, sometime there had existed a creature which was less than man, and in many ways less than an ape, at some point where the distant line forked and began to pursue constantly diverging trails. It had happened once, at some point in time, and evolution has a pattern we have not yet mapped, a stamp that surely may be repeated in different places, when the time of those places is right. I had always believed in the likeliness of simultaneous evolution, finding it far more plausible than since-sunken land bridges and fantastic ocean emigrations on crude rafts, to account for the presence of mankind in the New World and the islands. The only new concept was the timing, and this problem did not seem insurmountable now that I was at a place like this, a land untouched by change as the world aged around it. Could the old pattern have begun again, working here along the same old lines that had populated the rest of the world in forgotten ages? The same evolution, a million years behind?

My wild musings surprised me, as I realized what I had been considering. And yet I didn't scoff at the thought.

On the evening of the third day I walked out beyond the new Italian colony and turned from the path to ascend a rocky incline. The stones were soft beneath the heavy soles of my boots, and I carried a stout walking stick, using it as a third leg against gravity. Some small creature scurried unseen through the brush as I scrambled on to the flattened top of the hillock. A solitary beech tree twisted up from the undergrowth, and an owl hooted from the line of trees fringing a ridge to the north. It was raining lightly, and the wind was drifting higher than usual. I stood beneath the tortured limbs of the tree and lit a cigarette, looking out towards the west. I could not see far in the darkening mist, but I knew that somewhere out there were the mountains and canyons, the unmarked Chilean frontier and, somewhere beyond that, the place where I would find Hodson. I wondered what chance I would have of finding him if I were to set off myself, and the thought tempted my impatience. But it would have been more than hopeless. I had to wait.

Presently, aided by my stick, I clambered back down the incline and walked back to town through the soft, dark rain.

I encountered Jones on the stairs the next morning, and we descended together. I had intended to go to the breakfastroom, but I saw that it was occupied by three widowed tourists who had arrived the day before amidst cackling disorder. They were calling for separate bills and debating over who had devoured the extra doughnut. I believe they were from Milwaukee. I turned into the bar with Jones.

We sat at the bar. Jones had Pernod with his black coffee.

"Women like that make me ashamed to be a tourist," he said. The nasal tones still reached us, although we felt quite sure the ladies wouldn't come into the bar. "That's the trouble with tourists. They get some place and then, instead of relaxing and enjoying themselves they rush about trying to see everything. Laden with guidebooks and preconceived ideas of what they must look at. Now me, first thing I do is find a nice sociable bar and have a drink. Get to meet some of the people. That's the way to be a tourist." He poured some water into his Pernod and admired the silicone effect as it clouded. "Course, you're lucky. You can travel without being a tourist. Gardiner was telling me how you were a famous scientist."

"Hardly famous."

"What's your line?"

"Anthropology. I'm on a field trip for the museum."

"You don't work on atom bombs and things, huh?"

He looked vaguely disappointed.

"Decidedly not. My work lies towards discovering where mankind came from, before it is gone."

Jones nodded thoughtfully.

"Yeah, Still, I guess we got to have those atom bombs and things since the commies got 'em. Better if no one had 'em. You work for a museum, huh? I like museums, myself. Been in all the big museums all over the States and Europe. Not 'cause I think I got to, though. Just 'cause I like 'em. We got some fine museums in the States, you know. Ever thought of joining that brain drain? A scientist gets lots better money back home than you get over in England."

"I hadn't considered it, no."

"Ought to. I mean, science and all is fine, and that England's a great little island, but a guy's got to earn a decent living for himself, too. That's right, isn't it? You got to look after yourself first, before you can look after the rest of the world. That holds for science and politics and charity and everything."

"You have a point."

"Want something with that coffee?"

"No, thank you."

"I don't usually drink much at home, myself. But when I'm traveling, a little drink relaxes me. I like drinking in your country. Those pubs are fine things, 'cept they're never open when a guy's thirsty."

The barman refilled our cups, and poured Jones another Pernod.

"What you doing here, anyway?" Jones asked me.

I almost launched into a detailed explanation, but caught myself in time.

"Studying the natives, more or less," I said.

"That so? Ain't much to study, is there? I mean, they're sort of primitive."

"That's why I'm studying them."

"Oh," said Jones.

A boy was standing in the doorway, blinking. It was the boy from Graham's trading company. I raised a hand and he saw me and came down the bar.

"Mister Graham sent me over. Said to tell you that Hodson's man is here."

"I'll come with you," I told him.

"Want a drink before you go?" Jones asked.

"Sorry. I don't have time."

"Sure. Business before pleasure, huh?"

I left Jones at the bar and followed the boy out to the street. It was a bright morning, unusually warm. Half a dozen hawks were circling against the sun. I felt stimulated as we walked toward Graham's. This was what I'd been waiting for.

There were three horses tied in front of the trading post, and Graham was busily gathering the various supplies, referring to a handwritten list. He glanced up as I entered, and nodded toward the back of the room.

"There's your man," he said.

It was dark in the shadow of crates and shelves, and for a moment I didn't see him. Then, gradually, the outline took shape, and I believe my mouth may have gaped open. I don't know what I'd expected, but certainly not a man of such ferocious and terrifying aspect. He was gigantic.

He must have stood closer to seven feet than six, a massive column of splendidly proportioned muscle and sinew, wearing a *caterino* over chest and back, leaving shoulders, arms and sides bare. He was standing completely motionless, huge arms crossed over his massive chest, and even in this relaxed position the definition of his muscles cleaved darkly against the brown skin. The man's countenance was in accord with his body, his features carved from mahogany with a blunt chisel. A dark rag was knotted across his wide forehead, just above the eyes, the ends of the knot hanging loose and frayed and his hair a ragged coil over the edge.

Graham was grinning. "Quite a lad, eh?"

"Rather impressive. Any idea what tribe he could belong to? He doesn't look like any of the Indians I've seen around the town."

"No. I heard somewhere that Hodson brought him down from up north. The Amazon, I think. As his personal servant. Can't see why he'd want something like that around the house, though."

"And he can't speak, you say?"

"I never heard him make a sound. Dumb, I reckon. Brings a list of supplies and waits while I get it packed and loaded, then he's off again. Brings a cheque on Hodson's bank every few months to settle the account, but I don't think he knows what it is."

"Can you communicate with him?"

Graham shrugged.

"Sure. Sign language, same's I talk to any of them that can't understand English. Simple enough. Universal."

"Could you ask if I may accompany him?"

Graham frowned.

"Well, I can tell him you're going. Don't really know how I'd ask. No sense in it, anyway. He's got nothing to say about it. Can't tell you where you can go, and it wouldn't do to give him the idea he could. I'll just let him know you're going with him, and you'll have to do the rest. Keep up with him, I mean. Not that he might try to lose you, but I wouldn't be willing to bet he'd wait for you if you dropped behind. Probably wouldn't even notice."

"I see."

"You shouldn't have to worry about keeping up, since he's got two animals to lead. Can't go too fast. But he'll probably just keep right on going until he gets there, so it may be a long haul in the saddle."

"I'll manage."

"Sure. No worries."

Graham finished gathering the supplies into a pile by the door. The Indian paid no attention to either of us. He hadn't moved since I'd entered. I noticed that he carried a machete in his waistband and wore nothing on his feet. He fascinated me, and I could hardly take my eyes away from him.

"You can start loading these on the horse," Graham said to the boy. Then he held his hand up. "Wait. You better get Mister Brookes' horse over from the stables first. Get it saddled and ready to go before you load the pack horses." The boy went out. Graham went behind the counter and brought out my saddlebags and knapsack.

"Now we'll see what we can get across to him, eh?" he said. I followed him to the back of the room. The nearer I got, the bigger the Indian looked. I didn't actually get too near. Graham began making hand signs, simple symbols that I could have done as well myself. He pointed at me, at the Indian, and then out toward the horses. Then he made a few subtler movements. The Indian watched it all with absolutely no change of expression, no comprehension but also no disagreement, and it was impossible to know how much he understood.

"That's about all I can do," Graham said.

"Does he get the idea?"

"God knows."

"Should I offer him money?"

Graham frowned.

"I don't suppose he uses it. Probably doesn't know what it is. You might offer him something else, a present of some sort. Damned if I know what, though."

I rejected that idea as being too much like baubles and beads for the savages. Graham and I went back to the door. The Indian still hadn't moved. I looked out and saw the boy leading my horse around the side of the building. The animal wasn't too large and didn't appear frisky, walking with its head down. It had high withers and a long, arched neck.

"Not much to look at," Graham said. "You don't want a spirited animal on a trip like this. This one is placid and surefooted, it should be just the thing."

"I'm sure it will be fine," I said, wondering if Gardiner might have influenced the decision. The horse stood with wide spread legs and drooping back while the boy saddled it, but it looked sturdy enough—more bored than aged or tired.

I put my knapsack on. It felt comfortable. The boy began carrying Hodson's supplies out to the pack animals and loading them with quick efficiency, while Graham and I watched from the doorway. I lighted a cigarette, feeling a nervous energy tightening in my belly, a core of anxiety wrapped in the spirit of adventure.

Graham motioned to the Indian. The horses were ready. The Indian moved past us and over us, and went down the steps. He tested the straps and balance of the packs, his biceps ballooning as he tugged. Then he gathered the leads into one and moved to his mount. There was a blanket over the horse's back, but no saddle, and the Indian was so tall that he virtually stepped on to the animal. He arched his back and the horse moved off at a walk, the pack animals following.

I mounted and settled. Graham came down the steps. "Good luck," he said.

The anxiety was gone now. I felt fine. I felt like thundering out of town in a swirl of dust. But I heeled gently and we moved off at a walk, behind the pack animals, which was much more sensible.

V

The Indian paid no attention to me as I rode behind him. He seemed totally unaware of my presence, an eerie feeling once Ushuaia was behind us, and we were the only two people in sight. We went at a moderate pace and I kept about ten yards behind the pack horses, realizing again how much energy it takes to ride a horse over broken ground, even at such a slow gait. The Indian, however, seemed to use no energy. He rode with an easy grace, his long body relaxed and shifting to the horse's motion, a technique well suited to a long journey, functional rather than stylistic.

Although his horse was of a good size, it looked more like a burro beneath this vast man, and his feet almost brushed the ground.

The sun was abnormally bright and I began to sweat in my heavy clothing, and down my temples. After a while I shrugged out of the knapsack and balanced it on the pommel while I took the quilted windbreaker off and stuffed it in the saddle-bags and slid into the knapsack again. During these gyrations I dropped farther behind, and had to urge the horse into a trot to catch up. The ground was firm and the gait jarred me. I knew I was going to be stiff and sore in a short time, but discomfort earned in such a genuine way didn't bother me; the slight ache of bones and joints lends a certain awareness of one's body and of being alive. It would be a dull existence without pain.

The landscape changed gradually.

We had passed the farthest point of my walks, and I observed this new terrain with interest. The contours were lunar. Large, smooth boulders loomed on all sides and our path wound around and between them. There were few marks of civilization here. Indeed, few signs of life. A few stunted trees grew between and above the rocks, dull moss covered the stony surface, the odd wild sheep peered at us from impossible perches, an ostrich raised its curious head and turned its long neck until it resembled one of the twisted trees. I had had some idea of making a rough map of our journey, but gave the idea up without attempting it. The landmarks were all of a sameness that made recognition difficult—impossible, with my limited knowledge of cartography and compass reading. I knew only that we were heading westward, but not directly. The trail, where there was a trail, curved and zigzagged, following the broken face of the land. We were climbing steadily, the land rising and falling in changing pattern, but always drawing higher in the end. The sun pursued us until it drew level to the north of us, following its eternal path over the equator, and our truncated shadows shifted away from it. The light caught blinding points in the rocks. Time lost objective meaning for me, I was dulled by the heat and the motion and the unchanging contours, and did not even refer to my wristwatch. I'd had no breakfast, and my stomach was empty, but the effort of opening my pack and eating in the saddle was too great. My throat was parched, but I did not raise the waterbag. I slumped in the high Spanish saddle and rode on.

And then, some time in the afternoon, I became aware that the land had changed. It had been an unnoticeable transition, but suddenly we had come into the genuine foothills, the rising plain was behind us and we were ascending into the mountains.

There was no longer even the semblance of a trail, and the going was more difficult, the trees thicker and the rocks higher. The Indian seemed to know the way without having to pay attention, turning and detouring for no apparent reason, but never pausing or backtracking. My horse was placidly confident of his footing. Loose rocks clattered from beneath his hooves, soft mud sucked at his legs between spaces of bare rock, but he never faltered; he lurched but recovered instantly and smoothly. Graham had made a wise selection.

The sun had outdistanced us. It slanted into my face now, hotter than before. I turned to look behind, and found that the plains were already hidden by the folding hills. I knew that I was lost; that I could never have retraced our path back to Ushuaia. I wondered whether we had yet crossed the frontier into Chile. There was no possible way to tell, and it didn't matter in the slightest. Time and distance had both become completely subjective, and my mood was almost stoic; eventually we would be at our destination, and what more did I need to know or concern myself with?

It was in this mood that I nearly rode past the Indian before I noticed he'd dismounted; I didn't, in fact, notice until my horse had the sense to stop. I slid stiffly from the saddle and stretched. It must have been mid-afternoon. Our steady pace had taken us quite a distance, but the path had been so devious that it was impossible to estimate how much actual progress had been made.

We were in the shadow of a large, flat-sided overhang of rock, and trees grew all around, draped with thick yellow moss and stretching down to the dense shrubbery of the undergrowth. The moss stirred restlessly, and cast tangled, shifting shadows. I started to ask my silent companion whether we were halting very long, and then realized the futility of that. He was squatting beside the horses, thigh muscles bunched as great in circumference as a normal man's torso. There was a leather pouch at his waistband and he drew some coarse bark from it and commenced to chew it. The aromatic fumes hung on the air: Winter's-bark, stimulant and tonic, and apparently all the nourishment that vast body needed for this tedious journey. I watched his jaws work methodically and opened my own pack. I had no idea if there would be time to prepare a meal, and had a hasty bite of dried meat and a bar of chocolate. I would have had time for nothing more. I had not even fastened my pack again before the Indian stood up and approached his horse, stooping under the overhanging limbs. My muscles throbbed as I hauled myself back into the saddle, but my seat was all right. The Spanish saddle was very comfortable with its high, square cantel. I pushed my horse up level with the Indian as he started off, and volunteered with obvious gestures to take my turn leading the pack horses. He didn't actually refuse. He simply failed to acknowledge the offer, and a moment later I was once more trailing along behind.

Some time later, we came to a shallow stream bordered by steep, soft banks, and moved along beside it for a while. The water ran in the opposite direction, strangely rapid for such slight depth and bursting over the rocks that lined the bed. Trees burrowed their roots down to the water and mossy limbs stretched over in an arch. We weaved through the foliage and the moss clung to my shoulders, the soft earth gripped the horses' hooves. The Indian had some difficulty leading the pack horses here, and had to move slower. I was closer behind him, wanting to make sure we followed in his exact footsteps, close enough to notice the long scar that ran diagonally over his naked ribs, down to his hip. It was an old scar and not very visible against his dark, dust-covered skin, but it must have been a hideous wound when it occurred, a deep gouge with lesser marks on either side, not clean enough to have been caused by a knife or bullet and yet following a straight course that seemed to imply a purpose to the infliction. Perhaps the talons of some powerful beast, I thought, and wondered what animal might have dared attack this giant.

We came to a break in the bank, where the land had cracked and folded back in a gully, and here the Indian urged his mount down, leaning back from the waist as the horse slid down on stiff legs. The pack horses followed him down reluctantly and my horse stopped, tossing his head nervously and looking for an alternative route. I tugged the reins and heeled to little effect. The Indian was already moving away, riding up the center of the stream, and I felt a moment of panic thinking I might not be able to get the horse down and would be abandoned here; I heaved heavily on the reins, bringing the horse around and off balance. He sidestepped and missed the edge of the bank and we went down sideways, the horse snorting and kicking, and somehow managed to stay upright. I took a deep, relieved breath, and the horse shook his head, then started off again behind the others. The bed was strewn with rocks and the pack animals kicked spray up at me. It felt refreshing. We rode through the water for some time, perhaps an hour, and then ascended the far bank, lurching and heaving up through the slippery mud.

The land had changed once more on the far bank of the stream. We were traversing dense forest. The rocks and boulders were still there on all sides, but they were hidden and engulfed by the trees and shrubbery. The undergrowth was heavy, and I could not see the horse's legs beneath the knees, yet he carried on steadily enough on this invisible ground. Moss braided my shoulders and clung around my neck like Hawaiian leis. It was cooler here, the sun blocked out and the earth damp. I put my windbreaker on again. We passed through an open space and back into the shade, through patterns of light and shadow, moving chiaroscuro imprinted on the senses. I was still sweating, but the moisture was cold, and I was aware of my discomfort now, the blunted sensations of the hot afternoon sharpened unpleasantly. I became conscious of time again, hoping we had not far to go, and looked at my watch. It surprised me to find it was seven o'clock. We had been riding, virtually without pause, for ten hours. The Indian seemed as fresh as he had when we started, and who knew how long he'd ridden to reach Ushuaia that morning. It seemed impossible that anyone, even that extraordinary man, could have traveled through this terrain through the night, and yet we pushed on with no sign of a halt.

We emerged once more into an open space, a hill scarred with stumps. A waterfall sparkled from the ridge to the south and a fallen tree leaned like a buttress against the cliffs below. Halfway up the hill we passed a grave, an indented rectangle of earth and a weathered wooden cross lashed, leaning, against a stump. It amazed me. What solitary shepherd or recluse woodchopper had died in this forsaken place, and who had been here to bury him? Yet, in a way, this forlorn grave gave me a sense of security. I was not at the end of the world, man had been here before, if not civilized at least Christian, and they would be here again. In Ushuaia I had burned with the urge to get away from civilization and to explore undiscovered secrets in forgotten lands, but somewhere along this tedious journey those thoughts had modified and science had yielded to instinct. I would have been very happy indeed to have a drink with Clyde Jones at that moment . . .

We approached the top of the hill and yet another line of trees, silhouetted in tormented tangles against the darkening sky. Small birds watched from the safety of the limbs and butterflies waifed through the vines, catching the last sunlight in their brilliant wings. We drew near and I started at the sudden battering of wings, jerking around to look as a dark form rose up beside me, hovering for a moment and then rising slowly and heavily—a giant condor, a dozen feet between its wingtips, elevating from some disturbed feast. The Indian seemed as unaware of it as he was of me. I shivered and bent over the pommel. We brushed a tree, the rough surface scraping my cheek, but I was too exhausted to feel the pain, scarcely aware of the mountains ahead, capped with snow and fingers of white running down the slopes. They did not seem high, and then, dimly, I realized that we were high; that we had come to the peak of this range of hills, and a long valley was spread out before us.

I gripped the pommel and relaxed my aching knees, knowing I would be unable to go much farther, hoping we would be there soon, or that night would come and force a stop. It couldn't be long now, the mist was low and the light feeble. The horses were tiring, too, heads down and legs weary and uncertain. We were moving on level ground, crossing the flattened top of the hill towards the descent. A jagged arroyo yawned before us, we passed along the ridge and came out through a field of blasted and broken trees where the wind snarled. There was no shelter here, and the wind had conquered. It was moaning over us, and then, suddenly, it was raging and howling across the surface of the land. It struck without warning, nearly dragging me from the saddle. The horse whinnied and

I clutched at mane and pommel and leaned far over. Even the Indian seemed to sway in the unexpected blast. Streamers of yellow moss ran over the ground and a dead tree cracked and splintered. This was not the swirling wind of Ushuaia, but a straight shot from beyond the shoulder of the world, hauling the clouds behind it.

Clinging tightly to the horse, I faced into the wind. I caught my breath. I was looking out beyond those last rocks that stumbled from the edge of the land and sank beneath the towering walls of clouds, looking over the edge of the earth. For an instant the view was clear, and then the rain whipped in and the mists blanketed the sea. It was, in the lapse of seconds, black night.

Even the Indian yielded to this storm. He turned the horses back to the treeline and dismounted in the scant shelter of a rock castle, towers and pillars and spires of ancient stone, stroked smooth on the southern side and harboring tenacious moss on the north. The horses stood quietly, facing the rocks, their tails rippling as the wind curved around behind, while he unburdened them of their packs. This, obviously, was to be our home for the night, or the duration of the storm. I didn't know which; I didn't know if the Indian had intended to stop or if the storm had brought about the decision, and didn't care about the reason, so long as we had halted. I could scarcely slide from the saddle, every joint was stiffened and I ached through the length of my bones, as though the very marrow had petrified.

I unsaddled the horse and unpacked my sleeping bag and groundsheet, going through the motions mechanically. I hobbled the horse and put the feeding bag on as Graham had demonstrated, feeling hollow with hunger myself but much too weary to make the effort of eating. The horse shuffled off to join the others, dark outlines against the trees, grouped together. The Indian was wrapped in a blanket, lying close to the base of the rocks. I could barely see him. The end of his blanket was lifting as the wind tried to find us, curling around the edges and lashing through the columns, and then hurtling on to vent its fury in the trees.

I slid into the warmth of the sleeping bag, too numb to feel the hard ground under me, and looked up at the raging sky. Darts of rain stabbed my eyes and I turned toward the rocks. I thought for a moment of Susan, of the comfort of being with her in her flat, and decided I was mad to be here, as I drifted into sleep.

Some sound awakened me.

It was early and bright. The world was fresh and clean, and the wind had risen up above the clouds again. I sat up, all my muscles objecting, and saw that the Indian was already arranging the packs. I wondered if he would have ridden off and left me sleeping, and felt certain he would have, through indifference rather than maliciousness.

It was agony to slide from the sleeping bag, and I recalled my thoughts of the morning before—that I didn't object to genuinely earned discomfort—and decided that this principle could be taken too far. But necessity forced me on.

My horse stood patiently while I saddled him and removed the hobble. The Indian was already moving off through the broken trees as I painfully hauled myself into the saddle. My stomach muscles ached and my thighs throbbed as they gripped. I doubted that I could last through another day like the last, and yet there was no choice now. I couldn't turn back and I couldn't go on at my own pace, I had to follow the Indian at whatever speed he traveled, and pray we found Hodson before I collapsed.

Strangely enough, however, this second day was not so bad once it had started. We were descending now, and this threw new muscles and balance into use, fulcruming against the grain of the old stress, but my body was deadened and the pain was a dull constant which could be ignored. The muscles, being used, did not stiffen. I found it easier to keep my balance without conscious effort, and was able to eat dried meat and chocolate from my pack without slowing or faltering. Perhaps we traveled at a lesser pace, as well, for the horses must have been feeling the efforts of the long day before. Only the Indian seemed incapable of fatigue, and he was wise enough not to push the animals beyond their endurance.

At first I kept my mind from my discomfort by observing the landscape, and after a while my thoughts turned inward and dwelt on any number of unrelated subjects. When I came back to reality from these wanderings, I was surprised to discover how well my body was standing up to the rigors of the journey—far better than I would have thought myself capable of when I lurched painfully into the saddle that morning. There was a touch of pride and self-respect in this, and there might have been vanity as well, but for the example of the Indian riding on before me, relentless and enduring, and looking at him I felt that it was only luck that kept me going. I had no idea how far we'd traveled when, in the late afternoon, we came to Hodson's.

VI

We came around a fold in the hills and Hodson's house was below us, in the basin of a narrow, converging valley. The sun was in the west. It lighted the surrounding hilltops but hadn't slanted down the valley, and the house was shrouded in gloom. It was a bleak structure, rough grey wooden walls and a corrugated iron roof, protected from the wind by the shoulders of land that rose on three sides and a sheer rock face towering behind.

I was surprised. I'd expected something more, or something less—either a rough field camp or a civilized home, perhaps even a laboratory. But this was a crude, makeshift building, sturdy enough but poorly finished. Still, it fitted in with what I knew of Hodson. He wasn't a man who needed or wanted the fringes and frills of modern convenience; perhaps, with no income I knew of and only his limited personal funds, he could afford nothing else.

We followed a hard dirt track down the incline, where two rises rolled together. As the angle of vision changed, I noticed that the house seemed connected with the rock face behind—not leaning against it for support, but actually protruding from the rock, making use of some natural crevice or cave.

We had reached the bottom of the descent and turned toward the house when a figure emerged and stood by the door, watching our progress. A stocky man, solid on widespread legs. I recognized Hubert Hodson, from photographs taken a generation before, a little heavier, a little greyer, but the same man, sturdy and imposing in woollen shirt and heavy boots. His face was windburnt and tanned, and his brow was as corrugated as the roof above him. He was watching me, and he didn't seem pleased.

We halted in front of the house and the Indian slid from his horse. I nodded to Hodson. He nodded back and turned to the Indian, his hands moving rapidly. The Indian replied in the same fashion, and glanced towards me. I believe it was the first time he'd actually looked at me. Hodson made a final, terminating gesture, and walked over to stand beside my horse. His shirt was open halfway down, his chest hard and matted with hair. He looked more like a lumberjack than a scientist, and his obvious strength would have impressed me, had such feelings not been overwhelmed by observing the giant Indian.

"You wanted to see me?" he asked.

The Indian had apparently understood that much.

"Yes, very much."

Hodson grunted. "Well, you had better come in. Leave your horse, the Indian will take care of it." I thought it curious that he referred to his servant that way, instead of by name. I dismounted and handed the reins to the man, and he led the horses around the side of the house. Hodson had gone to the door and I followed. He'd started to enter the house, then stepped back to let me go through first, a perfunctory politeness that seemed to show a determination to keep our meeting on a formal basis. Courtesy had never been associated with Hubert Hodson.

"I saw you coming," he said. "Thought you'd most likely been lost in the mountains. A mistaken idea, obviously. Always been a fault of mine, leaping to the hasty conclusion. Well, I'm usually right, anyway."

The interior was as bleak as the outside. We stood in a barren room with home-made furnishings and bare walls, one small window throwing insufficient light. Two doorways led out at the other side, hung with curtains of strung beads. There was one battered leather chair, the sole acquiescence to comfort.

"Who are you?"

"Brookes. Arthur Brookes."

"You know who I am," he said. He held his hand out, another surface politeness. His grip was unconsciously powerful. "Afraid I can't offer you much hospitality here. Have a seat."

I sat on a straight backed chair that wobbled on uneven legs.

"This is luxury after a night in those mountains."

"Perhaps."

"Your servant sets an inexorable pace. A remarkable man. I don't know his name—"

"I call him the Indian. I expect you did, too. Mentally, I mean. Anyway, he can't speak so there's little sense in giving him a name. Always better to classify than denominate. Avoid familiarity. Once you label a thing you begin to think you know what it is. Clouds the issue. Trouble with society, they designate instead of indicating. Give everything a name whether it's necessary or not. Etiquette. Confusion. Nonsense. But I expect I'd better give you a drink, for all that."

This brisk monologue pleased me. I saw he was still the same Hodson I'd been given to expect, the same iconoclast and rebel, and that seemed to indicate that he would still be carrying on with his work—and furthermore, that he might be willing to talk about it. That was a paradox in Hodson. He denied society and civilization, and yet burned with the need to express his ideas to his fellow men, needing the objects that he scorned.

"I've some brandy. Not much. Plenty of the local stuff, if you can take it."

"That will be fine."

Hodson clapped his hands loudly. He was watching me with an expectant expression. A movement caught my eye at the back of the room and I glanced that way. I saw a young woman come through one of the beaded curtains, started to look away and then found myself staring at her. She was coming towards us, and she was absolutely splendid.

I don't believe I've ever seen such a magnificent physical specimen, and there was little cause to doubt my perception because she was wearing no clothing whatsoever. Hodson looked at me and I looked at the girl. She was tall and lithe, her flesh burnished copper and her hair so black that it reflected no highlights at all, an absence of all color. She smiled at me inquisitively, flashing teeth in a wide mouth and eyes as dark as her hair. It is extremely difficult to manage a polite smile of greeting in such circumstances, and Hodson was amused at my effort.

"This is Anna," he said.

I didn't know what to do.

"Anna speaks English. Anna, this is Mister Brookes. He has come to visit us."

"How do you do, Mister Brookes," she said. She held her hand out. Her English was flawless, her handshake correct if somewhat disturbing. "It is very nice to have a guest. I don't think we have had a guest before?" She looked at Hodson.

"Bring Mister Brookes a drink, my dear."

"Oh yes. Of course."

She smiled again as she turned away, her firm breasts in profile for an instant, and her buttocks inverted valentines rolling tautly together as she walked away. She left the same way she'd entered, moving through the beads with supple grace, not the acquired poise of a woman but the natural rhythm of some feline animal.

Hodson waited for me to comment.

"A charming young lady," I said.

"A trifle disconcerting, I suppose?"

"I must confess I was a bit taken aback. By her symmetry, of course, not her nakedness."

Hodson laughed.

"I wondered how you would—but no matter."

I felt I'd passed some examination, although I wasn't sure how he'd graded my reactions.

"She is an Indian?"

"Yes. Not a local, of course. From the Amazon. I found her there when she was just a baby—must be fifteen years ago or more. Bought her on a whim of the moment."

"Bought her?"

"Of course. What else? Surely you didn't think I stole her? Or does the idea of purchasing a human being offend your morality?"

I didn't like that.

"My morality is unequivocally subjective. But I notice you've given her a name. Unlike the Indian. Would that be significant, in any way?"

Hodson frowned and then grinned.

"It was necessary to the experiment. I had to give her an identity, in order to see how it developed. But, I must admit, it would be rather difficult to refer to Anna as, say, the subject under observation. Some matters defy even my principles."

Anna returned with two glasses, gave us each one and left the room again. Hodson pulled a chair over and sat facing me, balanced on the edge as though the interview would not be lasting very long.

"Now then. Why have you come here, Brookes?"

"I'm from the museum. You know Smyth, I believe. He sent me to find you."

"Smyth?" His face was blank for a moment. "Yes, I know Smyth. One of the more sensible men. Knows better than to scoff without comprehension. But why did he send you here?'

I took my cigarette case out and offered Hodson one. He declined. I wondered if a direct approach would be best. Hodson would certainly resent anything else; would slice through any oblique references with his sharp perception. It had to be direct. I lighted a cigarette and proceeded to tell him about the reports and Smyth's deductions. He listened with interest, hands resting over his knees, eyes shifting as though they reflected the thoughts behind them.

"And so I'm here," I said.

Hodson leaned back then, crossing his legs. "Well, I hardly started these rumors," he said. "I don't see any connection with my work."

"Just an idea of Smyth's."

"An erroneous idea."

"Surely you've heard these rumors yourself?"

"No reason to make that assumption. I am, as you can see, completely isolated here. My only contact with the world is through the Indian."

"Well, you've heard them now."

"What you've told me, yes."

"Don't they interest you?"

"Unfounded and fantastic."

"I thought so. Smyth didn't. And now that I've spoken with these people . . ."

He waved a hand.

"Genetics is my line. This wouldn't concern me, even if it were possible."

"Yes, I know your work. Tell me, what has kept you here for twenty years?"

"That same work. Research. Paper work, mostly. Some experimentation. I have a laboratory here, crude but sufficient. I stay here for the isolation and lack of distraction, no more. You were mistaken to assume that my research had any connection with the area in which I chose to pursue it." He drained his glass.

"You see, Brookes, I have the unfortunate trait of optimism. I overestimate my fellow man constantly. When I am surrounded by other men, I invariably try to give them the benefit of my work. It's disrupting, takes time and proves less than useless. That's why I'm here, alone, where my progress can continue peacefully and steadily. It's going well. You are, in point of fact, the first distraction I've suffered in years."

"I'm sorry if—"

He waved the apology away.

"I understand your interest," he said. "I've observed these people. Anna, for instance, is a fascinating study. One of the few people in the world who is completely natural and unspoiled. Been kept from the degrading influence of society. Not necessarily modern society, either. All society corrupts. If If I hadn't bought her she'd be ruined already, filled with superstitions and legends and taboos and inhibitions. Sometimes I actually believe that the so-called primitive man is more degraded than civilized man; more governed by superstructure. She came from a savage tribe and has become a superb woman, both physically and emotionally. Her nakedness, for instance. She is as immune to the elements as she is to shame, as innocent of the wiles of a modern world as she is the sacrifices and bloody religion of her parents. If I had met a woman like Anna when I was a young man, Brookes, I might have—oh well, I suppose I was born a misogynist."

Hodson was becoming excited. He was a talker, denied the opportunity for twenty years, and although he might not have wanted to, he was talking.

"Or the Indian," he said. "The intellect and the instincts of an animal, and yet I have his total devotion and loyalty—not an acquired trait, like patriotism, hammered into the young by conditioning, but a natural loyalty such as a dog gives to his master. It doesn't matter if the master is kind or cruel, good or bad. That is irrelevant. A most interesting aspect of natural man."

"Then you are studying these people," I said.

"What?" Hodson blinked. His face was flushed beneath the weathered skin. "No, not studying. A sideline. One can't help observing. It has nothing to do with my work."

"Will you tell me about that work?"

"No," he said. "I'am not ready yet. Soon, perhaps. It's a new field, Brookes. Unrelated to the study of primitive peoples. I leave that to the social anthropologists, to the do-gooders and the missionaries. To you if you like. You're welcome to them."

"And these rumors?"

"I may have heard something. Perhaps an aborigine or two just trying to live their own lives. They'd be enough to shock anyone who saw them, and of course no one has ever told them it's wicked to kill sheep."

"That, too, would be of immense interest."

"Not to me."

"You surprise me."

"Do I? That's why I'm here, alone. Because I surprise people. But I have nothing for you, Brookes."

He waved towards the window. The sun was coming in now, as it settled into the western junction of the hills, blocking a shallow parallelogram on the floor.

"You may seek your wild man out there. But you'll find no clues here."

And that positive statement ended the initial phase of our conversation. We sat in uncomfortable silence for a time. I felt a sense of futility and annoyance that, after waiting so impatiently in Ushuaia and then undertaking that arduous trek through the mountains, it had all come to nothing. I blamed myself for expecting more than I reasonably should have, and felt irritated at Hodson, even while I admitted his right to resent my visit. Vexation does not depend on justice.

Hodson seemed to be pondering something that didn't concern me or, more likely, something he didn't wish me to be concerned with. My presence both pleased and disturbed him, and he seemed undecided whether to treat me as the conversational companion he'd been without for so long, or the disturbance he wished to avoid. I felt it best to refrain from intruding on his thoughts, and sat quietly watching the dust dance in the oblong of light beneath the window.

Presently he clapped his hands again. Anna must have expected this, for she appeared instantly with fresh drinks, flashing that searching smile at me, undoubtedly puzzled at my visit and, I think, enjoying the change in daily routine. She moved off reluctantly, looking back over her shoulder with interest that was innocent, because she'd never learned that it wasn't.

Hodson began to talk again. His mood had changed during those minutes of silence, and he wasn't expounding now. It became a mutual conversation. We talked in general terms, and Hodson was interested to hear of some of the latest theories which hadn't yet reached him here, although he expressed no opinions and no desire to go into them in depth. I referred to some of his own earlier work in this context, and he seemed pleased that I knew it, but passed that same work off as misguided and outdated. This turn of the conversation came naturally, and brought us back to his present work, from a new angle, and he had lost his reticence now.

"For the past twenty years or more," he said, "I have been mainly concerned with the replication processes of the nucleic acids. I believe—I know, in fact—that my work has progressed far beyond anything else done in this line. This is not conjecture. I have actually completed experiments which prove my theories. They are immutable laws."

He shot a quick glance at me, judging reactions with his old desire to shock.

"All I require now is time," he continued. "Time to apply my findings. There is no way to accelerate the application without affecting the results, of course. Another year or two and my initial application will be completed. After that—who knows?"

"Will you tell me something about these discoveries?"

He gave me a strange, suspicious look.

"In general terms, of course."

"Do you have any knowledge in this field?"

I wasn't sure how much familiarity I should show here—how much interest would inspire him to continue without giving him reason to suspect I might be too formidable to be granted a hint of his secrets. But, in fact, my acquaintance with this branch of study was shallow. He was speaking of genetics, connected with anthropology only at the link of mutation and evolution, the point where the chains of two different sciences brushed together, invariably connected but pursuing separate paths.

I said: "Not very much. I know that nucleic acid determines and transmits inherited characteristics, of course. The name is used for either of two compounds, DNA and RNA. I believe latest thinking is that the DNA acts as a template or mold which passes the genetic code on to the RNA before it leaves the nucleus."

"That is roughly correct," Hodson said.

"Very roughly, I'm afraid."

"And what would result if the code were not transmitted correctly? If the template were bent, so to speak?"

"Mutation."

"Hmmm. Such an ugly word for such a necessary and elemental aspect of evolution. Tell me, Brookes. What causes mutation?"

I wasn't sure what line he was taking. "Radiation can be responsible."

He made a quick gesture of dismissal.

"Forget that. What has been the cause of mutation since the beginning of life on this planet?"

"Who knows?"

"I do," he said, very simply and quietly, so that it took me a moment for it to register.

"Understand what I say, Brookes. I know how it works and why it works and what conditions are necessary for it to work. I know the chemistry of mutation. I can make it work."

I considered it. He watched me with bright eyes.

"You're telling me that you can cause mutation and predict the result beforehand?"

"Precisely."

"You aren't talking of selective breeding?"

"I am talking of an isolated reproductive act."

"But this is fantastic."

"This is truth."

His voice was soft and his eyes were hard. I saw how he was capable of inspiring such respect in Smyth. It would have been difficult to doubt him, in his presence.

"But—if you can do this—surely your work is complete—ready to be given to science?"

"The genetics are complete, yes. I can do, with a solitary organism's reproduction, what it takes generations for selective breeding to do—and do it far more accurately. But remember, I am not a geneticist. I'm an anthropologist. I have always maintained that the study of man's evolution could only be made properly through genetics—that basically it is a laboratory science. Now I have proved that, and I demand the right to apply my findings to my chosen field before giving them to the self-immured minds of the world. A selfish attitude, perhaps. But my attitude, nonetheless."

I said nothing, although he seemed to be awaiting my comments. I was considering what he'd told me, and trying to judge the truth of the statements and his purpose in revealing them, knowing his tendency to jump to conclusions and cause a deliberate sensation. And Hodson was peering at me, perhaps judging me in his own way, balancing my comprehension and my credulity.

I don't know which way his judgement went but, at any rate, he stood up suddenly and impulsively.

"Would you like to see my laboratory?" he asked.

"I would."

"Come on, then."

I followed his broad back to the far end of the room. The beaded curtains moved, almost as though someone had been standing behind them and moved away at our approach, but there was no one there when we pushed through. The room beyond was narrow and dark, and opened into a third room which was also separated by curtains instead of a door. The house was larger than it appeared from without. At the back of this third room there was a wooden door. It was bolted but not locked. Hodson drew the bolt and when he opened the door I saw why the house had appeared to project from the cliff behind. It was the simplest, if not the most obvious, reason. It actually did. We stepped from the room into a cave of naked rock. The house, at this part, at least, had no back wall and the iron roof extended a foot or two under the roof of the cave, fitting snugly against it.

"One of the reasons I chose this location," Hodson said. "It was convenient to make use of the natural resources in constructing a building in this remote area. If the house were to collapse, my laboratory would still be secure."

He took an electric torch from a wall holder and flooded the light before us. The passage was narrow and angular, a crack more than a cave, tapering at a rough point above our heads. The stone was damp and slimy with moss in the wash of light, and the air was heavy with decay. Hodson pointed the light on to the uneven floor and I followed him some ten yards along this aperture until it suddenly widened out on both sides. Hodson moved off and a moment later the place was lighted and a generator hummed. I looked in amazement at Hodson's extraordinary laboratory.

It was completely out of context, the contrast between chamber and contents startling. The room was no more than a natural vault in the rocks, an oval space with bare stone walls and arched roof, untouched and unchanged but for the stringing of lights at regular distances, so that the lighting was equal throughout this catacomb. There was no proper entranceway to the room, the narrow crevice through which we had passed simply widened out abruptly, forming a subterranean apartment carved from the mountain by some ancient upheaval of the earth. But in the center of this cave had been established a modern and, as far as I could see, well-equipped, laboratory. The furnishings appeared much sturdier and more stable than those of the house, and on the various tables and cabinets were racks of test tubes and flasks and beakers of assorted shapes and sizes, empty and filled to various degrees. Files and folders were stacked here and there, just cluttered enough to suggest an efficient busyness. At the far side of the room there was a door fitted into the rock, the only alteration that seemed to have been made to the natural structure of the cave.

Hodson gestured with an open hand.

"This is where I work," he said. "The accumulation of years. I assure you this laboratory is as well equipped as any in the world, within the range of my work. Everything I need is here—all the equipment, plus the time."

He walked to the nearest table and lifted a test-tube. Some blood-red fluid caught a sluggish reflection within the glass and he held it up toward me like a beacon—a lighthouse of a man.

"The key to mankind," he said. His voice was impressive, the dark fluid shifted hypnotically. "The key to evolution is buried not in some Egyptian excavation, not in the remnants of ancient bones and fossils. The key to man lies within man, and here is where the locksmith will cut that key, and unlock that distant door."

His voice echoed from the bare rock. I found it difficult to turn my eyes from the test-tube. A genius he may well have been, but he definitely had a flair for presenting his belief. I understood the furor and antagonism he had aroused, more by his manner than his theories.

I looked around a bit, not understanding much of what I saw, wanting to read his notes and calculations but fairly certain he would object to that. Hodson had moved back to the entrance, impatient to leave now that I'd seen the laboratory, not wanting me to see beyond a surface impression.

I paused at the door on the opposite side of the chamber. I had thought it wooden, but closer observation showed it to be metal, painted a dull green.

"More equipment beyond?" I asked.

I turned the handle. It was locked.

"Just a storeroom," Hodson said. "There's nothing of interest there. Come along. Dinner will be ready by now."

It was curious, certainly, that a storeroom should be securely locked when the laboratory itself had no door, and when the entrance to the passageway was secured only by a key which hung readily available beside the door. But I didn't think it the proper time to comment on this. I followed Hodson back through the tunnel to the house.

A table had been set in the front room, where the initial conversation had taken place, and Anna served the food and then sat with us. The Indian was not present. Anna was still quite naked, and somehow this had ceased to be distracting. Her manner was so natural that even the absurd motions of placing her napkin over her bare thighs did not seem out of place; the paradox of the social graces and her natural state did not clash. The meal was foreign to me, spicy and aromatic with perhaps a hint of walnut flavoring. I asked Anna if she had prepared it, and she smiled artlessly and said she had, pleased when I complimented her and showing that modesty, false or otherwise, is a learned characteristic. Hodson was preoccupied with his thoughts again, eating quickly and without attention, and I chatted with Anna. She was completely charming. She knew virtually nothing outside the bounds of her existence in this isolated place, but this lack of knowledge was simple and beautiful. I understood full well what Hodson had meant when he'd suggested that, had he met a woman like this when he was young—was surprised to find my own thoughts moving along a similar line, thinking that if I had not met Susan—

I forced such thoughts to dissolve.

When the meal was finished, Anna began to clear the table.

"May I help?" I asked.

She looked blank.

"Why no, this is the work of the woman," she said, and I wondered what pattern or code Hodson had followed in educating her, what course halfway between the natural and the artificial he had chosen as the best of both worlds, and whether convenience or emotion or ratiocination had guided him in that selection.

When the table had been cleared, Anna brought coffee and brandy and a humidor of excellent Havana cigars, set them before us and departed, a set routine that Hodson obviously kept to, despite his avowed denials of social custom and mores. It was like a dinner in a London drawing room, magically transferred to this crude home, and seeming if anything more graceful for the transference. I felt peaceful and relaxed. The cigar smoke hung above us and the brandy lingered warmly within. I would have liked to carry on the conversation with this intriguing man, but he quite suddenly shifted the mood.

He regarded me over the rim of his brandy glass, and said, "Well, now that you see I have no connection with these rumors, you'll be impatient to get away and pursue your investigations along other lines, I assume."

His tone left no doubts as to which of us was anxious for my departure. Now that his exuberance had been satisfied, he was disturbed again—a man of changing moods, fervor followed by depression—feeling, perhaps, that he'd once more fallen victim to his old fault, the paradox of talking too much and too soon, and regretting it directly after.

He looked at his watch.

"You'll have to stay the night, of course," he said. "Will you be able to find your way back?"

"I'm afraid not. I hate to be a bother, but—"

"Yes. Ah well, perhaps it's for the better. At least my location remains a secret. I mean no personal offense, but already you disrupt my work. The Indian assists me in certain ways and now he must take the time to guide you back through the mountains. I'll know better than to make that mistake again, however. It should have occurred to me before that I must instruct him to return alone from Ushuaia." He smiled. "I can think of few men who would disagree with the Indian, if it came to that."

He said all this with no trace of personal ill will, as if discussing someone not present, and I could take no exception to his tone, although the words were harsh.

"The Indian may well be one of the most powerful men alive," he said. "I've seen him do things, feats of strength, that defy belief . . . all the more so in that it never occurs to him how remarkable these actions are. He's saved my life on three separate occasions, at great danger to himself and without hesitation. Have you noticed the scar on his side?"

"I did, yes."

"He suffered that in rescuing me."

"In what manner?"

Hodson frowned briefly, perhaps because he was recalling an unpleasant situation.

"It happened in the Amazon. I was attacked by a cat—a jaguar. He came to my assistance at the last possible moment. I don't fear death, but I should hate to die before my work is completed."

"I'd wondered about that scar. A jaguar, you say? Was the wound inflicted by fangs or claws?"

"I don't—it was a bit hectic, as you can well imagine. A blow of the front paw, I believe. But that was some time ago. Amazing to think that the Indian hasn't changed at all. He seems ageless. Invulnerable and invaluable to me, in such help that requires strength and endurance. He can go days without sleep or food under the most exhausting conditions."

"I learned that well enough."

"And you'll undoubtedly learn it again tomorrow," he said, with a smile, and poured more brandy.

We talked for the rest of the evening, but I could not lead him back to his work, and it was still quite early when he suggested that we retire, mentioned once more that I would want to get an early start in the morning. I could hardly disagree, and he clapped for Anna to show me to my room. He was still seated at the table when I followed her through one of the curtained doors at the back and on to the small cell where I was to spend the night. It was a narrow room with a cot along one wall and no other furnishings. There was no electricity and Anna lighted a candle and began to make the cot into a bed. This was disrupting again, not at all like the natural acceptance I'd felt at dinner, seeing her naked by candlelight, bending over a bed. The soft illumination played over the copper tones of her flesh, holding my eyes on the shifting shadows as they secreted and then moved on to reveal and highlight her body. She moved. The shadows flowed and her flesh rippled. Her firm breasts hung down like fruit ripe for the plucking, tempting and succulent. I had to tell myself that it would be a wicked thing to take advantage of her innocence, and think very firmly of Susan, waiting for me in London. I think man is naturally polygamous, although I don't know if this is necessarily a bad thing, and it took great resolution to force my thoughts away from the obvious.

She straightened, smiling. The bed was ready.

"Will you require anything else?" she asked.

"Nothing, thank you."

She nodded and left, and the room was stark and harsh with her departure.

I crawled into my crude bed.

I didn't sleep well.

It was still early and, although my body ached and protested from the rigours of the trek, my mind was active and alert. The thought of starting out again early in the morning was unpleasant, and I felt that very little had been accomplished by my efforts. Perhaps Hodson would tell the

Indian to set a more leisurely pace, but I couldn't very well suggest this after he'd already mentioned how inconvenient it would be to have the Indian wasting time as my guide. It was a distasteful thought, added to the futility of the journey.

Presently I began to drift towards sleep, my body overruling my mind and drawing me into a state of half-consciousness, half thinking and half dreaming. A vision of Susan occupied my mind and then, as the dreams became more powerful than the thoughts and my subconscious mind rejected the restrictions of my will, it became a vision of the splendid Anna which I was unable or unwilling to reject. I yielded to this night-time prowling of the id, the transformation of thought to dream.

I was asleep.

I awoke in instant terror . . .

The sound awakened me.

There was no gradual surfacing from slumber, I was fully conscious in that instant, and I knew it was no dream . . . knew, even in that first moment, what the sound had been. Gregorio's haunted words flashed back to me—a sound like no man has ever heard—and I knew that this was that sound.

It was a cry, a deep rolling bellow, quavering at the end, a sound that only vocal cords could have made, but that no vocal cords I'd ever heard could possibly have made. It was indescribable and unforgettable, the howl of a creature in torment.

I lay, trembling and staring at the dark ceiling. The candle was out, and my fear was blacker than the room. It seemed impossible that a sound, any sound, could have rendered me helpless, and yet I was petrified. I've always considered myself as brave as the next man, but this sensation was far beyond human courage—beyond human conception. I wanted desperately to stay where I was, motionless and silent in the dark, but I knew I would never forgive such cowardice, and I forced myself to move, inch by agonizing inch, as though my bones grated harshly together.

My cigarette case and lighter were on the floor beside the cot, and I fumbled for the lighter and ignited the candle. Shadows leaped against the walls and I cringed away from their threatening shapes, waiting for reality to form. It was some seconds before I managed to stand up and pull my clothing over the ice and sweat of my skin. Then, holding the candle before me like a talisman to ward off evil, I moved to the door and pushed through the curtains.

The house was too quiet.

Surely no one could have slept through that sound, and yet there was no stir of awakening. It was as if everyone had been awake beforehand and anticipated the noise. It had been very near, loud and vibrating, as though echoing from close confines, and I thought of the cave behind the house; felt strangely certain the sound had come from there; moved quietly down the corridor to the front room and then through the second passage that led toward the cavern entrance. Although the sound was not repeated, the silence was terrifying in its own way, a silence formed from that sound or an effect of the sound. I was stiff with dread, my backbone tingling and my flesh rippling until it seemed that snakelike, I was trying to shed my skin. If all fear is emotional, this fear was primordial, linked more to instinct than conscious knowledge of danger. I wanted to locate the source of the sound, but the dread was far deeper than any conception of what I might find, a repulsion that lurked secretly within me in some atavistic remnants of the past, some hideous racial memory awakened.

I forced myself forwards, through the second room. The door opening within the cave was open, and the tunnel beyond was dark. Light showed at the end, where it widened into the chamber, but it failed to penetrate the passage, and stepping into the darkness was like plunging into cold liquid qualms of panic. I don't know what resolution drove me forwards, what reserves of willpower summoned the mechanical motions of advancing, but I held the candle before me and walked into the corridor.

The pale light circled before me, floating over the contorted rocks in evil designs, and wavering on to meet the electric light at the far end, fading against the great brilliance and recoiling over the stoves, over a bundle of rags that blocked my path.

Rags that moved.

I would have screamed, had my throat worked, but I was frozen into motionless silence as the rags shifted and took shape, and I found myself staring into a face, a face twisted and wrinkled and human, swathed in a filthy shards, the eyes gleaming under the dark shelf of overhanging brow. It was a woman, ancient and bent and deformed. She had been coming toward me. Now she stopped and spread her arms wide, barring the way like some loathsome crucifix, the rags hanging from her elbows in folds that seemed part of her body, some membrane attaching her arms to her flanks.

She hissed, an exclamation, perhaps a word in some unknown language, rocking from side to side on crooked haunches, and another form loomed up behind her, brushed her aside and advanced on me. My heart stopped, then burst with a surge of blood that rocked my brain. I dropped the candle, and saw the Indian in the light that shot up from the floor, nostrils flaring and cheekbones casting oval shadows in the sockets of his eyes. His hand closed on my shoulder, the strength unbelievable, as if those terrible fingers could have closed effort, lessly through my bones. I fully expected to die at that moment.

The grip relaxed then. I was dimly aware that Hodson had shouted something from the laboratory; I heard a dull clang as the metal door beyond was closed. Then the Indian had turned me and was pushing me before him, back the way I'd come. I offered no resistance, and he was not unduly rough, although those hands could never be gentle. He walked behind me until we were back at my room, then pointed at the bed with all four fingers extended and stood in the doorway, bending beneath the frame, until I had crawled cringing on to the cot. When I turned he had left, the beaded curtains whispered his departure, and I collapsed in a limp reaction which it causes me no shame to recall.

It was some time before my mind was released from the emotions, and I was able to think. Then my thoughts came tumbling in disorder. What had caused that sound? What had taken place in the room beyond the laboratory? Who had the ancient crone been, what was her function, what would the Indian have done to me if Hodson had not shouted? Where was Anna? How on earth did this household fit together, what purpose did the members fulfill in whatever monstrous scheme was being conducted? I found no answers, and I don't suppose that I wanted those answers, that I was prepared to have such terrible knowledge etched on my mind, with my shoulder still burning from the dreadful clutch of the giant Indian, and that ghastly cry still vibrating in my memory.

Anna came to my room in the morning.

She acted as if nothing unusual had happened in the night, and told me that breakfast was ready. I was still dressed, the sweat dried on my clothing, but she didn't notice this, or comment on it. I got up immediately and followed her to the front room, where Hodson was already seated at the table. He looked tired and drawn. I sat opposite him.

"Sleep well?" he asked.

I said nothing. Anna poured coffee from an earthenware jug. Hodson's hands were steady enough as he drank.

"I found myself unable to sleep," he said, casually. "I often get up in the middle of the night and do some work."

"Work? What work?"

"I beg your pardon?" he said. His annoyance and surprise at my tone seemed genuine.

"What on earth caused that cry in the night?"

Hodson pondered for a few moments, probably not deciding what to tell me as much as whether he should answer at all, rather to satisfy my curiosity or castigate my impertinence.

"Oh, you mean just before you came to the laboratory?"

"Obviously."

"I wondered what brought you prowling about."

"And I wonder what caused that sound?"

"I heard it," he said. "Yes, now that I think of it, it's small wonder you should be curious. But it was merely the wind, you know. You've heard how it howls higher up in the mountains? Well, occasionally a blast finds a crevice in the rocks and comes down through the cave. It startled me the first time I heard it, too. I was tempted to find the fissure and have it sealed, but of course it's necessary for proper ventilation. Otherwise the laboratory would be as rank as the tunnel, you see."

"That was no wind."

"No wind you've ever heard before, Brookes. But this is a strange place, and that wind came from beyond where man has ever ventured."

I felt a slight doubt begin. I'd been positive before, but it was just possible that Hodson was telling the truth. I had noticed that the air in the laboratory was fresh, and couldn't doubt there were actually openings in the rock. But the doubt remained slight, with the sound still recent in my memory.

"I'm sorry if the Indian alarmed you," Hodson was saying. "I've instructed him never to allow anyone in the laboratory without me, you understand. He was just performing his duties."

"If you hadn't shouted—"

Hodson paused, his cup before his face.

"Would he have killed me?" I asked.

"For a scientist, you have a vivid imagination," he said. He shipped from the cup. "I'm no Frankenstein, you know. No mad scientist from a bad cinema film. Although, I must say, the mad scientists generally seem misunderstood by the clottish populace."

"Who was the old woman?"

"If it's any concern of yours, she's an old servant. Not actually so old, but these people age rapidly. She's past her usefulness now, but I let her stay. She has nowhere else to go. Surely you don't see evil implications in an ageing old woman, do you?"

His expression was scornful and angered me.

"Very decent of you to allow her to remain," I said. "And to supply her with such extraordinary garments."

His eyes reflected something that wasn't quite indignation.

"My affairs are my affairs," he said. "It's time for you to go, I believe. The Indian has your horse ready and is waiting for you."

At the door, I said, "I'm sorry for troubling you."

Hodson shrugged. Anna was standing beside him.

"No matter," he said. "Perhaps it did me good to talk with someone. And good luck with your investigations."

"Good-bye," Anna said.

We shook hands solemnly, as she must have thought a parting required. She remained in the doorway after Hodson had gone back inside. The Indian had led the horses around to the front of the house, and I saw they were both nervous, stamping and shying. When I placed my foot in the stirrup, my mount sidestepped away and I had to hop after him on one foot, holding mane and cantel, before I was able to get into the saddle. The horse had been very placid before. The Indian slipped on to his own horse and led the way up the track. I looked back and waved to Anna. She raised a hand rather timidly, possibly not acquainted with this gesture of farewell. Then she vanished into the house.

Well, that is that, I thought, as we wound up the track from the narrow valley. But I noticed one more thing. On the incline to the north a prominence of shrub jutted down toward the basin, and as we drew above it I saw that a strip, perhaps a yard wide, seemed to be broken and flattened, running from the top of the hill nearly to the apex of this growth, and where the strip ended some loose brush and limbs seemed to be stacked in a small mound, as if concealing something. A vague form, greyish in color, was just visible through this tangled pile. It appeared that something had been dragged down from the rim of the hill and hastily covered. I couldn't quite make out what it was. As we reached the top of the trail, and the land leveled out before us, I saw two dark shapes circling and starting a cautious descent, thick necks poised attentively, lowering their sharp beaks below arched wings. These repulsive carrion eaters sank slowly down towards the northern slope, and then the land shouldered up and I could see no more.

VII

I must have looked in fine shape indeed, judging from Graham's expression when I halted the horse in front of his store, filthy and unshaven and brittle with exhaustion. I expect I looked no worse than I felt. The pace of the return journey had not been noticeably less than the first, and had followed too soon to allow my body to harden from that initial exertion. And that incredible Indian hadn't even paused before turning back. When finally we reached the hardened beginnings of the trail that led through the tablelands to Ushuaia, he'd pointed in that curious, four-fingered fashion, turned his horse sharply, and headed back into the hills.

Graham helped me to dismount.

"All right?" he asked.

"Yes Just stiff and tired."

"You look like a wounded bandit who's been running in front of a posse for a week," he said.

I managed a smile, feeling the dirt crack along the creases of my face.

"Didn't expect you back so soon," he said. He looped the reins over the post and we went into the building.

"Neither did I. I wan't particularly welcome at Hodson's, I afraid."

Graham frowned. Inhospitality is virtually unknown in frontier territories. He said, "I always thought there was something queer about Hodson. What's he doing out there?"

"I honestly don't know."

I began pacing back and forth over the wooden floor, loosening my muscles. The knots were firm. Graham called the boy to take my horse back to the stables.

"How far did you go?"

"God knows. How fast can a horse travel in those hills? We must have been actually riding more than twenty-four hours."

"Yeah, that's right. God knows. But I'll bet that Indian covered the greatest possible distance in the time. It's amazing how these people find the shortest routes. Can't understand that Hodson, though."

He reached behind the counter and came up with a bottle; he handed it to me and I drank from the neck. It was brandy, and it felt very good.

"Well, what now?" he asked.

"I don't know. First thing, I want to crawl into a hot bath. Then I'm going to sleep through until morning. I can't make any decisions in this state."

"Good judge," he said.

I thanked him for his help, told him I would see him the next day after deciding what further supplies or assistance I might need, and limped back to the hotel. The desk clerk raised a polite eyebrow when he saw the condition I was in, and I asked him to have the maid heat a bath. I think he concurred with that judgement, and he asked if I needed any help getting upstairs. I managed on my own, however, and as soon as I was in my room I stripped my grimy clothing off and put a bathrobe on, then sat down on the bed to wait for the bath to be readied. After a moment or two, I lay back and closed my eyes, just for a second.

I never heard the maid knock, and when I awoke it was morning . . .

I spent the day relaxing and writing two letters, seated at a table in the bar. Jones, despite his reluctance to follow in the paths of his fellow tourists, had succumbed to a chartered flight to Cape Horn, and there were no distractions, other than my own musings as to how he was getting along with the three widows, and an admission that I would rather have liked to see Cape Horn myself.

The first letter was to Smyth. I considered for some time before I began writing, and informed him in detail of my interviews with Gregorio and MacPherson and my visit to Hodson's, stressing, I fear, the devotion to duty which the latter entailed. I sketched the nature of Hodson's work briefly, from what the man had actually told me, and asked Smyth for his opinion of the possibilities of that, from general interest rather than in relation to my own investigations, and stressing that it was a theoretical point because Hodson would surely not welcome further concern on my part. I mentioned the Indian and Anna in terms, respectively, of awe and admiration, and was surprised to find how greatly Anna had impressed me. My conclusion was that I considered further probing warranted, despite Hodson's avowed disinterest and lack of connection.

But I made no mention of that sound in the night.

Somehow, I found myself unable to express the feeling it had driven into me, and certainly there was no way to describe the sound itself, no comparisons whatsoever. And, now that I was back in the quiet hotel, I found myself almost willing to discount Hodson's connection with the rumors. There seemed to be no connection with his laboratory work, however advanced that might have been in its own right, and his explanation—the wind howling down the fissures—seemed reasonable enough, likely even, although it brought a chill to remember my certainty at the time. But it was far too subjective a feeling to symbolize by the written word, and I did not attempt it.

The second letter was to Susan. Before starting this, I re-read what I had written of Anna, and a sense of infidelity swept through me. I remembered how I had felt, watching her bend naked over the bed, with the candle light dancing over her flesh; how my loins had tightened with desire, and how close I had come to reaching out to her. I had never been unfaithful to Susan, and had never before felt the slightest urge or need, but there in the confines of that narrow cell, in that remote and forbidding land, I had struggled with an urgency so powerful—

Well. I had resisted, and I was very glad that I had, and I wrote to Susan with love.

VIII

My mind came back from that faraway place, through those eternal weeks. The waiter was taking the dishes away, concerned that we'd barely touched the food, but not mentioning it; aware that something was very wrong between us.

"Anything else, sir?" he asked, softly.

"A drink?"

"Yes. A strong drink," Susan said.

Susan had never drunk very much. I ordered large brandies, and she downed half of hers with the first swallow.

"I kept your letter," she said, as if she had somehow followed my thoughts. "The letter you wrote from Ushuaia. You still loved me when you wrote that, didn't you? Or was that a lie, too?"

"It was no lie. There is no lie, Susan. I love you now as much as then."

"Yes, whatever changed your mind must have happened after you wrote. I know there was love in that letter."

She drained the brandy.

"But I shan't ask you again."

"Another?"

"Yes," she said. She turned the empty glass in her hands. "No, never mind. I want to leave, Arthur."

"All right."

I signalled to the waiter.

"I want to leave alone, Arthur," Susan said.

"Susan. Darling—"

"Oh God. I can't stand this. I can't bear it. I'm going now."

She stood up and walked quickly towards the entrance. I pushed my chair back and started to rise, then collapsed back on to the seat. The waiter stood beside the table and Susan was getting her coat at the counter.

"The bill, sir?" the waiter asked.

I shook my head.

"No. Not yet. I'll have another brandy."

"Large, sir?"

"Yes," I said.

I'd been drinking a large brandy the day that Gregorio came into the bar at the Albatross, too. It was the second day since my return from Hodson's, and I'd sent the boy from Graham's store to fetch Gregorio, feeling that it might be to my advantage to put my proposition to him here at the hotel, rather than at his shack—to talk to him on my own ground, removed from the realities of Gregorio's life.

He stood in the doorway, beside the boy. I nodded and the boy pointed to me and went back out. Gregorio walked down the bar and stood beside me.

"Oh, it is you," he said. He didn't seem pleased. "I didn't remember the name." I had the impression that, had he remembered, he wouldn't have come.

"A drink?"

"Pisco," he said, shrugging. The barman poured the grape alcohol into a large tumbler. Gregorio was in no hurry to drink, and his feet shifted nervously.

"I've been looking for your Bestia Hombre," I said.

He nodded, expecting that. He lifted the glass.

"Pray God it doesn't look for you," he said.

"Will you help me, Gregorio?"

"I? How is that possible?"

"I'd like you to take me to the place where you saw it."

"No. I will not go there again." It was more a statement of unalterable fact than an assertion of refusal. He took his blackened pipe out and began to fill it with some exotic mixture from a rubber pouch.

"I'll pay well."

He looked balefully at me, struck a match and continued to regard me above the flame as he sucked the pipe into a haze of smoke. The contents blackened and curled above the bowl, and he pressed it back with a hardened thumb. A few shards escaped and drifted, smoking, to the floor.

"I need money," he said. "We all need money. But not to that place."

"You needn't do anything else. Just guide me there. What danger could there be?"

"Danger? Who knows? Perhaps none. But that place is . . . it is not a good place. It has very bad memories. I am no longer young and no longer brave. The dog was brave."

He shrugged once more.

"Well, could you show me on a map?"

"A map?"

I thought he hadn't understood the word.

"Mapa," I said.

"Yes, I know this word. But what map? There is no map of that place. Not with detail."

"Could you make a map?"

"Of no use to you. I have lived all my life here, and I am not young. I know the land. But to make a map—what is there to show on this map? It is rocks and trees and hills. How are they different? To me, perhaps, for I know them. But on the map it is the same."

This was true, of course. It had been a thoughtless request. And, anyway, I needed a guide with me, a man who knew the land and, preferably, knew where Gregorio had seen the creature. And that was only Gregorio.

"I have already been out there," I said.

"Yes."

"I have heard the sound of the thing. Gregorio, I have heard it, and I know you told me the truth."

His eyes were wide. I wanted to shock him.

"I heard it in the dark of night," I said.

"And still you wish to find it?"

"Yes."

"You are very brave, Señor. Braver than I."

"That is because I know there will be no danger," I said. "I was frightened when I heard it, yes. But it is a living thing. It is no demon or spirit, whatever it is, it is alive, and we'll be well armed. It can't hurt us." I tried to look confident, almost nonchalant, and Gregorio seemed to weaken slightly. He took the pipe from his mouth and drank, replaced the pipe and drew, cheeks hollowed and a deep line etched between his eyebrows.

"I would have a gun, too?" he asked.

I nodded. I don't honestly know if I had intended to carry a weapon, against my principles, but I do know I was relieved that Gregorio's reluctance made it necessary.

"I would like to kill it," he said.

"Only in self defense—"

"I would very much like to avenge the dog, yes." His jaw tightened. "But the dog is dead. It would not help the dog. It is my Spanish blood that has the desire for revenge." He leaned against the bar with both hands, head down between his shoulders. His shoulderblades were sharp beneath the canvas poncho, and his thoughts were sharp beneath his furrowed brow.

"I would be very much afraid," he said, without looking at me. The pipe bobbled in his teeth as he spoke.

"But you will show me?"

After a while he looked up.

"How much money will you pay me?" he asked.

But I knew that the money had very little to do with it.

We decided to leave in two days, which gave ample time to make preparations, and for me to recover from the physical effects of the last trek. Actually, I felt very well. I'd been exercising lightly since my return, so that my muscles hadn't stiffened much, and I felt that the exertion had hardened me sufficiently so that I didn't dread repeating the journey. Then too, this time I would be able to dictate the pace at which we traveled. Although I was eager to get to the area where Gregorio had seen the creature, I felt no need for haste now that definite arrangements were being made for departure, unlike the impatience I'd felt while waiting for Hodson's man to arrive without knowing when to expect him, when time and distance were unknown quantities. This time, we were able to plan accurately and take all the equipment and supplies necessary for a prolonged camp in the mountains.

Graham and Gregorio conferred on what we would need, and I left the decisions to them, with complete confidence in their judgements, hiring what I could and purchasing the rest according to their recommendations. For my own part, I bought only a change of clothing similar to what I'd worn on the first trek, and a pair of light sandals to alternate with the heavy boots. I'd paid so little attention to the rest that, on the night before our departure, I was surprised at the size of the pile that had accumulated.

We were taking two small Everest tents as well as sleeping bags, groundsheets and blankets for warmth and shelter; a large amount of food both for ourselves and the horses, along with cooking utensils which fitted neatly together when not in use, and a double burner Butane stove which Gregorio considered an unbelievable luxury, without disdaining it; a complete first aid kit and a spade and axe, both of which were hinged and could be folded to simplify transport and packing, and an ample supply of pisco which did treble duty as sustenance, warmth and medicine, and which I found myself growing rather fond of at a few shillings a bottle. Stacked together, these supplies made a considerable mass in one corner of Graham's storeroom, but he assured me that everything could quite easily be distributed between two pack horses and our own mounts.

He had already arranged for the hire of the pack animals and the same horse I'd ridden before, which I'd suggested, feeling confident in its reliability, and in my own ability to control it. Gregorio intended to use his own horse, the grey gelding, and I added the hire fee for one horse to what I was paying him as a guide.

Graham was dealing with a customer while I made the gesture of checking the supplies. Gregorio stood behind me.

"Well, we certainly seem to have everything we could possibly need," I said. "You've been very thorough."

Gregorio nodded, then frowned.

"What is it?"

"The guns?" he said.

I'd forgotten them, actually. I hesitated. I was afraid that Gregorio might do something rash out of hatred or fear or vengeance. But he was watching me expectantly, and I knew he couldn't be persuaded to go without a weapon. I didn't really blame him, either, and knew the idea of being able to defend ourselves would make us both feel better.

"Yes, I'll see about that now," I said.

Graham had finished with the customer, and I went over to the counter and inquired about hiring guns. Gregorio followed, as if he wanted to make sure.

"I never thought of that," Graham said. "I didn't know you'd be needing guns."

"I certainly trust we shan't."

"Well, I don't hire guns myself. All my regular customers have their own guns, and the tourists who want to do any shooting usually make arrangements through their travel companies."

Gregorio moved closer.

"There must be somewhere to hire them."

"Oh yes. But why don't you borrow a couple from Gardiner?" Possibly he resented the idea of sending me to a competitor. "Gardiner does some shooting and I know he has several spare guns. Want me to ask him?"

"I'll ask him," I said. It seemed a good idea, and I was certain he wouldn't object. "I'll go out to his place now."

Gregorio moved back towards the supplies, satisfied I was making an effort, and I went out to the street and found a taxi to take me to Gardiner's.

He seemed pleased, as usual, to have company, and gave me a drink while we discussed my trip to Hodson's and I told him a little about my plans for the second journey. When I'd finished, he asked if there was anything he could do to assist me. It was just the opening I needed, but somehow I felt rather ridiculous about the guns.

As casually as I could, I said, "I was wondering if I should take any weapons? What would you think?"

"Weapons?"

"Well, guns."

"For sport or food or protection?"

"Protection, I guess," I said, feeling foolish.

Gardiner smiled. "So you've come to believe those rumors, have you?"

"I don't know. I recognize the possibility."

He nodded thoughtfully, the smile gone.

"Might it be a good idea, anyway? There are foxes and such that might try to raid our supplies."

"A damn good idea, if you ask me," he said. "No harm in being safe. And, I must say, these rumors are a bit hair-raising, no matter what it is that's been killing Mac's sheep."

"What would you suggest I take?" I asked, feeling uncomfortable about asking a favor, and Gardiner saved me the necessity.

"I can lend you a gun, if you like," he suggested.

"I'd appreciate that, if it's no inconvenience."

"I've several spare guns. Not much to do these days but shoot, actually, and guns accumulate the same as golf clubs or tennis racquets or darts—whatever your game is, there's always a new piece of equipment that strikes your fancy. But I'm wondering what would be best for you? It's hard to decide when you have no idea what you might have to shoot." He seemed completely serious in considering this. "Shotgun or rifle, which would you prefer?"

"I'd be more comfortable with a shotgun, I think. But if you can spare two, Gregorio could carry the rifle."

"Sure. That solves that problem. Gregorio will probably be happier with a gun, too."

"Yes. He believes what he saw, whether I do or not."

Gardiner refilled our glasses and left the room; he returned in a moment with the firearms and handed me the shotgun. It was a superb gun, matched to the one hanging on the wall, hand engraved by some craftsman in Bilbao.

"Double twelve bore," he said. "Full choke on the left."

I admired the workmanship for a moment, then threw it into aim. I was roughly the same size as Gardiner and the balance suited me well.

"A splendid gun. This will do me."

"I suppose Gregorio can use this all right," he said, handing me the rifle. It was a .303 Savage, the lever action featherweight model, light and efficient in rough, wooded country where a longer rifle might be cumbersome. "It hits hard and it's fast," Gardiner said. He looked at me gravely. I suppose he'd sensed something of my nervousness, and he was quite serious when he said, "Just in case."

"Yes. Just on the off chance, eh?"

"I'll give you cartridges and shells before you leave."

"I'll pay you, of course."

He gestured.

"On the museum, of course."

"Oh, well, all right then. Better yet, have Smyth send me half a dozen bottles of that fine brandy he keeps."

"Certainly," I said.

I'd never known that Smyth kept brandy, fine or otherwise. There were many things I didn't know.

Gregorio was sitting on the front steps at Graham's when I got out of the taxi with the guns. He nodded appreciatively and I handed him the rifle. He worked the lever a few times, then threw it to his shoulder in quick aim. I could see he'd used a rifle before. He nodded again, satisfied.

"This is good. I will carry this?"

"That's right. But, Gregorio, you must promise me that you won't use it unless it's absolutely necessary."

"Necessary?"

"To our safety."

He smiled. His teeth flashed.

"Yes, I will promise that," he said. "But, if we find this thing, I think it will be most necessary . . ."

IX

We left early in the morning. It was raining and the dark clouds were torn by wind, strung long across the sky. Gregorio led the pack horses and I rode beside him, just stiff enough so that my muscles welcomed further exertion. Gregorio rode much the same as the Indian, although he used a saddle and boots, slumped slightly forward and relaxed. We both had our hoods pulled up against the rain and didn't speak much. I was concentrating on our route, and knew that we were following the same trail the Indian had taken from town, apparently the shortest or the only trail to the hills, such as it was. I was able to spot several landmarks I'd passed before, unusual rock formations and abnormally formed trees, the same impossible perch from which, perhaps, the same placid wild sheep observed our passage. We traveled slowly and steadily, and stopped for lunch before we'd reached the foothills; we rested for a few minutes and then pressed on again. Gregorio had lighted his pipe and the battered bowl jutted from his cowl, spluttering as the rain damped the burning mixture. The sky was dark, the weather foul. Where the low clouds were shredded by the wind darker clouds covered the gap from above. It looked as if it might rain for days.

When we reached the foothills and began to climb, everything seemed familiar, unlike the outstanding landmarks of the rising tableland, and I realized this was because everything was the same, curious and unusual formations repeated many times over until they became commonplace. I had no idea now whether we were still following the path the Indian had taken. Gregorio undoubtedly knew the land, but lacked the Indian's infallible sense of direction or familiarity, and he had to stop from time to time to get his bearings, relying on a visual knowledge which the Indian hadn't needed. We made frequent mistakes, and had to turn or backtrack, but they were not serious and our progress wasn't greatly hindered. Several times we stopped to stretch and sample the grape alcohol. The rain continued and it grew colder; the reins were slippery and the damp began to seep through my windbreaker, adding the unpleasant sensation and scent of wet wool to my discomfort. I was quite satisfied when Gregorio suggested we stop for the night, although I knew we had not made nearly as much progress as I'd made on the first day following the Indian.

We made a campfire, not bothering with the Butane stove or the tents until we'd reached a more permanent camping place, but sheltering against the rocks in our sleeping bags, talking for a while and then lapsing into silence. Gregorio's pipe glowed for a while longer and then we slept.

It was still raining in the morning. The fire was out and we had to relight it to make coffee. We ate our breakfast from tins while the horses watched with drooping ears. Progress was slower on this second day, as we climbed higher and the forest thickened around us. It was necessary to move in single file now, and I dropped to the back of the line. We had been traveling for several hours when we came to a stream. It was impossible to tell if this was the same stream I'd crossed behind the Indian, when I'd noticed that scar on his side, but if it was the same water, we had certainly come to it at a different place. The banks were shallow and we had no trouble fording it. I thought it was probably the same stream, but that we were farther to the north. On the opposite bank the land rose more sharply, and I began to anticipate reaching the top of the range—the same distance, roughly, as I'd made in the first long haul of some twelve or thirteen hours behind the Indian. But as we continued to rise higher and the land did not begin to level off, it strengthened my belief that our path lay farther north, where the mountain range extended towards the Pacific. Either that, or we were traveling much slower and more circuitously than I hoped.

In the late afternoon we came to the highest point of this slope, and the land lay below us on all sides. There were further mountains to the west, hazy and unreal in the rain. I asked how far we'd come and Gregorio told me we were more than halfway there. This was encouraging, but inspired no great desire to press on more rapidly. We went on a few miles beyond the top, to gain the shelter of the trees and hills, and made our second camp.

Sitting beside the fire, after dinner, Gregorio broke open the box of cartridges and silently began to load his rifle. He put the safety catch on but kept the gun beside him. The shotgun was in my pack, stock and barrels separated and carefully wrapped. I felt no urge to get it out. My foreboding had diminished, and the land no longer seemed so wild and savage on this second trek, at a slower pace and with a guide to whom I could speak. But I thought Gregorio might prefer me to be armed.

"Shall I get my gun out?" I asked.

He shrugged. "We are not very close," he said. "It is just that I am nervous. I have never before been in the mountains without a dog to awaken me if there is danger. I left my dog with a friend . . ."

I wondered if he still had the same dog that had fled when El Rojo died. But I didn't ask him.

We descended gradually throughout the morning of the third day. The rain had slackened somewhat, although the sky remained dark, gunmetal streaked with black. Progress was good and, although the land still lay below us north and south, looking back I could see we had come a considerable distance from the peaks. The land was fairly open and I was able to ride abreast of Gregorio, but he seemed in a solemn mood. He had the rifle slung across his back and looked like a Hollywood Hemingway bandit. We stopped late for lunch, and he didn't seem interested in the food but drank rather more pisco than usual to wash it down, then forfeited his after-lunch pipe in his impatience to get under way again.

A mile or so from where we had halted, he turned from the obvious flat route and led the way along an inclining shelf towards the north. Trees grew in a curiously straight line on our right, their limbs drooping wearily under the weight of hanging moss and pressing rain, and the ridge on our left dropped away sharply in layered rock. Presently, the incline became more gradual and then disappeared as the land rose to meet it in a triangle. I realized it had been a long canyon, and we had come to the end of it. Gregorio pushed his hood back, and the wind rippled his stiff hair. He was looking about, alert and concerned, and I wondered if we were lost.

Then he reined up, slipped the rifle from his back and held it across the pommel. The grey gelding pawed the ground.

"What is it?" I asked.

"We are there."

"Where?"

He pointed towards the trees at the head of the canyon.

"That is where I saw it," he said.

I nodded and dismounted. Gregorio looked down at me for a moment, then swung from the saddle.

"Will you show me?" I asked.

"I came here. I am not very brave about this, but neither am I a coward. I will show you."

He looked very Spanish suddenly, arrogant and proud. We tied the horses to a leaning tree and walked towards the trees. I remembered the darkness and silence he'd told me about, but didn't feel that sensation. It didn't seem a frightening place. Gregorio pushed through the brush, the short rifle held before him, and I followed. The trees inclined towards us and we were in an open glade. There was nothing there. Gregorio moved across the space, his boots sinking into the soft earth, head lowered and moving from side to side.

Suddenly he stopped very quickly. I came up beside him. His knuckles were white on the rifle, his teeth were white as he drew his lips back, and when he moved the toe of his boot I saw something else flash white on the ground. I knelt, and felt a sudden beat of sympathetic pain. It was the broken skull of a dog. A brave dog.

I wanted to say something, but one doesn't express those things. Gregorio stared at the skull for a moment, stone faced, and then he shrugged.

"It is done," he said.

There was nothing else there. He walked silently back to the horses.

X

We made our permanent camp some distance from that glade. That was our focal point and I didn't want to go too far from it, but Gregorio wouldn't have wanted to be too close to the scene so horrible in his memory, although there was certainly nothing there now. I'd searched methodically for footprints or patches of hair that might have been torn out on the thorns, but found nothing except a few more bones, scattered and picked clean. The scavengers had made a thorough job of their grisly feast.

Physically, the spot where we made camp was far more gloomy than the glade. Gregorio had chosen it for maximum shelter and convenience rather than scenic grandeur, although there was a certain unreal and eerie enchantment about the place. A brooding, timeless, unchanging mood clung to the rocks and trees, a smell of arrested decay that had begun but would go no further, as though a primordial swamp had been suddenly frozen for eternity.

It was an area enclosed by a rough oval of rocks and trees a dozen yards wide at the narrowest segment of the ring. The rocks were of all shapes and sizes, from boulders to stones, and the trees grew from all angles between them and around them, twisting to conform with the immovable rocks and bowing away from the constant winds. Several trees had grown together, joining at the trunks and limbs while boulders separated their roots; others had split around narrower rocks so that two trees shared the same roots. The stones were covered with slimy moss and fungus and sallow creepers dripped from the limbs.

I held the horses while Gregorio scrambled over the rocks, vanishing behind a curtain of swaying vines. He returned shortly, satisfied that the interior of that oval would be the ideal place to make our camp. It was enclosed from the wind, the trees arched into a roof overhead, and best of all a narrow stream ran through the space, appearing in a spurt of fresh water from between the rocks.

It was difficult to get the horses inside. They were reluctant to cross the barrier of rock and we had to lead them one at a time, clattering and sliding, but once they were inside they were safe and we didn't have to worry about them. They wouldn't cross the rocks voluntarily and it eliminated the need to tie or hobble them, as well as the effort of carrying water from the stream across the treacherous footing, as would have been necessary had we left them outside.

I erected the tents while Gregorio fashioned an interior barrier of rock and dead trees to keep the horses out of the living quarters of our strange dwelling, and used the folding axe to hollow a log into a feeding trough. Then I set up the stove and attached the Butane bottle while he built a circle of rocks in front of the tents to serve as a fireplace. The stove was adequate for cooking, but we needed a fire for warmth and light. Together we unpacked the rest of the supplies and covered them with a tarpaulin. Our camp was made, crude but adequate, and it was time to decide what the next step should be. I lit a cigarette and considered the prospects. Gregorio was gathering whatever dry wood he could find. Now that the destination had been reached, I felt a sense of futility. We were here, but had anything other than distance been accomplished? I don't know what spectacular clue I'd hoped to find, but there had been nothing, no sign of the creature's presence in the area and no reason to suppose he was still there. All I could do was wait and observe and hope, and that seemed a passive and remote approach. I decided to confer with Gregorio and waited while he used a chemical fire lighter to start the camp fire, and brought water for coffee.

The smell of coffee boiling in the open air is sufficient to raise the lowest spirits, and the prospect of lacing it with grape alcohol was even better. Gregorio seemed to have shaken off his depression by the time we sat huddled at the fire, tin cups steaming in the damp air. I felt peaceful again. It was the end of the day, but nightfall was not a definite thing under that overcast sky. The raindrops battered at the fuscous forest surrounding us, seeking entrance through the foliage and falling like moths to the firelight. It was dark and somber, a scene from a nightmare world. The little stream splattered from the rocks in peaceful contrast to the wind calling overhead, and the pungent odor of Gregorio's pipe drifted sharply through the scent of sodden vegetation and moldy earth.

Presently, feeling that I should do something constructive, I took out my map case and unfolded the best map obtainable of the area. It was sadly lacking in detail, with frequent gaps, indicating nothing more than approximate altitude. I asked Gregorio where we were, and he frowned over the map. A raindrop bounced heavily from the Straits of Magellan.

"Here. Somewhere here."

He stuck a forefinger in the center of one of the blank areas. It told me nothing except that we were over 5,000 feet above sea level.

"Well, are there any landmarks, anything to get an approximate bearing from?"

Gregorio thought for a moment, his finger moving over the map. "MacPherson's ranch is nearest," he said. His finger strayed northwards a vague distance but remained within the confines of the blank space. "Somewhere here. It was there I was traveling when I looked for work. When I saw it."

That was encouraging, and I kicked myself mentally for not finding out sooner where MacPherson's place was. The creature had been there several times, at least once since Gregorio had seen it, and this knowledge increased my hope that it still frequented this area. I modified my self-castigation by realizing I couldn't have found MacPherson's on this map, anyway, and hadn't known Gregorio was headed there, but decided I'd better tie up the other possibility into this framework.

"Do you know where Hodson's is?"

Gregorio shook his head. "I don't know that name. Is it a ranch?"

"No. Just a house. In a valley."

He smiled. "There are many valleys," he said. "I know of no house. Not north, I think. I know what is north from here, that is where I sometimes work."

I folded the map carefully and slid it back in the case.

"How shall I go about finding the creature?"

He shrugged, looking into the fire. The light danced off his face like sunbeams off granite.

"Wait," he said. "You must wait."

"But why should it come here?"

"Perhaps for two reasons," he said. He was smiling again, but it was a strange, tight smile. "One is the water." He nodded towards the stream. "It is the only water to drink on this side of the mountain. There are small streams that come and go and ponds that grow stagnant, but this is the only constant fresh water in some miles. It begins only a little way from here, and it ends just beyond. So, if this thing must drink, I think it will drink near here."

This revelation delighted me, although I felt very much the amateur for not thinking of such a simple aspect of the search, and I was grateful for Gregorio's good sense. He was still smiling into the fire.

"And the other reason?" I asked.

"Because we are here," he said.

It took a moment to understand what he meant. The fire was hot on my face, but a definite chill inched up my spine. Gregorio stood up and walked over to the supplies and packs, then returned with the shotgun and handed it to me. I saw his point. I bolted it together and kept it in my tent.

In the morning I set out to trace the stream to its source. Gregorio assured me it wasn't far, and that it emerged from a subterranean course through the mountains. I wore my heavy boots for scrambling over rocks and carried the shotgun. Gregorio volunteered to accompany me, but I didn't think it necessary since I was going to follow the stream and couldn't very well become lost since I could easily follow it back again.

The stream burst into the camp in a miniature waterfall, tumbling from a narrow opening in the rocks and falling a few inches with comical fury, a Niagara in the insect world. It was impossible to follow the winding stream around and under the rocks but that wasn't necessary. I crossed the barrier at the easiest point and walked back along the perimeter until I came to the spot where the water flowed into the circle. It was just a shallow flow there, and I saw that it must have been compressed and confined as it ventured through the rocks, to break out in such Lilliputian ferocity at the other side. But on this open ground it wandered through marshland with little direction, and it wasn't easy to follow its main course. Several times I found that I'd gone a few yards along a side branch which diminished and then vanished, seeping into the ground. There was still no danger of losing my way, however, since I was moving upwards and could still see the trees surrounding the camp, and as I walked farther the stream became wider and deeper.

I had been walking for ten or fifteen minutes when I heard the rumbling ahead, and knew I must be approaching the source. I was almost at the crest of the hill, and behind it a high cliff towered against the sky. The stream was much larger here, and when I came to the top I saw the waterfall, still above me on the next hill. It was an exact replica of the cascade in the camp, magnified many times over. The water surged from a long gash in the cliff and pounded down, defying the wind, in a torrent at the foot of the unassailable rock wall. The avalanche had worn the land away and formed a turbid pool at the base of the cataract, and this in turn spilled the overflow out to form the stream.

I hurried on until I was standing beside the pool. The spray dashed over me and the sound roared in my ears. It was a natural waterhole which any large animal would use in preference to the shallow stream, and I immediately saw traces of those animals. I recognized the tracks of fox, muskrat and wild sheep, and saw various other unidentifiable prints.

I moved around the bank to the other side.

And there, quite distinctly, I found a print that was almost human. I stared at it for some time, hardly believing I'd discovered it so easily and so soon. But there it was. It wasn't quite the print of a barefoot man. The toes were too long and the big toe was set at a wider angle than normal. But it was without doubt the footprint of a primate, and a large primate at that. My heart pounding, I searched for further evidence, but there was only the one print. From that point, the creature that made it could have easily leaped to the nearest rocks, however, and it was all the evidence I needed to convince me I was in the right place, and that all I needed now was patience. If I waited, concealed near the waterhole, sooner or later the creature would appear.

But that suddenly posed another problem, one I'd been deliberately ignoring until the time came. If and when I did find the creature, what would I do? Or what would it do? My problem was based on not knowing what it was, whether it was man or beast or both. If there was any chance it was a man, I couldn't very well trap it or use force to capture it. It was a tricky moral judgement, and one I was hardly qualified to make before I'd seen it, and decided, tentatively at least, what it might be.

I returned to the camp, excited and anxious to tell Gregorio what I'd found. As I slid down from the rocks, I thought for a second that he wasn't there, and then I saw him by the horses. He had the rifle in his hands, pointing at the ground, but I had seen a blur of motion from the side of my eye, and wondered if he'd been waiting with the rifle aimed at the sound of my approach. Once again I felt a foreboding that he might act rashly; I knew, without doubt, that if it had been the creature that had just scrambled into the camp, Gregorio would have used his weapon with no hesitation.

I didn't tell him about the footprint. I told him I'd been to the waterhole, however, and that I intended to wait there in concealment.

"When will you wait?" he asked.

"As soon as possible. Tonight."

"At night?" he asked, his tone not quite incredulous—more as though he couldn't comprehend such a thing than that he disagreed with it.

"I think the chance of seeing it would be better at night. And it will certainly be easier to conceal myself in the dark."

"Yes. Those things are true," he said, as if other things were also true. But he offered no discouragement, in the same way that one doesn't argue with a madman.

XI

There was a moon above the clouds and long shadows drifted across the land in skeletal fingers. By day that desolate cataract had been eerie enough, but in the moonlight the rocks seemed to take on a life of their own, grotesquely carved monsters that writhed and rolled in confused contortions, and would have been more in place on that moon which lighted them than on earth.

I lay face down in the forest, watching the water leap in silver spray from the pool. The shotgun was beside me and I kept one hand on the stock, the other on my electric torch. I lay very still, hardly daring to breathe, conscious of the soft ground and wet grass, the night noises cutting through the dull roar of the water, and my own heartbeats. I had no way of knowing how long I'd been there. My watch had a luminous dial, and I'd left it back at the camp, taking no chances with my concealment.

A sudden sound stiffened me. There was a scurrying in the brush beside me as some small creature passed by, not a dozen feet from my right hand, and emerged beside the pool a moment later. I relaxed, letting my breath out quietly. It was a fox, only a fox. It looked about, cautious and alert, and then began to drink. An owl peered down from a nearby tree, then turned round yellow eyes away, seeking a less formidable meal. I judged it to be about three o'clock and my eyes were heavy. I was about to concede that my first night's vigil would be ended without results, although I intended to stay there until dawn. A large cloud spun out across the moon, black with frosted edges, and all the long shadows merged over the pool. Then, whipped on by the wind, the cloud disintegrated and the light glided back.

I was instantly alert.

The fox had stopped drinking. It stood, poised and tense, pointed ears quivering. I had heard nothing, and felt certain I'd made no sound, but there was something in the animal's bearing that implied caution or fear. The owl had vanished, the fox stood silhouetted against the waterfall for several minutes. Then suddenly it darted to the side, toward the under-growth, halted abruptly and changed course. There was a louder stir in the trees as the fox disappeared. I rolled to my side, trying to follow the animal's flight without using the torch. Just above the spot where it had gone into the brush, a tree limb swayed, a heavy limb, moving as though it had just been relieved of a weight.

I pushed the shotgun out in front of me, thinking even as I did how I'd feared Gregorio might act rashly, and how that fear could well be extended to myself. And then there was time for thought.

The limb moved again, bending farther down and slowly rising until it merged with the limb above at one wide point. The point moved toward the trunk, blocking the light. There was something on that limb, something heavy and large, crouching. Then it was gone, the limb swayed, unburdened, and something moved through the dark trees, away from the clearing. The sound grew faint, and left only the wind and water to throb against the silence.

I did nothing. For a long while I lay perfectly still, waiting, hoping it would return and, at the same time, feeling relief that it had gone. Whatever it was, it had arrived with a stealth that had defeated my senses; I'd heard nothing and seen nothing, and was quite aware that it could just as easily have been in the tree above me. I rolled on to my back and looked upwards at the thought. But the tree was empty, the barren limbs crossed against the sky, and whatever had come, had gone. I didn't go after it.

Dawn came damp and cold. I got to my feet and stamped, then stretched, feeling a stiffness far more unpleasant than that caused by exertion. I lighted a cigarette and walked out of the trees. I could see the marks the fox had left beside the pool, and bent down to scoop some water and drink; I splashed my face and washed my hands. The second part of my vigil had passed very rapidly, and I can't begin to recall the intermingled profusion of thoughts that had occupied my mind.

Then I walked back along the route the fox had taken to the trees, looking at the ground and not knowing what I expected to find. A patch of undergrowth seemed to have been broken and I leaned over it. There was nothing on the ground. As I straightened up a drop hit me on the cheek, too heavy for rain, and when I wiped it my hand came away red. I thought I'd cut myself on a branch, and rubbed my cheek, then took my hand away and held it out, palm upwards, to see if there was blood. There wasn't.

And then, as I was watching, there was. A drop fell directly into my palm, thick and red.

I jerked back and looked up, but the tree was empty. The blood was dripping, slowly, from a small dark blot on the lowest limb. I couldn't quite make out what it was, although I felt a cold certainty that I knew. I broke a branch from the thicket and reached up, lifted the object and let it fall to the ground. I felt sick. It was the hindquarters of a fox, bloodmatted tail attached, torn away from the rest of the body.

I searched, but not too thoroughly, and I didn't find the rest.

Gregorio was squatting by the fire. He held a mug of coffee out to me as I walked over from the rocks. My hand shook as I drank and he remarked on how pale I was. It wasn't surprising. I'd spent a night without shelter on the cold, damp ground. I took the coffee into my tent and changed into dry clothing. I felt very cold now and drew a blanket over my shoulders, lighted a cigarette but found that it tasted foul and stubbed it out. Gregorio pulled the flap back and handed me a bottle of pisco. He seemed to want to talk, but saw I didn't feel like it. He didn't ask if I'd discovered anything, assuming perhaps that I would have mentioned it or, possibly, that I wouldn't mention it anyway. I drank the pisco and coffee alternately, my mind dull. The rain was smacking against the canvas without rhythm, a drop, a pause, two drops, three drops, another pause, and I found myself concentrating on the irregular tempo, a form of self-imposed Chinese water torture subconsciously devised to occupy my mind and avoid making conclusions and decisions. I shook my head, driving the stupor away and forcing my mind back into focus.

There had been something in that tree. That was one certainty, perhaps the only one. It had seemed large and bulky but the moonlight was tricky and I couldn't be sure of that. Just something. A large bird? I knew better and wondered why I was seeking alternatives to what I should have welcomed. I knew damn well what it had been, what I should have been overjoyed to know, and no amount of sceptical ratiocination was going to change that knowledge. Even had I logically thought differently, I still would have believed with the force of emotion.

I drank some more pisco and followed my thoughts.

Whatever it had been, it was powerful enough to tear that unfortunate fox apart. There were no marks of fang or claw, the fox hadn't been cut or bitten apart. It had been pulled in two with enormous strength. There had been no sound, save the rustling of the trees, no death howl or struggle. Either the fox had been stifled or destroyed so quickly that it could make no cry.

That struck a discord somewhere. I remembered the terrible sound I'd heard from Hodson's laboratory, and the sound, the same sound I felt sure, that the creature had made after it killed El Rojo. Why had it been silent last night? Had it heard me, detected my presence in some way and been frightened off? Or was a fox too insignificant a victim to warrant a victory cry? If it had sensed my presence, would it return? I might have missed my only opportunity. Why hadn't I used my torch? Was it caution or fear or . . .

Gregorio was shaking me.

I opened my eyes and was startled to realize I'd been half-conscious, between thought and nightmare. My teeth were clicking together, my stomach turned over, my forehead was burning. Fever laced me. Gregorio put his long, delicate hand on my brow and nodded thoughtfully. His concerned face drew near and then receded, swelled like a balloon and then shrunk away again. I observed everything through a haze, an unequal fog that parted on reality and then closed over again. I was only dimly aware of Gregorio's strong hands as he helped me into my sleeping bag, and then quite distinctly knew I was taking two of the small white pills Graham had recommended, could feel their roundness in my throat and taste the bitterness on my tongue. Reality paled once more, and yet my mind was alert on a different level and I wondered with lucid objectiveness whether I'd fallen prey to some exotic fever or merely succumbed to the wet cold of the night. Then I fell into disturbed sleep.

When I awoke it was evening. The campfire turned the canvas burnished gold. I watched the rough texture glow, aware of the minute details of color and grain on that clear, disinterested level of consciousness. Presently the flap parted and Gregorio looked in.

"Feel better?" he asked.

"I don't know." I didn't. "What's wrong with me?"

"Fever. Chill. Who knows? Not serious, I think. You must rest and be warm for a few days."

"What time is it?"

"I have no clock," he said.

My own watch was on the crate I'd used as a table. I nodded towards it and Gregorio handed it to me. It was ten o'clock.

"I intended to go back to the waterhole tonight."

He shrugged.

"That is not possible now."

"No, I guess not," I said. I felt relieved about it. After I was feeling well would be time enough; I would be unable to observe properly in this weakened condition and would undoubtedly become more seriously ill. And, perhaps feeling a need for more justification than my own physical failure, I told myself that the creature might well have sensed my presence and be wary. It was far wiser to wait.

I took two more pills, drank a glass of water, and slept more soundly.

I felt better in the morning. I still had a slight fever, but my head was clear, the curious dichotomy of muddled reality and sharply focused details had ceased. I was able to walk around a bit in the afternoon and force down some food in the evening, and decided I had fallen to a chill rather than some disease. But I was still weak and dizzy, and there was no question of returning to the vigil that night. Gregorio saw that the delay disturbed me.

"I could keep watch," he said, dubiously.

"No. That wouldn't do any good. I'll have to see this creature myself; you've already seen it."

"That is so," he said, and celebrated his reprieve with a mug of pisco.

I went to bed early and read, but found the strain of the kerosene lantern painful, the words blurred. I turned the light out and closed my eyes. I didn't feel sleepy, but sleep crept over me in modulated waves. I remember feeling annoyed that I was wasting this opportunity, and blaming my weakness for hindering the investigation; telling myself that I had to find the creature while it was in the area, that there might never be another chance to find it. I was determined to return to the waterhole the next night.

There was no need. It found us.

XII

I was awake and something was snarling outside the tent. It was the second time I'd been awakened by a sound in the night, but this time I didn't hesitate—this snarling did not petrify me as that other terrible cry. I slid from the sleeping bag and grabbed the shotgun. My eyes felt too large for their sockets, my mouth was dry. The snarl came again and I could hear the horses screaming. I pushed the flap open and let the gun precede me from the tent. The fire was burning low, and it was dark beyond. Gregorio came from his tent standing straight, the rifle at his shoulder, his eyes wild in the glow of the fire. He turned toward the horses.

The horses had gone mad. They were frantically milling about their enclosure. I moved to the side, to get a line of vision beyond the fire, and one of the horses leaped the rocks Gregorio had piled up. It was the grey. It charged towards me blindly and I flung myself to the side, heard the horse tear into my tent, saw the canvas flapping as I scrambled to my feet again. Another horse had attempted to leap the wide outer barrier and I heard its hooves clattering desperately for a footing, then saw it go down between the rocks, struggling to rise again. The other two horses were running in a mad circle around the enclosure, one after the other, following the circle. The second horse flashed past and I could see into the center of the corral.

Something crouched there.

The firelight barely reached it, outlining it dimly against the barrier. It stood on four legs, but the shoulders were higher than the haunches, its weight on the hindquarters as it circled, turning with the horses. As I watched, it drew its arms upwards and coiled.

"Something's in with the horses!" I cried.

And it moved. One arm swept out wide, hooking at a horse's flank. The horse reared, forelegs pawing the air as it rose, rose too high and toppled over backwards. It blocked the creature from my sight. I had the shotgun up and, man or beast, I would have fired. But I couldn't shoot without hitting the horse. Gregorio was frozen in position, the rifle leveled, his face grotesque. The horse flailed the air, fighting to get up, but the creature was on it, rending and tearing, its snarls muffled against the horse's flesh.

The shotgun boomed. It sounded unbelievably loud to my inflamed senses. I had discharged it into the air, whether by accident or design or instinct I don't know, and the hollow blast bounced from the surrounding rocks as the pellets laced through the trees.

The horse was up, bucking and rearing, and the creature turned toward me, squat and square, poised motionless for an instant. Then its long arms swung, knuckles brushing the ground, and I brought the shotgun down; for a moment I was looking at the creature down the barrels, my finger on the second trigger. I could have shot it then, but I was looking at its eyes. And it looked back at me, savage and fierce but also curious and startled by the sound. I couldn't pull the trigger. The creature wheeled about, its great bulk pivoting with amazing speed, and moved toward the rock barrier. I followed it with the gun; saw it leap into the shadows; heard the report of Gregorio's .303, sharp and crackling in contrast to the shotgun.

The creature went down, howling, twisting in pain. Then it lunged up again. Gregorio worked the lever, the spent shell sparkled, spinning through the firelight. The creature was in the trees when we fired again, and I heard the slug smack against solid rock. We looked at each other. The creature was gone.

Gregorio was holding the grey, one arm around its neck. He spoke softly and the horse lowered his head, trembling. The horse that had been attacked was dashing about the corral, white foam pouring from his mouth, lips curled back from square teeth. A great hunk had been torn from its flank and long gashes were open over its ribs. I saw that it was my horse, the one I'd ridden and become attached to, and felt my jaws tighten.

I moved back to the wreckage of my tent. The poles were snapped, the canvas spread over the ground. I found my trousers amidst the debris and pulled them on. The horse that had fallen on the barrier was still struggling to rise, wedged between two smooth boulders, whimpering in pain.

"Now you have seen it," Gregorio said.

I nodded.

"That was how the dog died," he said, with far more sadness than hatred. The grey's head came up, ears pricked, and he whispered soothingly. The fourth horse moved toward him uncertainly, head turned, looking at his injured companion. I pulled the canvas from our supplies and found the box of shot-gun shells, broke the gun open and reloaded the right barrel, then stuffed shells in the pockets of my windbreaker. I felt no fear now. Action had dispensed with dread. I felt determined and angry, and had no doubts that I'd use the gun if I had to. I knew that, whatever the creature was, it was not human enough to command human rights. I was not much of a scientist at that moment, but perhaps more a man. The smell of gunpowder was sharp on the thick air, a few leaves fluttered down from the blasted branches overhead. I walked over to Gregorio.

"You will go after it?" he asked.

"Yes."

"It is wounded."

I nodded. Gregorio had hit it once, and there are few animals a .303 won't bring down. I had no doubts that I could find it now.

"Someone should stay with the horses," Gregorio said.

"Yes. You must stay."

"It may be waiting for you."

"I'll be all right."

Gregorio regarded me with Indian eyes. He wanted to be brave, and he was brave. The grey gelding was still trembling under his arm and he nodded. That was right, someone had to stay with the horses. But he lowered his head and didn't watch me leave the camp.

I could hear the horse screaming in the rocks behind me. When I'd passed, he turned a wide eye upwards. His foreleg was snapped and he was lodged helplessly, looking for help we could not give. I called Gregorio and went on. The crack of his rifle came through the trees and the horse stopped screaming. I felt a cruel satisfaction when I found a smear of blood marking the creature's passage. It was large and dark in the light from my electric torch, and I didn't think he'd be moving very fast.

He wasn't. When I had crossed the rocks I saw him lurching up the hill that led to the waterfall. When he'd attacked the horse, he had uncoiled like a steel spring, fast and fluid, but he moved with a rolling, drunken gait now. His legs were short and crooked and he used his long arms for support as he ran. Perhaps his peculiar gait was not suited to traveling on open ground at the best of times, and the bullet had taken its toll of his strength.

I moved to the right, towards the trees, so that I would be able to cut off any attempt to disappear into the bush where he could move so much more silently and faster than I. But he didn't attempt that. He was following a straight course up the hill, as though not merely fleeing but moving towards a definite destination. I had the torch in my left hand and the shotgun cradled on my right arm. There was no need for stealth or caution as long as I kept him in sight, and I followed quickly. He was only three or four hundred yards in front of me, and I drew closer without great effort.

He reached the top of the hill and paused, then turned and looked back at me. He was silhouetted against the sky and his eyes gathered the moonlight. I knew he had the vision of a night animal, and was thankful for my torch. He watched me for a few seconds, his heavy head turning from side to side, then wheeled and vanished over the crest. I began to run, wanting to keep him in sight, but not worried. I was familiar with this terrain, and knew that the second hill stretched on for a long distance, that he couldn't possibly ascend it before I was over the first hill. I was breathing hard now, the soft earth sucking at my boots and slipping from under me, but I ran on and topped the rise.

The creature was not in sight. There was a small pool of blood where he had paused and looked back, and a few scattered dark patches beyond, heading toward the waterfall. But he had vanished. The far hill stretched away, smooth and rolling, with no concealment. The trees to the right had been in sight as I climbed. Behind the waterfall, the cliff rose sheer and unscalable. There was nowhere he could have gone except to the waterfall, and I moved down, walking slowly and cautiously now, my thumb on the torch switch and my finger on the trigger.

I came to the soft mud surrounding the pool and switched the torch on. A point of light reflected back from the cliff and I tensed, thinking it was those night-creature eyes, but it was only a smooth stone, polished by the waterfall. The beam played over the reeds and found nothing; then, at my feet, I found his prints. They were distinct and deep, moisture just beginning to seep in, the feet with wide angled toes and the impressions of his knuckles on either side. The tracks moved to the edge of the pool.

I turned the light on the water, but the broken surface revealed nothing. Very slowly, I walked around the bank to the far side and inspected the ground. There were no prints emerging from there. The creature had gone into the pool and had not come out. And yet, it was not in the water. There could be only one explanation, and I let the light flood over the tumbling cataract. The cliff was perpendicular, grey stone, the water sparkled down, and there, just where they met, a narrow rim of blackness defied illumination.

I walked up to the cliff, the water lapping at my feet, the gun level at my hip, and there I found the cave. It opened behind the waterfall, an aperture some three feet high, completely hidden in the light of day unless one stood against the cliff face. The pool was slightly higher than the cave floor, and the water ran inwards, several inches deep. There was a smear of red against the angle of rock.

I had found far more than the creature's waterhole, when I'd come to this cascade. I'd found its home.

Did it take a greater courage than I'd ever known I possessed to enter that black cavern, or were my senses and emotions too numbed with fever and excitement to feel fear? I know that I went into the Stygian darkness without hesitation, and that I felt very little at all. I simply did it, without thought or doubt. The only sensation I was conscious of was the water rivetting my neck and back as I stopped under it, and then I was kneeling in the cave. The floor rose and the water penetrated only for a few yards. I shone the torch before me. It flowed well into the tunnel, but the blackness stretched on in the distance. It seemed interminable, and I had the sudden fear that it emerged again at some point and that the creature would escape me. The thought forced me on. I had to crawl for a few yards and then found it high enough to stand, crouching. It was narrow, my arms brushed against the sides, and it was straight. There was little danger. I had the torch and the gun and the creature could only come at me from the front. If I was forced to kill it, I would be able to. I didn't want to, however. My anger at seeing my horse's agony had lessened, I was more the scientist than the hunter once more. I determined that I would make every effort not to kill it; if I was forced to fire, my first blast would be aimed at its legs. But perhaps it was already dying, had crawled home to suffer its death throes alone. If that were true, it seemed brutal to pursue it, but there was no way to know, and I moved forward following the beam of light.

The walls were slimy with greenish moss, cracked with numerous narrow fissures where the mountain had moved in ages past. It was very quiet. My heavy soled boots made no sound on the stone, and the drops of blood underfoot became fewer and farther apart. The cave widened gradually as I moved into the depths, fantastic formations of broken rock emerged from the walls, pillars and trellises jutted up and hung down from floor and ceiling. I approached them warily, but there was nothing waiting behind. The tunnel continued to follow a straight course and it seemed I'd been walking a long time.

And then the light hit rock ahead, spreading out fluidly to both sides. I thought for an instant that I had come to a dead end, and then saw that the tunnel turned at right angles, a natural geometric angle following a fault in the solid stone. I approached the turning very slowly. If the creature were waiting for me, it would be here.

I stopped a few feet from the turn; held the torch under the stock so that I had both hands on the gun and the light followed the line of the barrels, took a deep breath, braced myself, and stepped out wide of the corner in one long stride.

I stopped dead.

The creature was not waiting there. There was nothing there. Nothing but a green metal door . . .

The door swung open, heavy on its hinges. Hubert Hodson said: "I expect you'd better come in."

XIII

Hodson took the shotgun from me. I was too staggered to resist. I realized I'd passed completely under the mountain, and that we had inadvertently made our camp directly opposite Hodson's house, separated by the unscalable cliff but connected via the tunnel through the rock; that the door he'd claimed led to a storeroom actually opened into the tunnel. I followed

Hodson through the door, expecting to enter the laboratory, but in that respect I was wrong. There was a connecting chamber between, a small poorly lighted room with another green door in the opposite wall. That door was open and I could see the brightly illuminated laboratory beyond. Hodson closed the door behind us and turned the key. Heavy tumblers fell into place. He pushed me ahead of him, towards the laboratory.

A low snarl sounded beside me. I wheeled about, pushing Hodson's hand from my shoulder, tensed and then froze. The creature was in that room. It crouched in the corner, behind heavy steel bars, watching me with comprehension and hatred. All the details instantly impressed themselves on my consciousness as a whole, a single, startling tableau. The bars fitted into the wall on one side, and were hinged so that they could be swung open and closed again, forming a cage with three solid rock walls. The creature was in the cage, only a few feet from me, a grotesque caricature of man. Its chest was rounded, its shoulders stooped and heavy, its arms long. Short, coarse hair bristled on its body, but its face was smooth and brown, wide nostrils flaring and small eyes burning beneath a thick, ridged brow. I saw a dark, damp patch on its side, a few spatters of blood on the floor, and standing between us, one hand on the bars, stood the old crone. She had turned to look at me, and her eyes glowed with malevolence, with a hatred more intense and inhuman than that of the creature itself.

The creature lunged at me. One huge hand tore at the bars and the steel sang with vibration. I started to shout a warning to the old woman, but it was not after her. It ignored her. It reached out, groping for me through the bars, snarling with broad lips drawn back. I backed away and Hodson touched my shoulder.

"Come. We mustn't stay here. He knows you injured him and I wouldn't trust even those steel bars if he goes berserk."

"The old woman—"

"She will be all right," he said.

He pushed me toward the laboratory. The snarling became less violent and I heard the old woman speaking in some strange language—speaking to the creature. And the second metal door clanged shut behind us.

Hodson took me to the front room, motioned to a chair and began searching through a drawer. I saw him slip a hypodermic needle in his pocket.

"You aren't going to use that on it?" I asked.

He nodded and brought out a large box of medicinal supplies.

"A tranquilizer," he said.

"But it'll tear you apart if you get near."

"The woman can manage it," he said. "Wait here. I'll be back when I've repaired the damage you've done." He went back through the curtains. I sat down and waited.

Hodson returned, his shirt sleeves rolled up, poured two large drinks and handed me one.

"It wasn't a serious wound," he said. "He will live."

I nodded. Hodson sat down opposite me. The drink tasted strange on my dry tongue, and my fever was returning. There were so many things I wanted to ask, but I waited for Hodson to speak first.

"So this is the proper study of man? To shoot man?"

"Is it man?"

"Assuredly."

"It attacked my camp. It was killing one of the horses. We had no choice."

He nodded.

"Quite so," he said. "That is man's nature. To kill and to have no choice." He shook his head wearily, then suddenly laughed.

"Well, you've found my secret. Now what?"

"I don't know. It's still a secret. I'd like a chance to examine the creature."

"No. That isn't possible."

"You've already examined it completely, I suppose?"

"Physically?" He shrugged. "I'm more interested in studying his behavior. That's why I've allowed him to run wild and unrestricted."

"And yet it returns here? It comes back to a cage of its own choice?"

He laughed again.

"I told you. It is man's nature to have no choice. It returns because it is man, and man goes home. That is a basic instinct. Territorial possessiveness."

"You're certain it is human?"

"Hominid. Yes. Absolutely."

"Will you tell me about it?"

"It's a bit late for secrets."

"How can you be sure it's human? Hominid? As opposed, say, to some new form of ape? What is the definition, what criteria are you using?"

"Criteria? There is so much you fail to understand. There is only one definition of man. I used the absolute criteria."

I waited, but he didn't clarify. He sipped his drink; he seemed to be waiting for my questions.

"You discovered it here, I take it?"

"In a sense, yes."

"How long have you known about it?"

"For a generation."

"Are there others?"

"Not at the moment."

This was telling me nothing. I said: "Why have you waited so long, why keep this secret? What have you gained by your silence?"

"Time. I told you once before. Time is essential. I'm studying him as a man, not as a curiosity. Naturally I had to have time for him to mature. Who can gauge man's behavior by studying a child?"

"Then you found it when it was very young?"

"Yes. Very young indeed."

He smiled strangely.

"And when did you determine it was human?"

"Before I . . . found him."

"You aren't making sense," I said. "Why give me riddles at this stage? What is your definition of man?"

"I need no definition," he said. He was enjoying this. He wanted to tell me, his irresistible urge to dumbfound his fellow scientists returned, his countenance livened.

"I didn't exactly discover him, you see," he said. "I know he is man because I created him."

He regarded me through a long silence.

"You mean it's a mutation?"

"A very special form of mutation. It is not a variation, but a regression. What little I told you on your last uninvited visit was true, but it wasn't all the truth. I told you I'd discovered how to control mutation, but this went much further. In mastering mutation, I found it was the key to cellular memory—that the law of mutation be applied to unlock the forgotten replications."

He finished his drink. His face was flushed.

"You see, cells forget. That is why we grow old, for instance. Our cells forget how to replicate youth. But this knowledge, although forgotten, is still there, in the same way that things a man forgets exist in his subconscious mind. Exactly the same, on a different level. And as subconscious knowledge can be remembered under hypnosis, so the cells can be induced to remember by chemical treatment. And this, Brookes, is the very root of life. It may, among other things, be the key to immortality. We can teach our cells not to forget the replication of youth." He shrugged. "But man, as he is, isn't worthy of immortality, and I'm not interested in giving it to him. It will come. I am interested in man's evolution, and I've applied my knowledge in that field. I am the first and only man who has seen evolution as it occurs. Brookes, I am the creator of my ancestor!"

There was more than enthusiasm in his face. There was something akin to madness.

"But how—"

"Don't you understand yet? I treated the parents, chemically affecting their genes so that they carried a recessed heredity. The offspring, the creature you have seen, is regressed back through eons of time—carries the traits our cells have long since forgotten. I could possibly have taken it even further, back to the first forms of life, the single cellular creatures that existed in the dawn of life. But that, too, is of no interest to me. I limit myself to man."

He took my glass, crossed the room and refilled it.

"How do you classify this creature?" I asked.

He sat down again, frowning.

"I'm not sure. The ancestor of a branch of modern man. Not our branch, perhaps, but a parallel line. Man as he may have been ten million years ago. Or five million years. Time is essential but indefinite."

"And it was actually born of parents living today?"

"The father is dead. I'm afraid that his offspring—or his ancestor, whichever you prefer—tore his throat out several years ago." He said this with clinical detachment. "The mother—did you wonder why the old woman could control it? Why it came back here when it was hurt? She is the mother."

After a while I said, "Good God."

"Shocked or surprised?" Hodson asked.

"Surely it can't be right to create something so unnatural?"

He stared scornfully at me.

"Are you a scientist? Or a moralist? Surely, you know that science is all that matters. What does that old crone matter? What are a few dead sheep? Or a few dead men, for that matter? I have seen the behavior of one of man's ancestors, and isn't that worth any amount of suffering?" He was talking rapidly, gesturing with both hands, his eyes boring into me.

"And the further possibilities are countless. Perhaps, with time to work in peace, I will learn to reverse the process. Even that. Perhaps I will be able to progress cellular memory. To sidestep evolution. The knowledge must already be there, the cells simply haven't learned it yet; they learn it gradually as they forget the old knowledge. But it's there, Brookes. It was there when the first life crawled out of the sea. The future and the past, side by side. Think of it! To create man as he will be a million years from now!"

I was in two minds, on two levels. I didn't know whether to believe him or not on the superficial scale, but deeper, where I couldn't help but believe, magnetized by his voice, my reactions were divided again. The fact, and the possibilities, were wonderful beyond comprehension, but the details were appalling, the use of human beings in this experiment grotesque. To think of a living woman giving birth to that monstrosity in the cage was abhorrent. Perhaps, in some ways, I was a moralist, and certainly scientific interest struggled against a surge of repulsion.

"Think of it!" Hodson repeated, his eyes turned inwards now as he thought of it himself. His knuckles were white, tightening on his glass. He had been profoundly affected by this opportunity to speak of his discoveries, the overpowering urge to break the silence of twenty years. We had been talking for some time. A grey early light blocked the window; a bird was singing outside. In the surrounding hills day was breaking, day creatures awoke and night creatures slunk back to their warrens and dens, following the ways of nature, oblivious to the ways of science. But science was overtaking nature. I lighted a cigarette and drew the harsh smoke deeply into my lungs. I knew it wasn't a good thing, and it went far deeper than outraged morality.

"It can't be right, Hodson. Preying on these primitive people who don't understand what you are doing to them. That old woman—"

Surprisingly, he nodded in agreement. But not for the same reasons.

"Yes, that was a mistake. I'd misjudged the potency of my process and, more important and less forgivable, I failed to consider the theory of parallel evolution. This creature wasn't my first attempt, but it was the first to survive. The others didn't bear up to the strain, although the post-mortems proved most enlightening. But we learn from our blunders, and I have at least proved that all modern men did not descend from the same common ancestor. I suppose that was a worthwhile discovery. Evolution in the New World, at least in this part of South America, developed without connection to the rest of the world and, more surprisingly, at a different time in history." He had been talking softly, rather wearily, but now his oratorical tone returned, his eyes lighted once more.

"Twenty million years ago, sometime in the late Cenozoic era, and somewhere in Asia, the ancient primates divided into two branches. One branch led to modern apes, the other to creatures which became increasingly human. One million years ago, these creatures became *Homo*. Forty thousand years ago, they became *sapiens*. And they are our ancestors, Brookes. Yours and mine. But these men did not come to this part of the world. The same process of division occurred here, in much the same way and for much the same reason, but countless ages later in pre-history. The humans who developed here, like the New World monkeys, were different in many respects. Less advanced on the hereditary scale, because they emerged at a later point, and had to survive harsher conditions in some respects. The climate was the greatest factor responsible for the differences. The hominids developed in relation to this hostile climate, they became much tougher and resistant to extremes, able to exist naked in freezing wind and water. In that way they advanced faster, beyond our branch. But there were fewer natural enemies here, they were the predominant life form, and survival was gauged only against nature. While our branch of mankind developed tools, thumbs, uncurved spines, vocal cords and, finally, superior brains to enable them to exist against the powerful predators, these people had no need to advance along similar lines. Quite naturally, they did not. The physically stronger lived to breed and pass on those traits, while the intelligent, with no advantages in survival, succumbed to the evolutionary laws and advanced at a much slower rate. These creatures were as different from their Asian and European counterparts as llamas from camels, capuchin from rhesus.

"Who knows? Perhaps this branch was superior; given time they might well have developed into supermen. But they didn't have that time. Our branch had a head start and developed too quickly. We became travelers. We ventured down here from the north and the natives could not survive against us, or beside us. They died out. Perhaps we killed them, perhaps we brought disease unknown to them, perhaps our superior brains succeeded in acquiring all the available food. At any rate, they did not survive. But there was some interbreeding. That was selective and the offspring retained the qualities of both branches—the mind of one, the strength of the other. They were remarkably adaptable to life. The native branch ceased to exist, but the crossbreeds survived alongside the new branch. God knows how long ago this cross-breeding took place, perhaps fifty thousand years. They were still here when Darwin came, I know that. But, little by little, the native traits had weakened in the individuals. Although they may have been predominant at first, they were bred out by sheer weight of numbers, until only the odd throwback possessed them."

He paused, choosing his words, while I waited in dumb fascination.

"The old woman is one of those atavisms, as far as I know the last and only living human to bear a prepotency of the vanishing characteristics. That was why I selected her for my experiment. Her genes were closer to the past, the memory was not buried so deeply, and the ancient traits were predominant. That was why I selected her, and that was where I blundered.

"Do you begin to understand?" he asked.

Behind him, the window had silvered as the sun began to slant down the hills. I was burning with fever, and a different fever had set my mind alight. I nodded.

"The experiment succeeded too well," he continued. "The result—you have seen the result. It is human, because it was born of woman, but it is not human as we know the word. It is fascinating and fabulous, certainly the living ancestor of an extinct branch of mankind, but not our ancestor. Not yours or mine and only partially the old woman's. And thus it is a dead end, a creature whose offspring are already extinct. There is much to be gained by studying it, but little to be learned of man. I have formulated the theoretical descent of a being that no longer exists, but it is not much different to tracing the remote ancestry of the passenger pigeon or the dodo. You can understand the frustration of that?"

"But my God, what an opportunity—"

"Perhaps. But it is not my field. I will give it to the world when I have applied it to my own pursuits. Another experiment, eliminating the error. If only I can live long enough to see it through. With what I have already learned from this creature—from watching it grow and mature, with strictly clinical interest—" His mind seemed to be wandering now, his thoughts confused, divided between acquired knowledge and the further knowledge he anticipated. "It killed its father when it was twelve years old. It developed much more rapidly than man. I judge its lifespan to be a mere thirty years, certainly not more. But it will not grow old. This branch could not survive an old age, it will retain its physical powers until it has attained its normal lifespan and then it will die. And with it will die its genus. Perhaps the post-mortem will be interesting. The study of its life has been frustrating. It can't speak. It has vocal cords but they aren't capable of mastering more than bestial sounds. That was the greatest disappointment. Think of being able to converse, in your own language, with prehistoric man! It's cranial capacity is about 1,550 cubic centimeters—roughly the average of Neanderthal man, but its brain is relatively free of convolutions. Its branch did not need a mind, it needed strength and endurance. Did you see its eyes glow in the dark? The inner wall of the eye is coated with guanin, like most night creatures. Perhaps that is more valuable than thought to the creature. It hardly thinks at all. It feels, it acts by instinct. Its basic instinct seems to be to kill. Only the old woman has any control over it now. The Indian used to manage it by his great strength, but soon it became too powerful and vicious even for him to handle. It attacked me one day. That was where the Indian acquired that scar, of course. He saved my life, but even he fears it now. Only the old crone—it shows the basic instinct of motherlove—it killed its father, but obeys its mother without needing to understand her . . ."

I shuddered. There was something terrible in this regard of a beast for a human, and even more terrible knowing that the pitiful old woman regarded that monstrous creation as her child. I wondered, with absolute horror, if she had given it a name. I closed my eyes, uselessly. The horror was behind them.

Hodson stood up and took my glass. He brought it back refilled and I took a long swallow.

"You intend to continue this experiment? To create another creature like that?"

"Of course. Not like that, however. The next one must be our ancestor. The same process, with parents of our branch of mankind. It is only necessary to treat the male, although the regressed mutation occurs in the female. The Indian might be an ideal specimen, in fact."

"You can't," I said.

Hodson's eyes widened, amused.

"It's fiendish!"

"Ah, the moralist again. Do you consider the creature evil? Brookes, if you had been born a million years in the future—how would your behavior seem to the men of that distant time?"

"I don't know," I said, very slowly. I had trouble forming the words. Something seemed to weigh my tongue down, and the same weight pressed on my eyes. Hodson's eyes burned at me, and then they began to dull. The fire had left him, extinguished in his revelations, and he became solemn, perhaps knowing he had once again succumbed to his old fault; he had told me too much.

"Do you believe me?" he asked, smiling.

"I don't know," I repeated. I moved my head from side to side. It swiveled beneath a great burden, my neck faltered under the heaviness and my head dropped. I was staring at the floor. I could hear Hodson speaking, far away.

"It wouldn't have taken much imagination to think of these things," he said. "But it would have taken fantastic discoveries to actually do them. Perhaps I have merely been toying with you, Brookes. You know how I have always taken pleasure in shocking people. Perhaps this is all simply a hoax, eh? What do you think, moralist? Have I been deceiving you?"

I tried to shake my head again. It hung down, lower, my knees seemed to be rising to meet my face. The chair receded from under me. I fought under this enormous gravity, struggled upwards and stood before Hodson. He was still smiling. The room whirled and spun, his face was the only fixed point in my focus, my eyes were held on his grinning teeth.

"You're not well, Brookes?" he asked.

"I . . . dizzy . . . I . . ."

The empty glass was still in my hand. I looked at it, saw the points of light reflected along the rim; saw the tiny flakes of white powder in the bottom . . . Saw nothing.

XIV

I floated back through planes of awareness and Hodson's face floated over me, lighted from beneath with weird effect. I wondered, vaguely, why he had stopped grinning, then realized I was no longer in the front room, that I'd been unconscious for some time. I was dressed, but my boots were off. They were on the floor beside the candle that shot dancing light upwards, sweeping Hodson's countenance and fading out weakly in the corners of the room. It was the room I'd slept in on my last stay, and I was lying on my back on the cot.

"Ah. You are awake," Hodson said.

I blinked. I felt all right.

"What happened to me?"

"You fainted. You have a fever, apparently you've been ill. I didn't realize that, or I wouldn't have deliberately shocked you so outrageously. I'm sorry."

"That drink—you drugged me."

"Nonsense. You simply fainted. In your feverish state my little amusement was too much for you. Your perceptions were inflamed. Why, for a few minutes, I believe you actually thought it was the truth."

"You told me . . . those things . . ."

"Were all pure fabrication. Oh, there was a basis in fact; I have indeed experimented along those lines, but without success. I'm afraid I simply couldn't resist the opportunity to—pull your leg shall we say? Of course, had you been thinking clearly you would have seen the impossibility of such a tale."

"But I saw the creature."

"An ape. I assure you it was merely an ape. A curious cross-breeding of Old and New World primates, resulting from one of my experiments in controlled mutation. Unsuccessful, from my point of view, actually, since it's merely a hybrid, not actually a mutation—far less a regression." He chuckled at the absurdity of such a concept.

"I don't believe you."

Hodson shrugged.

"As you like. Your opinions cease to interest me, now that I've had my little game."

"Will you allow me to examine it then? There can be no harm in that, if it's just an ape."

"That, I regret to say, is impossible. The wound you inflicted upon it was more serious than it appeared. There were internal complications and my surgical skill is paltry. I'm afraid that the ape has expired."

"An examination of the body will satisfy me."

"I have no desire to satisfy you. If it weren't for you, the ape would still be alive. At any rate, the remains have already been dissected and disposed of."

"Already?"

"You have been sleeping for—" he regarded his watch, "some ten hours. Sufficient time to derive whatever scientific benefit can be found in examining a deceased hybrid. You may see my notes, if you like."

"Everything you told me was a lie?"

"Not a lie. What is a lie? A study in man's gullibility, perhaps. An objective observation of the effect of the absurd upon the credulous. You have undoubtedly heard how I used to enjoy shocking people with unfounded theories? My pleasure was not so much in the outraged reception of my statements, as in observing a man's reaction afterwards. This, in its way, was also a study of mankind. And that, Brookes, is my field, in all its manifold aspects."

I shook my head. It should have been so much easier to believe him now than it had been before. But, somehow, I couldn't quite do so. His tone lacked that enthusiasm and excitement it had carried before—an enthusiasm derived from success and pride in his accomplishments. And yet, I had not been thinking clearly, I'd been feverish and weak and susceptible to suggestion, and Hodson was a master of deliberate deception. I tried to reason, but my thoughts came helter skelter, my mind whirled, touching on valid points and then spinning on before I could follow a line of reasoning.

"Rest now," Hodson said, far away again. "You'll be able to laugh at yourself in the morning."

He took the candle with him. The room was black, and a sympathetic blackness began to nudge me towards sleep, a blank space growing larger in my brain.

The light had returned when I opened my eyes again.

Anna stood beside the bed, holding the candle. The curtains swayed behind her, the house was very quiet. She smiled down at me, looking concerned.

"You are all right?" she asked.

I nodded.

"I was worried for you."

She hovered over me uncertainly. She wasn't embarrassed, because she knew nothing of propriety or shame, but she seemed undecided.

"May I sit beside you?" she asked.

"Of course."

I slid over. Anna sat on the edge of the cot. I was still wearing my shirt and trousers and she was still naked. She curled one leg beneath her and placed the candle on the floor, stared at it for a moment and then moved it a few needless inches. Her smile was shy, although she did not know what shyness was. She placed a cool hand on my brow. My fever seemed to have left me now, but that cool palm felt very good and I placed my hand over hers. She leaned slightly toward me and her firm breast brushed against my forearm. I remembered how much I had wanted her the last time we were together in this little cell; realized that desire was stronger now than before; wondered if she knew, if she understood, if she had come to me because she felt the same way.

"I don't disturb you?" she asked.

"You do. Very much."

"Shall I leave?"

"No. Stay here."

It wasn't the playful teasing of a woman, she meant exactly what she said, honest and artless.

"You are not yet well—"

I moved my hand to her hip. Her flesh was silken warmth, her hair so black it seemed a hole in space, falling over her shoulders and absorbing the candlelight completely, without gloss or shine. My hand moved, stroking her thigh, and my mind avoided all thoughts of right and wrong.

"Shall I lie down?" she asked.

I pulled her to me and the length of our bodies pressed together. I could feel her smooth heat through my rough clothing, and her lips parted willingly against my mouth.

"I don't know how to do it," she said.

"You've never made love?"

"No. You will show me how?"

"Do you want me to?"

"Very much," she said. Her arms clung to me, timidly but firmly. I shifted, rising above her, and she lay back, watching and waiting for me. Her passion showed only in her eyes, and was all the more inspiring because she did not know the accepted motions of manifesting desire.

"Really? You never have?" I asked.

My hand moved on her gently.

"Never. There has been no one to teach me."

It cut sharply through my fascination. She hadn't come because she wanted me, but simply because I was the first man available to her. My hand stopped moving on her flat belly, she frowned, looking into my face.

"What is wrong?" she asked.

Another thought was toying with the edge of perception, a vague uneasiness that had seized its foothold in that moment of diminished desire. I wasn't quite sure what it was . . .

"Does Hodson know you've come to me?" I asked.

"Yes."

"He doesn't mind?"

"Why should he mind?"

"I don't—Anna, when I was unconscious—did Hodson do anything to me?"

"He fixed you. Made you well."

"What did he do?"

My heart was thundering, pumping icebergs through my arteries.

"What is wrong? Why have you stopped loving me?"

"What did he do?"

"I don't know. He made you well. He took you to his laboratory and fixed you so that you would be all right for me to come to . . ."

She said this as though it were the most natural thing in the world. The icebergs melted in my blood.

"Why have you stopped?" she asked. "Am I no good for making love?"

My mind erupted in horror.

I stood beside the bed, my boots in my hand. I didn't remember getting up. Anna was staring at me, hurt and disappointed, unable to understand how she had failed—a child punished without reason. But what reason could I give her? She was of a different world and there was nothing I could say. My breath came hard, but not with desire now. I wanted only one thing, to escape from that fiendish place, and Anna's graceful body had become loathsome to me.

I moved to the door. Anna watched me all the while. I couldn't even say farewell to her, couldn't even beg her not to give the alarm. She was still staring as I passed through the curtains and they closed between us. It was more than those curtains that stood between us. I went down the hallway to the front room. The house was silent, Anna made no sound behind me. The front room was empty and I moved quietly on bare feet. I didn't know what Hodson would resort to if he found me, didn't know if he would force me to stay, even if he might not kill me. But I felt no fear of this. The numb horror of the situation was too great to share its place with any other emotion, too great to be realized; and my mind froze in self preservation.

I crossed the room and went out of the door, started walking calmly across the narrow basin of the valley, almost sluggish in my determination. The night was black and cold, my body felt like a heated rod passing through the absolute zero of space, my course preordained and no friction to halt me. The ground rose and I began an angled ascent of the hills; I noticed objectively that I was climbing the same hill where the vultures had dropped down to feast the last time I departed from Hodson's. But this made no impression. Everything was external, my breath hung before me and the clouded sky was low, blanketing the hills as I climbed up to meet it.

My thoughts were superficial and purely functional, my mind rejecting the horror of the situation and concentrating on the task at hand, plotting the logical course. I had to ascend the hills, keeping in a northeastern direction which would bring me out east of the sheer cliffs which housed the tunnel, then descend the opposite side towards the north-west, compensating for the angle and coming out somewhere near the waterfall. The high, unscalable cliffs would be visible for miles as I walked down, and I felt certain I could find them, and find the camp in relation to them. I told myself I was safe now; there was no way that Hodson could find me.

Halfway up the incline I paused to catch my breath and realized I still carried my boots in my hand. I sat down and pulled them on, looking back toward the house as I tied the laces. The house was dark and quiet. Perhaps Anna was still waiting and wondering in that little room, or perhaps Hodson knew that pursuit would prove futile. The night was very dark, and there was no way he could follow me over that rocky land. Even the extraordinary Indian would not be able to track a man at night through such terrain. Hodson had no dog to follow by scent, no way to know what direction I'd fled in, no way to—

My fingers snapped the laces.

There was one way.

There was one being behind me with the senses and instincts of the hunting carnivore—one creature capable of silently tracking me through the blackest night—one creature whose eyes glowed with night vision and seethed with hatred—

I ran, mad with fear.

I ran. The broken laces slapped at my ankle, loose stones slid beneath my feet, trees loomed up suddenly before me and I crashed through in wild flight. I stumbled and fell, leaped up to fall again, banging against rocks and trees, tearing my fingernails at the roots as I heaved myself over boulders and caught at sapling limbs, crushing my shins and elbows without feeling pain. My mind was outside my body; I watched myself scramble through dark confusion; saw my forehead collide solidly with a rocky overhang and a line of blood seep down my temple; saw my balance tilt as I overstepped a ridge and tumbled down, legs still churning—and, all the time, apart from my body, my mind screamed that Hodson would have no qualms, that Hodson had no regard for human life, that Hodson would release the creature—

And then my mind was back inside my throbbing head, and I leaned exhausted against a mangled tree at the top of the mountain. I'd run for hours and for miles, or for minutes and for yards, it was all the same. My chest heaved so violently that it seemed the tree was vibrating and the land was running beneath my feet. I looked back. All the trees were vibrating. A razorback of land humped up in the center and crumbled at the edges, a solid wave of earth skimmed over the rock toward me, uprooting brush and trees in its wake, and the earth itself groaned in agony. Far away a deep rumble sounded for a moment, and then died out. The movement ceased and the moaning faded. The land looked different, the contours shifted and altered, but the same wind cried above and the same blood pounded through my bursting veins.

XV

Gregorio found me in the morning.

I was still walking, following some natural instinct toward the camp, the long night a blurred memory behind me, highlights and shadows in contorted chiaroscuro and strained awareness. My panic had left with the dawn, I was walking on calmly and steadily, placing one foot before the other in studied concentration. From time to time I looked up, but I couldn't see the cliffs; lowered my head and watched my feet; noticed that the broken lace was still flaying at my ankle but didn't think to tie it. Then I looked up again and there was Gregorio. He was on the grey, staring at me, his mouth open, and I saw him through the red-rimmed frame of hollow eyes.

He moved forward on the horse and I leaned against his knee.

"Thank God," he said.

He swung from the saddle.

"How did you find me?" I asked.

"I rode this way. I didn't know. I thought that I had killed you."

That made no sense, but I didn't want sense. I collapsed against him.

I was in Gregorio's tent. My own tent was still spread over the ground. Gregorio gave me a tin mug of water and I gulped it down, feeling it trickle over my chin.

"You are all right now?"

"Yes."

"I thought that I killed you."

"I don't understand. How—"

"When you did not return in the morning—when it was light—I followed your tracks. And the tracks of the creature. I followed to the waterhole and saw where you had gone into the cave behind the water. There were no tracks coming out. I called to you and there was no answer. I did not dare to enter and I returned to the camp. But I felt very bad because of this. I waited all day and felt bad because I had not gone in the cave. I drank pisco and waited and when it was night again and the pisco was gone I was not so afraid. I went back to the waterfall, pretending that I was brave and that it was shameful I had not gone into the cave. I called again and then I went past the water and stood inside the tunnel. I stood in the entrance but I had no courage to go farther. I could not see the sky and I had no torch. I called more but there were only echoes. I thought you were dead. Then I thought that perhaps you were injured and were too far away to hear me call, and so I fired the rifle three times so that you would hear."

He paused, his hands moving expressively and frowned as be sought the words.

"The noise of the gun and the echoes—they caused something. The noise inside the mountain. It caused the mountain to move. I ran out just in time. I saw the cave close, the rocks came together and the cliffs moved backwards so that the top slid down. But it slid on the other side, not on me. I thought you were inside, maybe you were injured, and that I had buried you. Thank God it was not so."

I nodded. "The vibrations. There were faults in the rock. I felt the mountain move last night, but I thought it was my imagination. Did it move very far?"

"I think far. I could not tell, it moved on the other side. To the south."

"Perhaps it is just as well," I said.

"If the creature was inside—" Gregorio began.

"Perhaps there are things that man should not know," I told him. And then I suddenly understood the full import of that, the full extent of what I did not know. Hodson's words sounded in my mind . . .

"It is only necessary to treat the male . . ."

Gregorio looked at me with concern. He thought I was sick again, because I was very pale.

Two days later I was well—as well as I will ever be. We rode back along the path of my flight, in the early morning. My horse was as placid as ever, despite the gruesome wound on its flank. It was a good horse, and I was glad it had survived. Gregorio was curious as to why I should insist on this journey, but there was nothing I could tell him. There was nothing I could tell anyone, and when we rode over the top of the hills my last hopes vanished. It was what I had expected, what I had known with terrible anticipation.

The narrow valley was no longer there. The sheer cliffs at the apex had slid back at a gentler angle, forming the Tarpeian Rock from which my hopes were hurled to their death, and the base spread out in broken rock and upheaved earth in a shallow triangle where the valley had been. There was no sign whatsoever of Hodson's house or the cave beyond. I looked down from the hills, but hadn't the heart to descend. There was nothing to be found amidst that wreckage that would help me, no way to discover which of Hodson's stories had been deception. After all, it might have been an ape . . .

It might have been. Perhaps he had done nothing to me in that laboratory. Perhaps.

There was only one way to tell, and the method was too horrible to contemplate; it shared a common path with madness.

"Shall we go down?" Gregorio asked.

I had a fleeting thought of Anna, innocent and helpless within the framework Hodson had built around her life, buried somewhere beneath those countless tons of stone. Had she still been waiting in my bed? It didn't seem to matter. I had no sorrow to spare.

"Shall we go down?" Gregorio asked again.

"It won't be necessary."

"This is all you wished to look for?"

"This is all there is, my friend."

Gregorio blinked. He didn't understand. We rode back toward the camp, and he watched me nervously, wondering why I would not look at him. But it had nothing to do with him.

It was raining, but there was sunlight above the clouds. A flock of geese passed overhead, flying in precise formation toward the horizon, following a call they did not understand. Birds were singing in the trees and small animals avoided our path. The world was moving on at its own slow pace, with its own inexorable momentum, and nature avoided us and ignored us. Perhaps, for a few moments while the land was rumbling, nature had acted in outrage and defense, but now it was quiet once more; now it would survive.

We broke camp and headed back to Ushuaia.

There was a letter from Susan waiting at the hotel, telling how much she loved me, and Jones told me how Cape Horn looked from the air . . .

The restaurant was closing.

The late diners had departed, the waiters had gathered in the corner, waiting for me to leave. Susan had gone. My glass was empty and I was alone. I signaled and the waiter came over quickly with the bill. He thought I was drunk. I overtipped him and went out to the street. It was late; only a few people hurried past. They were strangers, and I was a stranger. I began walking home, slowly and thoughtfully, accompanied by whatever horror I may, or may not, bear in my loins. I will never know.

There are some things it is better not to know.

JO FLETCHER
Frankenstein

◦━━◦

Jo Fletcher is the founder and publisher of the eponymous Jo Fletcher Books, a specialist fantasy, science fiction and horror imprint. She's also a poet, author and ghost-writer, following her earlier careers as a film and book critic and a Fleet Street journalist.

She has been published widely, both in and out of the genre, with her work appearing in numerous anthologies and magazines including, most recently, the Zombie Apocalypse! series. Her first poetry collection, Shadows of Light and Dark, *was short-listed for the British Fantasy Award. Her nonfiction includes* The World's Greatest Mysteries *and a number of ghost-written military and historical works.*

Fletcher's publishing career started in 1985 when she joined the fledgling independent publishing company Headline and masterminded the launch of Headline's fantasy, science fiction and horror list, introducing award-winning writers like Dan Simmons and Michael Bishop and Charles L. Grant's acclaimed horror anthology series Shadows to the UK. She left Headline in 1988 and worked for Mandarin (1988–1990), then moved to Pan Books to run the newly revitalized genre list. She took over the Gollancz science fiction/fantasy/horror imprint in 1994 after the untimely death of Richard Evans, and ran that until leaving in 2011 to start Jo Fletcher Books, then as part of the independent publisher Quercus and now, following Hodder's acquisition of Quercus and its imprints in 2014, part of the Hachette stable.

She has won a number of awards for her writing and her services to the genre, including the British Fantasy Society's Karl Edward Wagner Award, the World Fantasy Special Award—Professional and the International Society of Poets Award.

Snip and sew
From head to toe
A new torso,
Says Frankenstein.

Glue and patch
The latest batch;
To mix and match
Tries Frankenstein.

Blood and bone,
Then flesh fresh-grown;
The seed is sown!
Cries Frankenstein.

The brain is next—
The doctor's vexed:

A psycho's fixed
For Frankenstein.

A high IQ
He couldn't do
And that he'll rue,
Will Frankenstein.

The storm's amuck,
The lightning's struck,
The doc's in luck—
Oh, Frankenstein!

The lever's yanked,
The dials cranked,
The power's banked
By Frankenstein.

Now watch him rise
And blink his eyes—
The Monster's size
Dwarfs Frankenstein.

His doubts assuaged,
The Monster's made—
Now be afraid,
Dear Frankenstein.

For what's created
Can't be sedated
And hope's outdated—
Pray, Frankenstein.

The Monster walks
And sort-of talks,

But his brain baulks—
Poor Frankenstein.

And when he's killed,
The town is stilled,
Then Hell's revealed
To Frankenstein.

I guess 'tis best
That theories rest,
For damned the test
Of Frankenstein . . .

About the Editor

Stephen Jones lives in London, England. A Hugo Award nominee, he is the winner of three World Fantasy Awards, three International Horror Guild Awards, four Bram Stoker Awards, twenty-one British Fantasy Awards and a Lifetime Achievement Award from the World Horror Association. One of Britain's most acclaimed horror and dark fantasy writers and editors, he has more than 140 books to his credit, including the film books of Neil Gaiman's *Coraline* and *Stardust*, *The Art of Horror: An Illustrated History*, *The Illustrated Monster Movie Guide* and *The Hellraiser Chronicles*, the nonfiction studies *Horror: 100 Best Books* and *Horror: Another 100 Best Books* (both with Kim Newman), the author collections *Necronomicon* and *Eldritch Tales* by H. P. Lovecraft, *The Complete Chronicles of Conan* and *Conan's Brethren* by Robert E. Howard, and *Curious Warnings: The Great Ghost Stories of M. R. James*, plus such anthologies as *Horrorlogy: The Lexicon of Fear*, *Fearie Tales: Stories of the Grimm and Gruesome*, *A Book of Horrors*, *The Mammoth Book of Vampires*, the Zombie Apocalypse! series and the Best New Horror series. You can visit his web site at www.stephenjoneseditor.com or follow him on Facebook at Stephen Jones-Editor.

Acknowledgments and Credits

Thanks to Duncan Proudfoot, Claiborne Hancock, Neil Gaiman, Stephen Volk and Jo Fletcher for all their help.